AVA

AND

SHALOM

A NOVEL

KATE BIRKIN

AND MARK BORNZ

Viking Trade Press

Photograph of Czesława Kwoka attributed to Wilhelm Brasse, taken in 1942 or 1943, exhibited at Auschwitz-Birkenau State Museum.

For more information about Kate Birkin and her books, please visit https://www.katebirkinbooks.com.

LCCN 2025475052

ISBN-13: 979-8-9891841-2-5 (eBook)
ISBN-13: 979-8-9891841-3-2 (Paperback)
ISBN-13: 979-8-9891841-4-9 (Hardcover)
ISBN-13: 979-8-9891841-5-6 (Audiobook)

Praise for *Ava and Shalom*

"A deeply moving and truly unforgettable story of love and survival."
— ★★★★★ *The International Review*

"Exceptional and heartbreaking, crackling with poignant writing. These intensely gifted authors deliver a stunning reflection on the past."
— ★★★★★ *The Independent*

"Highly emotional with cataclysmic circumstances and a masterful narrative. Readers who can bear the heartbreak will reap an incredible story!"
— ★★★★★ *Historical Fiction Company*

"Sensational... Deeply personal... An emotional and moving story of human resilience through the deadliest conflict in history. Highly recommend!"
— ★★★★★ *Yarde Editorial*

"Unique storytelling and intricate characterization. Achingly beautiful and memorable. Prioritize this one. You won't regret it."
— ★★★★★ *NetGalley*

"Nothing I say will ever do this book justice, and it will stay with me forever. I will never forget the characters, the story, or the writing!"
— ★★★★★ *BooksGoSocial*

"Exquisitely written, deeply emotional. The characters leaped from the page, taking me on an emotional rollercoaster. I cried, felt hope, despair!"
— ★★★★★ *BookBub*

"This is not a book but an experience, encapsulating all the tears, sorrow, and depths of one's soul."
— ★★★★★ *Amazon*

"I could not stop crying! I have no words to describe this book!"
— ★★★★★ *Amazon*

"I've read so many books about WWII, and none compares to this amazing story. Kate Birkin will be revered for years to come as a "classic" writer. Her words create life and art. God gave her an amazing gift!"
— ★★★★★ *Goodreads*

Also by KATE BIRKIN and MARK BORNZ

The Consequence of Anna

COMING SOON!

To Kill a Singing Bird

Visiting the Village

Bad Luck Clementine

Dedicated to Sir Nicholas George Winton, who organized the rescue of 669 children from Nazi-occupied Czechoslovakia on the eve of World War II, thereby sparing them from the horrors of the Holocaust. Dubbed the "British Schindler" and knighted by Queen Elizabeth II in 2003 for services to humanity, his operation became known as the Czech *Kindertransport (children's transport)*. The survivors called themselves "Nicky's children," and by the time of Winton's death at 106 years of age in 2015, their descendants numbered over 6,000 around the world.

*Czesława Kwoka.
Auschwitz prisoner number 26947 and child victim.
Beautiful even with a bruised face from being beaten.
Confused and frightened but still brave.
Her mother nowhere in sight as she posed for her final photograph.*

Dear Reader,

The first time I saw the photo of fourteen-year-old Czesława Kwoka, a Polish girl photographed by fellow prisoner Wilhelm Brasse, it struck me with such great sadness and anger. An innocent little girl had been sent to Auschwitz with her mother, both of whom were murdered within three months.

There is so little known about her, other than she was from the small town of Wólka Złojecka, Poland, and she had been beaten just before the photo was taken. And I wanted to know more. I wanted to know who this pretty, blue-eyed little angel was before she found herself in this living nightmare. What was she like? What music did she listen to and what books did she read? What was her favorite color, her favorite candy? Did she have any hobbies, aspirations, or dreams? What about a sister, or a brother, or a crush on a boy?

So many unanswered questions.

And yet all that the world knows about her is captured in a few snapshots taken while she was a prisoner at Auschwitz. A prisoner at fourteen! That is her only story. Her legacy. And it is heartbreaking.

I began researching other photographs from the Holocaust, images millions of others have also seen, and it bothered me that so many had no story beyond the haunting stare into the camera lens. Who they once were, the lives they lived, and the love they shared before mercilessly taken away and murdered because of their race or religion. It troubled me to the point of losing sleep, and it moved me to action in the only way I knew how . . . by giving them a voice, creating their story for them. A melting pot of true accounts, all blended together. And not just about the Holocaust but also prior to it, when they lived on beautiful farms, owned successful businesses, had loving families and friends, and lived life to the full.

Ava and Shalom is inspired by all those people. A myriad of stories in honor of the millions of innocent victims who died during the Holocaust, like fourteen-year-old Czesława Kwoka. They were more than a haunting stare into a camera lens. More than the identification number on their prison uniform or tattooed on their arm. More than their injustice and suffering.

Yes, they were beautiful human beings, just like you, and they had lives, loves, and dreams . . .

Iceland
Norway
Sweden
Finland
Russia
Estonia
Latvia
Lithuania
Belarus
Ukraine
Ireland
UK
Germany
Poland
Czech Rep.
Austria
Slovakia
Hungari
Romania
France
Italy
Serbia
Bulgaria
Black Sea
Portugal
Spain
Greece
Turkey
N
W
E
S

"Hell is empty and all the devils are here."
– William Shakespeare

"There was so much innocent blood
hidden from the eyes of the rest of the
world. Enough blood to fill an ocean."
– Holocaust Survivor

Auschwitz-Birkenau
Concentration Camp
1943

The gates of Auschwitz loomed in the distance as the train, overflowing with humanity, screeched to a halt. The air was heavy with the stench of despair, the fetid smell of vomit, urine, and excrement permeating the cramped carriage. Within, hundreds of Jewish prisoners, their bodies weary and spirits broken, braced themselves for the unknown horrors that awaited them.

Ava and Shalom, twenty-two-year-old twin sisters raised in a loving German family, had only recently learned of their Semitic heritage. Once living fairy tale lives, they now found themselves in a horrible nightmare, in shock over how they ended up in this hellish camp. As if a theatrical oil painting of Gemini's twin stars, Castor and Pollux, dramatically personified into human form with eyes wide in fear, faces pale, skin stained with tears, dirt, and blood, they huddled close together, clinging to one another in the crowded boxcar like two mirror images embracing in a sorrowful kiss before death.

As the doors flung open, a flood of frightened souls poured out into the night, their faces etched with crippling dread and anxiety. The moon cast a ghostly glow over the scene, its light filtered through a thin veil of clouds creating an eerie, sinister atmosphere.

SS officers with vicious German Shepherds immediately began the process of sorting the prisoners. Their faces were cold and impassive and their voices harsh, barking orders that sent waves of panic through the crowd. Some of the people were destined to work until they collapsed from sickness or exhaustion, others marked for the gas chambers. Confusion, crying, and the sound of families being torn apart were everywhere.

The sudden crack of a gunshot elevated the fear. An older man, too slow for the officers' liking, fell to the ground, his life extinguished in an instant. Nearby, a woman clung desperately to her young son, refusing to let him go. She, too, met the same fate, her body crumpling to the ground as her little boy's screams pierced the night.

Another woman, grimacing in pain, stepped away from the line, clutching her swollen belly. When an older woman rushed to her aid, both were ordered back in line. She complained that the girl was starting early labor, and the officer responded with two more bullets. Both women lay still, their lives snuffed out in a cruel and senseless act.

Amidst this chaos, Ava reached over and held her sister's hand. Her grip was vice-like, her knuckles white with the force of her fear. Shalom's menses had started, blood running down her leg, and she thought of their adoptive German mother, how she would always make them a hot bath scented with vanilla and lavender when they were children, singing as she washed her daughters' hair. "Oh, Mama," Shalom cried out in desperation and sadness. Though she was now a young woman, she felt no different from that little boy who had just screamed for his dead mother.

An SS officer singled Ava and Shalom out among the crowd of terrorized Jews. "Are you twins?" he asked, his interest piqued.

Paralyzed, the sisters remained mute, praying silent pleas.

The officer pressed his gun firmly against Ava's sternum. "Are you twins?" he repeated, his scarred face, crooked rotting teeth, and bulbous nose a fitting motif to his heinous persona.

"*Ja (Yes)*," Ava managed to whisper, barely audible.

Dr. Josef Rudolf Mengele approached, his gaze scrutinizing the siblings with a chilling intensity. "Of course they are, you fool," he said dismissively to the officer. "Look at them." His eyes lingered with fascination on Ava and Shalom, a twisted smile playing on his lips. "And such pretty green eyes."

Both girls felt as if they were staring into the soul of a demon. A cold shiver ran down their spines.

More gunshots rang out, adding to the cacophony of death and despair. One of the fallen, only a few feet from where the sisters stood, was a man who had earlier offered Shalom his jacket, an act of kindness in a world devoid of compassion. Now, his lifeless body lay in the mud, the leather coat still carrying his scent.

Another man was shot for mere sport, his body refusing to fall despite the bullet tearing through his flesh. Two of the officers found amusement in his resilience, their laughter a grotesque soundtrack to the cruelty, and it irritated the one with the gun. He walked over to the man, shooting him point blank between the eyes. "*Die Ratte war stärker als er aussah (The rat was stronger than he looked)*," he said with a smirk, spitting on the dead man.

Josef Mengele, unfazed by the atrocities happening around him, as if it were just another day at the office, motioned for Ava and Shalom to follow. "You two are special," he said, his voice carrying an evil timbre. "I'm taking you to a place where I can examine you closer."

The twin sisters followed the doctor, stepping over bodies and through pools of blood. Their fate, now in the hands of a merciless man known for his monstrous experiments, seemed more uncertain than ever. As they walked, the camp's lights flickered ominously, casting long shadows that danced across the ground like specters of death, reminding them they had entered a realm where survival and hope were mere illusions.

No benefactors were there to help them.

No heroes were coming to rescue them.

No saviors could possibly save them.

Unless . . .

PART ONE

Berlin, 1997

I was twenty-five, fresh out of college, working as a correspondent at a major newspaper and doing side work for a TV news station. Despite my young age, I was already an accomplished writer, winning a few journalism awards and covering a story about the Cold War that aired on television. I met celebrities, went to wild parties, and navigated the social scenes from the sun-kissed boulevards of Los Angeles to the pulsating heart of New York. I was moving up in the world, and fast.

From the outside, everything looked as promising as a birthday present wrapped in shiny paper with a colorful bow. But on the inside, I was drowning. Beneath the facade, I was completely unhappy with my work and the direction of my life, fading into a chasm of dissatisfaction. I wanted to be a *real* writer, not just crafting narratives that filled the pages of a newspaper but creating something of significance. Something that bore weight, that whispered of truth, and that would leave an indelible mark on those who read it. But such paragons are not easily found; they are rare, hidden gems. To unearth one is like winning the lottery.

Only in my mid-twenties and already tapped out, my inspiration was gone. Like tumbleweed blowing across the Arizona desert, I searched for my oasis, but everything I came across was nothing more than a mirage, leaving me parched and desperate for a drop of meaning in a wasteland of mediocrity.

"Charlie!" my pop said to me in his large, Old English-style study after one of our weekly chess games, a cigar in one hand and a brandy in the other. Being a retired journalist who had traveled the world, his gruff and distinctive voice now dispensed advice like it was candy. "What you need is an adventure. A damn good one, too. One that will inspire you to write your book." He leaned in and looked me directly in the eye. "An account that puts fire in the bellies of people, teaching them something and making them feel again. The world has gone numb, son, and it needs an electrifying piece to shake 'em up." Exhaling a billow of smoke, he tossed back his brandy.

My pop was right. What I desperately needed to get me out of this funk was an adventure. One that would lead me to a genuine, salt of the earth, life-changing story.

Compelled by a fortuitous mettle, I made a rash decision that veered sharply from the path expected of me. It had to be done. Ignoring the protests of close family and friends–my pop being my only supporter–with a single, defiant stroke, I severed my connections to the familiar, quitting my job, ending my stale relationship with my girlfriend, and giving up my apartment. In a leap of faith and forfeiture of collective thinking, I bought a plane ticket to Germany to seek my providence elsewhere, in a new environment, one that bore the unspeakable scars of history, yet at the same time the triumphant and indomitable spirit of humanity. Being half Jewish, I had heard the Holocaust horror stories from my grandfather who survived Auschwitz-Birkenau, and I thought maybe there I would find my inspiration again, stumbling across something of value that hadn't already been written. I've always wanted to visit this place of tragedy and sorrow, anyway, and something was now drawing me there. Perhaps, amidst the shadows of the past and the solemnity of the Holocaust memorials, I would find the spark to ignite my passion once more.

Berlin welcomed me with open arms and a sky ablaze with promise on that glorious morn I arrived. It was there, on a serendipitous summer day in 1997, that luck intertwined my path with that of Gretchen Axmann. Gretchen rented a two-bedroom flat in an old Victorian home, and it just so happened she needed a roommate. Well, you can guess what happened next . . . I now had a place to stay. It didn't hurt that she was a beauty, as well, with a vivacious and quirky personality that made me laugh–the perfect antidote to my somewhat refined demeanor.

Soon Gretchen and I became more than just roommates; we became best friends and lovers. We partied with the locals in Berlin's nightlife, coming home at dawn. We slept till noon, crawling out of bed to go for a late *Frühstück (breakfast)* at Gretchen's favorite diner while lazily reading the newspaper. And we strolled leisurely through the park, hand in hand, lounging on the grass under the warm German sun. Neither one of us thought much about the future at that point, living in the moment, enjoying the fruits of each other.

Using the money I had saved, we bought new furniture for the flat, hung pictures on the walls, and put house plants everywhere. I grew a beard, let my hair grow long, and immersed myself in everything European culture had to offer. Gretchen was my personal tour guide and curator, and even taught me German as we lay in each other's arms in bed.

I remember one special night, with the moon shining through the window, the classical music serenading us in the room, and the wine coursing through our veins. She whispered to me, *"Ich liebe dich (I love you)*, Charlie John Rankin." I looked at her and replied, *"Und ich liebe dich (And I love you)*, Gretchen Axmann." That was the first time we said we loved each other, and it was in perfect German.

Those carefree days were such a fun diversion for me, and a refreshing change from my ex-girlfriend back home, who constantly hinted about getting married, or pestered me about buying a house, or pushed me about advancing my career. With Gretchen, there was freedom and no judgment, and I loved that. She was also an artist, and I think that's why she adored me; or at least liked the idea of having a writer as a boyfriend, finding it romantic. She also ran with the artsy crowd of Berlin; boy was that interesting and entertaining. We'd all go down to the local coffee shop and drink specialty java while reciting poetry, or crowd into someone's small apartment and smoke herb, or linger in bohemian shops and enclaves. True, I wasn't writing my groundbreaking story yet, but I was having the time of my life.

This breezy lifestyle went on for months, and I thoroughly enjoyed it, not having a care in the world, every day filled with whatever I wanted to do. It was great, until I grew restless. The endless cycle of hedonistic partying and next-day hangovers started to become tiresome and boring, and the insouciant way of life was losing its charm. I was running out of money, too, and that worried me. I figured I had maybe six months left to carve out my masterpiece before I'd have to pack it all in and head back to South Carolina. What an embarrassment that would be, proving the naysayers right. But it was either that or get a mundane job in Berlin to support myself, and that's not what I wanted. No, something important had drawn me here, and I knew it. But what?

Returning to why I had come to Germany in the first place, I reinvigorated my zeal to find my literary pearl. I visited all the tourist sights about the Holocaust, read historical books on it, and talked to those who had survived the death camps. But listening to their stories, though tragic and heartbreaking, did not compel me to sit down and write it all out. That is until the other shoe dropped . . .

My fun-loving, free-spirited, no-strings-attached blonde vixen came home one day from the doctor's office in tears. She sat down, her face in her hands, and mumbled in German that she was pregnant. Neither of us were expecting that, as we had been careful, but the Devil always laughs at our plans. At the time, with a new baby on the way, I saw my book spontaneously combust before my eyes, disintegrating into ashes before I had even penned the first word. I did love Gretchen, though, and I would not abandon her and our child, so I asked her to marry me.

Gretchen said yes, but she didn't want to move to South Carolina. That meant, for the time being, I was stuck in Germany, with no job, no direction, and no book. We had a simple wedding with a dozen of Gretchen's family and friends in a medieval German church, Gretchen wearing her grandmother's lace wedding gown and intricate gossamer veil, and me a rented vintage tux with a pink carnation. Afterward, we settled into married life.

I cut my hair, shaved my beard, and found a job as a drywaller at a construction company . . . I know, I know, but it paid the bills . . . and Gretchen opened a quaint little used bookstore nearby. She decorated it with colorful beanbag chairs, flowers and plants, and various knickknacks from the bohemian shops, serving her customers coffee and Danishes as they perused and read her books. Sometimes she bought more than she sold, though, and within a few weeks, our apartment was full of an assortment of tomes on a variety of subjects, ranging from French poetry to how to grow a prize-winning garden. Occasionally, she'd find a real gem, like the life story of Gustav Klimt, the nineteenth-century Austrian symbolist painter and one of the most prominent members of the Vienna Secession movement. He painted *The Kiss*–perhaps his most famous work–adding gold leaf, silver, and platinum to the piece depicting a couple embracing each other, their bodies wrapped in elaborate robes decorated in a style influenced by the contemporary Art Nouveau style. Gretchen, feeling inspired one day, tried to replicate it as a painting of us. Of course I didn't tell her, but it looked more like a Pablo Picasso disaster, or a child's watercolor portrait, than it did a work of art. Nevertheless, because I loved her, I complimented her profusely on it and proudly hung it above our bed.

During this sublime period, I surrendered and settled in, imagining myself years from now, speaking fluent German, eating Bavarian pretzels and bratwurst while surrounded by little blond children in lederhosen, crawling all over me and calling me Papa. And yet, still, the reason I originally came to Germany ate at me. I had all but given up hope of finding that elusive, erudite gold, until something pivotal happened, opening the unexpected door of fate in one of those miraculous ways.

Gretchen had asked the landlady, a sweet woman in her seventies everyone called Mrs. Kuchen, if we could remove some wallpaper in the second bedroom and paint it a pastel color in preparation for the baby. Mrs. Kuchen agreed, and when I peeled back a section of the paper, hidden beneath layers of time and paint I saw four names carved into the wall: Ava, Shaylee, Luka, Christian–Best Friends Forever, 1939. This bond forged in the crucible of history, promising eternal friendship at the beginning of a most epoch and harrowing time, intrigued me, as if desperately reaching across the decades to grab hold of my heart. As I stared at it, something strange, something outré, and even dreadful, came over me.

Later when I got the mail, I asked Mrs. Kuchen if she knew who these people were, and she looked at me with curiosity. "Tell me," she said, her German accent as strong and thick as molasses. "Your last name Rankin . . . is that related to the abolitionist Presbyterian minister, John Rankin, from the 1800s?"

"Yes," I said, surprised that she knew of him. "As a matter of fact, he's a distant relative."

"He helped 2,000 runaway slaves as a conductor on the Underground Railroad."

Her knowledge of American slavery intrigued me. "I know. My father taught me all about him when I was a young teenager."

"Hmm . . . You must be very proud to be related to such a man."

I nodded. "John Rankin was a true hero."

"*Ja (Yes)*, a hero," said Mrs. Kuchen, almost under her breath. I could see in her eyes that she was thinking of something. Or someone she knew. Someone important to her. "Your wife tells me you're a writer," she said, a soft smile touching her lips.

"Yes. I was a journalist in the States," I replied, sticking my hands in my pockets, embarrassed of my present situation. "I came here to write a book, but it never happened. I couldn't find that special story to inspire me."

She paused. "Why don't you and your wife come over for dinner tonight. I might have a story for you."

"We'd love to, but she's going to her mother's for the weekend," I said.

"Then just you. Eight o'clock." She smiled at me. "I think you will find that . . . how you say . . . inspiration you are looking for." With a quick wink, she turned and disappeared down the long hallway.

❧

That night, I brought a bottle of *Spätburgunder (Pinot Noir)* wine and some Allgäu Emmental cheese along with me to dinner. Mrs. Kuchen was most appreciative of my gift. She lived in the bottom half of the old Victorian home, which was separate from the upstairs flat. Her living room looked like something out of an 1800s-era movie set, with original decor—velvet wing-back chairs, silk curtains, Tiffany lamps, Art Nouveau styling. Being a quintessential German woman, she also made the best Germanic cuisine, which was such a treat. Though Gretchen was amazing at reciting poetry and making love, she could not cook to save her life, and I had forgotten how good unburnt food tasted.

While we ate dinner together, I was impressed with how elegant and charming Mrs. Kuchen was. Bright and witty, she made me laugh, and we talked into the night. When the Pinot Noir was finished, she brought out a special German liqueur in a green glass bottle, pouring us each a double shot. "Jägermeister is my favorite," she said, handing it to me.

I took a sip. "My wife had mentioned this drink to me before. It's good."

She smiled, gazing at me as if seeing into my soul. "You're in love, no?"

"Yes," I replied, smiling back.

Mrs. Kuchen leaned in closer, her large emerald eyes shimmering. "But have you ever been heartbroken?"

I thought for a moment. "No, I haven't experienced heartbreak yet."

She lit a cigarette and exhaled a billow of smoke, staring into the dancing flames of the fireplace, her mien turning rueful. "You will after the story I'm about to tell you."

As I observed her, lost in her cogitation, I could see something profound awakening in her mind. Something cataclysmal. I put the tape recorder on the table, and the second I hit "record," she came alive. There was a magic that settled around the room, and we both felt it. This meeting between us was meant to happen. Destiny, fate, kismet—all silent cousins listening as she spoke of two Jewish babies, Ava and Shalom, given to a German farmer and his wife in 1921. Secretly raised as German, for years everything was bliss, until their Jewish mother came back to the farm one evening, running away from the Nazis. The lie was eventually exposed, and all the demons were released from the abyss.

I sat there listening to her tale, absolutely mesmerized. Yes, this decorous, enchanting if not haunting lady—a keeper of secrets and stories—was right.

I had found my inspiration . . .

CHAPTER 1

Seventy-Seven Years Earlier

Germany, 1920

The two boxers had been fighting a grueling match. An intense fight, now in the thirteenth round. The agitated crowd, drinking and chain-smoking, yelling and thrusting their fists in the air, had picked their sides, hoping to cash in on their bets. Eckstein No. 5 cigarettes and Loeser & Wolff cigars filled the large room with a velvety blanket of smoke, hovering in the air like an apparition.

Ding! Ding! Ding!

The bell rang, ending the round, and each boxer retreated to his corner. A young woman dressed in marmalade-colored shorts that fit as snug as the tobacco leaf wrapper on the cigars she sold, strutted through the audience, selling her goods. Inebriated men whistled and shouted, catcalling until she disappeared.

Randolph Kowalski, a seasoned pugilist who had won many titles across Europe, was the favorite. Burly, broad-shouldered, solid on his feet, the Polish man with prominent brow and hairy frame was known for his strength and stamina, able to take a solid punch as well as release one. He reminded boxing fans of a bull, which is why they gave him the moniker, Randolph the Bull.

A muscular young German man named Albrecht Braun was the challenger. Untested but tall and strong, with lemon blond hair and chiseled face, he had a reputation with the ladies, several of whom were in the crowd that night, cheering him on. One in particular was absolutely smitten, and whenever Albrecht took a punch to the face, she would yell at his opponent, *"Tu ihm nicht weh, du polnisches Schwein (Don't hurt him, you Polish pig)!"*

The bell rang, and round fourteen began. Surprisingly, Albrecht Braun was winning the fight, having broken the Polish fighter's nose in the previous round, and cutting him below the left eye, now swollen shut. Though inexperienced and battered himself, he had studied his opponent well, noticing one important flaw in Randolph the Bull's technique: Every time the veteran fighter threw a jab, he lowered his shoulder slightly, leaving his chin exposed to the German's powerful right hand. Albrecht exploited that mistake mercilessly, and though Randolph the Bull was still standing, his endurance was under threat. The question was, could he turn things around with only two rounds left?

Interestingly, every time they answered the bell, the young German fighter always extended his arm to touch gloves in a virtual handshake, nodding out of respect, even though he knew he was winning. Randolph the Bull would swat it away rather than extend his in return.

"Shows you kindness and respect does not mean weakness," Hanz Wolff, a German farmer in the crowd, said to his friend, motioning at the gesture.

Ollie van Heinz saw it differently. The epitome of a white-haired Ichabod Crane, tall and skinny like a Q-Tip, with a large, crooked nose and mischievous smile, he had known Hanz since childhood. "I don't blame the Bull for snubbing him," he said, his prominent Adam's apple bobbing as he spoke. "Why shake the hand of the man who's trying to slaughter you?" He stuck the comic book he was flipping through back into his rear pocket. Ollie always had one on hand.

"It's *gute (good)* sportsmanship, that's why."

"*Nein (No)*. That's like shaking the hand of your enemy at war before he spills your blood."

Hanz took a large swig of his beer, swallowing down sudden unwelcome memories. "Not the same thing. This is sport. War is much different."

Ollie took his eyes off the fight and glanced over at his friend. Though they had both been in the Great War, which would later become known as World War I, only Hanz saw fierce combat, nearly losing his life in it. Ollie could almost see the terror-filled images of what Hanz had experienced as a soldier, now ricocheting in his head because of that comment.

"War is blood in the air, blood in the sea, blood in the field, and blood in the rich men's pockets," Hanz said, lighting a cigarette. "There is no comparison."

Both men thought of the ramifications the Great War had on them personally and for their country. The global conflict that raged from July 28, 1914, to November 11, 1918, pitting the Central Powers–mainly Germany, Austria-Hungary, and the Ottoman Empire–against the Allies, or Entente–mainly France, Great Britain, Russia, Italy, Japan, and, from 1917, the United States–had ended with the catastrophic defeat of the Central Powers. With the Kaiser's abdication, the creation of the new Weimer Republic, and the harsh terms of the Treaty of Versailles, signed on June 28, 1919, came severe hardship throughout Germany. Thousands of factories closed, unemployment and hyperinflation soared, many people lost all their possessions, and some even starved. Confusion, chaos, and anger escalated, resulting in violent uprisings. And that's why the boxing match in town that night had been so welcomed. Most of the men, living close to poverty, were able to forget their troubles for one night of excitement.

As they were talking, the German boxer pulled his left arm back to release another blow, but it was only a cunning trick. When Randolph the Bull went to block it, Albrecht Braun instead released a vicious uppercut with his right, landing squarely on the Polish fighter's chin. His head snapped back; he staggered to the side; a single gold tooth flew through the air, landing by Hanz's foot. The crowd went silent for a moment, holding its collective breath. Even Albrecht waited to see if the Bull would remain standing.

Ding! Ding! Ding! . . . Saved by the bell!

Each boxer retreated again to his corner, and Randolph's trainer brought out the smelling salts.

"Why don't you shake his hand now!" a man shouted from the crowd. Laughter followed.

"The Bull has been slaughtered!" yelled another. "Throw in the towel!" More laughter.

"I think he's right," said Hanz, looking at the Polish man's bloodied face. With his nose in the wrong spot, one eye closed and the other a mere slit, his mug was so swollen it looked as if he'd been attacked by killer bees. "Randolph the Bull underestimated the young German. He should quit now while he's still breathing."

The entire room was abuzz with commotion. And when the bell rang, the Bull answered it, lifting from his chair to meet his opponent for the final round. Again, the audience held their breath–a combination of fear for Randolph's life, and respect for his tenacity, stubbornness, and resilience.

"Good God, this is going to be murder," Ollie said.

"I don't think I can even watch," replied Hanz.

But of course, both men couldn't look away.

As the two boxers faced each other in the center of the ring, Randolph the Bull was the first to extend his arm, touching gloves with the German and nodding. The spectators began to chant Albrecht Braun's name, and then the slaughter continued, right to the very end of round fifteen. When the final bell rang, Randolph the Bull, still standing, released a wide, toothless smile at the crowd, then slowly fell backward, out cold on the canvas.

The crowd went absolutely wild.

Hanz looked down and stared at Randolph's tooth by his foot, twinkling at him, reflecting a light from some unknown source. Picking it up, he wiped it off and stuck it in his pocket.

⁓·c⳩⳨·⁓

With the fight over, Hanz and Ollie started making their way to a local tavern called *Die Teufelsnadel (The Devil's Needle)*. Popular within the small German town, it was often full, being one of only a few the town had to offer.

On one side of the street, a group of rabbis walked toward the Jewish quarter, while on the street corner outside the pub, a homeless older man and beggar, with long, gray beard and ragged clothes, stood shouting out scriptures at passersby. Holding a worn Bible in one hand and a shepherd's staff in the other, he resembled the image of Moses. Most people just ignored him, dismissing his proclamations. But occasionally a curious few would stop and listen, leaving a few coins in his hat sitting nearby.

As Hanz and Ollie drew close, he yelled out to them 1 Corinthians 15:41: "*There is one glory of the sun, and another glory of the moon, and another glory of the stars; for one star differs from another star in glory.*" He pointed at the luminaries in the night sky, and added, "Look how beautiful they are! Behold, the glory of God!"

Ollie laughed. "There's the nutcase, ranting about God again."

"You laugh at the glory of the Creator! How dare you!" yelled the older man, anger in his voice. "I will tell you what the Almighty said to Job . . . '*Where were you when I laid the foundation of the earth? Tell me, if you have understanding, who set its measurements? Since you know. Or who stretched the line on it? On what were its bases sunk? Or who laid its cornerstone, when the morning stars sang together and all the sons of God shouted for joy?'"* After quoting Job 38:4-7 from memory, the homeless man scrunched up his face and began to giggle in a demented way, dancing and waving his arms in the air, shouting out, "He made the earth, the sky, and the sea! He did, he did, he did!" Then he howled at the moon.

"The man may be mentally unwell, but he sure knows his Bible," Hanz said. "That was quite a profound scripture. God, declaring his awe-inspiring handiwork."

Ollie shrugged. "Don't know much about the Word of God. But the wife reads from it on Sundays and makes me and the kids listen. Last week she said overindulging in alcohol is a sin, and that drunkards won't inherit God's Kingdom. But if that's true, how can heaven be a paradise?"

Hanz only chuckled.

Nila Vogel, a little person who bartended at The Devil's Needle, tried to shoo the homeless man away. "Oh, hush, you crazy fool," she said, stepping out of the tavern to pour a bucket of hot water on the sidewalk, steam rising from the ground. Earlier, two drunken Germans had gotten into a brawl, one vomiting and the other bleeding on the doorstep to the pub. "Go rant somewhere else."

But that only encouraged the man further, moving him to recite Joel 2:30-31 about Judgment Day: *"And I will show wonders in the heavens and on the earth, blood and fire and columns of smoke. The sun shall be turned to darkness, and the moon to blood, before the great and awesome day of the Lord comes."*

Nila just shook her head and went back inside.

Hanz and Ollie entered the pub, waving at the regulars as they headed to their usual spot at the bar.

"After that intense fight, I think I need a splash of vodka in my lemonade," Ollie said, grinning.

Hanz laughed. "You mean a splash of lemonade in your quart of vodka." He took off his hat and got comfortable at the bar. "I've never known a man who could drink like you. A skinny noodle with a hollow leg."

Ollie often included vodka in his speech, using his favorite drink as a panacea for life's travails. He'd get a real serious expression on, squint his eyes, and say something like, "You need some vodka in your blood, *mein Freund (my friend)*. After a shot, or two, or three, everything will be all right." Or if someone was upset, he'd say, "No worries! No worries! Calm down, *mein Freund!* Just pour some vodka in your lemonade, and that'll fix it!"

The men at the bar would all laugh. It was something Ollie had coined, his own interpretation of the more common phrase, "When life gives you lemons, make lemonade." No matter how bad the situation, it always seemed to brighten the mood.

"You two lose any money on the fight tonight?" Nila asked, pushing strands of blonde hair out of her large, friendly brown eyes as she walked over to them. Though a grown woman, she stood only four feet three inches tall, barely visible from behind the bar.

"I didn't have any money to bet," said Ollie. "And Hanz never bets. He picked up an interesting souvenir, though."

Nila stepped onto a bench behind the bar, gaining an extra foot. "Oh yeah? What's that?"

Ollie nudged him. "Show her."

Hanz pulled Randolph the Bull's gold tooth from his pocket and placed it on the counter.

"Nice," said Nila. "From the winner or loser?"

"Loser."

"What are you going to do with it?"

Hanz shrugged. He had a habit of collecting eccentric things, some odd, some not. Like an old Roman coin he had found in his wheat field one day. Or a black pearl with the most beautiful hue—a mixture of onyx, deep purple, and a touch of some color with no name—that he found in an oyster. The coin might be worth something to a museum, and the pearl definitely worth something to a jeweler, but he had no intention of selling them. And now he had a gold tooth from a well-known professional boxer to add to his unique collection.

"I've got something to show you too," Nila said, a twinkle in her eye. "I came across it when I was visiting my mother in Berlin." She pulled out a leatherbound tome from under the bar and slid it to him.

Hanz glanced at the title of the book: *Frankenstein; or, The Modern Prometheus*. "Looks like a special edition of the original."

"It is. Found it in an old bookstore."

Hanz opened the cover and flipped through the first few pages of Mary Shelley's 1818 classic novel. He loved books, especially ones that had a knack for creativity and concepts that transcended any era or societal milieu. Often, when unable to find sleep, he would read for hours in the quiet of the night while his wife slept.

"It's yours, Hanz," Nila said, smiling even wider. Like all his friends, she knew of his love for literature.

He looked up at her. "Really?"

"*Ja.* My gift to you for the portrait you painted of me."

"But you paid me for that." Hanz didn't just love reading. He liked to paint, too, and play his violin. When not plowing in his fields, the farmer indulged his artistic passions in a makeshift art studio in his barn, selling some of his work.

"I know, but barely enough to cover the paint. Besides, I wanted to do something more. You're such a kind, *gute Freund (good friend)*, Hanz, and I wanted to show you my appreciation." More than once over the years, he had stepped in when some drunken boor started mouthing off at Nila, making fun of her small stature to the point of bringing her to tears.

Hanz started going through the book again. "I love it, Nila. *Danke (Thank you)*."

"*Gern geschehen (You're welcome)*. Now what can I get you boys to drink?"

"I'll have my usual vodka," said Ollie.

"Chartreuse, please," answered Hanz. "I feel like a *gute* French liqueur to go along with this *schönes Geschenk (beautiful gift)*."

"Coming right up."

As Nila left to retrieve the drinks, a sultry young woman named Gisela Lang walked over to the bar and smiled seductively at Hanz. He noticed her lips shining a candy apple red, and that her breath smelled of rum. "Handsome Hanz, how are you doing tonight?" she asked, leaning on the bar, wrapping her arm around his neck.

A grin born of flattery played at the corner of his mouth. "*Gute.* And you?"

"You know me—just looking for a *gute* time."

Ollie was lovestruck, smiling so big it hurt. "You look very lovely tonight, Gisela."

She ignored him. "How come you and I have never dated, Hanz?"

"Because I married Maria."

Gisela smirked. "That's right; you married that Austrian girl. But are you *happily* married?" Like the snake in the Garden of Eden, her tone attempted to inject doubt.

Hanz thought about his beautiful, deaf wife, Maria, with her long, curly, fiery red hair, sapphire blue eyes of wonder, and scarlet cheeks aflame on freckled skin. Such a good, sweet woman, too. He had met her right after the war when he was traumatized, broken, and lost. Rescued from his own private hell by an angel. A soulful and kind woman who seemed to never let her feet touch the ground. She reminded him of a mermaid, a Siren, and he would follow her to the depths of the sea. Without a doubt, Hanz Wolff loved his wife dearly. "*Ja*, I am happily married," he said. "Very much so."

Gisela kept pressing. "Took you a moment to answer."

He didn't reply.

"It was always curious to me why you married a deaf girl from Austria when there are so many pretty girls here in Germany." She pulled the pack of Eckstein No. 5 cigarettes from Hanz's shirt pocket, removed one and placed it between her lips, expecting him to light it. But it was Ollie who leaned forward, eager to oblige. "You even told me I was pretty, remember?" Gisela exhaled a billow of smoke over her shoulder. "Do you still think I am?"

"I sure do!" said Ollie.

"But does Hanz," she said, gazing at him with her enormous amber eyes.

"Everyone knows you're a *hübsche Frau (pretty woman)*," he admitted, staring down at his wedding ring–a simple gold band with Norwegian symbols. It had belonged to Maria's grandfather who had Viking roots.

Gisela looked at the wedding ring too. "You know, I have always wondered about deaf women. When a man makes love to one, she cannot hear his sweet nothings. And what does she do when he . . ." Gisela leaned in and whispered something crass into his ear.

Ollie overheard and turned red.

"Get your hand off my thigh, woman," was all Hanz said.

"*Mein süßer (My sweet)* Hanz, it's not on your thigh." She threw her head back and laughed.

"You tart, get away from him before I scratch your eyes out!" Nila demanded, returning with the drinks. She knew the woman was trouble. The whole town did. "He's a married man, you hussy!"

Gisela ignored Nila, like she did Ollie, then kissed Hanz on the cheek before sauntering off.

Ollie gawked at her like a pubescent teenage boy as she floated back to her table. "Wish she'd proposition *me* like that. And why is she always flirting with you and insulting Maria?"

"Because I'm the only one who says *nein (no)* to her."

Nila shook her head. "What decent woman flirts with a married man? She has no shame, that trollop. If I were tall enough, I'd grab her by the hair and drag her outside, then teach her a thing or two."

Ollie laughed. "Now that would be a fight I'd pay to see!"

Around midnight, Randolph the Bull walked in, surprising everyone. Though he had cleaned up some, his face was still badly cut, bruised, and swollen, and he probably should have been under observation in the hospital. Gossip and murmuring filled the room, people staring, some in admiration for the gladiator, others in disdain for the gambling losses they incurred because of him, turning their backs. But Randolph didn't care. He needed a cold drink and some hot food, so he ignored them all and looked around for a place to sit.

Hanz waved him over; there was an empty seat at the bar next to him and Ollie.

"*Verräter (Traitor)*," a disgruntled older man murmured at him. He had lost his pension check on the fight.

Randolph sat down on the stool and nodded at the German farmer for his goodwill.

"What can I get you, sir?" Nila asked, glancing excitedly at Hanz, having never met a celebrity before. After all, Randolph the Bull was a well-known, respected champion boxer throughout Europe, despite his loss that night.

"I'll have a Mampe Halb & Halb," he answered, his deep voice intimidating, just like his physique.

Hanz looked at him and almost laughed. Though he himself was drinking Chartreuse, he didn't expect the brawny boxer to order a liqueur as well. But then again, the German drink made from bitter oranges and 160 herbs, labeled *Halb & Halb (Half & Half)* because it was half bitter and half sweet, was so good it won the grand prize at the World Fair in 1904.

"And I'm hungry," Randolph said. "Go fetch me something to eat, woman."

"What do I look like, your personal chef?" Nila barked, scowling at him.

Randolph's face sobered. "*Nein*, ahh . . . I just need a *gute* meal."

"Then learn to ask with some manners."

"*Entschuldigung (Sorry)*."

Nila softened somewhat. "The kitchen is closed now, but there's some tasty roast beef in the back, just cooked today. I could make you a sandwich with a bowl of hot pea soup."

Randolph the Bull nodded. "Please add some sauerkraut with that. *Danke (Thank you)*," he said, winking at her.

Nila smiled, poured his Mampe Halb & Halb and left the bottle, then went to the kitchen to make his dinner.

"Damn," Randolph said when she was no longer within earshot, eyeing her as she walked away. "That one's a firecracker."

Hanz chuckled. "More like dynamite, *mein Freund*. Don't let her tiny size fool you."

"No, sir!" added Ollie. "Our little Nila is thunder and lightning in a bottle."

All three men laughed.

Hanz watched as the Bull downed a shot, then another, and another. "That was quite a fight tonight," he said. "Fifteen brutal rounds."

Ollie nodded enthusiastically. "It was, it was. A fight to remember."

Randolph glanced at them and grunted.

"But the young German seemed ready for you."

"I'll get him next time," Randolph mumbled.

"Don't worry," said Ollie. "Just add enough vodka to that lemonade, and soon you won't even remember you lost."

This time the Bull didn't laugh. Glancing at Hanz again, he said, "You look a bit like the man I just fought. Is Albrecht Braun your *Bruder (brother)*?"

"*Nein*, my younger *Bruder* is only sixteen years old," said Hanz, noticing the Star of David around Randolph's neck. "And my older *Bruder*, he . . . he passed away some years ago."

"Sorry to hear. Was it the war?"

Hanz simply shook his head and tossed back his drink.

Randolph could tell there was a sad story there. He examined Hanz more closely, taking note of his height and solid frame. "Have you ever boxed?"

"*Nein*, I'm just a farmer."

"And a mortician," said Ollie with a chuckle.

Randolph looked surprised. "No kidding. I'm sharing a drink with an undertaker? Holy Mother of God, I almost required your services tonight."

Hanz's father had served as the local mortician before one became available in town. He had trained his son to be the same, and even now many would bring their deceased loved ones to Hanz to prepare them for the wake that would take place at the surviving family's home. He didn't enjoy the work, but he performed the duty, nonetheless. "I only do that when called upon," he said. "I won't deny a grieving family member."

Ollie brought the conversation back to boxing. "I've thought about becoming a boxer myself," he said, nonchalantly taking a drink, trying to impress the Bull. "In the lightweight division, of course."

Randolph looked at Ollie and laughed, displaying his missing tooth. "Yeah, the *really* lightweight division."

Ollie laughed too. Feeling confident from the alcohol, he asked, "What makes a man want to go into a ring and try to kill another man with his bare hands?"

"Or be killed," added Hanz.

Randolph contemplated the question. No one had ever asked him that before. Downing a fourth shot of Mampe Halb & Halb, he stared at the empty shot glass and answered, "It's an addiction like this alcohol. Once it's in your blood, it excites, liberates, and poisons you all at once. You love it and hate it at the same time."

The men sat in silence for a moment, musing over their own love-hate addictions.

Three Italian girls walked past, and Ollie, now rather inebriated, whistled and shouted out to them in broken Italian, *"Posso sposare il tuo prezioso cane per stasera?"* His wife was from Sicily, and she had taught him a few words. He thought he had asked, "Would one of you beautiful women marry me for tonight?", but what he really said was, "I can marry your precious dog for tonight?"

The women looked confused, frowning and shaking their heads at the creep. Randolph, fluent in Italian, laughed like hell. He laughed so hard the sound bellowed through the entire pub, and when he translated for Hanz what Ollie had said, all three of them practically rolled on the floor.

This went on all night, drinking, joking, and laughing like they'd known each other all their lives.

At one point, and Hanz didn't know why, he reached into his pocket and pulled out the boxer's gold tooth. "Here," he said. "I believe this belongs to you."

Randolph the Bull stared at it as if trying to decide whether or not to take back an unfaithful lover. He remembered the day the dentist had added the gold veneer, and how it made him smile more because he liked how it shined. "What *gute* is that to me now?"

"Maybe it'll bring you better luck next time."

"I lost the fight, and the tooth. You keep it if you think it's lucky."

Hanz stuck the gold tooth back in his pocket. "You're a champion boxer, *mein Freund.* If that doesn't make this tooth lucky, I don't know what would."

And with that, a friendship began between a German farmer named Hanz Wolff, his skinny sidekick named Ollie van Heinz, and a professional boxer–a Polish Jew–named Randolph the Bull.

The Devil's Needle finally closed, but Hanz and Ollie didn't want to go home, and Randolph the Bull didn't want to go back to his hotel. Hanz for reasons he didn't want to talk about, Ollie because he was glad to have a night off from the responsibilities of his wife and four small children, and Randolph because he had nothing else to do before leaving the small town.

Before the three men left the tavern, however, Randolph said to Nila, *"Danke für die verwässerten Getränke (Thanks for the watered-down drinks)."*

That offended Nila greatly, and she would have slapped him had it not been for his already bruised up face. An argument ensued–she called him a rude beast; he called her a nag. Seconds later, as they stared each other down, they both broke out in laughter.

"How did you know I'm a beast?" he asked.

She coyly smiled. "Isn't it obvious?"

"I'll tell you what's obvious," Ollie said in a low voice to Hanz. "Those two like each other."

Though Randolph the Bull was a professional boxer who had traveled throughout Europe and made a decent income, deep down he was a simple man of few pleasures. Give him a roof over his head, a change of clothes, his Mampe Halb & Halb and a pot of hot stew, and he was a happy man. What was missing, however, was a woman after his own heart, and now that he could see the end of his fighting career on the horizon, he found himself searching for one. Something about Nila grabbed him, and though she tried to hide it, something about the Bull hooked her too.

"Instead of nagging me, maybe you can show me around your *schöne Stadt (beautiful town)* tomorrow," Randolph said, smiling with a gaping hole between his teeth, no longer shining with gold.

Nila blushed. "All right. You need some culture in that brute head of yours, anyway."

"*Ja, ja, ja, los geht's (Yeah, yeah, yeah, let's go),*" Hanz said to the Bull, interrupting the new lovebirds. He knew that his neighbor, Günther Nachtnebel, had a makeshift pub in his barn with a homemade distillery, and that's where he wanted to go next. It smelled like a barn but looked like a laboratory, its labyrinthine maze of copper and iron machinery producing the sweet secret nectar.

Several farmers were already there when they arrived, congregating like horses at a watering hole, and they eagerly joined them. Before long, all the men were staggering outside, gazing up at the German night sky sparkling with an infinite tapestry of lustrous stars–a poor man's diamonds–singing while Günther serenaded them on his hümmelchen. With warm bellies and lifted spirits, their troubles were far away.

One of the farmers made an enormous bonfire, and the inebriated men gathered around and started talking about boxing, each giving Randolph the Bull his two cents on fighting.

"You need to keep your head up, son," one farmer slurred. "That's the key."

"Are you crazy?" said another, swaying side to side. "That's how you get knocked out. He needs to keep his chin down."

A third offered his own boxing expertise. "Keep your fists high, then strike your opponent. Like this," he said, trying to demonstrate his technique, stumbling as he punched at the air. Everyone laughed when the man tumbled to the ground from his own punch.

Close to sunrise, the party was over. Randolph was passed out in the horse and buggy, still holding a bottle of moonshine and murmuring something about a rematch, and Ollie offered to drive Hanz all the way home. But Hanz refused, wanting to walk the rest of the way. Ollie saw the sadness returning in his friend's eyes and patted him on the back before leaving, trying to comfort him. "My prayers are for the little one you just lost, *mein Freund*," he said. "May God bless you and Maria with children someday."

"*Danke*, Ollie. Make sure the Bull gets back to his hotel safely. *Gute Nacht (Good night).*"

"I will. *Gute Nacht*, Hanz."

As he made his way down the long dirt road to his home–a house now steeped in mourning–moonshine coursing through his veins, the reverberations of the bell from the boxing match and his neighbor's bagpipes still tingling his skin, a sense of melancholy settled over Hanz, thinking about the infant he had recently buried. Small, pink, and scrunched up like a bud before bloom, the tiny boy had not survived this world. Oh, how his heart ached for the life his son could have lived, and for the love the child had both lost and taken with him into the cold earth.

The moon was out, full and white, like a polished pearl poking out from a deep black sea. A fog drifted in, floating halfway up the trees. And a chill settled in the air. Hanz tried to push the sad thoughts out of his mind, and that's when he saw her . . .

A ghost.

A young girl, not any older than sixteen, draped in a cloak.

He stopped, his hips seemingly locking in place, and stared at her in disbelief. Her small, pale face seemed to glow in the darkness, radiating an ethereal light against a backdrop of towering trees. Was she there as another somber reminder of his life's inherent sadness—a despondency that no amount of alcohol could quell?

Standing there on the deserted road, Hanz rubbed his eyes to better focus on this mysterious forest apparition. Perhaps she was the ghost of someone he had previously prepared for burial. Or maybe just a stranger reaching out from the other side. Regardless, he knew we all encounter a spectral presence at some point in our life, whether we recognize it or not. A prickly breeze on the nape of our neck, a soundless whisper that echoes in the heart, a fleeting shadow grasping at something just out of reach, or a long-lost lover forever etched in memory. Everyone was haunted in one form or another, either by the past or fear of the future, and no one was exempt from life's cruel, unbidden intrusions that curse us at will.

And yet, to Hanz's surprise, he felt no fear. Why am I not afraid, he questioned as their eyes locked in a prolonged, intense stare—hers glistening with an infinite, glossy dark hue, his a curious sky blue? When she didn't vanish, it occurred to him that he might be hallucinating. It wouldn't have been surprising. After all, his wife Maria had just suffered a terrible stillbirth, and due to complications they were told she'd never bear children again. She had since confined herself to bed, and their home had become a barren landscape, devoid of her once vibrant laughter. The stress of it all, the emotional exhaustion, and the overindulgence in alcohol that night could easily be playing tricks on his eyes.

Suddenly she cried out, "Help me, please! Help me!"

Startled, Hanz hurried over to her, and she collapsed into his arms . . .

The strong, musty smell of hay, manure, and farm animals saturated his nose when Hanz woke up late that morning. *What am I doing in the barn,* he wondered, lying on a bed of straw as the room slightly spun? It felt as if someone had driven an axe into his head, and his mouth had become the Sahara Desert. *I guess I passed out here last night.*

Hanz got up slowly, his stomach threatening to purge. The strange dream he had started filtering through the haziness in his mind, materializing into coherent thoughts. And then it hit him . . .

The girl! That was no dream; she was real!

Climbing up into the loft where he had let her spend the night, he looked around but she was nowhere to be found. *Hmm . . . was she a ghost after all?* No, she was definitely real. He remembered staying with her until she had calmed, asking her what happened and why she was in such distress, her face bruised and lip cut. But all she would say was, "My family is going to disown me," over and over and, "My life is ruined now," wringing her hands and sobbing. It almost seemed as if she wanted to say more yet was afraid. *Shame, regret, fear—they are powerful deterrents.*

People handle sorrow differently, and for Hanz it was the drink that softened the sharp spear of grief. Still, he was disappointed in himself–again–for drinking so much the night before. "A man takes a drink, the drink takes a drink, then the drink takes the man," his mother used to say, her words ricocheting in his mind.

Leaving the barn, Hanz went to the hand pump in the yard to splash water on his face, then headed to the farmhouse. As he opened the door, one of the cats brushed up against his leg, and he knelt to pet it. The house was quiet, and even though it was nearly noon, he knew his wife would still be in bed. A part of him wanted to undress and go lie next to her; another part wanted him to run and never look back.

When he entered their bedroom, Maria was lying on her side, the curve of her hip exposed from the brown linen sheet like a seashell poking up from the sand. Hanz reached down and gently caressed her skin with the back of his hand; she turned to look up at him. She didn't have to say anything; her sad eyes reflected it all.

The husband and wife in their mid-twenties had previously epitomized a happy German couple. That is until the tragedy suddenly struck, bringing a profound emptiness into their lives. An ache that infiltrated deep to their very core. They had yearned to start a family, to have children of their own, but the universe was determined to deny them that simple joy.

"Are you absolutely certain of this?" Hanz had asked Dr. Schultz that calamitous day. "She's now infertile?"

The doctor somberly nodded. "I'm sorry, *mein Freund.*"

Hanz observed his sleeping wife recovering in the hospital bed. Maria's womb had cradled their dream for nine months, and now it was all over. "I promised her a happy life with children," he said. "How can I tell her this now?"

Dr. Schultz patted him on the back and left the room.

When Maria later found out, she wailed and wailed. Never before had Hanz heard someone cry that way. For a woman who was deaf, the excruciating sounds that expelled deep from within her soul were spine-chilling.

Hanz chased that traumatic memory from his mind and slowly undressed.

"Sometimes I wish I had died during the delivery," Maria whispered, her voice small and sad. "At least I'd be with my child in heaven now." She began to cry.

Hanz lifted her chin to meet his gaze. "But you're alive, *meine Liebe (my love)*. You're alive, and I need you here with me among the living."

Maria just kept weeping.

Hanz simply held her.

⁓❧⁓

The following day, Hanz was working with the Jewish family who helped him maintain the vineyard. They had been working this farm for many years, and to him they were like his own family. One of them called out to him that a visitor was approaching, and when Hanz looked up, he saw the looming figure of his uncle Jürgen. A banker in Berlin, Jürgen Wolff had been wanting his nephew to sell the property and move with Maria to the city. They shook hands and walked along the field together.

"You really should have hired a *gute* German family to help you with the vineyard," Jürgen said, eyeing the Jewish workers with concern.

"Why?" asked Hanz.

"For appearances' sake."

Hanz rebuffed him. "'*From one man He made all the nations.*' Isn't that what we learned in church?" It was a scripture his wife often quoted whenever she saw bigotry or oppression of any kind.

Jürgen scanned the property. "It's a beautiful place here, Hanz; no one's going to deny that. But knowing Maria can never have children now, you should sell this farm and start over in the city. It'll be a new and easier life for you both. More comforts, no more hard labor in the fields, and I can get you a decent job with the bank."

Hanz contemplated his uncle's offer as he too scanned his property. "Maybe I'll consider it sometime in the future."

"The hell with future! You're not listening to me!"

"Why do you care, anyway?"

"Because I feel a responsibility for you, damn it! You're my *Bruder's* son, and his three children need my direction now."

"I appreciate your concern, Uncle Jürgen, but I'm a grown man now too, and I make my own decisions. This is my father's legacy, and my grandfather's before that. I promised I would carry it on. Besides, Maria and I are happy here."

"Happy?" Jürgen scoffed, cleaning his spectacles with his shirt. "She's now barren and depressed, and from what I hear, you're becoming a drunkard. With no children in your future, it's going to get lonely as hell out here, and you'll both spiral further until you eventually lose this place anyway."

"That's not true," Hanz said, frowning at his uncle's assertion. "Maria and I can still have a family."

"Oh yeah? How?"

"We can adopt."

Jürgen shrugged. "Perhaps. There are plenty of orphans who need homes. But it's too bad you couldn't have one of your own." They stopped at a small pond on the property where the water shimmered as if liquid mercury, the sun's reflection adding molten gold. Jürgen shook his head and said, "Bad luck follows this family."

"What do you mean?" asked Hanz.

"First your older *Bruder* commits suicide after shaming the family. Then your father is killed by his damn horse. And now this."

The subject of Hanz's brother Andrew had always been an open wound with him. He was only a young boy when Andrew took his own life, and he missed his brother terribly. The kind, soft-spoken older sibling had many secrets and demons but was always good to Hanz. After his death, not one family member ever spoke of him. As if he didn't exist. "Andrew suffered," was all Hanz said.

"*Ja*, and we all know why. Shame. Pure shame."

"Why was there no funeral?" Hanz asked. "I was young, and I don't remember. And why didn't my father prepare his body for burial?"

Jürgen didn't answer him. He only took out crumbs from his pocket and walked over to the edge of the pond to feed the visiting swans.

Just then, the wind carried with it *The Song of the Sea*, the archaic Hebrew poem from the Book of Exodus, where the Israelites exalted their God for saving them from Pharoah's army after crossing the Red Sea. The Jewish family was singing it as they worked, and it pulled Hanz in. As he listened to the powerful song, the invisible force created a division between him and his uncle, like the pillar of fire God had erected to guide and protect His people as they left Egypt and wandered through the wilderness on their way to the Promised Land. The sound grew stronger, his heartbeat quickened, and no sooner did his uncle wave him over to continue the debate over selling his property than Hanz abruptly turned and walked away, leaving Jürgen standing there, returning to help his Jewish workers.

～⚜～

Another week had passed, and Maria was up by dawn one morning, making breakfast in the kitchen.

"*Guten Morgen, meine Liebe (Good morning, my love),*" Hanz said, surprised to see her up and about so early as he entered the house. He had just finished talking to a grieving father in the yard. The man had brought his deceased nine-year-old son to the Wolff farm for burial preparation.

"What happened to that little boy?" Maria asked, having watched the men through the kitchen window.

"He drowned in the Tauber River. Poor lad went fishing by himself and fell in. His father said he couldn't swim."

"I want to help prepare his body."

Hanz hesitated. "Are you sure, *meine Liebe?* It might be better if you don't."

"*Nein*, let me help you," she said, placing a plate of eggs and sausage on the table and pouring a cup of coffee for him. "I want to."

After breakfast, the couple went to the special one-room building next to the barn where Hanz always prepared the dead bodies. A large metal table sat in the middle with the little boy on top, covered by a white sheet, his head forming a round bump under the material and his toes poking up at the end. He looked so small under there. So helpless. Lifeless.

Hanz and Maria both washed up at the sink using the pine tar soap made from the resin of the pine trees on their property. Used for centuries, its antibacterial and antifungal properties were well-suited for the task. Next, Hanz began the process he had been taught by his father, while Maria assisted, taking direction from her husband.

When Hanz first removed the sheet, they both stared at the little boy for a long moment. Was this what their own son would have looked like, had he lived and grown to this age, they each wondered?

Maria recalled the miraculous resurrection recorded in the Holy Scriptures at 2 Kings 4:34-35, where the prophet Elisha had restored the life of the son of a Shunammite woman. The boy had suddenly died, and after Elisha beseeched Almighty God in prayer, he got up on the bed and lay down on the child, putting his own mouth on the boy's mouth, his own eyes on his eyes, and his own palms on his palms. Soon the child's body started to grow warm, and the boy sneezed seven times, after which he opened his eyes. If only she could do the same, Maria wished. What joy she could bring to that grieving mother and father, wiping out their unbearable pain. Pain which she was all too familiar with.

Hanz was slow and deliberate as he gently washed the body, as if he were painting a portrait, dignity and respect in each stroke. He took this task extremely seriously, honoring the dead. Maria followed her husband's lead.

After the entire process was done, the boy's body washed and prepped, dressed and ready to be picked up, Hanz looked at his wife. She placed the back of her hand on the boy's cheek, tears falling down her own. When he came around the table to hold her, she buried her face into his collar, smothering her tears and wrapping her arms around him.

Strangely, in that moment, Hanz thought of the young girl he had met in the forest several days earlier. The one he had thought was a ghost. She too had fallen into his arms and wept, and he held her just as he was holding his wife now. Curious over who she was, why she was there, and where she went, he wondered if he'd ever see her again . . .

CHAPTER 2

Nine Months Later

Hanz Wolff was a good man.

Quiet, thoughtful, mild-mannered and slow to anger, his towering figure could easily be spotted miles away as he ambled along his property inspecting his crops, his stride slow and his gait conspicuous. The Great War had left him with a bad knee, but he was grateful to have survived.

Everyone in the village trusted and admired Hanz, forthright and principled as he was, never having told a falsehood in his life. That is until the day he received the precious gifts that resurrected Maria's spirit, restored joy to the farm, and fortified him with an unbreakable resolve to protect their newfound happiness—with his life, if necessary.

Yes, "Honest Hanz," the friendly farmer and mortician with a gentle hand, was prepared to take that lie to his grave . . .

∼◦⬩◦∼

In the hinterlands of 1920s Germany, where the musty tang of soil and the sweet redolence of pastures lingered in the air, the modest Wolff farm lay nestled in the countryside west of the picturesque town of Rothenburg ob der Tauber. The area was a Shangri-La of God's creation, surrounded by thousand-year-old linden trees growing in the forest, holding secrets of the land, their thick trunks covered in electric green moss at the base and their roots sunk deep into the ground, drinking from silver-blue streams bleeding through it.

Hanz and his deaf wife Maria had created a humble sanctuary in this empyrean setting, far removed from the looming chaos of city life. Shielded by straw hats from the relentless summer sun, they toiled diligently in the fields, their callused hands nurturing the meager crops and livestock that sustained their simple lives.

Rothenburg ob der Tauber, in the heart of Northern Bavaria, was several miles from the Wolff farm. Like a gem in a crown of rolling hills, seemingly conjured from the pages of a fairy tale, its monicker meant "red fortress above the Tauber"–an eighty-two-mile tributary that snaked its way through the land. The town was founded in 1274 and stood as a testament to medieval charm, with its winding cobblestone streets, enchanting alleyways, and whimsical half-timbered houses. These quaint abodes, with their playful facades, resembled gingerbread creations adorned with windows of plated sugar and shutters of white frosting, captivating every onlooker's imagination.

The town was also a fortified citadel, complete with preserved gatehouses and towers offering panoramic views of the surrounding countryside. Its defensive stone walls, lined with patrol paths, watchtowers, and front battlements bearing silent cannons, spoke of a time when Rothenburg stood as a sentinel against the tides of war.

In the bustling *Marktplatz (marketplace)*, the air was alive with the scent of sweet pastries and aromatic coffee from nearby cafés, mingling with the earthy fragrance of the morning's harvest. Vendors arranged their stalls with a cheerful diligence, laying out wares that ranged from handcrafted goods

29

to the freshest of local produce. The iconic *Rathaus (Town Hall)*, a magnificent Renaissance building, cast an observant eye over the square. Its 200-foot clock tower, standing proudly against the sky, chimed the hour, its sound echoing off the ancient walls and down the winding, narrow lanes.

St. Jakobskirche (St. Jacob's Church), with its intricate, late Gothic, Holy Blood altarpiece by the renowned woodcarver Tilman Riemenschneider, sat prominently close to the town center. It was within these hallowed walls that many lovers had exchanged their vows, under the watchful gaze of history and the Divine.

Throughout the day, the town pulsed with a life uniquely its own. Elderly locals, their faces etched with the wisdom of years, sat on wooden benches, exchanging news and playing chess. Their laughter and chatter added to the symphony of daily life, as children ran past them, their games and shouts permeating the neighborhood with youthful energy.

Down by the Tauber River, the reflection of the town shimmered on the water's surface. Fishermen prepared their boats, casting nets with the hope of a bountiful catch, the smell of fish and packing salt in the air; while women scrubbed clothes at the water's edge, their gossip and singing accompanied by birds chirping with flair.

Nightfall always brought a hush over Rothenburg ob der Tauber. The lamps flickered to life, diffusing a warm, golden light over the cobblestones. The town, cradled within its ancient walls, would then whisper tales of yesteryear to those who walked its paths—a living chronicle of resilience, beauty, and a spirit steeped in the annals of time.

Hanz tied his horse and buggy to a tree and walked to the heart of the town. He was there for a special reason that day—to buy his wife a replacement ring for the trinket band he had bought her when they got engaged. Married right after the Great War and unable to afford a wedding ring worthy of his bride, he wanted to rectify that flaw. Though he had sold a cow and two sheep to raise the money, he still didn't have enough, so he planned on selling one of his paintings to garner the rest. It was not the first time the German farmer had sold his impressive artwork to raise some cash. He even made violins and sold them too.

"Mein Freund!" Mr. Giovanni Mandolini greeted as Hanz opened the door to his art gallery, door chimes ringing. "Come in, come in!" It was still early, and the Italian owner was opening the curtains, letting the morning light flood the shop. "The other two pieces you brought me last month sold

the same day."

Hanz nodded, happy to hear they had sold. He pulled his new piece out of the protective leather cover–a painting of an orchard in the Bavarian Alps.

Mr. Mandolini lifted the canvas to the light to better inspect it. "Magnifico!" he said.

Hanz grinned.

"How do you make these look like photographs?"

"A lot of practice," said Hanz. "And patience."

The Italian art dealer hung it on the wall, went behind the counter, and pulled out the money. "You should go to France with your paintings," he said, handing the cash to Hanz. "Here in this tiny town, you will always be a farmer; but display your work there, and you'll become famous. Sell your land and take your wife to Paris; it will change your life."

Hanz thanked the man, accepted the money, and went on his way.

⁘

Stanley Horowitz was inspecting a two-carat diamond with his monocular loupe when Hanz entered the jeweler's store. The gemstone, emitting a mesmerizing sparkle, belonged to a Jewish woman standing with her back to Hanz, her posture tense as she anxiously awaited a fair price from the jeweler.

"I'll be with you in a minute, *mein Freund*," said Stanley, not looking up from the precious stone.

A Stollwerck chocolate vending machine stood conspicuously among the glass showcases full of glittering jewelry. Hanz had never seen one before and went up to examine the intriguing novelty.

"Go ahead and try it," Stanley encouraged, proud of his new contraption. "Put a coin from the dish in the top, and pull out your chocolate from the bottom. Compliments of the house."

"*Danke*," said Hanz. He smiled as the incongruous machine amid timeless treasures automatically dispensed its gift, putting the small chocolate bar in his pocket to give to Maria later.

Turning his attention to why he was there, Hanz stared through the glass of the display cabinet housing countless different rings, necklaces, earrings, and bracelets. An assortment of colors and styles winked back at him, twinkling like stars in the midnight sky. His eyes zeroed in on the sapphire ring he had picked out for Maria weeks earlier, relieved to see it was still there. But as he counted his money, to his chagrin he was short.

"How much will you give me for these too?" the Jewish woman asked Stanley, removing her diamond earrings and handing them to him. Her voice sounded familiar to Hanz. "They belonged to my great-grandmother, but I need the money now."

Stanley examined the earrings, just as he did the two-carat diamond. Buyer and seller agreed on a price, and the jeweler went to the back room to retrieve money from his safe.

As she waited, the woman glanced over at Hanz, her large brown eyes instantly changing from sad to surprised. "Hanz? . . . My goodness, is that you?"

Hanz, too, was caught off guard. "Josie . . ."

Josie Blum was her name. The two had been childhood sweethearts, each the other's first love. But her family was Jewish and his Catholic, so their parents put an end to the nascent romance before it had a chance to flourish. Josie was forced to marry a man she didn't love, whom her parents arranged through the Semitic tradition of shidduch, and Hanz went off to war. He found it ironic that on the day he was going to buy his wife a legitimate wedding ring, he'd meet the woman he first thought he was going to marry.

"It's *gute* to see you," said Hanz. "How are you?"

Josie removed a tissue from her clutch bag and wiped her nose. "Not so *gute*," she replied, her eyes returning to their former glum. "My husband ran off on me, and both my parents recently died from illness. I've had to sell what few valuables I have, and now I'm moving to Poland to live with my sister."

"I'm so sorry to hear that, Josie."

She steeled herself, bristling at his words, as if he were pitying her rather than showing empathy. "I saw your artwork for sale in Giovanni Mandolini's store," she said, shifting the focus away from her troubles. "It's outstanding. You've become quite the painter."

Hanz smiled. "*Danke.*"

"I still have the portrait you did of me when we were . . ." She stopped herself, unable to finish her sentence. The pain of their breakup was still raw, even after so many years.

"*Ja*, I remember," said Hanz. He had poured his heart and soul into that glorious painting years ago, her waist-length hair–black as night–flowing over her pale shoulders like a silken waterfall and her ebony eyes large and innocent.

"I'm taking it with me to Poland."

Hanz nodded.

"Remember when we used to lie on a bed of hay in the loft of your parents' barn, holding hands and dreaming of running off to Paris together? You were going to make violins and paint all day, selling your artwork in the market, and I was going to stay at home and raise our babies." She chuckled, mocking their youthful naïveté.

Hanz wondered why she was bringing this up, especially since they hadn't seen or heard from each other since before the war.

"You ever regret us not running off like we wanted to?" she asked, her eyes becoming sad again. "I do."

Though he loved Maria, Hanz too had often thought of the life he could have had with Josie, and how different it would have been living as an artist in Paris rather than a farmer in Germany. But there was no point in speculating about that now, and he chose not to answer.

Josie smiled, as if reading his mind. "How is your wife? Maria, right?"

"*Ja.* And she's *gute.*"

"Are you here to buy her something special?"

Hanz hesitated, then nodded.

"May I see what you picked out for her?"

He pointed at the sapphire ring beneath the vitrine glass.

"It's beautiful, Hanz. She's going to love it."

Stanley returned and handed Josie her money. As she counted it, he turned to Hanz and said, "I still have that ring for your wife, *mein Freund.*"

"I appreciate that," said Hanz, "but I'll have to come back for it another time. I miscounted my money and I'm short 6,000 Marks."

Josie placed 6,000 Marks on the counter. Both men looked up with surprise. "It's my gift to you, Hanz," she said, winking at him. "Have a happy life, and tell Maria I said *hallo (hello).*"

"*Nein*, Josie, I can't . . ."

"*Ja*, you can," she interrupted. Walking toward the door, she added over her shoulder, "Maybe someday you'll return the favor."

As Hanz guided his horse and buggy home along the winding dirt road, a rare and enchanting vision caught his eye: an albino fawn. Its seraphic beauty was stark against the green backdrop of the countryside, but the delicate creature was in distress, caught between the unforgiving rails of a farmer's fence.

Hanz immediately brought his horse to a halt. His boots crunched softly on the underbrush as he slowly approached the distressed animal, its spotless white coat shimmering like a ghostly specter in the sunlight. "It's all right, little one," he said in a calm voice. "I'm not going to hurt you."

The fawn's large, doe eyes, rimmed with the faintest touch of pink, met his gaze, frozen in fear and pain. With careful hands, Hanz worked to free it. The creature trembled but seemed to sense his compassionate intent, its panicked breaths slowing. Finally, with a gentle tug, the fawn was liberated, though it crumpled to the ground, its slender leg broken and unable to support its weight.

Hanz couldn't leave the baby deer to the mercy of wild predators, so he tenderly scooped it into his arms and brought it to his carriage, wrapping it in a blanket to keep it warm. The animal's eyes closed, comforted by the security of this stranger's care.

As he resumed his trek home, Hanz kept glancing back at the fawn, now resting peacefully. He knew this unexpected encounter had imposed on him a vital responsibility—to nurture this rare and beautiful creation back to health, just as he had done with himself and Maria.

The nine months that had passed since the tragedy seemed like an eternity. Maria was finally doing better, and life had gone somewhat back to normal. The bitter bite of winter, the promising renewal of spring, the warm kiss of summer—each season had progressively softened the scars as if God's hand were in the breeze, wiping everything clean. And even though the couple was still disheartened, the world seemed livable again, with hope resting on the horizon.

Hanz sat by the fireside in his favorite chair that evening, sipping on his vodka. As he gazed at his wife—a smoky blend of love and regret—she sat quietly on the sofa, knitting a sweater for him, manipulating the needles with innate precision while the dwindling daylight filtered through the living room window. A million crickets stridulated outside, and the burning wood in the fireplace crackled.

Hanz not only loved his wife but also admired her immensely. Bacterial meningitis had robbed her of the priceless gift of hearing when she was a child, but she did not let it define who she was, or how she'd live, or what her future had in store. No, as she grew up in her native Austria, she thrived with a silent strength, learning Austrian Sign Language but rarely using it, choosing instead to become proficient at reading lips, communicating with others as if she were no different from them. Though her speech had changed slightly over the years, she managed to retain most of her enunciation.

Growing up in a world of silence, Maria had found joy in the little things in life: The swaying wheat fields, undulating like a golden sea in the gusty breeze. The soft moonlight shining down on a babbling brook. The bumblebees pollinating the earth. The warmth of the sun on her face and the texture of the earth beneath her bare feet. She had an infectious spirit that touched everyone in her path, and her geniality made people smile. Not to mention her striking appearance–something to behold. With fiery red hair and unblemished fair skin, her beauty rivaled the Austrian Alps themselves.

An inspiration to all who knew her, Maria was not a victim of her circumstance but a master of her destiny. She did not think of all the things she couldn't do, but rather, all the things she could. Because Maria Wolff was not defined by being deaf . . . Being deaf was defined by her.

While remaining focused on her work, Maria sensed her husband watching her. "That's something rare and special to find an albino fawn," she said. "I remember reading somewhere that the American Indians consider a white deer to be sacred and a bringer of *gute* fortune."

"Interesting," replied Hanz.

"Too bad you didn't find it nine months ago," she muttered, crestfallen in tone.

The mood in the room turned doleful, and the couple sat in silence, sequestered by their melancholic thoughts.

"I heard Elise had a daughter," Maria finally said, breaking the reticence. Their neighbors were seeking to start a family too.

"*Ja*, Clovis came and told me."

"What a blessing for her." Maria put down her knitting needles and stared sadly into nothing. "I should have held our baby," she said, lamenting about the past. Unable to bring herself to hold their dead child the day they removed it from her womb, she had regretted it ever since. "Before you buried it, I should have."

Hanz recalled burying their stillborn son, planting a rosebush above the grave. For weeks afterward, Maria had knelt before it, whispering to herself and praying. It was hard to witness his wife in such pain. Getting up from his chair, he went over to the couch and sat next to her. "We have a life here, *meine Liebe (my love),*" he said softly, trying to be positive. "A home. You'll recover from this."

Maria, who had a personality to match her scarlet locks, could go from hot to cold in an instant. She pulled away and wiped her teary eyes. "*Nein,* we just share the same cage, that's all. If we don't have children, I don't want to live here anymore. And I don't even want to be married."

"Maria . . . I know you don't mean that."

She frowned and folded her arms over her chest. "I mean it, Hanz."

He looked at her for a moment, then reached into his pocket and gave her the chocolate bar he had saved for her.

"*Danke,*" she said, without a commensurate smile.

"I got it from a Stollwerck device called a vending machine. You should see it, Maria. You put a coin in it and out comes a chocolate bar."

She narrowed her eyes at him, thinking he was teasing her.

"It's true. Stanley Horowitz has one in his jewelry store."

Maria opened the wrapper and took a bite of the sweet confection, her mood instantly improving.

"I saw Josie Blum there, too. Poor girl. She was selling her jewelry because her husband left her, and then her parents both died. Now she has to move to Poland and live with her sister."

"Why were you at the jewelry store?"

Hanz smiled, caressing her cheek. Reaching into his other pocket, he pulled out a small velvet box. "I have something for you, *meine Liebe.*"

Maria blinked hard as he opened it, staring down at the sapphire stone ring in his hand. The indigo blue caught the dancing flames in the fireplace and sparkled.

"Something worthy of my *süße Braut (sweet bride).*"

"Oh, Hanz," Maria said, smiling widely. "*Es ist wunderschön (It's beautiful).*"

He placed it on her ring finger. "Let this symbolize a new beginning for us. Please say you'll keep trying for me."

Maria leaned in and kissed him, allowing a sense of hope to infuse her heart. "I will, Hanz. I will try for us both."

Maria retired early, and Hanz took out his cherished violin, an instrument he had made with his own two hands. He played one of Mozart's most famous works: *Violin Concerto No. 5 in A Major*, sometimes referred to by its nickname, "Turkish," due to some Turkish style elements in the final movement that added flavor to the piece. Written in 1775 in Maria's home country of Austria, it was one of Hanz's favorites. He loved Mozart and played the Renaissance great's five violin concertos often, and it saddened him that his wife could not experience the wondrous joy of music. Music from his own hand.

Before turning in for the night, Hanz went to check on the albino fawn convalescing in his barn. There, nestled in the cozy enclave of hay he had meticulously prepared for it, the tiny deer lay quietly slumbering, its pristine white coat shining under the glow of his kerosene lamp.

Hanz inspected its broken leg, carefully set with a homemade splint, mindful not to startle the quiescent creature. He remembered bottle-feeding it goat milk earlier, the fawn's trusting eyes locking onto his as it drank hungrily, and it made him smile. "Be strong, little one," he whispered to the genetic marvel. "Tomorrow will be a better day. For all of us."

The following morning, when Hanz opened the barn door, the familiar scent of hay, manure, and farm animals thrust through his nostrils. His horses, cows, sheep, goats, and chickens were all safely ensconced inside—he had brought them in the night before for protection from the threat of a storm. Their typical ease around each other was disrupted this morning, though, behaving rather oddly, as if they knew something fragile was in their midst. The last time this happened, a litter of kittens had been born in the loft, and now there was an albino fawn sharing their space. That must be it, he figured.

At the far end of the barn, Agatha, his usually gluttonous cow, faced away from her hay, her large brown eyes twinkling. Bucephalus, his beloved stallion named after Alexander the Great's horse, leaned his head over the stall, his velvety muzzle gently sniffing at something on the ground. Hanz's curiosity piqued, and he approached the object . . .

"What the . . . What in God's name . . . My God!"

Hanz couldn't believe his eyes. There, in a double wicker basket among the straw, lay two Sleeping Beauties! The twin girls–perhaps only a few days old–slept peacefully under the watchful care of Agatha and Bucephalus who seemed to know that two new lives had entered the Homo sapiens world.

As the early morning light filtered through the wooden slats of the barn wall, illuminating the babies' innocent faces, Hanz stared in shock at the astonishing sight, his azure blue eyes unblinking. His heart thumped in his chest. Where was their mother? Looking around inside the barn, he saw no one. *"Hallo?"* he called out. "Is there anyone here?" Running outside, he only saw the birds singing in the trees and heard the distant barking of a dog.

Hanz ran back inside the barn to inspect the babies. Wrapped in woolen blankets embroidered with the unmistakable Star of David, their peaceful slumber belied their mysterious arrival. With his heart still racing, he knelt beside the basket, and a tiny hand emerged, accompanied by a soft coo. He touched the baby's hand, and it opened its eyes, grasping his finger.

Overwhelmed, Hanz ever so gently picked up the infant. It felt like a small bag of warm mashed potatoes. Tender feelings came over him, and he softly spoke to it, just as he had done to the stillborn he held before burying it. The baby wriggled in his arms, and he smiled at the miracle of life.

As he placed the child back in the basket, a weathered note became visible, tucked between the newborns. Hanz read the letter, from a girl named Abigail Katz, her words resonating with despair as she pleaded with the German couple to care for her babies as their own. It detailed the young Jewish mother's plight: abandoned by her boyfriend, unsupported by her parents, disgraced and forced to give them away. She said she had heard Hanz and his wife had recently lost a child, and believed that her daughters would be loved and cherished by them.

Picking up the wicker basket, Hanz held it tight with both hands and rushed to the farmhouse.

⁓⁓

"Hanz, let me sleep a little longer," Maria mumbled as her husband shook her in bed. When he didn't leave, she slowly rolled over to face him, pushing her messy red hair away from her face.

"Look!" Hanz lowered the wicker basket onto the mattress. "Something *wunderbar (wonderful)* has happened!" he said, smiling the same way he had when they first met in Austria. The same way he had when he asked for her hand in marriage, and when he told her he inherited the farm.

Maria peered into the basket, her eyes growing wide.

"I found them in the barn, and there was a note that said a young mother had died giving birth to them." Hanz lied. "She was a teenager, and her strict parents don't want her illegitimate babies. The father is a teenager too, and he abandoned them."

"What? Slow down; you're talking too fast."

Hanz repeated what he said, slowing down so she could read every word off his lips.

"This is a dream," said Maria, as if trying to wake herself from it.

"*Nein, meine Liebe*, you're not dreaming! God has heard our prayers! We have two beautiful daughters now!"

Maria blinked hard to ensure she was indeed awake. "Where is this note, Hanz? I want to read it."

"I . . . I burned it." Again, he lied. But how could he tell his wife the truth? If Maria knew the mother was alive, she would try to find her. She would perpetually worry that someday the girl would come back for her children.

"Why would you do that?"

"Maria, the babies were left for us. And the note said to burn it if we accept them as our own."

One of the infants began to cry, and Maria picked it up. "There, there," she comforted, cradling it close in her arms. "Don't cry, little one. I'm here." To her utter joy, the baby stopped crying and reached out to touch her, staring up at her in absolute wonder.

～⚜～

Time froze on the farm that day as a surrealness enveloped the German couple, coming to terms with what this meant: These two precious Jewish babies were purposely left for them to raise and call their own. The horrendous stillbirth, the heartache and shattered dreams—all of it didn't seem to matter now. Finally they could live the life they yearned for, planning their future with newfound exultation rather than going through the motions with mundane rigor.

What a miracle!

But what about their neighbors? And the townsfolk? Abigail Katz had said in her letter that her parents sent her away to Poland when she started showing, and that no one in the village must know of her past pregnancy, or that Ava and Shalom–the babies' birth names–were hers. She wanted them to swear an oath to God that they would keep her secret. Their secret.

"Hanz, what are we going to tell people?" Maria asked, still unsure of this unbelievable providence.

"We'll say we got them from an orphanage," he replied, determined to take this secret to his grave.

Maria rocked the cradle he had built for the child they lost nine months earlier, the twin girls sleeping soundly in the wooden crib. "*Nein*, I want to say I gave birth to them. I want people to believe they are mine."

"But Dr. Schultz knows you can't bear children anymore."

"Doctors can be wrong."

"What are you saying–that we pretend you were pregnant and didn't tell anyone?"

"*Ja.*"

Hanz looked intently at his wife, his stern eyes and furrowed brow revealing the maelstrom of thoughts, plans, falsehoods, coverups, and repercussions thrashing about in his head. "I don't know, Maria."

"We'll say we kept it private because of the stillbirth. People will understand. Besides, we live out here alone in the middle of nowhere, and we only need to pretend for a few weeks since no one has seen me in months. I can stay out of sight for that long."

"What about the delivery?"

"It happened suddenly, and there was no time to go to the hospital." Maria gave him a smile of confidence, pulling him into her embrace to reassure him that this would work.

He reluctantly agreed.

"We have two daughters, Hanz," she whispered, tears welling in her eyes. "They're ours forever, right? Gifts from God."

"*Ja, meine Liebe.* Two precious gifts from God," he replied, tenderly kissing his wife.

CHAPTER 3

Hanz had to be sure. Though the letter from Abigail Katz had made her intentions clear, he was determined to talk to her, to look her in the eye and ascertain her veracity and fortitude. The gravity of the situation was too great—a life-changing outcome for her, for them—and before introducing the baby girls to the world as their own, he had to know that Abigail Katz was of sound mind, mentally and emotionally, and not making a rash decision under duress.

Saddling his horse Bucephalus, Hanz made the trip to Rothenburg ob der Tauber. The Jewish quarter was in the northern section of the town. Upon arrival, he tied his stallion to a tree and proceeded on foot, an entire world, both familiar and foreign, unfolding before him. Woodsmoke and roasted meats scented the air, and children played in the cobblestone streets, squabbling in Yiddish. His golden hair and pale skin were stark amid the dark locks and olive complexions, a vivid contrast to the Semitic heritage that surrounded him.

As he navigated the community, he wondered if, in the broad light of day, he would recognize the girl whose life was now intricately woven with his own in such a far-reaching way. A young boy with sidelocks and noticeably thick lashes approached with an air of curiosity. "Who are you looking for?" he asked, his innocent tone void of suspicion.

"Abigail Katz," replied Hanz.

With a knowledgeable nod, the boy pointed toward the river where she often washed clothes in the afternoon. Hanz thanked him and made his way down the cobblestone path, a strange symphony of emotions growing with each step—apprehension, gratitude, and a tangle of what might be guilt. As he neared the river, he heard the rhythmic sound of wet cloth meeting stone, a domestic percussion that set his heart racing. Finally, he spotted her. Abigail was knee-deep in the river, her skirt hiked up to avoid the water. Her eyes were focused, her hands working methodically as she scrubbed fabric against rock, a bundle of wet clothes resting in a basket on the riverbank.

"*Hallo*, Abigail," he greeted as he came near.

She looked up, and for a suspended moment the world fell silent around them. Her dark brown eyes glistened in the sun, searching through his, wondering why he was there. "Are they all right? Has something happened?" she asked in a rush of words.

"*Ja, ja, sie sind in Ordnung (Yes, yes, they're fine),*" Hanz said, removing his hat, holding it with both hands. "I just came to see how you're managing."

Abigail stepped out from the water, placing the wet garment in the basket. "You frightened me. I thought something was wrong." Her voice slightly cracked as she spoke, fighting back strong emotions.

"*Nein, alles ist gut. Sehr gut. (No, everything is good. Very good).*" Hanz softly smiled, thinking of the little girls, even as he examined their mother closely, discerning again how she was just a child herself. "But one is much smaller than the other."

Abigail hesitated, fearful he wanted to return the twins. Or at least Shalom. "Does that mean you don't want her?"

"*Nein*, not at all. We want them both."

Her intense gaze lingered on him, asking a dozen silent questions, yet relieved he wasn't there to bring back the babies. If the Jewish quarter ever discovered she had given birth out of wedlock, they would ostracize her. "How is your wife taking to them?"

"*Wunderbar (Wonderfully).* Maria loves them like her own. They've brought an indescribable joy to our home." He looked out at the calm Tauber River, winding its way through town, a silent witness to eons of human trials and triumphs, strengths and frailties. "But you should know what I told her. I did not show her your letter."

Abigail appeared confused.

"Instead, I told her a teenage mother had died giving birth to these twins, and neither her parents nor the teenage father wanted them. I know my wife, and if she thought you were alive, she'd try to find you. She'd forever worry that you'd change your mind in the future and want your daughters back."

That stung Abigail, the finality of it, as if she truly were dead to her girls.

Howbeit, she knew it was for the best.

"As for everyone else, no one knows your secret. *Our* secret. And they never will." Hanz glanced around and lowered his voice. "We'll say that Maria gave birth to them, and that we kept her pregnancy private because of her recent stillbirth. People will understand." He wiped his brow and ran his hand through his hair, once more grappling with the turmoil proliferating in his mind over the falsehoods and coverups he and Maria were embarking on. "And this is why I came to see you today. I wanted to talk to you before going down this path."

"About what?"

"About whether or not you know what you're doing. I need to hear it from your own mouth that you understand the seriousness of this. There's no going back."

As the sun held the sky in a warm embrace, Abigail appeared as if a fluttering bird caught in a gust. Hesitant yet impelled, her eyes carried the burden of her choice. "I understand, Herr Hanz."

"Abigail," Hanz said, his voice as gentle as the breeze, pressing her further, "I know what you wrote in your letter, but are you *really* certain this is what you want? I need you to be sure, because once we take them as our own, it must be forever," he added, ensuring the irrevocability was understood.

Abigail recalled that heart-wrenching day when her parents wanted her to give the babies to an orphanage in Poland. She couldn't bear to leave them to an unknown fate, and that's when she thought of Moses' mother, Jochebed. The Holy Scriptures tell how the Levite woman bravely defied the Egyptian Pharaoh who decreed that all Israelite boys be killed at birth to control the Hebrew population. She hid her son in a papyrus basket and placed it among the reeds by the bank of the Nile River, where Pharaoh's own daughter found him while bathing. Taking pity on the beautiful child, she named him Moses and raised him as her own. That act of love by his mother saved his life, and in an astonishing example of God's munificence and compassion, Jochebed became Moses' nurse and was able to see her son grow into a mighty man.

Likewise, Abigail had decided she would do the same for her daughters, placing the babies in a double wicker basket and leaving them for the Wolffs to find. Instead of the girls suffering in a rundown orphanage, they would be adopted by a childless couple who would shower them with love, raising them on a beautiful farm by the river. The one with the large porch and a porch swing, with sheep, goats, and chickens in the yard. A magical place. A place where, if her daughters couldn't be with her, perhaps they could be raised in a loving home near her.

"I am sure," Abigail finally replied, the simplicity of her answer belying the tremors in her heart. "I can't raise them. My parents were very angry, and they would never allow it."

Hanz recalled her bruised face and cut lip that night they met on the dirt road. No doubt her father had hit her, shamed by his daughter's shocking indiscretion.

"I'd be shunned by my village, too."

"Why choose a German family, though?" Hanz questioned. "Why not a Jewish one?"

"Even if I took them to a different village, the rabbi would eventually find out. Jewish communities talk. Besides, all I wanted was a loving home for them."

"You took a chance identifying yourself in the letter. Why?"

"Because I trusted you. After you helped me that night in the forest, I knew you were a *gute*, kind man." A tear traced a solitary path down her cheek, and she quickly wiped it away. "You will love and care for them, right Herr Hanz? You and Frau Maria?"

"*Ja*, Abigail, we will. More than words can say. Maria and I are forever in your debt. Forever grateful."

She allowed a brief smile to touch her lips, despite the obvious pain it masked.

Hanz observed her carefully, the lines of his face etched with the concern of a man who understood the weight of the world all too well. "And what of you, Abigail? What will you do?"

Her resolve seemed to fortify at his question, straightening her spine as if the very act could steel her for the journey ahead. "I will go on, Herr Hanz. I will live my life anew, and not repeat the same mistakes I've made."

"If you ever need anything, anything at all . . ."

"*Danke*," she interrupted. Plucking two wildflowers from the riverbank, she handed them to him. "For Ava and Shalom," she softly said, her voice thick with resignation, as if uttering their names for the last time. And with that, she picked up her basket and headed back to the village, leaving him standing alone at the water's edge.

Hanz watched her walk away, her sacrifice now flowing like a silent river through his veins, tugging on his conscience. An impulse goaded him to call after her, to offer something more tangible than words of gratitude, but he restrained himself. What could he offer that wouldn't further complicate things? Besides, he had accomplished what he came to do, impressed with her mental and emotional resilience under the circumstances, especially at such a young age. It reassured him about the future for his new family and the decisions that would come next. Without even realizing it, a subtle smile formed on his lips, and he headed back to Maria and their newborn twins.

$$\sim\!c\;\varphi\;\text{\ding{74}}\;\varphi\;\sim$$

As Hanz rode Bucephalus back to the farm, clutching the wildflowers, he reminisced about his life. About how he had gotten to where he was today. From first falling in love with a deaf woman, marrying her and becoming a farmer when his true aspirations were to be an artist, to now being a father . . .

While still a teenager, Hanz fought in the Great War. The War to End All Wars, as it was posthumously called. Among the carnage and the blood, when the heavens rained down Satan's fury on mankind, the sky a continual blaze of fire and metal, shedding tears of bullets and bombs that tore mercilessly into human flesh.

A fighter pilot in the German *Luftstreitkräfte (Air Force)*, Hanz flew the Fokker DR-1, a premier dogfighter of the time, celebrated for its unrivaled agility and maneuverability, and the same plane used by his famous comrade Manfred von Richthofen, the Red Baron. He loved flying that plane, soaring through the troposphere, free as a bird. But it wasn't a novelty of leisure; it was an instrument of war.

A newly trained pilot and reluctant gladiator, Hanz had not yet been engaged in air-to-air combat, and he certainly wasn't looking forward to his first dogfight. One fateful foggy morning on April 9, 1917, however, a day that would later become infamously known as Bloody April, he had no choice—the fight came to him . . .

"Bratakka-takka-takka!"

"Bratakka-takka-takka!"

"Boom!"

"Bang!"

"I've been hit!" he yelled out to no one.

Taken by surprise, the British Royal Flying Corps (RFC) had shot Hanz down, his plane spiraling out of control and plummeting to the earth. But God must have read this young man's heart, seeing that he was not a true killer, and decided to spare him because by some miracle, he had managed to survive, landing his wounded bird in an open field, half-conscious, his right leg shattered.

Hanz woke up in a French military hospital, a prisoner of war. He wondered how he had survived that crash. He could still hear the deafening sounds of the bullets whizzing past his head, taste the metallic bitterness of the gunpowder on his tongue, and feel the excruciating pain in his vitiated leg. At night, he'd wake up sweating profusely and screaming in the dark; and during the day, he'd dwell on those he knew who didn't make it home. One friend killed, two friends killed, three then four, one after the other, wiped out like ants on the ground, robbed of their youth, their future, their families.

After the war had ended, Hanz was repatriated. He was lucky, because most of his fellow prisoners of war weren't immediately released from Allied captivity, kept instead for a period of forced labor. But Hanz's permanent injury precluded that, and he went to Austria to convalesce. Not from his physical wound, which had already healed, but his mental and emotional ones, seeking to slay his new demons. His father had been to the Inntal Valley of Tyrol, a region known for its stunning alpine scenery, and told him of many intriguing tales about the history and beauty of the place. It was exactly what Hanz needed to suppress his bad memories, replacing them with good.

Known beyond the borders of Tyrol as the Capital of the Alps, Innsbruck is where Hanz stayed. With the mighty Nordkette mountains of the Karwendel Massif to the north and the Stubai and Tux Alps to the south, one's problems seemed so small and insignificant. Humbled before God, the creator of such magnificence, Hanz stared at them in awe.

While walking with his cane along an endless field of green one morning, he saw a young woman with flaming red hair, barefoot and shepherding sheep. So taken by the elysian scene he thought it was a mirage. "Am I dreaming?" he asked himself, blinking hard to focus.

"*Nein*," said an elderly voice behind him. "You're not dreaming, son.

That there is a rare *Fräulein (young lady)*. Only the Austrian Alps could produce such beauty."

Hanz turned toward the older man sitting quietly on a nearby rock. "Who is she?"

"Maria Jager is her name. The deaf girl who knows how to read lips and speak like you and me. Her poor mother passed away last year; the consumption got her. Now the *Fräulein* looks after her four younger sisters, two older brothers, and her father. She'll cook you a meal you'll never forget, and that's no lie."

Standing there, gazing at the young woman, her fiery locks tussling with the breeze, her cerulean eyes rivaling the bluest sky, her fair skin mocking the sun, Hanz was immediately lovestruck. *Mein Herr, sie ist wunderschön (My lord, she's beautiful)*, he thought. Without taking his eyes off her, he said to the older man, "I'm going to marry her," an all-knowing confidence in his voice. "She's going to be my wife."

The old man chuckled as he lit his pipe. "Spring is a time for new life and love to burst forth. God bless you, son, and may the *Fräulein* feel the same."

For the next week, Hanz walked down to that same field of green each morning, watching Maria Jager shepherd her sheep. The fact that she was deaf mattered none to him, and he wanted to meet her, but he had always been shy with women and didn't know how to approach. Then he saw the train in the distance, barreling through the valley. With her back to it, kneeling on the tracks to admire a solitary wildflower growing between the rails, the train was going to hit her if she didn't move!

Hanz immediately sprang into action and sprinted toward her. In the nick of time, he grabbed her, and they both rolled into the grass. When they came to a stop, she started to laugh.

"I saved your life," Hanz said, out of breath and still holding her, looking down into her heavenly face.

She read his lips and smiled. "I knew the train was coming. I could feel the vibrations in my feet."

Hanz was confused. "Then why?"

"Because I also knew you would save me."

The twinkle in her eye mesmerized him, and he spontaneously kissed her. He kissed her as if he had always kissed her. He kissed her as if it were the most natural thing in the world.

And so it began . . . From the beating drums of war, the screeching whistles of bombs, the whizzing hiss of bullets, and the screaming cries of soldiers, Hanz Wolff found peace, serenity, and contentment in the Inntal Valley of Tyrol, all in the form of a young, alluring Austrian woman who was deaf.

Before they knew it, six months of blissful courtship had passed, and the two lovebirds were completely besotted. One afternoon, as they promenaded through Hofgarten park, the imperial gardens once exclusive to the ruling elite and favored by the royals for hundreds of years, Hanz had something weighty on his mind. *"Es ist wunderschön hier (It's beautiful here),"* he said, coming to a stop on a bridge crossing the Inn River, a 317-mile tributary of the Danube that ran straight through the city center. "But I need to make a better living than working at the textile mill." He thought of the farm he grew up on back home, by the winding Tauber River, with the animals, the crops, and the small vineyard. "As you know," he continued, looking directly at Maria so she could easily read his lips, "when I was at war, my father's horse rolled over in the field and killed him. My mother and *Bruder* took on the farm, doing the best they could, but I just got word that my mother wants to move to my sister's in Hamburg now. Since my *Bruder* is still too young to be on his own, he'll be going with her."

Maria's expression turned timorous, and she looked down at the ground, anticipating what was coming next. "You want to return to Germany?"

He took her chin gently in his hand, bringing her gaze back to his. "*Ja,* but not without you, *meine Liebe.*" Pausing for the perfect words to match his emotions, he confessed, "Because when I am with you, I feel a happiness unknown to mortal man." Ever so softly he kissed her lips, gazing down into her face. "When I am with you, Maria Jager . . . I am home."

❦

The Wolff farm in the distance brought Hanz back to the present, and he stopped his horse on the dirt road to look at the surrounding area. As if something out of a scenic painting—like the ones he sold to the Italian art dealer, Giovanni Mandolini—the view was stunning. Rolling meadows, verdant forests, tranquil ponds, trickling streams, and the winding Tauber River accentuated the land's beauty. Much like the area where Maria grew up, minus the imposing Alps.

On the Wolff property itself, the small vineyard flared out on one side like the wing of a bird, with wheat and corn grown on the other. Between them was a small brook feeding the tiny pond where two white swans would often visit. Cows, sheep, goats, and chickens roamed freely over the farm, munching on grass and insects, and the barn provided shelter and storage. The farmhouse, built by Hanz's grandfather, stood solid overlooking it all. Made out of timber and stone, it had a large living room with stone fireplace, a well-equipped kitchen, a bathroom with Victorian claw-foot tub, and three bedrooms. A porch in front of the house spanned the length of it, with a swing that gently oscillated in the breeze.

The well-made German farmhouse was both a relic and an heirloom. Before the twins came into their lives, Hanz often wondered who would inherit it, along with the land. His younger brother Severin had always said he never wanted to be a farmer, toiling with the sun on his back and the dirt under his nails. But now he and Maria had two daughters, and it would all go to them. Their children, their legacy. It filled Hanz with joy, knowing there were roots again–the family tree would survive.

Years and years ago before Hanz was born, before his father was born, before his grandfather and great-grandfather were born, only the meadows, forests, ponds, and streams existed, flanking either side of the Tauber River. The land was wild, with no inhabitants. Prior to 1871, Germany wasn't even yet Germany but a conglomeration of many kingdoms and empires, often referred to as Germania, the Holy Roman Empire, and the Franks. But now eons later, countless German families cultivated and lived on the land, including the neighboring farms close by to the Wolffs.

On the south side, an older Jewish couple–the Friedmans–ran a goat farm. To the west, a German family–Clovis and Elise Steinburg with their newborn daughter and toddler son–grew wheat and barley. To the East, a young German man named Leon Dreisler, who had also survived the Great War, lived with his Jewish mail-order bride from Hungary–they raised cows and sheep. And in the North, another German farmer–Günther Nachtnebel, with his homemade distillery and his self-righteous wife Elvira–grew corn and soy.

And then there were a few in the area who didn't farm the land but just lived on it. Like Aadan Omari and his wife Chiumbo. A Black couple originally from Cameroon, Africa, they emigrated to France in their youth, only to settle in Germany. He was a skilled tile maker. And the eccentric Jewish widow, Willamina Benowitz, who lived with her mentally challenged adult daughter and five orphans whom she had magnanimously taken in. "I am a bountiful tree," she would say, "with deep roots and many branches for the lost little birds." And lastly, a wealthy Jewish woman, Nora Yurkovich, and her husband Maximillian, who lived in the fanciest home of them all. Her large house was on top of a hill overlooking all the other properties below.

These were Hanz and Maria's neighbors and friends, a diverse group who not only socialized with each other but also looked out for one another like family. And though Hanz's best friend, Ollie van Heinz, lived in Rothenburg ob der Tauber with his wife and kids, he'd often come by and visit too.

When Hanz finally got home, Maria was sitting on the porch swing, gently swaying with both infants slumbering peacefully on either side of her. Barefoot as always in the summer, her fingers stained dark magenta from picking wild berries in the forest, her hands were on the chest of each child, reveling in the sensation of their tiny heartbeats vibrating into her skin. She hummed an off-key, tender tune for her children, despite being unable to hear it, and smiled as her husband approached. "Where did you go?" she asked him. "I thought you were out in the vineyard."

"I went to Rothenburg," he said, admiring the angelic scene.

"Why?"

"To take care of some business. It's all settled now." He kissed her on the forehead and picked up little Ava, sitting down with his new family.

Later that evening, when Maria was tending to the newborns, washing and preparing them for bed, Hanz carefully folded Abigail's letter and the two woolen blankets embroidered with the Star of David. He took them down to a secret room next to the cellar, hiding them in a compartment in the brick wall.

Why he decided to keep them, he did not know . . .

CHAPTER 4

"*Hallo*, little flower," Maria said softly, cradling one of the twins in her arms as she nursed the baby with a bottle of fresh goat milk. Without taking her eyes off the child, she said to her husband, "I still wake up every morning thinking I've imagined it all."

A week had since passed, and a sense of surreal wonder yet lingered in the air. The couple's lives had sublimely changed, like a garden going into full, glorious bloom.

"Every time I see them," said Hanz, mirroring his wife, doting on the other baby with equal care and tenderness, "I think my eyes are playing tricks on me. Like I'm hallucinating. But then I blink, and they're still here, real as the morning sun."

"Do you think we can truly keep them?" Maria asked, the very thought of losing the babies now, causing her voice to tremble. "If they were taken from us, it would break my heart."

Hanz paused. He knew that beneath the veneer of joy, questions lay dormant, like seeds in winter soil, waiting for the right moment to sprout. But then the memory of his conversation with Abigail flashed through his mind. The weight of her trust, and the certitude in her mien, was enough to curtail his doubts. "They're ours, *meine Liebe*. No need to worry."

Maria's lips curved into a smile as she pressed a kiss to the baby's cheek. "Oh, Hanz, look at how beautiful they are. Like two little rosebuds, starting to bloom."

"*Ja*, they are. And their hair is already so dark," he observed, the morning light through the window accentuating the glossy ebony strands. He gently placed his hand on the baby's crown. "Quite a contrast to my blond hair and your red."

Maria, finding a plausible explanation to support a pretend family tree, said, "My grandmother was Russian, and her hair was so dark it almost looked blue. We can say they inherited it from my Slavic side."

The baby in Hanz's arms began to fuss, her little face scrunching up. Instinctively, he lifted her to his shoulder, rocking gently. "Shush now, little bird," he cooed, a soft patting rhythm on her back soothing her whimpering.

"They're identical, Hanz. If it weren't for Shalom being smaller, we'd never tell them apart."

"Except for Ava's birthmark on her neck," he said, a ray of sunlight illuminating the tiny, heart-shaped nevus.

Maria nodded. "We should change Shalom's name, though. People might wonder why a Christian couple gave her such a Jewish name like that."

Hanz agreed, pondering for a moment before reciting different names aloud. "Shalom . . . Sheila . . . Sherry . . . Shelly . . . Shaylee . . . That's it—Shaylee. It has a nice ring to it."

"Shhaayyllee," Maria said, slowly pronouncing the name after reading her husband's lips. "I like it. Ava and Shaylee, our little miracles." She smiled down at the treasure in her arms.

The kitchen, bathed in the soft glow of dawn, transformed into a domestic sanctuary. A tableau of hope for a newly created family where past losses were superseded by new beginnings, and a bond sealed not by blood but by karma's unexpected delivery echoed through the walls of their home and into the heart of their future.

When evening came, the ecstatic couple put the children to bed, then sat outside on the porch swing, drinking wine made from their own vineyard. Rain began to fall, and Maria walked out into the yard, undoing her bun and shaking her head to release her fiery red curls, the wind whipping them to-and-fro like threads of scarlet ribbon. As the sweet raindrops kissed her face, she closed her eyes and lifted her head to the sky, extending her arms to the sides while slowly spinning, laughing at the downpour.

Hanz watched his wife, smiling in fascination at her beauty and spontaneity. What an amazing woman!

Maria opened her eyes and waved to her husband to come join her.

"*Nein*," Hanz laughed, shaking his head.

"*Was, hat mein großer deutscher Mann etwa Angst vor ein bisschen Wasser (What, is my big German man afraid of a little water)?"* With a mischievous grin, she lifted the hem of her skirt, ready to run, then goaded him to catch her if he can.

Hanz took the bait and chased after her. She let him catch up, and the couple embraced, just as they always had in Austria when courting and falling in love.

"You are a wild, redheaded Siren, Maria Wolff," he said, pulling her in close, gazing into her cerulean blue eyes before kissing her in the pouring rain. "But I caught you out at sea, and now you are mine."

At the end of the night, as they lay in each other's arms in bed, Hanz listened to the sounds of his home—the gentle breathing of his wife and children, the creaking of timbers settling down, the distant rumble of the summer storm. It was the lullaby of his life, a life vastly enriched by the two new souls sleeping peacefully between them.

As slumber began to claim Hanz, Abigail's face again drifted into his mind, unwelcome but impossible to ignore. His eyes grew heavy, and his soul became light as air, floating somewhere between the woman he loved and the woman he owed. Somewhere between a blissful dream, a concealed secret, and a future mocking the unknown.

～⚜～

Hanz stood at the edge of the wheat field the next day, staring out at his property. Beyond it, the meadow went on for miles, resembling a blanket of green velvet flanked by thousands of trees. The breeze was cool. Cool and damp, with the scent of fresh rain still in the air.

At the fence line, his horses frolicked with each other, running up and down the length of it. The cows, goats, and sheep paid no attention to the steeds, their heads low to the ground, chewing on the healthy grass. And the chickens roamed about, pecking at the ground, squawking and acting superior. Three barn cats, all different colors with fluffy long fur, hid in the taller grass, eyeing the birds as if stalking their prey. But they knew better than to attack them, as the chickens were not afraid to fight back.

After watering the rosebush on the grave where their stillborn son lay— a weekly sacrament they maintained despite having a family now—Hanz looked over at the farmhouse and saw Maria through the kitchen window, washing dishes in the sink. When she lifted her eyes and met his, they both smiled. Having slept with the infants the night before, their warm, chubby bodies like soft dough snuggling against the couple's skin, was the most magical and wonderful feeling.

"Hey, mister!" a voice called out from the driveway.

Hanz turned around and smiled, catching sight of Ollie van Heinz, his dirty blond hair slicked back and his pants so loose they barely hung onto his bony hips. The two men took long strides and shook hands when they reached each other.

"What are you doing here?" Hanz asked.

"Whaddya mean what am I doing here? I'm your *bester Freund (best friend)*, remember?"

"*Ja, ich Armer (Yes, poor me)*," Hanz laughed.

"I had to deliver a parcel to the Yurkovichs." Ollie worked at the post office in town. "And Stella has a gift for Maria. She wanted me to drop it off." He handed Hanz a box containing an assortment of buttons of different colors–pearl, garnet, gold, and navy. His wife Stella was a seamstress.

"*Danke*," said Hanz, nervously glancing at the farmhouse. He knew it was time to tell people about Ava and Shaylee, and Ollie would be the obvious first choice to disclose such important news. Yet he hesitated, unprepared for his friend's surprise visit.

"Everything all right?" Ollie asked, noticing the pause.

"*Ja.* I'm glad you came," said Hanz, collecting his thoughts. "I have some *wunderbar* news."

"Oh yeah? *Wunderbar Nachrichten sind gut (Wonderful news is good)*. Tell me, tell me."

As the lie formed on his tongue, thick like honey, then shaped his lips to release the words from his mouth, a peculiar sensation enveloped Hanz. He suddenly felt lightheaded, like when he tossed back his vodka too quickly. "Well . . . last week . . . Maria had twins."

Ollie thought he was trying to be funny. Confused over why his friend would joke about such a serious subject, knowing how much heartache Hanz and Maria had gone through, he laughed uncomfortably. But then he could see in his friend's eyes that he wasn't joking. "Wait . . . Are you serious?"

"*Ja!* Can you believe it! Ollie, my Maria gave birth to twin girls!"

Ollie was flabbergasted. "Maria had a baby?"

"Two babies!" The falsehood had been seeded. Just like he told Abigail, there was no going back.

At first Ollie kept staring at Hanz in shock. Why wouldn't he have told him Maria was pregnant months ago? They were best friends, and he kept this happy news to himself all this time? Squinting, Ollie scratched the back of his head. He was no naïve bystander to how children came about, having four little ones of his own. Each time, he was there, in person, witnessing his wife give birth to the miracle of life, hearing that first bellowing cry from his child. And he knew better than any man about the months of anticipation that preceded it. With each pregnancy, his wife prepared everything well in advance, knitting all kinds of baby clothes and telling everyone who would listen about the soon-to-be-addition to their family. "Maria never even told my Stella," he said. "Women usually get all excited about these things."

"I know, I know," said Hanz, his chest tightening. He wasn't used to lying. It was much harder than he thought, especially deceiving his close friend like this. "But when we found out Maria was pregnant again, after being told she could never conceive, we didn't want to tell anyone. After what happened with our *Sohn (son)*, we wanted to wait until they were born."

Ollie could tell something wasn't right. Although he hadn't seen Maria in some time, he knew his friend too well. He knew Hanz was lying, and Hanz knew he knew. But obviously there was a reason for the falsehood, so Ollie gave his friend the benefit of the doubt and didn't challenge him, despite all the questions circling in his head. Lifting his bushy eyebrows, he relaxed his face and released a wide smile. "Well how about that! *Das ist die beste Nachricht aller Zeiten (This is the best news ever)!*"

Hanz exhaled. "*Ja*, we're incredibly happy."

"And *two* babies! God has blessed you!"

"*Danke, mein Freund.*"

"What are their names?"

"Ava and Shaylee."

Ollie slapped his knee. "If this doesn't call for a celebration, I don't know what does! Let's go to *Die Teufelsnadel (The Devil's Needle)!*" He gave Hanz a man hug. "Drinks are on me!"

Hanz first brought Ollie to the house to show him his daughters. Maria had been watching them from the kitchen window, so she was prepared, one baby against her shoulder in a white cloth diaper, the other sleeping in the wicker basket on the table. "Take off your dirty boots," she said to them as they entered. "I just cleaned the floor."

The two men obeyed, and Hanz handed Maria the gift from Stella. She opened the box and smiled at all the lovely buttons. "Tell Stella I said *danke*."

"*Ja*," replied Ollie. He slowly approached to get a better look at the angels. "Congratulations, Maria. Such incredible news."

Maria gave a half smile. Though she was fond of his wife, she didn't really like Ollie because he was always trying to coerce Hanz to go with him to the pub. That, and he talked so fast she often couldn't read his lips, which annoyed her. Sometimes she thought he even did it on purpose.

Hanz went over and kissed Maria's cheek. "I'm going into town for a bit. I won't be too late." He gave her a look of, 'it's okay–the news is out now, and everything will be fine.'

Maria nodded. "Tell Nila I said *hallo*."

✦

It wasn't just the Wolffs who had experienced a significant change in their lives. Six months ago, after Randolph the Bull had won his next fight, he quietly retired from boxing. And that's not all. He and Nila had run off together and got married in Venice, then came back and bought The Devil's Needle with Randolph's savings. Now the two of them owned the tavern and lived in the apartment above it. While she bartended, he worked as a cook in the kitchen.

When Hanz and Ollie walked into the pub, the Bull immediately saw them and beamed, the gap between his front teeth now double in size–his last opponent had knocked another tooth out. Raising his arms in the air, he exclaimed, *"Meine Freunde! Kommt rein, kommt rein! Nimm eine sitz! (My friends! Come in, come in! Take a seat!)"*

"Maria had twins!" Ollie blurted out.

"What did you say?" asked Nila, walking over to them. She had just finished serving food to another table. "Who had twins?"

"Maria. She gave birth to twin girls a week ago."

Nila looked at Hanz in disbelief, thinking perhaps Ollie was already drunk and speaking nonsense again.

"*Ja*, it's true," said Hanz, trying not to give any telltale signs of the deception. "We kept it all quiet until now, because of what happened before. But she carried them to full term."

"Isn't that *wunderbar* news?" asked Ollie. He was doing his best to support his friend.

Randolph the Bull slapped the bar. "That's not *wunderbar* news. That's goddamn amazing news!"

Hanz smiled. "*Danke.*"

"Congratulations," Nila said, seemingly in shock. "I'm so happy for you, Hanz."

Randolph appeared the most excited. He put a bottle of Chartreuse on the bar for Hanz, a bottle of fine vodka for Ollie, and a bottle of Mampe Halb & Halb for himself and Nila. "Drinks are on the house!" he exclaimed. "Handsome Hanz is now a father!"

"Let's make this a great night!" Ollie said, clinking glasses with each of them. "We're here among *die besten Freunde (the best of friends)*, and we're celebrating two new lives!"

"I guess that gold tooth of mine was lucky after all," said Randolph the Bull. Just like the day he first met the German farmer, he laughed like hell. He laughed so hard the sound bellowed through the entire pub.

⚜

"Had them at home, did you?" Dr. Schultz said later that week, surprised beyond belief. Hanz and Maria had brought the twins to Rothenburg ob der Tauber to see him. "This is incredible. I was certain Maria would never be able to carry a fetus again, let alone two."

"*Ja*, we are very grateful," said Hanz, glancing at his wife. "And they came so suddenly, we had no time to get to the hospital."

Maria nervously played with the new sapphire stone wedding ring Hanz had recently bought her. "I was at home for the last three months of my pregnancy, mostly in bed," she said, proffering an explanation as to why no one had seen her with a huge belly.

"Still, you should have come to see me when you found out you were pregnant," said the doctor. "Especially after what happened before."

"I know. You're right. *Entschuldigung, Doktor (Sorry, doctor).*"

"I'll examine you now to see how well you're healing."

"*Nein*, I'm fine. *Bitte (Please)*, Herr Schultz, just examine my babies."

The doctor hesitated. It was highly unusual for a woman to refuse a postpartum exam, and he felt as if he were violating his Hippocratic oath.

Nevertheless, he didn't press her on it.

Short and portly with salt-and-pepper hair, his thick spectacles magnifying his beady eyes, Dr. Schultz reminded Hanz of a wise old owl. He inspected Ava first, giving her a clean bill of health, then turned his attention to Shaylee, carefully examining her small form. "Hmm . . . *ja* . . . I see," he murmured to himself.

"What is it?" asked Hanz. "Is something wrong?"

When finished with his examination, Dr. Schultz turned to face the couple so Maria could read his lips. "She's obviously underdeveloped, as you can see. Probably due to selective fetal growth restriction, which occurs in ten to twenty percent of twin pregnancies. But it's nothing to be concerned about. With *gute* nutrition, she'll likely grow to normal size."

Hanz and Maria breathed a sigh of relief.

"Other than that, this little one is just as healthy as her sister." The doctor smiled as Shaylee gurgled and cooed. "And just as cute."

⁓◈⁓

As they made their way through the cobblestone streets of Rothenburg ob der Tauber, Hanz took a wrong turn with the horse and carriage, ending up in the Jewish quarter. Children with sidelocks played in the streets; women with head coverings bustled about doing chores; and men with beards, kippahs, fedoras, or shtreimels walked and talked.

Suddenly Hanz felt as if he had stolen Jewish property in his carriage. Priceless property, hidden in the same wicker basket he had found in his barn. Maria didn't notice her husband's panicked demeanor, her nose buried in a book.

As he tried to navigate his way out of the Semitic village, Hanz came to a stop to allow an elderly Jewish man to cross the street with his goats. That's when he spotted Abigail, mere yards away! She saw him too, and they held each other's stare. What an awkward, peculiar moment! One that cut through the air and crushed the illusion Hanz had created in his mind about his new family. The sounds around him faded, the buildings and people too, and instantly he found himself tightly bound to Abigail with an invisible lock and chain, her striking, dark eyes shining. Curious, longing. Begging that same painful question: how are my babies?

One of the twins woke and became cranky, waking the other, and soon the two newborns joined forces, wailing as if screaming for help to be rescued. The sound seemed to grow louder and louder with each second, all the while their young Jewish mother staring their way. And so Hanz waited, the reins in his hands, the goats in his way, his deaf wife oblivious to it all. It was as if a whirlpool had formed in that little Jewish community, sucking him in, refusing to let him go.

"Hanz, for goodness' sake, why have you stopped?" Maria asked, breaking his spell.

The goats had passed, and Hanz looked straight ahead, flicking the reins to make the horse trot, leaving Abigail standing there, listening to the cries of her newborn children.

❧

After dinner that evening, with the twins asleep in their crib, Maria retired early while Hanz went into his small library in the cellar. He had collected books of all kinds over the years, now filling three bookshelves, and often went down there to relax and travel to another world. Two worn-out leather chairs on a patterned rug, a coffee table, and a small cabinet with a bottle of Chartreuse, Jägermeister, vodka, and homemade wine from his vineyard—four choices depending on his mood and what he was reading—made the space cozy and pleasant.

Oliver Twist—a classic and a favorite of his—was his choice that night, along with Jägermeister. But no sooner had he sat down with his book and drink than Maria opened the cellar door, coming downstairs in her nightgown with two hot teas and Choco Leibniz biscuits. Named after the seventeenth-century philosopher and mathematician, Gottfried Wilhelm Leibniz, the most famous citizen of Hanover where the biscuits were made, they, too, were a favorite of Hanz's.

"I couldn't sleep," Maria said, placing the tray of treats on the coffee table.

Hanz smiled when he saw the Choco Leibniz. "*Danke, meine Liebe.*"

She gave a Mona Lisa smile in return, tinged with diffidence.

"What is it?" asked Hanz, reaching for a biscuit.

"Well . . . sometimes I wonder if you spend hours down here because . . ."

"*Ja?*"

Her expression turned rueful. "I often wonder if you occupy yourself with these books, your paintings, and your violin because I'm deaf and cannot communicate like normal people do. I have to read your lips, and I don't even know the sound of your voice."

"*Nein, nein, komm schon, meine Liebe (No, no, come on, my love)*. That's nonsense." He took her hand. "I adore you, and you know it."

As they held each other's gaze, a playful grin formed on his lips. "In fact, I would be fine with it if you couldn't speak, either."

Maria narrowed her eyes at him . . . And then they both laughed.

"Look at us," she said. "Happy and laughing again, all because of those two *schöne Kinder (beautiful children)*."

Hanz sat back in his chair and lit his corncob pipe. "And it feels so right, doesn't it? Like it's always been this way, and we've known nothing different."

Maria beamed. "*Ja*, it does. It was meant to be."

As they drank their hot tea and savored the Choco Leibniz, Maria noticed the book by her husband's side. "What are you reading?"

Hanz picked it up and looked at the cover. "*Oliver Twist*, by Charles Dickens. It's about an orphan raised in a workhouse who escapes to London and meets a gang of juvenile pickpockets. From there he gets into all kinds of trouble, and . . ."

"Hanz," Maria interrupted, shaking her head. "I've read *Oliver Twist*. You're not the only one who's taken to a book in their life."

He chuckled, always amused by her wit.

"Did you know that it has an alternative title? *The Parish Boy's Progress*."

"*Ja*, I did know that, *meine kluge Frau (my smart wife)*."

She smiled as she thought about Oliver and the other orphans. "With Ava and Shaylee's mother dead, and their father as *gute* as dead, we now have two Jewish orphans of our own."

"They *were* Jewish orphans," said Hanz. "Now they're German girls with Christian parents." The words, powerful as they were, seemed to float in the air, as if indicative of sacrilegious alchemy.

Husband and wife remained silent for a moment, mulling over the fragile lives they were now responsible for.

"We can never tell another soul, Maria. Never," said Hanz. "Do you understand?" Smoke from his nostrils circulated around his face as he exhaled, somehow making his appearance more solemn. Illusory, even. "From this day forward, we must swear a lifelong pact that you birthed these girls, no matter who suspects anything, or what the future holds."

Maria slowly nodded as if in a trance, her mind recreating the births, solidifying in her memory how it all played out.

Upstairs, one of the babies began to cry, breaking the spell. The lovely sound swelled through the entire house, adding a touch of magic to the moment.

"I'll go to her," Maria said. Picking up the tray, she walked up the stairs, adding over her shoulder, "Enjoy *Oliver Twist, The Parish Boy's Progress.*"

Hanz opened the book and stared at the first page. Instead of reading, however, he closed it and put it back on the bookshelf, then followed Maria upstairs. An irresistible desire to hold one of his daughters usurped all else.

❧

Late that night, a banging shook the front door, reverberating through the farmhouse. Hanz woke up, startled by the pounding, accompanied by a commotion outside with men shouting and dogs barking. The newborns woke too and began to cry; Hanz nudged Maria, telling her someone was at the door and that the babies needed her attention. While she tended to the twins, he stepped into his pants and went to the door.

"What in the devil are you all doing here so late?" Hanz asked, shirtless and barefoot. Even without his boots he towered over the men.

"Hanz, we have a murderer and thief on our hands," said Ulrich Göth, holding a rifle. He was the blacksmith in town. "The bastard stole a bunch of money from *gute* people and slit Constance Bodnar's throat for her jewels."

"Ear to ear!" yelled Dieter Marx, the local printer. "So savagely it looked like she had two mouths!"

"He also raped a young Jewish girl months ago," said Otto Schäfer, spitting on the ground in disgust. "She was too afraid to tell, but after they found Constance, she came forward and told her rabbi."

Hanz's ears perked up; a chill ran down his spine. With another piece of the puzzle revealed, things now made sense to him. No wonder Abigail gave up her babies. She must have been that poor girl raped by that deplorable creature, becoming pregnant by him, and the boyfriend story was just a lie. "Who did all this?" he asked the men.

"That supposed man of God who wandered here last year, asking everyone for donations to build a new church," said Ulrich. "Turns out he's an

61

escaped convict who killed a priest from Weikersheim and stole his identity. He tied the poor man's hands to the steering wheel of a car and pushed it into the Tauber."

Hanz blanched. He thought back to when that so-called priest had stopped by the farm weeks earlier, looking for the Wolffs to contribute to his holy calling of building a house of God. He quoted scriptures from the Bible, too, and Maria even invited him into the house for tea. That seemingly kind, soft-spoken man had committed these crimes?

"About a week ago, a fisherman found the real priest's body when he noticed the car in shallow water," added Boris Kraus. "That's when all hell broke loose."

"Why do you need me?" Hanz asked.

Ulrich motioned toward the small vineyard with his rifle. "Because he's hiding on your property. We chased him through the forest and lost him here."

Hanz dressed quickly, grabbed his pistol, and told Maria what was happening, instructing her to stay inside until he returned.

"Hanz, be careful," she pleaded, sitting protectively next to the wooden crib.

He looked down at the newborns who had fallen back asleep. How could such peaceful innocence in birth turn so wicked in life with some people, he wondered? Kissing his wife on the forehead, he returned to the men waiting outside. "What are you planning on doing when you catch him?" he asked the self-imposed posse.

"Hang him!" said Dieter.

Hanz led the men with their dogs to the barn first. No fugitive there. Next he took them through the entire vineyard, including the small cabin used by his Jewish workers during harvest season, but once more they found nothing. They even checked the outhouse.

"Anywhere else he could be hiding?" Ulrich asked.

Standing on an elevated piece of earth, Hanz scanned his entire property. The full moon shone like a bright candle in a dark room, illuminating the stretch of land. When his eyes gravitated back toward the farmhouse, his heart dropped, catching sight of a man's shadow crossing the large kitchen window . . . Oh my God! Maria! . . . "He's inside my house!" Hanz shouted.

The men ran like they were on fire. Overwhelming panic ripped through Hanz as gruesome images of Maria's throat slit ear to ear like Constance Bodnar caromed viciously through his head. And the babies, so tiny and fragile—would that evil man kill them too?

Bursting through the front door, out of breath and his heart thumping in his chest, Hanz feared the worst. But what he saw instead he'd never forget for the rest of his days . . . There in the corner of the kitchen, scrunched down and covering his head, talking to himself like a madman and crying deliriously, was the murderer and thief! Maria stood six feet in front of him, her eyes wild and unafraid like a mother bear protecting her cubs, a loaded shotgun in her arms, pointing at his head.

"*Gutes Mädchen (Good girl)*, Maria!" exclaimed Hanz. He took the gun from her and kept it pointed at the man. "How did you know?" he asked, keeping his eyes on the prisoner while turning his face so she could read his lips.

"I felt a draft from the bathroom window when he opened it," she said calmly. "And then there was an odor of vodka and sweat. I could have smelled that stench a mile away."

The other men stood behind Hanz, and for a moment they all stared at the convict like a rat caught in a trap. Dieter pushed through the group and kicked him in the face several times; everyone just watched. The man cowered and squirmed as blood spilled from his nose and mouth.

After tying his hands behind his back, the men hauled him outside like a bloodied pig being dragged by a pack of rabid wolves, taking him toward a large weeping willow tree in the yard. Hanz knew what came next. "Not on my property," he said.

"What difference does it make!" yelled Dieter. "He deserves to die for what he did!"

"I said not on my property! I won't have that memory burned into this land!"

"Let's take him back to the forest," said Otto. "We can do it there."

Hanz followed as the vigilantes cursed, punched, and shoved the beaten-up man down the dirt road toward Rothenburg. Along the way, they chanted, *"Toter Mann wandern! Toter Mann wandern! (Dead man walking! Dead man walking!)"*

They came to a stop at a massive linden tree a few feet off the road into the woods. The oldest and biggest in the forest, with a history that went back over a thousand years, the linden tree was not just a tree but also a subject of many myths and legends, acquiring sacred status in Slavic and Germanic cultures where it was seen as a symbol of love, peace, and justice. Revered since ancient times, important decisions and disputes were sometimes settled under the shade of a linden tree, reflecting the belief that truth could be revealed in its presence. A tree of truth and justice—yes, this was the spot.

Hanz remembered years ago, when he was a young child, that lightning had struck that same tree, and it had caught fire. In the morning it resembled a charcoaled hand rising from hell, reaching up to heaven, and when he touched its charred branches, black dust and ashes covered his hands. But to his surprise, by the following summer the tree had sprouted new branches, then leaves. The roots had remained, and the tree slowly grew back stronger than ever. Now it would serve as an executioner, with a large branch sticking out from the trunk like the arm of a Greek god. Perfect for a lynching.

Otto started a fire that lit up quickly, and the men stood around, talking and drinking vodka from their silver flasks as if attending a social event. As the flames flickered and crackled, Hanz observed the prisoner, half-conscious on the ground with his back against the tree, his face swollen and covered in blood. Dieter had cut off his nose, a medieval punishment called *Ungestalt (deformed)*, where the person so mutilated was no longer viewed as a human being after becoming hideously unrecognizable, provoking revulsion and rendering the victim a non-person and no longer a part of society. Extreme, yet very effective in deterring crime.

As Hanz stared at the man, the fake priest slowly lifted his head and met his gaze. In that instant, it dawned on Hanz that he was staring into the face of the twins' father, causing a chill to cut through the deepest part of him.

The men continued to harass the prisoner, and as they hurled their insults, throwing occasional rocks and sticks at him, the air seemingly became cold, mocking the flames. As if an evil presence had joined them. Like a demon, perched high on top of the tree, his dark wings spread out on either side, looking down at the fun and reveling in the affair. It was an otherworldly feeling, and Hanz didn't like it. Not a man easily frightened, the sensation made him uneasy, sprouting goosebumps all over his skin. He slowly looked upward, but saw nothing.

A young crow, appearing out of nowhere, landed on the branch that would soon facilitate the execution. It was Ingomar, the glossy black passerine bird that frequented the Wolff farm. Hanz had found it as a fledgling and named it after a first-century chieftain of the Cherusci–a Germanic tribe–and the crow often followed him around. Ingomar tilted his head from side to side, endeavoring to understand the goings-on of the humans below. He then let out a shrill squawk, as if to render his judgment.

"I saw a book in Rothenburg's library about medieval torture," Dieter said, proud of his first rhinotomy. "We could show the bastard what happens to men who rape and kill women."

Otto took a large swig from his flask. "What else do you suggest we do?"

"*I* know," said Boris. "We could gut him and pull out his entrails. If we do it right, he'll die slowly and in pain."

The fire was now a blazing monster, its flaming tentacles dancing on all sides like the writhing snakes of Medusa's hair. The inebriated men encircled the prisoner, angry and restless, with plans in their heart to extend the suffering all night.

Hanz looked into their eyes inflamed with rage, as if they were about to eat the prisoner rather than just inflict pain, and decided to speak up. "Hold on, now. You never said anything about torture. What this man did was unforgivable, but making him suffer isn't going to bring Constance Bodnar back, or undo the rape."

"What if it had been Maria?" Ulrich asked. "What if he had slit her throat for her jewels? Or what if that teenage girl had been your daughter?"

Hanz wouldn't speculate, afraid of his answer. "Engaging in torture makes us no better than him." He motioned at the tree branch. "We came here to hang an evil man for his wicked deeds, and that's all."

But the small group of men didn't listen, withdrawing their knives from their sheaths, ready to filet the murderer.

Hanz stepped in front of the prisoner and shot a bullet in the air. "There will be no more torture. He's already beaten to a pulp, and you took his nose. You found the man on my land, now string him up and be done with it!"

Ulrich, the leader of the group, glared at Hanz for a moment. He then nodded to Dieter, who threw a rope over the large branch, and Boris placed the noose around the felon's neck. Otto joined them, and all three pulled on the rope, lifting the man to his tiptoes.

"What did you do with the money and jewels?" Ulrich demanded. "Tell us, and we'll make it quick."

The masquerading priest remained mute. Why give them the satisfaction when he knew they were only going to hang him anyway?

"This is your last chance to confess your crimes before meeting your Maker. Perhaps he'll have mercy on your soul and spare you the torment of a fiery hell."

With no response, the men pulled on the rope, lifting him into the air. *"Gott, vergib mir (God, forgive me)!"* he yelled out, scaring Ingomar off the tree. His body jerked as his life force left him. It was over quickly.

Hanz wished he had brought his Bible with him to read an appropriate scripture, not only for the dead man but also for himself, to maintain his inner peace. Taking a man's life is a sad and unsettling thing, whether deserved or not, and he took no pleasure in it.

As the lifeless body hung in the air like a sinister scarecrow, the flames blazed higher and higher, licking against the night sky—a fiery doorway to hell, where murderers, thieves, and rapists were welcomed.

⁂

After the lynching, the men continued to drink and socialize. They spoke about the hidden loot that would probably never be found, they chatted about their work and their families, and they debated over the political and economic unrest now occurring throughout Germany.

Ulrich brought the conversation around to a happier event. "Congratulations, Hanz!" he said, patting him on the back. "It's too bad we had to find out about the *wunderbar* news on a night like tonight, but we're so happy for you and Maria. Twins, even! I could hear them crying from the bedroom; what a sweet sound."

"Danke," said Hanz, smiling nervously as the men raised their silver flasks to him. In the background, the dead fugitive hanging from the noose swayed gently in the breeze.

"It's a *gute* thing you have your farm and the vineyard," Otto said. "People are suffering right now, and with two new mouths to feed, living off the land is a blessing."

"Ja," said Hanz, looking over at the horizon. Signs of dawn were emerging, brilliant colors of tangerine and fuchsia sneaking up along the German

skyline, bleeding into dark sapphire. "Time to go home, *Herren (gentlemen)*."

The men agreed, each dispersing their separate ways.

When Hanz arrived home, Maria and the twins were fast asleep in bed, Ava and Shaylee curled up like kittens inside his wife's protective embrace. It made him think of Abigail, forced against her will by a man now hanging from a tree, then forced against her will to give up the heavenly product of that assault.

How ironic that something so beautiful could result from something so vile!

⚜

The sun rose quickly—the color of egg yolk—begetting a bright, beautiful morn. With her fiery red locks in a high bun and wearing a fresh apron, Maria bustled about in the kitchen, making her husband breakfast. The twins were in the wooden crib, satisfied with their fill of warm goat milk, and Hanz sat at the kitchen table, sipping his coffee.

Deep in thought, subconsciously frowning, Hanz was having flashbacks from the night before. Images of the twins' father filled his mind, bloodied and beaten with his nose cut off, lying on the ground like a sack of dirty refuse. The look on his swollen face when he had lifted his head to stare at Hanz, like a sick dog getting ready to die, was pitiful.

Maria halted his ruminations when she brought his breakfast to the table. "What did they end up doing to that man?" she asked, her eyes wide and curious.

"They hung him," was all Hanz said.

She picked up little Ava and held her against her chest, patting the baby's tiny back. "Did they hurt him first?"

He nodded.

"How badly?"

"Bad enough."

Maria went quiet for a moment as her husband ate his breakfast. "What a terrible thing," she eventually said. "Especially if the man had children."

Hanz stopped eating and gave his wife a level stare, her words jolting him. What made her say that, he wondered? He looked at Ava in her arms, and Shaylee in the crib, searching for any resemblance to the killer, and wanted to divulge the truth about the dead man, that he was likely the father of the twin girls left in their barn. He wanted to explain that even though the man had committed these horrendous crimes and deserved to die for them, he couldn't allow the men from town to hurt him further, watching as the father of their precious daughters suffered. Taking a deep breath, he said, "I have something to tell you, Maria."

She focused on his lips like she always did, sensing it was something important, not wanting to miss a single word.

But then, even as the truth rolled up his throat and hung on the tip of his tongue, Hanz could not release it. Instead, he said, "I never want to discuss this again," choosing then and there to remain silent, keeping the identity of the twins' real father a secret until his grave. "The man has been hung for his crimes, and if hell exists, then hell is where he is now. There's nothing more to say."

Before sundown, Hanz went back to the forest, cut the man down from the linden tree, and buried him.

⁕

The following morn, Constance Bodnar's corpse was brought to the Wolff farm for burial preparation. It was only days ago that Hanz had seen her in church, and now he was slowly walking around her lifeless body lying atop the cold metal table in his private morgue. He had known her since childhood–she and Josie Blum were best friends–and he could still remember her sitting in front of him in class, her blonde hair perfectly braided in the traditional *Gretchenfrisur (Gretchen hairstyle)*. Such a sweet girl.

"What do you want to be when you grow up?" he recalled her asking him one day in the schoolyard.

"An artist," he had told her. "What about you?"

"I just want to be happy."

"I can paint your portrait someday," Hanz offered.

"*Wunderbar.* Paint me on a bed of roses, with my hair flowing and the light shining down on me, like I'm a saint immortalized forever."

Hanz agreed. Little did he know then that someday he would be her mortician instead of her portraitist, not painting her but preparing her dead body, her hair flowing under the shining light in his morgue, with roses soon to be placed on top of her casket rather than laid beneath her.

Constance Bodnar had been born into a wealthy German family and married an architect from Munich, but unfortunately he died suddenly of influenza. Of course it devastated her, and that made her all the more vulnerable to a handsome, smooth-talking conman like the one they had just hung. What horrors ran through her mind when she first realized he was a predator, Hanz wondered, turning from a friendly priest into an abominable monster? What were her final thoughts as his cold knife sliced through her warm, soft flesh, spilling out her precious blood? The macabre image made him shiver.

Dieter Marx was right—Constance's throat had been slit ear to ear, so savagely it looked like she had two mouths. Her nails were all broken, and her arms and torso severely bruised. It was clear she had fought frantically for her life.

Whenever a body was this severely cut, bruised, or broken, requiring major repair, Hanz often pretended he was creating a new violin. A flick of the wrist, a stroke of the hand, a slice here and a stitch there. Yes it was odd, but it helped him get through it.

After gently washing Constance's body, Hanz slowly, painstakingly, began the difficult artistry of covering over her blemishes. Maria brushed and styled her hair, painted her nails red, and applied some lipstick. Together they clothed her in a white satin dress, and attached a pair of pearl earrings that had not been stolen, along with a ruby ring on her finger. She looked as lovely as she had that previous Sunday in church, except now she was sleeping—a saint immortalized forever.

The work never got easier for Hanz, especially when he knew the person. When it was all done, he remained behind for a moment, staring at Constance, seeing them together in the schoolyard that day. The memory made him sad, and as he turned out the light, the darkness enveloped him like a heavy cloak. Instantly a cold sensation ran through his entire body as if an icy, lifeless hand touched his bare back. Hanz panicked and fumbled to open the door, frantically trying to get outside. When he finally found his way out, he fell to the ground, his heart pounding in his chest.

CHAPTER 5

Word spread swiftly about the man who had been lynched, and though rumors were abound over who'd been involved, it was quickly forgotten–no local law enforcement repercussions. Instead, those who knew Hanz and Maria focused on the wonderful news about the Wolffs, friends and neighbors congratulating them, expressing happy surprise that Maria, whom everyone believed barren, had birthed two healthy babies. Hanz shared with everyone why they had kept her pregnancy a secret, and just as she predicted, everyone understood, empathetic over the couple's previous heartache.

"*Hallo*, Maria!" Nora Yurkovich greeted, standing on the Wolff porch, flashing a wide smile. "I came as soon as I heard the news. I thought to myself, 'My heavens, I have to see those babies!'" A small but stout Jewish woman, Mrs. Yurkovich thought it was not only her right but also her duty and responsibility to know everything that was going on, in and around Rothenburg ob der Tauber. Sixty-one years old but still with the spunk and vitality of a lively squirrel, she taught dance and etiquette to young girls in the Jewish quarter. She and her husband Maximillian had also traveled the world and brought several exotic animals back with them, each one a living souvenir from their adventures: A Siamese cat from Thailand, a saluki dog from Egypt, a bearded dragon lizard from Australia, and numerous exotic birds from the tropics.

"Mrs. Yurkovich, I was just thinking about you the other day," Maria said, a smirk on her lips. She knew the gossipmonger was there to find out all the juicy details about the Wolffs and their new babies. "I made some tea; would you like to join me?"

"I heard what happened to that man who came to Rothenburg pretending he was a priest," Abimelech Applebaum said the following week. He and his three sons–Malachi, Seth, and Aaron–were the Jewish workers Hanz hired whenever he needed additional help. "What a sickening, evil human being."

Hanz removed his sun hat and dusted it off on his leg, wiping the sweat from his brow. "Well he paid for his sins. Dead and buried."

Abimelech nodded. "I'm glad he was buried before sundown."

Hanz looked at him. He hadn't told anyone but Ollie and Randolph that he was there, let alone went back the same day to bury the man. "Why is that?"

"Because otherwise this land would be defiled before God." In Jewish tradition, leaving a body exposed on a tree after execution was considered a mark of disgrace and a way to symbolically accurse the deceased. However, the body must be buried the same day to avoid defiling the land.

Hanz thought for a moment. "Did you know the young Jewish girl he raped?"

Abimelech gave him a puzzled look. "*Nein.* Why do you ask?"

"Just curious."

"Only the rabbi and her parents know. It's best that way, for the girl's reputation. Don't you think?"

"*Ja.*" Hanz struck a match and lit his corncob pipe, puffing until the tobacco started burning. "I knew the woman he murdered. I went to school with her when we were children. It was difficult preparing her body for burial."

Abimelech scratched his long white beard, his dark eyes glazing over as his mind wandered into the past. "I was a sailor in my youth. Did I ever tell you?"

"*Nein,*" said Hanz, surprised, as Jews were not historically known to be seafarers.

Abimelech smiled, reminiscing. "Oh *ja*, indeed. I wasn't always a landsman. I wanted to travel the world, so I got a job as a sailor with a group of Gentiles, and let me tell you, the *schöne Dinge (beautiful things)* I saw would amaze you." He muttered something in Hebrew, something about the beauty of the sea and everything that resided in it. And then he became more somber. "One day, far out in the Mediterranean, a young man named Willy Wilcox said he didn't feel well. We called him Willy-Wi. No one thought it was serious, until the morning when we found him dead."

"Wow. What happened?" asked Hanz, exhaling a billow of smoke.

"None of us knew. We just gave him a traditional sea burial, wrapping his body in a canvas shroud and lowering it into the ocean. I said a Hebrew prayer, and we watched him sink to the bottom of the deep." Abimelech stared out into the distance, as if the sea were on the horizon. "I sometimes dream about him, down there in the cold water. And in the dream, he always opens his eyes and grabs me. It wakes me up every time, sweating and breathing hard." Scratching his beard again, he added, "Perhaps he didn't like my Hebrew prayer."

Hanz thought about the prayer he said on behalf of the dead man when he buried him in the forest. The Bible teaches that God is the Supreme Judge, so he figured it was the right thing to do. No one is born a monster, he reasoned, as we all come into this world an innocent babe. But then, sadly, some lose their way and do horrible things. I suppose I prayed for that babe he once was, he thought, and for the man he could have been. If that makes any sense.

Abimelech smiled, as if listening to Hanz's inner dialogue, then returned to work in the vineyard.

As he walked back to the farmhouse, Hanz thought about Willy-Wi at the bottom of the cold sea, and then again about the man he had buried in the cold ground. Despite the warmth of the hot summer day, a chill ran down his spine.

⁂

That night, Hanz had a nightmare. He was back in the forest, standing in front of the noseless cadaver hanging from the linden tree, swinging back and forth in the breeze. When he grasped the rope to cut the body down, the dead man opened his eyes and grabbed his arm. "Those aren't your daughters!" he screamed. "You're raising children belonging to a Jew, fathered by a murderer, thief, and rapist!"

Hanz woke up in a sweat, breathing hard, just like Abimelech did when dreaming of Willy-Wi. He looked over at Maria deep asleep beside him, and at the twins between them. Both little girls were wide awake, their eyes shining, watching him through the quiet darkness.

⁂

The weekend arrived, and Hanz sat at the bar of The Devil's Needle, slowly sipping his drink. Ollie was already sloshed, Randolph the Bull too, and both men drank and laughed like inebriated twin possums on a tree branch, interlinking arms and singing. The pub was alive with the chatter of people socializing, and music flowed to a small dance floor from a gramophone Nila had recently purchased. It smelled of seasoned sausages from the kitchen, earthy cigars from the men, and cheap perfume from the ladies. Yes, The Devil's Needle had become "the" place to be in Rothenburg on the weekends, being both a *Kneipe (pub)* and *Lokal (restaurant)*, and now also a *Tanzclub (dance club)*. Nila even had to hire two waitresses to help with the increased workload.

"This night is going to be the best ever!" Ollie slurred, lifting his vodka glass in a toast.

"You say that every time," Hanz mumbled. "And then I have to carry your bony drunk ass to the car."

Ollie and Randolph exchanged glances. Hanz had been in that sourpuss mood all night, making sarcastic comments rather than joining in the fun. But they didn't know what Hanz had learned about who the twins' real father was, and it kept bothering him, unable to shake it.

"C'mon, *mein Freund!*" Ollie said. "What's the matter with you? We're making happy memories here!"

Randolph slammed the top of the wood bar with his fist and let out a belly laugh. "Hell, *ja!* Memories of the first day of the rest of our lives!" Catching sight of Nila entering the kitchen, he called out, "Nila! Bring us a plate of those sausages with sauerkraut!"

"*Ja, ja,* don't worry," she sarcastically replied. "Just have fun with your *Freunde*; I'll do all the work tonight."

He winked and blew her a kiss.

She shook her head and smiled.

Turning his attention back to his friends, Randolph gestured to Ollie behind Hanz's back. Ollie nodded, and on a silent count of three, the Bull grabbed Hanz in a headlock while Ollie rubbed his knuckles on his head.

"Let me go!" Hanz demanded.

"Not until you change that grumpy mood," said Randolph. "We want *glücklich (happy)* Hanz back."

"Okay, okay! I'm *glücklich!* I'm *glücklich!*"

"Why are you *glücklich?*" asked Ollie, still rubbing. "Is it because you have me and Randolph as your *beste Freunde (best friends)?*"

Hanz tried to free himself, but Randolph's grip was too strong. "*Ja, ja,* that's why!"

"And we're like *Brüder* to you, right?"

"*Ja, Brüder!*"

"Tell us you love us," Randolph said.

"I love you! I love you! Now let me go!"

Randolph released his death grip, and he and Ollie practically rolled on the floor, laughing.

At first Hanz was mad, but then he broke out in laughter too. They all laughed hard, and Randolph apologized, patting him on the back. "No grumpiness allowed in *Die Teufelsnadel* tonight, *glücklich* Hanz! Tonight we drink and be merry!"

Hanz agreed, and the three men picked up where Ollie and Randolph left off, drinking, joking, and laughing like *beste Freunde und Brüder.*

Nila came through the swinging kitchen doors and watched them for a moment. The Three Musketeers—Athos, Porthos, and Aramis. With her hand on her hip, holding a tray of sausages and sauerkraut, she shook her head once more and smiled. "*Kleine Kinder (Little children),*" she said under her breath. "*Ungestüme, kleine Kinder (Rambunctious, little children).*"

❦

Hanz and Ollie, too inebriated to go home, slept it off in Randolph and Nila's back room. Hanz dreamed he heard one of the twins crying and woke, only to find Ollie passed out and snoring, his messy white hair sticking up like a rooster. Knowing Maria was probably worried sick by now, he nudged his friend to tell him he was leaving, but Ollie only rolled over on the couch and slurred, "Not tonight, Stella. I'm too sloshed." Hanz grinned, holding back a chuckle.

Grabbing his hat, he pushed open the intricately carved wooden door of The Devil's Needle, its medieval hinges creaking, and pulled up his collar to greet the cooler night air. Normally people were coming and going, but that late at night the street was empty. An eerie quietness, punctuated by three looming trees lurking in the shadows made the area seem ominous, while above on an abyss of ebony velvet, the stars shined with such an intense luster that Hanz swore they could be diamonds.

Bucephalus, patient and loyal as always, stood out front, watchful for his owner. When he caught Hanz's scent, he nickered softly and hoofed the ground.

"I'm sorry I made you wait so long, *mein Freund*," Hanz said, running his hand along the stallion's smooth, muscular back. "Too much of a *gute* time tonight."

Out of the shadows, the homeless older man who resembled the image of Moses suddenly appeared. But he wasn't standing on the street corner as usual, with a worn Bible in one hand and a shepherd's staff in the other, shouting out scriptures like a madman. Instead, he seemed rather docile. Normal, even. Acknowledging Hanz with a friendly nod, he stopped a few feet away from him and said, "Out of all the *Menschen (people)* in this godforsaken town, you are the only one who doesn't laugh at me. The only one who says a kind word."

Hanz reached into his pocket for some change.

"*Nein,*" said the man. "Not tonight. Tonight I am not a panhandler but a man like you, giving a kind word back." He extended his hand. "Let me properly introduce myself: My name is Silas Simpleton."

Hanz shook the man's hand; it was large and bony, with fingers stretching out like the branches of a tree. "*Gute* to meet you. I'm Hanz Wolff."

"Wolff . . . That's a very special German name that goes back centuries, *ja?* You should be proud of it."

Hanz simply nodded.

"Do you know who Christian Freiherr von Wolff was?"

"*Nein.*"

"He was one of the most eminent German philosophers in the early 1700s, and his life's work spanned almost every scholarly subject of his time. Perhaps he's your distant relative."

Hanz didn't know, giving a shrug.

"Some even deemed his demonstrative-deductive, mathematical method to be the peak of the Age of Enlightenment. And he was a strong proponent of natural law over moral law."

Hanz was impressed. There was much more to this vagrant than meets the eye. "You have quite an interesting last name yourself: Simpleton."

A soft smile touched the old man's lips. "*Ja.* It originates from England during a time when life was more elegant, more *schön (beautiful)*. Men wore top hats and women petticoats, and people were friendly and polite back then." His smile turned to a frown, and he shook his head. "In some ways it feels like yesterday when I was last there, and in others, a lifetime ago. How I ended up here in Germany, only the stars know."

The moonlight illuminated his face, and Hanz could see that one eye was quite different. Strange looking, as if a miniature galaxy existed within his orbital bone structure.

"It was a woman who did this," the man said, pointing at his eye after noticing Hanz staring. "*Ja,* even a nomad like me has a story. I was once more handsome than even you, Herr Wolff, and I made the wrong *Fräulein* jealous."

Hanz lit a cigarette; it glowed bright orange between the two men. "That's why she tried to take your eye?"

"*Nein.* It wasn't my eye she was after. It was my soul. Don't fool your-self—all *Frauen (women)* want your soul. The *gute* ones to take with them to heaven, and the *schlecht (bad)* ones to send you to hell." The homeless man chuckled, glancing up at the diamonds in the sky, his strange eye merging with the Milky Way. "I miss *Frauen,* though. Even the one who did this to my eye. Those were the days when I was passionately in love, intoxicated by their feminine wiles."

Hanz wasn't sure what to say, seeing him in this rare state of sanity.

And yet the soliloquy went on: "This life we live is funny. It's like we are all caught between two worlds, and our human spirit is always trans-forming, always getting brighter or darker. We're in a constant fight be-tween *gute* and *böse (evil)*. A holy war. An invisible struggle on the path of right and wrong, and everyone must walk it and choose."

Though it was impossible, a bizarre sensation swept over Hanz where he thought the man knew everything about him. An omniscient mind reader, aware of all his sins, iniquities, and bad choices; even the truth about Ava and Shaylee.

"Surviving is an art, you know. Like poetry." The older man crossed his arms over his chest and gazed intensely at Hanz, his galaxy eye orbiting the stars within it. Suddenly it was Plato standing before him, expounding his philosophical wisdom. "Birth, suffering, rebirth—over and over—it's the manifestation of life. The unstoppable metamorphosis that takes place, carving its masterpiece called humanity. Go with it, Herr Wolff. Go with it, and don't try to fight it, or you will lose."

What an unexpected encounter with the homeless man! Recalling the horrible things he witnessed during the Great War, Hanz found his voice and said, "But the suffering can be unbearable. It's difficult to 'go with it' when you're in a living hell."

"My dear boy, if you find yourself in a living hell, just keep living. Even as the flames surround you, keep marching forward like a Viking slaughtering his enemy, and you will find your way out of it." The older man paused for a moment, harkening back to the past again. "I have been around the world, met many people, and seen many things. Would you believe I was once a respected physicist? I even met Einstein while I lectured at the University of Zürich."

"You met Albert Einstein?" asked Hanz. Intrigued yet unsure if he could believe him, he flicked a piece of tobacco from his teeth.

"*Ja, ja.* Funny little man, he was. Obsessed with mathematics and physics, too. Did you know that when he was asked what it felt like to be the smartest man on earth, he answered, 'I don't know. You'll have to ask Nikola Tesla.'" He cackled, his laughter echoing down the street.

Hanz suddenly wanted to know more about this eccentric, homeless man named Silas Simpleton. Why was he living like he was? If everything he said was true, how did he end up a beggar on the street? What happened in his life that broke him, robbing him of his sanity? Maybe I can help him, Hanz thought. But then he changed his mind and thought of something else. "Silas, I have a question for you."

The old man's eyes homed in on Hanz, eager to impart his wisdom.

"Earlier you mentioned natural law versus moral law. What did you mean by that?"

"It's elementary, Herr Wolff. Natural law is based on objective moral truths inherent in nature and human behavior, discoverable through reason. Moral law is a set of rules and principles created by humans based on cultural or religious beliefs. Take a lie, for example. Is it reasonable to deceive when it protects someone, or is it still morally wrong?"

Hanz's heart skipped a beat. "Well . . . if it's carried out for *gute*, how can it be *schlecht (bad)*?"

"A lie is a lie is a lie, you know? The burden is, can you live with the lie?" The older man stroked his long, silver beard, thinking deeply. "But there are always two sides to a coin, as Christian Freiherr von Wolff would argue, and only a closed mind sees the one." Silas' eyes glazed over, and he began to recite scriptures. His special moment of sanity was gone, and he walked off into the shadows, mumbling to himself.

Hanz watched him disappear, somewhat in awe of the unexpected encounter with the homeless man. Adjusting the headstall on his horse, he climbed into the carriage and grabbed the reins, giving them a gentle yank. "There are always two sides to a coin," his mind echoed as Bucephalus trotted briskly toward home under the starry night. "Only a closed mind sees the one."

CHAPTER 6

The Wolffs were excited to get the twins baptized, and had made arrangements with St. Jacob's Church in Rothenburg ob der Tauber for the following Sunday after mass. As they sat in the old wooden pews of the historic Gothic basilica, waiting for the sermon to begin, Hanz cradled Ava in his arms while Maria held Shaylee. Maria had prepared for this special day through a labor of love, making matching outfits for the babies using fine linen, rich satin, and delicate lace, each child resembling a porcelain doll. The twins were quiet and peaceful in slumber, unlike the other babies crying in the church and making a fuss.

Maria scanned the congregation. A smile born of contentment and pride graced her lips; a deep sense of accomplishment lifted her soul. Being a mother and knowing the entire town believed the babies were hers was a feeling she could not put into words. She gazed down at the innocent features of little Shaylee, watching her sleeping daughter in awe. Shaylee's eyelids fluttered, and her tiny, plump lips puckered, sucking at nothing. Oh, how Maria wished she could breastfeed the newborns! Instead, she could only place a pacifier in the child's mouth; the baby latched on.

Ava woke and began to cry, and Hanz carried her to the rear of the church, gently patting and rubbing the child's back until she calmed. So tiny and light, she wriggled in his arms; so evocative was the love in his heart. When the child stopped crying, he rejoined his wife.

The priest ended his powerful homily with an affirmation of God's mercy and divine providence manifested in the miracle He performed for the Wolffs. "Have faith in the Creator, my children. Look at what he has done for Hanz and Maria. We watched them suffer; we grieved with them; we prayed for them; and now look!" he exclaimed, pointing at the twins. "Behold the power of God Almighty!" He gazed out into the congregation with deep conviction. "Always have faith in God, my children. His lofty eyes are on you, and you never know when he will grant you mercy."

Hanz, listening intently, looked down at the ground. Surely it was God's plan to have these two Jewish children given to them. What could it hurt to claim the twins as their own?

After the sermon and the babies' baptismal rites had been completed, several of the busybodies gathered around like a gaggle of geese, eager to see the little girls.

"Look at all that dark hair sprouting on their heads," Evelyn Koch said. "I'm sure it will turn strawberry blonde later."

"We didn't even know you were pregnant," said Gerda Neumann. "What a surprise."

"I thought I saw you in town not long ago, and you were skinny as a rail," Beca Adler claimed.

Maria nervously read their lips as the women chattered on, exchanging dubious glances.

"Listen to all of you," Tabatha Bach scolded. "It's like you're questioning where the babies came from. For goodness' sake, you sound like fools. Do you have to witness a woman give birth before you believe she has?"

"We're just curious, is all," said Beca, peering into the twins' adorable little faces.

Bertha Scheetz, a full-figured woman who always wore an overly decorative hat to church, pushed through the ladies, elbowing her way to the girls. "My goodness, they're little dolls from heaven, is what they are! Precious little cupcakes—I just want to eat them up! Now you give me one to hold right now, or I'll faint! Gimmie, gimmie!"

Maria smiled as the other women rolled their eyes, picking up Shaylee and lowering her into Bertha's chubby arms.

"Look at you," Bertha cooed. "You're an angel from above." She looked back at Maria. "Now give me the other one too. I want to hold them both."

Maria obliged, and Bertha held them close to her bosom, getting all teary-eyed.

Hanz approached and kissed his wife on the cheek. He stood tall and proud, like any good father would.

As the days unfolded, Hanz continued to nurse the albino fawn. The little deer had begun walking gingerly on its injured leg and was no longer afraid of him or its surroundings.

"I saved your life, little one," Hanz said one morning, holding it close as he bottle-fed the baby deer. "You were lucky I found you, too, or a wolf would have gotten you for sure."

The fawn stared at him with large doe eyes as it suckled on the bottle, its tiny tail wagging in delight.

Maria walked into the barn. She looked happy but tired, having spent most of the night up with the twins. When one would cry, the other would follow, but now they were both asleep. "The girls are finally down, so I came to visit our cute little *Freund*," she said, kneeling to pet its alabaster fur. "She's so beautiful."

"It's a 'he'," said Hanz, "and it will be a strapping buck someday."

"You think it will survive?" she asked, marveling at its soft blue eyes rimmed with pink.

"It should, with continued shelter, food, and care."

"If it does, then what? Are we going to have a white buck as a pet?"

Hanz chuckled. "Nature will run its course, and when he's ready, he'll be on his way."

"You're going to be sad when he goes."

"I know," said Hanz, already wistful about it. He thought for a moment. What a triumphant day that would be if, years from now, he saw the magnificent albino deer again—now a strong, healthy buck—staring back at him from the forest, quietly thanking him for its life.

"I'll go put some coffee on," Maria said. "I made some *krapfen (donuts)* too."

"*Danke, meine Liebe.* I'll be there as soon as this hungry little guy is finished."

But the baby deer didn't get that chance. Moments later, Maria yelled from the farmhouse, "Hanz, come quickly!"

The urgency in his wife's voice threw his mind into a panic, whipping up morbid thoughts. What happened? Were the girls sick? Did one of them die in the night? Dropping the bottle of goat milk, he bolted to the house as his heart thumped wildly in his chest.

"In the bedroom," Maria said.

Relief came over Hanz when he walked into the room and saw his children sleeping on the bed. What a beautiful scene: Ava and Shaylee, holding hands, peacefully snuggling side by side. The twin sisters had already developed an intrinsic bond, comforting each other by their mutual touch.

Hanz and Maria gently lay down on either side of them. Maria touched Ava's other hand with her index finger, and the infant subconsciously grabbed hold of it. "Hanz, look," she whispered, tears welling in her eyes.

He smiled and touched Shaylee's free hand, and she too grabbed hold of his finger.

As the adorable family lay still in that moment of beatitude, Hanz captured every detail on the canvas in his mind. Each shape, contour, line, color, and texture he memorized, preparing for the masterpiece he would later paint.

Every evening before entering the farmhouse after work, Hanz stood at the edge of the field, his boots caked with the rich, dark soil–evidence of another day of labor under the ever-faithful sun. His eyes scanned the horizon that kissed the embrace of twilight, while his mind was elsewhere, taking stock. So much had happened in such a short period of time, it was hard to believe.

And now Hanz and Maria had undeniably entered a new chapter in their lives, finding a sacred sanctuary they never thought possible–having a family. But that sanctuary was disturbed by the truth. Because somewhere not far from them was a wide-eyed girl who cried for her two daughters whom the couple now called their own.

A Jewish girl who had suffered immensely to bring them joy.

Abigail . . .

CHAPTER 7

Spring, 1922

A year had passed on the Wolff farm, and while the fields had yielded a bountiful harvest, Hanz and Maria focused on their greatest harvest of all—their family. The girls, now crawling and trying to walk, were a never-ending source of joy for the happy couple. And as their daughters' dark hair grew and their green eyes shined, the unspoken secret, like an invisible thread, continued to weave itself through the fabric of their lives, stitched into place but never discussed. As if Maria had truly birthed them.

"Mama . . . Mama," Hanz heard little Ava say as he sat in his favorite chair by the fireplace, sipping on a shot of Jägermeister. Maria was on the living room floor with the twins, changing their cloth diapers.

"Mama," Shaylee parroted.

Hanz looked at them in delight, then waved at his wife to get her attention, smiling widely. "They just called you Mama!"

Maria's face lit up, and she looked back at her girls gazing up at her. "Oh, Hanz, what did it sound like? Tell me, *bitte (please)!*"

He thought for a moment. "Like a little bird, *meine Liebe.* Like two little birds, calling for their mother."

Happy tears filled her eyes as she read his lips.

"Such a *wunderbar* sound, Maria. The sweetest I've ever heard."

The couple was so full of love in that special moment . . . The twins' first words!

"Come sit with them on my lap," Hanz said. "I want to hold my family."

Maria wiped her tears of joy, picked up their girls, and sat with them on her husband's lap. He wrapped his long, strong arms around them, and together they sat in familial bliss.

Hanz recalled what the priest had said during Sunday's sermon in St.

Jacob's Church, how there's a time for everything under the heavens. A time to be born and a time to die. A time to cry and a time to laugh. A time to grieve and a time to dance. A time to love and a time to hate, and so on. The meaning of that scripture in Ecclesiastes now hit home for him like never before. This was the Wolffs time to be born anew. A time to laugh, dance, and love. Yes, this was their time to rejoice!

Outside, an ominous-looking storm was fast approaching. The giant cumulonimbus clouds, dark and threatening, rumbled with thunder and crackled with lightning, angry at the earth. Ferocious winds bent the trees in the forest and whipped the tall grass in the meadow, resembling an emerald sea thrashing back and forth.

Within minutes it reached the house, and Hanz and Maria watched it for a moment through the living room window. The natural phenomenon escalated, and Zeus sent a bolt of lightning from heaven in a bright flash, striking Hanz's plow with an electrifying shower of sparks and fire, while Thor slammed his Mjölnir down in a deafening boom of thunder. Not to be outdone by the Greek and Norse deities, the Hindu god Indra followed with a deluge of rain.

"We better go into the cellar," Hanz said. "This is a bad one."

Maria quickly took the cherry pie cooling on the kitchen table, Hanz carried the twins, and the Wolff family descended into Hanz's library in the cellar. In no time the girls were fast asleep on one of the worn-out leather chairs, despite the mayhem outside, and while Maria cut the cherry pie, Hanz poured them both a glass Chartreuse. Together they sat on the patterned rug and enjoyed the moment.

Maria, a tender-hearted woman, shed more happy tears, and Hanz named each one as they fell. "This one is joy," he said, gently wiping it away. "This one is hope, and this one love." He knew Maria down to her very core, her essence. Her mind, her heart, her intentions and dreams. And she knew him the same way. Gazing into each other's eyes, their faces were happy, excited, and trepid all at once.

Above, the house shook violently as the thunderstorm overtook them, but the foundation held strong. And so it came to pass—the Wolffs had survived their first storm as a family.

But little did they know there would be many more to come . . .

Early the next morning, while mending the wooden fence that suffered damage during the storm, Hanz saw his neighbor, Clovis Steinburg, approaching. Haggard and drawn, his eyes vacant as if peering into some ghastly abyss, despair exuded from his pores.

"Hanz," he croaked as he got near, his voice soaked in misery. "Something terrible has happened."

"What is it, *mein Freund?*"

"It's Elise . . . She's gone . . . *Meine Sonnenblume ist tot (My sunflower is dead).*"

A shiver snaked down Hanz's spine. *"Gott im Himmel, Clovis! Was ist passiert? (God in heaven, Clovis! What happened?)"*

"A sudden illness took her. Dr. Schultz tried to save her, but it was too late."

"I'm so sorry."

Clovis wiped his tears. "Would you prepare her for burial?"

"Of course."

"*Danke* . . . I've given up, Hanz. I can't maintain the farm alone, not with my own health deteriorating. I'm going to sell it and move to America." Clovis was in anguish over the words he'd say next . . . "And I can't take my children with me. My baby daughter—I'm sending her to my sister in Berlin. She and her husband can manage another child. But Luka, my dear boy . . . I don't know what to do with him."

As Hanz looked empathetically at his friend, his pulse began to elevate, anticipating what his neighbor was thinking.

"Would you and Maria raise my *Sohn (son)?*" Clovis asked, swallowing hard, his eyes pleading.

The air seemed to thicken, each second stretching interminably as Hanz tried to assimilate the magnitude of this staggering request. A million thoughts ricocheted in his head.

"*Bitte*, Hanz. I cannot think of a better home for him. Or better parents."

Hanz hesitated, but the supplication in Clovis' gaze, the desperation in his plea, moved him to respond favorably with hope. "I'll talk it over with Maria. We'll let you know tomorrow."

⁓ↄ⸰ᴥ⸰ↄ⁓

Maria was kneading dough when Hanz walked into the kitchen. "You're back early," she said, her hands dusted with flour. "I haven't had time to make your lunch yet."

Hanz looked at his daughters holding onto the wooden lattices of their crib, wobbling as they stood. "We need to talk," he said, planting a kiss on each girl.

Sensing something serious, Maria wiped her hands on her apron and sat across from her husband at the kitchen table.

"It's about Clovis and Elise . . . He just told me she passed away from a sudden illness."

Maria's hand flew to her mouth, her eyes wide with shock.

"And Clovis is moving to America. His sister is taking little Hannah, and he asked if we would take Luka."

Again, Maria's eyes grew saucer wide. "What do you mean, 'take Luka?'"

"I mean to raise as our own, just like we did with Ava and Shaylee."

Hanz went on to explain how Clovis couldn't bring his young children with him across the Atlantic Ocean to a new land, especially with his own health failing and the uncertainty of his future there. And that this was yet another gift from God. An opportunity to grow their family.

Maria listened intently, knitting together the thoughts rampant in her mind as she considered the enormity of the decision before them. "So we would raise Luka as our own," she softly repeated when he had finished.

"*Ja*. Think of it, *meine Liebe*. We'd have a *Sohn*, and our daughters would have a *Bruder*. And when he grows, he could help me with the farm."

Maria nodded. "But to take on a young child who has known and lost his mother–it's not something we can decide lightly. It won't be easy for him."

"Luka is not a stranger to us," Hanz gently reminded her. "He will adapt quickly to his new family. And Clovis . . . he's desperate, Maria. He has no one else to turn to."

Maria met her husband's gaze, searching it for any remnant of doubt or reluctance. Finding none, a warm smile spread across her face. "Very well, then. We'll make room for another soul in this house of love."

⁓⋅⋐◈⋑⋅⁓

That afternoon, Hanz prepared Elise Steinburg's body for burial, going through the familiar process, step by step. Maria assisted him, since the Steinburgs had been their friends. They did not speak about how the woman lying on the cold metal table before them was the mother of the child they would now be raising. And yet it weighed heavily on their minds.

Afterward, Hanz said a prayer over the body, and the two of them held a wordless stare. Their neighbor's son was now their own . . .

Another unexpected gift born of someone else's suffering.

⁂

Hanz stood by the living room window later that evening, his gaze lost in the dusky horizon while his mind wandered through all the possible concomitants associated with adopting Luka. Watching Clovis retrieve Elise's dead body from his private morgue was heartbreaking, but now a young child's life lay in the balance.

The soft rustling of leaves interrupted his ruminations, drawing his attention to a familiar figure venturing into the yard. It was the albino deer he had saved, no longer the delicate fawn he had found entangled in the fence but now a yearling buck, adorned with splendid, twelve-inch deciduous antlers boasting six elegant points, hinting at the grandeur it would one day achieve.

Under the fading twilight, the buck's ivory white coat seemed to emit a ghostly radiance, creating a wraithlike aura around him. Hanz smiled, captivated by the beauty of the graceful animal. Another few years and it would be fully grown, with a massive crown of antlers branching out like the limbs of a sycamore tree.

A pang of melancholy washed over Hanz as he observed the exquisite creature. With its injured leg, once a fragile hindrance, now completely healed—a testament to the love and care he had given and the mercy of Mother Nature—its wild instincts beckoned it to roam the vast forest, disappearing for days, only to return to the familiar comfort of the Wolff farm. Soon it would not return at all, forging a new life in the wilderness.

Hanz fetched an apple and stepped outside to greet his Cervidae friend. The buck meandered closer, trusting their silent bond, and Hanz extended his hand, offering the apple. The deer accepted the gift, its muzzle gently taking the fruit as Hanz tenderly stroked its head.

"I see it in your eyes, *mein Freund*," he said softly to the animal, his voice laden with understanding and a hint of sorrow. "You long for the freedom of the forest, and it's calling you. I hope you stay one more summer before you must go."

As the albino deer slowly retreated into the embrace of the forest again, vanishing like a phantom into the shadows, Hanz watched, his heart heavy yet filled with hope. Like a worried parent, he sent a silent prayer into the night, asking for the deer's protection from the perils of both man and beast.

Turning back to the house, Hanz's thoughts drifted to the day he had found the young fawn, immediately preceding the discovery of his two precious daughters the very next day. The synchronicity of the events stirred something deep within him, a sense of wonder at the mysterious ways of life. In his heart, he knew that their paths had crossed for a reason, each leaving an indelible mark on the other's journey. Maybe the American Indians were right, he mused, gazing at the stars that now peppered the night sky . . .

A white deer is a bringer of good fortune.

In that moment, under the vast canopy of the heavens, Hanz felt a profound connection to the world around him, a sense of being part of something larger and more transcendent, more spiritual. The albino deer, a rare and beautiful anomaly, had become a symbol of hope and serendipity, a living reminder that in the midst of life's trials and tribulations, there are moments of unexpected grace and wonder.

✦

The next day, Clovis stood before the Wolffs, the very picture of a man whose world had been upended. "I wouldn't ask this of you if there were any other way," he said, clutching his hat between two rough hands.

"Don't worry, *mein Freund*," said Hanz. "We'll take *gute* care of him."

"*Ja*," added Maria. "Luka will be loved here, just like our girls."

The little boy, nearly four years old, shyly emerged from behind his father's back. His wavy blond hair, inherited from his mother, was so blond it was almost white.

"*Hallo, mein Junge (Hello, my boy)*," Hanz greeted, kneeling to his level.

Luka stared at him like a fragile bird, his eyes round and untrusting.

Hanz lifted him up, and the child's body went tense. "It's okay, Luka. I'm your papa now," Hanz whispered to him, feeling the boy's grip tighten around his shirt. Taking cautious steps, he slowly walked to the barn. "Look there," he pointed, putting the boy down.

Luka's eyes widened at the sight of a newly born lamb, nestled close to its mother on a bed of hay. He ran over to it, reaching out to pet its downy fleece, a smile forming on his lips.

"He likes you," Hanz said, observing the animal playfully reciprocate the affection.

Luka nodded, and the barn filled with a poignant blend of sounds and scents–a little boy's giggle, the earthy tang of hay, the cooing of doves, the subtle aroma of Maria's freshly baked bread wafting in from the house.

"There, you see? Life goes on, *mein Junge (my boy)*," said Hanz. "Even when we think it can't. I know this is all new and scary for you, but you're family now. This will be your home–a place of love and warmth. You'll be happy here."

The child looked up, his eyes locking onto Hanz's with an unspoken understanding. A promise of sorts that even a four-year-old boy could comprehend. In that tenuous moment, suspended between a painful past and an uncertain future, both Hanz and Luka knew they would make it work.

Clovis was watching from the entrance of the barn, a figure etched in woe. This was his world, his legacy, and he was giving it away, leaving it behind forever. As he turned to go, his eyes blurred with tears, erasing the image of his son in a haze of grief and loss.

❧

Later that evening, as Maria was tidying up the kitchen, wiping down the counters and sweeping the floor, Hanz came up behind her and wrapped his arms around her waist. She placed her arms atop his, and together they stood embraced in silence for a moment, smiling at the world's caprices.

Hanz reached over to the radio on the counter and turned it on, and though Maria couldn't hear the music, the happy couple slow danced in the kitchen, working their way to the living room. He spun her around and brought her back into his arms, planting a tender kiss on her lips.

Oh, so happy they were.

Where once they had lamented their barren home, void of laughter from children, now they rejoiced in it, having opened their world to two little girls with dark locks and green eyes and a little boy who had his mother's blonde hair. They were bound not just by the land they cultivated but also by the love they chose to give, freely and without condition, to a family now three children strong. A family not defined by blood but by the choices they made under the vast, indifferent heavens.

A family loved just the same.

CHAPTER 8

Summer, 1924

The summer zephyr danced through the yard, playfully blowing the laundry Maria was hanging on the clothesline one morning. Next to her, Ava and Shaylee played on the grass, speaking to each other in three-to-five-word sentences, while Luka sat on the porch, petting Rolf and Bruno, the Wolff's two sheepdogs.

A tall figure approached down the driveway, and Maria put her hand up against the sun, squinting at him until his face came into view. It was Severin, Hanz's younger brother, who had recently written to ask if he could come and live on the farm for a while, like he did when he was a teenager. Maria smiled and waved excitedly, then called out to her husband in the vineyard, "Hanz, your *Bruder* is here!"

"*Guten Morgen, meine Lieber (Good morning, my dear),*" Severin said when he got close enough for her to read his lips.

"My goodness, look how you've grown!" Maria said, giving her brother-in-law a big hug. "We weren't expecting you until next week!"

"*Ja,*" replied Severin, grinning ear to ear. "Slight change in plans; I hope it's okay."

"Of course, of course!"

Severin looked down at Ava and Shaylee on the grass, incredulous for a moment, struggling to align the images before him. "I can't believe you and Hanz had twins," he said. "That's a first in our family." He knelt to the girls' eye level and cooed in a soft voice, "*Hallo, kleine Lieblinge. Ich bin dein Onkel. (Hello, little darlings. I'm your uncle.)*"

Ava and Shaylee stared at him, wary of the stranger, unsure if they should release a gummy smile or start crying.

"I see you still have the same effect on the ladies, *Bruder,*" Hanz laughed, walking up to him. The two men shook hands, and Hanz pulled him in for a manly embrace before sizing his brother up. Seven years his junior, Severin was no longer a gangly teenager but a full-grown man, both in poise and stature.

Luka shyly came down from the porch. "Who's this, Papa?" It had taken several months after Clovis left him with the Wolffs, but eventually Luka started calling them Mama and Papa.

"This is my *Bruder, Sohn*. And your uncle Severin. Remember I told you he was coming to stay with us?"

Severin extended his hand to the little boy. *"Hallo, kleiner Mann. Schön dich kennenzulernen. (Hello, little man. Nice to meet you.)"*

"Hallo," Luka greeted in his small voice, shaking Severin's hand. "Papa says you're going to take me fishing."

"Ja, that's right. Now that I'm here, we'll have lots of *gute* times. Much to look forward to."

Luka smiled and nodded enthusiastically.

Maria noticed his shoes and shook her head. "Luka, your shoes are on the wrong feet, my sweet boy."

"But Mama, they're the only feet I have."

Everyone laughed.

Maria picked up Ava, Hanz picked up Shaylee, and Severin picked up his nephew. They all went into the house to catch up.

❧

"Tell me about Zürich," Hanz said later that evening, pouring two mugs of his homemade beer. The brothers were sitting in his makeshift art studio in the barn.

"Not much to tell, *Bruder*," replied Severin, chuckling ruefully.

"There must have been a calling, no?"

"That's a grand way to put it."

"What was the draw, then?"

An uncomfortable pause ensued, filling the space between them as a mix of estrangement and familiarity battled each other for dominion over the men.

"I know I left here suddenly, Hanz, and I'm sorry for that," Severin said. "It wasn't fair to you and Maria, especially after you let me stay with you all summer." He took a large swig of his beer. "And the truth is, Zürich never felt like home. I couldn't get used to it, and soon started wondering why I came."

"Well, it's *gute* to have you back," Hanz said, raising his mug toward his younger brother. "*Prost (Cheers).*"

The two men clinked glasses and downed their beer.

Severin looked about the place. I see you're still painting and making violins. Have you sold any?"

Hanz lit his corncob pipe and refilled their mugs with more beer. "*Ja,* quite a few, actually. Giovanni Mandolini sells my paintings in his art gallery in Rothenburg, and a rabbi in the Jewish quarter helps me find buyers for my violins. The extra coin is nice, but it's really just a hobby, to be honest."

Severin walked up to the easel and removed the tarp. Underneath was a painting of Maria smelling a pink rose in her garden—a near replica of John William Watehouse's classic 1908 oil painting, *The Soul of the Rose.* The beautiful, redheaded woman in Waterhouse's piece intrigued Hanz because she looked so much like Maria, and the famous painting created a feeling that the woman was trapped, both physically and metaphorically, drawing the viewer to her face and her sense of longing as she smelled the rose. Again, it made Hanz think of his dear wife and how she too was trapped, in a world of silence, longing for what she could never have.

Severin looked back at his brother in disbelief. "Is it the alcohol, or am I seeing this correctly?"

Hanz grinned.

"It's sensational, *Bruder!*"

"*Danke.*"

Hanz was very proud of that painting. John William Waterhouse was one of his favorite artists, who often incorporated a great sense of romance and sensuality in his women, whether in the form of naked flesh or simply a delicate look. His art was a visual narrative, telling stories of love, loss, and yearning, many of which were thought to be inspired by the poems of Alfred Lord Tennyson, the English poet appointed the Poet Laureate and member of the British royal household during Queen Victoria's reign. By using a warm palette of colors, mixing pinks, earthy oranges, and browns to help evoke a sense of summertime, with natural tones to accentuate the blush of Maria's cheeks, Hanz had successfully replicated the mood created by that renowned artist in that most impressive work.

Severin patted him on the back. "I've always admired you, Hanz. I know you wanted to move to Berlin and study art, but you went off to war instead."

Hanz covered up the painting. "Papa didn't give me much choice."

"Well, I'm going to do the same as you. I'm joining the military."

Hanz looked up at him. "Really?"

"*Ja.* You and Maria have the kids and the farm now, and you've built a *wunderbar* life here. But my aspirations are with the German army."

"Why?"

"Because soldiers are respected. And the military offers a structure, a purpose, that my life has lacked thus far. I can make a career of it, rising through the ranks."

"War has its costs, Severin. It's not all glory and uniforms. I almost lost my life, and permanently damaged my leg."

Severin grinned. "That's because you were a lousy pilot."

The two brothers laughed.

"Wait until Ollie and Randolph see you!" Hanz said, slapping his knee. "We'll go to The Devil's Needle soon and drink the night away! My *Bruder* is back, and there's much to celebrate!"

⚜

Hanz went to tuck the children into bed. Luka was already asleep, holding one of the wooden animals Hanz had carved for him, but Ava and Shaylee were waiting patiently, snug under the covers in their long cotton nightgowns Maria had made for them. They asked their father to read them a story, and Hanz sat in the chair next to the bed, opening the children's book, *Hansel and Gretel.*

Ava crawled out of bed and got into his lap. Shaylee did the same.

"How am I supposed to read like this?" Hanz protested. The little girls giggled, and as they laid their heads against his chest, curling up like kittens, his heart filled with joy.

Ava placed her little hand inside her father's; it felt like a tiny seashell. "I love you, Papa," she said, interrupting his reading.

"Me too, Papa," Shaylee echoed.

"And I love *you,* my little swans," he replied, tears welling in his eyes.

Days turned into weeks, and Severin, for all his past youthful brashness, slipped effortlessly into the mosaic of farm life. He toiled alongside Hanz in the fields, savored Maria's culinary delights, and doted on his nieces and nephew. Despite his dreams of military grandeur, it was evident that part of him had always yearned for this—this unspoken beauty of living close to the earth, of sharing love and laughter under a humble roof.

On weekends, the two brothers frequented The Devil's Needle, drinking and laughing alongside Ollie and Randolph the Bull.

"See this strapping young man here?" Randolph slurred one night, putting his arm around a drunken Severin. "He's going to be a heavyweight champion someday!"

"*Nein,*" said Hanz, leaning against Ollie to prevent him from falling over. "My *Bruder* would rather be an officer in the German army."

Randolph shook his head and downed his drink. "Too bad. The boy would make a helluva boxer!"

As Hanz drove the horse and buggy home that night, his younger brother passed out beside him, he noticed something white within the forest, almost glowing under the moonlight. Pulling on the reins, he stopped his horse and waited, and sure enough, as if summoned by some unknown force, the magnificent white buck he had come to know and love walked out from among the trees. The image caught his breath in his lungs, as he hadn't seen it in a while.

Encountering the albino deer on the road was a happy surprise for Hanz, as its visits to the farm were infrequent now. Rare, like the majestic animal itself. But each appearance was a gift, a precious moment captured in time, a fleeting connection to a world where the miracle of nature and the reality of life intertwined. Ever watchful for his albino friend, Hanz would notice the buck's arrival from afar, and whatever task occupied him—be it tending to the fields or mending a fence—he would set it aside, swelling with a mixture of joy and nostalgia. With a sense of urgency, he'd retrieve an apple or a handful of berries—treats he always kept handy for these special visits—and slowly approach. "*Hallo, mein Freund,*" he'd say, his voice a soft murmur, as if afraid to break the spell of the moment. "You've grown, haven't you." He would extend his hand, offering the treat, while his other hand gently stroked the buck's velvety muzzle—a touch that spoke of earned trust and recondite affection between man and beast.

And now, as he sat still in his carriage, gazing at the beautiful animal, Hanz could see there was something different in its eyes. Something wilder, more untrusting. The once sweet and innocent doe-eyed gaze of the little fawn that had looked up at him with repose and dependency had evolved into one born of survival and instinct. A penetrating stare from a creature that had embraced its true nature, wary and alert, attuned to every whisper of the wind, every rustle in the underbrush. The buck lowered its head to the ground, smelling the earth, then glanced back at Hanz again. Moments later, it vanished into the forest.

The fawn is gone, Hanz thought, and in its place the magnificent, regal beast has risen.

As it ought to be.

CHAPTER 9

Winter, 1925

It was the beginning of winter when the accident happened. When brown leaves were still in abundance but snow had begun to cover the ground like powdered sugar on a chocolate cake. Stanley Horowitz, the jeweler in Rothenburg ob der Tauber whom Hanz had purchased Maria's sapphire ring from, found Dr. Schultz half-conscious after a car accident. He had swerved to miss a deer and lost control on the icy road, hitting a tree.

From the impact, the doctor had been thrown through the windshield, his lower body still in the car while his upper body lay across the hood. Hanz was returning from town in his horse and buggy when he came across the wreckage. Pulling off the road, he ran over to help, but the doctor had lost a massive amount of blood as his torso had nearly been severed in two. Hanz knew right then and there that the doctor had mere moments left on this earth.

This was the second time that tree would claim a life, the first being the phony priest lynched by the men from town after he had raped a young Jewish girl, murdered a woman for her jewels, and scammed the townspeople of their money. Standing over the dying man's body, Hanz contemplated how the doctor would not have been killed had that tree burned to the ground the day it was hit by lightning when he was a child. It was a strange cogitation that lingered in his mind.

"Tell Roberta not to make a fuss about my funeral," Dr. Schultz moaned. "And that . . ." He coughed blood as he took a breath. "*Ich liebe sie (I love her).*"

"I will," said Hanz, holding his hand.

The doctor looked up at him, a knowing gaze in his eyes as his breathing became more labored. "Who is . . ."

Hanz leaned in closer. So close that his ear almost touched the dying man's lips. "Who is what?"

"Who is the real mother of those twins, Herr Hanz?" he asked in a rush of strangled words. "Are you ever going to tell them the truth?"

Taken aback by his question, Hanz just stared at him. It was obvious Dr. Schultz had never believed the lie. Seconds later, his eyes became empty–a candle with no flame–and he exhaled his last.

Hanz kept holding his hand, wondering if the doctor had ever told anyone, or if the secret was now dead with him.

"He's gone," Stanley Horowitz said. He closed the doctor's eyes that were still staring hauntingly at Hanz, and covered his head with a scarf, saying a quick prayer that God remember the man. Turning to Hanz, he asked, "What did he mean, 'Who is the real mother of those twins, and are you ever going to tell them the truth?'"

Hanz's mouth went dry. "I don't know. He was dying–it could mean anything."

Stanley nodded. "*Ja*. A man in shock will often ramble nonsense."

In the near distance, the buck that caused the doctor to swerve off the road was watching. The same albino deer Hanz had saved, standing still like an apparition, its coat the same color as the snow and its majestic deciduous antlers now fifteen inches and ten points strong. It stared at the three men for a moment, then disappeared into the woods.

⁂

"Papa!" Shaylee called out in the yard, catching sight of her father as he got home. She and Ava ran over to him, and Hanz got on one knee, scooping them up and cradling them in his arms, their tiny faces pressed against his cold cheeks. Luka was busy playing in the snow, a mixture of mud and slush covering his clothes. He noticed his father's face–usually lit up with a smile–appearing downcast and sad.

Maria stood behind the screen door, a thick wool shawl over her shoulders. "Get in the house now, children. And take off those grubby boots and clothes. A bath is waiting for you before dinner."

Hanz kissed the twins on the forehead and told them to listen to their mother; they scooted inside. He picked up Luka and carried him to the porch, helping him remove his boots.

"You're late for dinner," said Maria. "I was worried."

"Where's Severin?" Hanz asked, entering the house.

"He went to Nuremberg to sign up for the *Reichswehr (Reich Defense)*."

Taking a deep breath, Hanz spoke slowly to ensure his wife could read every word off his lips. "Dr. Schultz has been in an accident. He lost control of his new car and hit a tree. I think he was trying to avoid the albino deer, because I saw it nearby." He stared at her, his eyes large and bloodshot.

"Oh no. How badly is he injured?"

Hanz glanced over at the twins playing with their dolls and Luka with his wooden animal, patiently waiting in the living room by the fireplace, ready for Maria to give them their bath. "He's dead, Maria. I was with him when he took his last breath."

She gasped and covered her mouth.

Though they didn't speak, their eyes acknowledged the corollary outcome. Aside from Abigail, who would never disclose their secret, the doctor was the last scarlet thread connected to the lie.

Hanz's emotions were in utter turmoil. He would never wish harm to Dr. Schultz, and yet for the last few years there had been a constant fear the doctor might reveal that their daughters, whom he loved more than life itself, could not be his and Maria's. "It's terrible to say this, but . . . I can't help feeling almost . . ."

"Relieved," Maria said, supplying the word.

Hanz nodded. He sat down at the kitchen table, dropped his head into his hands, and to his surprise, gave way to tears, weeping like a child. He cried for many reasons: for the burden he carried, for the death of a good man who was also his friend, and for the sweet taste of freedom from the worry he had slept with every night till now.

Maria knelt beside him, placing her hands on his lap, shedding a tear of her own. "No one would blame us for this strange sense of relief, Hanz. Dr. Schultz knew I couldn't carry a child, and that twins would be impossible. All this time we've been worrying ourselves sick that he would eventually tell people."

Hanz wiped his eyes and looked down at his wife. Removing a lock of fiery red hair from her face, he kissed her forehead.

"I'm sorry he's gone too, but now it's over, and no one will ever know. They're our daughters, Hanz, and they'll think that for the rest of their lives, as they should." A determined expression crossed her face, and she grabbed hold of his hands. "They're *my* daughters, and a gift from God. I birthed them, and now no one can say any different."

Maria was the one who slept deeply and often had lifelike nightmares that seemed as if premonitions. But that night Hanz had one too. A remarkable vision, both awe-inspiring and frightening.

He dreamed he was sitting on Bucephalus on top of a mountain, and a ring of fire blazed in the valley below, surrounding a battlefield where thousands of men were fighting like red and black ants at war. Throats were being slashed, heads severed, abdomens disemboweled–a gruesome sight indeed! And when Hanz looked closer, the soldiers were not men at all but monsters, gargoyles, and reptiles in silver medieval armor. What kind of abomination is this, he wondered!

Oddly, Joan of Arc, the patron saint of France who led the French army in a momentous victory against the English at Orléans in 1429 during the Hundred Years' War appeared. How bizarre. Why would she be there? Hanz gasped as he witnessed the creatures catch her, tie her to a stake, and set her on fire, her soft, pale flesh disintegrating into ashes, floating in the sky.

The firmament was scarlet, and the moon refused to give its light. On the other side of the valley, on top of an even higher mountain, the leader of the beastly army came forward riding a huge, muscular steed with elaborate metal headgear, sharp points on all sides. His appearance was unusually fearsome, and he watched the battle below while holding a swastika flag in his hand, flapping in the wind. To the right of him, the kings of the earth sat at a round table, doing obeisance as they dipped their bread in a bowl filled with the blood of the innocent.

Hanz scanned the battlefield again, and suddenly the albino fawn appeared, standing all alone in the middle of the mayhem, wounded and afraid. The ashes from Joan of Arc's cremated body fell softly all over it, and one of the gargoyles took notice, intent on slaughtering the helpless animal. A powerful anger consumed Hanz, and he stormed into the battle on his righteous stallion, determined to save the baby deer. No fear, no hesitation, no doubt, he knew what he had to do, galloping through the bloodshed toward the vicious gargoyle before it was too late. The white fawn lifted its head, its doe eyes pleading, hoping, believing Hanz would save its life once more.

Above the entire scene, the heavenly constellations spun like an intricate clock. On the inside was a council of members, each watching in horror at what humanity had become. They began to sing, and the unknown song was like a million grieving instruments, angelic yet powerful, rocking the ground like an earthquake.

In the commotion of it all, the monsters, gargoyles, and reptiles intercepted Hanz, throwing him from his horse. They dragged him to another stake, tied him to it, and lit him on fire, just like they did to Joan of Arc. Hanz looked down to see the albino fawn in his arms. He wept as they burned, knowing he had failed them both.

Waking up in a sweat, breathing hard, Hanz gently shook his wife. "Maria . . . Maria," he said, sitting up in bed.

She roused, feeling his clammy hand on her skin, and turned on the bedside lamp to read his lips. "What is it?"

"I had a terrible nightmare. Like the one about the demon soldiers you had last year." Maria had woken up screaming one night, dreaming the fiendish creatures were marching through pools of blood, looking for Ava and Shaylee. "I could taste the evil, Maria. I could taste it."

"It's the stress," she said, gently caressing his furrowed brow, smoothing over the tension on it. "You're still in shock over what happened to Dr. Schultz."

"*Nein*, this is something else." He paused, thinking. "A symbolic message, maybe. Or a warning."

"About what?"

"I don't know. But the things I saw in that dream will haunt me for the rest of my life."

"You poor, sweet man." Maria kissed his lips. "I'm sorry you had such a nightmare; I know how frightening they can be. Try to get some sleep now." She turned off the lamp and nestled back into his embrace.

Outside, the moon in all its full glory shone through the bedroom window, a thin veil of clouds creeping past it. Hanz lay back down, and as he stared at the shadows on the ceiling, he thought of what his good friend, Aadan Omari, had once told him: "There are two worlds out there. The one that we see, and the other that lives in the fabric of our time. Occasionally, that other world seeps into this one, and we catch a glimpse of it. Or a glimpse of what's to come."

CHAPTER 10

Summer, 1927

The benevolent period that followed was a long stretch of time the Wolffs would forever hold sacred. Nestled in their agrestic German farm west of the quaint town of Rothenburg ob der Tauber, life unfolded in the rhythm of changing seasons and the cadence of hard but fruitful labor. Hanz and Maria had found an unexpected heaven that had descended upon them in a wicker basket, bundled in wool and marked by the Star of David, followed by yet another unanticipated gift at the pleading of a misfortunate neighbor. The farm, once a quiet place haunted by the ghosts of children they could not conceive, was now filled with joy, laughter, and the pure delight of two giggling little girls and a little boy who followed his father everywhere.

Ava and Shaylee had just turned six, and Luka almost nine. While Hanz worked in the field or the vineyard, sometimes he'd pause and see them playing in the yard, and he'd whistle to get their attention. The sound was a unique resonance, musical in tone, like a tropical bird singing in a tree, and whenever they heard it, they'd immediately run to him.

Nighttime brought its own familiar sounds, the stillness in the house punctuated by the occasional creaking floorboard and the clittering of crickets outside. Whenever a storm rolled in, lightning flashing through the bedroom windows transforming ordinary furniture into menacing shapes and rumbling thunder sounding like giants walking across the sky, the children would scamper into their parents' bedroom. Without a word, Hanz and Maria would lift the covers, allowing them to crawl in.

Often Hanz would read to his children, both to educate and entertain, teaching them life's lessons while expanding their incipient imaginations. Gazing at their papa wide-eyed, full of amazement, they'd listen in awe to his enchanting tales.

"Would you save us from *der große böse Wolf (the big bad wolf)?*" Ava asked one evening, her cute little voice laced with trepidation.

"Of course, *Schätzchen (sweetheart)*."

"What about a dragon?" asked Shaylee.

"*Ja, Liebling (darling)*, even a dragon."

"But what if it had huge teeth, big red eyes, and could breathe fire?" Luka asked.

"Even then, *Sohn*."

"How would you kill it, Papa?" Shaylee asked, always the inquisitive one.

"I would make a large sword and be brave, slaying it to save my children."

"But Papa, you would be risking your own life," said Ava.

Hanz smiled at his three children. "That's just what papas do, *meine Schützlinge (my precious ones)*."

◆

"Hanz, what have you done now?" Maria asked one afternoon, narrowing her eyes at him as he entered the kitchen, a mischievous grin on his face.

"It's a surprise, *meine Liebe*. Come with me." He covered her eyes and carefully led her outside.

Maria smiled at her husband's romantic playfulness. He was always looking for ways to brighten her day.

"Almost there," Hanz said. He winked at Luka in his overalls rolled up to his knees, and Ava and Shaylee in their matching pink and white checkered summer dresses, all of them standing excitedly beside an object in the yard, covered by a tarp. When he had Maria positioned exactly where he wanted her, Hanz said, "Okay, open!" releasing his hands from her eyes.

Instantly the children ripped the tarp off the object, revealing two brand new bicycles leaning upright against their kickstands. "Surprise, Mama!" they exclaimed in unison, jumping up and down.

Maria looked stunned. For months she had been telling Hanz how she missed cycling through the long, twisting roads where she grew up in Austria, with the mighty Nordkette mountains of the Karwendel Massif to the north and the Stubai and Tux Alps to the south as the backdrop. The

Wolffs didn't have the Alps by the farm, but the long dirt road through the forest and meadows, and the winding Tauber River alongside it, provided plenty of stunning scenery for a bike ride.

"Oh, you lovely man!" Maria said, giving him a hug and kissing his lips. She gazed at the bicycles in amazement.

"Come on, let's try them out," said Hanz. He grabbed a bike and gave the other one to his wife, and they started cycling around the yard, laughing and whistling like they were children again. Luka, Ava, and Shaylee ran barefoot alongside them, trying to keep up, the girls squealing as their parents drove round and round. Hanz headed down the driveway toward the dirt road, and Maria followed. "Watch over your sisters, Luka," he called out over his shoulder. "We'll be back soon."

Maria blew kisses to her children as they ran behind them as far as they could before losing their breath. They watched their parents disappear into the distance, swallowed whole by the blazing marmalade sun, setting on the horizon.

Later that night, after finishing his work in the barn, Hanz quietly entered their bedroom, expecting Maria to already be asleep. Instead, she was wide awake, reading a book by the bedside lamp. "Can't sleep, *meine Liebe?*" he asked, undressing and getting into bed.

"*Nein.*" She put her book away. "And with all that cycling today, I should be sleeping like a baby."

Hanz grinned. "You know what the Bible says . . . No rest for the wicked."

Maria pinched him.

"I'm just teasing you," he laughed. "Come here, my *Fräulein.* Let's be wicked together."

Maria giggled and opened her arms wide.

❧

Malachi Applebaum and his wife Ursula, along with their two little girls, Jeta and Zelda, moved from the Semitic quarter in Rothenburg ob der Tauber to the farmhouse on the south side of the Wolff property. They had owned a bakery in town, but Ursula's parents—the Friedmans—were getting older and needed help with their goat farm, so the Applebaum's sold the bakery and relocated to the country. Malachi used to work on the Wolff farm with his father and two brothers before getting married, and with his daughters close to the same age as the Wolff girls, the two families—one Catholic and one Jewish—saw each other frequently.

One weekend, the Grimaldi Family Circus came to town. The Wolffs and Applebaums all crammed together in Hanz's horse and carriage, eager to go see it.

"Papa, why do those men have those funny fur hats on their heads?" Ava asked as they entered Rothenburg, pointing at a group of Ashkenazi Jews wearing large black shtreimels.

"It's because they're members of Hasidic Judaism," said Jeta. "Papa, tell her what they're made out of."

Malachi smiled at his young daughter. "Most are made out of thirteen tail pelts from sable, martens, or fox. The shtreimel symbolizes the unity of God since there are thirteen letters in the Hebrew word for 'One.' Other shtreimels contain twelve tails to symbolize the twelve tribes of Israel."

"Interesting," said Hanz. "I did not know that." He pulled on the reins to halt the wagon, allowing the Ashkenazi men to cross the street. One of them nodded a silent 'thank you', and Hanz couldn't help but stare at his furry hat. Ava and Shaylee stared too, but Luka couldn't care less.

Although many families were still struggling to recover from the post-WWI economic disaster brought on by hyperinflation, the circus served as a welcome temporary respite. People were everywhere, with clowns, fire-eaters, and jugglers entertaining them.

"Hanz!" Randolph the Bull shouted as the Wolffs and Applebaums neared the entrance to the large circus tent. He and Nila were waiting for them.

"*Gute* to see you, *mein Freund*," said Hanz. He leaned over and kissed Nila on the cheek. "And you too, *mein Lieber (my dear)*."

Randolph and Nila greeted Maria and the Applebaums, and the Bull turned his attention to the little girls, picking them up and swinging them in the air as they giggled with delight. Not to leave Luka out, he shadow-boxed the young lad, then gave him a man hug and messed his hair.

"We have front row seats for everyone," Nila said, leading the way. "Randolph's and my treat."

Hanz and Malachi thanked them.

Ollie van Heinz was already seated with his wife and four children, all of them eating popcorn. Each child looked like a tiny version of their father.

Everyone politely greeted, and they all waited excitedly for the show to begin.

The Grimaldi Family Circus did not disappoint. Gargantuan elephants decorated in Middle Eastern attire, rolled on balls and stood on their heads. Roaring lions, tigers, and bears obeyed their taskmaster, jumping through hoops and doing tricks. Funny chimpanzees and clowns engaged in silly antics while riding ponies, making people laugh. And tightrope walkers, trapeze artists, and acrobats performed death-defying feats.

"Did you ever want to run away with the circus?" Hanz asked Ollie, giving him a teasing nudge.

Ollie tossed a piece of popcorn into the air, catching it with his mouth. "Sure, what child doesn't?"

"What would you have been?"

"A clown!" Randolph bellowed, his laughter echoing across the circus tent.

A lion was let out of its cage, and the ringmaster snapped his whip, forcing the beast to do some more tricks.

"I don't like how these animals are being treated," Maria whispered to Hanz. "They look abused, and they should be free, roaming the jungle rather than forced to entertain humans. God did not create such *schöne Lebewesen (beautiful creatures)* to be caged, whipped, and starved."

Hanz thought of the barn cats at the farm, how they roamed the meadow freely, frolicking and doing as they pleased. Maria was right–these poor, majestic beasts, stolen from their natural habitat, were being abused.

Just then, the lion roared and the crowd gasped. Hanz looked around, and that's when he noticed a young woman staring intently their way. She wasn't watching the circus act; she was watching his daughters . . . Her daughters! . . . Abigail!

He hadn't seen her since that awkward moment when he took a wrong turn and ended up in the Jewish quarter after taking the girls to see Dr. Schultz when they were babies. That was six years ago, and suddenly he felt like he had stolen Jewish property in his possession again. Priceless property, whose rightful owner was mere yards away.

Hanz looked at Ava and Shaylee, pointing and laughing at the circus spectacle, oblivious to it all. When he looked back at Abigail, she was gone.

CHAPTER 11

Autumn, 1933

When the Great Depression began after the Wall Street Crash of 1929, the country spiraled into a tailspin as foreign investors withdrew their German interests. The Wolff family weathered the storm, sheltering themselves from the economic collapse by living off the land. The farm not only sustained them during this arduous period but also engrained a strong work ethic in the children, strengthening the family as one cohesive unit. Maria had taught the girls how to feed the hens and gather their eggs without startling the birds, how to wash clothes against the washboard in circular motions, and how to clean the farmhouse and prepare various meals. Hanz had taught Luka how to direct the horse that pulled the plow, how to tend to the cows, sheep, and goats, and how to maintain the vineyard. Their willing hands fumbled initially but grew surer with time.

And yet still, the girls' unique appearance becoming more and more apparent in a community of blond-haired, blue-eyed citizens continued to raise a few curious eyebrows. "Miracles of nature," Maria would explain, attributing their daughters' dark hair and green eyes to a mysterious blend of distant relatives. Although the gossip flitted like sparrows from one neighbor to another, no one ever suspected the concealed secret behind Ava and Shaylee's heritage.

A secret contained in a handwritten letter and two woolen blankets, safely hidden away.

⁓⸰❦⸰⁓

The farm was abuzz with excitement during the grape harvest. Every year, once the last of the clusters were picked from the vines, Hanz and

Maria would mark the occasion with a traditional, Old World, foot stomping ceremony, crushing a pile of grapes in a large stone vat with their bare feet. This year, Ollie and his family, Randolph and Nila, and the Applebaums—Malachi, Ursula, Jeta, and Zelda—all joined in, making the event an especially happy one. The children loved it, jumping up and down, squishing the grapes between their toes.

"Thank goodness for modern methods of winemaking," Ollie said as he took his turn in the vat. "This is hard work."

"*Ja*," said Hanz, chuckling as he waited for his tall and skinny friend to inevitably slip onto his butt. "But it makes for better wine than using the machines because human feet provide a soft, even pressure, which is ideal for gently breaking the grape skins without damaging the seeds. The wine has a more refined balance of flavors and tannins, as a result."

No sooner had Hanz spoken than Ollie slipped, soaking himself head to toe with grape juice. Everyone laughed.

After the centuries-old tradition of foot treading was over, they all cleaned up and gathered for a meal, drinking wine from last year's batch.

"This is one of the best harvests yet," Hanz said, raising his glass in a toast. "*Danke* for helping out."

"*Gern geschehen (You're welcome)*," said Malachi. "I remember harvesting this vineyard with my father and brothers. Those were *gute* times." Sadly, Abimelech had since passed away, and Seth and Aaron moved to Berlin. "May all our families be blessed with happiness and long life." He lifted his glass and said in Hebrew, "*L'chayim (To life)!*"

Everyone joined in and cheered.

At the end of the night, Ollie and Randolph the Bull remained behind with Hanz as the Applebaums, Ollie's wife and children, and Nila went home. The three men stood in front of a bonfire, drinking vodka and talking, their silhouettes against the flames resembling a short and stocky wall—Randolph; a tall, muscular tree—Hanz; and an even taller string bean—Ollie.

"Today was a *wunderbar* day, but I fear for the future, *meine Freunde*," Hanz said. "The country is changing, and not in a *gute* way."

Ollie took a swig from his flask. "What do you mean?"

Hanz looked over at the small cabin at the edge of the vineyard used by the new seasonal workers. After the Applebaums had moved on, he hired another Jewish family to help out when needed. "Now that the Nazis are in power, the Jews and other minorities are being singled out and mis-treated. People are being desensitized, watching as the government treats them like animals."

When Adolf Hitler came into power on January 30, 1933, Nazi anti-Jewish policy had one goal in mind: to make the Jews leave Germany. Legal measures were quickly implemented to expel them from society and strip them of their rights and property while simultaneously engaging in cam-paigns of incitement, abuse, terror, and violence. For example, on March 9, 1933, organized attacks on Jews broke out across the country. Two weeks later, the Dachau concentration camp opened near Munich, where anyone considered an enemy of the Third Reich would be sent. And on April 1, 1933, a general boycott against German Jews was declared, where Nazi *Sturmabteilung (Storm Troopers)* stood outside Jewish-owned stores and busi-nesses to prevent customers from entering. One week later, a law was passed to purge the civil service, judicial system, and public health system of any officials who had Jewish origin. Then on May 10, 1933, ceremonial public book burnings of any work considered "un-German" took place across thirty-four towns and cities–a powerful statement of Nazi intoler-ance and censorship. Many were torched solely because their authors were Jews.

Ollie looked confused. "It's too bad this is all happening," he said, scratching his head. "But why does it bother you so much? You're German, so it doesn't affect you."

Randolph subconsciously balled his fists. "Doesn't affect him? Are you *verrückt (crazy)?* Ollie, an injustice to one man is an injustice to all."

Hanz agreed.

"At *Die Teufelsnadel,* those arrogant *Sturmabteilung* sometimes don't pay for their drinks, knowing they can get away with it. And if they see anyone Jewish, disabled, or different from their Aryan ideals, they bully them. They even had Nila in tears one time, and it took everything I had not to kill the bastards."

A silence settled in, the men just staring at the fire, until Ollie tried to lighten the mood by changing the subject. "Remember how I used to scrib-ble down poetry on the napkins at *Die Teufelsnadel?*"

"*Ja,*" said Hanz.

"I found one stuffed in my shirt pocket the other day. I wrote it after my mother died; it's pretty *gute.* You want to hear it?"

"Sure, sure," Randolph said.

Ollie cleared his throat, straightened his back, then recited his poem . . .

'The first blessing is the sweet kiss of a mother to her babe.
In her warm bosom, she holds her child.
Her love is like a shield, protecting him from harm.
But only for a while, until the babe becomes a man.
Yet in her mind, she always sees that first embrace,
That first kiss on your soft cheek,
That first day when you opened your eyes.
For although you may now be a man, her child you will forever stay."

Hanz smiled and patted Ollie on the back. "That's quite a poem, *mein Freund.*"

When they both looked over at Randolph the Bull, he was crying. "That's the most *schönes Gedicht (beautiful poem)* I have ever heard," he sobbed. "Oh, sweet Mama, I miss you so."

Hanz and Ollie couldn't help but laugh.

❧❦❧

The first time the twins had met Aadan Omari, they were only babies, staring up at him in curiosity. And then when they were six years old, they thought he was magnificent, staring up at him in awe. The only Black man they had ever known, dressed in his white African linen robe and leather sandals, his wide smile flashing bright ivory teeth against his deep dark skin, they thought he was Jesus Christ.

"Are you Christ our Savior?" Ava had asked him one day.

Aadan laughed, his baritone voice resonating through the air. "*Nein,* little one," he said, kneeling to her level. "Why do you think I'm him?"

"Because Papa said he was a handsome man dressed in a white robe with leather sandals."

Now the girls were twelve, and they had become very fond of Aadan and his wife Chiumbo. They loved visiting Aadan's workshop, too, because he would teach them ceramic artwork, particularly how to make decorative masks. Ava and Shaylee would use their own faces for the mold, and then paint the masks a variety of colors and designs. Some were regular clowns with stars and hearts on rosy cheeks, others Pierrot clowns with white faces and crying eyes. Some were pretty fairies with dainty features, others mischievous elves. Whatever they fancied in the moment, they'd create, using their imaginations to the full.

Aadan also taught them doll making, and Shaylee quickly mastered the craft. Her dolls were quite enchanting, with little silk outfits, accessorized by hats and ribbons, lace and bows. So unique and lovely were they that Hanz even took some of them to The Devil's Needle, where Randolph and Nila agreed to sell them.

One day Hanz went into the room where Shaylee was working on her latest dolls, adding her and Ava's own hair from when their mother last gave them a haircut.

"Papa!" she said, excited to see him. "Why don't you pull up a chair and help me."

He sat down and watched her for a moment, smiling at her meticulously taking great care with the fine details of her creation.

"You can apply some pink color to this one's cheeks," she said, handing him a doll, "and give her red lips."

While Hanz assisted his daughter, he noticed a doll sitting by itself on the windowsill. It was different from the rest, wrapped in a plain shawl with no makeup or fancy accessories. "What's that one supposed to be?" he asked, motioning at it as he worked.

"Oh, that's the woman in the forest," said Shaylee, briefly looking up.

"Who?"

"The woman who comes by the farm sometimes and hides behind the trees. Maybe she's a ghost; I don't know."

Hanz looked at her, a shiver running down his spine as a sense of déjà vu hit him. The last time a ghost came by the farm, it was Abigail Katz. "Has she ever spoken to you?"

"*Nein.* But Ava tried to approach her once to say *hallo*. The woman just ran away."

Hanz stood and walked over to the window, looking out at the forest. "Dinner is almost ready, *Schätzchen (sweetheart)*. Wash up and don't make your mother wait." Kissing Shaylee on the cheek, he left the room.

CHAPTER 12

Summer, 1936

"*I think that I shall never see*
A poem lovely as a tree.
A tree whose hungry mouth is pressed
Against the earth's sweet flowing breast;
A tree that looks at God all day,
And lifts her leafy arms to pray;
A tree that may in summer wear
A nest of robins in her hair.
Upon whose bosom snow has lain;
Who intimately lives with rain.
Poems are made by fools like me,
But only God can make a tree."

The years had passed swiftly on the Wolff farm, and the twin girls had grown from inquisitive children into vivacious teenagers, now fifteen years old. Their brother, almost eighteen, was becoming a strapping young man. The three of them, along with the neighboring boy, Christian Hoffmann—the same age as the girls—all lay under the massive weeping willow tree in the yard one afternoon. It was the weekend, and the foursome were looking forward to a day of no chores and unbridled adventure.

"*Das ist wunderschön (That's beautiful),*" Ava said after her sister finished reciting Joyce Kilmer's famous 1913 poem.

"*Ja,*" replied Shaylee, emotionally moved by it. "But not as beautiful as a tree itself. Look at this *wunderbar* creation."

Everybody stared up at the branches draping over them like the Hanging Gardens of Babylon.

"I wonder what God thought when he made trees," Luka said, stretching his arms and legs out on the grass. "He must have been mighty proud of himself."

"Of course," said Shaylee. "And that's what the poet was saying–that only God can create something so glorious."

"I wrote a poem not long ago myself," Christian said proudly, "about my mother's bird."

Luka propped up on one elbow. "Oh yeah? Let's hear it."

Christian stood and cleared his throat, his face taking on a serious expression . . .

> *"To cage a bird, binding its lungs,*
> *Stealing its voice of songs unsung.*
> *Like angels' wings, clipped will bleed,*
> *We cut the rose for selfish greed.*
> *A rock, a stone, a jewel, or gold,*
> *No animal should ever be bought or sold.*
> *Nor hunted, trapped, killed, or caged,*
> *Or like the precious bird, made our slave."*

Ava and Shaylee, both impressed, clapped their approval. Luka, however, smirked and said, "Roses are red, violets are blue, I hate your stupid poem. The end."

At first Christian took offence, but then both young men howled with laughter.

As the leisurely day continued, the four teenagers ate a hearty lunch on a blanket under the willow tree. Maria had cooked a feast the night before, and now they had a choice of leftover traditional German dishes, including *Sauerbraten (pot roast)* for sandwiches, served on rye bread with sauerkraut, *Frikadellen (meatballs)*, *Kartoffelsalat (potato salad)*, and veal *Schnitzel (cutlet)*, washing it all down with grape juice from the Wolff vineyard. Afterward, the conversation turned toward their future dreams.

"What does everyone want to be when they grow up?" Luka asked, lying back on the blanket, staring up through the branches of the willow tree again.

"I'm going to be a librarian and own my own library," Shaylee said, sure of her future vocation. She opened the book she had brought–*Wuthering Heights*, by Emily Brontë–and began flipping through its pages. "It'll be full of the most exquisite leatherbound books, with *schöne Gemälde (beautiful paintings)* on the walls, and unique and peculiar things scattered throughout."

"Like what?" asked Christian.

"Like a stuffed turtle with two heads. Or a human skeleton with a fish tail attached. Or a pirate's wooden leg . . . Things like that."

"Sounds more like a creepy museum than a library," Ava laughed.

"I'm going to call it, *Die Schwarze Perle (The Black Pearl)*."

Ava put on the new sunglasses her father had bought her for her birthday, knowing that she idolized Hollywood movie stars where the fashion trend was popular. Lifting her chin in a celebrity pose, she said, "I'm going to be a famous movie star in America."

"*Ja, ja*, we know," said Shaylee. She had heard it a hundred times before.

Christian had a crush on Shaylee, and all he really wanted was to marry her someday, keeping her all to himself. But trying to come up with something interesting, he said, "I'll probably move to London and be a detective like that character, Sherlock Holmes. I'll go after the body snatchers and solve crimes nobody else can."

"The proper term is 'resurrectionist,'" Shaylee said, "not body snatcher."

"Or maybe I'll buy my own boat, be my own boss, and fish on the Tauber River. I'll take it all the way to the North Sea and meet Zeus, God of the Sea."

"You mean Poseidon," Shaylee corrected again, rolling her eyes.

"What about you, Luka?" Ava asked. "What are your plans for the future?"

"I'm going to join the military," he said, chewing on a twig.

"Why?" asked Christian, "when you could take over your father's farm?"

"I'd rather have a career like Uncle Severin. I'll look mighty fine in that uniform, too, and have my pick of any *Mädchen (girl)* I want. They'll all be fighting over each other to kiss me."

"Ahhh, *wunderbar*," Christian said in a long, amorous sigh, glancing at Shaylee. "I can't wait to kiss a *schönes Mädchen* myself."

Luka grinned. "Why don't you kiss Shaylee right now? We all know you want to."

Without hesitation, Christian leaned over and quickly kissed Shaylee on the cheek. Her face instantly turned beet red, and before anyone could say anything, he jumped up and ran toward the river, yelling out over his shoulder, "Last one in the Tauber is a rotten egg!"

"Christian just kissed you!" Ava teased. "Now you have to marry him!"

Shaylee blushed even harder.

A chorus of giggles filled the air as the three siblings ran after their neighbor. When they reached the river, its surface shimmered like diamonds in the midday sun. Wildflowers of various hues blossomed along the riverbank, adding to the natural splendor.

As the friends cavorted in the cool, calm water, splashing and laughing about, they did not notice they were being watched. In the near distance, the woman in the forest stood surreptitiously behind a tree, covered in a shawl, watching the girls and smiling, tears glistening in her dark brown eyes.

The sun cast its golden tendrils across the Wolff farm, caressing fields of wheat that swayed like an amber ocean. As it started its faithful descent, painting the sky shades of fuchsia and lavender, Hanz and Maria saw their teenage children returning home from their day of leisure by the river.

"Look at them, Hanz," Maria said, her eyes tearing up as they sat on the porch swing, enjoying the evening. "I can't believe how fast our babies are growing. Ava and Shaylee have turned into beautiful young girls, and Luka a handsome young lad. Overnight, it seems."

Hanz agreed, observing his children with fatherly pride. His girls were getting taller by the day, their features maturing, their innocent faces slowly giving way to the first glimpses of the women they would become. Shaylee had sprouted past her once smaller form, too, now within inches of Ava. And Luka was already on the precipice of being a man. Husband and wife looked at each other and shared a ubiquitous smile.

That night, as the Wolff family ate dinner together, everything in the world seemed right, wrapped in the quiet grace of love and life's simple joys. These were the cherished moments for the family. Before the war, before the heartache. Before Adolf Hitler became possessed and tried to rule the world, setting it on fire . . .

CHAPTER 13

The following week was a busy one. On Monday, a mare had delivered a difficult birth. Thankfully, both mother and baby survived, and Hanz let his daughter Shaylee name the colt. Since she had been reading *King Arthur*, she chose Camelot. On Tuesday, Hanz and Luka helped their neighbor Malachi repair a section of his barn that had long been neglected, and on Wednesday the Wolff family were invited to the Applebaums for dinner. Randolph the Bull came by on Thursday, asking if Hanz could help him with some carpentry work at The Devil's Needle–a brawl had broken out recently and damaged some of the furniture, and with Hanz's skill making violins, he was an expert with woodwork. Of course, Ollie was there too, supervising while drinking and storytelling, getting in the way. Friday came around, and Hanz and Luka spent a long day working in the fields and vineyard, while Maria and the girls cleaned the farmhouse top to bottom. Saturday was the church picnic, and by Sunday evening, all Maria wanted to do was relax and have a simple dinner with her family.

When it was time to help prepare the meal, however, her daughters were nowhere in sight. She sent Hanz out to look for them, his sheepdogs Rolf and Bruno faithfully by his side, and he found them by the small pond, engaged in a peculiar activity. Shaylee was floating in the water in a lavender dress, arms to her sides, palms up, staring at the sky, while Ava was wearing a similar dress and crown of wildflowers, tossing petals on her.

Hanz stopped and grinned, watching the enchanting scene for a moment, puzzled yet charmed. "What in God's green earth are you two doing?" he finally asked as he approached.

Ava laughed. "I think she's lost her mind, Papa. She wanted to reenact a scene in one of her favorite paintings."

Shaylee slowly rose from the water like a ghost. "Oh, Papa, isn't it obvious? I'm Ophelia in Shakespeare's *Hamlet*."

Hanz shook his head in amazement. "Look at you, all soaking wet. You're going to catch pneumonia like this."

"But Papa, don't I look marvelous? I feel like I'm literally coming out of his painting."

"Whose painting?"

"Sir John Everett Millais. He painted *Ophelia* in 1852, floating in a stream with wildflowers all over her before her tragic death. It's so beautiful, Papa, and I wanted to be her."

Ava giggled, removing her crown of wildflowers and placing it on her father's head.

Hanz smiled. "Your mother needs your help with dinner, and if I don't bring you back to her, there'll be a Shakespearean tragedy for sure."

As they walked back to the farmhouse, Ava and Shaylee linked arms with their father, one on either side of him. At one point, Hanz spun each girl, and they twirled like a tiny ballerina in a jewelry box. The sun had nearly set, and as the girls' flowing homemade dresses fluttered in the breeze, the two dogs nipped at the fireflies lighting up around them.

Shaylee hugged her father and said, "Look at us, Papa, with our pretty dresses and the lightning bugs all around us. It's *wunderbar*, isn't it?"

Hanz, still wearing the crown of wildflowers, kissed the top of her head. "*Ja*, my little swan. Pure magic."

❧❦❧

"*W*ow, *ist das mein kleiner Bruder (Wow, is that my little brother)?*" Hanz asked, smiling at Severin in the kitchen. His brother was on military leave and had come for a visit a few days later.

Severin stood at attention, clicking the heels of his shiny leather boots and saluting. "*Jawohl (Yessir)!*"

Hanz laughed.

"You look very sharp in your uniform," said Maria, giving an approving nod.

"*Danke*," Severin replied with a wide smile.

Hanz noticed the bottle in his brother's hand. "What did you bring?"

"Jägermeister. I have fantastic news."

Maria removed a roasted duck from the oven. "Did you finally meet a lovely *Fräulein?*"

"Even better–I'm now an officer in Hitler's new *Wehrmacht (Armed Forces)*."

"*Wunderbar!*" exclaimed Hanz.

Maria gave Severin a congratulatory hug. "Of course you are. You're young, intelligent, and of *gute* Aryan blood. The military needs men like you."

Severin kissed his sister-in-law on the cheek.

Ava and Shaylee walked into the kitchen. "Uncle Severin!" they greeted in unison.

Opening his arms, he welcomed them in for a simultaneous embrace. "*Meine schönen Nichten (My beautiful nieces)*, I brought you gifts."

The girls smiled with delight as he gave them both a silk scarf and leather gloves. They asked him a million questions, having not seen him in a while, and he smiled back as he attentively answered each one. They had a special bond.

Luka came in moments later. He shook Severin's hand, staring in awe as if the uniform had turned his uncle into a god. "I'm going to join the Wehrmacht like you, Uncle Severin. I'm going to be the bravest and strongest *Soldat (soldier)* ever."

"*Ja*, I have no doubt," Severin replied, patting his nephew on the back. He gave him a stainless steel Swiss pocketknife with a swastika on its handle.

Luka beamed.

Hanz popped open the liqueur, grabbed two glasses, and led his brother outside to his makeshift art studio in the barn. "Tell me the news, *Bruder*," he said, pouring them each a shot.

Severin downed his drink. "I've heard rumors through my commanding officer that Hitler has plans to eradicate all the Jews."

Hanz turned pale. "What?"

"There's talk among the Nazi Party leaders that the world would be better off without them." Severin walked over to the barn door and stared out at the land. "Already there are many anti-Semitic boycotts and laws, as you know."

"But they're *gute* people. What have they done?"

His brother didn't respond.

Ava and Shaylee, his Jewish neighbors, and even Abigail Katz flashed through Hanz's mind.

"It won't happen now," Severin added, "but someday it will. It's crazy, I know, but from what I'm hearing, they're going to round up all the Jews across Europe. Every single one of them."

⚜

After Severin left, Hanz went to see his good friend and neighbor, Aadan Omari. Besides being a skilled tile maker—some said the best in the country—he was a very wise man, and Hanz greatly respected him. Often he spoke of stories from Africa, sharing them with his German friend, each one carrying a moral or ethical theme.

Hanz brought his violin with him, knowing that Aadan loved music. The native African man played an idiophone called a slit drum, which his chieftain grandfather had made in Cameroon. Carved out of a tree trunk, the percussion instrument was a mostly closed hollow chamber with three slits in it, the edges of which were different thicknesses to produce varied pitches when struck. Known to have been developed by multiple ancient civilizations including Africans, Aztecs, and Indonesians, these unique instruments were used for both ritual and entertainment purposes. Similarly, when strategically situated for optimal acoustic transmission along a river or valley, they were used for long-distance communication.

"When you play that drum, I can envision a leopard staring up at the moon," Hanz said as they sat under a European beech tree. "Or an elephant getting ready to charge, protecting its young."

Aadan laughed, his smile a flash of white against his ebony skin. "And when you play that violin, I see the leprechauns dancing."

Hanz laughed too.

After their musical interlude, Aadan took Hanz into his workshop to show him his latest creations. The new tiles, freshly baked in his kiln, were stacked by shape and size and still warm to the touch. Penny round, hexagon, pinwheel, square, and basketweave were the popular styles of the day. The finished tiles, painted an array of colorful designs, were laid out on a table for display.

"Beautiful," said Hanz, inspecting the artwork. "No wonder they say you're the best tile maker in the country."

Aadan smiled. "*Danke*. But I've been doing this for over thirty years now; I better be *gute*."

"What is Africa like?" Hanz asked as he focused on a particular group of tiles that were clearly of African motif.

Aadan's face lit up in a way Hanz had never seen before. "Much hotter and dryer than Germany, with different landscape, yet very beautiful. The animals are both dangerous and magnificent. Elephants, rhinos, and hippos; lions, cheetahs, and leopards; gorillas, baboons, and crocodiles; zebras, ostriches, and giraffes," he listed off like a walking encyclopedia. "So many different species it's mind-boggling. And the people are just as varied, but kind and friendly with each other. Much more so than here."

"Why did you leave?" Hanz asked.

"Making the tiles brought me to France, and then my *Bruder* said the restaurants in Germany would pay double for my work, so Chiumbo and I moved."

"By the way, you never did tell me what your African name means."

The sage man with skin dark as night smiled again. "Omari comes from Swahili, and means 'God the Highest.' It also has Hebrew origins, meaning 'speaker or chief', and Arabic, meaning 'flourishing, thriving.'"

"A name to be proud of, for sure."

"*Ja*. And Aadan is a Somali form of Adam." He paused, his shimmering eyes focusing intently on Hanz. "We are all sons of Adam, are we not?"

"*Ja*, we are. But unfortunately, not everyone sees it that way." Hanz told Aadan the rumors his brother Severin had disclosed to him, about how the Nazis were planning to round up and exterminate all the Jews across Europe. "I still can't believe it," he said, even though the signs were already there.

"Believe it," said Aadan. "The German empire has done it before."

"What do you mean?"

"In Africa. Decades ago, under Kaiser Wilhelm of the Second Reich."

Aadan went on to explain to Hanz how European imperialists had long sought to exploit the African continent, with its wide-open spaces, rugged, romantic beauty, and wealth of resources. In fact, by the early 1880s, England, France, Belgium, Portugal, and other countries had already inaugurated colonies throughout the land. Many were shockingly brutal, exploitative, and dehumanizing, resulting in tens of thousands of tribespeople slaughtered.

The Second Reich enthusiastically joined the scramble for Africa in 1884. Fearful of being shut out, a special conference was convened in Berlin for the European powers to cooperatively carve up the spoils, resulting in a treaty enacted "in the Name of God Almighty," for an orderly territorial invasion. Germany received four territories across the breadth of the continent: Cameroon, Togoland, a section of East Africa, and a main coastal presence in Southwest Africa.

It was there, Aadan continued to expound, in Southwest Africa, that German settlers with lucrative plantations, governmental backing, and military protection viciously exploited the local Herero and Nama indigenous tribes. They saw them as subhuman, racially inferior, and fit for enslavement. Men were beaten and murdered, women frequently raped, ancestral lands and livestock routinely stolen. And when Herero and Nama warriors finally joined forces to revolt against the white oppressors, exacting a brief victory, they were soon met with devastating retribution. Berlin dispatched 14,000 troops to the area with modern cannons and Gatling (machine) guns, wiping out the uprising in what became known among the soldiers as *Vernichtung . . . extermination.*

The Germans didn't stop there, either, annihilating the native civilians as well. Even women and children were mercilessly put to death. And in an act of incomprehensible malevolence, those who yet survived were driven into the scorching dry Omaheke section of the Kalahari Desert, where soldiers first poisoned the wells. Starved of food and water, emaciated with ribcages bulging to the limits and faces gaunt and ghostly, thousands more died.

Aadan had to stop there to compose himself before continuing. He had Herero relatives who suffered what came next . . .

Miraculously, some of the tribespeople had survived to this point, only to meet a more horrific fate. Because they did not die quickly enough, they were seized by soldiers and stacked into human heaps atop makeshift pyres of bushes and branches, and while still alive and whimpering, set on fire.

Eventually the Germans realized they were killing off all their local slave labor, so a shift in policy came down from Berlin. After all, how could an imperialist power maintain its colonies without a local workforce to exploit? So from then on, the native peoples were no longer exterminated but rounded up instead, then sent to concentration camps to serve German industrial and infrastructure ambitions.

When Aadan had finally finished this unbelievably heinous yet true lesson in German history, Hanz was visibly shaken. *"Mein Gott, Aadan, was für eine Gräueltat (My God, Aadan, what an atrocity),"* he said.

"Ja. It was genocide. But genocide never just happens. There are always signs in advance that, if ignored and go unchecked, allow it to take place."

Hanz nodded, recalling once more the rumors Severin had heard. "Do you think something like that can happen here?"

Aadan gave him a level stare. "I know it can, and most likely will," he said, a forlorn look in his dark eyes.

⁂

Saturday night arrived, and Hanz and Ollie went to The Devil's Needle to visit Randolph and Nila. As always, the Bull met them with a toothless smile and waved them over to the bar. Now thick around the middle and graying at his temples, he no longer resembled the intimidating boxer who fought fifteen brutal rounds with the younger, stronger, Albrecht Braun. Instead, he looked more like a lovable teddy bear.

Randolph poured both men their favorite drinks–Chartreuse for Hanz, vodka for Ollie–along with a shot of Mampe Halb & Halb for himself. Nila was busy serving customers.

"How are you, *mein Freund?*" Hanz asked, taking a seat along with Ollie at the bar.

"*Gute, gute.* Nila keeps me fat and happy," he chuckled, patting his stomach. "But like you *Herren (gentlemen)* once warned me, she's thunder and lightning in a bottle. Drives me crazy and keeps me on my toes."

They all laughed.

"What about you men?"

Ollie answered first. "The wife's after me to take her to Paris," he said, downing his shot. "How can a mailman afford that?"

Randolph poured him another. "Take her to a French restaurant instead. When there, surprise her with a bottle of Guerlain Shalimar. That'll make her happy."

"What the hell is that?" asked Ollie.

"Eau de parfume, of course. An intoxicating fragrance of eternal romance, designed for the woman who is sensual, sophisticated, and uninhibited."

Hanz and Ollie looked at each other, then back at the Bull, nearly breaking out in laughter. It reminded Hanz of the night he first met the fighter, when the brawny pugilist had come into the bar and surprised him by ordering a liqueur–Mampe Halb & Halb–after being beaten half to death in the ring.

"It's very, very French," Randolph added. "In Paris, you smell it in the theaters, at the opera, and even in the streets." Now on a roll, he continued as if he were the proud perfumer who created it. "And there's a love story behind it, unlike any other. More than 300 years ago, Shah Jahan, the Mughal Emperor of India, loved a woman named Mumtaz Mahal. Some say he loved her unto madness, and that empires, victories, and riches were dust compared to her. When she died, he built one of the world's greatest wonders in her memory–the Taj Mahal at Agra. But while she was alive, he built her the glorious gardens of Shalimar, which means 'abode of love' in Sanskrit, the likes of which had never been seen before."

At this point, Hanz and Ollie were gobsmacked. What happened to their friend? Who invaded his body? Did Albrecht Braun come into The Devil's Needle and give him another blow to the head?

"So you see, *mein Freund*, if you take your wife to a romantic French restaurant, give her a bottle of Guerlain Shalimar, and tell her that beautiful love story . . . it will save you a lot of money."

All three men burst out laughing.

After another round of drinks, Randolph said to Hanz, "Those little dolls Shaylee makes still sell well in here. When I place them by the cash register, parents will buy them for their children. Your daughter's quite talented."

"She takes after her proud papa," Ollie said, patting Hanz on the back. "He's always making or painting something in his barn."

"Bring me more if you like, and I'll sell them quickly for her."

"*Danke*," said Hanz. "She'll be happy."

The Bull nodded. "Anything else new on the farm?"

"*Ja.*" Hanz downed his drink. "Severin dropped by a few days ago. He's now an officer in Hitler's Wehrmacht."

Randolph frowned. He had nothing good to say about that. "Hopefully he can influence them for the *gute*, rather than being influenced himself for the *schlecht (bad)*. You heard what those Nazi SS bastards did to that Jewish man in Fürth, right? Humiliating him, making him walk naked through town, holding a sign that said he was a filthy Jew who had relations with a German *Fräulein*. They were engaged to be married."

Hanz nodded. "*Ja*, the Nuremberg Laws are a disgusting travesty of human rights."

Implemented on September 15, 1935, the Nazi regime had announced two new laws related to race: the Reich Citizenship Law, and the Law for the

Protection of German Blood and German Honor, together known informally as the Nuremberg Laws because they were first announced at a Nazi Party rally held in that German city. They believed that the world was divided into distinct races not equally strong and valuable, with the so-called Aryan German race the strongest and most valuable of all. Furthermore, they thought Jews belonged to a separate race inferior to all others, and that their presence threatened the German people, requiring separation from other Germans to protect and strengthen the Fatherland. As a result, only racially pure Germans were allowed to hold citizenship, and *Rassenschande (race defilement)* was banned, prohibiting intermarriages and sexual relations between Jews and people of German or related blood, later clarified to prohibit Roma (Gypsies) and Black people as well.

"I've never spoken freely about being Jewish," Randolph said. "In fact, I'm not even a practicing Jew, and I attend a Catholic church with Nila so she doesn't have to go alone. But with everything that's happening now, I have this uneasy feeling we should sell this tavern and leave Germany."

"We'd sure miss you around this place, if you did," Ollie said. "It wouldn't be the same without you and Nila."

Hanz thought about what his brother Severin had told him. Before he could bring it up, however, the Bull said, "Bah! I don't want to think about anything tonight. I just want to eat a good meal with *meine Freunde*, and drink until I forget my worries."

"I'll drink to that!" Ollie cheered, raising his glass. "Here's to *gute Essen (food)*, *gute Unternehmen (company)*, and *gute Laune (spirits)!*"

Randolph refilled their shot glasses and looked at his wife who was cleaning off one of the booths. "Nila, bring us three roast beef sandwiches with au jus on the side!"

"What do I look like, your personal chef!" she barked at him.

The men laughed, harkening back to the night the two lovebirds first met.

Nila winked at her husband, then headed to the kitchen to prepare the food.

Four SS officers walked in and sat at a booth across from the bar, interrupting the fun.

"Whatever it was, it wasn't me!" Ollie shouted out to them, always the jokester.

They looked at him with zero expression, paying his wisecrack no mind.

"The air gets chilly whenever they come in," Randolph said. "You ever notice that? It's like standing near a tomb."

Hanz discerned an angst in Randolph the Bull. For the first time ever, he saw something in his friend's eyes that he never thought he'd see . . .

Fear.

Fear like an animal caught in a trap.

And then something peculiar happened that he couldn't make sense of. He thought of the albino deer he had saved all those years ago. The little fawn that had grown into a large white buck with enormous antlers and became well known in the area. An unspoken pact had existed among the hunters not to kill it, and as he looked at Randolph's reaction to the Nazi officers, he could see that buck in his mind's eye, with a rogue hunter pointing a rifle at it, right between the eyes. A second hunter was telling him not to shoot it, that it was rare and special to the forest and needed to live so its offspring could survive. Hanz wondered why this had crossed his mind, and it bothered him.

Nila returned with their food, and while the men ate, she went to take the Nazi officers' orders. The tavern, once jovial and happy, had changed in mood, the presence of the SS sucking the oxygen out of the room.

"Those men sitting at the bar look odd," the commanding officer said, taking a drink of his beer.

The other officers looked.

"The tall, solid one resembles a Viking with a Roman face. And the tall, skinny one looks like Olive Oil, the *Frau (wife)* of that American cartoon sailor called Popeye."

They all laughed.

"The short, stocky one, however . . . Now *he* looks like a Jew."

"Apparently he was once a boxer," said one of the officers who had been to The Devil's Needle multiple times before. "But I don't know if he's Jewish."

The commander's face turned ugly. "I know a dirty Jew when I see one."

"He and his wife own this place. She's the dwarf who just served us."

"Is that right," said the commander, smirking. "It is in the best interests of the Fatherland that all such deformities be cleansed." Narrowing his wicked gaze at Randolph the Bull, he added, "And I'm very much looking forward to that day."

CHAPTER 14

Autumn, 1938

Hanz received an unexpected and disturbing visit from Stanley Horowitz one chilly October morning. The jeweler and his family, along with all the other remaining Jews who hadn't already left Rothenburg ob der Tauber, were expelled by the Nazis from the medieval town. With only minutes to pack, they took whatever they could and left the rest behind. Their homes and businesses were confiscated in the name of the Third Reich.

"Hanz," Stanley said, walking toward the German farmer whom he had sold various pieces to over the years, the most expensive being the sapphire stone wedding ring for Maria.

Hanz looked up from his work in his makeshift art studio in the barn. He was painting what he had seen weeks prior, before everything had exploded in town, the memory so remarkable that he wanted to capture it on canvas. To him, it was a piece of history. Something he considered profound, moving him to record it the only way he knew how–through paint. Three SS officers in full Nazi uniform with numerous military pins, *Schirmmützen (peaked caps)*, and shiny black boots were walking through the *Marktplatz (marketplace)* that day, coming face to face with three rabbis in long black coats, beards with prominent sidelocks, and black shtreimels. Both groups stopped suddenly and stared at each other in a voiceless duel, loathing what they saw. Opposing forces, like night and day, oil and water, heaven and hell. A striking scene that Hanz was now trying to recreate in minute detail. "Stanley," he said, surprised to see him there.

The jeweler and his wife and daughter were temporarily staying at the Yurkovichs–Nora was his best customer. Why he came to see Hanz Wolff, he wasn't sure. Perhaps it was because he needed to believe that there were still good German folk in this country who had no ill intention or hatred toward the Jews. Sitting down on a bale of hay, he took off his glasses, rubbed his eyes, and said, "I don't know why I am here."

Hanz could see the anguish in his face. He covered his painting and asked, "What's wrong, *mein Freund?*"

"They've finally done it. The Nazis—they've forced us out of Rothenburg. All Jews have now been expelled and are forbidden from returning."

Hanz shook his head.

"They've stolen our homes, our businesses, our lives. Now they want our souls."

"I'm sorry, Stanley. *Das ist schrecklich (This is terrible).*" Hanz examined the defeated man. Stanley Horowitz had always reminded him of Albert Einstein, but now his steel gray hair was even more unruly, his sidelocks had been cut off, and his clothing ripped. It was clear he had been roughed up. "Do you want some hot tea? Maria made some with the lavender she grows in her garden. It will help you relax."

"I think I need something stronger than tea."

Hanz nodded and fetched a bottle of vodka, pouring him a double shot.

Stanley downed it and reached for the bottle.

Hanz gave it to him, then threw three more logs into the fire burning in the cast iron stove he had installed years ago for those chilly days when he'd paint in his art studio.

"How long have I known you, Hanz?" Stanley asked.

"Since I was a boy."

"You were never a boy," the jeweler said, remembering Hanz as a quiet child, always under his father's strict thumb while the other children played freely. "Your papa put you to work in the embalming room while you were still wet behind the ears. That's not the life of a boy."

Hanz warmed his hands above the stove. "When my older *Bruder* took his own life, my father said I needed to become tough, because life was cruel. He said my *Bruder* was too soft, always babied by my mother, and that working with him in that room would make a man of steel out of me."

"And did it? Are you now a tough man made of steel?"

"*Nein,*" said Hanz, lighting his corncob pipe. Thinking about how traumatizing it was to see a dead body so young, he added, "But it taught me how fragile life is. And how when the death angel comes for you, all that's left is cold flesh and bones and five quarts of blood."

Stanley was beginning to feel brazen from the alcohol. "I think the death angel is coming for the Jews. He's watching in the shadows, waiting for Satan's command. But you know what? I spit on the death angel! I curse him to hell! We are the chosen people, and we walked out of Egypt under God's mighty hand! Arrogant Pharaoh was destroyed along with his army, and haughty Hitler will end up the same with his Nazis!"

Hanz watched as Stanley became erratic, thrusting his fist in the air as he went on an extended tirade. The man was close to having a nervous breakdown. "Stanley! Get a hold of yourself!"

The jeweler calmed. Staring at nothing for a moment, he turned sad and reflective. "My whole life I have felt like a balled-up fist. Working harder than any man I know. I have been through many trials, and I've conquered them all. But this one I cannot win. This one will be the end of me. If I cannot feed my family, I have no life."

Again Hanz remembered what Severin had told him two years earlier, that Hitler had plans to eradicate all the Jews. Not just in Germany but across Europe. "You should take your family to America. Start over there."

"At my age? *Nein*, my whole world is here."

"From the rumors I've heard, things are going to get worse for the Jews."

Just then, Ava and Shaylee came outside. "Papa, Mama says lunch is ready," said Shaylee.

"Hi, Mr. Horowitz," Ava politely greeted.

"*Hallo, Mädchen (girls)*." Stanley watched the teenage twins in curiosity. A strange look came over his face.

"What is it?" Hanz asked.

"There was a Jewish woman and her family who were expelled along with us. Abigail Katz is her name. I've never noticed it before today, but your girls look so much like her."

Hanz took his pipe out of his mouth, and the two men stared at each other for an awkward moment. "What did he mean, 'Who is the real mother of those twins, and are you ever going to tell them the truth?'" he recalled Stanley Horowitz asking him when Dr. Schultz spoke those last words before dying in that car accident. Dismissing the memory, he asked, "Would you like to join us for lunch?"

"*Nein, danke*," said Stanley. "I need to get going." As he left, he stared at Ava and Shaylee sitting on the porch steps, waving at him goodbye.

Two weeks later, on November 9 and 10, 1938, a series of devastating pogroms were unleashed against the Jewish population in Germany and its annexed territories. The event came to be known as *Kristallnacht (The Night of Broken Glass)* because of the shards of shattered glass that littered the streets after the vandalism and destruction of Jewish-owned synagogues, businesses, and homes.

Extremely violent and organized, Nazi Party officials had disguised the attacks as the spontaneous responses of German people to the assassination of German diplomat, Ernst vom Rath, in Paris. Herschel Grynszpan, a seventeen-year-old Polish Jew, had shot the diplomat after thousands of Polish Jews were expelled from the Reich, including his parents who had been residents in Germany since 1911. This provided the perfect opportunity for Propaganda Minister, Joseph Goebbels, to promote the lie that world Jewry had conspired to commit the assassination. From there, the Nazi *Sturmabteilung (Storm Troopers)* and Hitler Youth led mobs through the streets of towns and cities across the country, most wearing civilian clothes to support the fiction that the riots were expressions of the outraged German public.

An estimated 7,500 Jewish-owned businesses were looted, hundreds of synagogues burned, and countless Jewish cemeteries desecrated. Men, women, and children were attacked and terrorized in their homes, forced to perform acts of public humiliation, and beaten with hundreds raped and killed. Additionally, some 30,000 Jewish males were rounded up by the SS and Gestapo and taken to Dachau, Buchenwald, Sachsenhausen, and other concentration camps. This was the first time Nazi officials made massive arrests of Jews simply because they were Jews, without any further cause for arrest.

When it was all over, the Nazis made an immediate and outrageous declaration that the Jews themselves were responsible for the pogroms, imposing a fine of one billion Reichsmark (400 million US dollars). They confiscated all insurance payouts, leaving the Jewish owners personally responsible for their losses.

Two of the Wolff's neighbors came to talk to Hanz a week after the pogroms. It was Leon Dreisler, the farmer to the east who had also fought in the Great War, taking a Jewish mail-order bride from Hungary thereafter;

and Günther Nachtnebel, the farmer to the north, with the homemade distillery and wife nobody liked because of her sanctimonious manner. The two men were going to Munich to hear a speech by Adolf Hitler and wanted to know if Hanz would join them.

At first Hanz said no; he was not interested in politics, and certainly didn't like the Nazi Party and its leader. But then he thought about what had happened during *Kristallnacht*, what had happened in Rothenburg just two weeks prior to it, and what Aadan Omari had told him two years earlier about the atrocities committed in Africa by the Second Reich under Kaiser Wilhelm, stating that it could happen again here. He changed his mind and agreed to go with Leon and Günther, and the three men took the train to Munich.

As they disembarked at the city station, it immediately struck them how different things were there compared to the normally peaceful atmosphere in and around Rothenburg. German soldiers proliferated the streets; swastikas and Nazi symbolism covered the buildings; civilian supporters were abuzz with excitement and anticipation. It was as if an invisible force had lulled everyone and everything into a hypnotic trance, awaiting their Führer's direction. People young and old, from all walks of life had come to hear the words of the man named Adolf Hitler.

Hanz watched as *der Führer und Reichskanzler (the Leader and Chancellor of the Reich)* slowly walked up the steps to take his place on the large outdoor platform. Physically unimposing, with dark, greasy hair combed to one side and half-mustache under his nose, he certainly was no bastion of intimidation. Yet when he stared out at the crowd, his eyes a bottomless pit of animus and rage, his tongue seeping with deadly venom, the monster began to emerge. And then, when he started speaking, his thunderous voice echoing with rancor and hatred, the monster transformed into a larger-than-life god.

This was not the first speech Adolf Hitler had given, mesmerizing the crowd with his inflammatory speaking style and dramatic gestures. No, he was in fact a seasoned and gifted orator, able to command and direct the emotions and impulses of his audience at will. It was how he came into power in the first place . . .

After World War I ended, Germany experienced great political turmoil. Racist and anti-Semitic groups sprang up on the radical right, blaming Jews for Germany's defeat in the war. These factions opposed the new Weimar Republic that replaced the monarchy, along with the harsh terms imposed by the Treaty of Versailles. They were against capitalism, socialism, communism, democracy, and human rights, and advocated for the exclusion of anyone who did not belong to the German *Volk*, or race.

Hitler joined one such group—the German Workers' Party. Attracting notice with his public speaking skills, he soon found himself the leader of the group, and in 1920 changed their name to the *Nationalsozialistische Deutsche Arbeiterpartei (National Socialist German Workers' Party)*, dismissively coined "Nazi" as an insult by its opponents. He formulated a twenty-five-point party platform that rejected the overbearing Versailles settlement, demanded the unification of all people of pure German blood, stipulated the creation of a Greater Germany ruled by a strong central state, and endorsed the acquisition of new lands and colonies for the "master race." Citizenship and rights would be denied to all non-Germans, particularly Jews.

The Nazi Party had little popular support at first, even being banned by German authorities in 1923 after a failed attempt to seize control of the government by marching on Berlin with the hopes of launching a nationwide uprising against the Weimar Republic. Hitler was convicted of high treason and sentenced to five years in prison, of which he served only eight months. From then on, he decided the only way to promote his world view and personal mission of creating a master German race, which he wrote about while in prison, publishing a book called *Mein Kampf (My Struggle)* upon his release, was through democratic means. He promised Bavaria's leaders that he'd only seek power through elections, and in 1925 they lifted the ban, thereby allowing Hitler to reestablish the Nazi Party with renewed vigor and control.

Under Hitler's leadership, the party grew steadily, absorbing other radical right-wing groups and slowly attracting support from influential people in the military, big business, and society at large. He emphasized propaganda to attract attention and interest, staging many meetings, parades, and rallies, using posters and newspapers to create stirring slogans, and displaying eye-catching uniforms and emblems to impress.

It wasn't until the crisis of the Great Depression beginning in 1929, however, that the Nazi Party made significant inroads. Germany's subsequent economic collapse resulted in widespread unemployment and poverty, with a commensurate increase in crime, driving anger and fear among the people. Perfect fodder for the arguments and agenda of the extreme right.

By 1930, the Nazi Party saw a sharp rise in support, becoming the second largest party in the *Reichstag (Parliament)*, and by 1932, they became the largest. More and more Germans came to agree with Hitler's propaganda that parliamentary democracy was destroying the country by catering to special interests, and that the nation needed a strong leader to unite the Fatherland and rule in the peoples' interest instead. Of course, anti-Semitism was not emphasized in the party's general campaign messaging.

Finally, on January 30, 1933, Paul von Hindenburg, president of the Weimer Republic, who tried and failed to rule by presidential decree, gave in to Hitler's demands and made him Chancellor in a coalition government. His advisers had assured him that the conservative members could control Hitler since non-Nazis dominated parliament, and that in time they could use Hitler's mass following to amend the constitution and create an authoritarian state.

Once he became Chancellor, however, Hitler moved quickly to seize governmental control. Using emergency decrees, violence, arrests, intimidation, and false promises, the Nazis abolished all other political parties, declaring Germany a one-party state with Hitler as its supreme leader. From there, the tentacles of Nazi power expanded under a program called *Gleichschaltung (Coordination)*, controlling economic, social, and cultural life, purging Jews and suspected political opponents from government, legal, and educational institutions. And then, when President Hindenburg died in August 1934, the German armed forces came under Hitler's control as well. At that point he declared himself Führer and Reich Chancellor—the absolute ruler of the German people.

Now it was 1938, and Hanz was there in Munich to hear Adolf Hitler himself. As he listened to the leader of the Nazi Party give his speech that day, shivers kept running down his spine. Hanz did not cheer like the mass of people around him, but instead kept shaking his head, shocked by the lies and hatred spewing from this madman's mouth:

"Jews are poisonous vermin plotting to destroy the Aryan *Volk (people)*!

"Jewry must be seen for what it is—a deadly bacillus infecting the land!

"Pogroms are not enough; we must permanently eradicate them!"

Was Hanz hearing correctly? . . . Yes, he was . . . These were the outrageous assertions thundering from the microphone from a man possessed. It frightened Hanz, thinking about his two beautiful swans, Ava and Shaylee. And it deeply disturbed him, realizing without a doubt that Aadan

Omari was right: Genocide *could* happen here, just like it did in Africa decades ago.

Putting on his hat, Hanz nudged his two friends, Leon and Günther. "I'm leaving," he said. "I cannot listen to this madness any longer." As he pushed through the crowd, Hitler's booming voice echoed behind him.

The voice of a demon who would change mankind's history forever . . .

132

PART TWO

CHAPTER 15

Summer, 1939

Eighteen years had passed since the Wolffs received their tiny gifts wrapped in woolen blankets with the Star of David intricately woven into the fabric. Like chapters unfolding in an unwritten book, each month a sentence, each season a paragraph, the Jewish twins Ava and Shalom, raised as Ava and Shaylee by their adoptive German parents, blossomed into striking young women. Their unique appearance, now even more of a stark contrast to the blond and red-haired German couple, continued to spur gossip in the nearby town of Rothenburg ob der Tauber. When the busybody townspeople asked questions about them, Hanz simply smiled and replied, "God took the best of me and Maria and produced two priceless gems."

Living on the farm continued relatively benign for the Wolffs. Ava and Shaylee still lived at home, but Luka was now in Berlin, preparing to join the Wehrmacht. Untouched by the geopolitical shadow darkening the world beyond their small haven, life was good for the Wolffs. Life was happy. And yet, storm clouds were gathering on the horizon . . .

❧❦❧

"Papa, I can't sit still much longer," Ava said one afternoon, adjacent to her twin sister Shaylee. Their father was painting another portrait of them—his greatest opus yet—now that they were young adults.

As the soft light of the afternoon sun illuminated his makeshift art studio, and the musty smell of animals and hay mingled with the distinct fumes of oil paints, Hanz's brushstroke moved deftly across the canvas, capturing his daughters' physical likeness. Though identical, they had several differences, like a stone broken in two—symmetrical down the center but different around the edges. Ava was five feet seven inches tall, Shaylee five foot three. Ava had chestnut-colored hair and a sultry gaze; Shaylee's hair was dark auburn with eyes warm and friendly. Whereas Ava had feminine curves, Shaylee was lissome-framed with a fragile form. Every detail, every subtlety—nothing was missing.

Hanz took great care when painting the differences in the sisters' eye color, too. Ava's were an exotic emerald green, or maybe lime with a tinge of yellow. The best way to describe them in a word would be chartreuse. Which was ironic, because Hanz's favorite drink was Chartreuse, a French liqueur made with 130 herbs and botanicals, first produced by the Carthusian monks at Grenoble, France, in 1797. He would look at his daughter and say, "Your eyes are like two shimmering pools of Chartreuse," hugging her affectionately. "Which reminds me, it's time to go visit *Die Teufelsnadel* for a drink."

Shaylee's eyes were just as pretty but in a different way. More hazel green than emerald, with hues of brown and gold, the inside of her iris was a different color than the outer rim, giving her eyes a vibrant, multicolored appearance.

Somehow their father's artistic skill also captured the essence of the girls' individual characters and personalities. Ava was spirited, flirty, and adventurous. Always holding your stare before looking away. Always wearing red lipstick while sucking a sucker. Always throwing a kiss and then laughing. She smoked in secret, thinking it avant-garde, and had no time for art and books like her sister, dismissing them as insipid. She absolutely loved big-screen movies and Hollywood movie stars, though, and fantasized about being an actress herself, with a contract from MGM and her name in marquee lights . . . "Starring AVA WOLFF."

On special occasions, the Wolff family would drive in their new car to Munich, Frankfurt, or Berlin, and Ava would insist on seeing the latest Hollywood picture show. When back home, she'd make her sister reenact certain scenes with her until Shaylee couldn't take it anymore, escaping downstairs to her father's small library—her favorite hiding spot. Afterward, Ava would put a record on the gramophone, apply her scarlet red lipstick, and dance while staring at a photo of Rex Harrison, Clark Gable, or Cary Grant, dreaming of marrying a handsome leading man who would take her away from the farm to a beautiful home in America where she'd wear Chanel No. 5 perfume, a cocktail dress, and her hair in a sophisticated coiffure. There, she and her husband would invite all their fabulous famous movie star friends over for parties on weekends, socializing around a turquoise-colored swimming pool, with everyone drinking martinis until sunrise.

Yes, with those chartreuse eyes and certain *je ne sais quoi*, there was no doubt Ava Wolff could be a Hollywood movie star, possessing both a sultry character and demure charm. Like an orchid basking in the light of a full moon.

Shaylee, on the other hand, was her sister's polar opposite. Quieter and more reserved than Ava, unless she perceived an injustice, she had an introspective depth and inquisitive nature. Like a little elf inspecting a forest, she was always hunched over a book, gleaning what she could from it, or studying her surroundings, drawing sketches and taking notes.

Kind and sweet with a sincere heart, Shaylee displayed great empathy for others. She loved cooking in the farmhouse with her mother, and caring for the animals with her father. One of her favorite pastimes was writing down unique words that described different vibrant colors. Like quercitron (a shade of yellow), smaragdine (emerald green), ponceau (vivid reddish-orange), mazarine (deep purplish-blue), and her favorite, cattleya (from the beautiful pink, white, yellow, and orange Cattleya orchids).

Unlike Ava who had posters of American movies and movie stars on her bedroom walls, a vanity covered with makeup and perfumes, and magazines all over the floor, Shaylee had turned her room into a magical cocoon using her own imagination. She painted her walls with the scenery from her sketches and the characters in her books: leprechauns in funny hats, ballerinas with wings, majestic unicorns, and the like. On her shelves she had tomes of every kind, from fairy tales to ancient history to modern science, placing dried flower petals between the pages.

Shaylee loved art and classical music. Whenever she went into town, she'd spend her entire day in a gallery or bookstore, seeking to feed her inner aesthete. Often she'd come home with a new book and spend the next few days under a tree or in the hammock, reading nonstop. These were her favorite moments, lost in a phantasmal world of knights and dragons, princes and maidens, faraway lands and dramatic tales–exquisite fodder for a rich imagination. When her mother would call her to help with dinner, breaking the enchantment, she'd run to the farmhouse and say, "Oh, Mama, you interrupted the most exciting story!"

Yes, Shaylee Wolff was an intellectual, an academic, a thinker. She wanted to see the world, visit ancient libraries, and read every good book ever written.

As his hand continued to move with calculated fluidity, each brushstroke adding another layer of life to the portrait, Hanz's mind wandered back to the period of his own formative years. A time wrought with a paradoxical blend of youthful innocence and a dawning awareness of the stringent norms that governed the society he was part of. He was not like the other boys. His interests and dreams were different. Often his glimmering eyes would fixate on the mundane—the intricate patterns of leaves against the sky, or the way sunlight would speckle the Tauber River in the morn—and it was those seemingly inconsequential details that he yearned to capture with charcoal and paint. His father, a stern man of few words and strict rules, never understood this magnetic pull toward art that seemed to consume his son. "*Verrückt (Crazy)*," he would mutter, his brows furrowing in paternal disappointment. It was an era where the practicality of life choices was esteemed above the yearnings of the human spirit.

And then there were those harrowing days when Hanz stood next to his father, helping him with the dead bodies, preparing them for burial. "*Bitte*, Papa, I don't want to do this anymore!" he would say, desperately trying to avoid that gruesome task. But his father would force him, and his terrified eyes would witness what no young child should. For years he'd have nightmares over it, haunting his sleep into adulthood. And even now, when he performed the service for grieving relatives of the dead, it was never easy, and he never got used to it.

When the Great War broke out, Hanz joined the German military instead of pursuing his true passion. Not because he wanted to but because his father expected him to. "*Es ist eine Ehre, seinem Land zu dienen (It's an honor to serve your country)*," were his parting words when Hanz left for training.

As a young man, this decision felt less like an honor and more like a subjugation. Hanz's art was relegated to stolen moments—sketches scrawled on the back of discarded paper, secretly birthed in the dim light of his military barracks. And then the premature demise of his father added another layer of complexity to his life, as he found himself inheriting not just a piece of land but a legacy, laden with unvoiced expectations. When his mother took his younger brother and departed for the domestic convenience of the city, it left Hanz with the dual responsibilities of husbandry and viniculture. Which, as it turned out, served him well when he got married. But even after exchanging vows with Maria and becoming the stewards of their shared agricultural destiny, the artist in him never died.

"Papa, how much longer!" Ava complained, shifting slightly in her chair, trying to get comfortable in her pose. "I have to go practice my beauty pageant walk."

Shaylee's countenance remained tranquil, her appreciation for the moment and the artistic process evident. She understood the significance of these sittings, not just as a subject for her father's art but as a cherished memory they were creating together.

As Hanz added the final touches to the painting, he took a step back, observing his work. The portrait captured more than the physical beauty of his daughters—it was a window into their souls, a frozen moment in time that spoke of their journey from childhood to womanhood. Filled with both satisfaction and a hint of sadness at the end of the session, he announced, *"Erledigt (Done)!"*

"Es ist wunderschön (It's beautiful), Papa," Shaylee said, gazing at the finished artwork. She kissed him on the cheek. "What a talent you have."

"Ja, Papa," said Ava, kissing his cheek as well. "It looks like a color photograph."

As the three stood in front of the canvas, Hanz put his arms around his girls. "This will probably be the last one," he said, holding back the strong emotion churning in his chest. "It won't be long now before you're both married and on your own."

"Oh, Papa," Shaylee replied, leaning her head into his shoulder. "How can you be so sure? Maybe I'll stay here forever and never marry."

"Or maybe you can all live with me in my Hollywood mansion," said Ava, smiling coyly.

The girls began talking among themselves about the upcoming beauty pageant Ava was going to compete in during the Rothenburg ob der Tauber town festival. Meanwhile, Hanz quietly put his paints away, cleaned his brushes, and covered the painting to protect it until it dried. He knew this was the last one he would paint of his beloved swans as young, single, innocent girls.

He could feel it in his bones.

"Luka, your place is *wunderbar!*" Shaylee exclaimed as she, Ava, and Christian walked into his new apartment, their arms full of groceries, decorative knickknacks, and fresh flowers. Luka had rented the upstairs flat in an old Victorian home in Berlin prior to commencing military training for the Wehrmacht. He wanted a place of his own to exercise his freedom before being assigned to an army barracks, as this would be his only chance to bring girls home. Up until now, however, his only visitors were his two sisters and his childhood friend, Christian Hoffmann, who had come to spend the weekend.

Ava walked over to the window and pushed it open. "You can see the entire town square from here."

Luka stared at her from the couch. Though he had seen his sister a million times before, the way the outside light reflected off her eyes mesmerized him. "You have the most unique eye color I have ever seen," he said aloud, almost by accident.

"Papa calls them chartreuse after his favorite drink," Shaylee said, placing the fresh flowers in a vase, "but they're really smaragdine."

"Huh? What the heck is smargaree?"

"Smaragdine," Shaylee said slowly, pronouncing each syllable clearly. "It's a shade of emerald green."

Ava rolled her smaragdine eyes. "My sister and her silly words—she couldn't just say 'green.' She literally writes down pages and pages of words no one has ever heard of."

"Words themselves are poetry, Ava, when used in the right way."

"Roses are red, violets are blue, now that we're here, do you have any beer?" Christian rhymed off, slapping his knee.

Luka laughed. "You're a poet and didn't even know it! In the fridge, *mein Freund.*"

Christian retrieved four beers from the small refrigerator, handing one to each of them. Ava put a jazz record on the gramophone, and they all took off their shoes and started swing dancing, doing their best renditions of the Lindy Hop and the Jitterbug—both a symbol of rebellion and freedom from the Nazi regime's attempts to suppress what they considered degenerate and vulgar pop culture from America taking root among the German youth.

"Let's call Adolf and invite him to our party!" Ava joked.

"Nein!" said Luka. "If he found out you had a jazz record, you'd be taken away for interrogation, and my career in the Wehrmacht would be over before it started."

"Ja, ja, relax. Who would want to watch that penguin waddle, anyway?" They all laughed.

Young and carefree, with their entire lives ahead of them, the foursome danced until out of breath and out of beer. It was the beginning of a new era for them. A time of freedom with no adults to tell them what to do—they were the adults now. It felt terrific. Magical.

Later, as they all finished decorating the spare bedroom where Ava and Shaylee were going to sleep, Luka pulled out his stainless steel Swiss pocketknife with the swastika on the handle that his uncle Severin had given him when he was eighteen. The others stood around and watched as he carved each of their names into the wall, immortalizing that special weekend forever. "Ava, Shaylee, Luka, Christian—Best Friends Forever, 1939," he echoed when finished.

They all looked at each other and smiled. *"Ja!* Forever!"

～ce❦ze～

With summer in full swing, the Rothenburg ob der Tauber yearly festival arrived. The day was perfect, with white fluffy clouds sailing high above the horizon, and the sky so prodigious and blue it appeared to have swallowed the ocean whole, reflecting it from above. People of all ages walked around the marketplace, children on the shoulders of their fathers, elderly couples smiling and holding hands, still very much in love. Vendors hawked their wares, buyers haggling with sellers, and street performers entertained the public, a mime and two clowns making the children laugh.

The highlight of the festival was a beauty pageant. Young women from all around Bavaria came, hoping to claim the coveted crown. Ava jumped at the chance to enter, but Shaylee was too shy, so she declined and supported her sister instead.

For weeks prior to the event, Ava went to their Jewish neighbor's home for instruction. Mrs. Yurkovich, now seventy-nine years old, had long since retired from teaching dance and etiquette to young Jewish girls in town, but she agreed to help Ava, instructing her how to walk, talk, hold her head up high, and answer pageant questions intelligently. She firmly believed that the young Wolff girl would win, not because of Ava's obvious physical beauty but because of her own most excellent training.

Multiple German soldiers were in the medieval town that day, enjoying the festivities. Among them were two members of the *Schutzstaffel (Protection Squadron)*—Starholf Steiner and Fritz Köhler. Decked out in their conspicuous SS uniforms with shiny black boots, crisp collars, and patent *Schirmmützen (peaked caps)*, the handsome, tall young men could have been brothers, both with lemon blond hair, eyes so light they approached silver, and jawlines like the edge of an axe. They had spent the last year together at the *SS-Junkerschule (SS-Junker School)* in Bad Tölz of Lower Bavaria, where SS officer candidates received leadership training, political and ideological indoctrination, and military instruction. The training stressed stringency and ruthlessness as part of the Schutzstaffel credo, which helped foster a sense of superiority and self-confidence.

Starholf Steiner had been a member of the Hitler Youth, embodying the ideals of the regime with his Aryan good looks and pedigree. Not only was he indoctrinated by the Nazi propaganda but he also firmly believed in it. Painfully reserved, incredibly ambitious, with the backing of his wealthy, influential family, he had the natural air of a man born to old money. A shoo-in as an officer in the Schutzstaffel.

Fritz Köhler, also from a wealthy Germanic family, was a know-it-all who could be pretentious at times, not to mention annoying. But his dirty jokes made his friends laugh, and his family connections secured him with the Schutzstaffel as well.

Starholf and Fritz had been putting up more Nazi propaganda posters throughout the town that afternoon, and now that they were done, they wanted to enjoy the day's entertainment. They mingled with the locals, watched the performers, ate sausages smothered in sauerkraut and horseradish mustard, and Starholf even purchased a gold pocket watch from the jewelry store that used to be owned by Stanley Horowitz before the Nazis expelled him, stole his business, and transferred it into Aryan hands.

"It's a *gute* thing they've already forced all the Jews out of this *schöne Stadt (beautiful town)*," Fritz said, pulling a silver flask of *Wodka Gorbatschow (Gorbachev vodka)* from his pocket. He took a large swig and handed it to his friend. "The last thing we need are a bunch of rats running around, spoiling the fun."

Starholf stopped fiddling with his new pocket watch and took a swig, handing the flask back. "*Ja*. Keep it Aryan pure."

As they continued walking through the crowd, Starholf noticed a group of young women on a stage. "Look, the beauty pageant," he said, beelining toward it. Fritz put his silver flask away and followed.

The girls had already competed on talent–Ava did a ballet dance Mrs. Yurkovich taught her–and were now modeling their swimwear. The crowd grew larger, particularly with men, whistling and cheering as each girl strutted up and down the runway, showing off her feminine form. Ava wore a one piece "mini-skirt" style bathing suit with a low flirty back, thin straps, and tight skirt. Pink with polka dots and a white bow on each hip, it was both flattering and cute.

"That brunette is beautiful," Starholf said as Ava sashayed down the catwalk. When she got close enough for him to see her emerald eyes, the ground beneath his feet moved and the beat of his heart quickened. "I don't believe in magic," he once told his grandmother who loved fairy tales. "Ah, but one day when you see her, you will," she had replied, winking at him. Though he had dated many pretty women since then, only now did he fully understand the magic his grandmother spoke of.

"She's a little too skinny for me," said Fritz.

Starholf grinned. "Well I know how to fatten her up. For nine months, at least."

Both men laughed.

Ava was the only brunette among the girls, and a curvy blonde came next.

"Now that's what I'm talking about," Fritz said, ogling the young woman. "An Aryan *Mädchen* with childbearing hips. I bet she's a tornado in bed."

"If so, you couldn't handle her."

"Why not?"

"Because when a *Mädchen* even talks to you, you start stuttering."

"*Ja, Ja, lustiger Typ (Yeah, yeah, funny guy),*" said Fritz, giving him a friendly shove.

The last event of the pageant was the evening wear and interview. Rather than purchasing Ava a new dress, Maria had sewn one from a beautiful silk tablecloth her mother had made in Austria before she died. It had great sentimental value for Maria, and she thought it fitting to convert the material into a lovely gown for her daughter. Pale blue like the sky that day, with lavender wildflowers woven into the material and delicate lace on its edges, the sweeping gown was strapless, baring Ava's arms, shoulders, and upper back, flowing down her body like the Afqa waterfall feeding the River Adonis. A purple belt and white satin gloves accessorized the gown.

Hanz, too, participated in his daughter's vision of beauty. Again, rather than buying jewelry from town, he made her a necklace with matching earrings from deep purple glass, melting, molding, and polishing them until they looked like amethyst diamonds. With her dark hair done up and lips stained in red, Ava was stunning.

The judges whittled the contestants down to five girls–Ava among them–and began the final interviews to judge personality, intelligence, and communication skills. Shaylee had tutored her sister for days on a wide variety of topics in preparation, and luckily Ava gave an educated response to an uncontroversial question.

Fritz nudged Starholf after his favorite girl performed well in her interview too, despite her question being politically charged. Her answer made it clear she was a Nazi supporter. "Hey, let's bet on who wins," he said. "I put fifty Marks on my curvy blonde."

"You're on," replied Starholf. "My money's with the brunette."

The crowd of people waited in anticipation for the judges to make their final decision. Ava beamed on stage, head up, back straight, hand on her hip with one foot slightly forward, exuding confidence like Mrs. Yurkovich had taught her. Yet inside she was dying with anxiety. From where she stood, she could see her parents in the audience, taller than most, smiling proudly and waving at her. Shaylee was next to them, holding hands with her boyfriend Christian, nervously awaiting to see if her sister had placed. And Luka was absent, unable to leave his military base.

"Hanz, I can barely take this!" Maria said, putting her arm around Shaylee while clutching her husband's hand. She started second-guessing her decision to make Ava's gown. "Maybe I should have bought her a nice dress instead."

Hanz looked at his wife so she could read his lips. "*Nein, meine Liebe.* Look at our girl. *Sie ist wunderschön (She's beautiful)* and looks like a movie star. The crowd favors her, too."

Just then, a man dressed in a navy blue suit and orange bow tie walked up to the microphone. Opening a small envelope, he announced the third-place finisher–the blonde girl Fritz had favored.

"Ha! Too bad, *mein Freund*," said Starholf.

Then the man looked at the crowd and smiled. "And the winner of the 1939 Rothenburg ob der Tauber beauty pageant is . . ."

Maria could not hear the results, so she watched her husband's reaction, then turned to the stage to see her daughter's.

Ava gasped when she heard her name. Tears of joy immediately fell, and she covered her face with her hands as the other girls rushed over to congratulate her. A white victory sash was placed around her shoulder, a shiny crown on her head, and a bouquet of roses in her arms. Slowly she walked down the runway, the crowd whistling and cheering.

"She won!" Maria exclaimed, crying. "My baby won!"

"*Gute* girl, Ava!" Hanz shouted.

Shaylee screamed for joy, jumping up and down, and Christian whistled through his fingers.

"*Bezahlen auf, Verlierer (Pay up, loser),*" Starholf laughed.

Fritz begrudgingly handed him the fifty Marks.

As Hanz hugged Maria, an older woman grumbled to herself a few feet away. She was the grandmother of the runner-up. "Never thought I would live to see a Jew win a German beauty contest," she murmured. But Hanz heard her, making his ears grow hot and his heart race.

⁕

"**P**apa, I won!" Ava said with unbridled excitement, now down from the stage and with her family. She threw her arms around her father's neck. "I can't believe I won!"

"I had no doubt, *Schätzchen (sweetheart)*. And now you must promise me you'll write when you go to America and become a big star," Hanz teased.

"Oh, Papa," Ava said, laughing.

With tears still in her eyes, Maria kissed her daughter on the cheek and hugged her. "I'm so proud of you, baby. After all that hard work, just look at you now."

"I knew you'd win," said Shaylee, hugging her sister too. "Your answer was the best, and the crowd cheered the loudest every time you walked down the runway."

Christian agreed.

Mrs. Yurkovich walked up to the Wolff family. "Congratulations, young lady," she said, filled with pride of her own for being the winner's esteemed instructor.

"Mrs. Y, *dankeschön so sehr (thank you so much)* for all your training," Ava said. "I couldn't have won without you."

"You're welcome, dear. You were the only one who was elegant, dignified, and wholesome." She frowned, shaking her head. "Some of the bathing suits worn by those other girls were a shame. An outright shame."

Gertrude Schumacher walked past the Wolff family with a few other girls, all of whom were also in the pageant but didn't even crack the top five. "Well, well, well," she said, arms crossed with a sore loser's smirk. "I can't say the best beauty won. What were the judges thinking? I've seen better evening gowns at a funeral."

Ava turned on her heel and smirked back. "Don't worry, Gertrude. Once you learn how to shave that mustache off, I'm sure you'll place next year."

"Why, I oughta slap your face!"

"Why don't you kiss my *Arsch (ass)* instead," Ava retorted, turning her back to the girl.

Shaylee and Christian laughed as Gertrude and her friends scowled and walked off.

"Ava . . .," said Hanz, disappointed in his daughter's language. "I raised you better."

"It's all those American films, Papa," said Shaylee, shaking her head at Ava. "I fear they've completely corrupted my once-innocent sister."

❧

Mrs. Yurkovich offered to treat the Wolffs to dinner to celebrate her win. Or rather, Ava's win. Though all the Jewish residents had already been expelled from Rothenburg ob der Tauber, she was bold enough to enter the town, unafraid of any dirty looks from someone who might know her. Besides, her money was just as good as anyone else's, and since she lived in the country, the owner of the restaurant she liked tolerated her. Ava, Shaylee, and Christian gladly accepted her offer, knowing the wealthy lady would wine and dine them, but Hanz and Maria declined, preferring instead to go home. They thanked Nora for her generosity, and left the young adults with their neighbor.

On the drive back, Hanz drifted into melancholic musing. Though he didn't say it, he knew days like this were rare, and soon they'd become just memories. His beautiful twin daughters were now at an age where their minds, hearts, and personalities had converged into their own independent identities, and soon there would be young men who'd pluck his beloved swans from the pond.

Over the years, he and Maria had done their best, lovingly and tenderly nurturing and teaching their girls to be the young women they were today. Along with their brother, he had homeschooled them himself, with his own books, in a makeshift classroom in his basement library. Not only on reading, writing, and arithmetic but also on life. On morality, honor, kindness, and goodness. On respect and consideration. And sadly but necessarily, on evil and the dangers in the world.

Maria, too, had taught her beloved girls. She showed them how to cook, clean, and sew. How to make jewelry and quilts, and even soaps and perfumes from the flowers that grew in their own garden. Together with her husband, she poured her heart and soul into raising them. Neither could be any prouder of the result.

As the car steadily made its way down the long dirt road, Hanz thought about how his daughters were like his arms and legs. Body parts he couldn't live without. Though it was a happy day, his heart still ached, thinking of the time when they'd both marry and leave his home. Never once did he see them as someone else's children, either. A Jewish woman's children. No, Ava and Shaylee were his and Maria's own flesh and blood, and always would be.

And yet, despite that truth, the lie resurfaced. The falsehood that Maria had given birth to them from her own barren womb. The deception he had buried long ago, so deep in the dirt and rocks that he hoped it would never emerge again. "The truth is like a light," he remembered his grandfather saying many times. "You can block it out for only so long, and then it breaks through."

Like a murdered soul whose bony hand reaches out from the grave for vengeance, that's exactly what happened that day. "Never thought I would live to see a Jew win a German beauty contest," still rang in his ears. Only just a few words from an old lady, but powerful enough to tear down a towering house of denial.

And what of that Schutzstaffel officer Hanz noticed, whistling and howling at Ava while his friend looked on—another uncomfortable and perverse moment. Had that soldier known the truth, he never would have cheered for her. In fact, Ava wouldn't have even been allowed in the pageant. With the country becoming more and more anti-Semitic, poisoning the minds of the people about the Jews, it felt as if someone had firmly pressed a rifle into his chest, ready to pull the trigger. What did it all mean for the future? For his daughters?

Maria had a permanent soft smile on her face, holding Ava's crown in her lap. "You look worried," she said, glancing at her husband.

"*Nein.* Just a bit tired, *meine Liebe.*"

"I'll make some *Knödel (boiled dumplings)* and honey tea for us, and we can turn in early."

Hanz nodded and smiled.

On the winding dirt road that carved through the forest like a long snake, the shimmer of the Tauber River came into view, reflecting the dying sun's rays. They were now only moments from their home. Hanz breathed in the warm summer air and exhaled, letting himself relax. His daughter had just won the beauty pageant of Rothenburg ob der Tauber, and he wasn't going to let some bitter old stranger ruin the day. Reaching over, he held his wife's hand. How perfectly it fit into his.

CHAPTER 16

It was the end of summer in Germany, and soon the trees would start changing from evergreen to a blaze of candy apple red, pumpkin orange, and tart lemon yellow. With the echoes of war and the creeping tentacles of Nazi propaganda infiltrating the land, the outside world grew increasingly chaotic. A gloominess began to stretch over the Wolff's idyllic existence, threatening to shatter the fragile happiness they had known. Alas, the Nazi regime was about to plunge Germany into a nightmare of conflict and oppression . . .

Ava and Shaylee sauntered side by side along the beaten path toward their favorite picnic site by the Tauber River one afternoon, picking up acorns, pine cones, and dead leaves as they walked, examining the intricacy of each one before tossing them into the gusty breeze.

"Did Mama tell you Luka was promoted to sergeant?" Ava asked, glancing at her sister's reaction. "Uncle Severin put in a *gute* word." Now a colonel in the German military, Severin had used his influence to help his nephew Luka, taking him under his wing after he joined the Wehrmacht.

Shaylee seemed disinterested.

"You should be happy for your *Bruder*. Uncle Severin, too. They're making a career for themselves."

Shaylee narrowed her eyes at her twin sister. "The Nazi Party mistreats the Jews. They've already kicked them out of Rothenburg."

"That has nothing to do with Luka and Uncle Severin," Ava said, glancing up at the sky. "It's out of their hands."

"The Jews have done nothing wrong to justify this disgusting hatred toward them. They're innocent, and it's wrong what's happening."

Ava shrugged. "There's nothing we can do about it."

"I wish there were," said Shaylee. "I wish I could help them."

"Luka and I are going to a rally at the *Rathaus (Town Hall)* tomorrow. They're going to broadcast Hitler's speech from Berchtesgaden. They say he's mesmerizing, and the people love him because he gives them hope for a better future."

Shaylee shook her head. "I've heard one of his speeches before. He sounds like a madman."

When the sisters reached the familiar spot, Shaylee laid out a blanket, and Ava prepared the food in the picnic basket. Christian approached from across the field, waving as he got near, and Luka joined soon after, on military leave for a couple of days, bringing with him some homemade beer. Before long, the four of them were all eating and discussing the future of Germany.

"Adolf Hitler has brought in a new German order to replace the incompetent and inefficient democratic system," Luka said, getting on his nationalistic pedestal. "It's based on an authoritarian political structure with a supreme leader, and all German citizens must unselfishly serve the state. Individualism is to be sacrificed for the greater *gute* of all."

Christian took a drink of his beer. He hadn't yet been drafted, and worked as a fisherman on the used boat he took a loan out to purchase. "You're being brainwashed, *mein Freund*. What you're saying sounds like a societal hell."

"I agree," said Shaylee. "Adolf Hitler does not impress me; he scares me. That man has evil running through his veins."

Luka laughed. "My dear, small-minded sister, what do you know about politics?"

"I know one thing: The worst part of politics is when the poor are forced to defend the rich who are responsible for their poverty."

"She's right about that," said Christian.

"Hitler has *gute* intentions for Germany," Luka insisted. "I admire the man."

Christian scoffed. "The ultimate goal of the Nazi Party is to seize power through Germany's parliamentary system and install Hitler as dictator, which they've already done, and create a community of racially pure Germans loyal to their Führer, who would lead them in a campaign of ethnic cleansing and world conquest. It's complete madness, and if you ask me, demonic."

"You better be careful how you talk," Luka warned. "You'll be in the Wehrmacht soon too."

Everyone went quiet for a moment, letting the tension subside. Shaylee broke the silence: "We have *Freunde* that are Jews. They're our neighbors, and very nice people. None of them have ever hurt anyone."

"You don't understand," said Luka. "If there is to be prosperity in Germany again, if we are to be a great nation, then the weak must be removed."

"Jesus helped the weak, cured the sick, and even raised the dead. He didn't 'remove' them."

"Well that was a long time ago. And unless we make changes, we'll end up like the Roman Empire–nonexistent."

Ava decided to join the debate. "A strong leader makes a strong country," she said matter-of-factly, parroting the sentiments she heard at the rally. "We need a lion to lead us, not a sheep."

"That's right, Ava," concurred Luka, giving his sister an approving wink. "Adolf Hitler is not only a strong leader but also a brilliant man with genius ideas for Germany. He's like a light."

Shaylee grimaced, her hazel green eyes incredulous over her siblings' naïveté. "And the Bible reads that Satan disguises himself as an angel of light, misleading many."

⁕

After the picnic, Ava and Luka went home while Shaylee and Christian stole away to the abandoned cabin in the woods. They had been going there for months, seeking privacy from the prying eyes of the world. The rundown, single-room hut was once a secluded hunter's shelter, and they claimed it as their own, cleaning it up, putting curtains on the window and fixing the door. Later, they brought in a new mattress for the old bed frame, along with clean sheets and blankets. A small table and two chairs were already there, as well as a stone fireplace and a rare bear rug on the floor. It was in this romantic getaway that the two would-be lovers played house, spending time together and watching the sunset, sometimes staying overnight.

"Hurry, Christian, make a fire," Shaylee said, shivering as she rubbed her arms up and down. "It's freezing in here!"

Christian stuffed wood into the fireplace with kindling underneath it. He lit a match, and soon the space filled with warmth, the crackling fire adding to the amorous atmosphere. They stripped down to their knickers–Shaylee in her cotton panties and bra, Christian in his long johns–and sat on the bear rug in front of the fire, wrapped in each other's arms under a blanket. Christian escalated the cuddling by removing Shaylee's bra, and the osculation became more heated until he was on top of her, her breasts exposed, nipples puckering in the air.

"I want to make love to you," he whispered as he kissed her neck, sending shivers down her spine.

"We can't," she whispered back, breathless from his touch.

He pressed his body more aggressively against her.

"*Nein*, Christian," she protested, even as she kept kissing him. When he didn't listen, she pushed him off her.

Christian looked at her, frustration manifest in his eyes. "You're driving me crazy, you know that? You keep lying here half naked with me, but you won't go any further than kissing." Propping himself onto his knees, he stared down at her, the faint moonlight filtering through the window illuminating her arresting face with sparkling hazel green eyes, and her carob hair covering her pale shoulders. "You're so beautiful, Shaylee," he said. Leaning down, he planted more kisses on her forehead, her cheeks, her eyelids, and then back to her lips again, whispering, "*Ich liebe dich (I love you).*"

The words that came out of his mouth startled them both. It was the first time he said he loved her, even though he had thought it many times. Somehow in that moment, it didn't seem so scary to say it out loud.

Shaylee's heart melted, and her doe eyes went soft. "I love you too, Christian," she said, butterflies fluttering in her stomach.

Spontaneously, he pulled her up and formally got down on one knee, his hands holding hers. "Shaylee Wolff, I'm madly in love with you, and I want you to be my wife. Will you marry me?"

Of all the times he had joked about marrying her, even as children, Shaylee never took him seriously. But now she could see how serious he was. "*Ja*, Christian Hoffmann, I will marry you. I will be your wife."

He stood, tenderly cupping her face in his hands. "It means a simple life, Shaylee. I'm a fisherman, and I will never be rich. But I'll always love and take care of you."

Her eyes brimmed with tears, seeing not just the boy she grew up with but the man she would spend her life with. "I don't need riches, Christian. Only your love."

A storm was brewing outside, lightning illuminating the sky in flashes of silver, followed by rolling thunder that seemed to shake the very earth. Yet inside the cabin, the world was reduced to the crackling fire and the newly engaged couple embracing, sealing their promise with a kiss—a symbolic oath of newfound commitment and love.

"I've dreamed of this since we were children playing by the river," Christian whispered, his voice thick with emotion. "I always knew it would be you."

"Me too," said Shaylee, "ever since you kissed me under the willow tree when we were fifteen."

"I swear I'll make a *gute* husband for you."

"I'm not worried, because I know my papa will kill you if you don't," she teased.

"And I promise we'll be happy." He held her closer. "We're going to live to a hundred years old, with ten children and grandchildren around us."

Nearby, lightning struck the ground so hard it sounded like the sky splitting in two.

⁓⚜⁓

As Shaylee tiptoed into the farmhouse late that night, stealthily making her way to her bedroom, her mother intercepted her, sitting in the darkened living room with an aura of quiet disapproval about her. She turned on the light, startling her daughter. "Shaylee, I don't want you staying out so late with Christian like this," she chastised.

Shaylee sighed, annoyed that her mother had waited up for her. "I'm eighteen, Mama. I'm not a child anymore," she said, her voice carrying the defiance of newfound adulthood, though her mother couldn't hear it.

"If he wants to keep you out all night, he needs to marry you."

Shaylee's hazel green eyes seemed to brighten in the semi-darkness. As excited as she was about Christian's proposal, she didn't want to share it until he had bought her a ring.

"It's not decent for a *Fräulein* to stay out so late, especially when you don't even come home until the next day sometimes," Maria continued, her tone not just one of reprimand but of deep-rooted worry, characteristic of a mother's protective instinct.

Shaylee looked down and murmured her reply.

"Look at me when you talk. You know I have to read your lips."

"Sorry, Mama. It's just that I feel like you're treating me as a child."

"You will always be my child, *meine Lieber (my dear)*."

Shaylee softly smiled. "We got caught in the storm and took shelter, waiting for it to stop."

"Shelter where?"

Shaylee hesitated. "Oh, Mama, stop worrying. Christian is an honorable man. Can I please go to bed now?"

Maria exhaled, conceding for now. "We'll talk about this in the morning."

Shaylee walked up to her mother and kissed her on the cheek. *"Gute Nacht (Good night)*, Mama."

"Gute Nacht," said Maria, holding her daughter's hand for a moment before letting go.

Maria remained seated, lost in thought long after Shaylee's footsteps had faded. Where had the time gone, she wondered? It seemed only yesterday the twins were eating their porridge at the kitchen table in the morning, legs dangling in the air from their high chairs. And now in the blink of an eye, her two baby girls had grown up into beautiful young women.

Over the years, she had always indulged her children, making them pretty dresses, baking their favorite cookies and cakes, granting their whims and fancies. She loved them so much her heart warmed just looking at them. Countless treasured memories were now hers because of these angels from heaven. They hadn't just added to her life—they became her life.

Sitting alone in the quiet of the night, her mind wandered through the memories of her twin daughters' childhood, the years flashing by like scenes in a play: The day Hanz brought them in from the barn, altering their lives forever. Holding them close as if the sun and moon were in her arms. Bathing their tiny, chubby bodies in the sink as they splashed and smiled up at her. Their first steps, their first words. The day they first called her "Mama," and her husband "Papa." The many picnics they had as a young family by the pond where the swans would visit, and the joys each new milestone would bring. She remembered the day her daughters first said, "I love you, Mama," and how she wanted to live in that moment for the rest of her life. Even the scary and sad times she recalled, like when Ava almost drowned in the Tauber River, or when Shaylee had been so sick with pneumonia she almost died. And now her girls were on the cusp of a new chapter in life, one filled with love and its accompanying trials. They weren't ready, she thought. No one ever is.

As the moon sailed high in the sky, Maria finally stood, her movements slow and reflective, and made her way to join her husband in bed, the echoes of her own youth whispering through the corridors of her heart.

CHAPTER 17

September 1, 1939

Germany invaded Poland.

The horror of World War II had begun.

Anti-Semitism escalated, beyond that which anyone had imagined . . .

⚜

A month after the declaration of war, the Nazi Party organized a grand parade through Berlin's main east-west thoroughfare, Unter den Linden, to celebrate their swift victory over Poland. Crowds, dense and eager, lined either side of the famous street all the way up to the iconic Brandenburg Gate. Waving Nazi flags and cheering, the sea of people stood facing the spectacle, with children perched high on their fathers' shoulders and the elderly cheek by jowl with the youth. The ether vibrated with excitement, a collective breath held for the pomp and circumstance unfolding.

Goose-stepping soldiers marched in rigid formations, their boots hitting the pavement in a hypnotic rhythm. Military vehicles, symbols of the regime's power, followed in their wake. The air was filled with the resounding notes of martial music, wind and percussion instruments bellowing out patriotic tunes, fueling the heightened state of euphoria among the masses.

Within the throng of boisterous Germans stood Ava, her heart beating in sync with the drumming, her eyes wide with a mix of wonder and apprehension. She had traveled by train to witness this momentous event, the likes of which she had never seen before, and planned on meeting up with her brother afterward. In his full military garb, Luka was assigned a role in crowd control, a visible reminder of the strict order that governed the day.

Severin, with his higher rank, enjoyed the privilege of riding in one of the jeeps.

As several tanks rumbled past, German soldiers atop them waved to the crowd. Suddenly, one soldier's *Schirmmütze* fell off, and he jumped down from the armored vehicle to retrieve it. Without thinking, Ava ducked under the rope, scooping up the cap and extending it back to him. Her piercing emerald eyes locked onto his sky blue gaze, and instantly the clamor around them dissipated. Time stood still; the world stopped spinning.

"Wie heißen Sie (What's your name)?" the soldier asked. A dimple popped in his left cheek as he grinned, curiously out of place on his chiseled, square jaw.

Her heart fluttered like a trapped bird. "Ava Wolff."

"Ava," he echoed, his gaze lingering. "I've seen you before. You're the beauty queen of Rothenburg ob der Tauber."

She blushed.

"I'm Lieutenant Starholf Steiner, with the Schutzstaffel."

Ava smiled as an exhilarated rush came over her body. The electricity ran through him too, and he spontaneously reached out to move a strand of hair from her eyes, her silky lock between his fingers giving him goose-bumps as he tucked it behind her ear.

"Where do you live?" the lieutenant asked, already stepping backward to rejoin his unit.

"Outside of Rothenburg ob der Tauber," she answered, barely audible. "On my father's farm."

Leaping back onto the tank, he turned and called out, "Nice to meet you, Ava Wolff, beauty queen of Rothenburg! *Ich hoffe auf ein Wiedersehen mit Ihnen! (I hope to see you again!)"*

They kept smiling at each other as the armored vehicle disappeared down the street.

"He's an SS officer," warned a woman with curly blonde hair and un-trusting eyes, holding her newborn. Her buckteeth were all the more prom-inent between lips lacquered with candy apple red lipstick—something Hitler himself frowned upon, preferring Aryan women to display natural beauty void of makeup. "I would be careful, if I were you."

"Why?" asked Ava, still in a daze, caught in the afterglow of the dreamy encounter.

"Because they're heartless, that's why. The Schutzstaffel drink their enemy's blood for breakfast."

"*Gute* thing I'm not their enemy, then."

The parade reached its crescendo with the arrival of the senior Schutzstaffel contingent, marching ominously ahead of a sleek, midnight black Mercedes-Benz 770 cabriolet. Inside the state vehicle stood the Führer himself, Adolf Hitler, giving the Sieg Heil salute. When the people saw the car approaching, it sent them into a frenzy of ecstatic cheers and salutes, as if taken over by a diabolical fever, losing their minds to some unknown madness. The deafening audible vibration of the crowd went right through Ava's bones.

"The people sure love him," said another woman in joyful tears, her arm extended in the Nazi homage. "That man is directed by the gods."

Soon Hitler began his tyrannical speech in a celebratory and highly mendacious accounting of the conquest of Poland. From the enormous stage, his fiery eyes, booming voice, and pumping fists captivated the crowd, spit ejecting from his mouth as he disgorged his hateful propaganda. Whenever he paused to take a breath, the people roared with approval.

At the end of his thunderous vitriol, Hitler repeatedly shouted into the microphone, *"Eine neue Welt ist in Sicht, und sie gehört dem deutschen Volk! (A new world is on the horizon, and it belongs to the German people!)"* The Führer finished with a fiendish vow: "I am going to remove all abominations from Europe, starting with the Jew parasites! They are the worst of the vermin, and must be eradicated!"

And with those satanic, venomous words, the cheering became so loud and out of control that it frightened Ava.

❧

The aftermath of the parade left the streets of Berlin buzzing with an electric energy, but Ava found herself unnerved by the spectacle she had just witnessed. The display of military might and fervent national pride had revealed a sinister underbelly—a chilling insight into a regime driven by hatred and blind allegiance. As Hitler's maleficent words echoed in her mind, a sense of foreboding enveloped her, though her guileless innocence struggled to comprehend the full extent of the baneful path their nation was treading.

"We don't serve Jews," the hostess said loudly as Ava walked into the restaurant where she was meeting her brother Luka. The stark declaration cut through the room, drawing stares from several patrons.

"I'm . . . I'm not Jewish," Ava stammered, jolted by the imputation. "I'm German."

"You look Jewish to me."

Luka had just walked in. "A Jew?" he said, insulted. "Are you crazy? This is my sister, and she's one hundred percent German, like me."

The waitress gave Ava another dubious look-over.

"Can you not see my military uniform, you idiot?" Luka continued. "What German soldier would eat with a Jewish *Mädchen?* Get us a table before I have you arrested."

"*Es tut mir leid, Sir. Sofort (I'm sorry, sir. Right away),*" said the hostess. She ushered them to a booth near the window.

Ava leaned forward and whispered to her brother, "Do I look Jewish?"

"You look like a one-eyed monster," he answered, holding back a laugh.

She tried to kick him under the table. "I'm serious, Luka. I've heard people say that before about Shaylee and me."

"That's ridiculous," he scoffed. "You both have dark hair and fair skin, which means you could be German, French, Russian, Turkish, or several other nationalities. That hostess is jealous because you're far more beautiful than her."

Ava pulled out her compact and stared into the mirror at her large green eyes and dark hair. "I often wonder why Shaylee and I didn't turn out like Mama and Papa. He's blond, she's a redhead, and they're both much taller than we are."

"Maybe you and Shaylee are adopted like me," he teased, scanning the menu for something to order.

"You think?"

Luka put down the menu. "I was joking, you silly *Mädchen.*"

"And yet you look more like them than we do."

"Not all children resemble their parents. Besides, why would they lie about that?"

"I don't know."

After the waitress took their orders, Ava's eyes floated around the diner. The barstools were occupied by several older men—longtime regulars— smoking and drinking coffee as they each perused the newspaper. A group of young soldiers congregated at the back, laughing and talking boister-ously, imbibing more alcohol than they should. And a strange couple, void of conversation, sat in the middle of the room, the man consuming his food while the woman stared blankly at him as he ate.

"Did you two attend the rally?" asked a girl with short blonde hair two booths behind them.

"*Ja*," replied Luka with a wide grin.

"Heil Hitler!" the girl said, smiling flirtatiously back at him.

"*Ja*, Heil Hitler!"

The food arrived, and the two siblings ate like they'd never seen hot food before. As Luka dipped his meatloaf into the horseradish, he looked at his sister and said, "I saw you talking to that SS officer today. He seemed pretty smitten with you."

Again, Ava's heart fluttered like a trapped bird.

"What did he say?"

She smiled. "He asked for my address."

"Seriously?"

"*Ja*. But he was just flirting with me, which he probably does with all the girls. I doubt I'll ever see him again." She took a drink of her soda. "A woman in the crowd warned me about the Schutzstaffel. What do they do?"

"They're an elite corps assigned to carry out Hitler's most important objectives. It's a very prestigious position in the military, headed by Hein-rich Himmler himself. They only select those of pure Aryan blood who are absolutely loyal to the Führer, the Nazi movement, and the Fatherland, supporting Hitler's vision of the long-term future for the Third Reich."

Ava picked up the newspaper left on the table next to them and scanned the headline: *Adolf Hitler's New Germany*. "What did you think of the parade today?"

"Impressive," said Luka. "With Hitler as our Führer, the survival and greatness of our nation is secure."

"But don't you think it's extreme to vow annihilation of another group of people to achieve that goal?" Ava was starting to question the Nazi agenda, just like her sister Shaylee.

"Ava, you have to pick a side," said Luka, standing at the crossroads of duty and conscience. "Either you're for Adolf Hitler and his ideals, or you're against him, and that's like going against a tidal wave of fire."

"I don't like Hitler and what he stands for," Maria said in the kitchen, fearful that her daughter might get caught up in the frenzy of the Nazi propaganda. "Luka is in the military and must toe the party line to a certain extent, but Ava's only a civilian. You need to talk to her."

Hanz, sitting at the table, had a terrible sinking feeling in his gut, recalling last year when he himself went to a Nazi rally in Munich with Leon Dreisler and Günther Nachtnebel to hear Hitler speak.

"Hanz, did you hear me?" Maria asked, noticing his mind was elsewhere.

He looked up. "*Ja, meine Liebe*. I'll talk to her."

The evening air was cool and crisp as Hanz went outside to sit on the farmhouse steps, his corncob pipe in hand. Despite the twilight sky painting a serene watercolor across the horizon, his thoughts remained turbulent while he awaited his son and daughter's return from Berlin. Two hours later, they pulled into the driveway.

"I don't want you going to those rallies anymore," Hanz said as soon as Ava stepped out of Luka's car.

"Why, Papa?" she asked, walking up to him. She kissed him on the cheek. "It wasn't dangerous, and Luka was there. I even saw Uncle Severin driving in a jeep during the parade."

"I'm a man of God, and the Bible says we should be peacemakers. Adolf Hitler is a man of war, and a devil who spews nothing but hatred." His words were a lamentation for the path his country was taking. A path he didn't want his family to follow.

Luka removed their suitcases from the trunk and carried them up the steps. "We know you're a man of God, Papa. But religion and politics don't mix."

Hanz stood, towering over his adopted son. "And politics should reflect the laws given by the Creator, not those invented by evil men."

"The world is changing," said Luka with a thread of defiance as he continued into the house. "You either change with it, or get stomped on as it runs you over."

Hanz shook his head, disappointed in his son's perspective, regretting that he initially supported Luka's choice to join the military. Turning back to his daughter, he implored her again, his voice softening. "You're an adult now, Ava, and you can make your own decisions. But I'm asking you to please not go to those rallies anymore." Memories of the day he found Ava and Shaylee as babies, their true heritage hidden in the symbols embroidered on their blankets, along with a heartbreaking letter from their Jewish mother, once more flooded his mind.

Ava, still clutching the Nazi pamphlet from the rally, wondered why her father was so worried. What did he know? What could he see? Whatever it was, the depth of love, wisdom, and concern in his manner was crystal clear.

Hanz gently took the pamphlet from her hand and struck a match, setting it ablaze. The paper curled and blackened as its hateful words disintegrated in the flame. "Please promise me you'll never attend another one of those rallies again," he repeated, on the verge of tears.

Ava took her father's hand, seeing the strong emotion in his eyes. "I won't, Papa. I swear."

Hearing those words was a balm to Hanz's troubled soul. He grabbed his darling swan and pulled her into his embrace, hugging her tightly.

CHAPTER 18

Spring, 1940

While the Nazi military machine prepared for its next European conquests, the Nazi propaganda system continued to poison its people. Like a venomous snake rearing its ugly head from a deep, dark hole, frequent rallies were held across Germany, sweeping the land and producing a blazing inferno of rage, bigotry, and hate. The aura of the Führer reached that of an omnipotent god, and the Sieg Heil salute became as common as a handshake between friends. Those caught in the middle of the thunderous insanity could not escape its grip, and those standing from a distance tried to look the other way. In every city and town, Nazi soldiers wearing impressive uniforms and black, shiny boots stomped the ground–rhythmic, loud, all-consuming–and if you listened closely, you could hear the steady, eerie hum from miles away.

Despite the evil spell infecting the land, Ava kept her word to her father and didn't attend any more rallies. But one bright, sunny day, the rallies decided to make a house call, disguised in the form of SS officer Lieutenant Starholf Steiner. So besotted was he of the dark-haired, green-eyed beauty he had met in Berlin that he searched all the farms outside of Rothenburg ob der Tauber, until he finally found the Wolffs . . .

"I have a feeling this is going to be the best summer yet," Ava said to her sister, lying on a blanket by the small pond where they always used to picnic as a family. Felix, Bastian, and Axel–the three new sheepdogs Hanz had purchased after Rolf and Bruno died–lay in the grass nearby.

"Why do you say that?" asked Shaylee, fixated on one of her books. She had brought three, going back and forth between them–*Strange Creatures of the Sea, The Lands of Éire and Alba,* and *Haunting Stories of Lore.*

Ava picked up a long piece of straw grass and put it in her mouth. "Because I can feel it in my bones, that's why."

The day was as picturesque as a Claude Monet painting–tranquil, long and lazy, with a clear, baby blue sky stretching across the expanse above, and the springtide sun warming the fertile earth below. Deciduous trees sprung new pickle green leaves, boasting survival of winter's arduous passage. Wildflowers sprouted in the fields, efflorescing anew, imbuing the air with the faint, delicious fragrance of vanilla and lavender, their colorful blooms heliotropically turning in the field. And the calm waters of the silvery pond shimmered in the warm breeze, teeming with renewed aquatic life. If you were a bird, however, warily human-watching from a tree, your focus would be on the two slender, fair-complected twin sisters with dark hair lounging on a colorful patchwork quilt with German images sewn into the material, little girls in dirndls (traditional dresses) holding hands with little boys in lederhosen (traditional leather shorts with suspenders) stitched into the patches of red, black, and gold.

"Shaylee, look!" Ava said, noticing the two white swans several yards away. Half a dozen cute little cygnets, fluffy and light gray, were tucked within the mother's feathered pinions. "The babies have hatched and the mama has them under her wings."

But Shaylee was now engrossed in *Strange Creatures of the Sea*, captivated instead by the images in her book. A rare, sixteen-foot goblin shark, with its elongated flat snout and highly protrusible jaws containing prominent nail-like teeth, graced the first few pages. And a gigantic lion's mane jellyfish, seven feet in diameter with 150 tentacles stretching 118 feet long, followed next. Named after its orange and gold bell and hair-like tentacles that remind people of the color and texture of a lion's mane, the translucent Cyanea capillata composed of ninety-four percent water was extraordinary indeed.

Ava picked up *Haunting Stories of Lore* and, opening it to a random page, began reading aloud. "When the young bride found out her love had died at sea, she cut off her waist-length red hair and threw herself from the cliff, her body disappearing into the crashing waves below. And now, 300 years later, if you visit the castle on the high cliff on the eve of that tragic day, after sunset when the fog rolls in you'll see a faint ship offshore, the ghost of a young man standing on its bow, hoping to reunite with his bride. On the cliff, the bride will be waiting for him, her white wedding gown flowing in the breeze, her haunting cries echoing in the night."

Shaylee looked up. "That's the story of Emma and Jack. I love that tale. He was a fisherman who went out to sea, trying to earn enough money to buy a silver comb for his bride's long, flowing red hair. But he got caught in a storm and never returned."

"That's why she cut off her hair before jumping to her death?"

Shaylee nodded.

"That was dumb to jump. Why kill yourself over a man?"

"She was in love, and sorrow overtook her. She didn't want to live without him."

Ava closed the book, spit the straw grass from her mouth, and retrieved a cigarette she had hidden in her lipstick pouch, trying her best not to cough as she lit it. She picked up her sister's other book and stared at its title. "*The Lands of Éire and Alba*. Never heard of them."

"Éire is Gaelic for Ireland, and Alba is Gaelic for Scotland," said Shaylee.

"I suppose you'll be moving there someday, knowing your dreamy fantasies about faraway lands. Papa says it just rains there all the time, and the men live in the pubs, drinking grog."

"There's much more to Ireland and Scotland than that. The castles, the history, the culture—it's beautiful there; and *ja*, I do want to visit someday."

"To catch a good-looking Irishman?" Ava teased. "Or maybe a Scottish highlander?"

Shaylee touched the bracelet her boyfriend and secret fiancé had recently given her. "I'm in love with Christian, and you know that."

"Puppy love," said Ava, now flipping through the book's pages, contrasting the metropolitan centers of Dublin, Galway, Glasgow, and Edinburgh with the countryside and surrounding towns. "Aside from a lot of green, these places look rather lonely and boring, if you ask me."

Shaylee grabbed her book back. "I didn't ask you, did I."

Ava laughed. "You and your silly books." She stared at her sister for a moment, trying to understand her love of the written word. "What's your favorite quote from one of your beloved writers, anyway?"

Without hesitation, Shaylee replied, "'I am out with lanterns, looking for myself,' by Emily Dickinson."

"What does that mean?"

"It means she was on a quest of self-discovery, searching for her own identity and purpose in this world. Trying to figure out who she was."

"I already know who I am," Ava scoffed. "I don't need to go searching."

Shaylee looked at her sister in a way that was almost condescending. "Fashion magazines, Hollywood gossip columns, red lipstick, and swing dancing are not things that define you, Ava. They're only things you like. In ten years, you'll be a different woman than you are now, perhaps even with new likes. Then again in twenty, and thirty, and forty, and so on. Life changes, and so do we, whether we realize it or not."

"Maybe so, but I have dreams now, and I hope they come true."

"*Ja*, I know," said Shaylee, shaking her head. "Fickle dreams of being a movie star and meeting womanizers like Rex Harrison and Clark Gable."

Ava pretended she was offended and about to faint, placing the back of her hand on her forehead. With her best Southern American drawl, she cried out, "Sir, you are no gentleman!"

Shaylee, recognizing Scarlett O'Hara's line in *Gone with the Wind*, responded with Rhett Butler's reply: "And you, Miss, are no lady."

Both girls laughed.

After they ate lunch—chicken sandwiches and sweet tea, lovingly prepared by Maria—Ava lay back on the blanket to take a nap, while Shaylee scanned the picturesque landscape the siblings had known since childhood. Noticing the two swans, she watched and smiled as the mother coaxed her babies into the pond for their maiden swim, the father remaining protectively close by. Then, out of nowhere, a young man appeared from across the field. An officer, dressed in his uniform, tall and lean, waving as he approached. "Ava," said Shaylee, nudging her sister. "A soldier is coming."

Ava opened her eyes and sat up, squinting into the distance. Seconds later, her stomach knotted and her face flushed. "Oh my goodness, Shaylee, it's him!"

"Who?"

"That handsome officer I met in Berlin!" Quickly Ava sprang to her feet, patted down her dress, and ran her fingers through her windblown hair. Lieutenant Starholf Steiner, the man who had unexpectedly entered her life during a fleeting visit to Berlin, was now here, in the very heart of her childhood home. She hurried across the verdant field to meet him.

Shaylee picked up the blanket and her books, trailing behind her sister.

"Starholf," Ava said breathlessly when she reached him. "What are you doing here?"

"*Hallo*, Ava." He removed his peaked cap and smiled at her. "I've been looking for you."

"But . . . that was six months ago when we met. I didn't think I'd see you again."

He looked at Shaylee as she caught up to them. "And you must be Ava's sister. I'm Lieutenant Starholf Steiner; nice to meet you."

Shaylee smiled.

For an awkward moment they all just stood there, twin sisters side by side, staring shyly at the unexpected soldier, and the soldier staring surprisingly at mirror female images.

"I didn't know you had an identical twin, Ava."

"Oh, *ja*. Sorry. This is my sister Shaylee."

Starholf nodded as he glanced back and forth between them, his mind registering their slight physical differences. Shaylee was doing the same, studying his face, comparing it to how Ava had described him: Ice blue eyes–almost translucent–thick blond hair, and a jawline that could cut glass. Multiple Nazi insignias sparkled on his uniform, and he wore a swastika ring on his middle finger. Impressive but intimidating; and yet, Shaylee also sensed a refined persona about him, as if he were related to royalty.

"What have you been up to since Berlin?" he asked Ava, his gaze softening.

"Thinking about you every day," said Shaylee.

Ava's cheeks flushed scarlet.

"It took me a while to find you. In fact, I've been to every farm within a thirty-mile radius of Rothenburg. It would have been easier if you had just told me which farm," he chuckled.

"Would you like me to show you around?" Ava asked.

"*Ja, danke*." Starholf extended his arm, and she inserted hers, her heartbeat still racing.

Shaylee watched them leave. Felix, Bastian, and Axel reappeared and watched as well, wondering who the stranger was.

<hr>

The conversation flowed easily as Ava gave Starholf the grand tour of the Wolff farm. The serene beauty of the countryside, the vineyard, the calm pond with the swans and their babies, and the winding Tauber River added to the enchantment. Even the war seemed a distant shadow as they promenaded. And though it was only their second meeting, it felt as if the young couple had known each other their entire lives.

"I come from a long line of German ancestry," Starholf said proudly. "A pure, Aryan bloodline. Everyone in my family has the *Abstam-mungsnachweis (genealogical certificate)* to prove it."

"I'm afraid I can't say the same," Ava confessed. "I have some Slavic on my side. My great-grandmother was Russian."

"That's why you have the dark hair."

Ava remembered Shaylee mentioning that the Nazi regime did not consider Slavic people to be of pure Aryan race but contaminated with Mongol blood during the Middle Ages. "Maybe your family wouldn't approve of my Slavic side."

He grinned at her. "Let me worry about that."

"Seems like they'd want you to pursue a pure German girl."

"I *am* pursuing a pure German girl," he replied, putting his arm around her. "What they don't know won't hurt them."

As they kept walking, they found themselves a fair distance along the bank of the Tauber River. Ava recognized they had long since passed the extremity of the Wolff property line, and brought her suitor back to the dirt road between Rothenburg and the farm. The massive linden tree that was well known in the area stood imposingly a few feet off the road in front of them, staring them down as if to command, *"Anhalten (Halt)!"* Starholf stopped to admire it, gazing at its twisted trunk and branches, lifting his eyes to the light scattering through the leaves like rays shooting through water.

"In Japanese, they call this phenomenon *komorebi*," he said. "It means, 'sunlight that filters between leaves.'"

"That's beautiful. Do you speak Japanese?"

"*Nein*," he laughed softly. "But my best friend in elementary school was Japanese, and he taught me a few words. We were like *Brüder* back then."

"Not anymore?"

The smile dimmed from Starholf's face. "*Nein.*"

"Why not?"

"Because," he said, picking up a branch, breaking it in two and tossing it aside. "My father was not going to allow his only *Sohn* to associate with anyone other than people he approved of. When he found out about Toshiko, he ended our friendship, taking me to a different school."

"How sad," said Ava, thinking once more about her Slavic side. "Did you ever see him again?"

"*Nein*. I tried to contact him when I was a teenager, but his family had moved." Starholf changed the subject, noticing an "X" carved into the trunk of the tree. "What's this 'X' mark mean here?"

Ava ran her finger along the smooth grooves cut into the rough bark. "My papa did that," she said, as if it were something to be proud of.

"Why?"

"Years ago, when Shaylee and I were just babies, a man pretending to be a priest was hung from this tree by a mob of vigilantes. As the story goes, he had murdered a real priest in another town, stole his identity, and swindled the money from the congregation in Rothenburg, which he collected by promising to build them a new church."

Starholf shook his head.

"He also slit a local woman's throat for her jewels, and raped a young Jewish girl."

"No wonder they hung him. He deserved it. Was your father one of the men in the mob?"

Hanz had never told the full story to his daughters. Despite being only a spectator, he was not proud of being present that night. "*Nein*, but afterward he carved the 'X', saying that it was a mark of significance because a man who had been born innocent, had sadly lost his way, and then his life, because of poor choices."

"Interesting," said Starholf. "What about the money and the jewels?"

"As far as we know, they've never been found. But the story has become legend around here, and sometimes you'll see people searching the forest for the stash."

Just then, Ingomar, the black crow Hanz had found as a baby and nurtured back to health, landed on the very tree branch that had been used for the lynching. He stared at the couple in curiosity, then let out a large, screeching caw, spreading his feathered wings and flying away.

❦

That evening, as Shaylee hung her newly sewn moss green velvet curtains, Ava lay on her bed, flipping through a fashion magazine while listening to a record on the gramophone. Dinner had been eaten, and their parents were relaxing on the porch swing, enjoying another splendiferous sunset bleeding vermilion red, tangerine orange, and saffron yellow.

"You need to be careful with this soldier," Shaylee said to her sister as she stepped back to admire her drapery work. "SS officers have been known to be cruel."

Ava looked up from her magazine. "You met him. Did he come across as a cruel man to you?"

"I'm just saying be careful."

"Luka and Uncle Severin are in the military too."

"*Ja*, in the regular army. Not in Hitler's Schutzstaffel."

Ava scoffed. "You're just jealous."

Shaylee turned to face her sister, reflecting genuine concern. "*Nein*, Ava, I'm not. You know as well as I do that the SS and Gestapo are a heartless bunch led by a dictator."

"I think Starholf is . . . different," said Ava, looking back down at her magazine.

"If he were, he wouldn't be an SS officer to begin with."

"He has the face of an angel. I can't imagine him doing anyone harm."

"Remember what Papa told us about being courted. If a man shows unkindness and intolerance toward others, he will eventually do the same to you."

Ava ignored her and went over to the gramophone. Turning up the volume, she began to dance, pulling her sister in, spinning and giggling without a care in the world. Only her excitement for a tall, handsome young soldier filled her mind.

❧⸙☙

Starholf came back to the Wolff farm the following day, asking Ava's parents if he could take her into Rothenburg ob der Tauber for dinner. Hanz and Maria were initially against it, given the true heritage of their daughter and the reputation of the SS, but with the disappointment on Ava's face and the confusion on the young soldier's, they conceded and decided to allow it. But on one condition: their other daughter had to come along as a chaperone. Little did they know, however, that Shaylee wanted to be alone with Christian that night, and on the way into town, Ava dropped her sister off at his boat.

Starholf took Ava to her favorite café in Rothenburg. They sat at a little table on the cobblestone patio, with flowers on one side and a trickling fountain on the other. Near sunset, the golden ball on the horizon cast a warm glow on the ancient stones and timbers of the romantic, storybook town.

"What's it like being in the Schutzstaffel?" Ava asked. As an SS officer, he represented everything she and her sister had been taught to fear and distrust. And yet as he sat there, he also seemed disarmingly human.

Starholf's deportment momentarily changed from a man courting his love interest to an austere military officer. "It's a life of discipline and duty, *Fräulein* Ava. But there are also moments of pride and joy."

"My *Bruder* Luka and my uncle Severin are in the Wehrmacht, and Luka told me the SS are an elite group that carry out Hitler's most important objectives."

"*Ja*, it's true," said Starholf, winking at her. "You should be proud to be courting one."

Ava smiled. "And what about the Gestapo? Where do they fit in?"

"The Gestapo are the *Geheime Staatspolizei (Secret State Police)*. They're under SS control, responsible for investigating political crimes and opposition activities." Starholf made it sound oh so noble, when in fact the Gestapo would go door to door, looking for Hitler's enemies—socialists, communists, trade union leaders, and others who had spoken out against the Nazi regime. Some were just beaten and arrested, others killed. It's how Hitler had managed to nearly wipe out all opposition, thereby leaving the Nazi Party as the only formal political entity in the country. Democracy in Germany was dead. "Too bad for the Gestapo that they don't get to wear these fancy uniforms, though," Starholf said, winking at Ava again. "But it's much more effective for them to be plain-clothed and blend in than to announce themselves in a uniform."

As innocent as she was, Ava didn't fully understand the forces of terror that had been created in Nazi Germany under the Schutzstaffel and Gestapo, headed by ruthless SS chief, Henrich Luitpold Himmler. Or the cruel and barbaric methods they used to achieve their egregious goals. No, she was simply a young woman, infatuated with a young man in uniform, dreaming of a happy life. "That day at the parade in Berlin, you were with a bunch of other Nazi officers," she said. "Are they all your *Freunde?*"

Starholf cut into his steak. "I wouldn't say they're *meine Freunde*. Acquaintances are more like it, and a few are my superiors."

Ava noticed that before he spoke, he'd look intently at her, thinking over his words. He did it every time, and she found it both intimidating and attractive. "I don't really know much about politics, but I do know there are certain people who are discriminated against, simply because of their religion or race. Why is that?"

Starholf frowned. "To be honest, I don't want to talk about it. As an SS officer I have a responsibility, a job to do, and I do it. I leave the politics to the Führer and his inner circle. Besides, it's not a topic to discuss at dinner."

But Ava pressed him further, thinking about her sister's warning, and the warning from the woman with curly blonde hair, buckteeth, and lacquered red lips who spoke to her at the Nazi celebration in Berlin. "After I first met you at that parade on Unter den Linden in Berlin, a woman came up to me and said I should be careful about you."

"Why?"

"She said the Schutzstaffel drink their enemy's blood for breakfast."

Starholf laughed.

Ava was about to tell him what Shaylee had said too, that the SS and Gestapo are a heartless bunch led by a dictator. But instead she held her tongue, not wanting to go too far, or create a wedge between him and her sister.

Starholf looked at the dark-haired, green-eyed beauty sitting across the small table from him. Sensing her reservations about courting an SS officer, he wanted to quell her concerns. Taking her hand, he said, "I don't make the rules, Ava. But as you know, on a farm the fields must be plowed, the crops planted, and the cows milked. The one who owns the land makes those decisions, and the workers get it done. It's the same with politics. I swore loyalty to the Third Reich and its Führer, as have my family, and I perform a service in carrying out that oath. It's a matter of honor, and so far it has served me well."

"My sister likes to quote from famous philosophers, and what you just said reminds me of one: 'Dictatorship naturally arises out of democracy, and the most aggravated form of tyranny and slavery out of the most extreme liberty.'"

"Plato," said Starholf. "He also said, 'At the touch of love, everyone becomes a poet.'" A wonderful smile spread across his face, making Ava blush. Pausing, he considered his next words, wanting to ensure she'd be comfortable with him going forward. "I have a personal life too, Ava. Separate from my work in the Nazi Party, and I have no intention of blending them. Like most people on this earth, I simply want to be happy. And I want to raise my own family, making sure they're safe and happy too." With that, he took a drink of his wine and finished the last piece of his steak.

Shaylee's concerns, and the blonde woman's warning in Berlin, instantly vanished from Ava's mind.

"Do you think your parents will find out about your sister not being with us?" Starholf asked, redirecting the conversation. "You both might be in trouble."

Ava shook her head. "Shaylee and I have been doing this since childhood, helping each other out. They won't know."

"Shame, shame," Starholf said, waving his finger at her.

"You're an SS officer; I doubt you're so innocent," Ava retorted, eyeing him from above the rim of her wine glass.

Starholf narrowed his eyes at her and grinned. "*Nein*, I'm not innocent. But a girl needs a man who has lived a little, and though I am still young, I do have experience. And you know what else I have? Dreams. What are your dreams, *meine schöne junge Fräulein (my beautiful young lady)*? What have you always wanted?"

"You might think it's funny, but I've always wanted to be a movie star. I'd love to move to America–Hollywood, specifically–and see my name in lights."

"That's very far from Germany, especially for a young, inexperienced woman. Wouldn't you be afraid?"

"I'm afraid of nothing except being bored," she replied, citing a Greta Garbo quote of her own.

"The Wild West, with all those cowboys and Indians." Starholf put on his best American accent. "Y'all better watch out, folks! Ava Wolff is going to be on the silver screen!" He sat back and spread his arms out in the air, looking up as if introducing her name in marquee lights.

"Oh, stop."

He reached over and touched her chin. "*Ja*, I do believe you could be an actress. You're certainly pretty enough. But you know," he added, becoming more serious, "life in Hollywood can be very hard."

"What do you mean?"

"I believe the best place for a woman is at home with her family, where she'll be loved and protected, not with a bunch of rich moguls who gawk at, grope, and abuse her. And the few who do make it often regret what they had to do to achieve success, unless they had powerful connections to begin with. I'd never want a woman like that to raise my children."

"What kind of woman are you looking for?"

Starholf's gaze and tone softened again. Leaning forward, he took her hand and said, "Someone about your height, with chestnut hair, emerald eyes, and ivory skin. Know anyone like that?"

Ava smiled so big her face hurt. "Maybe."

The lovestruck couple continued talking and laughing, enjoying each other's company into the night. As the restaurant began shutting things down, Starholf paid the bill, and they leisurely walked the cobblestone street toward his car. When they came upon a dimly lit area, he pulled her in, gently pushing her against a stone wall. Looking down into her face, his eyes tracing every beguiling detail, he asked, "Is there any way I can talk you out of going to America?", his sapphire blues latching onto her emerald greens. Leaning in, he brushed his lips against hers, so tenderly she barely felt them, and when his sweet breath teased her thin neck, goosebumps followed. "Ava . . .," he whispered amorously into her ear, returning to her lips with a fervid kiss. "That day I saw you at the beauty pageant, the only dark-haired beauty on stage, looking like an angel, I knew I had to make you mine."

Slightly dizzy, Ava shivered.

Starholf removed his jacket and put it on her slender shoulders to warm her. Wrapping his arms around her, strong yet gentle, he kissed her passionately. Once more, the world around them seemed to pause, holding its breath as they stood on the cusp of promise and possibility. Starholf kissed her in a way that no man ever had, and deep down she knew ever would. Her mother had warned her about men like him. The ones who could so easily break your heart. And yet Ava didn't care.

In fact, she dove right in.

❧

"They're seeing each other almost every day now," Maria said, a worried expression on her face. She was making herself some herbal tea for a persistent, achy fatigue.

"I was hoping it wouldn't become serious between them," replied Hanz, lighting his corncob pipe. "But it looks like it has."

Maria sat at the table. "Hanz, you have to talk to her. We must stop this, and you know why."

"Stop two people falling in love?"

"But what if somehow the secret gets out?"

"Stop worrying, *meine Liebe*. No one will ever know."

Maria frowned. "How can you be so sure?"

Hanz puffed on his pipe while petting Axel lying by his feet. Felix and Bastian were roaming around outside. "Maybe this is a *gute* thing," he said, looking at it from a totally different perspective. "Think about it. If Ava married an SS officer, people would never suspect she's a Jew. It would actually be a protection for her, as crazy as that sounds."

Husband and wife stared at each other, long and deep, and in that moment the letter from Abigail Katz wandered into Hanz's mind. It was time to burn it, he thought. Along with the woolen blankets embroidered with the Star of David. Yes, later that night, when Maria went to bed, he would take the lantern and go down into the secret room next to the cellar, remove the letter and blankets from their hiding spot, and take them outside to burn.

It was way past time.

⚜

The whirlwind courtship that followed was dazzling for Ava. Restaurants, theater performances, parties, Nazi parades–Starholf put her on his arm and took her to them all. One weekend, he brought Ava to meet his parents. They were throwing a VIP party at their mansion in Berlin, and he was expected to be there.

The Steiners were a wealthy family who lived in an affluent neighborhood that prided itself on its exclusivity and prestige. Their home was a turn-of-the-century Neo-Baroque manor, two stories high on twenty acres of land, with spectacular vistas and views. Vaulted cupolas, rows of colonnades, lavish entryways, and walls made of stone were distinct features of the palatial home. Interior design denoted by luxuriant fabrics and furniture, frescos on walls and ceilings depicting mythological scenes and historical triumphs, Persian rugs and exotic vases on marble floors, opulent ornaments and embellishments were all part of the extravagance. Two giant staircases curved up to the second floor as you entered the grand foyer, and a magnificent stained glass window sparkled from the sun's rays at the top.

Oh, heavens, it was incredible!

As Starholf led Ava through the house, her saucer eyes took it all in, like Alice the first time she entered Wonderland. She had only ever seen homes like this in magazines, and the contrast with her parents' simple farmhouse was overwhelming. When they got to the rear of the mansion that opened to a stunning, manicured garden in the backyard, Ava got nervous, observing the crowd of people.

This was no small gathering. Politicians, bankers, celebrities, high-ranking SS officers—the elite of Germany—were there, dressed to the nines, cocktails in hand, mingling, laughing, shaking hands and making deals. A ten-piece band was playing popular Aryan music by favored German composers, like Richard Wagner—Hitler's favorite—and Anton Bruckner. And a buffet of delectable foods a mile long, with a fountain of sparkling champagne a mile high, was on display.

Ava looked down at her modest dress and felt inadequate compared to what the other women were wearing, each gown more striking and expensive than the next. As if competing in a Berlin beauty pageant or attending a movie premier, the wives and girlfriends of the honored guests tried to outshine each other, their showy updos and fancy jewelry accompanied by fake, two-faced smiles.

"Starholf, I'm not dressed for this event," Ava whispered, squeezing his arm in apprehension.

He stopped, took her hand, and kissed the back of it, the dimple in his left cheek popping as he grinned, his blond, sleeked-back hair shimmering under the terrace lights, his confident, firm grasp on her hand making her feel safe. "Don't be silly, you're absolutely beautiful. The prettiest woman here, by far. Just follow me and stay by my side."

Ava smiled; the trepidation in her stomach dissipated. As she gazed into his reassuring blue eyes, her heart filled with love. She would follow this man to the ends of the earth if he asked her to. And with each passing moment, the idea of becoming a movie star floated away like a midsummer night's dream.

⌘

"You're lucky, you know," said a female voice that evening, her eyes projecting an envious stare.

Ava had gone to the powder room to reapply her lipstick when the short, blonde woman with unbelievable curves followed her in. "How so?" she asked, releasing a friendly smile.

"Being with Starholf. All the girls are after him. What makes *you* so special?"

The bathroom, with its opulent marble counters and gilded mirrors, suddenly felt too small, the air perfumed with a mixture of expensive scents and uncomfortable tension. Ava turned to the mirror, her reflection staring back at her—a farm girl amidst Berlin's elite—her simplicity and diffidence now stark among the wolves.

The churlish woman smirked and turned to the mirror too, applying her own orange-red lip stain, proud of herself for knocking Ava down a notch.

"I'll tell you what makes her so special," said another woman exiting a stall. Tall, slender, and elegant, with high cheekbones that, like Starholf's jawline, could cut glass, she came to Ava's defense. "Perhaps it's because, unlike you, she's a doll. Look at her; she's beautiful."

The short, blonde woman made a face and left.

"That's right, scram!" said the defender. She winked at Ava and laughed. "I'm Gwyneth, by the way. Starholf's older sister."

"Oh . . .," said Ava, caught between discomfort and gratitude. "I'm Ava Wolff. And *danke*."

"I know who you are. And don't mention it—Berlin is full of envious cows like her." As Gwyneth washed her hands in the sink, her gaze remained fixed on Ava in the mirror. "But really, though, what did you do to catch such a prize as my *Bruder*? It's not every day a girl from the countryside captures the heart of a Steiner."

Ava's hand trembled slightly as she capped her lipstick, wondering if another attack was imminent. "I suppose we just . . . found a connection."

Gwyneth arched an eyebrow, her curiosity unsated. "A connection, hmm? Well, love, in our circles, connections are everything. But they can also be fickle. Especially during a war. Loyalties are often tested, and alliances can shift. Remember that."

"I will," Ava timidly replied. She wanted to believe that what she and Starholf had was immune to the whims of society and the brutalities of war. But Gwyneth's words were a blunt reminder of the fragile bubble they were in.

Gwyneth straightened, her demeanor softening. "You have a *gute* heart, Ava. It's rare and . . . refreshing." She paused, weighing her next words judiciously. "Just be careful, darling. Our world–it devours the naïve."

Though raised to be pompous, commensurate with her station in a filthy rich family of Germanic nobility, Gwyneth turned out to be smart, sassy, and down-to-earth–a saving grace in an otherwise haughty upbringing. She'd soon become Ava's good friend. "And like I said," she added, "don't let those creatures bother you. Starholf knows his mind. He knows what he likes, and he's told me he likes you. So, welcome to the family." She gave Ava a big hug.

⚜

"She has *wunderbar* Aryan features," Starholf's mother said, observing Ava across the terrace with a calculated interest that vacillated between approval and skepticism. She and her son were by the champagne fountain, talking as Gwyneth introduced Ava to another guest. "Fair skin, beautiful green eyes, feminine form. But that dark hair–where did that come from?"

"What does it matter?" Starholf asked, his voice carrying a hint of defensiveness. His mother's approval meant everything to him. "The Führer himself has dark hair."

"True enough."

"Be *gute* to her, mother. I think she's the one."

Mrs. Steiner looked at him, analyzing her son's lovestruck countenance as if reading tea leaves. "My dear boy, how many times have I heard that?"

He took a sip of his champagne and smiled. "Ava's not like the others. There's something about her. Something . . . different."

"A farmer's daughter, though," she tsked.

"You were the daughter of a teacher before father met you."

Mrs. Steiner looked over at Ava again. "She is very sweet, and a pretty little thing–I'll give you that."

"And she makes me laugh. I love that about her."

"Just remember, *Sohn*, you're one of the most eligible bachelors in Germany right now. Our family is rich and of noble birth, and you're a high-ranking SS officer with a shining career ahead. Be careful who you choose to have by your side."

"She's the one, mother," Starholf insisted.

Mrs. Steiner pointed at the two young officers who had approached Ava, talking and flirting with her. "Well you better go to her, then. Before someone else catches her eye."

⁓❦⁓

Starholf took Ava on a surprise trip, traveling first class by train to Cologne. Dressed in an expensive outfit he had bought her—a cream silk suit with matching hat and pearl earrings—Ava sat by the window watching the beautiful landscape passing by, while he sat next to her, stealing kisses along the way.

Founded in 38 BCE, the historic, cultural, and economic capital of the Rhineland was rich in museums and galleries showcasing masterpieces from renowned artists and Roman antiquities. The High Gothic architecture of the 515-foot twin-spired Cologne Cathedral was its famous landmark, home to other art treasures and a massive gilded shrine containing ancient reliquaries. Starholf had picked the destination after consulting with his sister Gwyneth, and planned everything himself in detail, from staying in a luxurious hotel, dining in the finest restaurants, to visiting all the must-see sights and attractions of the city. Ava had never dreamed of such a pampering.

On the last day of the romantic excursion, Starholf brought Ava to a picturesque spot overlooking the Rhine River and glimmering city lights below. "Ava Wolff," he said, getting down on one knee, "I have fallen deeply in love with you." He opened a small velvet box containing the most beautiful diamond ring she had ever seen. "I want to spend the rest of my life with you. Will you please marry me?" The threat of tears glistened in his eyes.

At that moment, Ava didn't think of her dreams of being a movie star, or meeting Rex Harrison, Clark Gable, and Cary Grant. She didn't think of Hollywood or seeing her name in marquee lights. All those hopes and aspirations no longer seemed to matter, and all she wanted now was to lie next to Starholf Steiner for the rest of her life, being with him, holding him, kissing and loving him. "*Ja!*" she exclaimed, happy beyond words. "*Ja*, I will marry you!"

Starholf placed the dazzling ring on Ava's finger, then stood and picked her up, spinning her around and around. As they both laughed, she strangely recalled when her sister had said that in ten years she would be a different person, perhaps with new likes. Shaylee was right, except for one thing . . . It didn't take ten years; it took less than one.

⁓⸗⟶⟵⸗⁓

Life always surprises you. The threads of destiny weave patterns unforeseen, and whenever you think the road you have chosen has been set, often you find yourself on another.

Ava and Starholf had courted for only three months before he proposed. The heirloom ring belonged to his grandmother, whom he adored while she was alive, and though his aristocratic parents, guardians of their lineage prestige, wanted him to marry an upper-class girl of the same status, eventually they warmed up—somewhat—to the charming and beautiful Ava Wolff with intense green eyes, thick ebon hair, and infectious spirit.

And so it was . . . A wealthy, highborn, high-ranking German officer and a common yet striking farm girl from disparate worlds, madly in love. A fairy tale indeed. Though Ava initially had dreams of moving to America and seeing her name in the marquee glow of Hollywood's glitter, she instead agreed to marry a man she believed to be her happily-ever-after prince.

And he would have been, had the gates of hell not opened and let all the demons out . . .

CHAPTER 19

Ava and Shaylee, Luka and Christian—now conscripted into the Wehrmacht—went to a restaurant in Rothenburg ob der Tauber. The two men had been granted military leave to attend Ava and Starholf's wedding in a few days, and they all sat in a red velvet booth by the window, catching up over dinner. Music played on the jukebox, and the soothing atmosphere belied the mayhem engulfing the world outside.

"What's wrong, Luka?" Shaylee asked, noticing her brother's somber mood.

"Nothing."

"You seem rather distant."

"I'm fine."

"Leave him alone," said Ava. "He's probably thinking about how to better serve the Fatherland. I'm sure someday he'll marry his uniform."

Christian laughed.

"Maybe I will," Luka replied, bitter in tone. "And when I die, they'll bury me in it. Perhaps the Führer himself will say my eulogy." He abruptly stood and left.

Shaylee looked at her sister with concern. "What's wrong with him? He didn't even finish his dinner."

"I don't know," said Ava, watching her brother through the window as he stormed down the street. An odd expression shrouded her face, and Shaylee wondered if some kind of rift had formed between her two siblings.

The evening wore on, and Christian eventually drove the girls home. Shaylee went to bed, but Ava quietly went to the barn. She had found her brother's scribbled note in her room, telling her to meet him there.

"Are you really going to marry him?" Luka asked, standing in the shadows, his messy hair covering one eye and his military outfit rumpled. After leaving the restaurant, he went by himself to The Devil's Needle, coming home intoxicated.

"You're drunk again," said Ava, her silhouette framed by the doorway as she observed his inebriated demeanor.

"So what? I have *gute* reason to be." Ever since Ava and Starholf became engaged, Luka started acting strangely, keeping to himself, sleeping less and drinking more. "Answer my question."

"Of course I'm marrying him. I love him." Ava picked up the kerosene lamp and walked into Hanz's makeshift art studio to inspect her father's latest project–another sweeping landscape of the Bavarian Alps. So lifelike were his paintings that he had no trouble selling them in Giovanni Mandolini's art gallery in Rothenburg ob der Tauber. In fact, over the years, the Italian owner couldn't get enough of them, with customers on a waiting list, even during the war. "Why did you want me to meet you here?" she asked, looking back at her brother.

Luka just stared at her, a wall of silence, impenetrable and cold.

"If you don't answer, I'm leaving."

"Why did you let me fall in love with you?" he finally blurted out.

Ava wasn't expecting that. As she stood there, stunned, in the shadowed confines of the barn, a place where secrets and confessions mingled with the scent of hay and oil paints, it began to rain outside, heavy drops pelting the barn roof, sounding as if beef sizzling in a frying pan.

"After what we did in the loft that summer . . .," continued Luka. "I thought you were in love with me too."

Ava cared deeply for her adopted brother, but at the same time had a certain fear of him, his persona becoming more agitated and forceful since joining the Wehrmacht. "That wasn't love, Luka. That was experimenting. I was sixteen, we were drinking, and we fooled around a bit."

"*Nein*, it was more than that . . . It was more than fooling around a bit, and you know it."

She could smell the strong vodka on his breath, becoming more uncomfortable by the second. "I'm your sister, Luka. We're siblings."

"Not biologically. I was adopted."

"What difference does that make?"

"It must have made a difference for you to let me do that to you." Memories of those encounters of lost innocence flooded his mind, exploring her, feeling up her thighs, her breasts, becoming familiar with her curves and erogenous zones. He could still hear her moaning from his touch. It had been a forbidden love that turned into obsession for him, and he wanted no one else but her. Often he found himself thinking of their wild and unbridled kissing. And when their bare stomachs touched, Ava would allow him to touch her 'there', too. Kissing deeper still, he would push against her, the heat from his lust nearly burning him alive. Afterward, they would say nothing as they both dressed. What was there to say? Luka had become infatuated with Ava; and Ava, curious about sex, welcomed the romance but always felt guilty and ashamed afterward.

"We were stupid kids back then," she said, bringing him back to the present.

He stepped closer to her, his eyes pleading for mercy, his voice thick with emotion. "I have loved you since we were children, Ava."

"What happened between us was a mistake. You have to know that. You need to find someone else and build a life with her, not me. Stop this silly infatuation and move on."

"You've bewitched me, and I want no one else now."

Ava shook her head, realizing the repercussions of her summer fling with her adopted brother were more serious than she'd ever imagined. Curiosity had led them down a path from which there was no return, and the secret they shared in the deepest corners of their hearts now loomed over them, shining a spotlight on unspoken truths, suppressed desires, and a wound that refused to heal.

Walking over to the barn entrance, Ava looked up at the darkened sky, its heavy clouds still drowning the earth. She crossed her arms to warm herself from the chill in the air, thinking of their past lovemaking for a moment, now regretting it immensely. "I'm sorry I've hurt you, Luka. But you need to think more clearly about this and realize it could never be. Can you imagine if Mama and Papa found out what we did? They'd be horrified."

"What if I tell them?" Luka asked defiantly. "What if I tell Starholf?"

Ava turned and walked back to him, slapping him in the face. Hard, saying nothing, staring at him in silence . . . One second . . . Two . . . Three . . . Four . . . Five . . . Six . . . "I'm going back inside the house now," she said calmly. "There's nothing more to say here, and you will take what we did to your grave. Do you understand?"

Luka grabbed her, and in a state of emotional delirium, tried to force himself on her, kissing her passionately.

"Stop!" she yelled.

But he didn't, pulling her into him, squeezing her tight. She tried to fight him as his mouth made its way up her neck and found her lips, while his hand ran through her hair. When he tried to slide his other hand up her skirt, she pushed him away with such force he stumbled back, a slight smile on his face, thinking she had enjoyed the kiss.

Ava glared at him. "Never again," she said, running out into the rain.

Luka picked up his vodka bottle and stared at the portrait of Ava and Shaylee that Hanz had painted the previous summer, now mounted like a prized possession in the art studio. From the illumination of the kerosene lamp, Ava's face seemed to glow. The painting haunted him, just like the woman in it, and he became angry, throwing his bottle to the ground, shattering it to pieces. He called out her name in the darkness, his lament bleeding with pain. "Avaaa!"

Ava stopped on the farmhouse porch, drenched from head to toe. She listened to his cries for a moment and shuddered, then disappeared into the house.

CHAPTER 20

Three days later, the happy union between Ava Wolff and Starholf Steiner arrived. Despite the objections of Starholf's parents, wealthy as they were, preferring a much more extravagant venue for their only son, Ava insisted that their vows and reception be held on the farm, and the groom acquiesced.

Hanz had built a quaint gazebo for the ceremony, next to the majestic weeping willow tree in the yard. The same tree that was almost used to lynch a man when Ava was a baby. Rows of chairs sat in front for the bride and groom's family and friends; circular tables with linen tablecloths, fine dishware, and silver cutlery were carefully arranged; and hired waiters served catered German delicacies to the honored guests. A special *Schwarzwälder Kirschtorte (Black Forest cake)* was made for the wedding cake, courtesy of the baker in Rothenburg ob der Tauber. Maria and Shaylee had hung lights and decorations everywhere.

Ava walked into the living room wearing her wedding gown and lace veil.

Stunning!

Starholf's sister Gwyneth had done her makeup, Shaylee had painted her nails, and Maria had styled her daughter's hair in a sophisticated French braid with volume on the sides and curled tendrils on the front, modeled after one of Ava's favorite actresses, Hedy Lamarr. Matching pearl earrings, necklace, and bracelet, once owned by Maria's mother, completed the look.

Hanz had been waiting for her, and when he saw his beloved swan, his heart melted away.

"Well, Papa, what do you think?" Ava asked.

Tears filled his eyes. "Words cannot describe the vision I see before me."

"Oh, Papa."

He reached out for her, and she came into his loving embrace.

"I want to tell you something before we go out there," Hanz said.

"Papa, please don't make me cry before I get married."

Hanz wiped his eyes. "I want you to know that you are so loved, Ava. *Mein süßes, schönes Mädchen (My sweet, beautiful girl)*. More than you can ever know." He paused, gathering his thoughts. "And that wherever you are, you are never alone or lost, because my love will always be with you. Let it guide you, protect you, and keep you strong."

Just then, the music started playing. Hanz opened the door, and everyone turned around and watched as Ava Wolff walked down the aisle, her proud papa by her side.

⚜

After the wedding vows and formalities were over, the guests bestowed their well-wishes on the happy couple, then started mingling with each other. Before long, Randolph and Ollie had escaped their wives and were huddled together with the father of the bride.

"Congratulations, Handsome Hanz," Randolph said. Instead of shaking his hand, the Bull gave him a bear hug so tightly he nearly picked him off the ground.

Ollie, nicely dressed with his hair sleeked back but his pants too short, patted Hanz on the back. "Seems only yesterday when I stopped by with Stella's gift for Maria, and you shocked me with the *wunderbar* news about her birthing twins. Now those tiny babies are *schöne junge Frauen (beautiful young women)*."

"It's true," said Randolph the Bull. "And when they were little girls, I remember picking them up and swinging them in the air at the Grimaldi Family Circus. Now Ava is married. How can this be?"

"How do you think *I* feel?" Hanz asked. "It's like I was changing their diapers only this morning. I'm getting old fast, *meine Freunde*."

"We all are," said Ollie, eyeing the variety of alcohol on the table with a crooked grin. "But you know what I always say . . . Add a splash of vodka to your lemonade, and you'll feel young again."

Hanz laughed. "You mean a splash of lemonade to your quart of vodka."

"*Ja, ja*," said Randolph. "The skinny noodle who can outdrink anyone!" He grabbed Ollie by the scruff of the neck and gave him a friendly shake. "Let's go celebrate this *wunderbar* day with some fine vodka for an old man

185

with a hollow leg, Chartreuse for an old man who'll no doubt soon be a grandfather, and Mampe Halb & Halb for an old man who used to be a champion fighter!"

By the early morning hours under a canopy of stars, Hanz and Maria were sitting alone together on the porch swing, gently oscillating as they held hands and gazed out at the remnants of the wedding. With everyone now gone, the yard seemed so quiet and empty, the echoes of laughter and merriment replaced by a profound stillness. No people, no chatter, no music–only the chirping of crickets, the occasional rustle of field mice, and the wistful hoot of a distant owl.

"Well, it's done," Maria said, her cerulean eyes glossy with emotion. "One daughter married and gone."

Hanz stood and reached out for his wife's hand. "*Ja*. Now come dance with me, *meine Liebe*."

Maria smiled as she read his lips. "But there's no more music."

"We don't need music."

She took his hand, following him to the gazebo. There, amidst the soft glow of the moonlight, they embraced and began to dance, cheek to cheek, their movements slow and graceful, a silent waltz played by a symphony of love. Her feminine scent intoxicated him more than the earlier consumed libations; his masculine aftershave and alcohol-infused breath elevated her pulse. The softness of her breasts pressed against his chest awakened his carnal desires; the strength of his arms holding her waist gave haste to thoughts of lying next to him in bed.

As they continued to sway where their daughter had said her vows, Maria reflected on the events of the day. She smiled at the radiant vision of Ava in her head, wearing the same wedding dress and pearls she herself had worn when she married Hanz. How stunningly beautiful her daughter looked in that satin gown, which she had modified to fit Ava's smaller frame. Standing beside her handsome groom, decked out in his military uniform, they were a sight to behold. It had made Maria cry, realizing her little girl was no longer hers but his. Strangely, in that moment, echoes from the past ricocheted across the yard and into her ears: "I want to say I gave birth to them. I want people to believe they are mine," she recalled saying to Hanz when Ava and Shaylee were first brought to her. Those sentiments from long ago were so strong, so ardent, fusing so deeply into her heart they became true.

Hanz squeezed her hand to get her attention, breaking her deep ruminations. "I wonder when Shaylee will be next," he said. "They've been courting for quite a while now." Christian, now on a meager monthly salary from the Wehrmacht, still couldn't afford a proper ring, so Shaylee hadn't yet told her parents they were already engaged.

"I don't even want to think about it," said Maria. "Losing one is enough for now."

Hanz nodded, his grin mirthless. The thought of both his darling swans no longer living with them left a lugubrious mood in the air.

"When Christian does ask for her hand in marriage, you could always say *nein*," she half-joked.

He chuckled.

"What."

"You know as well as I do that when two people are in love, nothing will stop them." He spun her, pulling her back into his embrace.

Maria smiled. "When my papa said I was too young to marry, you told me to meet you at the end of my street at midnight."

"And you said *auf Wiedersehen (goodbye)* to your little sister and crawled out your bedroom window with your small suitcase."

Maria laughed. "It's a *gute* thing level heads prevailed, because if we had gone through with the elopement, my papa would have hunted you down and killed you."

Hanz laughed too. "No doubt."

"And yet here we are, still together after all these years, having raised two daughters and a son." Maria looked at her husband with deep love in her eyes. "*Danke*, Hanz."

"For what?"

"For marrying me, even though I was deaf. For staying with me, even though I couldn't bear children. For giving me Ava, Shaylee, and Luka. You've made me so very happy, giving me a *wunderbar* life."

He tenderly kissed her lips. "It's not over yet; we have many years together still." Hanz noticed Maria's brow was damp with perspiration. "Are you okay, *meine Liebe?* You're sweating." He pressed his hand against her forehead. "And you're hot, too. Do you feel a fever coming on?"

"I'm all right," she replied, snuggling closer into his chest. "Just dance with me a little longer."

Hanz went into Rothenburg the following morning to pick up some supplies. Every time he entered the medieval town, it seemed as if there were more Nazi soldiers with rifles hanging from their shoulders, swastika flags hanging from windows and buildings, and nervous apprehension hanging in the air. Minding his business, he quietly bought what he needed and left.

On his way home, Hanz decided to check in on his good friend, Aadan Omari. As much as it had pained him, he had no choice but to tell the African man prior to Ava and Starholf's wedding that he couldn't invite him and his wife Chiumbo, simply because of the color of their skin. With the groom being a member of the Schutzstaffel, the Steiner family and friends would have been appalled had they seen a Black couple at the Aryan celebration. Not that Hanz cared, but it was his daughter's special day not his, and he didn't want to ruin it.

Aadan was outside, busily loading luggage into his vehicle when Hanz arrived. He stopped and looked up, his countenance unusually serious.

"How are you, *mein Freund?*" said Hanz, releasing a warm smile as he approached.

"Hanz, I'm glad you stopped by," Aadan replied. "How was Ava's wedding?"

"*Wunderbar.* And again, I'm so sorry I couldn't have you and Chiumbo there with us. Please forgive me."

"*Nein, nein,* don't worry about it. I understand."

Hanz looked at the luggage. "Going on a trip?"

"More than a trip," said Aadan. "I'm leaving."

Hanz gave him a puzzled look.

"The country, *mein Freund.* I'm leaving Germany. Chiumbo is already in Switzerland with our daughter and her husband, and I'm going to join them there. I was just about to come your way to say *auf Wiedersehen* to you and Maria."

"What? Why?"

"A few days before Ava's wedding, Chiumbo had gone into town. Some SS officers saw her and began calling her ugly, racist names."

Hanz shook his head.

"Then one of them grabbed her, slapping her to the ground."

"Those bastards!" said Hanz.

"They humiliated her, and several townspeople stood by watching, saying nothing. A young boy even ran up and kicked her, emboldened by the Nazis' abuse, which made the soldiers laugh."

"Is Chiumbo all right? Did they hurt her?"

"She's fine now, but very shaken."

"I'm so sorry, Aadan."

"It has already started, Hanz."

"What has?"

"Remember what I told you four years ago? About what happened in Africa and how it could happen again here?"

Hanz nodded.

"There were clear signs then, *mein Freund*, and the Nazis were only three years in power. We should have left when *Kristallnacht* happened, and now Hitler has an iron grip on the country and has started a war. This is going to end very badly for anyone not considered part of the Aryan race."

"What about your tile business? And your home?"

"I will arrange for its sale from Switzerland. If I don't do it now, they'll soon take it from me anyway."

Hanz ran his hand through his hair, visibly upset. "This is so sudden. I can't believe you're leaving."

"There's no place for us here anymore. Just like you had no choice in not inviting a Black couple to your daughter's wedding, we have no choice but to leave a country ruled by an absolute madman. History has taught us a chilling lesson, and for the sake of my family, I will no longer ignore it."

Hanz helped his neighbor put the last of his things in the car, and when Aadan extended his arm for a farewell handshake, Hanz pulled him in, embracing his friend as if saying goodbye to his own father. "You've been a *gute Freund* to me, Aadan. I'm sad you're leaving, and I will miss you."

"I will miss you too, Hanz. Please say *auf Wiedersehen* to Maria for me and Chiumbo."

"I will."

"And take any tiles you wish from my workshop. There are plenty with colorful designs that I think Maria will like."

"*Danke.*"

Aadan got into his car and waved as he drove off. Hanz watched, teary-eyed, as his African friend disappeared down the long dirt road.

CHAPTER 21

The summer Ava and Starholf got married was unlike any other German summer. Aside from the war, even the weather had a different feel that year, as if it were afraid, aware of something ominous to come. All the people could feel it too, and they talked about it among themselves in the streets, in the barbershop, the butcher shop, and elsewhere. Though not a cloud in the sky, a storm was coming, and it was going to be a bad one.

A week after their honeymoon, Ava was fanning herself in the couple's enormous bedroom suite on the second floor of the Steiner mansion. For days now there had been no wind, no rain, only humidity and heat. It reminded her of the spa steam room in the posh hotel they stayed at in Paris.

The bedroom was luxurious and glamorous, like a fancy apartment all on its own. Flowing, taupe velvet curtains; lavish Persian rugs and tapestry wall hangings; antique European furniture; a low-hanging chandelier, shimmering like diamonds; and an enormous four-poster canopy bed with satin sheets, comforter, and pillows. Ava practically lived in that room, rarely venturing out through the rest of the house, as she was not yet comfortable with the enormity and grandeur of it all.

They had returned from their honeymoon with many purchases from the finest Paris boutiques, and Ava was busily sorting through them that afternoon. Wearing one of the dresses Starholf had bought her, she stared at herself in her full-length floor standing mirror, admiring the layered white chiffon gown, cinched at the waist. Twirling in it, she giggled, imagining she was a Parisian model for Coco Chanel.

Starholf came out of the bathroom with a towel wrapped around his waist, steam trailing behind him from the shower. "Now that is a *schöner Anblick (beautiful sight),*" he said, smiling at his new bride. "Look at you. You take my breath away." Pulling her into his embrace, his spicey aftershave permeated the air. "You're the prettiest *Fräulein* I have ever seen. And it's a strange beauty, too."

"What do you mean, 'strange?'" asked Ava.

"You have a beauty that teases me. Mocks me. It's a monster with a will of its own."

She threw her head back and laughed. "Come, now. You're talking silliness."

Starholf's face took on a serious expression. "I'm not joking. It's no secret my family wanted me to marry a rich duchess. But I saw you, and you bewitched me, as if I've known you from another life. You changed my destiny."

Ava held his gaze for a long moment. "You sound like you regret meeting me."

"*Nein.* On the contrary, I fall more in love with you every day." A tendril of Ava's hair hung down over her face, and he gently brushed it aside. "I've never felt this way about anyone. That's why I saved you from that insignificant farm and married you."

"Insignificant farm?" Ava echoed, slightly offended. "We had cows, sheep, goats, and chickens. A wheat field and a corn field. Even a small vineyard. I'd hardly call that insignificant."

"*Ja, ja, Sie wissen was ich meine (Yeah, yeah, you know what I mean).* I saved you from farm life. From marrying another farmer."

"It wouldn't have been so bad, baking bread and making babies."

"Oh, you'll still be making babies, I promise you that," he said, pinching her bottom.

She pulled away, giggling.

"Get me that emerald necklace I bought you that matches your eyes."

Ava retrieved the fancy box from the mahogany armoire and handed it to him. He opened it and fastened the necklace around her thin, elegant neck. Standing behind her in the full-length mirror, blue eyes met green in the glass reflection.

"You've married into a powerful family, Ava. By marrying you, I have changed your life."

She reached up with both hands and touched the jeweled piece. "I know."

Starholf wrapped his arms firmly around hers, pinning them to her chest. "You're no longer the peasant Ava Wolff from the countryside. You're now the sophisticated Ava Steiner, with a noble family name to protect."

It was the first time Starholf had spoken to her in such a denigrating way, insulting her as a peasant. His eyes even had a sinister glint, causing a chill to run down her spine.

He turned her around to face the oil painting on the wall–a portrait of them he had commissioned before they left for Paris–he in his Nazi uniform decked with shiny military pins, standing behind her as he was now, and she sitting down in a royal blue gown, dripping with jewels. "That's who we are, Ava: Mr. and Mrs. Starholf Steiner. You must never embarrass me, or my family."

The conversation was starting to make her uncomfortable. "Of course not. I would never do that."

He slid his hands from her arms to her neck, the glint in his eyes becoming dark, almost evil. "And if you ever cheat on me, the consequences will be disastrous."

"Starholf!" She pulled away from him. "Why are you saying that!"

"It had to be discussed. My family's reputation must always be upheld, and my wife must always be loyal to me," he repeated.

"Of course! I would never, ever cheat on you!"

Starholf changed back to his normal iconic cool, his expression relaxed again. "Calm down, *Schätzchen*. They're just words. A simple exchange between husband and wife." Brushing it off, he changed the subject. "Did you send your sister her gift?"

Ava's mouth was dry, her bearing off center. That so-called 'simple exchange between husband and wife' shook her. "*Ja*," she replied.

"Did she like the dress?"

"She loved it. She'll be the best dressed *Mädchen* at the library."

It amused Starholf that the conversation made her uncomfortable, and he gave her a reassuring hug. "You know what you and your sister remind me of?"

"What."

"Two timid Siamese cats." He released her and smiled. "That's what I thought the first time I saw you together at your father's farm. Cats hiding in the field."

Ava put her hand on her hip. "I'm not timid. Shaylee's the shy one."

"You're still more reserved than most. You think you're gregarious, but really you're demure. Demure like a swan."

"My papa always called Shaylee and me his swans," Ava said, thinking about her father, a towering figure with blond hair and kind blue eyes. She missed her parents.

"Demure like a swan with eyes like a cat," Starholf said. "Anyway, it's time to get ready."

"Aww, do we have to go to that party tonight? I wanted to do a Parisian fashion show for you."

"You can do it tomorrow."

She sighed, looking up at him with puppy dog eyes. "Can't we just stay in this time?" Since they had first started dating, there was always a Nazi event, gathering, or party to attend. "I just want to lounge around in this beautiful room, eat dinner with you alone, and do my fashion show for you. Those Nazi parties are so boring, anyway. So staunch and cold."

"What about dinner with my family?"

Ava pulled on a pair of white satin gloves. "We eat with them every night as it is. And that huge dining room table is so long it's like eating off the roof of a house."

Starholf laughed. He enjoyed her down-to-earth personality and the funny things she would say. "You're going to have to get used to it, *Liebling (darling)*."

"I know. It's just that sometimes I'd like to have dinner with you alone." Wrapping her arms around him, she leaned her head against his bare chest. "It's more intimate."

He finally gave in. "Okay, my demure Siamese cat. I'll have Clarence bring us some food, and you can do your little fashion show. Start with the sexy red dress; that's my favorite."

Ava almost squealed as she ran to the armoire. "Close your eyes, and don't open them until I say."

He obeyed, smiling in anticipation.

Moments later she said, "Okay open," twirling around him seductively.

"Wow!" exclaimed Starholf, mesmerized by what he saw.

She smiled at his reaction, her chest swelling with glee. Oh, how she loved him then! With his tall, regal presence, and those wolf blue eyes. She loved him so much it hurt.

"Ava Steiner, what are you doing for the rest of your life?" he asked, a sweet little nothing he started saying to her while on their honeymoon.

"Starholf Steiner, I'm staying close by your side," she answered, as always.

He pulled her in and kissed her. "First desert, then the fashion show, then dinner," he said, picking her up off the ground. "In that order."

She laughed as he carried her and tossed her on the bed.

⁓⸾⸾⸾⁓

At the Wolff farm, Hanz was in the vineyard, finishing up his work, and Maria was in the kitchen preparing dinner. The barn cats played in the meadow, trying to catch field mice as the sunset, superlative as ever, transposed from bright orange to a blistering red, fading into lavender before dying into tomorrow. All the birds were already nestled in the trees, wings folded and resting, while the blue-emperor dragonflies, orange-tipped grasshoppers, and short-winged lightning bugs began their dusk rituals.

Shaylee and Christian met halfway along the familiar path; she was going to his parents' home for dinner. When they saw each other, she ran into his arms, and he spun her.

"Where did you get that dress?" he asked, putting her back down.

"Ava bought it for me while in Paris. Do you like it?"

"*Ja*, it's beautiful." Christian paused as he looked her over. "Shaylee, you know I'll never be able to afford things like that, right? I can't give you the lifestyle Starholf gives Ava. That man lives like a king, and she's now his queen."

Shaylee put her arms around his neck and kissed him. "Like I told you before in our secret cabin, I'm not marrying you for your coin. I'm marrying you because you're the last thing I think about before bed, and the first thing I think of when I wake up."

He smiled.

"Remember the story of the Women of Weinsberg?"

"Kinda. Something about women carrying men on their backs."

"*Ja*. In 1140, King Conrad III of the Holy Roman Empire went to war against the Duke of Welf and defeated him. With the Bavarian city of Weinsberg under siege, the wives of the castle negotiated a surrender which allowed them to leave with whatever they could carry. The king granted them that concession, and foregoing all material possessions, each woman took her own husband on her shoulders and her children under her arms, carrying them out. The king's advisors told him to stop them, that this was not what was meant. But the king laughed and accepted the women's clever trick, sparing the lives of all Weinsberg citizens and setting the city free. 'A king,' he said, 'must always honor his word.'"

"Quite a story," said Christian. "I remember it from school now."

"They took their men and their children. Not any valuables, only their loved ones. And that's how I feel about you, Christian. All I want is to lie next to you for the rest of my life. Oh, and those ten children and grandchildren you promised."

He laughed. "You sure?"

"Well, maybe not ten."

Christian grinned, looking down at her, kissing her tenderly. "It's going to be a *wunderbar* life, isn't it."

Shaylee linked her arm in his, and they continued walking. "As the Americans would say, 'It's going to be the berries!'"

CHAPTER 22

Autumn, 1941

Another year had passed since Ava and Starholf's wedding, and the once peaceful landscape of Rothenburg ob der Tauber had become eclipsed by the nefarious viscera of war. The relentless march of the Third Reich, fueled by Adolf Hitler's tyrannical regime and its perverse ideology of German racial purity, cast a shadow of dread across Europe. By the fall of 1941, the German assault had swiftly invaded and subjugated Poland, Denmark, Norway, Luxembourg, the Netherlands, Belgium, France, Greece, and Yugoslavia, adding to their previous annexations of Austria and Czechoslovakia. Britain had successfully held the Third Reich at bay, and the Nazis turned their attention to Russia instead. The air was thick with fanaticism and cruelty, gripping the hearts of those who dared to stand against the tidal wave of evil. In every city and town, the presence of fear, distrust, and a desperate instinct for survival was palpable, leaving no corner untouched by its chilling hand.

Severin was acutely aware of the unfolding horror. His uniform, crisp and authoritative, seemed to weigh heavily on him as he entered Hanz's barn. "They're going to start rounding up Jews throughout Germany," he announced, his voice tinged with a tenebrous urgency. "And not just in the cities, but also the countryside." He had come to warn Hanz, knowing well his brother's fondness for his Jewish neighbors.

Hanz was tending to Bucephalus, his faithful horse. "Bucephalus" literally meant "ox-headed," and Alexander the Great had chosen that name for his own horse due to the mark on its thigh that looked like an ox's head. One of the most famous black stallions of classical antiquity, the impressive creature was of the best Thessalian strain, or more specifically, an Akhal-Teke, one of the most beautiful and ancient equine breeds descended from the Turkoman horse. When Bucephalus died in what is now Punjab, Pakistan, after the Battle of the Hydaspes in 326 BCE, Alexander was so grieved that he named one of the many cities he founded after him—Alexandria Bucephalus.

"What are they going to do with them?" Hanz asked.

Bucephalus nickered softly, sensing the tension.

"I don't know. Expel them, I suspect. Some to work camps, others to the Jewish ghettos in Poland, probably."

Hanz looked up at his brother, disbelief etched across his face. "This is absolute madness."

"*Ja, so ist es (Yes, it is)*," Severin agreed. "I told you years ago this was going to happen."

"God help us all," replied Hanz, that same sick feeling again rising in his stomach, like an ungodly kraken awakening from the abyss.

Severin looked around the barn, his eyes landing on the tools, the hay, the mundane details of a life far removed from the barbarity of a regime he no longer believed in. "You need to be careful, *Bruder*. Watch over your family, and do not take any risks. These are treacherous times, and the penalty for harboring Jews is death."

Hanz nodded, his mind racing with the implications of his brother's warning. The world he knew was unraveling at a frightening pace.

As Severin turned to leave, the brothers shared a look that spoke volumes. It was a silent exchange of trepidation, regret, and a deep, unspoken understanding of the perils that lay ahead.

⁂

After Severin's visit, Hanz went to see his Jewish neighbor, Malachi Applebaum. Malachi was sitting outside his barn, practicing on his Hohner harmonica that his father-in-law had given him before he and his wife passed.

"*Hallo, mein Freund*," Hanz said as he dismounted his horse.

"Hanz, nice to see you," replied Malachi. He walked over and shook his hand.

"I've come to bring you grave news, I'm afraid."

"What is it?"

Hanz paused, gathering his thoughts. "As you know, my *Bruder* is a colonel in the Wehrmacht. He came to warn me today that the Nazis are going to start rounding up Jews across Germany, sending them to work camps and the Polish ghettos."

Malachi's wife came outside, having noticed Hanz speaking to her husband. "*Hallo*, Hanz. How's Maria?"

"*Hallo*, Ursula. Maria is fine, but she has bouts of illness that seem to come more frequently these days."

Ursula shook her head. "That poor woman. Tell her I said *hallo*, and please let me know the next time she's feeling ill. I'll come over to cook and clean."

"*Danke*," said Hanz. "That's very kind of you."

"Oh, it's nothing. That's what we do, right? Help each other, as God wants us to."

After Ursula returned to the farmhouse, the men continued their discussion.

"I've heard that rumor before, Hanz. What am I supposed to do? Take my family and leave everything behind? My land, my animals, my home?"

"*Ja*. It's not a rumor this time, *mein Freund*. My *Bruder* would not have warned me, otherwise. And look what's already happened. It's three years ago now that they expelled all Jews from Rothenburg, followed by the riots of *Kristallnacht*. The war hadn't even started then."

"The countryside is different. They need farmers to supply the people with food."

"Malachi, *bitte*, for your family's safety, you must flee Germany. Go to neutral Sweden. After all this madness has passed, come back. I will look after your home and your animals until then."

Malachi, stubborn as a mule, refused to go. "I'll take my chances, putting my faith in God," he said with firm conviction. "The Almighty delivered my forefathers from Egyptian slavery, and he will save us from Nazi tyranny."

As Hanz rode Bucephalus down the road, Malachi's harmonica bellowed auspiciously through the air. Hanz went to warn his other Jewish neighbors too—Nora and Maximillian Yurkovich, Willamina Benowitz, and Leon Dreisler, whose wife was Jewish—but they all had the same stubborn reaction.

True to Severin's word, the crimes perpetrated against the "Undesirables" by the Greater Germanic Reich escalated, bringing untold pain and suffering to its victims. Rothenburg ob der Tauber and surrounding area was no exception. Hailed as "the most German of German towns" by Nazi ideologists who organized regular day trips to the medieval attraction from across the Reich, it was seen as the epitome of all that was quintessentially German. As a result, it was also a prime target for cleansing the area of its vermin.

Hanz and Maria sat down for dinner one evening when a sudden, frantic knocking came through the front door. The couple looked at each other, confused, wondering who that could be. They rarely had company, and when they did, it was always prearranged.

Hanz wiped his mouth with a napkin and rose from the table. When he opened the door, the last person on earth he ever expected to see again, disheveled and out of breath, stood before him . . .

Abigail Katz!

Her dark brown eyes were wild with terror. The same two eyes that had haunted his dreams for years, fearful of their return. Staring at him as if she had escaped hell, with the Devil now on her tail, her words caught in her throat like thorns. But none were needed. Anguish, doom, and horror screamed from her pores in the darkness of the night, begging for asylum.

Hanz, too, was speechless, his mind reeling from the shock. He panicked, thinking of his beloved swans, Ava and Shaylee . . . Why would their birth mother come here? What menace has followed? Would her sudden presence finally expose the lie?

"*Bitte*, Herr Hanz!" she implored in ragged gasps, her voice desperate. "You must help me! The Schutzstaffel killed my entire family, and they're coming this way! Help me!"

As Abigail Katz stood on the threshold of the Wolff farmhouse, pleading for mercy, Hanz was unsure of what to do. His brother's warning about harboring Jews rang in his ears.

"*Bitte*, I'm begging you!" she almost screamed. "You promised once that if I ever needed anything . . ."

That promise made years ago, when Hanz had wanted to offer something more tangible than words of gratitude for the gift Abigail gave them, echoed through his conscience like a clarion call. Now he had to make a choice: Would he honor that promise and help a desperate woman, risking everything–his family, their safety, their future? Or would he turn her away, condemning her to a fate too horrific to imagine? For a few heartbeats, Hanz wrestled with his conscience, the weight of his choice bearing down on him . . . He made his decision . . . A decision that would once again entwine their lives and lead them down a path fraught with danger and uncertainty.

"Quickly, come with me!" He grabbed Abigail's hand and ran with her to the barn, their hearts pounding in sync with each dramatic stride. Dogs barked in the distance–a harbinger of the approaching villainy–and multiple flashlights crisscrossed the field, accompanied by the ominous glow of headlights from a car slowly creeping down the road.

Once inside the barn, Hanz's hands trembled slightly as he lit a kerosene lamp, its flickering light casting eerie shadows on the wall. He moved swiftly to a trap door in the middle of the barn and opened it. "Get in," he urged, "and don't make a sound until I come back."

Abigail was shivering. "How do you know they won't search in here?"

Hanz grabbed a worn blanket from a nearby shelf and handed it to her. "Because my *Bruder* is a colonel in the Wehrmacht, my *Sohn* is a sergeant, and my son-in-law is an SS officer. They know me and won't think I'm hiding a Jew."

"But they have dogs, Herr Hanz. They might smell me."

"Abigail, listen to me. They're most likely coming by to ask if I've seen or heard anything. I'll give them some alcohol and keep them busy in conversation until they leave. You don't have to worry; you're safe in here."

Abigail appeared just like that night when he had found her on the side of the road as a distraught teenager, lost in a world that had turned against her. Déjà vu. Overcome with grief, she fell into his arms, her sobs echoing the deep chasm of loss. "My husband, my son, my parents–they shot them all, Herr Hanz," she cried. "They shot them all right in front of me."

Hanz held her for a moment, the sorrow in her voice piercing him. Her tears soaked into his shirt, each one a testament to the atrocities she had witnessed. "Abigail . . .," he said softly, gently releasing her. "You must hide now, and I must go back into the house. The soldiers will be here soon, and then they'll be gone. Trust me."

With a nod, Abigail composed herself and descended into the ground. Hanz closed the trap door, rubbed cow manure over it to throw the scent from the dogs, then extinguished the kerosene lamp and hurried back to the farmhouse to wait for his pernicious visitors.

❧

"Hanz, what's going on?" Maria demanded, standing on the porch steps. "Who is that woman?"

"I can't explain right now; the Schutzstaffel will be here any minute. Do not say a word about her. Her life, and ours, depends on it."

She gasped. "You're hiding a Jew? Hanz, why would you risk our lives like this!"

"Maria, you must trust me. *Bitte.* Let's go back inside and continue our dinner like nothing has happened. When the soldiers arrive, they'll see a *gute* German couple eating and spending time together." As Hanz was speaking, the approaching car was almost upon them. "Hurry."

Boots crunching on gravel soon penetrated the hush, followed by a sharp knock on the door. A foreboding tension gripped husband and wife, as if they too were somehow targeted to be rounded up, despite their Aryan background. Hanz squared his shoulders and stood from the table to face the night's second intrusion, his chair scraping against the wood floor like fingernails on a chalkboard. Maria's heart raced, her eyes wide with trepidation.

"*Guten Abend, mein Freund (Good evening, my friend),*" the commander greeted, his voice carrying a false cordiality.

"*Guten Abend,*" Hanz replied.

The soldiers–three of them–entered the home uninvited.

"We're making the rounds, looking for filthy Jews," said the youngest of the three, his eyes alight with a disturbing zeal.

The eldest soldier ambled through the house, arms folded behind his back, intrusively checking each of the rooms before returning. "There was a woman who escaped our grasp by boat," he reported with a sneer, as if it were his personal failure. "We found the boat in the Tauber near here, and searched the fields, but the scum eluded us."

Hanz retrieved a bottle of schnapps, his mind tumultuous with thoughts of Abigail hidden mere yards away. "We just sat down for dinner," he said, pouring the men a drink. "If you're hungry, you're welcome to join us. *Meine Frau ist eine wunderbare Köchin (My wife is a wonderful cook).*"

"*Danke,*" the commander responded, gesturing for his men to take a seat.

Maria prepared three more plates, carefully watching everyone's lips.

"My *Bruder* Severin is a colonel in the Wehrmacht, and my *Sohn* Luka is a sergeant," Hanz said, trying to portray a proud Nazi supporter.

"*Ja*, we know them," the commander replied. "*Gute* men. The Fatherland needs more like them."

The younger soldier, devouring his food, kept staring at the painting of Ava and Shaylee that Hanz had put his heart and soul into when they were eighteen. Previously on display in the barn art studio, it now hung above the fireplace mantel in the living room. "Your daughters?" the soldier asked, motioning at the portrait.

"*Ja*," said Hanz.

"*Schöne Mädchen.* Strange, though, how different they look from their parents."

The commander and the elder soldier turned to look. "That's German *Frauen* for you," said the soldier, winking at Maria. "Their beauty knows no bounds."

"Where are they?" asked the commander.

"My daughter Ava is in Berlin," Hanz answered. "She's married to Lieutenant Starholf Steiner of the SS."

"You don't say!" exclaimed the commander. *"Wunderbar!"*

"And the other?" the younger soldier asked, keenly interested, his odious gaze sending a shiver down Hanz's spine. "What's her name?"

"Shaylee. She's out with her boyfriend."

The elder soldier laughed. "Look at the poor boy," he said, pointing at the younger man. "You just broke his heart."

As the evening painfully dragged on, Hanz and Maria's pulse beat a frenetic rhythm, each laugh from the soldiers a reminder of the danger lurking outside, hidden beneath the floorboards of the barn. They did their best to engage in the social facade, showing hospitality until their unwanted guests were finally ready to leave.

"Well, we didn't find any dirty Jews here tonight, but at least we won't leave hungry," said the younger soldier. *"Prost!"* he toasted. All three men clinked glasses and laughed, downing their schnapps.

After the Schutzstaffel left, immense relief washed over the Wolffs.

But now Hanz had to explain to his wife who the Jewish woman in their barn was, and why she came to them—a German family—for help. Turning to face Maria, her eyes still wide with fear and confusion, searching his for an explanation, he took a deep breath and crafted a story he hoped would shield the truth and protect them all.

"The woman in the barn," he began, his voice steady despite the turmoil inside, "is the daughter of the jeweler I bought your ring from in Rothenburg. Her family was murdered by the Nazis, and she managed to escape. I couldn't leave her to the mercy of the soldiers."

Maria's expression softened slightly, a mixture of compassion and worry etching her features as the gravity of the situation sunk in. "But Hanz, the danger we are in now. If they find her, they could kill us all."

"I know. I couldn't turn my back on her, though. We must help her, just for a little while. They're not going to find her," he said, hoping his words would ease her anxiety.

With a slow nod, Maria accepted his explanation and reassurance, though the concern never quite left her eyes. Hanz knew he had just woven a fragile web of deceit, but it was necessary to protect both his family and the secret of Ava and Shaylee's birth.

Lighting a kerosene lamp, Hanz went to check on Abigail. The night was cold, the stars a faint glimmer in the overcast sky, and as he entered the barn, the lamp diffused a warm, flickering glow in the dark space. Abigail sat huddled on the makeshift bed of hay in the hideaway, her figure small and forlorn in the dim light.

Hanz approached with a plate of food and a jar of fresh goat milk, setting it down in front of her. "You must eat, Abigail. To maintain your strength."

"What does it matter?" she cried. "My entire family is dead. I might as well join them." Her words turned to sobs, murmuring a Yiddish prayer between her tears.

When Abigail had calmed, she told Hanz her tragic story. After being expelled from the Jewish quarter in Rothenburg ob der Tauber just prior to the war, her family found sanctuary in a vacant farmhouse abandoned by another Jewish family who fled to America. But that night, the Nazis came calling, unrestrained in their murderous intent. She barely escaped with her life, bullets whizzing past her as she ran to the river.

Hanz's heart ached as he listened to her woeful tale. "I'm so sorry, Abigail. It's a miracle you survived." He handed her a bottle of homemade wine, hoping it might offer some small comfort. As she took it, her large, brown eyes met his. Eyes that were a striking, dark version of Ava's and Shaylee's, his daughters.

Her daughters.

The realization hit Hanz anew, the secret he had kept for so long now staring back at him from Abigail's face.

Leaving the barn, Hanz stepped out into the chilly night, his mind a whirlpool of conflicting emotions. He was torn between his compassion for Abigail's plight and the complexity of the lies he had woven to protect his family. The young, frightened girl he had once encountered had grown into a beautiful woman bearing the unmistakable resemblance to his daughters. This truth, hidden for years, now felt more real and pressing than ever. As did the danger it brought with it.

As he walked back to the house, the night air whispered secrets, and the stars blinked in silent understanding. The burden of his decision weighed heavily on him—a secret shared between him, the night, and the woman hidden in his barn.

⁂

Inside the farmhouse, Hanz and Maria continued to wrestle with the predicament they now found themselves in. Their conversation, usually filled with the day's small joys and challenges, was now a somber discussion of fear and moral quandary. What were they to do with this Jewish woman seeking refuge in their barn? How could they help her without endangering themselves and their family? And most pressing of all for Hanz, what would happen when Abigail saw their daughters, Ava and Shaylee, the children she had birthed but never raised? Shaylee would be home later, and Ava would be visiting from Berlin; it was inevitable they would sooner or later meet. Would seeing them open the floodgates of truth, which in itself could destroy their family?

Their debate was abruptly cut short by the sound of gunshots echoing in the night. Hanz ran outside, only to discern they came from his neighbor's farm and not his own.

Oh no! . . . Please, God, no! . . . Malachi!

Hanz frantically saddled Bucephalus and galloped toward the Applebaum property. When he got to the fence line, the grim reality hit him—he was too late. The Schutzstaffel were already there, tormenting Malachi, his wife, and their two daughters, dragging them outside into the yard, beating and forcing them to their knees. In the headlights of the Nazi vehicle, Hanz saw it all . . .

Jeta hurled an insult at the younger soldier who groped her, and the older one hit her in the face with his rifle butt, knocking her out cold. Zelda screamed when she saw the blood gushing from her sister, and she too was knocked unconscious. Ursula went hysterical and attacked the man for assaulting her daughters, only to be pistol-whipped back to the ground, then shot in the head by the commander. Finally, Malachi himself stood and rushed the men, taking six bullets before dropping.

Powerless and unable to save them, Hanz watched in absolute horror as his dear friends were brutally slaughtered and their daughters taken away, simply because of their faith. He fell to his knees and wept, overcome by grief.

Distraught beyond words, Hanz then picked himself up and galloped to his other Jewish neighbors, fearful the Nazis had already been there earlier. Thankfully, they were all fine, albeit shocked to hear the terrible news. When he arrived home, he vomited in the yard before entering the house.

So disturbed by the atrocities he had witnessed, Hanz could not find the words at first. When he eventually told Maria, she fainted in his arms. "I tried to warn you, *mein Freund*," he cried to himself as he carried his wife to their bed. "Why didn't you listen!"

～⸙～

In the dead of the night, Hanz remained awake, sitting on the farmhouse steps and smoking his corncob pipe, waiting for Shaylee to come home. It reminded him of when he did the same for Ava, waiting for her to return from Berlin after attending a Nazi rally. Earlier the stars were out, and now they refused to give their shine, turning the sky into a wall of black tourmaline stone, with only a sliver of a moon hanging like a deadly sickle. How fitting, he thought.

Terrified over what he knew was only the beginning of the nightmare, Hanz thought of the Applebaums. He had known Malachi and his family for over fourteen years, and they often visited, sharing with each other the fruits of their labor–milk, cheese, beef, wine–and celebrating their moments of joy. Their wives were close friends too, as were their daughters. How did the world become so wicked, he wondered? Where was God in all this? Why doesn't He do something?

Hanz's sad cogitations drifted to Abigail, hiding in his barn. She too had witnessed a horrifying massacre that day, except those murdered were more than friends–they were her family. A panic surged through him. "Those Nazi bastards must never know my daughters are Jewish," resounded in his mind. "But what if they find out?" the voice in his head cruelly postulated back. Before he could ruminate further, Shaylee interrupted his thoughts, sneaking in through the back door. Hanz got up to intercept her.

"Where have you been?" he asked, firm in his tone. "It's late."

"With Christian," she answered.

"Where is he?"

"He walked me home and left. He has to report back to his unit in the morning." She noticed the worry and sorrow in her father's face. "Papa, what is it?"

Hanz hesitated as he tried to maintain his equanimity.

She became frightened. "You're scaring me now."

"The Nazis have started rounding up Jews throughout Germany. They murdered Malachi and Ursula Applebaum tonight, and took Jeta and Zelda away."

Shaylee blanched under the kitchen light. "*Nein*, Papa!" She began to cry.

Hanz held his daughter close. "A Jewish woman also came to us for help. They murdered her family too, and I hid her in the barn."

She looked up at him. "Who is she?"

Hanz repeated the same story he told Maria.

"What are you and Mama going to do?"

"I don't know yet. But it's a much more dangerous world for Jews now, and I want you coming home before dark."

"Why, Papa? We're not Jewish."

Hanz held her tighter. "*Sei ein gutes Mädchen und tu einfach was ich sage (Be a good girl and just do as I say)*."

Morning arrived, and everything seemed as it always was on the Wolff farm.

Except it wasn't.

Nothing was the same, nor would it ever be again . . .

Hanz and Maria sat at the kitchen table, their hands wrapped around cups of coffee that had long since turned cold. Still in shock over what happened the night before, the gruesome images played over in their minds, irreversibly altering the last vestige of their once utopian existence. Nevertheless, the couple decided they would shelter the Jewish woman hiding in their barn. How could they possibly turn her away, especially since her entire family had also been murdered? Yes, the penalty for harboring Jews was death, but their Christian conscience left them no choice—the poor woman had nowhere else to go.

"After I bury Malachi and Ursula, I'll prepare the secret room for her," Hanz said. "She can live down there until we figure something else out."

The secret room was constructed by Hanz's grandfather when he built the farmhouse, wanting a safe, inconspicuous place to hide his family in the event of danger. Situated next to the cellar, it was a self-contained lair with a cast iron fireplace for warmth, piping into the living room chimney above, and a water tap in the corner with drain in the floor for bathing and limited bodily waste. Access was gained through a wooden hutch serving as a decoy, and unless you opened its front doors and pulled out its uniquely designed shelving unit containing linens and dishes, thereby exposing the entrance, it was just another piece of furniture.

Maria nodded, despite her apprehension. "If they find her here, they'll kill us all, Hanz," she repeated for perspicuity. "Not just her."

His expression reflected the same acknowledgment of the dangerous path they were choosing. "I know, Maria. I know."

When Shaylee entered the kitchen, she saw the angst in her parents' faces. Hanz explained to her their decision, instructing her never to go down into the secret room or engage with the woman in any way. He expounded that she must never speak a word of it to anyone, not even her sister.

"Why, Papa?" she asked.

Hanz trusted his daughter Ava, but not her SS officer husband. "Because if Starholf finds out, the woman is dead . . . And likely so are we."

Shaylee's pale complexion turned a shade paler, like that of the albino fawn. "He would never do that, Papa. He loves Ava."

"*Ja, Schätzchen*, but he loves his family's position and wealth, the Fatherland, and the Nazi regime more."

⁓⧼⧽⁓

Hanz lit a kerosene lamp and opened the hutch door that evening, leading Abigail down the creaking wooden steps into the secret room next to the cellar. He and Maria had diligently cleaned and rearranged the space for their unexpected guest, trying to make it as hospitable as possible under the grim circumstances. Prior to this day it had never been used, but now it would be a homeless Jewish woman's temporary abode.

The secret room, with its low ceiling and brick walls, felt both confining and safe. Hanz motioned for Abigail to sit on an old leather love seat he had brought down earlier, while he started a fire in the cast iron stove. After lighting the kindling and nurturing the flames, he tossed in some logs sitting in a pile next to it, and soon the fire was ablaze. "*Dort (There),*" he said, rubbing his hands together, claiming victory over the dampness. He glanced back at her with a kind smile. "The room will be nice and warm as you sleep."

She gave no response, still shivering from being hidden away for hours in the cold ground beneath the barn.

Hanz fetched a quilt from the closet and draped it around her shoulders.

"*Danke,*" Abigail whispered, looking up at him like a frightened little bird, her large brown eyes reflecting the dancing flames. In that wordless stare held a desperate plea, received with a quiet reassurance from the man she directed it to, letting her know he would do all he could to help her without her even having to ask.

"There are more blankets in the closet," Hanz said, breaking the intensity of her stare. "And when you're tired," he added, pointing at the small bed in the corner, "the sheets are fresh and the mattress soft."

Abigail looked at the single bed pressed against the wall. Just two nights prior, she had lain in her own bed with her husband and their five-year-old son snuggled between them. Instantly the floodgates opened, and the torrent of pain and grief returned, knowing they were now both dead, along with her parents—her entire world cruelly snatched away in a heartbeat. "I can't believe my family is gone," she once again sobbed. She would in fact be screaming in agony if it weren't for the emotional exhaustion.

"I'm sorry, Abigail," was all Hanz said, his voice thick with empathy. He wished he knew how to comfort her.

Maria knocked on the doorframe at the top of the stairs. "I have bread and cheese, and some hot tea," she said, timidly walking down a few steps, as if an intruder in her own home.

Hanz met her halfway and took the tray of food. "*Danke, meine Liebe.*"

She looked down at Abigail sitting on the loveseat, then at Hanz, holding his gaze in a questioning stare before returning up the steps.

Hanz placed the tray on the wooden table beside Abigail. "You must be hungry. You should eat."

She stared at the food but didn't answer, didn't touch it. "Did you ever tell her the twins were mine?"

He nervously glanced back at the staircase. "*Nein.*"

Abigail flashed her teary eyes up at him. "How are they, my daughters?"

"*Es sind schöne junge Frauen (They're beautiful young women).* Happy and healthy. Ava is married now, just last summer. She lives in Berlin with her husband. Shaylee will be married soon too, no doubt. She has a steady boyfriend."

"You changed her name."

"*Ja.* A German girl with a Jewish name would have raised questions."

Abigail mechanically picked up a piece of bread and ate it, staring into nothing as she chewed. "After I eat, I will go to bed and try to sleep. When I wake in the morning, for a moment I will think this was all just a nightmare. And then to my utter horror, I will realize it was not. Pray for me, Herr Hanz. Pray for me, because unless God himself helps me, I will not survive this nightmare."

CHAPTER 23

In the weeks that followed, the burning fire of chaos that ignited in the countryside around Rothenburg ob der Tauber had finally started smoldering, as the Nazis moved their murderous anti-Semitic scourge to other areas. A semblance of peace settled in like a hesitant morning fog, and life on the Wolff farm, for the most part, returned to normal. Except for one inconceivable fact . . .

The woman who had given birth to Hanz and Maria's beloved twins was now living under their roof!

Before, when Hanz looked at the hutch that concealed the hidden entrance to the secret room, he only saw the place where they stored their linens and dishes. But now, he saw so much more. Just passing by the hutch made his heartbeat elevate.

Each time Hanz went down into that room, it was a stark reminder of the perilous situation now part of their lives. The smell of the brick became bothersome, the fire in the fireplace daunting, and the look in Abigail's eyes discomfiting. Her despondent gaze, watching his every move, spoke volumes of the hardship she was enduring, and she remained quiet, perhaps even cold and a bit rude, saying very little. The daily ritual of descending into the secret room to bring Abigail sustenance became a pilgrimage of sorts for Hanz, the creaking wooden stairs a gateway into a world of sorrow and survival in the face of unimaginable loss.

Whenever it was safe enough and Shaylee wasn't home, Hanz would take Abigail outside for some fresh air and sunshine, timorously keeping watch. At night, Abigail would wail, calling out to her dead husband, five-year-old son, and parents. Hanz had to warn her not to do that, in case the soldiers unexpectedly came back. He felt bad for trying to suppress her outcries, as if she weren't entitled to them.

Eventually Abigail did learn to grieve in silence, and Hanz introduced her to a method of communication they could follow. A type of Morse code between them. Hanz had a cane he'd use when his bad knee bothered him, and he told her he would hit the floor with it three times if there was danger around and she needed to be quiet. She, in turn, could hit the ceiling with a broom handle three times if she needed anything.

One evening, as Hanz carried down a tray of food—a meal prepared by his daughter Shaylee, her daughter Shalom—Abigail initiated the conversation. "You sold my father a violin years ago," she said, reminiscing about those wonderful times with her family when her father would play Bach, Beethoven, and Brahms violin concertos as if he were Yehudi Menuhin, his favorite contemporary violinist. "He said it was the best violin he ever played."

Hanz smiled, surprised that her father was one of his previous customers, and encouraged that she was finally opening up and engaging with him.

"Do you know how to play it yourself?"

"I do."

"How did a farmer learn how to make, let alone play, such a beautiful instrument?"

"My grandfather was a violin maker, and he taught me his craft. I've been making custom violins and selling them ever since."

"I would like to hear you play sometime," Abigail said. "*Danke* for the food."

Hanz nodded and returned upstairs.

❧⟡☙

"What does she say to you?" Maria asked, lying next to her husband in bed that night.

"Nothing," said Hanz.

"All this time, and she has said nothing?"

"Well, tonight she told me her father had bought one of my violins. And she asked if I would play for her sometime."

Maria laid her head on his chest, listening to the strong cadence of his heartbeat. "I don't want you playing for her."

Hanz lifted her chin so she could see his lips. "Why not, *meine Liebe?* It would cheer her up, and God knows she needs that." He was actually looking forward to playing his favorite instrument for a new audience. An audience of one, yet with special significance. Abigail's request to hear him play was a sign of hope, too, a willingness to find solace in the beauty that could still exist amidst the ugliness of their world.

"Because," Maria said, closing her eyes. "I don't like the idea of you playing your violin for another *Frau*."

Hanz reached over and turned out the lamp; darkness instantly eclipsed the room. As he lay there, he thought about those nights when Abigail would sob, her wailing echoing throughout the house. He wondered if she was now crying in silence, and that bothered him, regretting telling her not to weep so loudly. It reminded him of the bird he loved when he was a little boy, and how his father became annoyed at its chirping, cruelly putting the bird in the barn to suppress its song. That's how he now felt about what he did to Abigail, cruelly suppressing her voice.

⚜

"**W**hy does your wife never come down to bring my food?" Abigail asked one morning.

"She prefers I do," was all Hanz said, putting her breakfast on the table.

"Why?"

"The whole thing frightens her. And lately, she doesn't feel well."

"She's ill?"

"*Ja.*"

"What's wrong?"

"We're not sure. It comes and goes, and some days are worse than others."

Abigail thought for a moment. "I could give you a recipe that will help her. It was from my grandmother, and it's a broth full of healthy herbal ingredients. Your wife should eat it every day."

"*Danke.* That's very nice of you. If you write it down, I'll give it to Shaylee and she can make it."

Abigail watched as Hanz slowly walked back up the steps and closed the door behind him. When she heard the second door from the hutch close, it made her think of the dollhouse her parents had given her as a child. She loved that huge dollhouse, which at one time had belonged to her bubbe (grandmother) as a little girl. At night before she went to bed, Abigail would close all the windows and doors of the dollhouse and lock her dolls inside, pretending it was for their own protection. The irony of her current situation was not lost on her; she, too, was now locked away for her protection, albeit in a far less enchanting prison. Now she knew how the dolls felt—trapped, in a place not of their choosing.

After finishing her breakfast, Abigail opened one of Shaylee's books that Hanz had brought her to help pass the time. This one had little hand-written notes inside, scattered among the pages like breadcrumbs, inscribed by Shaylee herself. Abigail studied her daughter's cursive strokes in fascination—a window into Shaylee's mind—tracing her finger over the words. Oh, how she longed to get to know her twin daughters in person! To hug them, talk to them, tell them how proud she was of them. Would that day ever come?

Abigail's reflections turned to Hanz and Maria, the two people she had entrusted her precious daughters to, all those years ago. Clearly she had chosen well, as this German couple had stepped into the void left by her absence, providing her children with the love and stability she could not, raising them to womanhood. "Happy and healthy," they now were, as he had assured her. And to risk their own lives by saving hers—an act of self-lessness and bravery—was also a testament to the kind of people they were.

She wondered if she'd be able to survive all this, though. When she was pregnant with Ava and Shalom, she was so scared and alone she didn't know what to do, at times thinking she would die from heartache. But they were born, she found them a home, and life went on. Now her entire family was gone, and she once again thought she would die from grief. But little by little, life was moving forward. And though they were not hers, she still had two vibrant daughters in the world. They would want her to fight through this, she thought. So fight she will.

CHAPTER 24

In secret, Shaylee joined an underground resistance group, helping Jews and others escape Germany. To her, doing nothing about the iniquities taking place against them was the same as being complicit. The clandestine group had observed her many times at the library in Rothenburg ob der Tauber before cautiously striking up a conversation to ascertain her affinity for or against the Third Reich. Once they were certain of her views, they approached to recruit her. All she had to do was act as a mule, delivering information.

Christian joined the Resistance too. Despite being in the Wehrmacht, he loathed the anti-Semitic Nazi policies, sickened by their murderous barbarism. In fact, he wouldn't even be in the German army if it weren't for mandatory conscription. Being close to Nazi leaders also provided him with information he wouldn't otherwise have access to, which was a great advantage for the Resistance, having someone on the inside.

The routine was always the same: Shaylee would meet her handler in Rothenburg's marketplace to receive instructions on smuggling a family out of Germany, then take the train to Nuremberg where she'd deliver them to her next contact. Names were neither given nor asked; just dates, times, and locations, in case someone was caught.

Christian was on military leave when Shaylee's next mission was arranged. He insisted on driving her to Nuremberg rather than her taking the train.

"Where are you going in that pretty scarlet dress?" Hanz asked the morning of, looking up from the violin on his lap. He was polishing the wood in preparation for a sale, listening to the radio in the background. "Isn't that the one Ava bought you in Paris during her honeymoon?"

"*Ja,*" said Shaylee. "Christian is taking me on a day trip to Nuremberg."

"Are you sure that's a *gute* idea, *Schätzchen*? There's a war going on."

"Don't worry, Papa, I'll be safe. He's in the Wehrmacht."

Just then, Christian honked the horn. She kissed her father on the cheek and hurried out the door.

As they drove toward Nuremberg, Christian and Shaylee spoke about the mission, going over the details. Nervous yet exhilarated, they were both proud to do their part, knowing they were making a difference.

"And what do you do if you sense you're being watched or followed?" Christian quizzed her.

"Find a crowd, blend in, and discreetly lose the instructions hidden inside the book I'm carrying."

"*Gute*. And what if the contact doesn't show up?"

"Go to the hotel across the street, call the number they gave me, and let it ring three times then hang up."

"*Ja.*"

When they reached Nuremberg, Christian dropped Shaylee off a block from the meeting point, parking the car far enough away so as not to be conspicuous, yet at the same time able to rush in and scoop her up if necessary. She walked the rest of the way, hyperaware of her surroundings and the people coming and going.

Each time Shaylee went on a mission—this was her ninth—her senses heightened in a way she'd never before experienced. Her eyes noticed everything, her ears perked up at the slightest sounds, her nose captured the scents wafting through the air, her tongue tasted them, and her feet seemed to feel the sidewalk moving with each step. In that pretty scarlet dress, with her hair styled in a sophisticated bun and her lips stained a matching red from one of Ava's lipsticks, she imagined herself playing a noble character in one of her books. A feminine spy. A heroine. A vigilante, even, fighting for what was right in the face of evil. It was almost a game to her, a chance to live vicariously as someone else, despite the risks. And yet, she knew if caught, it would mean the end.

Shaylee also knew that her parents would be extremely upset if they ever found out what she was doing. Maria would be aghast and forbid it, and Hanz would punish her for it, even though he himself was hiding a Jew. The double standard wouldn't matter, as their daughter was too precious to them.

When she reached her destination—the entrance of a department store—

Shaylee stood there and waited, the book in one hand and her clutch purse in the other. Passersby politely nodded, a few men stealing a backward glance at the pretty young *Fräulein*. Catching her reflection in the store window, she noticed how much she looked like Ava. Yes, they were identical twins with only slight differences, but in that elegant dress and sultry makeup, Shaylee could actually *be* Ava, pretending she was acting out a scene in a Hollywood movie. The realization made her grin.

"Shaylee, is that you?" a voice asked, approaching from behind and grabbing her arm.

She turned around. Her heart almost stopped.

"Lord, it *is* you!" His grip tightened. "What are you doing here?"

"Starholf . . ."

Decked out in his SS uniform, holding a briefcase with a swastika on the front, Starholf was in Nuremberg on official Nazi business. "I thought you were Ava at first, but I know she's at home."

"*Ja*, I ahh . . . I came to buy something for Mama, and Rothenburg doesn't have what I'm looking for."

"How did you get here?"

"I took the train."

Starholf looked her up and down. With the exception of his and Ava's wedding, he had never seen his sister-in-law all dolled up like that. Normally she wore simple cotton dresses and was makeup free. "*Du siehst wunderschön aus (You look beautiful)*."

Shaylee blushed.

Spontaneously, he reached over and lifted her chin toward the sunlight. The corners of his lips turned up, finding her appearance both stunning and amusing. It was unsettling, almost creepy, making Shaylee uncomfortable, wondering what was going through his mind.

"What is it you're going to buy your mother?" he asked.

For whatever reason, Shaylee thought of Maria working in her garden, her fiery red hair aglow under the sun, tussling in the breeze as if flames. "A mother-of-pearl hair comb," she answered, trying to remain calm. "She has those lovely red curls, and it would be so nice if she had something other than bobby pins to put her hair up."

"*Wunderbar.* I'll help you find it, and then we'll go for dinner."

Shaylee hesitated, staring at him. She'd have to abort the mission, and that could cost the family their lives. Not to mention that Christian was waiting for her down the street. "*Nein*, I can't," she said. "Christian is on leave for a couple of days, and I'm meeting him in Rothenburg this evening."

"I see." Starholf's icy blue eyes appeared questioning.

An awkward pause ensued, and a chilly breeze kicked up, teasing Shaylee's neck, giving her a shiver. She looked over at the people socializing in the coffee shop across the street, her mind scrambling over what to say next.

Starholf followed her eyes. "You know, back in the 1800s, people used to drink coffee while talking about politics, religion, and life like it was art. It wasn't just a social thing but a cultural one, where participants engaged in intellectual sparring and expression of ideas."

Shaylee's eyebrows raised.

"*Ja*, your brother-in-law knows more than just military strategy and expensive champagnes. I read a lot, like you."

She forced a tense grin.

"There was this one writer . . .," he said, trying to recall the man's name. Seconds later, he snapped his fingers, pleased with himself that he remembered. "William Allingham, *ja*. He was an Irish poet and editor in the 1800s, best known for his published work called *Diary*, in which he recorded his lively encounters with other *gute* writers and artists. It's quite interesting. And no doubt many of those conversations were held in a coffee shop, just like that one."

Up ahead, Shaylee saw a group of people crossing the street. A man wearing a black fedora with a white feather was in the middle, like the eye of a storm, his intense gaze locking onto her as he approached. She had been told her contact would be wearing that hat, and he had been told his mule would be outside that department store wearing a scarlet dress and holding a book. The closer he got, the more Shaylee's heart pounded.

Starholf's voice faded away, their surroundings too, and it was just Shaylee and her contact barreling toward her, as if two stars about to collide. Thinking quickly, she noticed a shiny, cream-colored Opel Kapitän cabriolet, driving past them. "Wow, nice car," she said, pointing at it. "You should buy one of those for Ava. She'd love it."

Starholf turned and looked. "*Nein*," he said, looking back at her with a smirk. "The Americans bought Opel in 1931, and last year they refused to switch to munitions manufacturing for the Reich. That will be rectified soon. But regardless, my family only drives Mercedes."

The handler was now only several paces away. Shaylee could see the tense expression on his face, and it made her panic. But then a lover's quarrel broke out across the street, loud and conspicuous, with the woman shouting at the man, waving her hands and pointing at him. She slapped him, yelling in French about how he had cheated on her and that she regretted moving away from France, leaving her dear mother and little sister to be with an unfaithful scoundrel. Everyone within earshot looked, including Starholf.

In that precise moment, the Resistance contact grabbed Shaylee's book in one smooth motion without stopping, exchanging it with another as if a magician. It happened so fast that if you were watching and blinked, you'd have missed it. Like a phantom hallucination, he then vanished.

Almost in shock, Shaylee slowly exhaled, her knees threatening to buckle, her knuckles white from clutching the new book in her hand. This was the first time the exchange was so unpredictable, so risky, and the fear of it going terribly wrong sunk deep into her bones.

Starholf shook his head in disgust. "What kind of woman embarrasses her man like that in public? Disgraceful. Ava would never do that to me." Looking back at Shaylee, he noticed her change in demeanor. "Are you all right? You look a little pale."

"*Ja, ja,* I'm fine," she said, collecting herself. "But I should get going. Otherwise I'll be late meeting Christian."

"Okay. Come to Berlin soon. Your sister misses you." He leaned down and kissed her cheek. "*Auf Wiedersehen (Goodbye),* Shaylee."

"*Auf Wiedersehen,*" she said over her shoulder, briskly walking away. "Give Ava my love."

～⚜～

Shaylee and Christian sat in silence in a private booth at the back of a restaurant, both numb over the gravity of what had almost gone wrong. The eatery was nearly empty, save for a group of nuns who huddled together at another table. Surprisingly, they seemed unafraid, despite the Nazi regime's persecution of religious orders, with many priests and nuns facing imprisonment, torture, and even murder. Shaylee met eyes with one of them; they both nodded and smiled.

After the couple ordered their food, Christian leaned over and whispered, "Of all the people to bump into, it had to be Starholf! What are the chances!"

"I know," said Shaylee, her heartbeat still elevated.

"The man is such a Nazi bloodhound, too—I'm surprised he didn't smell the information on you. Or at least sense that you were lying."

She nodded. "When I saw my contact coming toward me, I thought it was all over." Her hazel green eyes grew large and glossy. "But the exchange was the only thing that mattered, and even though I panicked, a surge of courage forced me to stay the course. Thank goodness that couple across the street started arguing, otherwise the contact would have kept walking."

Christian reached over and held her hand. "The bravery you showed was incredible. That information will mean the difference between life and death for that family, and you had a part in it."

Shaylee's eyes drifted off somewhere, staring into the deep past where life and death were as fickle as they were now.

"Penny for your thoughts?" Christian asked.

"I was just thinking about my father's *Freund,* Aadan Omari, and the tragic, heartbreaking stories he told us about the Africans who were stolen and forced into slavery."

"What made you think of that?"

"When you said that information will mean the difference between life and death for that family. It was true during the slave trade too."

Shaylee went on to explain how cornrows—the distinct style of tightly braided hair along the scalp that originated in ancient Africa dating back to 3000 BCE—emerged as a powerful tool of covert communication and resistance during the transatlantic slave trade. Enslaved individuals used cornrows to create secret messages and maps, as well as conceal small items essential for survival or escape along the metaphorical Underground Railroad—a secret network of routes and safe houses used by enslaved people in the American South to escape to freedom in the North. Specific braid patterns represented different information, from escape strategies and routes to take or avoid, who could be trusted or not, where to meet and when, or simply to communicate feelings and acknowledgements.

Christian was fascinated. "Can you imagine the fate of your life depending on understanding such a hidden code?"

Shaylee nodded. "The difference between life and death, as you said."

"*Ja.* And by delivering that information today, which was also written in code, you too have become a conductor on an Underground Railroad. One that saves people from Nazi tyranny."

The waitress came over with their food: thick, hot tomato soup–a wonderful blend of sweet and creamy–with freshly baked bread and chilled wine. As Christian dipped his bread in the soup, he took note of the book on the table that the Resistance contact had given Shaylee. "*Faust*, by Johann Wolfgang von Goethe," he said, staring at the cover. "That's a famous book. I wonder why they picked that one."

The tragic play of a scholarly man named Faust, who became dissatisfied with his life and made a pact with the devil Mephistopheles, giving his soul after death in exchange for unlimited knowledge and worldly pleasures, was apropos. In fact, with its themes of ambition, knowledge, and the pursuit of power, the Faust legend resonated with the German intellectual and cultural landscape, and would later be used to explore the nature of the Nazi regime and the German population's complicity in the Holocaust. Interestingly, a printed edition of the play could be found in the personal libraries of many Jews, demonstrating its renowned popularity.

"I think they picked it as a deliberate reference to Hitler making a deal with the devil," Shaylee said, taking a sip of her wine. "A madman driven by his ungodly desire to rule the world."

"I'd never want to rule the world," said Christian. "Just give me a beautiful day, a *wunderbar* meal, and someone to love." He winked at her. "That's all I need to be a God-fearing, happy man."

After dinner, the young couple went for a stroll down *Weißgerbergasse (White Tanner's Street)* in the heart of Nuremberg's *Altstadt (Old Town)*. Named after the white tanners who once lived and worked there, skilled artisans who specialized in processing animal hides into white leather–a valuable material used for various purposes, including clothing, shoes, and other goods–the cobblestone street lined with colorful half-timbered houses and well-preserved medieval architecture could have been right out of Rothenburg ob der Tauber. Though the evening was charming and tranquil, signs of the treacherous world they lived in were everywhere. Nazi propaganda decorated buildings, fresh graffiti spewed hatred toward Jews, and military planes flew sporadically overhead.

Two Nazi soldiers walked past them as they ambled along, giving Christian the Sieg Heil salute, followed by three women in nurse uniforms, chatting about the increased workload at the hospital. A new mother struggled to soothe the wailing baby in her arms, her husband nowhere in sight. And a street vendor hawked his goods, trying to make a sale to anyone he could.

When they got to the end of the street, a gray-haired woman stood near the curb, asking a German man for directions to a home where she was to be interviewed as a nanny. A car drove by and splashed water on her, causing her to shake her fist and curse at the driver.

"Oh no," Shaylee said. "That poor woman."

Christian grinned, finding it funny. He pulled Shaylee in close and whispered in her ear, "Don't worry. Little old nannies are invincible. I bet she has a superhero cape under that tweed jacket and turtleneck sweater."

Shaylee giggled. But when they reached the woman, she offered her handkerchief to dry off with. The woman thanked her for her kindness.

Unlike the drive to Nuremberg that morning, fretting about the mission, the drive home to Rothenburg was peaceful. Christian could tell Shaylee was still thinking about what had happened earlier with the Resistance contact, though, and reached over to hold her hand. "Everything is *gute*," he said. "The exchange was successful, and by this time tomorrow, that family will be safe in Sweden."

⚜

A week later, Ollie and Randolph the Bull were at the Wolff farmhouse. Ollie had witnessed Shaylee doing something in town earlier that greatly worried him. While delivering the mail, he happened to see her, in the broad light of day with people all around, sitting on a bench in the marketplace. Wondering why she was there, he smiled and started walking toward her to say hello, only to stop in his tracks when a man sat next to her, placed a book between them, then got up and left without his book. When Shaylee put the book in her bag and left too, Ollie immediately knew what had taken place. It was so obvious, and he went to The Devil's Needle to tell Randolph.

It angered Hanz that this underground Resistance group, that everyone knew existed, was risking his daughter's life in such a blatant way. And Shaylee clearly had no real understanding of the dire consequences she would face if caught: Imprisoned, beaten, tortured for information, perhaps raped, and ultimately hung or shot as an example. The images made him nauseous.

As they waited for Shaylee to get home, the three men sat at the kitchen table, playing cards to lighten the mood. Hanz glanced down the hallway where his wife, feeling unwell, was fast asleep in their bedroom, and then at the floor where another woman—the one he was risking his own life for—was hidden beneath their feet. He hated having to keep Abigail locked away all day like that, occasionally letting her out in the yard while nervously keeping watch. When he'd lead her back into the secret room and shut the door behind him, it felt as if he were a jailor bringing his prisoner into the dungeon.

How long could he hide her like this, he wondered? Should he tell Ollie and Randolph? The war could go on for years still—maybe it would be wise to contact the Resistance himself, getting Abigail false papers and smuggling her to the North Sea, putting her on a boat to Sweden to escape Germany.

He looked at the painting of Ava and Shaylee above the fireplace mantle in the living room, the light of the flames reflecting off their innocent faces. There was no denying the uncanny similarities between them and their birth mother, and it galvanized his resolve to stay the course. After all, he and Maria owed this woman so much. No one knows she's here, he thought, not even his best friends, and the likelihood of anyone finding out is far less than the likelihood of her getting caught if he tried to smuggle her out.

Ollie smiled as he reshuffled the deck and dealt the cards. He was on a winning streak. "This is *wunderbar*, taking your money so easily like this," he laughed, downing his shot of vodka.

"*Ja, ja*," said Randolph. "I'm sure your wife will be happy."

"*Nein*, I'm not telling her. I'm going to use it to buy some more comic books." He winked at the Bull. "What she doesn't know won't hurt her."

Randolph grinned as he studied his cards. "Not so fast, *mein Freund*. This time you're going to lose."

"Ha! You and a thousand card sharks couldn't beat me!" Ollie bragged, the alcohol feeding his overconfidence.

"You both sound like women yapping," said Hanz. "Shut up and play."

Shaylee walked through the door, and all three men stopped and turned to look at her.

"*Hallo*, Ollie. *Hallo*, Randolph," she politely greeted. Removing her coat slowly, she sensed something was wrong.

"Where have you been!" Hanz demanded.

She stared at her father, startled by his tone of voice. "What do you mean? I was at work."

"At work doing what, Shaylee? Ollie saw you in the *Marktplatz*."

"*Ja*, I . . . I . . ."

Hanz hit the table with his fist, bouncing the cards and nearly causing their drinks to spill. "Don't you dare lie to me!"

"Papa, why are you so angry?" She started to quiver. "You're frightening me."

"You *should* be frightened!" He stood, and in two strides was directly in front of her, grabbing her slight shoulders, giving her a shake. "Do you know what would happen if they caught you with the Resistance! Do you!"

Shaylee's mouth went dry. She thought they'd been so careful. So discreet.

Hanz looked at his friends for support. "Tell her!"

"Your father's right," Ollie said, a concerned look overshadowing his comical features. "It's extremely dangerous. You can't be involving yourself in such things."

"You could get yourself killed, little one," added Randolph.

"Or worse!" Hanz yelled. "Raped and tortured, and then killed!"

"Papa!" Shaylee ran to her bedroom, crying.

Hanz removed his belt and followed her. He was going to put the fear of God into his daughter, lest she do it again and he lose his beloved swan to the evil Reich. Ollie and Randolph looked at each other, wondering if they should intervene.

As he entered Shaylee's room, Hanz slapped the leather against the wall, inadvertently striking some of her ceramic decorative masks on the dresser, shattering them to the floor. "Anyone could have seen you!" he yelled, his voice booming and tremoring with equal measure. "Anyone! That obvious exchange could have cost you your life!"

Shaylee stared at her father in fear. She had never seen him so angry before.

"You are forbidden from meeting with that group again!"

"But Papa . . ."

"You heard me!"

"I'm making a difference!" she asserted, desperately trying to plead her case. "I'm helping save lives, like you saved Abigail! Just last week, another family made it safely to Sweden! They lived, Papa! They lived!"

"I don't care!"

"You have to let me continue!" Shaylee almost screamed. "We have to help these people!"

"*Nein!*"

"Then why are you helping Abigail? Why just her?"

Father and daughter locked eyes. What could he say? The hypocrisy was evident, but he couldn't tell her the truth.

"Christian is in the Resistance too. He has access to important Nazi information."

Hanz could not prevent the Nazis from murdering innocent people, but he could prevent his daughter from becoming one of their victims. Walking over to her, he raised his belt high as if to strike, his large frame looming over her fragile form. "If I ever find out you did that again, so help me God, Shaylee Wolff, I will whip you black and blue! Do you understand!"

Shaylee's eyes became large, and she slowly nodded.

Maria had woken and went to see if her daughter was in her room. "Hanz, what are you doing!" she said, alarmed by the scene.

He lowered his arm and turned to her. "She was helping the Resistance."

Maria's eyes grew large too. "Shaylee, *nein!*"

"Who was that man who gave you the book?" Hanz asked.

"My handler," replied Shaylee.

"What was in it?"

"Instructions to help another family escape Germany."

"Where is it now?"

Shaylee pulled the book out of her bag and gave it to him with trembling hand.

Hanz read the letter inside it. "And who was to receive this?"

"I'm supposed to take it to a man in Nuremberg in two days. He'll be wearing a blue tie, sitting at a table in a French restaurant called *La Maison de la Lumière (The House of Light).*

He stuck the letter back inside the book. "Go to bed!"

Maria put her arms around her daughter, holding Shaylee tight as she sobbed into her mother's chest.

✧

All three men went to the makeshift art studio in the barn. Hanz started a fire in the cast iron stove, opened a bottle of vodka, and the drinking and talking resumed. The alcohol affected each of them differently, with Hanz opening up and sharing more than he normally did, Ollie becoming more animated than usual, and Randolph the Bull taking on a reminiscent bearing. And yet, the three personalities, as diverse as they were, seemed to relax each other, complement each other.

"When I was a young lad, I had glorious dreams of becoming a champion boxer," Randolph said, now intoxicated. "And I did it, didn't I." He leaned on Ollie for support. "I fought the best and won."

"You did, you did," echoed Ollie, patting his friend's burly back. "Luck was on your side."

"Luck?" Randolph looked insulted. "I fought with everything I had; there was no luck involved." He balled his fists and shadowboxed the air, stumbling when the air struck back.

Hanz retrieved a small wooden box containing all the eccentric items he had collected over the years. Next to the Roman coin and black pearl was the Bull's gold tooth that Albrecht Braun had knocked out during that fight two decades earlier, landing by Hanz's feet. "Well this sure brought me luck," he said, showing it to them.

Randolph stared at it the same way he did that night Hanz offered it back to him in The Devil's Needle, then let out his hearty belly laugh. "I said it before and I'll say it again, Handsome Hanz. That tooth brought you more luck than it ever did me!"

The camaraderie lasted deep into the night, with the conversation turning more serious, politics and world events providing plenty of fodder. Each man expressed strong opinions and ideas about current affairs, discussing at length what happened that day, and how Hanz was right to be angry with Shaylee.

"What should I do?" he finally asked them, the alcohol in his veins second-guessing each potential option he came up with. "Should I deliver the information in that book, or should I burn it?"

"You have enough on your plate, *mein Freund*," Ollie slurred, finishing off the bottle of vodka. "Burn it and tend to your own family."

"*Nein*," Randolph quickly rebutted, opening another. "That message must be delivered. Another family's life depends on it."

Ollie and Randolph began to argue over what to do, both raising their voices and jutting out their chests in a testosterone-filled duel.

"You skinny, dumb piece of German *Nudel (noodle)!*" Randolph yelled. "You wouldn't know what to do if God himself told you!"

Ollie threw his hat to the ground. "You hairy, bullheaded Polack! No wonder they call you the Bull! You don't just look like one; you have the brains of one too!"

Randolph stepped forward, and Ollie quickly jumped behind Hanz.

"Shut the hell up, both of you," Hanz said, keeping them apart. "This is not about you. It's about that family. Now shake hands and make *gute*."

"I wouldn't shake his hand if you paid me to!" Randolph said, scowling.

"And I wouldn't shake yours if you paid me!" said Ollie, peeking around Hanz.

Randolph looked at him, frustrated. "I just said that."

"And?"

"Huh?"

Confused and inebriated, everyone paused. Seconds later, they all burst out laughing.

The two men finally shook hands and hugged each other.

"Hot under the collar, we both are," said Ollie. "That's all."

"A man after my own heart," Randolph agreed, raking his fingers through his dark, unruly hair. "Nothing wrong with being passionate over what you believe in."

Hanz went to the cabinet where he kept the alcohol. He pulled out a bottle of vintage Jägermeister, and they all cheered.

As the conversation resumed—peacefully—Hanz stared at the flames behind the glass door of the stove, his three sheepdogs by his side. Still grappling with his decision, he looked down at Felix, Bastian, and Axel sleeping by the warmth of the fire. What a blessing it was to be a dog, he thought. Carefree days, unconditional love, oblivious to the hatred and evil impelling man's injury to man.

"You know what you should do?" said the happy-go-lucky Ollie. "Flip a coin." He pulled his latest comic book from his back pocket and began perusing through it.

"Flip a coin over such a critical decision?" Hanz questioned.

"*Ja!*" said Randolph, coming alive. He grabbed Ollie's comic book and rolled it up, pointing it at Hanz. "But whatever it reveals, you must follow through."

The crazy suggestion harkened Hanz back to that night he saw the homeless older man who looked like Moses, speaking in a rare state of sanity, expounding his philosophical wisdom about life. He had said that we're all in a constant fight between good and evil. A holy war. An invisible struggle on the path of right and wrong, and everyone must walk it and choose. "There are always two sides to a coin," Silas Simpleton had concluded when Hanz questioned him about natural law versus moral law. "And only a closed mind sees the one."

"Give me a coin," Hanz said, looking up at his friends.

Ollie reached into his pocket and pulled out a 5 Reichsmark silver coin engraved with the Nazi eagle, handing it to him.

Hanz flipped it into the air. The silver shined for a flicker of a moment, catching the light of the flames before landing by his feet.

Looking down at the coin, he had his answer . . .

❧

Two days later, Hanz took the train to Nuremberg. Dressed as if a businessman on his way to work, he discreetly surveyed the other passengers on the car, nervous over the book he was carrying. A nun with two young children—a boy and a girl—sat directly in front of him, and if he had to guess, he'd say the kids were Jewish. The nun looked nervous too, and he felt bad for them, hoping they'd make it safely to their final destination.

As the train rolled through the German countryside, Hanz stared out the window to try to relax. The bucolic scenery was stunning, with charming rivers and lakes accentuated by trees turning their vibrant colors of fall. This is my homeland, he thought. Such a beautiful place to live. How could it now be possessed by such evil?

The train stopped, and two men from the Gestapo got on, systematically going seat to seat, asking to see the passengers' papers. The nun panicked—obviously she was not the little boy and girl's mother—and she whispered frantically to the children. Hanz couldn't hear what she was saying, but the little girl was terrified and peed herself, and the little boy paled like a ghost.

Hanz leaned over and quietly said to the children, "*Komm setz dich neben mich (Come sit next to me).* I'm going to say I'm your papa, *ja?* Just for today."

The frightened children looked at the nun with wide eyes, and she nodded for them to go. They sat on either side of Hanz, and he put his arms around them, whispering that everything would be all right.

"*Papiere (Papers),*" demanded the Gestapo, eyeing Hanz and the two children.

Hanz smiled courteously and handed his ID card to the man.

He examined it and said, "*Danke,*" then noticed the book on the seat. "Interesting read?"

"*Nein,*" Hanz said, his heart pounding in his chest. "A waste of time, but

I promised my wife. She wrote it."

The man laughed and moved to the next seat.

When the Gestapo left the train and it began to move again, Hanz looked down at the little girl. Never would he forget the look of anxiety and terror in her eyes. A look that no young child should ever have. A look that would haunt him for the rest of his life.

❧

Hanz entered *La Maison de la Lumière* restaurant and sat at a table by the window. He looked around but didn't see anyone wearing a blue tie, so he ordered a beer and waited. After an hour, three Nazi soldiers walked in, and his heart once again thumped wildly in his chest . . .

"Hanz!" Severin exclaimed, surprised to see his brother there. "What are you doing in Nuremberg?"

"Oh, I ahh . . .," Hanz stammered. "I needed a special paint they don't sell in Rothenburg. It's a short train ride so I figured I'd come here and pick it up."

"My *Bruder*, the farmer who paints and makes violins," Severin laughed to his peers.

The other soldiers paid him no mind, and they all sat down in a booth. Severin insisted he join them, and Hanz reluctantly agreed, keeping the book inconspicuously by his side.

While the men drank and ate their food, busily conversing about their lives and the war, Hanz kept glancing around, watching for the Resistance contact. It had been two hours now, and no one wearing the distinct blue tie had entered the restaurant. But then, just as Hanz thought the trip had been for nothing, a small man with spectacles, a top hat, a newspaper tucked under his arm, and yes, a bright blue bow tie, walked through the door. He sat down in the corner by himself and appeared to be waiting for someone. That must be him!

The sounds around Hanz faded, and he became acutely aware of the book resting on his lap. The letter inside it gave instructions on helping a family of eight—two grandparents, a husband and wife, four children—detailing how, when, and where to bring them to safety. Their very lives depended on that letter, on Hanz, and on the man in the blue tie.

"Hanz . . . Hanz," said Severin.

"Oh, sorry . . . What?"

"I asked you how *meine schönen Nichten (my beautiful nieces)* are."

"*Ja, ja, gute.*" Hanz tried to seem relaxed, forcing a grin while the sweat accumulated on his brow and upper lip. "Ava is enjoying married life, and Shaylee is busy with her books and dreams."

"*Wunderbar.* I saw Luka yesterday, too. He has a promising career in the Wehrmacht ahead of him."

"*Ja,* especially since his uncle is a colonel," one of the soldiers ribbed. The other soldier laughed.

"I'm very proud of him," was all Hanz said.

"And so you should be," replied Severin. *"Prost!"*

All four of them clinked their beer mugs.

The man in the blue tie appeared impatient to Hanz. How am I going to get this book to him without being obvious, he wondered? I can't let him leave without delivering it–that could mean the end for that poor family. As he sat there trying to figure out a plan, conflicted feelings raged inside. Two days earlier, he was about to take the belt to his sweet daughter for wanting to do exactly what he himself was doing now. And what he was doing with Abigail. Yet still, despite the hypocrisy, he was glad he had stopped her. This was no easy thing, and if he got caught, so be it. If Shaylee got caught, however, his entire universe was over.

When Severin and his peers ordered another round, Hanz decided it was time. Taking a deep breath, he excused himself to go to the bathroom, and as he walked past the man in the blue tie, he slid the book onto his table.

"Sir, what's this?" the man asked.

Hanz stopped and turned around, his heart pounding so hard he thought the entire restaurant could hear it. "You don't want it?"

The man laughed. "Why would I want your book?"

People at the next table noticed the strange interaction and stared.

Embarrassed, Hanz apologized and took the book back. Once inside the bathroom, he splashed cold water on his face and stared at himself in the mirror. What are you doing, he asked his reflection? You're just a farmer. A farmer who paints and makes violins. You cannot save the whole world, so stop trying and focus on your own family instead.

"You all right?" Severin asked, entering the bathroom to relieve himself. "You seem stressed."

Hanz dried his face. "It's Maria. Her health has gotten worse lately."

"Hmm. Sorry to hear." Severin noticed the book on the sink as he stood at the urinal. "What's your book about?"

"Nothing. Just ahh . . . a silly story to keep me occupied on the train. I'm going to go home now, Severin. Maria is waiting."

"Okay, *Bruder*. Give my love to her. I'll come by the farm and visit soon."

Hanz nodded and left the bathroom, going straight to the front cash to pay his bill.

"I'll be with you in a minute," the waitress said, busy pouring some drinks.

Another man came over to the cash too. A man wearing a blue tie! "They have *gute* food here, no?" he asked Hanz. Placing some bills on the counter, he said to the waitress, "*Danke*, Anneliese." She simply nodded, and he promptly left.

Shaken by the unexpected encounter, Hanz watched the man through the window as he disappeared down the street. When he turned back to the cash, the book he had placed on the counter was gone.

⚜

"They caught a member of the Resistance," Severin said later that week. He had come to the farmhouse for a visit, just like he promised he would when he saw Hanz at the French restaurant in Nuremberg. In full Nazi uniform, his presence was intimidating as he sat at the kitchen table with his brother, waiting for Shaylee to serve them dinner. Maria wasn't feeling well and remained in bed.

Shaylee had made *Eintopf (stew)* that day, a remnant of the *Eintopfsonntag (Stew Sunday)* campaign that the Nazis pushed when they came into power. On the first Sunday of each month, every German family was asked to replace their traditional roast with a thriftier "one-pot" meal—an *Eintopf*—and set aside the savings for charity. Collectors around the country would knock on doors to accept the money, and the government even released promotional photos of Adolf Hitler sitting down to a steaming pot of stew, sending a clear message that everyone was doing it, and participation was a national obligation. Though the campaign had since died off, the stew was still popular. Shaylee's *Eintopf* was made with potatoes, vegetables, and beef from their farm.

"Why are you telling me about the Resistance?" Hanz asked, taking a spoonful of the hearty soup.

"Because when interrogated, the man said a farmer's daughter had been helping them."

Shaylee didn't look up, but she momentarily stopped eating.

Hanz glanced at her as he nonchalantly poured himself a shot of vodka. "That could be anyone. You know how many farmers there are in this country?"

The sudden silence in the room was deafening. And uncomfortable. The warmth and cordiality common within the Wolff family seemed to have vanished.

Finally Severin came out with it: "Was it you, *Bruder*? You and Shaylee? The man said he was supposed to meet the daughter in a French restaurant in Nuremberg called *La Maison de la Lumière*, but another man showed up instead."

Hanz dabbed his bread in the stew and took a bite, thinking about the Resistance member in the blue tie who had briefly spoken to him in the restaurant before taking the book. He seemed like a nice man. A good man.

"They tortured him, you know. First they beat him up badly, and crushed his fingers in a press. Then they hauled him up to the ceiling with a pulley and whipped him, letting his body drop to the floor several times to break more bones. When he still didn't talk, they used electricity."

Shaylee got up and ran to her room.

"Enough!" said Hanz. "I won't have you talking like that in my home, in front of my daughter!"

But Severin continued. He had to. If his brother and niece were involved with the Resistance, he had to scare them enough that they would never do anything like that again. "When they finally got what they wanted out of him, they beat him some more, and then hung him from a meat hook."

"Ich sagte halt den Mund (I said shut your mouth)!"

The two men stared at each other. Knowing his brother would never admit to it even if he were involved, Severin said, "Hanz . . . I'm only telling you this because that's what happens to those who help the enemies of the Third Reich and get caught. Remember that."

CHAPTER 25

"*Papier! Papier!*" a newspaper boy shouted out in the streets of Rothenburg ob der Tauber. "Hot off the press!"

Hanz waved him over and paid for the *Völkischer Beobachter (People's Observer)*. When he looked at the front page, Adolf Hitler's foreboding eyes stared back at him. What an unsettling image, he thought. And his message was even more sinister. Worse yet, the masses throughout Germany seemed to give credence to the Führer's madness, and in these times of chaos and war, they placed more trust in his perversions than in the Holy Bible itself. Or even in logic. Or humanity. Or the rapprochement between peoples for the sake of peace. No rational answer to the irrationalism of this race ideology, which incited hatred and annihilation, could be found.

Hanz crossed the street and went to The Devil's Needle for breakfast. The tavern was already busy with a patchwork assortment of people, and when Nila saw him, she smiled and came right over with a pot of hot coffee.

"*Guten Morgen (Good morning)*," she greeted. "You're visiting town awfully early today."

"*Ja*," said Hanz. "I brought another painting to Giovanni Mandolini."

Nila stepped onto the bench behind the bar and poured him a cup of coffee. "You look tired."

"I am tired," he said, adding cream to his hot drink.

She noticed the worry in his face. "Maria not getting any better?"

Hanz shook his head. Besides hiding and tending to Abigail, he was now also taking care of his wife, who had once again fallen ill. This time gravely. It worried him that Maria was not recovering from her mysterious ailment like before, and the doctor from Rothenburg failed to diagnose why.

Nila frowned. "Such a sweet woman, she is. I'll pray her for, Hanz."

"*Danke.*"

Randolph the Bull came out of the kitchen, his missing front teeth always prominent as he beamed his usual smile. "Hanz!" he exclaimed, coming up to him at the bar.

Normally Hanz would light up too, but today he only gave a soft smile. "*Guten Morgen, mein Freund.*"

"You want some breakfast? I just made some scrambled eggs, sausage, and fried potatoes."

Hanz nodded.

Randolph glanced at the newspaper with the image of Hitler on the front page. His smile dissipated. "I keep telling Nila we should sell this place and leave," he said in a lowered voice. "Especially now that Jews have been banned from Rothenburg." He scratched his stubby beard and gave her a disappointed look. "But she won't leave this damn tavern."

"Why should we leave?" Nila asked defiantly. "We worked hard to buy this place, and I'm not letting any bully run us off."

Hanz ate his breakfast, then picked up supplies and began the drive home, worrying about the women in his life. Why was Maria always getting sick, he wondered, his brow furrowing? Such a helpless feeling, like slowly drowning. It seemed only yesterday he had met her in Austria, where they walked hand in hand, strolling through the beautiful imperial gardens of Hofgarten park in Innsbruck, talking about their future. And yet a lifetime had happened in what seemed like a blink of an eye. Who would have ever thought he'd be in the situation he is in now, taking care of a sick wife, protecting the identity of his daughters, and illegally harboring a Jew—their birth mother? Concealing Abigail in the secret room was as surreal as it was frightening, and if it weren't all so serious and draining, he would have laughed at fate's malicious jokes bearing gifts wrapped in irony.

❦

Halfway home, Hanz came across a ghastly scene. A dead man on the side of the road had been set on fire! Crumpled up in the fetal position, his charred remains were still smoldering. Obviously he had been hiding too, and the Nazis found him, exacting a barbaric punishment.

When Hanz stopped the car to inspect the corpse, he noticed something in the Jewish man's arms that shocked him to his core. A child! The two bodies appeared to be fused as if they were one. A cold sweat came over Hanz, followed by nausea, and he stumbled back into his car, praying the rest of the way home.

The following week, Ava and her husband came with Luka and Severin to the farmhouse for dinner. Shaylee had prepared a traditional German feast of Bavarian pot roast and Fränkische bratwurst with sauerkraut, and everyone sat around the kitchen table catching up. Maria mustered the strength to get out of bed and visit too, since it was a rare occasion for them to be all together like this as a family. Laughter and conversation filled the house, proffering a semblance of normalcy in a time of great despair.

Afterward, the men went outside for a smoke while the sisters cleaned up in the kitchen and conversed with their mother. It was a joy for Maria to see both her daughters under her roof again, listening with a mother's pride to them chattering like best of friends, hearing about the goings-on in their lives. Ava loved living in Berlin, and she and her husband were trying for a baby. Shaylee skirted around questions about her and Christian, directing the conversation instead to her job as a librarian.

Outside, Hanz stood on the porch, leaning against the railing, thinking about what he had seen the previous week alongside the road. Who was that poor man and child? What was their story? Where was the mother? And where had they been hiding before they were found? In his mind he could see the man begging for the life of his son, if not his own, and yet still the Nazis killed them both. It was as if a wormhole had opened and sucked Hanz through, dropping him into a parallel but evil universe.

Hanz's thoughts drifted to Abigail in the secret room next to his cellar. What was she doing at this very moment, he wondered? Could she hear them talking? Strangely, despite the atrocity he had witnessed, and the fact that two men from the Wehrmacht and an SS officer were there on his porch, he wasn't anxious about having a Jewish woman hiding in his home. Perhaps it was because the men were family, although Starholf he didn't trust. Or maybe because they had no reason to suspect anything, and no cause to go into that room.

Severin struck a match on his boot and lit a cigarette. Though he was talking, he could see Hanz's mind was elsewhere. "*Bruder*, did you hear what I said?" he asked, snapping his fingers to get his brother's attention.

"They're rounding up the Jews like sheep now."

Starholf chuckled. "We should just shoot them on the spot rather than take them away. Why waste the time and resources?"

"Many of the Schutzstaffel are already doing that," said Luka. "They arrest some, and others they kill. There's no rhyme or reason. No rules."

"When they don't cooperate, that's what happens," said Starholf. "Most of the dirty sheep follow orders, but the stubborn goats are difficult and like to argue." He smiled. "There was one Jewish rat—a rich one—demanding we leave his home. After we shot his wife and daughter in front of him, his arrogance turned to sobbing."

The SS officer's casual brutality, and the ease with which he spoke of murder, sent a chill through Hanz. This was the man whom he gave his daughter to in marriage. How could this happen? He looked over at the two innocent, graceful swans swimming peacefully in the nearby pond, and it made him think of Ava and Shaylee, his beloved twin daughters whom he had always called his darling swans. Moral disgust rose from the pit of his stomach and vomited out his throat toward his son-in-law. "Stop!" he yelled. "I've heard enough!"

All the men looked at him.

"Hanz, with his heart of gold," Starholf laughed. "The Good Samaritan."

Father-in-law and son-in-law stared at one another, the tension palpable, neither backing down until the uncomfortable stalemate was broken when Shaylee stepped outside. "Let's go to the gazebo," she said, holding a tray of desserts. Ava was right behind her with a tray of tea and dishes, and everyone walked to the large weeping willow tree in the yard where Hanz had made the charming structure for his daughter's wedding.

"This is where we got married," Ava said with a happy smile. She sat on her husband's lap and kissed his cheek.

"*Ja*," said Starholf, gazing at his wife. He turned to his father-in-law and extended an olive branch for the previous awkward friction. "*Danke*, Hanz. You did a *wunderbar* job on this gazebo."

Hanz nodded, once more thinking of the killer masquerading as a priest from twenty years ago, imagining him swinging from the weeping willow tree next to them had he allowed the vigilante men from town to lynch the felon there on his property. Like a mental thorn, he could never seem to dissociate that man from that tree.

With dessert finished, Maria picked up an empty tray and collected some of the dishes. As she walked back to the farmhouse, she collapsed in the yard.

"Mama!" Shaylee screamed.

Everyone ran over to her.

"Maria! Maria!" exclaimed Hanz, his heart pounding as he gently shook her. He picked her up from the ground and rushed to the house.

"Take me to the bedroom, Hanz," she mumbled, half-conscious. "I don't feel well."

⁓⦕⦖⁓

With Maria fast asleep in bed, Hanz bid farewell to his family outside the farmhouse. Ava and her husband, and Luka and Severin, had rented hotel rooms in Rothenburg ob der Tauber, with plans to depart for Berlin together in the morning. Hanz asked his brother to stop by the doctor's office before leaving town, requesting that he come to the farmhouse to see Maria. Though she now appeared to be all right, he wanted to play it safe.

Shaylee made a plate of food for Abigail, and Hanz brought it to her in the secret room. "Shaylee cooked this," he said, smiling as he placed it on the wooden table, the aroma of pot roast and bratwurst suffusing the air. "It's delicious."

"*Danke*," she replied.

He stoked the fire and added a few more logs. "How are you feeling?"

Abigail didn't answer, making him feel foolish for asking. How would anyone feel after going through what she did?

"I brought you some more books, too," he said, retrieving the bag he left at the foot of the steps. "I have a little library in the cellar, and if you want, I can show it to you later."

"How was your visit with your family?" Abigail asked numbly.

Hanz had told her they were coming, kindly asking her to remain quiet. "*Gute*. It's not often my *Sohn*, my two daughters, my son-in-law, and my *Bruder* are all together at the same time." He almost felt criminal calling Abigail's biological daughters his daughters, as if he were stealing them from her. "I say 'my daughters', but I mean 'your daughters' too."

She nodded, sitting on her small bed, nervously wringing her hands. "You had told me your *Sohn* and *Bruder* are in the Wehrmacht, and your son-in-law is an SS officer. Has there been any sign the Nazis are still searching for me?"

Again, Hanz thought of the grisly scene on the side of the road. "*Nein*, Abigail. They're not looking anymore. No one is going to find you. You're safe in here."

She looked up at him, gratitude in her gaze. "*Danke*, Herr Hanz. You and Frau Maria have been nothing but kind to me, and I am very grateful. I know you have put yourself and your family in great danger by helping me."

Hanz sat down in the chair across from her. There was so much to talk about, so much to share. But the atmosphere was all wrong. It wasn't a time of visiting and sharing but only survival. A protective instinct stirred in him, to comfort her and show humanity in a time of inhumanity despite the risks involved.

"Are you ever going to tell my . . . I mean . . . your daughters about me?" she asked. "About who I really am?"

"*Nein*. That would be too shocking for them, after believing all this time that my wife and I are their real parents. Their whole lives they grew up thinking they're German."

Abigail paused for a moment, lost in the past, a rare smile gracing her lips. "I remember seeing them as young teenagers when they were fifteen years old. I had followed them to the river and hid behind a tree, watching as they swam all day with two boys. It was so beautiful to see, and my heart filled with such happiness." Tears rolled down her cheeks as the images played out in her mind.

Hanz recalled the doll Shaylee had made of the woman in the forest when she was twelve years old, telling him that she and Ava would sometimes see her watching them. "*Ja*, they often went down to the river with my *Sohn* Luka and their *Freund* Christian. They were thick as thieves back then. Christian is now Shaylee's boyfriend."

"They had also worked as housemaids for the Wagners in Rothenburg when they were eighteen," said Abigail.

"That's true. How did you know?"

"Because I worked there too for a while. When I found out they were Wagner housemaids, I applied for the same job so I could see them up close. I almost fainted the first time they spoke to me."

He smiled.

"All day we folded clothes, mopped floors, and polished cutlery. I watched them and memorized their faces, their voices, their nuances." Abigail's tears were flowing now. "And at the end of the day, when I went home, I cried. They had no idea I was their mother."

Hanz reached over and held Abigail's hand. "I remember Ava and Shaylee telling me about a lovely Jewish woman they worked with. That was you."

She nodded. "I had no choice but to give them to you, Herr Hanz. I didn't want to, but I had no choice." Abigail covered her face with her hands and wept.

Hanz thought about the trauma she went through, first being raped by a vile man, then having to give her babies away. "You were only a child yourself. You did the right thing."

She wiped her tears. "Now everyone thinks they're German, which is *gute*. Giving them to you saved their lives twice. First as babies, then as young women."

"*Ja*, thanks to you."

Abigail looked at Hanz with strong conviction in her eyes. "I used to feel bad that they didn't know of their Jewish heritage. Now I don't. I don't ever want them to know the truth."

Hanz slowly nodded, while upstairs Shaylee was calling, telling him her mother needed him. For a moment they both listened to her voice; then he stood and went to his ill wife.

⁕

The doctor from Rothenburg ob der Tauber knocked on the farmhouse door the following morning. He examined Maria, just like he had before, yet remained confounded. Despite her alarming decline in health, his assessment brought no new insight, her diagnosis remaining elusive. "Must be a stubborn flu," he concluded for lack of a better verdict, "which precipitated her weakness and caused her to faint." After giving Maria some medicine and advice, he was on his way.

While his wife slept, Hanz stepped out onto the porch and scanned his sprawling property, smiling at the wildflowers in the field defying the morning frost. Winter had not yet arrived, but it was lurking somewhere in the shadows, a chilly breeze giving indubitable evidence of its encroachment on fall. He didn't mind the cold slowly creeping in; it was Mother Nature's way. In fact, fall and winter could be beautiful too, with the majestic deciduous trees turning from vivid green to a stunning amalgam of bright crimson, marigold, and amber, transmogrifying into long-limbed skeletons feigning death, only to resurrect again into new perennial goliaths bursting with life in the spring. In the meantime, winter provided its own unique beauty, with the fields covered in a resplendent blanket of fluffy white snow like frosting on a cake, and the small junipers, colossal European silver firs, and symmetrical Norway spruces standing as if Apollo in a white tunic or Aphrodite decorated in diamonds and pearls.

Hanz reminisced about winters past, when the children were small and the family would hunker down while Jack Frost cast his magic spell over the land, hypnotizing it to sleep. He would cut wood to keep the fireplace burning and the farmhouse cozy, Maria would knit sweaters and weave quilts, and the children would make snow angels in the yard. When they were snowed in, they would read stories, play games, or listen to the radio. The children would watch and giggle as Hanz and Maria slow danced barefoot in the kitchen, and sneak into their parents' bed to snuggle. This was their routine during the long winter months while spring hibernated somewhere far off in the mountains.

As the sun warmed the chilly air, Hanz put his worries about Maria aside and went to the barn. He had begun making another violin and wanted to finish it before the snow started falling. Picking up a chisel, he continued carving away at the wood, letting his creative side take over, much the way he did when he painted. There was a method to his artistry, and he loved becoming lost in the process, his movements slow and deliberate, his senses heightened. The feeling in his fingertips intensified as he caressed the wood, watching it take form, conjuring it into a voluptuous curve like a woman's hip. To him, he was making a Soil Stradivarius.

After a while, Hanz abandoned his violin and quietly left the barn. As the orange ball against the blue orchid sky emitted its faithful rays, and the birds chirped a melancholy song, he sensed something staring at him, its eyes burning into his flesh. Hanz stopped and turned, and there, at the edge of the forest, stood a massive albino buck, fully grown with twenty-inch antlers fourteen points strong. It was magnificent! A glorious vision lasting only a glimmer of a moment before vanishing from whence it came.

Without a doubt, Hanz knew it was the offspring of the albino fawn he had saved all those years ago. Was it now there to pay him homage? Had he not saved that baby deer, its progeny would not be thriving in the forest today. The impact of that realization would remain with him forever.

Hanz stood there for a moment longer, hoping the extraordinary beast would return. Sadly, it did not, and he walked back to the farmhouse where a myriad of worries awaited him . . .

Maria.

His daughters.

Abigail.

The lie.

❧

"Hanz, nice to see you," Nora Yurkovich greeted the following afternoon as she answered her door. "What a lovely surprise."

"*Hallo*, Mrs. Y," he replied.

"Where's Maria?"

Hanz took off his hat and held it in his hands. "She's still not feeling well."

Nora frowned. "Goodness, that poor woman. Hasn't she suffered enough? . . . Come in, come in."

Hanz stepped inside the fancy home on top of the hill overlooking all the other properties below.

"How are those lovely daughters of yours?" Nora asked, taking his hat and coat.

"*Gute, gute.*"

"They always remind me of porcelain dolls. So graceful and delicate."

"*Ja.* That's why I call them my swans."

"Indeed," said Nora. "It's too bad you didn't bring your violin. My *Sohn* and his wife are visiting, and they adore your music."

"Unfortunately, I'm not here on a social call," Hanz said. "I came to warn you and your husband instead."

"Warn us about what?"

"Nazi danger. Your husband should hear it too; is he home?"

"*Ja*, he's in the living room." Nora led him down the marble-floored hallway lined with plants of various kinds, with multiple exotic birds in intricate metal cages of all shapes and sizes–some even as tall as Hanz. When they entered the large living room, Maximillian was sitting on the leather couch, smoking his pipe and reading the Torah. Their Siamese cat from

Thailand stared at Hanz with its striking blue eyes, their Saluki dog from Egypt sat quietly by its owner's feet, and their bearded dragon lizard from Australia watched curiously from its tank.

"Hanz," Maximillian said, closing the Torah and getting up to shake his neighbor's hand. "We weren't expecting you."

"I know. Sorry, *mein Freund*, but I wanted to stop by to talk to you and your wife."

"He thinks we might be in danger," said Nora.

Hanz nodded. "My *Bruder* told me the Nazis are escalating things now, rounding up all the Jews throughout Germany. I think it's wise that you finally leave for Sweden before they arrest you."

"Why? What crime have they committed?" asked Caleb, walking into the room with his wife on his arm. He was the Yurkovich's only son.

Maximillian patted Hanz on the back. "My *gute* man, *danke* for your concern. But the Gestapo already came here a few months ago, snooping around and asking questions. When I showed them our papers and told them to leave, they did."

The unconscionable crime Hanz's son-in-law had related two days prior, where the Schutzstaffel shot a Jewish man's wife and daughter simply because he told them to leave his home, ricocheted in his head.

Mrs. Yurkovich agreed with her husband, dismissing Hanz's warning, waving her hand in the air as if it were a magic wand rendering any threat impotent. "We'll be all right. Besides, who'll look after my plants and animals if we leave? My birds are spoiled," she said proudly, smiling at her neighbor. "Are you going to come over and take care of my babies?"

Hanz wanted to shake them. They had no idea of the danger they were in. Why were they being so stubborn? Don't they remember what happened to the Applebaums?

"You're staying for dinner, *ja?*" Nora asked. It wasn't a question. "I'll have my cook put something together for Maria, too. You can take it home to her when you leave."

Hanz reluctantly agreed, thinking about how to articulate how critical it was for them to leave. He even contemplated telling them about Abigail, how the Nazis slaughtered her family too, and she was now a fugitive hiding in his secret room. But he held his tongue, fearful that if the Yurkovichs were eventually arrested, they would share any information they had to spare their own lives. When staring in the face of death, people can be un-predictable, and giving up a Jew and the German harboring one would be valuable information indeed.

Dinner was like all the others the Wolff family had at the Yurkovich home over the years. Pleasant, cordial, laughing and enjoying each other's company. At the start of the meal, Maximillian raised his wine glass in a toast and said in Hebrew, *"Baruch ata Adonai, Eloheinu melech ha-olam, borei p'ri hagafen. (Blessed are you, our God, Sovereign of the Universe, who creates the fruit of the vine.)"*

As the evening progressed, Hanz himself relaxed, glancing about the large house, the many fond memories coming back to him. He reminisced about bringing Ava and Shaylee there for ballet lessons when they were young girls, their cute little tutus and leotards making him smile. Mrs. Yurkovich had been an instructor then, working in the Semitic quarter of Rothenburg ob der Tauber, teaching young Jewish girls dance and etiquette. She also had a small dance studio in an upper room of their home for private lessons.

"Our family has lived in this house since the mid-1800s," Maximillian said with pride. "May there be many generations more." Again, he raised his glass in a toast and said in Hebrew, *"L'chayim (To life)!"*

Everyone did the same.

"I too wish that for your family," Hanz added, the worry returning to his brow. "And that's why I came to warn you today." He thought he'd try one more time to convince them to leave. "Things are happening very fast now, and the smart Jews are leaving. *Bitte, mein Freund,* take your family to Sweden until this madness is over."

Caleb was getting annoyed with Hanz. "The smart Jews or the cowards? My parents aren't leaving, so stop the fearmongering. We are German like you, and also God's chosen people. As long as we put faith in him, he will protect us like he always has."

Hanz internally cringed. Those were the exact same sentiments Malachi Applebaum had expressed before the Schutzstaffel came and shot him and his wife. Nora and Maximillian, however, smiled proudly at their son.

As he left to go home, Hanz thanked the Yurkovichs for their hospitality and wished them well. He rode Bucephalus down the hill toward his farm, and when he glanced up at the twilight sky, he saw Ingomar circling above, watching him, following him. It reminded Hanz of that fatal night the murderer, thief, and rapist posing as a priest was hung from the massive linden tree close to his home two decades ago. Ingomar was there that night, too, sitting on the very branch that facilitated the execution. He was only a small fledgling at the time, and now his wingspan was so large it made a shadow on the ground as he flew overhead.

Like a dark premonition.

A week later, Ava invited her family to stay with them for a few days at the Steiner mansion in Berlin. Maria was still sick, so Shaylee went alone via train, and Luka picked her up from the station. As they pulled into the circular driveway surrounding a large fountain with Roman and Greek statues, they both stared in awe at the stunning estate, flabbergasted at the grandeur of it all.

"This house is like a castle," Shaylee said.

"Who would have thought my sister would marry into such money," replied Luka. "She doesn't really love him, though. It's all about status with Ava." He rang the doorbell, and a sonorous echo reverberated inside.

Seconds later, the butler opened the door. "This way," he said.

Brother and sister followed the aloof man, his dress and mannerism prim and proper. He walked them down the long hallway adorned with oil paintings of the Steiner family line, then led them into another lavish room. "Miss Shaylee Wolff and Mr. Luka Wolff," he formally announced.

"Shaylee, you're finally here!" Ava exclaimed, running up to embrace her, taking her hands and spinning her. Oh, how happy she was that her sister was going to visit for a while!

Luka, standing off to the side, opened his arms and waited for Ava to give him a hug too.

Starholf approached with a bourbon in hand. That night, he was not in uniform, and his face was relaxed and warm–much different from the usual Schutzstaffel persona. He greeted his sister-in-law with a kiss on her cheek, and shook Luka's hand.

"I'm not used to seeing you out of uniform," Luka said. He didn't like Starholf, jealous of the man, but he had learned to hide his resentment.

Starholf chuckled. "*Ja,* my mother insisted."

"I think you look rather dashing," said Ava, smiling as she gazed dotingly into her husband's light blue eyes.

"I want to see the library," Shaylee said. Her excitement was obvious, as if a little girl in expectation of her favorite doll.

"I'll give you a tour of the entire house, not just the library," replied Ava. She linked arms with her sister. "Let's go!"

"Don't be too long, darling," said Starholf, making Luka a drink. "You know my mother and her rules about being on time for dinner."

The girls scurried off, hand in hand, just as they always had when they were children. Ava left the prodigious Steiner library for last, and as she opened the double doors, Shaylee's jaw dropped to the floor. "My goodness, it's glorious!" she exclaimed, her eyes wide as she slowly looked around at the intellectual gold mine.

"Told you," said Ava, grinning.

Floor-to-ceiling shelves covered the high walls, with thousands of books of every kind. Each tome was cataloged by subject, title, and author, and a rolling library ladder allowed easy access to every one of them. An enormous mahogany desk sat at the end of the room, with two diamond-tufted leather couches, a large spinning globe, and a fully stocked bar.

"I could easily live in here," Shaylee said, in complete heaven.

Ava laughed. "I'm sure you could, judging by how much time you spend in the library in Rothenburg. Poor Christian, he fell in love with a girl who's already given her heart to a bunch of books."

Shaylee noticed a single portrait in a gold frame, of a beautiful woman stretched out on a red velvet chaise longue, wearing a flowing lavender chiffon gown, with two white Egyptian saluki dogs sitting on either side of her. "Starholf's mother is looking *hübsch und elegant (pretty and elegant)* there."

Ava smirked. "*Hübsch und elegant, ja.* But cold as ice." She went to the bar to make them drinks. "I think she wanted Starholf to marry some princess. Thank goodness at least his sister Gwyneth is friendly to me."

Shaylee pulled an old, leatherbound book off the shelf and brought it to the couch. "Don't they know you *are* a princess? A princess who grew up on a farm."

Both women laughed.

"Look at us," Ava said, handing her sister the drink. "Seems like only yesterday we were little girls playing with sheep and goats, milking cows, and swimming in the Tauber. Now I'm married."

"I should be too."

"*Ja,* and I'm surprised Christian hasn't proposed to you yet. It's obvious how much he loves you."

Shaylee hesitated. "Actually, he has."

"What? When?"

"Just over two years ago. I didn't tell anyone because he didn't have a ring at the time, and Papa wouldn't have approved. Then the war started right after. With Christian's monthly salary in the Wehrmacht so small, he still can't afford one, especially since he has to pay off his boat."

"Shaylee, why didn't you tell me? Starholf would have given him the money."

"*Nein*, Ava, *nein*. Christian would never accept; he has too much pride. We'll get married when the time is right. And I don't want you telling Mama and Papa, either. Promise me."

"I promise."

Shaylee took another sip of her drink, feeling the alcohol warm her body. "What about you? Are you and Starholf still in love?"

The green in Ava's aventurine eyes brightened. "Oh, Shaylee, I love him so much it hurts. We have a glorious life together, and I can't wait to start our own family. In fact, I have some special news of my own to share."

Shaylee grabbed her sister's arm. "Are you pregnant?"

"*Ja!*" Ava squealed. "I'm pregnant!"

Instantly Shaylee jumped up and hugged her. "How long have you known?"

"A few weeks."

"And you're only telling me now?"

"We were going to announce it last week at the farmhouse, but when Mama fainted, it didn't feel right to bring it up. We thought we'd tell them tonight, too, but she's still sick and they didn't come."

"You need to call her, Ava. When she finds out she's going to be a grandmother, she'll will herself better; I just know it. My heavens, she'll jump out of bed and celebrate!"

"I sure hope so. I hate seeing her ill like that."

Shaylee smiled and hugged her sister again. "Ava, you're going to be a mama soon! I can't believe it!"

Just then, the butler opened the double doors to the library. "Mrs. Steiner sent me to fetch you two. Dinner is served immediately."

While Shaylee was still in Berlin with Ava and Luka, Hanz went to see how Willamina Benowitz was doing. He hadn't checked in on the eccentric Jewish widow in a while, and with her hands full, taking care of not only her mentally challenged adult daughter but also the five orphans she had altruistically taken in, he wanted to see if she needed anything. When Hanz arrived, however, what he found was a grisly apocalypse.

There, scattered in the yard, were seven dead bodies—four shot in the head execution style, three in the back while trying to run. Just like when he witnessed the Nazis murder Malachi and Ursula Applebaum, Hanz stood there in shock. What did any of them do to deserve this? They were good, decent people, just trying to live their lives, and now here they lay, slaughtered like sheep. Crushing his eyes shut, he visibly shook.

The murders were clearly recent, perhaps even today, and Hanz immediately got back on his horse and galloped toward the Yurkovich home. The Schutzstaffel were just arriving as he neared the house, so he stopped Bucephalus and watched from behind a tree. His heart sank as five men in Nazi uniforms, with black shiny boots and guns drawn, exited the two cars and pounded on the door. When Nora opened it, the SS officers barged in and brutally dragged each family member outside, including the cook and the maid. Meanwhile, the commandant shot the cat and the dog.

God, why did none of my Jewish neighbors listen, Hanz thought! I told them all they must leave!

Unable to intervene, he could only watch in horror what happened next . . . Déjà vu . . . As if in slow motion, yet also very fast, Maximillian told the Schutzstaffel to leave his home, just like he did the Gestapo months earlier. They responded with a bullet between his eyes. Caleb tried to wrestle a gun from the officer next to him, only to be shot in the chest. The cook and the maid tried to run; both were shot in the back.

Nora fell to her knees, wailing in Hebrew, and her daughter-in-law ran into the house. The SS commander followed her and dragged her outside again, tossing her to the ground and kicking her in the back, her face hitting the dirt.

When it was all over, Nora and her daughter-in-law were taken away. Hanz, numb from head to toe, sat on the ground beneath the tree and wept. Then slowly, painstakingly, he went to bury Maximillian, his son Caleb, and the cook and the maid.

Inside the house, Hanz released the lizard and the beautiful parrots, hoping they could survive on their own. He then went back to Willamina Benowitz's home and buried five more innocent souls.

~c⊗ï⊗ɔ~

That night, when Hanz brought Abigail her dinner, he tried to hide the fear in his eyes. She thanked him for the food, as always, and he left. Closing the hutch door behind him, his insides tightened.

At one time Hanz was confident that the Gestapo or the Schutzstaffel would never raid his home. But now, with all of Germany losing its mind and the atrocities escalating, he wasn't so sure.

Was anyone safe?

~c⊗ï⊗ɔ~

The tragedies in and around Rothenburg ob der Tauber did not end there. Hanz went into town the next day to see his friends, Ollie van Heinz, Randolph the Bull, and Nila. He wanted to tell them what happened.

"What's wrong," Ollie asked. He was already at The Devil's Needle when Hanz walked in, and could tell his friend was in distress. "Is it Maria?"

"*Nein.* It's the Yurkovichs and the Benowitzs. The Nazis paid them a visit like they did the Applebaums."

"Oh no," said Nila.

Hanz went on to explain what he had witnessed. Ollie, Randolph, and Nila were aghast, not because this was anything new but because it had hit close to home again. The Bull looked at Nila, once more silently conveying his fears, his eyes pleading with hers to sell the tavern so they can leave Germany.

For the rest of the afternoon, the four of them conversed and comforted each other. Nila went to the kitchen to make the men her famous roast beef sandwiches with au jus and sauerkraut, and Randolph served Hanz his Chartreuse, Ollie his vodka, and himself his Mampe Halb & Halb. The atmosphere was calm and safe, until suddenly the front door of The Devil's Needle burst open . . .

A Nazi raid!

Several soldiers stormed in, guns at the ready. The same four Schutzstaffel officers who had visited the tavern five years prior, eyeing Hanz,

247

Ollie, and Randolph at the bar, were among them, demanding to see everyone's papers. When the commander approached the Bull, he smirked. "I remember you, Jew. *Hände hinter den Rücken (Hands behind your back)!*"

"I'm not Jewish," Randolph said, refusing to comply.

The commander nodded to one of his men, and the soldier hit Randolph in the head with the butt of his rifle, knocking him to the ground. Randolph tried to get up, but the soldier hit him again. And again. And again. The Bull lay semi-conscious on the floor, blood spilling from his head, nose, and mouth.

Soldiers entered the kitchen, and Nila screamed. The commander followed and walked straight up to her, pointing his Walther P38 pistol at her forehead. "It is in the best interests of the Fatherland that all such deformities be cleansed," he said, repeating the same Mephistophelian words he had uttered when he first saw Nila. Smiling, he pulled the trigger, and Nila collapsed.

By now Hanz and Ollie were horrified, hands on their heads, standing side by side. If it weren't for the two soldiers pointing a rifle at each of them, Hanz would have intervened.

The commander returned and approached Hanz. "I remember you too," he said, standing inches from him. "The Viking with a Roman face. Except now I can see in your eyes that you feel sorry for these vermin."

Hanz said nothing. He knew that talking back or showing disrespect would give them further license to kill.

The commander laughed at his silence, then looked at a frightened Ollie. "What about you, Olive Oil? You feel for those rats too?" He pressed his pistol into Ollie's stomach. "Let me see your papers."

Ollie fumbled to get his ID out of his breast pocket, then handed it to him.

The commander briefly looked it over and handed it back. Returning to Hanz, he said, "I don't have to check yours, do I. It's obvious your bloodline comes from *gute* German stock."

After the Nazis finished checking everyone's papers, confirming their Germanic ethnicity, they left as quickly as they came. Randolph was the only one they took with them, an officer on either side, dragging the Bull out as he looked over his shoulder at Hanz until the door closed behind him.

All the other customers ran from the tavern, leaving Hanz and Ollie alone. When they went to the kitchen and found Nila's lifeless body in a pool of her blood, both men broke down and cried.

Once they collected themselves, the two friends wrapped Nila's body in a blanket and took it to Hanz's car.

"I can't believe she's dead," Ollie said, still in shock.

"I'll take care of her," said Hanz, his voice thick with emotion. "If her mother agrees, I'll bury our Nila in a peaceful spot on my land."

"Randolph is going to be so heartbroken when he hears about it. If they kill him, at least his hell will be over."

Hanz stood there numbly, staring into nothing. "*Nein*, Ollie. Where they're taking him, his hell has just begun."

⁓⌇⌘⌇⁓

Hanz spoke with Nila's mother in Berlin, giving her the tragic news. Mrs. Vogel was a widow with no money for a casket or burial plot, so she was grateful he offered to take care of everything.

In the one-room morgue next to the barn, Hanz began the process of preparing Nila's lifeless body for its eternal resting place. This would be the hardest one he ever did. Even harder than when his father used to force him to work in that room as a young boy.

As he scrubbed his hands with the pine tar soap, he thought of the many happy memories he had at The Devil's Needle with Nila, Randolph the Bull, and Ollie. The men were the Three Musketeers—Athos, Porthos, and Aramis—from French author Alexandre Dumas' 1844 novel, and she was their D'Artagnan. So much love, laughter, and joy, ending in tragedy. So many future memories stolen from them.

When he gently unwrapped the blanket covering Nila and saw the blood still seeping from the bullet wound, Hanz broke down and cried again. Poor, sweet Nila, he thought as he began to clean her body. Murdered simply because she was born with achondroplasia. A little person with a huge heart. A beautiful human being.

Hanz stayed up all night making her casket, carving roses into the wood and applying a deep, dark lacquer until his hands were stained bronze. When it was dry, he buried his dear friend near his stillborn son.

Once the last heap of earth was packed down, Hanz prayed over Nila's

249

grave, then placed colorful primroses at the head of it. The wildflowers reminded him of a poem he once read, called *To A Primrose*, written in 1796
by Samuel Taylor Coleridge to mark his first encounter with the flower . . .

Thy smiles I note, sweet early Flower,
That peeping from thy rustic bower
The festive news to earth dost bring,
A fragrant messenger of Spring.

But, tender blossom, why so pale?
Dost hear stern Winter in the gale?
And didst thou tempt the ungentle sky
To catch one vernal glance and die?

Such the wan lustre Sickness wears
When Health's first feeble beam appears;
So languid are the smiles that seek
To settle on the care-worn cheek,

When timorous Hope the head uprears,
Still drooping and still moist with tears,
If, through dispersing grief, be seen
Of Bliss the heavenly spark serene.

And sweeter far the early blow,
Fast following after storms of Woe,
Than (Comfort's riper season come)
Are full-blown joys and Pleasure's gaudy bloom.

The poem celebrated the beauty and resilience of the first spring primrose, comparing it to the feeble yet hopeful signs of recovery from illness
or despair. Given the despair running through Hanz now, and the illness
consuming his wife, it seemed rather appropriate. Many years ago in Celtic
Ireland, people even considered the primrose to be sacred, believing it to
be the key to heaven. And yet, they also thought primrose would protect
them from evil fairies.

Ollie arrived at the farmhouse. He stood next to Hanz, both men quietly paying their respects, when suddenly a rustling noise came from the
nearby bushes. To their surprise, not one but three white deer showed
themselves, including the massive albino buck Hanz had seen recently.

"*Was für ein Anblick (What a sight),*" Ollie said, his eyes bloodshot and his face drawn. "Ghosts of the forest."

"*Ja,*" said Hanz. "I saw the buck just over a week ago."

"They've come to say *auf Wiedersehen* to Nila too."

Hanz nodded as the three albino deer stood in the clearing in the near distance, side by side like him and Ollie. Moments later, they slowly turned and went back into the forest.

"Just think, those *wunderbar* beasts are alive because of you. Because you saved that baby fawn twenty years ago."

"I wish I could have done the same for Nila and Randolph," Hanz replied, his voice cracking.

"I know you do, *mein Freund.* Nila is gone, but hopefully Randolph is still alive. Yesterday when they took him, it made me think of a lion with his mane shaved off. The Bull is a prideful, strong man, and they humiliated him, treating him like a pest. God help him, wherever he is now." Ollie looked up at the sky. "Why is it the *gute* must die and the evil ones gain fame for their atrocities?"

Hanz wiped his eyes. "*Ja, es ist wahr (Yes, it's true).* Unfortunately, bad men are immortalized for their crimes, and *gute* men are buried and forgotten along with their courageous deeds."

CHAPTER 26

aria's health deteriorated rapidly over the next few weeks, and the Wolff farm took on a gloomier atmosphere. In addition to grieving over the cold-blooded murders of Nila and his Jewish neighbors, Hanz was afraid for his wife's life. Frustrated by the doctor's inability to diagnose her in Rothenburg ob der Tauber, he took her to see a specialist in Frankfurt. Perhaps a more experienced and learned physician could determine what was wrong.

"Everything will be fine, *meine Liebe*," Hanz assured on the drive there, giving her hand an affectionate squeeze. "Soon you'll be back on your feet, babysitting your grandchild."

Maria nodded, her eyes betraying the skepticism her voice dared not speak. Wishful thinking, she feared. Though the news of Ava's pregnancy had brought her immeasurable joy, she wondered if she'd still be alive when the baby was born.

They didn't have to wait long for a diagnosis when they arrived at the hospital. More than just a stubborn flu, Maria had contracted extrapulmonary tuberculosis. It explained her weight loss, chills and fever, achy joints and bones, weakness and general discomfort.

"Given her symptoms, the doctor in Rothenburg should have known this," said Dr. Bauer, shaking his head. "Makes me wonder where he got his training."

"But you can treat it, right?" Hanz asked while Maria changed from her hospital gown back into her clothes. "She'll get better."

Dr. Bauer hesitated. "Tuberculosis has proved immune to the antibiotics we currently have, so there are no guarantees. But with rest, isolation, fresh air, and *gute* nutrition, it's possible she could improve. There's a sanatorium here in Frankfurt, but . . ."

"But what?"

"There's a war going on, Herr Wolff. If it were my wife, I'd send her to the Desert Sanatorium in Tucson, Arizona. The arid climate and abundant sunshine there are beneficial for the treatment of TB. She'll get the best care there."

The stress on Hanz's face turned severe. "America? *Nein,* that's too far. I can't do that to her. And if that's the only treatment, she'll get better quality care at home than from strangers in a depressing sanatorium."

"Then I recommend you take precautions and avoid physical contact as much as possible."

Maria read the doctor's lips as she approached the two men. "Oh no. Have I infected my husband? Could my daughters have gotten this from me?"

"Not likely," said Dr. Bauer. "Extrapulmonary TB affects the organs other than the lungs. But it could potentially spread to the lungs, becoming miliary TB, in which case it would be contagious."

"Will I get better?" she asked.

"*Ja, meine Liebe,*" Hanz interjected quickly, glancing at Dr. Bauer as he helped Maria with her jacket. "The doctor said lots of rest, fresh air and sunshine, and healthy food will spring you back in no time."

She looked at the specialist for confirmation.

Dr. Bauer managed a quick, unconvincing smile.

～⚜～

The revelation of Maria's illness—an eidolon that had lurked in obscure shadows, now given a name—cast a pall over the Wolff household. On the one hand, they finally had a diagnosis for her mysterious illness that had previously eluded them. Yet on the other, there was no surefire prognosis or path to recovery. In fact, the treatment was really just a hope and a prayer, sprinkled with good luck.

Concerned over the news that her mother had an acute case of tuberculosis, Ava returned from Berlin, joining her sister Shaylee in a vigil of care and affection around Maria's bedside, doting on her as if she were a child, just like she used to do for them. The two girls tried hard not to cry as they looked down into their mother's sickly face, her complexion excessively pale and her bright freckles void of their vibrancy.

Ava poured water into a large bowl to sponge-bathe her, while Shaylee applied salve to her dry lips. The water pitcher, hand-painted by Maria with lovely flowers, reminded Shaylee of her mother's garden, and she walked over to the bedroom window to look at it. The blooms, however, had long since turned shy and withdrawn, no longer blooming. The surrounding greenery had browned and wilted, appearing dead. The melodies of the songbirds could not be heard. And the sky above was depressingly dull and gray, instead of that vivid blue that always lifted one's spirit. "I wish it were summer," Shaylee said in a quiet, melancholy voice, her arms crossed over her chest. "That way we could bring Mama outside into her *schöner Blumengarten (beautiful flower garden)*."

"*Ja*," said Ava, gently smoothing the damp sponge over the alabaster speckled landscape of her mother's arms and shoulders.

Shaylee took the towel and followed behind her sister, drying her mother's skin so she wouldn't catch a chill. The care they were giving made her think of the famous novel she had recently read, called *The Magic Mountain*, written by Nobel Prize winner Thomas Mann in 1924. Considered one of the most influential works of twentieth-century German literature, the story reflected the author's experiences and impressions during a period when his own wife, Katia, suffered from a respiratory illness and resided at the *Waldsanatorium (Forest Sanatorium)* in Davos, Switzerland. As he visited her and became acquainted with the team of doctors and patients there, it inspired his novel.

The book, rich with allegorical characters and a sweeping critique of the dangerous totalitarian political forces that shaped Europe during Mann's lifetime, explored how one finds the true beauty of life only after experiencing suffering and tragedy. The premise of the story was strikingly similar to what happened to Maria, where the protagonist visited his cousin in a tuberculosis sanatorium and contracted the disease himself. Likewise, Maria had visited several orphanages in the past—notorious for tuberculosis outbreaks—and the doctor said her lowered immune system from the bacterial meningitis she suffered as a child predisposed her to the illness. Remaining dormant in her body for years, the Mycobacterium tuberculosis she came in contact with had now become active with a vengeance.

With the sponge bath finished, Ava placed a thick quilt over her mother to keep her warm. She brushed her long, fiery red hair, then Shaylee braided it in the traditional *Gretchenfrisur (Gretchen hairstyle)* that Maria liked. Afterward, they each read a letter Maria had received from two of her younger sisters in Austria–Brigitte and Karina. Maria had always been there for them when they were children, looking after her siblings when their mother died of consumption, and now they wanted to come and look after their older sister in return. Hanz had written back, though, telling them it was not a good idea for obvious reasons, not the least of which he was hiding a Jew, which of course he didn't disclose.

"You're going to get well soon, Mama," Ava reassured, as if saying the words out loud would magically make it so. "Aunt Brigitte and Aunt Karina even said you will in their letters."

"That's right, Mama," added Shaylee. "Your body needs time to heal, that's all."

Maria smiled, listening to her daughters trying to cheer her up with their gifts of hope and optimism. "Tell me a favorite memory of yours growing up here," she said, thinking about those halcyon days when she and Hanz had raised their girls–her greatest gift of all.

The twins glanced at each other, as if their mother were saying goodbye in some reminiscent way. Ava answered first: "I have so many *wunderbar* memories, Mama. It's hard to pick only one."

"Me too," said Shaylee, recalling the childhood joys they shared. "We had so much fun."

"But I always loved our family picnics by the pond," Ava continued, "where the two swans would visit. And the dinners, with everyone together, talking and laughing."

"And when Ava and I would curl up on Papa's lap, falling asleep as he read stories to us," added Shaylee.

"*Ja*. Or when you and Papa would dance in the kitchen, or cuddle with us kids on the couch. Even as a little girl, I knew there was something special between you and Papa. I didn't know what love was, but I could see it in you both, and it made me feel *gute*."

"I loved watching Papa paint you," Shaylee said. "It was magic to me, how he transferred your image onto the canvas. I used to stare at you while you remained still, thinking you were the most beautiful woman in the world. Papa was a king, and you, his queen."

Tears dampened Maria's eyelashes as if she were swimming in an ocean of happy memories. She looked at her daughters with immense emotion, her heart aching with love and pride. "You both turned out to be such beautiful, sweet young women, inside and out. How blessed I am to be your mother." She asked for a drink of water, and while Shaylee helped lift her head, Ava poured the water into a cup and guided it to her lips. "*Danke, meine Lieblinge (my darlings),*" Maria said. Exhausted, she drifted off.

Ava and Shaylee left their mother's side, quietly shutting the bedroom door behind them. They held each other close, just as they had as little girls, and silently cried.

⁓⊱✦⊰⁓

After the Wolff family had eaten, Shaylee prepared an extra plate of food for Abigail and handed it to her father. Ava was now also aware of the Jewish woman Hanz was harboring in that secret room, and she had promised never to tell her husband Starholf. Both girls reasoned that their papa was doing what was right in God's eyes, and though they knew it was dangerous, they nonetheless supported him.

"Can I bring you anything else? Anything you need?" Hanz asked, handing Abigail the plate of food with a jar of homemade wine.

"*Nein*, Herr Hanz. *Danke*," she replied. "You're very kind."

He turned to leave.

"I hear them talking and laughing sometimes," she said. "Can you tell me more about them?"

Hanz hesitated. He didn't think it was a good idea to encourage Abigail's curiosity about Ava and Shaylee–it would only make things more difficult for her–but he obliged and sat down across the table from her. "What would you like to know?"

Abigail's dark eyes, reflecting the flickering flames from the fireplace, turned a shade brighter. "Now that they're grown, how are they different from each other?"

Hanz paused, an emotive warmth curling the corners of his lips as he thought about his darling swans and how their individual personalities had developed over the years. "Shaylee . . . Shalom . . . is rather quiet and a deep thinker. She notices everything around her, and embraces life as if it were a painting in which she lives." Hanz chuckled–he loved that about his daughter. "And she reads one book after another. The library in Rothenburg is her second home."

"She gets that from me," said Abigail, her voice laced with pride. "The

256

reading, I mean. I love my books too." Her demeanor manifestly improved, talking about these two young women as if she had raised them herself instead of given them up to a German couple two decades earlier. "And Ava? What is she like?"

Hanz grinned. "She's more outspoken and a little cheeky at times. Restless, too, always wanting to do something. She's not into the arts like her sister, but she adores American movies and glamor magazines."

"Which one is married to the SS officer?" Abigail asked, her expression turning serious.

Hanz glanced away for a second. "Ava. His name is Starholf. They love each other, and he treats her well." How sad, he thought, that his son-in-law could not do the same for others. "They're also going to have a baby in the summer."

"A Nazi fanatic unknowingly married to a Jewish *Mädchen*," Abigail said, frowning. "How ironic." She looked directly at Hanz with a castigating stare. "Knowing her heritage, you should never have allowed her to court him."

Her rebuke stung, and he felt guilty, regretful. Desperate, even, knowing that Abigail was right. Despite being raised German, if anyone ever found out Ava was in fact Jewish and married to an SS officer, a tragic outcome would be certain.

Abigail stood and paced the room. "I'm putting everyone in jeopardy by staying here. It's not right, and I should leave," she muttered to herself, her inner conscience scolding her. "If they find me . . ."

"They won't," Hanz interposed.

She stopped, her frightened gaze piercing right through him.

"They came that night you escaped, remember? They ate dinner with me and my wife, drank my schnapps while they laughed and joked, and never suspected a thing. Why would they? I have family members in both the Wehrmacht and SS. We just need to keep you out of sight until the war is over."

Abigail went and stood by the fire, staring into the flames frolicking about as if Terpsichore laughing at her plight. "Each day down here is so long, Herr Hanz. My mind won't stop worrying, and I keep thinking they're going to break down the door at any moment and shoot everyone like they did my family."

Hanz studied her petite form throwing a shadow against the wall, noticing her long dark hair like his daughters'. The sheen of her locks reminded him of the coat on a black stallion he had once owned, and he had the strongest urge to walk over and caress the softness of it between his fingers. Orthodox Jewish women covered their hair around other men when they were married, and even did so if they later became widows. Hanz could understand why. "You're torturing yourself, Abigail," he said. "This war will not last forever. Be strong and have faith."

Her eyes bolted to his. "Faith? I have seen my son, husband, and parents brutally murdered in cold blood for their faith. Countless others have suffered the same for their faith. What *gute* is faith?"

Hanz had no answers. No one did. What could anyone say to make sense of a world gone mad and a Creator gone missing? If God did have His reasons for not stepping in, they were inscrutable to him.

"Even if I do survive this nightmare, what then?" she rhetorically asked. "My family is gone. *Meine Freunde* are gone. I have nothing." Hearing herself say the words triggered a new but familiar wave of emotion, and she lowered her face into her hands and cried.

With the crackling fire the only sound in the room, Abigail lay down on her bed, curled up in the fetal position, her ebony locks flowing across her feminine shoulders like the whorls of the Tauber River.

Hanz stared at her, wishing he could paint what he saw. Quietly he returned upstairs.

⁓⚜⁓

The days became a blur, and Hanz found himself adrift in a turbulent sea, impotent against the illness consuming his wife. She was getting worse, not better, and he couldn't take it anymore. It was time.

"Maria," he said one evening at her bedside, tracing the lines of exhaustion that framed her face, the pallor of her skin a stark contrast to the vibrant woman he had married. "I'm sending you to a tuberculosis clinic. You need proper care from trained physicians."

Maria sat up in bed, rubbing her eyes. "*Nein*, Hanz. I don't want to leave my home."

"You must, *meine Liebe*. I've thought it all through. You're still strong enough to travel, so we have to take advantage of that while we can."

Everything Maria both needed and loved was on or near their small farm, and the thought of leaving it to convalesce in some cold clinic with other sick strangers was not what she wanted. She'd miss her daughters and son too much, her husband, the familiarity and comfort of her home—especially the kitchen, with her beloved grandmother's hand-painted dishes, copper pots and pans—and even the farm animals. She'd miss her entire life as she knew it, and who knows for how long she'd be gone.

"I'm not going," she repeated.

"*Ja*, you are," said Hanz.

Maria wanted to fight, to be the feisty and passionate woman she was, but the fire inside her was flickering like a candle in the wind, the disease ravaging her body marching mercilessly forward, taking no prisoners, giving no quarter. Closing her eyes, she lay back down and asked, "Where are you sending me?"

Hanz wished it were somewhere close where he could visit. A clinic in Europe, perhaps even the *Waldsanatorium (Forest Sanatorium)* in Davos, Switzerland, where famous author Thomas Mann had sent his own wife Katia. But like Dr. Bauer had said, there was a war going on, and nowhere was safe. "Tucson, Arizona," he told her. "There's a clinic there where the dry climate will be *gute* for you, and Dr. Bauer said the medical staff are excellent. He knows the chief physician, and he's already made arrangements for you to arrive."

"America?" Maria asked in amazement. "That's so far away."

"I know, *meine Liebe*. But you'll be back in no time."

She gave him a tired smile, as they both knew that wasn't true. "Will you promise to write to me?"

"Of course. I'll be sending you many letters." Hanz stared at her then, with her wide eyes glossy and curious, her fiery red hair tousled about her pillow, her lips parted, showing her two front teeth with one slightly chipped on the corner—a physical anomaly he had always loved. In that moment, he didn't see a sick woman lying before him. No, he saw a beautiful girl he had fallen in love with all those years ago in the Inntal Valley of Tyrol, Austria. He saw, as always, the wild, redheaded Siren.

"You'll probably be at The Devil's Needle every night with Ollie and Randolph once I'm gone," Maria teased. "Acting like a single young buck again."

Hanz laughed. "If it makes you feel any better, I'll invite them here to drink instead."

"*Ja, gute.* But no one is allowed in my kitchen with their grubby boots on. Especially Ollie. He'll probably break one of my fine dishes that my grandmother gave me."

Hanz grinned, thinking of his lanky best friend, always so clumsy and mischievous, never without a comic book. Often he'd point his finger at Randolph with his thumb up, pretending it was a six-shooter, then pull the trigger. Randolph would play along and feign being shot. "Ollie's going to be jealous of you. He's always talking about visiting America someday, living as a cowboy."

"Then I'll have to tell him all about it once I'm well again and back home," said Maria. "We'll have a celebration and invite everyone."

Hanz tenderly caressed her cheek. "And what a beautiful day that will be, *meine Liebe.*"

⁓

Three days later, Maria was at the train station with her family, a single suitcase in one hand and her sun hat and ticket in the other. She was using a cane Hanz had made to help her walk, and yet still she labored. With great sadness, she hugged her daughters and son goodbye. Ava and Shaylee sobbed like little girls, and Luka wept too, all of them as if little children again, clinging to their statuesque mother with her arms open wide like an eagle's wings, gathering her young together.

Hanz boarded the train with Maria to help her find her seat and stow away her luggage. For a long moment, he sat there beside her, wishing he could go with her. "Ollie showed me a comic book about cowboys and Indians in 1800s Arizona," he said. "The land was full of funny cactuses."

Maria leaned her head on his shoulder. "I never thought I'd say this, but I'm going to miss that Ollie van Heinz."

Hanz continued in his best American accent. "Don't be breaking my heart and running off with some handsome cowboy, now."

Despite the sad moment, Maria laughed. She reached over and held his hand. "You've always said that when you are with me, you are home. I feel the same way, Hanz. You are my home, and now it will feel like I'm without one, until I am with you again."

The conductor began checking each passenger's ticket, announcing that the train would be leaving in ten minutes. Hanz hugged Maria and kissed her on the forehead, telling her that he loved her. As he got up to leave, she grabbed his arm and pulled him back down, her expression both sad and grateful. "Hanz," she whispered so softly he barely heard her. "That Jewish woman you're hiding in the secret room . . . Abigail . . . She's their mother, isn't she."

For a moment Hanz stared at her in shock. Then his brow relaxed, and he slowly nodded.

"I knew it. I could sense it in her demeanor. And I could see my daughters' likeness in her face."

Husband and wife held each other's gaze.

"Take care of our girls, Hanz," Maria said, lifting her chin and forcing a smile, struggling to be strong. "And our son. Don't let anything bad happen to them."

"I won't, *meine Liebe*. I promise."

CHAPTER 27

In the weeks following Maria's departure to Arizona, the Nazi terror continued to accelerate against the "Undesirables." Jews, Roma, and others were being arrested nonstop and transported to concentration camps, or simply shot. All this while Hanz was harboring Abigail in his basement. Though he remained calm, the intensity of the doom and gloom kept approaching like a train barreling his way.

Despite the dire circumstances, Hanz wanted to make Abigail feel at home. Not only through hot meals, books, and conversation, but also through tokens of kindness. So one night, he brought her a special surprise.

"What's this?" she asked, taking the small box from him.

He smiled. "A gift. Open it."

Like an excited child on her birthday, Abigail opened the box to find a little bundle of fur. "Oh my goodness! I can have a kitten?"

"*Ja.* One of the cats had them recently. It's old enough now to be taken from its mother." Even with barn cats, Hanz was kind and considerate, not wanting to traumatize the kitten or its mother. "Do you favor another color? There's also white, brown, orange, and calico."

"*Nein.* This black one is so cute," she said, holding it against her cheek and kissing its tiny nose.

Hanz thought for a moment as he watched Abigail fawn over the kitten. "Isn't it sad how human beings judge others over their differences?" he asked. "Instead of embracing God's variety, they're threatened by it."

Abigail agreed. "It's true. Such a shame that God's gift of color could be seen as bad."

"As an artist, I often think how dull and drab life would be without color. Only one hue of paint would make artwork a waste of time. If all gemstones were blue, or red, or green, they would lose much of their value.

And if there were only one shade of flower, how tragic that would be." He shook his head. "*Ja*, it is such a shame that humans take for granted the *wunderbar* blessing of variety."

Abigail's face softened. The words coming out of Hanz's mouth touched her deeply. "*Dankeschön so sehr für diese (Thank you so much for this),*" she said with gratitude. "I get so lonely down here."

"I could visit more, if you wish."

"That would be nice. I would enjoy that." From the warmth of the conversation, and the softness of the kitten in her arms, Abigail began to cry. "I'm sorry. It's just that . . . my *Sohn* . . . he loved kittens. I miss him so much."

Hanz put his arms around her. She wept on his chest for a long while.

~c◆x~

As he lay awake in bed that night, Hanz heard Abigail singing. Her sweet voice came through the floorboards, the notes soft and delicate, streaming out like silky ribbons flowing from her heart. But then the song turned to sorrow and despair.

The pain in her voice was palpable, as if the melody were a language all on its own, communicating in a vernacular only a musician would know. An unspoken lyric of deep emotion.

How in the world will I survive this pain, the notes cried out? I will die soon, just like my family.

As her song encircled him, resonating through his body, Hanz stared out at the moon through the window. Bathed in white the color of milk, glowing with the intensity of a star, the heavenly body seemed to have lowered to better hear the mournful cry.

Once it was over, a sense of wonder enveloped Hanz. The connection he now felt toward Abigail through the song was as if she were lying right beside him, the moonlight washing over them, her black diamond eyes transfixed on his. And suddenly a powerful sensation joined the wonder, like how the wind blows across the oceans, lakes, and rivers, creating waves. The same strong sensation as the gravitational pull of the moon, creating the ebb and flow of the tides.

Yes, Hanz wanted to pull Abigail into his embrace, like the waves and tides.

CHAPTER 28

Spring, 1942

Hitler's boots echoed ominously down the hallway as he tramped toward the Great Room at the Berghof, his summer residence. Ensconced in his delusions of grandeur, he silently reveled in his ambitious plans manifesting with rapid success throughout Europe, spreading out like veins with razor-sharp edges. I possess the absolute power and the unstoppable will to do what I want, he internally boasted. I will cleanse the land of its vile and dirty things and show no mercy. From sea to sea, like a hungry dragon, I will release my fury and annihilate my enemies from the face of the earth.

The Berghof was Hitler's retreat in the Obersalzberg, a scenic mountainside area above the town of Berchtesgaden in the Bavarian Alps. It became the Führer's second seat of government in the Third Reich, alongside Berlin, where the Nazi leaders built villas, SS barracks, administration buildings, and underground bunkers. Politicians, heads of state, and military leaders from all over the world met, dined, and negotiated at Obersalzberg before and during the war, including British Prime Ministers David Lloyd George and Neville Chamberlain, the leader of the Italian Fascist party, Benito Mussolini, and the Duke and Duchess of Windsor.

The oversized chalet, intended to impress, was decorated with opulence. Expensive Persian rugs, Gobelin tapestries, antique furniture, and famous artwork–both bought and plundered–made its way there. Hitler had a great interest in architecture and an earlier career as a struggling artist, and was heavily involved in the design and furnishing of his favorite home. He spent more time in the Berghof than he did in his Berlin office.

The Great Room was where Hitler received his important visitors. It was huge and had an enormous picture window that looked out at the majestic vista of the Untersberg Mountain in Austria. The large window could be lowered into the story below, leaving it open to the air, and on a clear day he could see Fortress Hohensalzburg, the centuries old medieval castle overlooking the city of Salzburg.

When Hitler entered the Great Room, immediately everyone stood and saluted him. Among those present were several of his key inner circle: Joseph Goebbels, Reich Minister for Propaganda and Public Enlightenment. Hermann Göring, Commander in Chief of the Luftwaffe and one of the primary architects of the Nazi police state in Germany. Heinrich Himmler, Reich Leader of the dreaded Schutzstaffel. And Martin Bormann, one of Hitler's closest lieutenants and his private secretary. A few other SS officers were present as well, including Lieutenant Starholf Steiner. He was honored to be invited there, and it was a great privilege to be among these esteemed, top Nazi leaders. What a stepping stone for his career!

Hitler sat at the head of the large mahogany table and paused. A dozen pair of steely blue eyes stared at the dark-haired man with small mustache and foreboding mien, wondering what their Führer was thinking.

"I am very pleased with the latest reports," Hitler finally said. "Despite the Americans joining the war, the Fatherland will prevail." His German Shepherd, Blondi, walked up to him, seeking his attention. Hitler was very fond of his canine friend and took her everywhere, even allowing the dog to sleep in his bed.

The officers exhaled a collective sigh of relief, hearing praise from their Führer rather than rebuke. They nervously glanced around at each other as they somewhat relaxed in their chairs.

"We must not let up, however," Hitler continued, his gaze hardening at the men around the table. "And the Jewish problem must be dealt with more expediently." Hitler expounded what the Nazis called the *Endlösung der Judenfrage (Final Solution to the Jewish Question)*, meaning the deliberate and systematic mass murder of European Jews–complete extermination. This solution had first been proposed in July 1941 by SS General Reinhard Heydrich, authorized by Hermann Göring. The methods of implementation, its scheduling, and planning were left to Himmler, Heydrich, and the different protagonists of the anti-Jewish policies.

Hitler continued spewing his vitriolic hatred like a demon explaining the rules of hell. "I don't care what you do, or how you do it. The young, the old, the pregnant woman, the small child, the elderly man with a limp and the old lady in her bed–round them all up. If they resist, shoot them on the spot and leave them there. They are all rats, and you must treat them that way." He stopped for a moment and walked over to the open window, staring out at the stunning panoramic view. "When I was younger, I wanted to be a professional painter," he said, reflecting wistfully on his youth, a sad, pathetic smile carving into his lips. "That's all I thought about."

The men at the table exchanged confused looks.

Hitler turned and gazed admiringly at *Venus and Amor* adorning the wall, by Paris Bordone, the Italian painter of the Venetian Renaissance. "But they all said *nein*. Every one of them." His smile morphed into a wicked smirk. "Now no one says *nein* . . . No one."

Starholf observed Hitler staring at the painting. He found it funny that such a small man with a bad haircut and stupid-looking mustache could be so powerful, like a modern-day Napoleon Bonaparte. It made him grin without even realizing it.

Hitler caught the amusement on Starholf's face. "What's so funny, Lieutenant Steiner?"

Starholf panicked. "*Ah . . . nichts (nothing), mein Führer.*"

Hitler walked right up to him, his eyes blazing. "But you were grinning."

"*Bitte vergib mir (Please forgive me).*"

"That depends. What made you grin?"

Starholf scrambled over what to say next. "I was just thinking about a joke I told recently."

"*Wunderbar.* Please share this delightful amusement."

Starholf's heart pounded so hard he thought it would explode from his chest. "A fellow officer had asked me why Jewish men wear a kippah. I told him it's to prevent their brains from splattering when we shoot them in the head."

Hitler laughed, and the rest of the men joined in.

~∽❧∾~

While Starholf was in the Obersalzberg, Ava invited her sister to Berlin. Shaylee took the train from Rothenburg, and the two siblings planned to spend some quality time together in the Steiner mansion: Breakfast on the terrace overlooking the estate, lunch in the backyard on the patio, and dinner in the formal dining room. Morning strolls through the luxurious garden, laughing and talking about their lives, and leisurely afternoons in the impressive library, picking boy and girl baby names. Ava was overjoyed about becoming a mother, and Shaylee about becoming an aunt. It was all going to be such fun.

From the minute Shaylee arrived, it seemed as if the two sisters had successfully banished the war, resurrecting their carefree days as teenagers on the Wolff farm. Ava gave the grand tour of the property.

"How long has this estate been here?" Shaylee asked, scanning the prodigious grounds as they walked.

"Decades, since the late 1800s," Ava answered. She knelt beside a rosebush and selected a bloom with vibrant red petals, bringing it to her nose. Cutting off the stem, she stuck it in her hair.

Shaylee did the same. "To think that a farm girl's children will grow up in a palace like this. How many would you like to have?"

Ava placed her hand on her stomach, a small baby bump barely showing. "It depends. Starholf wants a *Sohn*, so we'll probably keep trying until we have one."

"You could have a dozen *Mädchen* before a boy arrives."

"Oh my God, Shaylee, don't say that!"

Both girls laughed, linking arms as they continued their stroll, finding themselves in the middle of the garden.

"Mama would have loved this," said Shaylee. "To be here with us. It would have given her such joy."

Ava agreed, and tears welled in the siblings' green eyes. They subconsciously held hands—a habit they had formed since that first day Maria saw them as babies only a few days old, snuggling and holding hands, comforting each other with their mutual touch.

Shaylee looked around at the exceptionally manicured oasis. A large ivy-covered gazebo—triple the size of the one at the farmhouse and much more elaborate—sat in the center, with a huge fountain pond in front. Sculptures of Greek heroes and gods stood throughout, keeping a vigilant eye. And vivid flowers of every kind—pink chrysanthemums, red snapdragons, purple bigleaf hydrangeas, yellow creeping buttercups, orange tulips, golden daffodils, lazuline bluebells, Teddy Bear sunflowers, and Sweet Juliet roses—swanked their pulchritudinous charms. When in full bloom, the entire scene was magnificent.

"When you and Christian get married, you should have the ceremony here," Ava offered, wiping her eyes.

Shaylee walked over to Zeus and touched his chin. "Whaddya think, mister? Should we get married here?" she asked, looking deep into the face of the Greek god. "Hmm . . . You think so too, do you?"

Just then, Ava felt a tickle in her stomach, and she gasped. "Shaylee, the baby moved!" She waited a moment, hoping it would return.

"What did it feel like?"

"Like a caged bird, wanting out." Ava recalled before the war, before she was married and pregnant, when she and her sister were with Luka and Christian, lounging under the large willow tree in the yard at the Wolff farm. "What was that poem Christian recited to us under the willow tree when we were young teenagers?" she asked.

"The one about his mother's bird?"

"*Ja.*"

Shaylee knew that poem off by heart now, and she recited it . . .

> *"To cage a bird, binding its lungs,*
> *Stealing its voice of songs unsung.*
> *Like angels' wings, clipped will bleed,*
> *We cut the rose for selfish greed.*
> *A rock, a stone, a jewel, or gold,*
> *No animal should ever be bought or sold.*
> *Nor hunted, trapped, killed, or caged,*
> *Or like the precious bird, made our slave."*

"That's incredibly deep for a young man to write," Ava said. "I didn't realize it at the time, but it's beautiful. Meaningful, too."

"He's brilliant in that way," said Shaylee. "He has a *wunderbar* mind, when he wants to."

"You really love him, don't you."

Shaylee thought of Christian's kind eyes and gentle ways. "I do. And when the time is right, we will marry."

The baby moved again, and Ava put her sister's hand on her stomach. "Feel it?"

Shaylee nodded, fascinated.

"Soon I'll be holding my baby in this very garden, and you'll be here too, helping me," Ava said, a soft glow about her face as she smiled.

Shaylee smiled too, happy for her sister. And yet, for some odd reason, one which she did not understand, an unease formed in the pit of her stomach. A dread. She tried to ignore it as the two sisters kept holding hands, taking the long path back to the Steiner mansion.

After a gourmet lunch of poached salmon, sweet potatoes, fresh greens, sparkling apple cider, and an assortment of fruits and pastries–all indicative of wartime wealth and privilege–Ava brought Shaylee to the nursery to show her the lovely room. She had decorated the walls with a lavender wallpaper, hung purple silk drapes, and added cute baby furniture. Stuffed animals and toys were strategically placed for whimsy and charm. And in the middle of the room sat an elaborate wooden crib, carved with great detail into a large swan, its folding wings on either side serving as a baby change table. The swan was painted white, and its two eyes held real sapphire stones.

"My heavens!" exclaimed Shaylee. "This nursery is fit for a prince."

Ava smiled with pride. "Starholf couldn't believe I did all this by myself. He almost scolded me about it, telling me this kind of work is beneath his wife."

"Where did you find that *schöne Krippe (beautiful crib)?*"

"It was Starholf's when he was a baby."

Shaylee admired the artistry and craftsmanship. Whoever created it was truly talented.

"Let me show you his matching music box."

Ava took her sister to a small table by the window where another intricate carving sat. The unique box had been made by the same craftsman, and when she opened the lid, up rose a danseur and a ballerina in a swan costume. A beautiful rendition of Tchaikovsky's *Swan Lake* played as the figurines turned together.

"Starholf was certainly spoiled," Shaylee said. "It looks like something out of the Imperial House of Romanov."

"I know," agreed Ava. "He was treated like royalty as a child."

"Don't be surprised if the indulgent child resurfaces when he doesn't get his way."

Ava looked at her sister. "What's that supposed to mean?"

"Just that he probably has a side to him that's cold as ice. Being over-indulged as a child can give you a sense of superiority and entitlement as an adult. And he is in the Schutzstaffel, after all. They're known to be ruthless at times."

"Against our enemies, maybe. But he'd never treat me badly. He loves me and would do anything for me."

"*Ja*, because you're not Jewish."

Ava's face tensed, the conversation turning from lighthearted to more serious. "That's part of his job, Shaylee. As Germans, we're supposed to despise our enemies."

"They're not our enemies. And it's obscene what's happening to them."

Ava sighed. "I'm not saying it's right, but I have no control over that. I just want to take care of my family and live my life."

"Sticking your head in the sand does not make things go away."

"That's why you joined that ridiculous resistance group, right? To smuggle them out of Germany. Papa even forbade you but you're still doing it. You're putting your life at risk to help strangers, Shaylee, just like him. If you get caught, they could shoot you."

"What if it were you, Ava? What if the Nazis broke into this beautiful paradise and dragged you from here, taking you to a work camp? How would you feel?"

Ava contemplated for a moment. "That's a silly question, because it would never happen."

CHAPTER 29

Hanz brought dinner down to Abigail, as he had been doing since she first arrived. She stood behind the chair and waited for him to place it on the table, graciously thanking him. This time, however, as he was about to walk back up the stairs, she quietly said, "Hanz . . ."

He turned.

"I was thinking," she continued, fighting her trepidation. "Since Shalom . . . Shaylee . . . is away visiting her sister, why don't you eat dinner down here tomorrow?"

"With you?"

Abigail released a warm smile. "*Ja*, of course with me."

Hanz loved the idea. Whenever Shaylee wasn't home, dining by himself was a lonely experience, and he often thought of inviting Abigail upstairs to eat with him. But it was too dangerous. If surprised by the Nazis, they'd have to scramble to get her back in the secret room, and with no time left, he'd have to explain why there were two settings of dinner on the table. "Are you sure?"

"*Ja*. I would like your company."

Hanz too smiled. "All right. Tomorrow it is, then."

Abigail looked like she wanted to ask him something else, yet was afraid to.

He picked up on it. "What is it?"

"Umm . . . Before we have dinner . . . I was wondering if I could take a hot bath upstairs. It would be so nice to soak in a tub."

Hanz glanced at the water tap and buckets in the corner that were used for bathing. "Of course," he said, notwithstanding the same risk. "Tomorrow I'll fill up the bathtub with hot water for you."

"*Danke.*"

He nodded and left.

That night, Hanz lay in bed, staring at the ceiling. He was thinking about how he hadn't eaten dinner with anyone other than his daughter for so long, and that it almost felt like he was cheating on his wife. The flickering shadows cast by the moonlight through the window only exacerbated the feeling, dancing across his bedroom wall like specters of his life with Maria before she became deathly ill. Each movement seemed to whisper accusations, questioning the legitimacy of the budding connection he felt toward a new woman. And yet, beneath the compunction burned an excitement. A yearning for companionship, for the warmth of shared laughter and conversation once again—something he hadn't realized he missed so dearly until now. Yes, he was really looking forward to this dinner. Specifically because it was with Abigail.

Hanz listened to the nocturnal sounds interrupting the silence of the night, suddenly seeming so loud. The familiar hoot of an owl echoed somewhere in the yard, a small animal rummaged for food, and the breeze rustled the leaves on the trees as if they were clapping. Despite the distractions, however, his thoughts kept coming back to the Jewish woman lying in bed just beneath him in her personal bunker. Likely she was wearing the satin white nightgown he had bought her in town. How incredibly erotic she must look, with her olive skin and dark hair contrasting the silky white fabric. Closing his eyes, his carnal desires awakened.

Abigail, too, stared up at the ceiling that night, wondering what Hanz was doing. What he was thinking. She found him to be such a kind and gentle, soft-spoken man. Handsome in a way that was new to her, with his rawboned face and intimidating height conferring a powerful presence. She recalled how, over the years, she would sneak over to the Wolff farm, wrapped in a cloak and scarf, trying to get a glimpse of her daughters Ava and Shalom. When the twins were small, they would play with their toys on the porch or run around in the yard, engrossed in their own little world while she watched from behind a tree, tears flowing, arms aching to hold them, lips begging to kiss their chubby cheeks. Invariably, she would catch sight of Hanz and Maria, as well, who were always close by, usually holding hands and showing other expressions of affection. The German couple seemed so in love.

In those moments, among the waves of joy she experienced seeing her little girls, a tinge of jealousy would also prick at Abigail, knowing this happy couple had taken her place in raising her children. And now, in another twist of fate, she was living in their home and beginning to have feelings for that same man. It must be because of the tragedy she had suffered, Abigail reasoned, and that Hanz had risked his own life to save hers. But then again, he was such a handsome man, and there was something very lovable in the way he treated her.

❧❧❧

While Hanz worked in the field the next day, he whistled a jolly tune that inadvertently matched his mood. Subconsciously it morphed into the same whistle he used to do for his daughters when they were young—musical in tone, sounding like an exotic bird. With Shaylee away visiting her sister in Berlin, he had the entire house to himself, and he was going to spend the evening with Abigail.

Eventide came quickly, and Hanz began preparing their dinner. While the food was cooking, he filled the Victorian claw-foot tub in the bathroom with hot water, laying out fresh soaps and towels. Abigail was sitting on the love seat, patiently waiting for him to summon her, and when he opened the hutch door leading to the secret room, she excitedly ran up the stairs.

As she bathed in the caressing, soapy hot water—a luxury she hadn't had in so long—Abigail heard Hanz banging around in the kitchen. She smiled, thinking how endearing that was. The men in her family would never dream of cooking; that was women's work. While the savory aromas wafted into the bathroom, she leaned back in the tub and exhaled a reposeful sigh, closing her eyes as the rejuvenating power of a simple, hot bath penetrated her weary bones, bestowing its salve. I will thoroughly enjoy this moment, she thought. Enjoy this night of peace and tranquility.

For who knows how long it will last . . .

❧❧❧

When Abigail returned to the secret room, a beautiful dress lay waiting for her on the bed. Hanz had purchased the gift in Rothenburg ob der Tauber after she agreed to let him paint her portrait, and he wanted to do it with her in that stunning dress. "*Schönheit passt zu Schönheit (Beauty befits beauty),*" he had told the store clerk when he examined the gown. "I'll take it."

The elegant garment with matching shawl was a wonderful surprise for Abigail, and as she put it on, she felt like a princess—something she hadn't felt for an eternity. It was a poignant reminder of the simple pleasures and joys that had been stripped away by the conflict engulfing their country, momentarily transporting her back to a time when life was defined by beauty and grace, not survival and secrecy.

When Hanz came downstairs with dinner, he too was cleaned up, his transformation from a rugged farmer into a suave gentleman, striking. His overalls had been replaced with black trousers, a crisp white shirt, and a neatly tied bow tie, and his hair was sleeked back with his face clean-shaven. He looked more like the painter he had always aspired to be than the farmer he had become, his appearance evoking an air of sophistication and artistic flair. Tanned skin from working long hours in the sun reflected a manly glow, and his spirit, once burdened with worry, now exhibited renewed hope.

"*Wow, du siehst schön aus (Wow, you look beautiful),*" Hanz said when he saw Abigail in her new dress.

She smiled. "*Danke. Du siehst sehr gutaussehend. (Thank you. You look very handsome.)*"

He put the tray of food on the table and came closer. "May I kiss you on the cheek?"

"You may," she said, her heart skipping a beat.

Hanz leaned in and gently pressed his lips to her cheek, just underneath her eye. The kiss was longer than he had intended, her silky skin and feminine scent intoxicating him, as if he had consumed too much moonshine from the homemade distillery in Günther Nachtnebel's barn. As he pulled back, they stared at each other, enamored by the chemistry that seemed to ignite so naturally between them, all from a simple, anodyne gesture of mutual friendship.

Abigail finally looked away, breaking the intensity of the moment. "My goodness, Hanz, you made a feast," she said, turning her attention to the food he brought. Gefilte fish, kneidel (matzo balls), brisket, and kugel—all traditional Ashkenazi dishes—covered the table. "How did you know how to make all this?"

"I asked Shaylee to get me a Jewish recipe book from the library in Rothenburg."

Abigail was impressed, not only by his culinary feat but also his respect for her culture and heritage. "And you made chocolate babka—that's my favorite!" She picked up a piece of the moist, deeply flavored brioche-like cake wrapped around a dark fudge filling and topped with cocoa streusel crumbs, sinking her teeth into it. "Oh my God, I'm in heaven!" she mumbled with her mouth full.

Hanz laughed. He turned on the radio and lit some tapers, poured two glasses of wine, and together they sat down for a candlelight dinner to classical music by Beethoven.

"Mmm, this is so *gute*," Abigail said, taking a sip of the wine. The light from the candles reflected in her dark brown eyes, making them look like polished onyx stones.

"*Ja*, I've been saving that bottle for a special occasion," said Hanz, bringing the glass to his nose to inhale its succulent bouquet. "It's from my best harvest."

As the evening progressed, the conversation flowed easily. Exuberantly enjoying each other's company, they bonded on a deeper level, revealing their likes and dislikes to each other, what they were passionate about, and what they hoped for in the future. Though they had interacted for months since Maria left Germany, this was the first time they shared an intimate meal together, yet it seemed like they had shared a thousand. They both felt as if they were in a cocoon, not in denial of what was happening outside in the real world but allowing themselves a night of blissful respite.

They conversed about their favorite artists, musicians, and composers, focusing on the nineteenth century. Hanz expressed his admiration for the works of Austrian artist Gustav Klimt, his favorite being *The Kiss*, and English painter John William Waterhouse, favoring *The Lady of Shalott*. Abigail concurred, adding her esteem for the works of Jewish painters like Moritz Daniel Oppenheim and his *Marriage Portrait of Charlotte de Rothschild*, and Jozef Israëls with his *Alone in the World*. It was ironic how similar the two of them were, and they reveled in the experience, elevating their friendship into romantic territory.

A pause in the lively conversation came when they ran out of famous nineteenth-century artists to critique. Abigail smiled at Hanz and said, "I also love *your* paintings. Especially the ones you showed me of Ava and

Shalom. I mean . . . Ava and Shaylee."

"Ha!" he laughed. "You're just being kind to the man who cooks your meals."

"*Nein*, I'm serious." She reached out and put her hand on his. "Your talent is outstanding."

Hanz gazed into her large, dark brown eyes. As innocent as it was, he savored her touch, hoping it wasn't the wine that made her do it. "Maybe we should move to Paris," he said, his own eyes shimmering with delight. "I could paint there and sell my art, and you could be my muse. I had a chance to do that once when I was younger, but I never took it."

Abigail's demeanor suddenly changed, and she removed her hand.

His smile faded. Who was he kidding? The Nazis had infested Paris too; there was nowhere safe, nowhere to escape. And this wasn't a courtship, either. He was still married, and the woman in his secret room was not there by choice but by circumstance, having nowhere else to go. Her life depended on him.

"Abigail, I . . ." Hanz hesitated, unsure how to continue. "I want you to know that you're not just a responsibility to me. These past several months, getting to know you, albeit under these circumstances . . . It's been a lifeline for me too."

Abigail looked at him, her eyes searching his face for sincerity. She found it there, in the gentle furrow of his brow and the softness of his gaze. "Hanz, I . . ." She paused, gathering her thoughts. "I never imagined when I left my daughters in your barn that I would find myself here, with you, sharing a meal together, sharing our stories. It's given me a glimmer of hope in a time when I thought all hope was lost."

The air between them shifted, charged with an emotion neither of them fully understood but embraced deeply. In that moment, the secret room was no longer just a hiding place from the storm raging outside but a sanctuary of human connection, overlaid with an amorous milieu.

Hanz got up and retrieved his violin. Abigail had previously asked him to play for her sometime, when she was reminiscing about her father playing for her family and disclosed that he had bought one of Hanz's violins, saying it was the best he ever played. At the time, Maria didn't want her husband to play for another woman, and Hanz respected her wishes. And then when Maria became ill and had to leave for Arizona, it took him a while to even play for himself. But now, in the confines of that secret room, he wanted very badly to play for Abigail.

She watched in fascination as Hanz conjured the music she had almost forgotten. Bach, Beethoven, and Brahms—the same violin concertos her father had played—and others sang from the bowels of the instrument, ranging from the softest pianissimo to the loudest fortissimo. The farmer she saw before her was transfigured into a virtuoso whose hands could coax the most beautiful sound from wood and strings as easily as they tilled the earth. The joy that had seemed lost to the past was now resuscitated anew, forged in the crucible of war and woven through with the threads of loss. Both Hanz and Abigail felt it . . . The music, and its power to heal.

After the brief concert, Abigail turned the radio back on, and to Hanz's surprise, reached out her hand to him. "Dance with me," she said, her exotic beauty hypnotizing. "Then you can work on my portrait."

He stood and took her hand—like Maria's, how perfectly it fit into his—and led her to the imaginary dance floor in front of the fireplace. While the flames flickered their excited approval, his other hand pulled her in close, covering the small of her back. Torso to torso, her petite, delicate frame felt incredible in his arms, arousing his carnal desires once more to the point where the ground had disappeared and they were floating. Abigail laid her head against his chest, and neither one spoke, cherishing the intimacy. Hanz knew, despite everything—the war, the risks, the life and love he had shared with Maria—that he was falling for this Jewish woman hiding in his home.

When the song ended, Hanz removed the cover from his easel in the corner, and Abigail sat on the stool by the fireplace. As he began to paint, one side of her shawl slipped off her shoulder, and he told her to leave it—he wanted to capture that subtlety in his painting.

Finally, with the last brush stroke for the night completed, Hanz walked over to her. She stood and looked up at him with her mesmerizing brown eyes, silky olive skin, and full lips. Gently he pulled her shawl back over her exposed shoulder, her soft skin sending shivers through his body. Somehow his mouth met hers, and the fervent kiss lasted and lasted. Unexpected as it was, the encounter was as natural as breathing . . .

And as powerful as lightning.

Early the next morning, Hanz sat alone in his kitchen, drinking his coffee, an electricity still flowing through his body. He smiled as the morning light flooded the room, thinking about the night before. The sensation he was feeling was akin to the one he had as a teenager with Josie Blum, and then again when he married Maria.

Hanz wanted to go back downstairs and have breakfast with Abigail. Then lunch, then dinner. He wanted to talk with her, be around her, smell and touch her. When they shared their love of the arts, it made him feel alive again, that anything was possible, even with the madness of the world outside. And when he played his violin for her, his spirit soared. Being deaf, Maria could never appreciate the skill her husband had; she could only watch and imagine the sound. But Abigail not only heard the music; she was also emotionally moved by it. In her eyes, Hanz wasn't just a simple farmer but a talented and accomplished musician and artist–something he had always strived to be.

Hanz recalled when Abigail's shawl had innocently slipped off her shoulder, and how it added such a sensual appeal when he was painting her portrait. And afterward, when he pulled the fabric back onto her shoulder, his fingertips touching her silky skin sending waves of electricity through his body, culminating in the most powerful kiss he had ever experienced. Though he was a married man, he couldn't deny his feelings, and he wanted to share them with her. He knew he would never act on them, but he wanted her to know.

⁓⦿⁓

For the rest of the time while Shaylee was away, Hanz and Abigail were inseparable. Every day he went down into the secret room, and they ate and conversed together. Hanz would play his violin for Abigail, and he finished painting her portrait. They laughed and danced, unaware of the time, the day, the year, or even that there was a war going on outside.

One night their deep conversation extended long into the early morning hours, and before they knew it, the sun was starting to rise. Abigail heard faint tapping on the roof. "Is that rain I hear?" she asked, her eyes lighting up.

Hanz looked toward the ceiling. "*Ja*, I believe it is."

"It's been so long since I've felt the rain."

"Why don't we go outside, then?"

She hesitated. "Are you sure it's safe?"

"You know I would never put you in harm's way."

"I know, Hanz. I know you wouldn't."

Their eyes met—sky blue gazing at dark ebony—and in that intensity was an all-knowing, wordless acknowledgement of their strong feelings for each other. Hanz put her sweater around her bare shoulders and led her up the stairs, and after double-checking to make sure no one was around, motioned for Abigail to come outside.

As she stepped into the yard, the world seemed to pause in anticipation. Abigail welcomed the cool, gentle caress of the raindrops on her skin. Closing her eyes, she lifted her face and arms to the heavens, her smile a beacon of pure, unadulterated joy. She spun slowly, embracing the downpour as it drenched her clothes, her hair, her very soul. Happy tears mingled with the rain, and she whispered, "*Danke*. This is heaven for me."

Hanz stood back, his heart swelling with a mixture of pride and sorrow. To see her like this, so alive and radiant, was a stark reminder of the harshness of her confinement. Though he had taken her outside for fresh air and sunshine on many occasions before, it was always under a veil of anxiety, fearful of being seen. The potential threat of a nosy neighbor, a coincidental passerby, or God forbid, a Nazi soldier, was ever-present, casting a shadow over their moments of freedom.

But tonight, there was no fear. The rain was their ally, its steady drumming a protective shroud. Hanz watched as Abigail twirled and danced, her laughter a melody that rivaled the music he played for her. She was a vision, her dark hair plastered against her face, her eyes closed in sheer bliss as she reveled in the simplicity of the moment.

When the rain abruptly ceased, Abigail stilled, looking up to see a brilliant rainbow arching across the horizon. Beside it, the rising sun painted the sky with hues of pink and gold. The dual phenomenon was breathtaking, a gift from the heavens.

"Such beautiful light," she said, her voice filled with wonder as she absorbed the scene. The natural light was a stark contrast to the artificial illumination in the secret room.

"*Ja*, one of many kinds," he replied, his gaze fixed on her rather than the sunrise.

"How do you mean?"

"There's sunlight, moonlight, starlight, and planet light. There's the angel of light, and the light of God. Each one has its own magnificent brilliance."

"You forget one," said Abigail, her face softening in such a way that reminded Hanz of the teenage girl he saw all those years ago.

Curious, he asked, "Which light did I forget?"

She reached over and held his hand. "The light of love."

That very morning, after Abigail had returned to the secret room, Hanz made himself a cup of coffee. Looking out the large kitchen window, he saw his son being dropped off by a carload of fellow soldiers. Luka appeared disoriented, staggering as he got out of the vehicle. When he reached the front door, he stumbled through it, reeking of booze and cigarette smoke.

"Not an honorable look on you, *Sohn*," Hanz said, shutting the door behind him.

Luka sat down at the kitchen table and tried unsuccessfully to pull off his black military boots. "*Sohn*," he mocked. "I'm not your *Sohn*. I'm the child you took in who nobody else wanted."

Hanz looked at him, taken aback by what he said. "What? Where did that come from?"

"It's the truth, and you know it." After hearing of Ava's pregnancy, Luka had become increasingly bitter, staying out all night and getting drunk, fighting in bars and looking for trouble. It was bad enough that she had married Starholf in the first place, but Luka had clung to an imaginary thread of hope that the marriage wouldn't last, opening the door for him to be with Ava again. Now that hope was shattered.

"Stop talking foolishness, *Sohn*. Your mother and I have always wanted you, and always loved you."

Luka's head felt like it was splitting open, and as he leaned back in his chair, the room started spinning.

"Here, drink this," said Hanz, placing a cup of black coffee on the table for him. "And shouldn't you be at the barracks?"

"I didn't want my commanding officer seeing me like this again, so I came here," Luka said, sitting up straight to take a sip of the hot beverage. "I've already gotten into enough trouble with him."

Hanz sat down at the table. It was obvious his son was going through something, and he wanted to help in any way he could. "What's going on, Luka? Did you break up with a *Schätzchen*, or something?"

"*Nein*, my *Schätzchen* doesn't want me," he said bitterly.

"Well you need to smarten up and pull yourself together. You're putting your health at risk with this behavior, and you're jeopardizing your career."

Luka's eyes widened. "Who the hell are you to tell me that? You're harboring a Jew and playing house with her! You're risking your farm, your family's honor, and even your life for a dirty rat!"

Hanz stood, the coffee in his hand spilling from his cup. "Don't call her that."

"I'll call her whatever I want!" Luka yelled, scowling at Hanz. "You're an embarrassment to Germany for what you're doing!"

"You're not even supposed to know about it."

"Yeah, well, I do. I overheard Ava and Shaylee talking about her. Sooner or later, you're gonna get caught."

Hanz slowly sat back down. There was no point in debating it with Luka, especially when he was agitated and drunk. But he would not allow his son to be disrespectful in his home. "When you're under my roof, *Sohn*, you'll show me the respect I've earned."

"You actually care for her, don't you," Luka said in disgust. "While Mama is away in America, trying to heal, you're salivating like a starving hyaena lusting after a rat."

"What did I just tell you!"

Luka looked at the portrait of Ava and Shaylee hanging above the fireplace mantel, and the anger eating him alive momentarily quelled. "I care for someone too," he said. "A forbidden love, like yours." He dropped his head and started to cry.

Hanz softened. He could see his son was hurting, and it all stemmed from some girl. It usually does. "Who is this *Fräulein*?"

Luka slowly looked up. "Ava."

"Ava who?"

He hesitated . . . "Ava your daughter."

Hanz blanched, as if an invisible hand just slapped his face. "What kind of sick joke is this?"

"It's no joke, Papa." Luka knew he was saying too much, but the alcohol gave him courage, and he wanted to get it all off his chest. Maybe by some miracle, his adoptive father would understand. Perhaps even accept it. He continued, slurring his words, "I do see you and Mama as my parents, and Shaylee my sister. But with Ava, it's different. I don't see her as my sister. Not really."

Hanz stared at Luka in shock. He didn't see the scared little boy he had taken in, loved and cherished as his own flesh and blood, nurtured and raised to manhood. No, instead he saw an intoxicated stranger who had walked into his home uninvited and sat at his kitchen table, spewing unholy nonsense.

"I have been in love with Ava since I was a child," Luka confessed, feeling liberated by finally saying it out loud. "And she was in love with me. At least for a while."

Hanz tried to control the shock, the anger, building up inside him.

Emboldened by laying all the cards on the table, Luka took it a step further. "Ava and I . . . we've even been together."

"Nein!" Hanz yelled, slamming his fist on the table. Coffee spilled everywhere.

Thick tears rolled down Luka's cheeks. "Afterward, she said it was a mistake, but I know if I hadn't been adopted by you and Mama, Ava and I would be married now."

Hanz was stunned, flabbergasted, his face and neck turning flush.

"I'm telling you this because I thought you'd understand. You have fallen for a Jew, which is forbidden. And I have fallen for Ava."

"She's your sister!" Hanz yelled.

"Nein, she's not. Not by blood, anyway."

"You grew up together!"

"So what!" Luka yelled back. "I'm in love with her, and I always will be!"

Listening to his son's words, a rage came over Hanz in a way it never had before. As if he himself had been violated. "Did you rape her!" he demanded to know, his heart pumping wildly in his chest.

"Nein. She initiated it. She said she wanted to know what it was like to be touched."

Suddenly Hanz saw red. The world he had tried so hard to give his children—a place of peace, safety, and love—was all in vain. Everything was upside down and nothing made sense. Had he fallen into a deep sleep, and all this was a bad dream? Was Maria still here, and Abigail with her own family? Were the Nazis and the war just part of the nightmare?

With his rage on fire, the gentle giant's temper exploded, and he grabbed Luka by the collar of his uniform, punching him in the face. But Luka fought back, and both men thrashed about, wrestling each other, trying to gain the advantage. The kitchen table turned over, chairs flew across the room, and dishes shattered on the floor. From the thunderous vibrations reverberating across the floors and walls, the portrait of Ava and Shaylee above the fireplace mantel fell to the ground, cracking its frame.

And still they fought, neither one caring about the corollary damage to each other or the farmhouse. Years of unspoken, pent-up resentment resurfaced in them both, erupting like two competing volcanoes. For Hanz, it was the pain of his own son dying, replaced by a boy who grew up in his dead son's shadow, now becoming the man who soiled his daughter. And for Luka, it was the pain of his own mother dying and his father giving him away, now forbidden by taboo to have the woman he loved.

Though Luka fought like a cornered badger, he was no match for the towering, big-boned German farmer. When Luka fell to the floor, he tried to crawl away, but Hanz pulled him back by his leg, dragging him outside and tossing him to the dirt. Felix, Bastian, and Axel ran up to them, barking a frightened yelp. The chickens in the yard clucked a distressing trill. And the horses in the barn released a nervous neigh.

"Take it back!" Hanz yelled, standing over him. "Take back what you said! It's all lies!"

"Never!" Luka shouted, out of breath. "It's all true. Your precious swan is sullied!" He spat blood, then surprised Hanz with a swift kick to his bad knee, toppling him to the ground.

Hanz grabbed Luka and laid a beating on him within an inch of his life. He would make this wicked imposter suffer for everything he had said and done, ruining the pure image of his innocent daughter, his beloved swan.

Suddenly a voice cried out from the porch, "Hanz, stop! Hanz, you're going to kill him!" It was Abigail. She had heard the arguing between father and son, and the dramatic fistfight that followed, and came up from the secret room.

Hanz had his fist cocked, ready to release a blow that could level a brick wall. But Abigail's plea locked his elbow in place.

Luka, lying bloodied on the ground, half-conscious, glared up at Abigail with disgust. This was the woman who had replaced his mother? A Jew rat?

What a disgrace, he thought.

Hanz stood and pointed at him like God banishing a demon to hell. "You're right. You're not my *Sohn*," he said, wiping the blood from his mouth with the back of his other hand. "Don't ever come back here. You've shamed me and my daughter, and I never want to see your face again."

Luka staggered to his feet, glowered at Hanz, then turned and ran away.

⁂

"Heavens, what happened to you!" Gisela Lang asked, her bleached blonde hair in curls and her silk white slip leaving little to the imagination.

Luka stumbled in through her door. After the fight with his father, he hitched a ride on a hay wagon to her apartment in Rothenburg ob der Tauber. "When does your husband get back?" He knew the high-ranking SS officer was currently in Berlin.

"Not for a couple of days," she said, looking around to see if anyone noticed before closing the door.

Luka had met the salacious woman, still blessed with her youthful beauty, when he was on military leave and went to The Devil's Needle. Flirting escalated to a one-night stand, and soon they were having an affair. He'd visit Gisela whenever he was on leave or stationed close by, as her husband was rarely home.

"What happened? Why are you all beaten up?"

Luka went over to her bar and poured himself a shot of Jägermeister, tossing it back and pouring another. "I got into a fight with my father. I mean . . . the man who raised me." Staring at himself in the bar mirror, he grimaced at the inflicted damage. Two black eyes, a broken nose, his lips swollen and bloodied. If it weren't for that Jew he was harboring, Hanz might have killed him, he sardonically thought.

"Why were you fighting?"

"Never mind." He noticed Gisela's painted face, framed in blonde curls, with her amber eyes adorned in false lashes and her lips stained in red. "Why are you all dolled up, anyway? It's not even noon yet."

"Ahh . . . Luka, we're not married, you know." She had a visitor the night before, and had sent the young soldier out to get them food for breakfast.

Though fully aware of their unspoken agreement, their mutual use of one another in a game where the rules were clear–no promises, no expectations–Luka scowled at her. "You're cheating on your husband with me, and you're cheating on me with someone else." He laughed. "Why should I be surprised?" Walking up to her, he raised his hand to strike.

"Stop!" she yelled.

He glared at her and lowered his hand. "Whore!"

"Maybe . . . But you wouldn't have it any other way, would you," Gisela said, releasing a sultry grin. She liked that he was jealous. Her husband never was, barely showing her any attention, even though other men always chased after her.

Luka backed away. He was sickened by Gisela, sickened by himself, and in a twisted, perverse way, thought this was what he deserved–shame and humiliation for loving his sister Ava, even though they had biologically different parents. Being disowned by the only father he ever knew added salt to the wound, and with the only mother he ever knew, thousands of miles away, deathly ill and perhaps even dead by now, he felt totally alone in the world. Returning to the bar, he tossed back another shot of Jägermeister. Then another, and another, until everything became a blur. "My adoptive grandmother used to say, 'A man takes a drink, the drink takes a drink, then the drink takes the man,'" he laughed. "Well come and get me, Jägermeister, because I'm all yours!"

"There are worse ways to die than alcohol," Gisela said. She joined him at the bar, pouring herself a glass of wine.

The young soldier who had spent the night came back, knocking on the door with a bag of food in his hand.

Gisela didn't answer, and eventually the soldier left. "I'm not hungry anyway," she said, taking a drink of her wine.

Luka let out a laugh. "Like a dog in heat, they come for you." He went over to the couch and sat down, leaning his head back. By now, the alcohol was circulating in his veins, working its magic, assuaging his emotional pain. "You remind me of the harlot who rides a wild beast in the Book of Revelation."

"And are you the wild beast?" Gisela asked, approaching him like a ballet dancer, her movements languid and deliberate. She sat beside him on the couch, placing her hand on his thigh.

"Perhaps." As he lifted his head to focus his blurred vision on her, something bizarre happened. In his drunken state, Luka saw Ava sitting beside him, with *her* hand on his inner thigh, seductively smiling and flirting with him. "Come here," he said, pulling her close.

"You poor boy," Gisela replied, kissing his neck, her warm breath titillating his skin. She unbuttoned his shirt and inserted her long, manicured fingers to caress his chest. "What's troubling you? Let me help."

Luka grabbed her by the hair and stared deep into her face, seeing Ava's emerald eyes. "All I wanted was to love you!" he cried. He began kissing her, wildly, passionately, picking her up and taking her to bed.

⌘

Hours later, Luka woke up in a haze of confusion. "Where am I?"

Gisela lay naked next to him, smoking from an opera length cigarette holder. "You're in my home, love."

"What time is it?"

"Midnight. You slept the day away."

Luka sat up; the room spun. "I need some water."

"There's a pick-me-up on the nightstand beside you. Sip it; you'll feel better," she said, exhaling smoke through her nose.

"What's in it?"

"Two raw eggs, tomato juice, and salt."

Luka drank it quickly.

"I said sip it." Gisela shook her head. "You better not throw it up on my bed, now."

He lay back down and closed his eyes, still feeling drunk.

Gisela observed him for a moment. Beauty and charm were her currency in a transactional world, but she had stumbled upon information that could be useful to her. "What's this about a Jew hidden at your father's farm?"

Luka opened his eyes. "What?"

"After we made love earlier, you passed out, mumbling something about your father hiding a Jewish woman. You sounded mad."

"I must have been dreaming," Luka said, his heart thumping. Though he was angry at Hanz—furious, in fact—he would never want to get his father in trouble.

"You sure about that?" Gisela got up and put on her satin nightgown,

286

then walked over to her vanity and sat down, her long, thin legs crossed to one side. "You said quite a lot."

He sat up and stared at her as she brushed her blonde locks. "It was just a dream," he repeated, his pulse now hammering in his ears. "My father wouldn't do that."

She looked at him in the mirror. "You seem awfully nervous about something that was just a dream."

"What are you trying to do, stir up trouble? Do you know the penalty for harboring a Jew?"

Gisela continued primping in the mirror, removing her false eyelashes, the Ferris wheel in her mind spinning. "Why are you so protective of Hanz, anyway? He's not even your real father, and he just beat the hell out of you. Clearly there's no love lost between you two."

Luka's gaze hardened as he contemplated her question, the swirling mix of love, loyalty, and anger vying for supremacy over his emotions. "Because he still raised me. No matter what, I owe him that."

"Family ties in a time of war . . . They can be both a blessing and a curse, can't they?" She started painting her nails, humming an unknown tune. "Hanz and I have history, you know. Years ago, when I was a teenager, I had a crush on him. But he married Maria instead. It always irritated me that he chose a deaf woman over me."

Luka's mouth went dry, and the room spun again. Obviously, in his drunken state, he had confessed what he knew, and now he was panicking.

Gisela met eyes with him in the mirror. "Who's Abigail?"

Luka almost threw up the elixir she gave him. "Never heard of her."

"You know we're supposed to report anyone harboring Jews, right? It's a crime not to."

Luka got angry. "Look! There's no Jew being hidden at my father's farm, okay! If you tell anyone there is, I'll kill you!"

Her eyes lit up, and she cackled. "Don't worry, darling. I'll never tell."

CHAPTER 30

Three days later, Hanz was working in the far end of his field when he saw two military vehicles coming down the dirt road. By the time he rushed back to the farmhouse, they were pulling into his driveway. He had no opportunity to warn Abigail.

"Heil Hitler!" the SS commander said as he exited the first vehicle. He was a lot shorter than the four soldiers who jumped out of the second, with a deep scar across his left cheek, a glass eye, and a permanent demented grin on his face.

"*Guten Morgen (Good morning)*," Hanz greeted.

"Are you Herr Wolff?"

"*Ja*, how can I help you?"

"I'm Lieutenant Matteo Schröder of the Schutzstaffel. There's been a report that you're harboring a Jew," the commander said straight away, staring at Hanz to gauge his reaction.

"Really?" Hanz feigned amusement. "That's ridiculous. Who told you that?"

"It's not important who told us. What's important is if it's true."

"Well, considering that my *Sohn* and *Bruder* are in the Wehrmacht, and my son-in-law is an SS officer, it's rather strange that someone would lie about me hiding a Jew," Hanz said, hoping to put an end to the search before it even began.

"Exactly," replied the commander, turning his logic against him. "And I know who your family in the Reich are."

Hanz forced a nervous smile. "Regardless, you're free to inspect my property. There's no one here but me and my animals."

"I don't need your permission." Lieutenant Schröder snapped his fingers, pointing at the house, and the four soldiers immediately ran inside. "Who else lives here?"

"Just my daughter. She's in Berlin right now, visiting her sister."

"No wife?"

"She's in America recovering from tuberculosis."

"My condolences," said the commander, already dismissing her as dead.

The soldiers searched through the entire house, room by room, including the attic and the cellar. Hanz sat quietly at the kitchen table, his heartbeat racing, fearful one of them would open the hutch door and discover how to access the secret room. They searched the barn, and when they found Hanz's artwork and the latest violin he had been working on, Lieutenant Schröder questioned him on it, curious how a simple farmer could have such artistic talent. He even forced Hanz to play his violin to prove his musical ability, suspecting that perhaps the instrument belonged to the Jewish woman they were searching for. Lastly, they combed the surrounding fields and woods, looking for any shred of evidence that the report they had been given was true. But they found nothing.

"My apologies, Herr Wolff," Lieutenant Schröder finally said, walking into the kitchen. "Looks like you were telling the truth, and the report was a lie."

Hanz stood, expecting to escort him outside where the soldiers were smoking, waiting for their commander. "No harm done."

"These false allegations sometimes happen." The SS commander looked up at the portrait of Ava and Shaylee above the fireplace in the living room. "Your daughters, I take it?"

"*Ja.*"

"*Schöne junge Frauen (Beautiful young women)*. Did you paint that one too?"

Hanz nodded.

"Which one is married to Lieutenant Steiner?"

"Ava. She's on the left."

"A farmer who paints and builds violins," the commander chuckled. When he grinned, his glass eye created a sinister countenance. "That's very unusual, but what kindles the soul of another German man is of no concern to me." He looked at Hanz, examining his features and physical stature. "You know, Herr Wolff, you could actually be the poster child of the Aryan race. Golden hair, blue eyes, tall and strong. How many generations does your German bloodline go back?"

Hanz inwardly cringed. "I'm not certain." At that moment, he hated being German, simply from hearing such praise from this monster, and wished he had a different life. One with Abigail, in a different country, in a different time. The last few days he had spent with her were a private paradise in a world gone to hell.

"I bet a thousand years," said the commander. He shook Hanz's hand, and as he was about to leave, suddenly he heard a noise . . .

"Tap, tap, tap," came through the floor next to the hutch. Abigail was thinking of Hanz and issued their Morse code signal to get his attention.

"What was that!" the commander demanded.

Hanz's heart plummeted into his stomach. The patter—so innocuous yet so damning—seemed to reverberate off the walls, a death knell to the sanctuary protecting Abigail. "This old house is full of noises, Lieutenant," Hanz explained in a desperate Hail Mary. "Floorboards creak all the time."

The SS commander's eyes narrowed in suspicion. "Houses don't tap in code, Herr Wolff." He lifted his hand, ordering complete silence while he listened with a predatory gaze . . .

"Tap, tap, tap."

Hanz closed his eyes. Their private paradise was over.

❧

Lieutenant Matteo Schröder carefully examined the hutch and its uniquely designed shelving unit, discovering how to access the secret room. *"Unglaubhaft (Unbelievable)!"* he exclaimed, impressed as much as he was infuriated. He called the soldiers back in, and within minutes, the hutch was demolished. Seconds later, they ripped Abigail from her haven, kicking and screaming.

Outside, the soldiers viciously beat Hanz, while inside, the commander viciously beat Abigail. During the scuffle, she had knocked him over, and his glass eye popped out of his head, infuriating him. Hanz could hear her screams, and the more he fought to save her, like quicksand the more he sunk, bludgeoned to near death. "Abigail, I'm coming!" he yelled out as he lost consciousness.

With Hanz incapacitated in the back of a military vehicle, and the SS commander finished with his assault on Abigail, the Nazis went down into the secret room again, searching for any other useful evidence.

"Look what I found!" one of the soldiers said, waving a letter in one hand as if it were a golden ticket, holding two woolen blankets embroidered with the Star of David in his other. "They were hidden in the brick wall."

Lieutenant Schröder took the worn-out, yellowed paper and read the words from a desperate seventeen-year-old teenager, his permanent demented grin widening into a wicked smile. *"Wunderbar!"* he laughed. Walking over to Abigail whimpering on the floor, curled up in a fetal position, he kicked her to get her attention. "This letter is yours, no? I see your name at the bottom."

Abigail said nothing.

"You gave birth to twin *Mädchen*, and you couldn't keep them, so you gave them to the farmer and his barren wife."

Still, she remained mute.

The commander kicked her harder, and she covered her head. "Tell me or I'll go shoot the farmer," he threatened, standing over her body. Though the letter left no doubt, he wanted to hear her confess.

Abigail began to weep. *"Ja,* I gave them to the Wolffs. I had no choice."

Lieutenant Schröder laughed. "A German farmer raising two Jewish rats. This is the most incredible thing."

The soldiers laughed too.

"And one of them is now married to Lieutenant Steiner!" the commander roared, laughing so hard his eyes watered.

When the guffawing finished, the SS commander got serious again. "Send out an immediate arrest warrant for the two vermin."

"What should we do with the farmer and his Jew?" asked one of the soldiers. "Shoot them?"

Lieutenant Schröder thought for a moment. *"Nein.* Let's make Lieutenant Steiner decide."

❧

"Come in!" Starholf beckoned, sitting behind his desk in Berlin, the firm knocking on his office door sounding urgent. He had just returned from his trip to the Obersalzberg, invigorated by the meetings he was privileged to attend, especially the one at the Berghof with the Führer and his inner circle.

The door swung open, and two high-ranking SS officers walked straight up to Starholf's desk. "Heil Hitler!" they said, giving the Nazi salute, thrusting their arms in the air as if striking their enemy.

"*Guten Nachmittag (Good afternoon),*" Starholf said, returning the gesture.

The men didn't reply.

"What's this all about?" asked Starholf, a bit surprised at their aggressive posturing.

The senior officer spoke up. "Yesterday, a Jewish woman was arrested at a farmhouse outside of Rothenburg ob der Tauber. The farmer was hiding her in a secret room."

"*Gute.* But what does that have to do with me?"

The two officers glanced at each other. "The farmer is your father-in-law."

Starholf stared at the man is if he were crazy. Then he laughed. "Hanz? That's funny. Clearly you've made a mistake, *mein Freund.*" He took a drink of his coffee, thinking one of his staff was playing a practical joke.

"It's true. His *Sohn,* Luka Wolff, a sergeant in the Wehrmacht, told his lover, who then reported it."

Starholf almost choked on his coffee. "Is Hanz dead?"

"He should be, but *nein.* Lieutenant Matteo Schröder made the arrest, and he left that decision to you."

Stunned, Starholf didn't know how to react. Should he be angry? Or perhaps afraid of being disciplined by association? Hanz was a good man, he thought, but how could he do this? A strange prickling crawled all over his skin. "My wife will be very distraught over this news. What an embarrassment for me, as well."

The SS officers remained stoic, showing no empathy.

Starholf stood. "I must go tell her."

"Sit down, Lieutenant Steiner," said the senior officer.

"What, there's more?"

"*Ja,* we are also here because of your wife."

"Ava knew nothing of this," Starholf said, his heart rate elevating further.

"After the vermin was arrested, the soldiers searched the house, and they discovered why she was being hidden."

"And what the hell has that got to do with my wife?"

"They found two woolen blankets embroidered with the Jewish symbol and a letter from a teenage *Mädchen* explaining why she couldn't keep her newborn twins. She brought them to the farmer's barn and left them there, knowing his wife was barren."

Starholf panicked, his face turning pale.

"This Jewish woman confessed to being that teenage girl, and she's your wife and her sister's real mother."

"Impossible!" Starholf yelled.

"Your wife's real name is Ava Katz, and her sister is Shalom."

Starholf thought he was going to throw up and excused himself to the bathroom in his office. It took him a minute, but after splashing cold water in his face, he composed himself and reemerged.

The senior SS officer continued where he left off. "As a fellow, high-ranking Schutzstaffel patriot, we are giving you the benefit of the doubt that you were unaware of this crime. You may accompany us to pick up your wife, if you wish. We have not yet located her sister, but she will be found and arrested too."

Starholf's knees became weak. He didn't mention that he dropped Shaylee off at the train station that morning before coming into work; all he could think about was Ava. "My wife is pregnant with our first child," he said almost under his breath, still in shock.

It made no difference to the officers. "Of course you'll be granted an immediate divorce, and the child and it's mother will be taken away and dealt with accordingly."

Starholf silently prayed that somehow this was still all a terrible mistake. In his mind he saw Ava's beautiful face, smiling at him adoringly with her shining green eyes that had stolen his heart. "We're going to have a baby, darling," he recalled her saying that beautiful sunny morning when she disclosed the happy news to him. They had made love right after, intoxicated with each other and the promise of their wonderful future. How blessed they were, he thought that day. And now it has all come crashing down.

For the final dagger, the senior SS officer removed Abigail's letter from his breast pocket and laid it on the desk. As if it were rife with leprosy, Starholf didn't touch it, but his searing sky blue eyes read every word. It was all there in black and white, detailing a young Jewish girl's plight, pouring out her heart on why she couldn't keep her twin babies, and how she wanted the German couple, Hanz and Maria Wolff, to raise them as their own.

With a heavy sigh, Starholf exhaled, accepting that within mere moments, his entire life had drastically changed, his glorious dream becoming a horrible nightmare. "Let's go," he finally said, heading for the door. "I need to talk to her before she's taken in."

❧

When Starholf and the other two SS officers arrived at the Steiner mansion, Ava was in the nursery. So engrossed in the delightful task of further decorating the room for their unborn child, she didn't notice her husband standing in the doorway, staring at her.

"Goodness, Starholf, you scared me!" she said, glancing up from the box she was sifting through. It contained numerous keepsakes from her childhood that she wanted to place in their baby's room. Like photographs of her and Shaylee as cute little girls, and their pet sheepdogs Felix, Bastian, and Axel as rollicking puppies. Or her half of the matching doll set Maria had made for them. And little wooden farm animals Hanz had carved for his darling swans.

Starholf just kept staring at her as if he'd never seen this woman before.

"What's wrong?" Ava asked, noticing the distress on his face. "You look like you've seen a ghost."

"Come downstairs," Starholf demanded. "I want to talk to you."

"About what?"

He didn't answer, turning to leave.

Confused, Ava wondered why he was acting so cold toward her. Something was terribly wrong, because usually he would pick her up in his arms and kiss her, telling her how much he loved her. She got up and followed him downstairs to the living room.

"Sit down," Starholf said, his voice a commanding baritone instead of the kind and loving tenor she was used to.

Ava sat on the couch and stared up at him, wondering what she had done to upset him. She found it odd that no one else was around—not her mother-in-law, father-in-law, or even the household staff, as if everyone had been dismissed.

Starholf got right to the point. "Your father was caught hiding a Jew," he said with disgust.

Ava's heart instantly pounded in her chest. She had always feared they'd find out one day, and knowing the penalty was death, she panicked. "What? *Nein*, Starholf, tell me they didn't kill him!"

"Her name is Abigail Katz, and she was living in a secret room next to his cellar."

"Is he still alive? Starholf, tell me! Please tell me he's alive!"

He didn't answer, becoming more agitated. "Did you know?"

Ava was now terrified. The austere expression in her husband's eyes, not looking at her but through her, was chilling. Threatening.

"I said did you know!" he yelled.

Slowly she nodded and began to cry. Ava stood and tried to hug him, but he pushed her away. In shock, she shrunk to the floor, sobbing.

For a flicker of a moment, Starholf's comportment mollified, his voice softened, and he appeared sad. "They found a letter hidden in the room, Ava. The woman had left two newborns in your father's barn twenty-one years ago when she was a teenager. Twin girls named Ava and Shalom." He picked her up from the floor and held her tight, giving way to his own tears. "She's your mother," he said, his voice cracking. "You're Jewish, and your mother is Abigail Katz. That's why Hanz was hiding her in his home."

"*Nein!*" Ava wailed. "That can't be! . . . Mama, *nein!* . . . Papa!"

"Your father's still alive," said Starholf, feeling sorry for her. "But *ja*, Hanz and Maria adopted you and Shaylee as babies."

After a moment, Starholf kissed her on the forehead and let her go. "Get your jacket," he said, becoming rigid and cold again. "SS officers are waiting outside for you."

Ava felt the room spin. "I'm not leaving you. I'm not leaving our home."

He retrieved her jacket and took her by the arm, pulling her outside.

"Starholf!" she pleaded, trembling at her husband. The rose she had placed in her hair earlier–the same one she plucked from the garden when Shaylee was there–fell to the ground. "I love you! Please don't let them take me! *Bitte!*"

Starholf appeared tortured, an internal war between the woman he loved and the ideology he served raging inside him. Having no choice but to vindicate one and betray the other, he surrendered his wife to the Nazi regime.

As the SS officers put her in the back of the vehicle, Shaylee's words echoed in Ava's head: "What if it were you, Ava? What if the Nazis broke into this beautiful paradise and dragged you from here, taking you to a work camp? How would you feel?" Traumatized by her sister's prophetic supposition, she screamed, "Starholf, help me! You're my husband; please help me! My God, I'm pregnant with your child!"

Starholf only turned his back as the car drove off. He lit a cigarette and exhaled a billow of smoke, tears rolling down his cheeks. The crimson rose from Ava's hair lay still on the cold ground, and he picked it up, smelling its sweet scent. "*Auf Wiedersehen,* Ava," he said aloud, crushing the rose in his hand. "*Auf Wiedersehen.*"

CHAPTER 31

"There was this Polish Jew, very *gute* looking, who I had to take to Sachsenhausen," said *SS-Oberführer (SS-Senior Leader)* Zimmermann. It was the commandant's birthday, and though it was only afternoon, he was inebriated, which loosened his lips. "Long, strawberry blonde hair, and *wunderbar* backside."

The other SS officers listening to him at the party grinned.

"It was a shame having to drop her off. In fact, I wanted to keep her as a servant, but my miserable wife said no!"

The men laughed.

What the commandant left out was that he had raped her in his office before taking her to the concentration camp. A high-ranking SS officer disclosing he had sex with a Jew would have been seen as illegal and degrading, so he didn't boast about his crime. He had contemplated taking her home to work for him as a maid, a cook, or whatever—it didn't matter—which would have provided him ample opportunity to be with her as often as he wanted, but it would have been risky, not only because his wife would keep a close eye on him but also because he would be severely reprimanded if caught. No, to take a beautiful Jewish woman as a lover, he would have to do it carefully under auspicious circumstances.

"I'll tell you this, though, *meine Freunde*," SS-Oberführer Zimmermann concluded, slurring his words. "Had I lowered myself to bed the dirty creature, I would have had to bathe in bleach!"

All the men roared with laughter.

Christian was the only one who didn't find the vile jokes funny. Though not an SS officer, he had found favor with Zimmermann and was invited to attend the commandant's birthday party in Nuremberg. An entire pig had been roasted and served in the SS-Oberführer's honor, along with other delicacies and desserts rare during a time of war, and expensive Italian wine was flowing freely. Christian had accepted the invitation to be respectful and to indulge in the food and drink normal Wehrmacht soldiers were not accustomed to.

The German escorts hired for the party entered the room, and the men gawked in excitement as the scantily clad women fluttered around from one officer to the next. One of the girls with large blue eyes, dark eye shadow, and thick, flaxen hair done in an elaborate bun, placed her hand on the commandant's shoulder. "Do you have a smoke?" she asked with a seductive smile, her bloodred lipstick shimmering under the chandelier light.

Ogling her with his creepy smile, he handed her a cigarette and lit it, all the while their eyes never wavering from each other.

"You look like a man who needs someone to help you de-stress," she said.

"You can see that, can you? Well you're right, I do." He took her by the hand and led her upstairs to a room, closing the door behind him.

Christian wasn't interested in the women at the party—his heart belonged to Shaylee. As he was about to leave, he overheard Lieutenant Matteo Schröder talking with another SS officer, bragging about the arrest he had made. Yesterday, he caught a German farmer outside of Rothenburg ob der Tauber hiding a Jewish woman in his home. The funny part was, they found proof she was the mother of his adopted twin daughters.

"Turns out one of them is now married to Lieutenant Starholf Steiner," said Lieutenant Schröder, his glass eye sparkling as he cackled. "Can you believe that? Poor bastard thought he married a *gute* German girl, only to find out she's a dirty Jew."

"He'll be a laughingstock for the rest of his life," said the second officer.

Christian felt the ground beneath his feet move. A sudden panic ricocheted through his entire body, and he slowly made his way to the door. All the years of wondering how two dark-haired, lissome-framed twins looked so different from their blond and red-haired, big-boned, statuesque parents, now made sense. As did the fact that Maria never had any more children . . .

Ava and Shaylee were adopted, just like Luka!

As soon as Christian stepped outside, he sprinted to his car.

The drive to Rothenburg ob der Tauber was only an hour, but to Christian it felt like ten. Each mile was an agonizing stretch of uncertainty and dread, his heart pounding in his chest, his mind racing with horrifying images of what might be happening at the Wolff farm and the Steiner residence. But Shaylee had left Berlin by train that morning, rendering him a glimmer of hope. Perhaps when she arrived in Rothenburg, she decided to stop at the library before returning home. She could spend an entire day lost in her books. He silently prayed the whole way there.

As Christian entered the medieval town, its quaint beauty and splendid architecture now seemed like a cruel facade, hiding the monstrous truth of the wicked ideology lurking inside its walls. Each Nazi flag hanging from a building was another Mephistophelian gasconade from the evil regime. When he turned the last corner, he saw the woman he loved leaving the building with her bicycle she had stored there, attaching her small suitcase to the rear rack. "Thank God!" he exclaimed aloud. Bringing his car to a screeching halt, he demanded, "Shaylee, get in!"

Startled, she looked up. "Christian, what are you doing here? I thought you were in Nuremberg."

He nervously looked in his rearview mirror. "I was. Now get in!"

"What about my bike?"

"Leave it! I'll explain later!"

She took her suitcase and got into the passenger side, and he sped off.

"What on earth is this all about?" she asked, concerned over the urgency. "Is something wrong with Papa? Or Ava?"

His complexion had turned pale, his brow tense and creased. "*Nein*," was all he said, driving out of town like a madman.

"Where are you taking me?"

Christian knew Shaylee could not go home—not now, not ever—as the Schutzstaffel would likely be waiting for her. Yet where was he going to take her? He would have to get her out of Germany, but how? "For now I'm taking you to a house hidden in the forest. It belonged to a wealthy Jewish family before they were arrested, and the home is now unoccupied. We'll stay there until I can figure out what to do next."

"You're scaring me," Shaylee said, staring at him with her large, hazel green eyes.

There was no use not telling her, of trying to soften what he himself had just found out, and yet somehow always knew. "Shaylee . . .," he said, glancing at her.

"What . . . Tell me."

"I think you and Ava were adopted, just like Luka."

She looked at him like he was crazy.

"Think about it. You and Ava look nothing like Hanz and Maria."

"So what? Mama had a Russian grandmother with dark hair and green eyes. I told you that."

"You also told me Dr. Schultz said she could no longer have children after the tragic stillbirth."

Shaylee's heart started palpitating.

He reached over and held her hand. "Was Hanz hiding a Jewish woman at the farm?"

"*Nein.*" She lied.

"Shaylee, she's been arrested. And they found documentation explaining why your father was helping her."

"Why?"

"Because that Jewish woman is your mother."

❧

Shaylee was in shock.

Her world had ground to a halt, free-falling into an abyss, the inconceivable words from Christian's mouth echoing in her ears, refusing to coalesce into a coherent thought. "Mama," she whispered as images of Maria flooded her mind, happy and healthy, cuddling with her and Ava when they were small. Her tears would not stop.

Eventually the car veered off the main road, entering a narrow path that led through dense woods. The canopy of trees overhead formed a dark tunnel, mirroring the suffocating sensation tightening around Shaylee's chest. As the vehicle approached a clearing, an old, elegant house came into view, hidden away from the prying eyes of the world. Its stateliness stood in stark contrast to the simplicity of the Wolff farm, yet it seemed so lifeless, its soul stripped bare by the savagery of war.

Christian brought the car to a gentle stop and turned to face Shaylee. "We'll be safe here for now," he said, trying to comfort her. "I'll figure out a way to get us out of Germany. But you need to be strong, Shaylee. Can you do that for me?"

She didn't answer, wiping away her tears. No longer the carefree girl who dreamed of adventures and exploring the world, the harsh reality of war and the burden of her newfound identity pressed heavily on her shoulders.

"Stay here," he said. "I'll go inspect the property."

As he stepped out of the car, Christian hesitated a moment and looked around. The vacant house was dark and haunted looking, and electrically charged particles in the earth's upper atmosphere triggered the rare celestial phenomenon of aurora borealis, dancing like phantom aliens across the German sky. Though the colorful show was impressive, it only heightened the spookiness.

Cautiously Christian walked up the concrete steps to the house. The door was locked, which he found odd since the owners were taken away in haste and by force. Removing his jacket, he placed it against a decorative pane of glass on the door and punched through it, then reached inside and opened the door.

The broken glass crunched under his feet as he slowly entered the lavish home. With only the moon and stars giving their light, and an eerie silence surrounding him, Christian could almost feel the family who once lived there, as if their ghosts had remained. Their portraits hung on the walls, their clothes hung in the closets, and their shoes still lay on the floor. Their home was a miniature palace, with beautiful furniture and rugs, each room decorated with a skillful eye, the love and care of its owner obvious. And now it was forgotten and abandoned.

Christian went back to the car and got Shaylee. She sat on the velvet couch in the living room while he started a fire in the enormous stone fireplace, and soon the flames were blazing, warming the room with its heat and light.

Shaylee's mind raced back to the countless moments of her childhood, searching for clues, inconsistencies, anything that would make sense of this overwhelming revelation. But all she could see were the faces of Hanz and Maria, the German parents who had raised her, her sister, and her brother with unconditional love and kindness. "Why didn't they tell us?" she asked, the question hanging in the air, laden with years of untold truths and secrets.

Christian sat beside her and took her hand. "I don't know. Probably because they loved you and Ava so much, they wanted everyone to believe they were your biological parents."

Shaylee's eyes flashed up at him, as if only now realizing her sister was in the same predicament as her. "Christian, you have to go get Ava! They'll be looking for her too!"

"It's too late, Shaylee. She's already been arrested by now. It was sheer luck that I found out about this, and that's why I came to get you right away."

"How do you know she's been arrested?"

"Because she's married to an SS officer. They would have gone straight to Starholf's home."

"This isn't happening," Shaylee whispered, her eyes wide and frightened.

Christian thought for a moment, trying to piece things together. "What do you know about this Jewish woman who birthed you? And why would she give you and Ava to Hanz and Maria?"

"All I know is that she escaped when the Nazis killed her family, and she came to the farm for help. Papa said her father was the jeweler in Rothenburg who sold him Mama's wedding ring. Her name is Abigail Katz."

"Does she look like you and Ava?"

Shaylee paused, thinking about Abigail's features—her hair, eyes, frame, and complexion—realizing they were similar to hers and Ava's. "*Ja*, I suppose," she reluctantly admitted. The woman she thought was her mother was deathly ill in America, her father and sister had been arrested, and she had just found out that everything she knew and believed about herself was a lie. "I'm dreaming, and none of this is real," she said. "It can't be. Tomorrow I'll wake up and think, what a horrible nightmare." Laying her head on Christian's shoulder, she quietly wept.

Christian put his arm around her. "I'm sorry, Shaylee." He stared into the fire, knowing it wasn't just her life that had been altered overnight, but his as well.

≈✦≈

That night, the young couple crawled into a foreign bed with a large canopy on the second floor, naked under a thick, red tapestry comforter. Shaylee lay in his arms, and neither one spoke. Christian kept staring at the ceiling, trying to figure out a way to smuggle her out of the country. Smuggle them both out. Hitherto, they had both worked with the Resistance to help those persecuted by the Nazi regime escape Germany, and now he had to devise a similar plan for themselves, except they were wanted criminals. Traveling over land would be extremely risky. He could take his boat through the winding Tauber River to the Main tributary and then the Rhine, he thought, following it all the way to the North Sea. From there they would sail to England and begin a new life. Would that work? Maybe, maybe not. For now, however, they would live in this large, abandoned house, trying to squeeze as much life out of these perilous days as they could. When he had carefully planned and prepared everything, only then would they attempt the voyage that would save Shaylee's life. And his.

Shaylee put her hand on his stomach. "Christian . . ."

"Ja?"

"All this time, I wanted to wait until we were married before making love. I don't want to wait anymore."

He looked down into her face, glowing in the moonlight streaming through the diaphanous curtains on the window. "Are you sure?"

She nodded, and they began to kiss. Soon the passion became intense, unrestrained, even frantic, as if this were their last night on earth and in the morning they would die.

Christian kissed her entire body—lips, neck, breasts, stomach—touching every inch of her warm, silky skin. And when his knees parted her thighs, it was the most natural thing in the world.

With the rhythm of their lovemaking inaugurated, arms and legs intertwined, both became lost in the rapturous dance, fusing together into one. Christian made her feel loved and alive, and Shaylee made him feel alive and loved, each transcending the parlous circumstances they found themselves in. While the newfound lovers consumed each other, just outside, in the chaos of the world around them, every single Jew was either being arrested, shot, hung, burned alive, or taken to a death camp and gassed.

CHAPTER 32

The day after Ava's devastating arrest, Starholf visited the jailhouse where the Nazis held his father-in-law. Hanz sat quietly in the interrogation room, staring straight ahead. Even in that dramatic situation, with his insides in utter turmoil, he seemed calm, cool, and collected. Not for a second did he regret what he had done. In fact, he would do it all over again, from raising his beloved swans to helping their birth mother, regardless of their religion, race, or culture. Now he must face the consequences.

Starholf entered the room, decked in his military uniform, his face clean-shaven and his hair newly shorn. He dismissed the guard so he could speak to Hanz alone, and instantly a tension flooded the space between them. You could almost touch it, like two powerful, opposing magnets repelling each other. "Look at you," he said to him, scolding in tone. "You're lucky to be alive."

Hanz didn't reply. His body was black and blue, his left eye swollen shut, and his mouth and head bleeding. He had three cracked ribs and a badly broken nose. He had been slapped, spat on, and pistol-whipped, and when he tried to protect Abigail from being assaulted, the soldiers nearly beat him to death, hitting him over the head with their rifle butts.

"How stupid could you be," Starholf continued.

With his right eye still open, Hanz looked at his son-in-law, showing no emotion.

"Why didn't you burn that letter years ago? Why would you keep those filthy Jew blankets embroidered with that symbol?"

Hanz thought back to the night he stood before a small fire flickering in the firepit in the yard, intent on destroying them. But when he held the weathered note from Abigail Katz and the woolen blankets embroidered with the Star of David, something strange happened. Like magical rings of folklore that, when touched, tell stories of the past, confessing their secrets, an overwhelming sensation came over him. He was holding sacred and priceless relics—items to be protected not destroyed. Where once they seemed as if damning paper and cloth, an alien alchemy transformed them into steel and stone, embedding into his flesh, intermeshing with his soul. And not just his but also his daughters', like an invisible umbilical cord connecting the twins to their own flesh and blood. Rather than burning them, he poured water on the fire instead.

While Starholf clasped his hands behind his back and paced the room, Hanz looked down at his own hands. The callused hands that had worked hard his whole life, earning a living from the land, nurturing crops and livestock. The same two hands that had held and buried a stillborn son, cradled and raised twin baby girls, and caressed and loved a beautiful wife until she got sick and had to be sent across the ocean to America. His son-in-law's berating voice disappeared into the background—a faint babble from a nugatory man—as he studied the oil paint still on his fingers from painting Abigail's portrait. He wanted so badly to go back to that night, in their familiar cocoon, enjoying dinner and drinking wine together, conversing about art, playing his violin, and dancing to classical music. Staring into her dark brown eyes, becoming lost in them. In his mind he could see her sitting on that stool in that flattering new dress, smiling at him as he painted her portrait.

In an unexpected and peculiar turn of events, Hanz had fallen in love with this Jewish woman while his wife was away recovering. Though it was under lamentable circumstances, and not a pleasant arrangement for her to have to hide, they both endured and comforted each other, bonding over art and music, becoming friends, their mutual feelings developing into something more. The fact that she was the birth mother of his daughters also had a significant impact. Yes, falling for another woman while still married was completely wrong, but the stress and loneliness had been too much to bear alone, fostering fertile ground in his heart for the seeds of love to grow again. It didn't mean he didn't still love Maria, but only that he had developed feelings for Abigail too. Deep feelings. And now she would never know.

"Hanz, help me!" echoed in his ears, remembering Abigail screaming as they dragged her from the secret room. "Help me, *bitte!*" And then the

SS commander mercilessly beat her. He would kill that Nazi pig with his bare hands if given the chance.

Hanz shuddered. Never did he think his own adopted son would be the catalyst to betray them all, angrily shooting off his mouth in his intoxicated slumber. Betraying not only him and Abigail but also, unwittingly, his sisters Ava and Shaylee too. They could have lived protected from the satanic Nazi turpitude until it was safe for Abigail to emerge. They could have, and no one would have been the wiser.

But the Devil wouldn't have it.

In fairness to his son, Hanz recognized that he, too, had made a grievous mistake, letting his rage get the best of him. He could have handled Luka's confession of his feelings for Ava better, in a calmer and more understanding way. But he didn't, and tempers flared, leading to a god-awful outcome. Now it may cost the three women he loved their lives.

Starholf's eyes were bloodshot. Though he was very much part of the Nazi totalitarian regime and oppressive demagoguery, his world had been shattered as well. The morning of the arrest, none of them knew what was coming their way. They had a wonderful breakfast together, and then he drove Shaylee to the train station. Hours later, he had no choice but to hand over his wife to the Schutzstaffel. "You did this, Hanz," he said, appearing grief-stricken for a moment. "You did this to yourself, and you did it to your daughters."

"Where are Ava and Shaylee now?" Hanz asked, his very question causing his heart to instantly pound.

"Ava was arrested yesterday at my home. Shaylee they haven't found yet."

"I thought Shaylee was with her."

"She was, but I drove her to the train station before they came."

"They didn't catch her in Rothenburg?"

"*Nein*. It seems she's in hiding, and someone is likely helping her." Starholf scoffed. "The Wolffs are *gute* at that, aren't they. But regardless, she will be found."

It must be Christian, Hanz thought. "You could do the same for Ava. You could save her. Get her out of Germany."

Starholf became sour and staunch again. "*Nein*, I can't."

"Why not?"

"Because I'm an SS officer loyal to the Führer. And I won't help a Jew."

"That Jew is your pregnant wife."

"Enough!" Starholf shouted.

Hanz saw another man materialize before his eyes. A wicked creature who liked the taste of blood. "Where are they going to take Ava?"

"To a work camp," said Starholf, clenching his jaw. "Most likely the women's camp at Ravensbrück."

A large stone of distress sunk to the pit of Hanz's stomach, and he just sat there, staring into nothing.

"Look at me," Starholf said.

Hanz looked up.

"Know that this is killing me too." For yet another fleeting moment, his demeanor softened, his eyes glazing over. "I loved Ava deeply."

"Then help her!" Hanz pleaded. "Help the woman you love! My God, Starholf, she's carrying your child! Will you see them both destroyed for your Nazi ideals!"

Starholf leaned in, speaking directly into Hanz's ear as if to torment him. "Again, I ask you . . . Why did you keep that letter and those blankets? Why didn't you burn them? You have deliberately killed your precious swans."

For the first time in his adult life, Hanz lost his composure and began to sob, holding his head in his hands. "I don't know why I kept them!" he wailed. "I don't know!"

⁓⦿⦿⁓

When Starholf left, the guard brought Hanz back to the crowded holding cell where the other prisoners were also awaiting their fate. Most, if not all, would go straight to a concentration camp because the Nazis considered criminality an illness and prisoners beyond reform. For those who did remain in a "normal" prison, after they served their sentence the Gestapo would likely be waiting for them, taking them to a work camp as well.

The holding cell, cold and damp with no natural lighting, stank of vomit, sweat, and urine. Hanz found a corner and sat down, leaning his head against the cement wall, hoping his beaten and exhausted body could find sleep. But the maelstrom of bleak thoughts racing through his head like a wild stallion running for its life would not let him.

"Hey Blondie," said a dastardly looking man.

Hanz opened his eyes, sensing the inmate was addressing him.

"That's right; I'm talking to you."

Judging from his tone, Hanz figured he was violent. He just stared at the man.

"What are you in here for? Who'd you kill?"

Still, Hanz didn't answer.

"Hey! I said I'm talking to you!"

"I didn't kill anyone," said Hanz. The last thing he needed was to get into another fight.

The Irishman smiled, his teeth nearly black from decay, his greasy hair falling over his face and his dark eyes amused. "Sure, sure," he chuckled. "We're all innocent in here."

"*Nein,*" said another prisoner, staring at nothing. Small and harmless looking, his tone reflected deep remorse over his crimes. "We're all sinners who deserve what's coming to us."

The Irishman ignored him and kept his focus on Hanz. "You're German, right? Why would they put one of their own in here? You had to have done something gruesome. Tell me."

"I was harboring a Jewish woman," was all Hanz said.

The Irishman laughed. "What did she look like?"

No reply.

"Must have been pretty to want to save her. A pretty little Jew, locked up for your own private pleasure. I hope she was worth it," he added, making a disgusting sexual gesture.

Hanz glared at him. "You're awfully small to provoke a man who could kill you with one punch." He held the cretin's stare. "Like a little monkey harassing a lion."

The other prisoners laughed.

"You think I'm scared of you?" asked the Irishman. His expression suddenly changed, becoming unnervingly deranged. "Let me tell you why I'm in here. I killed a young, fresh whore when she complained I was being too rough with her. After they saw the bloody crime scene, they sent me to an insane asylum, and when a nun came to teach me about God's forgiveness, I strangled her with her rosary necklace." The Irishman smiled as if his crimes were a badge of honor. "But you know, I was actually doing God's work. I saved the whore from a life of sin, and the nun wanted to go to heaven anyway." He laughed and laughed.

Hanz just stared at the depraved man, feeling pity for the young girl and the nun, as well as all the others who no doubt fell victim to him after crossing his path.

"You know what else is funny?" he asked, his demented giggle magnifying his unhinged behavior. "They're going to hang me for killing a prostitute and a nun while they massacre an entire race of people."

"You won't be laughing soon, you stupid fool," said a tall, skinny prisoner with a chilling stare void of life, just like the corpse he had left behind when the authorities caught him. "Being hung is like Satan's tail grabbing hold of your neck and cutting off your head, pulling your soul into hell. And that's what you deserve, you filthy pig."

"Just ignore the imbecile," said another prisoner. "He doesn't get along with anyone."

"That's a bloody lie!" the Irishman yelled. "I like the American Indians. They helped my countrymen during the Irish famine." He opened his shirt and showed his tattoo of an Indian chief in full feathered headdress.

"Shut the hell up," said another prisoner. "Since you've been in here, you've told that stupid story twenty times. You just want to show off that dumb tattoo."

More than a million people had died during the Great Irish Famine of 1845 to 1851, either from starvation or hunger-related disease. Another million emigrated to England, Canada, and the United States, in vessels nicknamed "coffin ships" because of the malnourished and disease-ridden Irish refugees on them. Astonishingly, in 1847, a group of Choctaw Indians in Oklahoma had heard about the famine and collected $710, sending it to Ireland to help. What made the donation so remarkable was that many Choctaw themselves were living in poverty after being brutally removed a decade earlier by the U.S. government from their homeland in Mississippi, Louisiana, and Alabama and relocated to what is now Oklahoma—part of the forced mass migration of Native Americans that would later be remembered as the Trail of Tears.

"It's true, though!" said the Irishman. "Way back, many were starving in my country, including my grandparents who almost died. But when a group of Choctaw Indians collected money and sent it to help, they lived. Ever since, the Choctaws and the Irish have been good cobbers. Best of friends. I would never kill an Indian."

"And yet you kill helpless women," another prisoner said. "You're nothing but a coward and a psychopath. Too bad your grandparents didn't die. Then you wouldn't have been born and there'd be one less scumbag in the world."

The Irishman jumped up and attacked him. "I'll cut your throat while you sleep, you bastard! I'll slit you ear to ear!"

Hanz stood and got between them. When the Irishman saw the German farmer's full size and felt the strength in his arms, he backed away, mumbling incoherently in Gaelic.

"They should have taken that lunatic to Hadamar," another prisoner next to Hanz said when the commotion was over. "Patients in that mental hospital never leave."

Almost 15,000 men, women, and children were killed in the Nazi Euthanasia Program carried out at the Hadamar Psychiatric Clinic—one of six such killing centers. Aimed to restore the racial integrity of the German nation, "life unworthy of life" was eliminated because of mental, psychological, or physical disabilities that represented a genetic and financial burden on German society. Resident physicians and medical staff directly administered lethal drug overdoses or asphyxiated the unsuspecting victims with carbon monoxide in a gas chamber made to look like a shower room.

"My name is Enzo Grimaldi, by the way," the man said, extending his hand to shake Hanz's. "Joseph Grimaldi was my great-great-grandfather—a legend among clowns."

Hanz nodded. He had heard of that name before. Joseph Grimaldi, an English actor, comedian, and dancer, was the most famous and popular clown of the Regency era. His performance style had its origins in the Italian Commedia dell'Arte of the sixteenth century, but in the popular Harlequinades of the early nineteenth century he emerged as the founding father of modern clowns.

"My brothers and I still perform as clowns in a circus," said Enzo. "Well, we did before the Nazis changed all that."

Hanz thought of the colorful masks Ava and Shaylee used to make in Aadan Omari's ceramic workshop when they were young. Regular clowns with stars and hearts on rosy cheeks, and Pierrot clowns with white faces and crying eyes—how apropos. The memory bore through him like a nail right into his heart.

Enzo continued to talk, explaining what happened to him and his Jewish family. "We traveled throughout Europe, performing in many cities. Everything was fine until we came to Germany. One night there was a raid, and the Gestapo arrested all the Jews." He leaned back against the wall, releasing a regretful sigh. "The funny thing was, I had a feeling something bad was going to happen. An omen, if you will. We all had falsified documents indicating Aryan heritage, but I still kept my Star of David necklace. That morning, it broke and fell between the floorboards, and suddenly I got cold. Really cold, as if winter had consumed my body." He looked at Hanz. "Strange, right? It was a warning, I tell you. A warning, and I wasn't smart enough to heed it."

"I took my children to see the Grimaldi Family Circus in Rothenburg ob der Tauber about fifteen years ago," Hanz said. "Was that your family?"

"*Ja*," said Enzo. "When my parents were still performing."

"That was quite a show."

All this time, the Irishman was still staring at Hanz from across the room, studying him with eyes like two shiny black stones. "I have seen you before, Blondie," he said, his crazed grin returning. "*Ja*, I remember now."

"Leave him alone, you nutcase," said Enzo.

"I never forget a face. He was there too."

"Where?"

"At the insane asylum."

"I've never been to a mental institution," Hanz said, dismissing the madman.

"And I never forget a face. If it wasn't you, then it was someone who looks exactly like you." The deranged Irishman started giggling again, singing in a gleeful voice, "I killed a whore and a nun, and I didn't use a gun. They sent me away, but I'm back today. Now I'm going to hell, so ring the bell!" He stopped singing and looked at Hanz as if possessed. "I'll be waiting for you there, Blondie. I will be waiting for you in hell with open arms," he said, laughing wildly again.

⁓⸙⁓

The following day, they brought Hanz back to the interrogation room. This time his brother Severin was waiting for him. "Hanz," he said, his countenance reflecting both disappointment and distress. Though Severin was a Nazi officer who carried out his orders, the man before him was not just any prisoner who had unlawfully shown mercy to a Jew. No, this man was his only brother, whom he cared deeply for. Inside, Severin felt as if a piece of timber splitting in two.

"*Bruder*," replied Hanz, happy to see friend not foe.

Severin shook his head as he examined his brother's swollen face. "They did a number on you, didn't they."

Hanz gave no reply.

"It's a wonder the Schutzstaffel didn't execute you on the spot. They're trained to kill without hesitation, especially those who betray the Fatherland."

As Hanz looked over his brother's uniform, eyeing the fancy pins on his breast pocket, he pondered what was coming next. "I'll be given the death penalty, won't I."

Severin nodded.

The tragedy of it caused Hanz to tear up. Not for himself but for the women he loved whom he'd no longer be able to save.

"If there was something I could do, *Bruder*, you know I would." Severin became upset, knowing his brother was going to die soon. "But your actions, no matter how noble they seemed to you, have sealed your fate. The risk you took was beyond foolish."

"Risk? What do you know of risk, Severin? You talk to me of danger from the safety of your uniform, while I've lived with it, day in and day out, under my own roof."

"And look what it got you."

"Innocent people are being ripped from their lives and murdered like animals. Innocent people, *Bruder*. Doesn't that affect you?"

Severin removed his *Schirmmütze*, the symbol of his military allegiance and the gulf it created between him and his brother. "This is the law now. Fighting against it is futile."

A momentary silence ensued, charged with the unsaid, with years of brotherhood that no conflict could entirely erode. Severin leaned back, his eyes fixed on Hanz. "I'm going to try something. God help you that it works."

Hanz looked up, his eyes latching onto his brother's as if two sibling lions preparing for war. "What can be done?"

"I'm going to plead temporary insanity on your behalf. I'm going to tell the judge you've been an upstanding, loyal German citizen your whole life, and you've suffered from severe grief and depression since Maria acquired tuberculosis and had to leave to the US. It clouded your judgment and led you to commit this crime that you otherwise wouldn't have."

Hanz looked away. "I committed no crime."

"Listen to me!" Severin yelled, gritting his teeth. "I'm fighting for your life, here! They'll either hang you or put you up against a wall and riddle your body with bullets!"

"I don't even care, anymore!" Hanz yelled back. "I can't save my daughters and Abigail, so I don't care!"

Severin frowned at his brother's stubbornness. "I warned you about this a year ago, *Bruder*. I told you to be careful, to watch over your family and not take any risks. And I told you what happened to that man from the Resistance when they caught him. But you didn't listen."

"What did they do with her?" Hanz asked, afraid of the answer. "Where's Abigail?"

"I heard they took her to Auschwitz."

"So she's still alive," said Hanz under his breath, grasping at a thread of hope despite the horrific rumors he had heard about Auschwitz. "Why didn't they take her to the women's camp at Ravensbrück?"

"I don't know; I don't make the rules." Severin stood, placing his *Schirmmütze* back on his head. "But tomorrow in front of the judge, I'm going to stick my neck out as a colonel in the Wehrmacht and plead for your life. And when the judge questions you in court, I want both your answers and your face to be swimming in remorse. Do you understand?"

Though his head barely moved, Hanz nodded.

⚜

"Hanz Wolff, you have been charged with harboring a Jew," the judge said from his judiciary bench in the People's Court of Berlin several days later. In his late seventies, with steel-colored hair and a searing gaze to match, he fixed his attention on the accused. "How do you plead?"

"Guilty," Hanz answered unequivocally, impenitent of his alleged crime. Abigail's face flashed through his mind, her brown, doe-like eyes shining as she smiled. The image was so vivid and clear, it made his heart ache over failing to protect her.

An obtrusive chatter rippled through the courtroom until Judge Leonardo Von Alvensleben silenced the audience. "It's one thing to harbor a Jew, Herr Wolff, but it's entirely another to raise her children as your own. Did you father these twins?"

"*Nein, Herr Vorsitzender (Mister Chairman)*. They were abandoned as infants in my barn." As he said the words, a strange sensation overtook Hanz. He was speaking a truth he had concealed for over twenty years as if it suddenly mattered none. Like opening a forbidden tomb that had been sealed for eons.

"Why didn't you take them to a Jewish orphanage?"

"Because my wife had suffered a tragic stillbirth," Hanz explained. He paused, remembering when he had held the diminutive infant in his hands before burying it. The child who would have been his son. How different things would have been had he lived. "Afterward, she was deemed infertile, and that's why we decided to keep the twin girls. At the time, we thought it was a gift."

"A Semitic gift," Judge Von Alvensleben scoffed, shaking his head. "And then years later, you allowed one of them to marry an SS officer, knowing of her Jewry. Lieutenant Starholf Steiner comes from a long line of dignified German families of noble birth. How dare you attempt to taint his bloodline with a dirty Jew."

Again, the gallery erupted in chaos.

"Enough!" the judge ordered, slamming his gavel down. The crowd went silent, and he returned to Hanz. "You are deserving of death, Herr Wolff. Death for the crime of harboring a Jew."

A sudden dizziness slapped Hanz in the face. Severin's head dropped to the floor.

"Your *Bruder*, Colonel Severin Wolff of the Wehrmacht, has told me you suffered a mental breakdown, becoming temporarily insane after your wife had to be sent to America to recover from tuberculosis. He wrote in his statement, and I quote: 'It clouded his judgment and led him to commit this crime he otherwise wouldn't have.' Do you agree with your *Bruder?*"

Silence . . .

"Herr Wolff, I asked you a direct question!"

With his eyes to the ground, Hanz forced out, "*Ja, Herr Vorsitzender.*"

Judge Von Alvensleben leaned back in his chair, staring at Hanz with contemplative eyes. Seconds later, he said, "We'll recess for an hour, and I'll come back with my judgment," striking his gavel and exiting to his chambers.

Hanz and Severin were forbidden from leaving the courtroom, remaining seated in silence, side by side. Surprisingly, it brought back fond memories for Hanz, recalling when he was a teenager and his brother a young boy, sitting like that in church. He would try to make Severin laugh, whispering jokes about the priest or the choir, or the woman with the funny hat, or the man asleep from boredom and snoring like a pig, until his mother would throw a scolding look his way. Hanz would turn and make a funny face at Severin, who would giggle. And now, here they were, sitting side by side again but as grown men, two blond-haired, blue-eyed brothers, one in a prison uniform, the other a Nazi uniform.

"I have met someone," Severin said, breaking the silence.

Hanz looked at him. "*Wunderbar.* I'm happy for you, *Bruder.*"

"We're planning to be married soon, and I was going to ask you to be my best man." Severin became emotional, holding back tears, finally ready to say what he had been avoiding. "If the sentence is death, I'm going to ask if I can take your body back to the farm. I'll bury you beside your *Sohn* in Grandfather's suit that Grandmother gave me when he died, and I'll put a picture of Maria in the breast pocket."

"*Danke,*" said Hanz, the reality of the situation now bearing down on him.

"Is there anything else you want me to do for you, Hanz?" He knew that once the judge ruled, he would likely never see his brother again.

Hanz thought for a moment. "Bury me with my violin, and the last painting I did of Ava and Shaylee–it's hanging above the fireplace. Place my hand over the pocket with Maria's photo in it, and when the coffin is in the ground, sprinkle flowers on it from her garden."

"What do you want me to tell Maria when I write to her at the clinic in Arizona?"

Hanz thought carefully about this one. "Lie to her," he said. "Tell her that Ava and Shaylee made it to Sweden. Until you know for sure what happened to them, I want Maria believing they're safe."

"And what about you? What do I tell her?"

Closing his eyes, Hanz lowered his head and ran his fingers though his hair, not wanting to say the rest. Wanting it to be just a bad dream. Wanting to wake up at the farm, take a breath of fresh country air, and tend to his animals, his crops, and his vineyard. When he lifted his head again, he said, "Tell Maria that I died doing what was right in God's eyes . . . And tell her that my last thoughts were of her."

Judge Von Alvensleben had said he'd recess for only an hour before coming back with his judgment, but three had passed. The wait was unbearable, making Hanz's stomach burn from worry, causing a metallic taste in his mouth. This must be how the Roman gladiators felt, he thought. Thumbs up, you live. Thumbs down, you die. Those who survived the battle entered and left the Colosseum through the "Gate of Life." Those who died left through the "Gate of Death," also known in Latin as *Porta Libitinaria (Door of Death)*.

Finally Judge Von Alvensleben returned.

"All rise," said the bailiff.

The audience rose.

"You may be seated," said the judge as he took his place. "Except for you, Herr Wolff."

Hanz remained standing, though his knees threatened to buckle.

As the silver-haired judge sat on his elevated judiciary bench and stared down at the accused, it appeared as if God himself were about to render his judgment on mortal man. "Like I said, Herr Wolff, you deserve to be executed for your crime. But instead, I'm sentencing you to two years of house arrest."

The gallery went wild.

"Silence!" exclaimed the judge, slamming his gavel again.

Everyone obeyed.

"You're a farmer, but also an undertaker; are you not, Herr Wolff?"

"*Ja, Herr Vorsitzender.*" Hanz suddenly recognized the man holding the gavel. It had taken him a while to place the face, but like a veil lifting to expose what was hidden, he remembered shaking the judge's hand years ago. Leonardo Von Alvensleben had been to the Wolff property with his mother as a younger man, when Hanz and Maria first took over the farm. The judge's father had died in the medieval town of Rothenburg ob der Tauber, a place the senior Von Alvensleben and his wife had adored, and he wanted to be laid to rest on a small burial plot he had purchased overlooking the Tauber River. Hanz had been hired by the family to prepare his body.

The kind way Hanz had treated the judge's mother, and the outstanding job he did on his father, was enough to make Judge Von Alvensleben spare his life in return. A stern judge who ordered death as easily as lighting a match, had shown rare leniency for personal reasons.

"I must warn you, however," Judge Von Alvensleben added, "that violation of this judgment, or any other involvement with Jewry, will result in your certain death. Furthermore, from this day forward, your farm outside of Rothenburg ob der Tauber now belongs to your *Bruder*, Colonel Severin Wolff of the Third Reich, whom you owe your life to."

Hanz was both stunned and grateful when he heard the sentence. As they released him into the custody of his brother, murmurs from the gallery could be heard, hurling obscenities at him. They wanted blood. The court guard removed his handcuffs, and Hanz walked behind his brother toward the door.

"Traitor!"

"Jew lover!"

"Son of Satan!"

He was spat on and cursed all the way to the courtroom entrance, and when the two large doors of the People's Court of Berlin opened and the natural light flooded in, Hanz choked back tears. He hadn't seen sunlight in days, and though he was living a nightmare, the sunshine gave him the sweet gift of hope.

⁓⚬⚔⚬⁓

As Severin drove them home, the two brothers barely spoke, each sequestered in his own morbid thoughts. Waves of nausea kept hitting Hanz as he agonized over the fate of his daughters and Abigail. Scenarios of what could have happened had the judge been less forgiving occupied Severin.

Upon arrival at the farmhouse, Severin put a record on the gramophone in the living room and went to the small bar to grab a bottle of vodka. Pouring two shots, he handed one to Hanz. "What a nightmare that was," he said, removing his peaked cap and military jacket, tossing them over a chair.

Hanz nodded. The very earth had opened and swallowed his family whole.

"I can't imagine the pain you're going through, *Bruder*."

Both men downed their shot, and Severin grabbed the bottle, pouring two more.

"But don't be trying to play the hero again. You heard the judge; they'll execute you next time. To be honest, I wasn't even sure if they'd let you go *this* time." Severin paused. "And another thing: Though they awarded me your farm, you know between us, nothing has changed. It's your land, Hanz. I have no use for it, and even if I did, I would never take it from you."

Hanz was quiet, already thinking of how he could save the women he loved. As the music from the gramophone floated through the air, reminiscent of happier times, they both sat on the couch to process the day.

"Let's get drunk and forget our troubles for a while," Severin said. "There's nothing we can do about that Jewish woman and her daughters, but at least you're alive."

"You mean *my* daughters," said Hanz, giving his brother a level stare.

"*Ja*, sorry . . . Your daughters."

Hanz downed his shot and looked at the portrait he had painted of Ava and Shaylee, sitting above the fireplace mantel, faces so innocent and pure. Another wave of nausea mixed with utter hopelessness enveloped him, and he almost broke down again. My swans, he thought. My beautiful swans. Please God, deliver them from evil.

"Want me to stay here for a while?" Severin asked. "I could request military leave for a few days."

"*Nein*," replied Hanz.

Severin poured them both another drink. "Listen, *Bruder* . . . I know you love Ava and Shaylee; how could you not? You and Maria raised them from birth. And they're my nieces, damn it. As their uncle, I love them too. But we have to be strong now. These are treacherous times, and the value of human life is fickle. I don't want to squash any hope, but I'm not going to lie to you, either. The truth is, they're both going to end up in a concentration camp, along with Abigail Katz, and there's nothing you or I can do about it."

Hanz got up and stared out the window. For some strange reason, he thought of the albino fawn he had rescued over two decades earlier, just before he found the twins in a wicker basket in the barn. He reminisced about nurturing that fawn into a full-grown, majestic buck, and in his mind's eye he saw the magnificent, white beast moseying toward him in the yard, coming to him for a treat. Oh, how he longed for those halcyon days to return!

Once he had consumed enough alcohol, Severin was ready to share a revelation of his own. One that would tie pieces of the puzzle together.

"I'm going to tell you something, *Bruder*, and it's going to shake you to your very core. But it's time you know."

Hanz turned and looked at him. "Tell me what."

"Sit down first."

He walked over and sat in the chair across from Severin.

"Remember that summer I stayed here when I was sixteen?" Severin asked, his mannerism now appearing extremely nervous.

"Of course I remember."

"There was a reason why I left so abruptly without saying *auf Wiedersehen*."

The music on the gramophone ended, and Severin got up to lift the needle from the record, turning the machine off. With his back still to his older brother, he made a shocking confession: "That summer, I had an affair with a pretty Jewish *Mädchen* and got her pregnant. We were both so young and didn't know what to do, and like a coward, I got scared and ran away to Zürich." Regrettably, he had even hit her when she told him the news, bruising her face and cutting her lip. "Once I learned she had given birth to twin daughters and adopted them out to a farmer and his wife, I came back."

Hanz froze.

Severin turned around to face him, ashamed and remorseful, his bloodshot eyes shedding tears. "I never once imagined that farmer and his wife were you and Maria, Hanz. I swear. Hell, why on earth would Abigail bring them here, knowing you were my *Bruder*?"

Hanz struggled to keep his temper in check. "All these years, and you never told me? Why!"

"Because I didn't think it mattered. And only when I found out who the Jewish woman was that you were hiding, did I realize who Ava and Shaylee really were. But regardless, Hanz, they're still *your* daughters, not mine. You and Maria raised and loved them, and they loved you back. I'm just happy to be their uncle."

"That's the reason Abigail left them here!" Hanz yelled in utter shock and disbelief. "Because of you, you bastard! And this whole time I thought that murderer we hung was their father!" He stepped forward to grab Severin and punch him, but a gunshot stopped him in his tracks, cutting through the air . . .

"Bang!"

Severin reached for his Walther P38, ready to withdraw it from its holster, and both men ran outside. Instinct told Hanz the gunfire came from his barn, and when he got there, his heart almost stopped. *"Neiiinn!"* he yelled in anguish.

Luka lay on the ground in Hanz's makeshift art studio, bleeding from his chest next to a portrait of Ava, a 9mm Luger in his hand. But he was still alive.

Hanz fell to his knees and took him in his arms. "Why, Luka!" he cried. "Why!"

Tears streamed down Luka's face, and his eyes glazed over. "I went to *St. Jakobskirche* in Rothenburg, Papa . . . I went to beg God to forgive me for what I have done." As he spoke, blood came out of his mouth, and he coughed, gasping for air.

"*Nein,* my *Sohn.* It's not your fault. The fault is mine, and I'm sorry," Hanz wept.

Severin knelt and held his nephew's head up.

"I saw Jesus when I was there . . . He looked like he did in that painting you once showed me . . . Remember?"

"I remember," said Hanz, recalling when he had shown him Sandro Botticelli's famous painting of Jesus from a book on Renaissance artists. "*The Man of Sorrows.*"

"That's who I am, Papa . . . I'm a man of sorrows too . . . And now I lay in your arms, just as Jesus did in Mary's."

From Luka's visage and labored breathing, Hanz knew he only had mere moments left with his dear son. He tenderly wiped Luka's tears away, even as his own poured out like rain.

Luka looked up at Hanz with mournful eyes. "You were always my father, Papa," he said, gurgling blood. "And I'm sorry for what I said to you before."

"And you've always been my *Sohn,* Luka," said Hanz, holding him tight. "I love you, and I always have."

Luka's strength left him, and his eyes slowly closed. "Forgive me, Papa. Forgive me for telling them . . .," he whispered, exhaling his last. As his arm went limp and fell to the side, his hand opened, and a small figurine he had been clutching fell to the ground . . . A wooden horse, carved by Hanz and given to his son when he was a little boy.

Hanz buried his face in his dead son's chest and sobbed.

CHAPTER 33

Without delay, Ava was taken to the Ravensbrück concentration camp located on the edge of a small village, approximately fifty miles outside of Berlin. Staffed by male SS administrators and female guards, the facility was designated almost exclusively for the imprisonment and exploitation of female prisoners in the Third Reich. It had a capacity of 3,000 inmates, but the number of women incarcerated there far exceeded that, making the work camp conditions unbearable.

Prisoners were assigned a category with its own colored triangle, sewn on the left breast of their uniform: red for political, green for criminal, black for asocial, purple for Jehovah's Witnesses, and yellow for Jews. This allowed the Nazis to easily distinguish between the different inmates, with some singled out for harsher work and treatment than others. Forced labor took place in the camp itself, in the immediate local area, or in nearby subcamps, with a variety of different jobs depending on the day and the prisoner. If you were lucky, this would include cooking and cleaning, making and repairing clothing, or other factory work. If you were not, it meant backbreaking travail on building projects, or sex work in brothels.

Upon arrival, Ava went through the registration process along with the other new prisoners. She still couldn't believe what was happening, praying the whole time that she would wake from this horrendous nightmare. "Those are mine," she said, resisting the female guard trying to remove her wedding ring and the necklace Starholf had given her for their anniversary.

The supervisor—a large, brawny woman who suffered no insubordination—walked over and slapped Ava so hard she fell to the ground. "Not anymore, they're not. Lieutenant Steiner wants them back."

Next they forced her and the other women to strip naked and enter a shower room. Terrified of the rumors they had heard about people being gassed by the Nazis, several of the women panicked and started screaming, banging on the locked door until, moments later, water sprayed from the showerheads. Head shaving followed the frightening ordeal, and Ava cried as her thick, dark locks fell to the floor, thinking about how Starholf had loved running his fingers through her long, gorgeous hair. Each prisoner was then given a gray-blue striped uniform with an inverted colored triangle for their category and an identification number for their new name. Lastly, they were assigned to a barracks where prisoners slept in three-tiered wooden bunks, with only one unsanitary bathroom containing three toilets. Ava noticed Yiddish writing on the walls—names and heartbreaking messages from past prisoners—as they entered the cramped housing. She couldn't read them, but the words screamed out ghastly utterances, nonetheless, making her skin crawl.

Soon Ava found herself working in the hard labor unit. With Ravensbrück constantly under some form of construction, they needed young, healthy workers to spend long hours digging sand, moving it from one area of the camp to another, flattening out areas of the ground. The fact that she was pregnant made no difference.

As the guards passed back and forth nearby one morning, supervising the workers, Ava tried to strike up a conversation with a Roma woman. The Nazis considered her an asocial, giving her a black triangle, and referred to the Roma people as *Zigeuner (Gypsies)*. "How long have you been here?" she asked.

The woman looked at Ava and shook her head, continuing her work.

"She doesn't speak German," said a young girl next to her. She glanced over her shoulder at the guards. "And I wouldn't talk, if I were you. Don't give them a reason to punish you."

Ava stared at the girl, with her head shaved like everyone else and her hands and face filthy. How was it possible someone so young could be sent here? What could this ingénue girl possibly have done to deserve this? "What's your name?" she whispered.

"Seraphina."

"How old are you?"

"Twelve."

"Where are your parents?"

"They're dead," said Seraphina, not looking up as she worked. "The Nazis killed them outside our home. They shot my six-month-old baby

Bruder too. My mother tried to hide him in a drawer, but when he cried, they found him and shot him in the head. I escaped, but they captured me the next day and sent me here."

Ava almost started crying as she listened to Seraphina relate her ineffable story as if reading off her resume. "I'm so sorry," she managed to utter.

The young girl just nodded, her face betraying no emotion, as if she had built a fortress around her heart, a place where sorrow could no longer penetrate because it was already filled to the brim. And yet, despite her stolen innocence, replaced with grief far too profound for someone this young, Seraphina's dark brown eyes exuded a kindness and resilience that even the Nazis' sanguinary hatred could not extinguish. She reminded Ava of the Jewish sisters she had grown up with—Jeta and Zelda Applebaum—when they were that age. Her childhood friends who had been taken away by the Schutzstaffel after they murdered their parents too, simply for being Jewish.

"You're not alone," Ava said firmly, reaching out to gently squeeze Seraphina's dirt-caked hand. "I'm here now. We'll look out for each other, okay?"

Seraphina's eyes flickered with a glimmer of something Ava hadn't expected to see in such a desolate place: hope. It was faint, as fragile as a candle flame in a storm, but it was there, an attestation to the indomitable spirit of the human soul, regardless of age. "Okay," the girl whispered back, a slight smile touching her lips for the first time since her arrival. "*Danke.*"

As they returned to their backbreaking labor under the watchful eyes of their captors, Ava's thoughts drifted to her own family, to the loved ones she had been ripped away from. First she reminisced about her marriage to Starholf, and how blissfully happy they were until it vaporized into a bitter bane. Then she thought of Hanz and Maria, the only parents she ever knew, and her siblings Shaylee and Luka. And lastly, she wondered about Abigail, her Jewish birth mother.

I, too, am Jewish, Ava thought as she scanned the desolate landscape of Ravensbrück, its barbed wire fences cutting into her psyche. Adopted and raised by a German couple named Hanz and Maria Wolff, I'm Jewish, and my mother's name is Abigail Katz. My life has been a lie.

The realization always hit Ava anew—and hard—whenever she contemplated it.

Like a tsunami decimating a beach.

CHAPTER 34

Aweek had passed since Christian and Shaylee arrived at the abandoned Jewish home in the country. The time they spent in that lovely mansion, though short, would have been something out of a storybook had it not been for the circumstances that brought them there. Anxiety and trepidation lurked behind every smile, every laugh, and every intimate moment they shared, knowing the Nazis were hunting and killing Jews and others, treating them less than human. Now they, too, were being hunted.

That morning, Shaylee woke up early, unable to sleep, and stared at the oil painting of the wife and mother of the home, mounted on the wall. The woman's expressive eyes seemed to reflect many emotions, and to Shaylee, they settled on disapproval, as if she and Christian were the ones who usurped her palace. Beneath the portrait was the woman's vanity where she would prepare herself for the day, her makeup, perfumes, and a gold hand mirror with matching hairbrush still on the table. Her fine silk robe lay draped across the chair, ready to be claimed by the new queen.

Shaylee got up and put on the silk robe, then walked down the winding staircase to the foyer. She made her way through the living room to the back of the house where double French doors opened to a splendid terrace with stone steps leading into a large garden. Manicured shrubs and trees, flowering plants, stone sculptures, and a glorious fountain in the middle welcomed all visitors. It reminded her of the garden at the Steiner estate—not as grand or elaborate, but impressive, nonetheless.

At the top of the stone steps, Shaylee stood there and looked out at the view, inhaling a deep breath of fresh air scented with the bouquets of blossoming angiosperms. The early morning breeze nipped at her nose and stained her pale cheeks the color of a pink carnation, and she pulled her robe tighter around her neck to chase away the chill. It had gently rained overnight, and the droplets on the grass shimmered like a billion diamonds scattered across the lawn under the burgeoning daylight. Up in the firmament, stars were faintly visible, refusing to surrender to the day, while the rest of the expanse slowly brightened, turning from navy to powder blue. The sun was still hiding behind the horizon, but offered hints of its rays, teasing the land with its approaching warmth.

Though it was a breathtaking morn, a mix of numbness and fear superseded Shaylee's appreciation for its beauty. What would become of her when the Schutzstaffel found them, she wondered? And what has become of her twin sister, Ava? Shaylee could only imagine the horror her poor sister must be going through, ripped from her utopian life with Starholf. Was she now in a concentration camp? Or perhaps dead? And what about her father? His wife had been taken from him, and now his daughters. Was he too in a concentration camp or dead? It no longer mattered to Shaylee that Hanz and Maria were not her real birth parents. To her, they were still her parents, in every sense of the word. Loving their children, nurturing them, raising her, Ava, and Luka to adulthood. Yes, Hanz and Maria Wolff had been her entire world, and genealogy meant nothing.

"Oh, Papa! Oh, Mama!" Shaylee whispered on that lonely terrace, hot tears streaming down her cold cheeks. "I miss you both so much!"

⁓✽⁓

Christian woke in the four-poster canopy bed to find Shaylee missing from his side. Yawning and stretching, he smiled, recalling the intimacy they shared the night before. Getting up, he put on the husband's robe–a brown satin garment with long sleeves–and went to look for his fiancé. Knowing her penchant for books, he figured she'd be in the library.

Hundreds of interesting tomes lined the shelves, but Shaylee wasn't there. As the morning light flooded the room, Christian randomly grabbed a book and scanned its pages, only to realize it was written in Hebrew. A Jewish holy book–probably the Torah. Instantly he was struck with a sense of unease, accompanied by a strong dose of reality. This was no vacation home they were staying at. This was a hideout, the previous owners were probably dead, and they would be too if found.

He pondered that for a moment, trying to assess and rationalize the situation, preventing the fear from taking over. We're a long way from town, in the middle of a forest, and they've already arrested the family who lived here, he reasoned. Why would the Nazis come back? They would have already searched the house for money, jewelry, gold and silver, so there's nothing left that interests them. We're safe for now. And yet, as he sauntered toward the living room in his search for Shaylee, the exquisite paintings on the walls and expensive Persian rugs on the floors smirked at his confidence.

Christian walked up to the life-size family portrait hanging above the stone fireplace in the living room. The husband was decked in his Yom Kippur garb–a kittel (long white robe), a tallit (prayer shawl), and kippah on his head–sitting like a king in his castle on a lavender velvet wingback chair, with a proud grin on his face. His wife stood to the right of him, wearing a modest white dress and sheitel (wig), with her hand on his shoulder. And his three children sat submissively by his feet–a son about nine years old; a daughter, maybe thirteen; and a little girl no more than four. It was a lovely painting, and they all looked so happy and alive, as if they were about to step out of the frame and exclaim, *"Mazel tov!"*

What really happened in this home, Christian wondered? And where was that Jewish family now? Were they sent to a death camp? Or murdered in the yard? "If they resist, shoot them on the spot," he had heard the Schutzstaffel say more than once. He shuddered at the thought of what took place that day, when the SS officers arrived like a catastrophic storm and set their world on fire. He could almost see the officers breaking down the door, beating the husband on sight, the wife screaming and the children crying, "Mama! Mama!" Sadly, it would be a scene played out in countless Jewish homes across the country, with innocent people beaten, raped, and murdered by sadistic monsters belonging to an unholy, demonic regime.

The only reason Christian knew of this property was because he and another soldier were sent to pick up the vehicles after the family had been removed. Never in his wildest dreams did he think he'd ever be back, this time as a fugitive, hiding his fiancé who also turned out to be Jewish. Regardless, they had no choice but to stay there while he figured out what to do. Escaping the Nazi tentacles would not be easy.

"Christian," Shaylee said, interrupting his ruminations. "You're up."

He turned around. "*Ja.* When I woke and you weren't there, I came to find you."

"You look handsome in that robe," she said, giving him a wink.

"And you look beautiful in yours."

She coyly smiled. "I found some pickled vegetables and canned fruit in the cellar. I made you breakfast."

He walked up and pulled her in, kissing her forehead. "Sounds like heaven. I'm starving."

Shaylee took his hand and led him to the dining room. As if it were Thanksgiving, she had everything formally laid out on the long, black walnut table under the romantic kerosene chandelier, neatly served with fine china and silverware. Sardines and crackers, green beans, pickled artichokes, and for dessert, canned peaches. To them, it was a feast.

"How much food did you find?" Christian asked, washing down his meal with a cup of hot coffee.

"Loads. The wife did a lot of canning."

"*Gute*," he said, wiping his mouth with the linen napkin. "Who knew sardines and artichokes tasted so delicious together."

She laughed. "When I found her stockpile, I was ecstatic. You'd think I'd found gold, the way I screamed. I'm surprised I didn't wake you."

Christian grinned. "We'll live like kings, now."

"How long do you think we'll stay here?"

"After last night, I'd like to stay forever," he joked, putting his hand on her thigh.

She let out a small giggle, swiping his hand away. "Seriously. How long?"

Christian took a sip of his coffee. "I figure if we wait a month or two, the Schutzstaffel will believe we made it into Sweden, and they'll stop searching for us."

"You really think we'll be safe here that long?"

"I do," he said. "They have no reason to return." As the words left his mouth, Christian noticed the exquisite painting on the dining room wall and the Persian rug on the floor.

～⚜～

After breakfast, the young renegade couple decided to take a bath. The upscale home in the forest had indoor plumbing sourced from an artesian well, with a unique kerosene-heated water tank, and Christian filled the Victorian claw-foot tub in the swanky bathroom. They both disrobed and got in, gently washing each other with scented soap.

When the water cooled, they dried themselves off and went through the previous owner's walk-in closet, trying on different outfits. Christian settled on a cream shirt and dinner jacket with black wool pants, and Shaylee wore a periwinkle cowl-neck satin dress. The fancy, fresh attire lifted their spirits, and like husband and wife preparing for a night out at the opera, arm in arm they walked out the double French doors leading to the terrace.

The sun was bright that day, the sky clear, and the birds were singing a happy song. As if newlyweds strolling in the private garden of their matrimonial home rather than fugitives running for their lives, the two lovers flirted and laughed, forgetting their troubles for a while.

"It's so gorgeous here," Shaylee said, leaning her head on Christian's shoulder as they lazily perambulated through the garden. The floral redolence of roses, lilacs, and jasmine drifted through the air. "If this were our home, I can't imagine being violently ripped from it. How terrible that must have been for that family."

"I know," said Christian.

"And why? Because they're Jewish? It's completely insane."

"Let's not think about that now."

She looked up at him. "I'm sorry. You're right. Let's just enjoy this perfect day."

They stopped walking, and Christian gazed down into her guileless, hazel green eyes. "I love you, Shaylee. Always have. You're such a beautiful, innocent soul, inside and out."

She bashfully smiled. "Not so innocent anymore, am I."

"I love that we make love."

"Me too," she whispered, blushing.

He tenderly kissed her.

They continued their casual amble through the garden, coming upon the decorative fountain. Four cherubs sat around the stone bowl, with another in the middle holding a bouquet of roses. Water spouted from each of their mouths into the trickling reservoir below, their playful expressions and eternal youth seemingly mocking the gravity of the situation.

Christian put his hand in his pocket, and to his surprise he felt a coin. He pulled it out and held it up. "Make a wish," he said, a smile adorning his lips.

Shaylee looked at the coin glistening under the sun, then closed her eyes, opening them seconds later.

He did the same and tossed it in, watching it arc through the air before disappearing into the fountain with a soft plink. "What did you wish for?"

"You know I can't tell you, because then it won't come true."

But Christian already knew her wish, because it matched his own: Escape Hitler, escape the Nazis, escape Germany, and start a new life, far, far away.

The days went by like leaves in the summer breeze, and before they knew it, a month had passed. In the beginning, living at the mansion in the forest engendered severe anxiety, not just because they were hiding from the Nazis but also because of what had happened to the Jewish family who owned it. Shaylee would often bite her nails and pace the rooms, fearing the same fate, or cry over what her sister and father must be going through, if they were even still alive. And Christian would rack his brain on how to smuggle them out of Germany, and what to do if the Nazis returned. Both had many restless nights, adrenaline surging with every unexpected or unexplained sound in the house, and each dreaded waking in the morning to guns in their faces, surprised by a Schutzstaffel ambush.

But none of that happened. Instead, they were able to master their angst, enjoying each other at night, and developing a routine during the day. In the mornings, they would eat a simple breakfast on the terrace, take a bath in the claw-foot tub, and go for a leisurely stroll in the garden. In the evenings, they would play dress-up using the previous owners' bountiful wardrobe, eat a humble dinner in the dining room, and read books to each other in the library. Christian would recite poetry, which made Shaylee laugh; Shaylee would read history, which made Christian fall asleep. They explored every inch of the mansion, discovering the stored bottles of wine, which made the same canned food and pickled vegetables easier to stomach; and they found an art room in the attic, with easels, canvases, and paints, which made Shaylee miss her father more. A cute white rabbit showed up on the terrace one day, timid yet unafraid, and Shaylee fed it vegetables while petting its velvety hair. She named the bunny Herbert, and it became her pet.

One evening before dinner, Christian sat on the chaise longue in the master bedroom, waiting for Shaylee to come out of the walk-in closet with her chosen outfit. "What's taking so long?" he asked, already dressed in a slate tailored worsted wool suit. "Just pick one and let's go eat. I'm starving."

Shaylee slowly emerged, tears welling in her eyes. She had found the wife's silk wedding dress in a sealed garment box, along with the lace veil. The gown was stunning, and she looked like an angel descended from heaven. "What do you think?" she asked, nervous over his reaction.

Christian held his breath as he rose to his feet. "Come here . . ."

She floated over to him.

He gazed into her mesmerizing eyes through the gossamer veil. For a moment, they only stared at each other, until he lifted the veil and kissed her lips. "God, you're so beautiful. Look at you."

Shaylee smiled, her heart melting like butter.

"Let's get married now. Let's go into the garden and say our vows. Who knows what tomorrow will bring, so let's not wait any longer when we both love each other."

To Christian's surprise, Shaylee said yes.

He lowered her veil, and arm in arm they slowly walked to the terrace as if walking down the aisle of *St. Jakobskirche*, the medieval Gothic basilica in Rothenburg ob der Tauber. In a private ceremony in front of the glorious fountain, Shaylee held a flower arrangement she made from the blossoms in the garden, and Christian held a Bible from the library. They each recited their vows, witnessed by five stone cherubs, while the setting sun painted the sky a spectacular variety of colors as if God himself were presiding over their union.

Christian cleared his throat, his voice steady yet laden with emotion. "Shaylee, my love, my life, in this Garden of Eden, amidst the beauty of creation, I take you to be my wife. I vow to love you, to cherish you, to protect you with every breath in my body. In the face of darkness, I will be your light; in the grip of despair, I will be your hope. Together, we will face whatever comes, bound by the love that has brought us to this moment."

Tears glistened in Shaylee's eyes as she listened to his oath before saying her own. "Christian, my heart, my soul, standing here with you, under the canopy of heaven, I take you to be my husband. I vow to stand by you, to lift you up when you fall, to be the joy in your laughter and the comfort in your sorrow. Our love will be the beacon that guides us through the storm.

I love you, now and forever."

After exchanging their vows, Christian lifted Shaylee's veil and sealed their pledge to each other with a kiss. The future was uncertain and rife with peril, but in that wonderful moment, it was perfect, offering nothing but hope and promise.

⚜

Christian opened his eyes early the next morning. An unsettling feeling had woken him, as if a demon had whispered in his ear. He couldn't shake it, and he didn't know what it was, like when someone is watching you but you don't know who.

Glancing over at Shaylee, naked and sleeping peacefully beside him, he calmed. All it took was one look–her beauty instantly disarmed his disquietude. They had said their wedding vows yesterday, notwithstanding the absence of a priest, or a best man and maid of honor, or even formal wedding bands. Afterward, the unmarried married couple made passionate love. What a special day for them both, consecrating their commitment, their love. If only it could have stayed that way forever.

If only.

It was early yet, and the birds hadn't started chirping, so Christian closed his eyes, trying to will himself back to sleep. As he lay there, the foreboding feeling returned. What was it, he wondered, annoyed by its presence? Moments later, he panicked . . .

Like a herd of wild horses stampeding in the distance, a soft rumble touched his ears, steadily growing.

"Shaylee, wake up!" Christian yelled, jumping out of bed. "Vehicles are coming!"

They both scrambled to get dressed, and Christian grabbed her hand and ran to the dumbwaiter in the hallway that connected the first and second floors. Shaylee was terrified and started crying.

"You must be quiet!" he said, stuffing her inside. "And do not get out under any circumstances until I come for you!"

"What about you! Where are you going to hide!"

"Somewhere else!" He kissed her, shut the door of the dumbwaiter, and ran back to the bedroom to tidy it up and make the bed. Then he ran to the kitchen, hiding any evidence of recent food preparation, quickly picking things up and putting them away. Lastly, he ran to the dining room, removing the empty wine bottle and dishes they had left. Normally they kept the home clean and tidy for this very reason, with no evidence of someone living there, but it was their wedding day yesterday, and they had let their guard down.

Christian could now hear the military vehicles coming up the driveway. When the Schutzstaffel got out, they lingered by their cars for a moment, talking and laughing as they finished smoking their cigarettes. It afforded Christian the opportunity to run back upstairs and hide in the armoire inside the walk-in closet. The Nazis would have no interest in going through Jewish clothing, he thought.

As he was about to step inside, he remembered Herbert, the bunny rabbit Shaylee had been feeding. She had brought the pet inside the house the previous day, putting it in the next bedroom. If the Nazis found it, they'd know someone had been there, and would search every inch of the home. He had no choice but to take his chances and go get it, grabbing the rabbit by the neck and tossing it out the window.

Christian made it back to the armoire just as the Schutzstaffel opened the front door. Out of breath, he silently begged God to protect his wife.

"Take only the expensive art and Persian rugs," the SS commander ordered his men. "Leave the rat portraits."

Both Christian and Shaylee could hear their own heartbeat pounding in their ears as the men walked through each room, taking what they deemed valuable. When one of the officers stopped directly in front of the dumbwaiter to light another cigarette, Shaylee almost gave herself away, breathing hard and shaking like a leaf. Another officer entered the walk-in closet where Christian was hiding, and he thought he was done for. But the Nazi simply looked around in disgust, and said, *"Rattenkleidung (Rat clothes)."*

At the end of the looting, one of the SS officers pulled out his Walther P38 pistol and fired five shots into the Jewish family portrait hanging above the stone fireplace in the living room. Each family member, including the three children, now had a bullet hole through their forehead.

Finally there was a deafening quiet. Had they gone? Christian dared not come out until absolutely sure, waiting for the rumble of the military vehicles to fade into nothing. Then he exited the armoire and ran to the dumbwaiter in the hallway, opening the door. Shaylee fell into his arms, shaking uncontrollably.

"It's okay," Christian said, holding her tight. "They left. We're safe now."

Shaylee burst out sobbing.

As they surveyed the house in the aftermath, all the exquisite paintings and Persian rugs were gone.

⁘

"Do you think they'll be back?" Shaylee asked that night, still shaken by the whole ordeal.

"*Nein*," said Christian. "Now that the paintings and rugs are gone, there's nothing valuable left."

They were holed up in the attic, which seemed safer, since there was a small balcony with a telescope, allowing them to see across the landscape for miles. Christian had brought up a mattress for them to sleep on, and they ate a dinner of sardines with crackers, accompanied by a bottle of wine.

"That was so frightening," Shaylee said, the flickering candlelight refusing to imbue a romantic ambience. "One officer was so close to me outside the dumbwaiter, I could smell the alcohol on his breath."

Christian crossed the room and stepped out onto the balcony, looking through the telescope again, checking for anything of concern. Satisfied, he came back in. "We have to be better prepared, though, just in case, for some reason, they do return. We're lucky they didn't burn the house down before they left."

⁘

After the initial shock wore off, the newly married couple resumed their normal routine. The world and all its madness seemed so far away while they continued living somewhat of a fantasy.

But in truth, they were both in denial. Though they appeared to be safe inside their bubble, unbeknownst to them, only a few feet away in a cold, shallow grave, lay the Jewish family who had once lived in that same home, slept in that same bed, and wore those same clothes, never knowing they would be buried alive in their own garden.

CHAPTER 35

bigail Katz had now been at Auschwitz for two months. Every night as she lay in her crowded wooden bunk, she relived that dreadful day when the Schutzstaffel found her, tearing apart the hutch in the living room at the Wolff farmhouse and storming into the secret room, dragging her out kicking and screaming. She could still hear Hanz calling to her as the SS commander brutally beat her, until his voice went silent from the beating of his own. Had they since killed him? Surely they had, as harboring a Jew was punishable by death. Hanz had tried to do a good deed and paid for it with his life. She would never see that kind, gentle man on this earth again.

And what about her daughters–Ava and Shalom? With their heritage now exposed, where did the Nazis take them? Could they perhaps be here in Auschwitz too, without her even knowing?

Abigail regretted going to the Wolff farm that night, knowing she had ruined three lives, including those of her girls. Oh, why didn't I just run to the forest and find the Jews hiding there, she kept asking herself? The Wolffs would all be alive and well today, untouched by this evil plague. Oddly, she even thought of Maria, wondering how the woman was doing at the tuberculosis clinic in America. Fighting her own battle, but protected from all the sadness and despair happening in Germany. That is until now. Soon she'll receive a letter from Severin, explaining that her husband had been executed for hiding a Jew, and that her daughters know the truth and have been sent to a concentration camp. The heartache saturating the land will stretch its cruel tentacles across the Atlantic Ocean and touch her too.

What that letter won't reveal, however, is the wonderful relationship she and Hanz had developed. How he played his violin for her, as if magic exuded from his fingertips. How he painted her portrait, as if he were a

Renaissance great. How they talked into the early morning hours about music, art, and life, enjoying each other's company, dancing, and even sharing a kiss. She had found her twin flame in the blond-haired, blue-eyed German farmer, and that would remain unsaid too.

334

CHAPTER 36

As the days at Ravensbrück continued, Ava did as she was told, trying her best to remain unnoticed and out of trouble. The soft skin on her hands was now blistered, and her body perpetually ached from the hard labor. She constantly wanted to scream, but other women had been severely disciplined–even shot–for less, so she endured until the feeling waned. Every night she cried herself to sleep, praying she would wake up in the morning in her own home, with Starholf lying next to her in bed, holding her in his arms as she related the disturbing nightmare she had had. But instead, she woke to the sonorous vibration of the camp gong, the smell of vomit and excrement, and the whimpers of other prisoners crying.

One early morn, Ava awakened to a little girl, no more than three years old, snuggled up to her for warmth and comfort. She had no idea where the girl had come from, or who her mother was, and before she could inquire about it, a guard came and ripped the child from her arms. Ava never saw the little angel again.

Later that same day, one of the female guards approached her at the work site. "You speak German, no?"

Ava nodded.

"Do you speak that Jew gibberish too?"

"*Nein*, I do not speak Yiddish," Ava corrected.

"Why not?"

"Because I was raised German."

The guard examined her more closely, studying Ava's face and feminine form. "You're easy on the eyes. Maybe I can give you a better job."

"What kind of job?"

"Come with me."

Ava followed the female guard–she had no choice–afraid of what was lurking behind her next assignment. She had heard of the women they had forced into sex work, and her pulse raced with each step she took.

When they got outside the main entrance of the camp, a pile of dead bodies lay on the ground, as if a parcel ready for pickup. These were the latest "selection" victims that the SS authorities had shot, considering them too weak or injured to work. Ravensbrück did not have its own gas chamber and crematorium yet–they would come later in the war–so bullets were the chosen execution method and the corpses had to be disposed of elsewhere.

As they passed the ghastly sight, Ava was both shocked and repulsed. No one would believe me if I told them what I just witnessed, she thought. Does Starholf know about this? Naked bodies–male and female, young and old–piled on top of each other in a macabre scene from a morbid abyss. It reminded Ava of a painting Shaylee had once shown her, called *The Raft of the Medusa*, an icon of French Romanticism painted in 1819 by Théodore Géricault. The artwork depicted the aftermath of the 1816 wreckage of the French naval frigate Méduse, which had run aground, with only fifteen of the 147 people who were set adrift on a hurriedly constructed raft surviving the starvation and dehydration that followed. The artist had visited hospitals, asylums, and morgues where he could view, firsthand, the color and texture of flesh from the dying and dead.

And now, seeing these cadavers firsthand herself, Ava knew how the artist could capture the scene with such authentic realism. How different death looked from life, she thought. That miraculous spirit we are all born with, that unique light we carry, is stolen by the sting of death, and what is left over is cold and baleful, as useless as a common stone in a forgotten stream.

Suddenly Ava could hear the priest in St. Jacob's Church in Rothenburg ob der Tauber giving one of his past sermons, quoting from the Bible . . .

"O death, where is thy sting? O grave, where is thy victory? The sting of death is sin; and the strength of sin is the Law. But thanks be to God, which giveth us the victory through our Lord Jesus Christ." – 1 Corinthians 15:55-57

Ava said a silent prayer for the dead souls as she kept walking. When they reached their destination–the camp commandant's residence in the SS housing section–the female guard knocked, and they waited on the porch.

"Ah ha," said the commandant, opening the door, his sinister eyes and creepy grin scanning Ava head to toe. "This is the one you told me about."

"*Ja*, commandant," replied the female guard. "And she's a hard worker."

"*Gute, Gute.*" He grabbed Ava's chin and turned her head side to side to get a better look at her face. Her baby bump didn't seem to bother him. "*Ja*, she can work here. She'll be my new housekeeper."

The female guard escorted Ava to the basement where she would now be living. She hadn't felt hot water touch her skin in so long, and as she bathed in the small shower, she caressed her growing stomach. Her baby was moving more often these days, and at night she softly spoke to it, telling her unborn child how much she loved it. She had been told by some of the women in the barracks that they'll take it away from her, though. That once the child is born, she won't even get to hold it. Maybe I can escape before then, she thought. But how?

As she lay in her tiny cot that night, Ava thought about her father Hanz, and her sister Shaylee. She wondered if either were still alive. Likely not. "Maybe it's for the best if I die soon too," she whispered to no one in the darkness. "That way the nightmare will be over."

❦

Working as the commandant's housekeeper was worse for Ava than the hardest labor they could have ever given her. Despite her pregnancy, he raped her regularly. Each violation was a theft of her dignity, her autonomy–her very essence–with her condition evoking in him a grotesque fascination rather than any semblance of empathy or restraint. At first Ava fought it, but that only seemed to heighten his sick pleasure, so eventually she capitulated and let it happen, closing her eyes in detachment to a place within her mind where his filthy touch could not reach while she waited for it to be over.

"You've bewitched me with your pretty face, *Fräulein*," the commandant would always say as he grunted on top of her with his foul, sweaty body. "And I like your belly too," he added–his vile perversion degrading Ava further.

In truth, it was nothing short of astonishing that she hadn't already suffered a miscarriage, given the treatment she had endured. Prior to living in the commandant's residence, meal rations were meager and the quality poor. Sometimes they had to take their chances with food that was almost rancid, or not eat at all. And the arduous labor over long hours was extremely difficult for anyone, let alone a pregnant woman. Then when the abuse from the commandant started in her new job, that added a whole new dimension of stress and despair. And it wasn't just sexual assault but physical battery too. Like the time when she had made a minor mistake and he slapped her to the floor, kicking her so hard she thought for sure her pregnancy was over. But that unborn child kept clinging to life, just like its mother.

One afternoon, Ava overheard the commandant gossiping with another SS officer. He made a comment that stuck a knife into Ava's heart, dropping her to her knees . . . Starholf was already engaged to be married again!

As if in a trance, Ava picked herself up and slowly walked to her living space in the basement. She smashed a glass on the sink and sliced her wrists without even so much as a wince. Lying back on the cot with her arms extended on each side, her blood pooled on the floor like a scarlet halo while she stared at the ceiling and waited, ready to step into the unknown, leaving behind a world too cruel to bear. As her life force ebbed away, memories of that wonderful day when Starholf had found her after searching for months, going farm to farm outside of Rothenburg ob der Tauber, shimmered like a mirage on the horizon of her fading consciousness, culminating in their first kiss.

"Ava . . .," he had whispered amorously into her ear after she said she wanted to move to America to be a movie star. "Is there any way I can make you stay?"

"If you kiss me like that again, I'll reconsider," she had replied.

How perfect that day was, she thought, clinging to the remnants of that love, allowing it to cradle her spirit as it left her body . . .

✦

Ava woke up in the prisoners' infirmary. When she hadn't answered the commandant's beckon, he went down into the basement to beat her, only to find his housemaid almost dead by her own hand.

"Where am I?" she mumbled, groggy and in pain.

As her blurred vision began to clear, rows of beds holding broken bodies caught between the living and the departed came into focus, echoing with soft moans of the sick and the dying. The stark, antiseptic smell mingled with the miasma of their suffering, hovering in the air like a persistent brume.

Suddenly Ava recalled what had happened, as memories of her failed escape from her pain surged back. She had wanted to leave this world, where to live was to suffer and to die was to find peace, but her request was denied. *If only I had cut deeper,* she thought, staring down at her bandaged wrists, tears welling in her eyes.

I wish I were dead.

⁓⌇⌇⁓

A week later, Ava was released from the prisoners' sickbay. As the female guard escorted her outside, the bright sunlight hit her eyes, causing her to squint and blink repeatedly. Seconds later, she thought she was hallucinating Starholf emerging directly out of the sun. She rubbed her eyes to focus, and then she heard his voice . . .

"*Hallo,* Ava."

Ava shook all over. Her knees went weak. She fainted to the ground.

They put her in the back of Starholf's car, and when she regained consciousness, she was sitting beside her husband, her love, her savior. "Starholf, *sie came (you came)! Gott sei Dank (Thank God)!*" she cried. "I knew you would come back for me! I knew this was all a terrible mistake! *Danke,* Starholf! *Danke!*" She grasped onto his arm with both hands, leaning her shaved head into his shoulder, crying uncontrollably. "I love you so much!"

Starholf acted unmoved, smoking his cigarette, staring straight ahead.

"I'm so happy you changed your mind! I knew you still loved me!" Ava couldn't stop weeping for joy. "I'm going home! I'm finally going home!"

As the chauffeur kept driving away from Ravensbrück, Ava swam in overwhelming bliss. "I thought you were engaged to another woman," she said, her head still pressed into his shoulder. "I heard the commandant say that, but it was a lie. You've come for me and our child." She put her hand on her distended belly and looked up at him, her large emerald eyes battling between sadness and elation, wondering why he was so quiet.

"Ava . . .," he finally said. "I'm not taking you home. And *ja,* I am engaged to be married again, this time to a real German girl." Though he had loved her, Starholf wanted to move on from the embarrassment of Ava Wolff as quickly as possible, putting it all behind him. He had endured enough of the other SS officers' relentless jokes, some of them leading to fisticuffs.

That same crushing vise that had gripped Ava's heart when Starholf handed her over to the SS officers at the Steiner mansion returned, squeezing the life out of her again, and she began to tremble. "What? . . . I thought you were here to take me home . . . Where are you taking me, then?"

He didn't answer.

"Starholf, you're scaring me. *Bitte!*"

"How would I have known she was a Jew?" Starholf said to the chauffeur, as if to absolve himself of this abhorrent blunder. "She grew up in a *gute* German family and looked like a beautiful *Fräulein*. Her *Bruder* and uncle served in the Wehrmacht. She could have fooled anyone."

The chauffeur nodded in the rearview mirror.

"And that farmer—how dare he let this humiliation happen," Starholf continued, clenching his teeth as he cursed under his breath. "He knew all along."

Ava started to cry again, hearing those stabbing, hurtful words spoken to the chauffeur as if she weren't even there. The man she loved, whom she thought had come back for her, to save her from this hell, instead just added to her unbearable suffering. She let go of his arm, slumping back in her seat, once more wishing she were dead.

As the car wound through the pastoral countryside, Ava's mind churned in wretched misery. The serene landscape, with its lush fields and quaint farmhouses, seemed to taunt her unending tragedy. She looked at Starholf, searching for any sign of the man she once knew, the man she had loved with all her heart, but instead only saw a stranger, a man obscured by the veil of ideology that had ensnared him. "Why, Starholf?" she asked, her voice a mere whisper, a fragile thread of sound in the oppressive silence of the car. "Why must our love, our family, be sacrificed on the altar of such madness?"

Starholf, cold and detached, didn't answer.

Tears streamed down Ava's cheeks. "I loved you more than life itself. I believed in us, and in our future together."

Starholf turned and looked at her long and hard. "This is the world we live in, Ava. I thought you were German. Your father should have never allowed us to court, let alone marry."

"He let us because he could see how much we were in love," Ava said in a small, woeful voice.

"In love with a lie," replied Starholf, staring out the window as if gazing at a memory.

"Is Papa still alive?" Ava expected the worst. Why wouldn't she? Hope was no longer her bastion.

"*Ja.* Your uncle came to his rescue, and the judge confined him to house arrest on his farm. He's lucky."

From the depths of despair, she had been tossed a crumb. "Where's Shaylee?" she asked, envisaging her sister in a similar affliction at some other work camp.

"We don't know."

Ava looked up at him. "She escaped?"

Starholf flicked his cigarette butt out the window and lit a new one. "Seems that way. Christian is missing too; he must be helping her. That traitor is dead when they find him."

Like a phoenix rising from the ashes, Ava's hope resurrected anew, and she pleaded with Starholf to escape together, just like Shaylee and Christian.

He swiftly cut her off. "*Nein*, Ava, that's impossible. You're a Jew, and I will not abandon my family and my country."

"But *I'm* your family," she entreated. "I'm carrying your child."

"And that's why I took you out of Ravensbrück. I'm starting a *new* family once I'm remarried."

"I don't understand."

Starholf knew of the *"Lebensborn (Fount of Life)"* program the Nazi regime had implemented to increase Germany's Aryan population. Based on their racial ideology and theories of eugenics, they wanted to create future generations descended from those deemed "racially valuable." Originally intended to provide single, pregnant, Aryan women with financial assistance, adoption services, and private maternity homes away from the judgmental eyes of family and friends, the program soon became radicalized in the context of the war. Many foreign women were impregnated by German SS, military, and civilian personnel, and the Lebensborn program assumed control of these children if the mothers' health and Aryan ancestry could be established.

Because Ava was Jewish, however, Starholf had to improvise with his own personal Lebensborn program, arranging for a German family in the country to be Ava's guardian until she gave birth. Then the child would be taken from her, just like the thousands of children with the appropriate racial features who were kidnapped from ethnic Germans living in foreign countries and repatriated to the Third Reich. "My fiancé cannot have children," he said. "If you have a boy, we will be raising him. If you have a girl, she'll be given to the German family I'm taking you to."

Ava's heart pounded so wildly in her chest she thought she was having a heart attack. She recalled Starholf's sweet words to her one morning after they had finished making love: "We can have as many daughters as you want, but I must have at least one *Sohn*," he had said to her, gazing deeply into her shamrock eyes.

Everything around her suddenly spun out of control, and in her severely enervated state–physically, mentally, emotionally–Ava once again fainted.

CHAPTER 37

Upon arrival at the large countryside estate outside of Berlin, Ava met Olga, the head housekeeper. An austere, burly woman in her early sixties, her posture rigid and her expression unyielding, she exacted strict obedience from those she ruled over and wasn't afraid to strike someone. Scanning Ava up and down, she shook her head in disgust and said, "You're dirty," grabbing her nose and adding, "and you smell like a horse that's been rolling in its own manure."

Olga took Ava to the basement to get her cleaned up and ready for work. The room was dim and damp, with stone walls, cement floor, and no windows for natural light, imposing the atmosphere of a cold and wet medieval dungeon. Four cots sat side by side in a row, and one toilet, sink, and shower were situated in the corner in the open—no privacy.

Ava did as she was told, scrubbing herself with pungent soap under a broken showerhead dispensing lukewarm water at best. Olga stood there watching, staring at her swollen stomach and malnourished body, showing not an ounce of empathy. On the contrary, she frowned in distaste, looking down her nose at Ava, flummoxed that the homeowners would even want a baby from a dirty Jew, notwithstanding the father's German roots and status.

As Ava dressed in the maid's uniform given to her, Olga silently evaluated her character. She had seen many come and go, each with their own story, their own silent battles, and knew the importance of resilience, of bending without breaking. If it weren't for Ava carrying the child who would be adopted out to the owners of the home, Olga doubted she would have even been brought there, let alone survive. Regardless, once the child was born, Ava would be returning to the work camp. Olga had heard it herself from the homeowners.

Next, Olga expounded the house rules, emphasizing the punishment for breaking them. She warned Ava about attempting to escape, too, as one other servant had recently tried. "If you're lucky enough to get past the dogs," she said with a confident smirk, "you'll still end up catching a bullet."

The other three housemaids stared at Ava as she came across each one while Olga led her through the large house. Their disconsolate gaze, deep and forsaken, followed her with curiosity whilst their hands never stopped working. It reminded Ava of an American movie she had once seen, where the eyes of a possessed painting eerily moved left to right, stalking the person walking by.

When they passed through the living room, Ava noticed a silver-framed photo on the cherry wood table. This was the German family who would potentially claim her child: a tall, blonde wife; an even taller blond husband; and three small sons.

"The last time Frau Johannmeyer was in labor, she almost died," Olga said, noticing Ava's attention on the photo. "Now she can no longer bear children."

Ava thought of her mother, Maria, and even Starholf's new fiancé. How sad, she thought, when a woman was robbed of a fruitful womb.

"That's why you're here," Olga continued as she kept walking. "She longs for a daughter. I'd pray that you deliver her one, if I were you."

Finally they came to the laundry room at the back of the house. "Here we are," said Olga, opening the door. They walked inside, and she pointed at the dirty clothes in one pile, sheets and towels in another. "This is your job for today. All this must be washed, dried, and ironed. Do you understand?"

Still in shock over Starholf abandoning her, yet grateful for her change of fortune compared to the work camp, Ava obediently nodded.

Olga showed her how to use the strange contraption sitting conspicuously in the room, called an automatic washing machine. It had an open steel drum with a rotating device inside to agitate the clothes in the water, which would then be manually fed through two rollers called a ringer. Fascinated, Ava had never seen such a machine before, as they had always washed clothes by hand using a basin and washboard at the farm, or in the Tauber River, and the servants washed their clothes at the Steiner mansion. Now she was a servant and would be doing the same.

"I will be back in the evening to fetch you," Olga said. She handed Ava a small paper bag containing a stale piece of bread and an apple bordering on rotten. "This is your lunch. Now get to work."

Inside her new prison cell, Ava looked around. Several rows of wooden racks stood by one of the walls for hanging wet clothes to dry, and a small couch sat against another. A table for sorting and folding was on the left side of the washer, and an ironing board with iron was on the right. The outside wall had a locked door leading to the backyard, along with a small window.

Ava longingly stared out the window at the children's toys scattered across the lawn, and then at the forest in the distance. What she wouldn't give to be free again, she thought, back at the Steiner mansion, lounging in the garden with her husband, awaiting the birth of their first child. Or even more so at the Wolff farm, safe and secure in the embrace of Hanz and Maria, her beloved parents.

Exhausted, Ava looked at the couch, as inviting as a glass of cold water on a blistering hot day. Everything hurt, and all she wanted to do was rest. She hesitated, staring at the doorknob, wondering if they would check on her, but exhaustion overruled her fear, and she decided to take the risk. Covering herself with one of the cotton sheets, she curled up on the sofa for a few minutes; how good it felt compared to the hard wooden bunks at the work camp. Maybe it was the quiet in the room, or the mellifluous melody of the songbirds outside, or simply the relief of no longer being at Ravensbrück, but within seconds, she fell into a deep sleep.

When Ava woke hours later, she panicked. The sun was already low on the horizon, and she hadn't even started on the laundry yet, let alone the ironing. The last thing she needed was to be disciplined by Olga, the draconian head housekeeper—that would not be pleasant.

Vigorously she went to work, and by some miracle managed to finish everything by the time Olga returned to fetch her. What's more, Olga was even pleasantly surprised how much Ava had accomplished, scrutinizing her work with a rare smile, expecting Ava to have failed the challenge, considering it was her first day and the washing machine was new to her.

Soon Ava had a daily routine. First she'd be assigned to work in the kitchen, assisting the family chef. After lunch, she'd be brought to the laundry room to wash, dry, and iron clothes. The second Olga left her there, locking the door behind her, Ava would lie down on the couch and try to rest for a while, then get up and tackle the large workload.

One afternoon, the unexpected happened. A little boy walked in through the locked door that opened to the backyard. He had been playing there with his brothers and scraped his elbow. "I'm bleeding," he said, trying hard not to cry—his father had taught him that vulnerability was a weakness.

Startled, Ava only stared at the boy, her eyes wide and her breath caught in her throat. That was the first time she had seen that door open, and she didn't know what to do. Would she get in trouble, accused of trying to escape? Instantly it dawned on her that the door was only locked on the inside—an incredible revelation that could lead to her freedom.

"I need help," said the little boy, confused why this woman was just standing there doing nothing. "I've cut my elbow, and it's bleeding." He lifted his arm to show her. "See?"

Ava's heart raced; her knees threatened to buckle. "Let me get a damp towel," she said. Collecting what she needed, she knelt to his level. "What's your name?"

"Peter."

"That's a special name." Ava started cleaning the wound. "There was a famous emperor named Peter the Great."

"What's an emper?"

"Emperor . . . It's a ruler, a king. Peter the Great ruled over all of Russia, long before you and I were born. He had fifteen children, and was six feet eight inches tall." Ava almost started crying, thinking of her sister Shaylee who had told her that.

"I wanna be that tall when I grow up."

"I'm sure you will be. Tall and strong, like Peter the Great." Each time Ava glanced at the open door, her pulse elevated.

"Then I'm going to join the Wehrmacht, like my papa did before he got injured."

Ava finished tending to his wound and stood, staring down at the little boy.

Peter inspected his elbow. Satisfied, he fixed his bright blue eyes on her from under a head of messy blond hair. "Who are you, anyway?"

"My name is Ava. I'm one of the maids."

"You're much prettier than the others."

"*Danke,*" said Ava. She smiled, but inside she was afraid, not knowing what would become of her if the boy talked to his parents about her. Would they punish her for speaking to their son? Would they take away her laundry room job? No doubt they would at least lock the door from the outside too, preventing any future chance of escape. "Peter . . .," she said as he stared up at her with curiosity.

"Uh-huh?"

"It's probably best if you don't tell anyone that you hurt your elbow in the backyard. Otherwise, your parents might not let you play there anymore."

"All right. I'm gonna go back outside now. *Auf Wiedersehen*, Ava."

As he closed the door, Ava heard it click, automatically locking. That gave her an idea. What if the next time Peter, or one of his brothers, came in, she was able to apply some tape to the latch, preventing it from locking again? That would allow her to escape to the forest!

Next time she'd be prepared.

⁓⁕⁓

That night, in the suffocating space of the basement, Ava lay in her small cot next to the other three maids. A berth amidst strangers, her bed felt more like a raft adrift in a sea of sorrow than a place of rest and recuperation. The child inside her belly was moving more than usual, reminding her of her plight, and she started to cry.

"Hush, or you'll get us all in trouble," whispered Eleanor, a light-skinned Jewish woman like Ava, lying in the cot beside her.

Ava sat up. "You don't understand. If you knew what happened to me, you'd be crying too."

Eleanor sat up as well. In the dimness of the faint light emanating from a dying candle by the toilet, her face was a canvas of loss and defiance. She looked at Ava with both empathy and superhuman resilience, and said, "My husband, two daughters, and baby boy were all shot right in front of me. As my girls were screaming for their mother, four Nazi soldiers took turns gang-raping me. They left me for dead, and when I regained consciousness, I found myself a slave for a German family who supports the very regime who committed these crimes. But do you see me crying?"

Ava stared at Eleanor, gobsmacked by her traumatic story. It rendered her speechless, dwarfing her own pain.

"Crying will get you nothing. There is no sympathy for people like us here. It would be easy for me to give up, but instead I choose to hope. Every day I convince myself to keep going, trusting that this barbaric nightmare will soon come to an end. You should start thinking this way too or you won't make it. Feeling sorry for yourself will buy you nothing but misery. You must only think of enduring and saving yourself."

Ava wiped her tears and lay back down, reflecting on what Eleanor had said. Her eyelids grew heavy, and she finally found sleep.

⚜

Ava dreamed of the flower garden. Not the elaborate one at the Steiner mansion but the modest patch that grew at the Wolff farm. She dreamed she was lying in the soft grass next to her twin sister Shaylee, and they were admiring the shape-shifting clouds floating across the azure blue sky, talking and laughing.

It was such a glorious, peaceful day, with the bucolic scenery green and the vibrant flowers in bloom. The birds were alive and singing in the trees, and the swans floated on the surface of the pond. So real was the dream that Ava could even smell the scent of her sister's perfume, Coty L'Aimant. With top notes of bergamot, neroli, peach, and aldehydes; middle notes of geranium, rose, orchid, jasmine, and ylang-ylang; and base notes of vetiver, musk, vanilla, sandalwood, tonka bean, and cedar, the eau de parfum was captivating. *L'aimant*, which means both "Loving Her" and "The Magnet" in French, certainly lived up to its appellation. Oh, how she missed that scent!

When a soft rumble traversed the ground, Ava noticed her father Hanz, sitting on his tractor, smiling and waving at his own beloved swans. I'm home, she thought! I'm really home! But then Maria called out from the farmhouse that dinner was ready, and instantly Ava knew something was wrong. Her mother was sick in America; how could she be calling out to them? Am I dreaming, she questioned?—a dream inside a dream. Suddenly the earth began to shake violently by her feet, and the paradisaic fantasy vanished . . .

"Get up! Get up!" Olga barked, kicking the end of each bed for the maids to wake.

As Ava sat up, nausea churned in her stomach. She would do anything to go back inside that dream and stay there.

"And you, you're coming with me," Olga said directly to Ava. "Herr Johannmeyer is back and wants to get a *gute* look at you."

"Why?"

"Never mind why. You don't ask questions; you just obey."

Ava waited her turn to use the toilet and sink in the corner, then quickly dressed and followed Olga to Edmund Johannmeyer's den. He had been away on business when Ava first arrived. As she stood there in front of his oak desk, awaiting the master of the home, she felt like a young girl who had been sent to the principal's office for misbehaving in school.

Edmund entered the den. "And what do we have here?" he asked, walking straight up to Ava, his eyes fixed on her like glue.

"This is the woman Lieutenant Steiner brought you, Herr Johannmeyer."

"*Ja, ja,* I know," he said, inspecting her top to bottom as if auditing a racehorse he was interested in buying. "Starholf was right; she certainly doesn't look Jewish." He grabbed Ava's chin and turned her head side to side to look closely at her features and bone structure, just like the camp commandant at Ravensbrück had done. "Why is it you look Aryan, *Fräulein?*"

Once more stripped of her dignity, examined and judged not for who she was but for the potential value of her unborn child, Ava answered, "My parents were German," wishing it were true. "Hanz and Maria Wolff."

Edmund laughed. "*Ja,* I heard about that too. Jewish babies raised by German farmers—quite something. Except that doesn't make them your biological parents, does it."

"If she does have a girl, it will be lovely, Herr Johannmeyer," said Olga, as if coming to Ava's defense, promoting her as a prodigy. "Such fine, delicate features and porcelain skin."

"I'd rather have a full-blooded German with blonde hair," replied Edmund. He walked around to the back of his desk and sat down, looking up at Ava, deciding what to do. "But of course you're right, Olga. I'm sure the child will be beautiful, regardless. Starholf also has perfect Aryan features, and the dominant genes always crush the weak ones. This *Fräulein* will do." With his cold verdict given, he turned his attention to the mail on his desk.

Ava fought hard not to cry. Before being dismissed, she quickly said, "Why would you separate a mother from her child," her voice barely audible.

"What was that? What did you say?"

She mustered the courage to speak further, desperately appealing to his compassionate side, if he had one. "I said why would you separate a mother from her baby? It's cruel. How would you and your wife feel if someone did that to you?"

Olga stepped forward and slapped Ava's face, knocking her to the floor. "You're not to speak unless spoken to," she reprimanded, hovering over Ava like a gladiator waiting for the emperor's signal to inflict the final death blow. "How dare your insolence!"

Ava stood and wiped the blood off her lip, saying nothing more.

Unfazed by Olga's aggression, Edmund Johannmeyer dismissed them both. "Take her away."

Ava again cried that night, despite Eleanor's attempt to fortify her. She cried for how it used to be, how it should still be, and for what it will never be again. Thoughts of Starholf gently caressing her pregnant stomach as if it were a priceless vase filled her mind, exacerbating the heartache. It was bad enough he had discarded her, causing her immense suffering at Ravensbrück, but now he had arranged for her to lose her precious baby too. The hopelessness was so overwhelming it hurt to breathe, like a massive wave crashing over her, collapsing her lungs and taking her far out to sea.

Can you die from sadness, she wondered?

And if so, how long does it take?

The daily routine resumed, and Ava carried on.

One afternoon in the laundry room, Edmund's wife walked in unexpectedly. Just as Ava had heard from the other maids, Frau Johannmeyer was wearing a prosthetic baby bump–a pretense for the public whenever she left the house. The two women stared at each other across the room, one carrying a child in her womb, the other pretending to. A weird encounter, the air thickened, heavy with a cacophony of unspoken thoughts and emotions as Frau Johannmeyer's face revealed her disdain, pronouncing judgment on Ava as if she were a dissolute intruder in her home. Ava, in turn, froze, fearful of another threat, as if the woman might cut out her child right then and there.

As they stood locked in an odd duel of sorts, between the powerful and the weak, the privileged and the poor, the winner and the loser, to Ava it seemed like Frau Johannmeyer was angry at her. Angry that she was carrying the woman's baby, somehow hiding it in her belly until birth. Her penetrating gaze frightened Ava, almost as if Frau Johannmeyer sought to peer into her soul, to lay bare and expose what Ava had that she did not, yet so desperately desired. The stare transcended all boundaries, reaching into the realms of envy, yearning, and the pain of motherhood denied. True, she already had three boys, but a girl was what she truly longed for. The fact that she needed someone like Ava to deliver her one made her hate her for it.

Unnerved, Ava instinctively put both arms around her stomach, as if protecting her baby from the Wicked Witch of the West in *The Wizard of Oz*.

"I didn't want to meet you at first," Frau Johannmeyer finally said. "I wanted to wait until the baby was born, pretending all along that I was pregnant with her. But something changed in me, and I wanted to see the Jew, face to face, who will be birthing my baby girl."

"I could have a boy," Ava said, looking down at the ground.

"*Ja*, and then your ex-husband will take him. But if it's a girl, she's mine."

Ava's breath caught in her lungs, a sea of tears threatening to break the levee.

Frau Johannmeyer continued staring at Ava for a long, excruciating moment. Then just as quickly as she had come, she turned and left.

⁂

"You did not polish the silverware!" screeched a voice in the kitchen.

"But Frau Olga, I did polish it," pleaded Ingrid, one of the Jewish maids.

Olga grabbed her by the arm, yanking her over to the silverware set in the dining room. "I can still see the tarnish!" And yet, each piece shined, catching light from some unknown source.

"I scrubbed hard; I swear," said Ingrid, staring at the cutlery.

"Lying rat!" She slapped the small, fragile maid.

Whenever the Johannmeyers went on holiday, Olga turned into a vicious tyrant. She relished being the boss, put in charge of everything by Edmund, mutating from a cold head housekeeper to the primordial she-demon Lilith. Dictatorial and harsh, the new master of the house gave vivid meaning to the axiom, 'absolute power corrupts absolutely', personifying it consummately.

"Do it again," Olga demanded, standing over her like Goliath of Gath.

Ingrid, cowering under her tormentor, timidly picked up a silver spoon that already sparkled and repolished it.

"Not *gute* enough," said Olga. She enjoyed victimizing the poor girl, slapping her a second time. "Again!"

Once more Ingrid polished the same spoon, handing it to her overlord for inspection.

"Still tarnished!" Olga yelled, kicking her this time. Hard.

Ingrid almost toppled in pain. "*Bitte*, stop! I did what you asked, now leave me alone!"

Enraged at her subordinate's audacity to talk back, Olga became bug-eyed. Losing all self-control, she picked up a miniature bronze sculpture of Hitler sitting on the dining room table and struck Ingrid on the head with it, felling her to the floor. Olga didn't stop there. She kept hitting, over and over with the bronze weapon, unable to discern that she was now killing the girl. Even when Ingrid's excruciating screams ceased, Olga kept on striking, as if in a trance.

This whole time, unbeknownst to the rabid despot, Ava stood in the adjoining room, hand over mouth, witnessing the horrific murder. A terrifyingly morbid sensation swept through her entire being, unable to fully process what she saw. Though she had seen dead bodies at Ravensbrück, and heard the grisly stories of those murdered, like the Applebaums, the Benowitzs, the Yurkovichs, and the families of Seraphina and Eleanor, to actually behold such a gruesome crime, where a crazed woman beat someone to death and then kept hitting the dead body as if beating a bag of wet towels with a stone, the victim's blood spilling everywhere, transcended even the most macabre scenarios. In that moment, completely traumatized, Ava felt as if her own body were being beaten, bruises appearing all over her skin by proxy.

When Olga finally stopped, panting and sweating, she dropped the bronze sculpture and stared at Ingrid lying motionless in her own blood.

"Look what you made me do!" she yelled, not an iota of remorse. Lifting Ingrid's lifeless body by the arms, she dragged her backwards down the hallway.

Ava, now crouching behind a piece of furniture, lest she be seen, covertly followed to observe what Olga would do with the body. When she saw her take it outside, she watched from a second-floor window as Olga tossed Ingrid in a wheelbarrow and hauled her into the open field behind the house. An hour later, just like that and for no reason at all, this poor Jewish maid ended up buried in a shallow grave.

For the rest of the day, Ava robotically did her work, emotionally stunned. She couldn't stop mulling over what Eleanor had previously said: "There is no sympathy for people like us here," the words ricocheting in her head. True to that assertion, in all of Europe the Jews were now fair game—murder, rape, theft, slavery, you name it—and no one would intercede to stop it.

Ava recalled past conversations held at the Steiner mansion during cocktail parties and dinners, where the guests would converse about the increasingly severe discriminatory, anti-Semitic measures implemented by the Nazis when they first came into power. Jewish citizens had been harassed and subjected to violent attacks long before the war even started, actively suppressed and boycotted, stripped of their citizenship and civil rights, and eventually completely removed from German society, crippling them both economically and socially. Starholf had thought it was funny that the Nuremberg Laws, implemented in 1935, prohibited Jews, and later Roma and Blacks, from having sexual relations, let alone intermarriages, with racially pure Germans. "What decent Aryan would even consider such a disgusting thing," she remembered him laughing. "Especially when we have beautiful German *Fräulein* like Ava."

To her, it was all just politics then, and she didn't concern herself with these topics, absconding from the debates at the first opportunity. Now, however, having suffered under these very policies and laws as a Jew herself, a victim of unspeakable atrocities, and witnessing or hearing the same from many others, there was no doubt in her mind that the Third Reich was inhabited by legions of demons.

Demons led by devils named Barbaric, Abhorrent, Wicked, Monstrous, and Inhumane.

Now seven months pregnant, Ava made a pivotal decision. She knew she had to escape, or she'd end up like Ingrid after birthing her child. Every day in the laundry room, she kept her eye on the locked door that led to the backyard, hoping the little boy would open it again. Except this time, she would flee.

And then it happened . . .

"My *Brüder* are being mean to me," Peter bemoaned one afternoon, walking through the door. "They won't let me play with them."

Ava froze, just as she had when she last saw that door wide open, staring at freedom like a hungry wolf.

"Would you play with me, Ava?" he asked, looking up at her with his bright blue eyes.

Ava mentally recovered, like a ray of sunshine piercing through the gloom. "I would love to, Peter, but I have work to do," she said, slightly trembling. She glanced at the small roll of tape she had placed on the windowsill next to the door, days earlier. "You don't need them to play with, though. You could pretend you're a pirate and climb a tree, making it your ship. That's what my *Bruder* and sister and I would often do."

Peter smiled. "Will you come and sail it with me when you're finished your work?"

"Well that depends on where you want to sail."

He thought for a moment. "Egypt! My papa showed me pictures of the big stone forts there, called permids!"

"Pyramids, *ja*," said Ava, smiling at the cute little boy. "Let me think about it while I finish my work. All right, Captain Peter?"

"All right!"

Beads of sweat formed on Ava's brow and upper lip, anticipating her next move. "But before you go and get our ship ready, you need to wash your hands. They're dirty, and a pirate captain needs to set a *gute* example for his crew."

When Peter happily went over to the sink to wash his hands, Ava rushed to the window and grabbed the roll of tape she had stolen from the kitchen, ripping a piece off and placing it securely over the door latch.

"*Danke*, Ava," said Peter, scampering back outside. "I'll get our ship ready now." When he closed the door, there was no click.

❧

The wait was agonizing, but midnight finally arrived, heralding the moment that would either mark the beginning of Ava's salvation or her undoing. With the other two housemaids fast asleep, she quietly got up and dressed, then tiptoed up the steps to the basement door. Earlier, just before Olga had shut it, Ava had placed a strip of tape over the latch in the same way she had on the laundry room door, preventing it from automatically locking. Risky though it was, knowing there would be hell to pay if she were caught, she had to take the chance. Besides, Olga wasn't herself lately, making mistakes she normally wouldn't make. After killing Ingrid, whom Edmund Johannmeyer was secretly sleeping with, he castigated her, upset that he now had to find someone else to groom for his lascivious encounters. Olga took it personally, and it affected her work. Paradoxically, it seemed to make her even more obsessed with catching one of the other maids doing something wrong rather than softening her toward them. Perhaps she had gotten a taste for blood and wanted more.

At the top of the steps, Ava reached out and grabbed hold of the doorknob, pushing on it gently. Like magic, the door opened, and she paused, allowing her eyes to adjust before proceeding. All the lights were off in the large home, and the darkness lay like a blanket, thick and almost palpable. God forbid she'd get this far, only to knock something over.

Like a timid spelunker about to enter a dangerous cave, Ava bit her lip and made her way through the house, stopping in the kitchen to grab some raw meat. When she reached the laundry room, her heart thundered against her ribcage so loudly she thought it would wake the entire household. Seconds later, she was at the door leading to the backyard, her hand on the doorknob, slowly pushing it open . . .

Freedom!

Was it really this easy? Or was someone playing a sick trick on her, allowing her to get this far before ending her laughable escape?

Standing under a canopy of cheering stars, Ava stared up at the full moon for a moment, almost in disbelief. The large, creamy white ball in the midnight sky shone like a gigantic pearl, exhorting her on, promising to guide her way. A rooster crowed, either warning the hens or joining the applause, and as the dogs ran up to investigate the trespasser, she tossed them the raw meat, suppressing their barks with a juicy feast.

Without further delay, Ava approached the fence and opened the creaking gate. Walking as fast as she could, even half running, she crossed the field, stopping for a moment beside Ingrid's shallow grave before disappearing into the forest. The trees whispered around her, leaves rustling in a symphony of clandestine support as she pushed forward, driven by the primal need to protect the life within her. Despite no food, no water, no shelter, no plan, and no idea where she was or where she was going, she didn't care. All she knew was that she had escaped and was now running for her life.

And for her child's . . .

Ava had traveled on foot for hours, and by dawn emerged from the other side of the forest, finding herself on the outskirts of a small town. The early morn was markedly quiet as she made her way through the cobblestone streets, still walking fast. Placing her hand on her stomach, she was so grateful to have escaped. To be out of the cruel clutches of Olga and the abominable plans of her ex-husband.

Side-stepping puddles of water on the road, avoiding wide-open spaces and anything that looked public, Ava nervously glanced around. She wondered where she was, wishing it were Rothenburg ob der Tauber, a town she was well acquainted with; that way she could walk back to her father's farm. She imagined Hanz waiting for her at the end of the driveway, waving his arms as she ran to him, collapsing in his embrace, crying out, "Papa! Papa!" and no more, unable to speak of the horrors she had been through as she wailed in the loving grasp of her father's strong arms. The mental vision made her so homesick she became physically ill, and she had to stop, lean over, and vomit on the side of the road.

As the morning light began to show itself, chasing away the dark, the skyline turned the color of raspberry and egg yolk among the cirrocumulus clouds. A single car approached up ahead, and Ava quickly hid behind a tree until it passed. Pregnant, starving, and exhausted from walking all night, she needed to get out of sight and rest, but there was nowhere that appeared safe. That is until she came across a modest home that looked vacant, with a white picket fence and a child's Bavarian cottage playhouse in the back.

Ava rubbed her eyes. Was she hallucinating?

She hurried to the home, unlocked the gate, and surreptitiously advanced to the playhouse. The inside of it was just as charming as the exterior, with a miniature pretend kitchen, a tiny bed, a small table with two chairs, and a red velvet couch next to a bookshelf filled with children's books. Unicorn tapestry hung on one wall, and forest fairies and elves on another. She and Shaylee would have loved something like that as children, she thought. They would have practically lived in it.

Several bottles of soda and a box of cookies sat on the counter. Ava immediately opened a bottle and almost finished it all in one drink–nectar from the gods for her parched throat–and devoured one cookie after another. And yet there was more: She found a jar with money in it–probably the child's weekly allowance. A fancy gold watch–no doubt forgotten there by the father. And some makeup–red lipstick, mascara, and powder, likely snuck in there by the girl to play with, mimicking her mother like all little girls do. These items would certainly come in handy later.

By now Olga would have discovered Ava missing, and there would be a search party out for her. Ava pictured that she-demon running around the Johannmeyer house, calling out her name and cursing that she had gotten away. She would be disciplined again for this, since she was the head house-keeper responsible for the maids.

With her thirst and hunger pangs satiated, Ava curled up on the small bed to rest, covering herself with the blanket. Like Snow White in the cot-tage of the seven dwarfs, she had found sanctuary and planned to stay there all day, then leave at night under the cover of darkness–to where she did not know. "Don't worry, little one," she whispered as she caressed her dis-tended belly, her eyes becoming heavy. "Mama loves you and will always protect you. We're safe now. Everything will be all right."

By the time Ava awoke, it was nearly dusk. She had slept most of the day and was starving again, feeding now for two. More cookies and another soda were her only sustenance, but she was grateful for at least that.

At first she dared not open the door to see if anyone was outside, lest she give herself away. She couldn't hear anyone, though, and the playhouse was far enough from the house, so she opened it to take a quick peek. Again, there appeared to be no activity in the home.

Once it was dark, Ava went outside and discovered the garden, grab-bing a cabbage, three tomatoes, and two carrots, wiping them clean and eating them. With food, shelter, and a false sense of security, it was an easy decision to stay the night. And then another. And another. Besides, she reasoned, no one was home, and she needed to build her strength for the next leg of her escape.

At 3:00 a.m. on the third night–the witching hour–voices could be heard in the yard . . .

"Maybe she's hiding in the playhouse, sir."

"*Ja*, go check if she's there."

"What do you want me to do if she is?"

"Drag her out by her hair and bring her to me. I'm going to shoot the vermin through her belly!"

"*Ja*, Lieutenant!"

Ava woke up in a panic, kicking and screaming in bed . . . It was only a bad dream. Yet how real it seemed.

For the rest of the night, Ava couldn't sleep, so she lay there in the darkness, thinking about her next steps. With only two months before her delivery, time was crucial. She needed to find a safe place to have her baby, a place with an experienced woman who could serve as a midwife and help her through it. There was a risk she would be reported to the authorities, all alone and looking rather suspicious with her shaved head and maid's outfit, but what choice did she have?

Dawn arrived, painting the sky in hues of hope, and Ava ate more garden vegetables, along with some cookies and another bottle of soda. With her circadian rhythm now disturbed from so much trauma, causing sleep-wake inversion, exchanging diurnal habits for nocturnal ones, she needed to wait a few more hours before becoming drowsy again. Then she'd sleep the rest of the day, eat the remaining food, and leave at night.

To pass the time, Ava picked up one of the children's books on the shelf–*Hansel and Gretel.* The large, leatherbound book by Jacob and Wilhelm Grimm was a childhood favorite of hers as well. As she turned the pages, she reminisced about that wonderful evening when she and Shaylee were little girls, giggling as they crawled up on their father's lap, laying their heads against his chest and curling up like kittens, listening to him read them the story.

"I love you, Papa," she remembered saying to him, interrupting his reading.

"Me too, Papa," Shaylee echoed.

"And I love *you*, my little swans," he had replied, his eyes welling with tears.

Oh, Papa, how I miss you so, Ava lamented as she turned the page!

Suddenly the door opened. "What are you doing in my playhouse?" a little girl's voice pinged.

Ava's head shot up; her heart fell to the floor; adrenaline surged through her body.

"And that's my book you're reading."

"Um . . . *Ja,* I know . . . I lost my cat and was looking for her." Ava thought she was going to faint.

"Maybe she's hiding in your belly," the little girl giggled. "That's why your tummy is so big."

"*Nein* . . . I'm . . . I'm going to have a baby," Ava said, looking past the girl to see if anyone else was coming.

"I know, you silly goose. My mama's tummy is big too. I hope she has a boy; that way I'll have a *Bruder.*" The little girl stepped inside and closed the door. She put a round metal canister of Scho-Ka-Kola chocolate on the table, also known as *Fliegerschokolade (Aviator Chocolate)* because it was given to Luftwaffe pilots to help them stay alert during bombing raids, and went to the miniature pretend kitchen to retrieve her tea set. "Would you like some tea with our chocolate?" she asked cordially.

Ava nodded.

Pouring imaginary tea from her teapot into each of their cups, the cute little girl handed her guest a triangular wedge of the creamy candy.

"*Danke,*" said Ava. As she took a bite, her eyes teared up. Chocolate was rationed for civilians during the war, and she hadn't tasted the sweet confection since the Schutzstaffel ripped her from her home at the Steiner mansion.

"Why are you crying?" the little girl asked, taking a sip from her teacup. "Don't you like my chocolate?"

Ava wiped her eyes. "*Ja,* it's delicious."

"I'm Helen. What's your name?"

"Ava."

"That's a pretty name." Helen gave her another wedge of the Scho-Ka-Kola chocolate. "This is for your baby."

Ava smiled. "*Danke;* you're very generous."

"I know. Do you like the tea?"

She nodded. "Helen, where are your parents?"

"They're unpacking. We just got back from Grandma's."

As the two unlikely acquaintances continued their morning tea and chocolate in the playhouse, Ava sat there with her shaved head and dirty clothes, examining the little girl in pigtails. No more than five years old, with lemon blonde hair, cerulean blue eyes, and scrubbed clean cherub cheeks, she was a paragon of a sweet little German girl. The Third Reich could even make a propaganda poster of the two of them, showing a dirty Jew being secretly poisoned by an Aryan child serving her tea. The thought made Ava shudder, and she suddenly felt nauseous. For a moment she even hated the girl for what she looked like and what she represented. But then she quickly remembered it wasn't Helen's fault. *"From one man He made all the nations,"* rang through her mind, recalling the biblical truth of Acts 17:26 she had learned as a child in church.

As little Helen clicked teacups with her visitor and giggled, Ava realized if she had a daughter, she'd likely look the same, given Starholf's strong Aryan features. Instantly her resentment turned to love, and she wanted to hold this little girl, crying as she rocked her in a motherly embrace. Instead, however, Ava remained calm and composed. She didn't want to scare the child. If Helen went and told her parents, Ava would be caught, and either sent back to the Johannmeyers, or worse, Ravensbrück. Despite her trepidation, she kept playing with Helen all morning, until her mother called her in for lunch.

"It was fun having tea with you, Ava. You can stay in my playhouse for as long as you like."

Just before Helen opened the door, Ava grabbed her hand. "Do you like kittens, Helen?"

"Oh, *ja*, I love them!"

"My cat is having kittens tomorrow, and if you don't tell your parents that I'm here, I'll give you one."

"You promise?"

"I promise. But only if you keep our secret. Do you promise to keep our secret?"

She nodded vigorously.

"*Gute.* When we have tea tomorrow morning, you'll get your kitten."

"*Danke*, Ava!" exclaimed Helen. "I can't wait!"

"But remember, you can't tell your parents about me or the kitten until tomorrow."

"I won't!"

"Heellenn!" her mother called out again. "Come in for lunch, dear!"

The little girl left, and the rest of the afternoon went by agonizingly slow. Frozen in fear, Ava kept thinking that at any moment the Schutzstaffel would come barging through the playhouse door, dragging her out, kicking and screaming, just like in the nightmare she had. But they didn't; Helen had kept their secret.

In preparation for her journey, Ava applied some of the red lipstick, mascara, and powder she had found. Wearing makeup would help her look more like a German civilian than a runaway Jew, she reasoned. She then stuffed the remaining cookies into her pockets.

Nighttime finally arrived as the sun began its descent over the horizon into tomorrow, and Ava ventured out into the quiet town. She took the makeup, the money in the jar, and the gold watch with her. When she came across another home with clothes on the clothesline, she also stole a dress to replace her maid's outfit, a wool jacket, and a red beret, changing into them quickly.

Ava looked up at the stars twinkling like polished crystals on a bed of black sand, seemingly cheering her on like they had the night she escaped the Johannmeyers. So vast and beautiful, they took her breath away, reminding her of the midnight sky at the Wolff farm. When she got to the edge of the town, she could see city lights far away in the distance, and decided that was her next unknown destination. A car approached her from behind, but she didn't hide; she just kept on walking.

"Do you need a ride?" a man asked, pulling up beside her.

Ava exhaled. Thank God it was a taxicab. "*Ja*, I do."

"Where are you going?"

She pointed at the city lights.

"*Gute*, I'm going to Dresden too. Do you have the fare?"

That's where she was–outside of Dresden. "*Ja*."

He nodded toward the back seat. "Okay, get in."

Ava got into the cab, and away they went. As the car sped off, she turned, looking out the back window, watching the town getting smaller and smaller, and by default, the Johannmeyers' country home farther and farther. Relief spread through her body from head to toe like the warmth one feels when a cloud moves off the sun.

Now that she knew where she was, Ava had renewed hope. She felt stronger, braver, as if she were now in control rather than her captors. How grateful she was that she had mustered the courage to take things into her own hands and escape the Johannmeyers rather than succumb to the cruelty of her situation. She was indebted to Peter, too. Had that little boy not come through the locked door to the laundry room, she'd still be slaving away, day and night for an evil master, awaiting the birth of her child, only to have it ripped away and given to the very villains who oppressed her. And then what? Of course they wouldn't want her around her stolen child, so back to Ravensbrück they'd send her. Or maybe Sachsenhausen, or Dachau, or Auschwitz, or any number of other horrific work camps.

"What's waiting for you in Dresden?" the cab driver asked, examining his new customer in the rearview mirror.

Ava had to think quickly. "Oh, umm . . . It's personal, really."

"*Fräulein* with child, walking along the road by herself after dark, leaving town . . . Is everything all right?"

"*Ja, danke.*"

As she met eyes with him in the mirror, he held her gaze, scrutinizing her further but saying nothing. It made Ava's unease return. Did the cab driver suspect something? Was he feigning concern for her wellbeing, fishing for information that would expose her? Had he heard there was an escaped Jew on the loose? Nervously she withdrew the compact from her pocket and powdered her nose, trying to appear normal.

"Marriage is hard, but you can't just run away, *Fräulein*," the man continued, assuming Ava had a domestic dispute with her husband. "Trust me; with a wife who thinks she wears the pants, and four *Kinder (children)* to feed, I know. That's why I'm working so late."

"It's more complicated than that," said Ava. "My husband is very abusive."

"Oh, I see."

A long silence followed, which Ava welcomed.

The cab driver kept glancing at her in the rearview mirror, noticing a fading bruise from when Olga had slapped her, thinking it was from her husband. "You're lucky," he said, breaking the silence, "because I dropped off my last fare in that town. Otherwise I wouldn't have been there, and it's a long walk to Dresden. Especially for someone in your condition."

Ava simply nodded. She didn't want to encourage further conversation.

The man frowned, as if a father angry at his son-in-law. "When a husband mistreats his wife, it's a reflection of his own defective character. I'm sorry he hurt you, *Fräulein*. Must have been bad to make you up and leave at night like this with nothing but the clothes on your back."

"*Danke* for your kindness," was all she said. The cab driver was right, though. Ava used to grieve over what her husband had done to her. To them. But now, after all she'd been through, she felt much differently. Instead of utter wretchedness and despair, rage and hatred consumed her. Starholf had all the money in the world, authority and connections, and a beautiful, loyal wife who was carrying his innocent, unborn child. And yet that was not enough to move him to protect her and their baby, putting them on a boat to Sweden where they could be safe. No, instead he chose an ungodly regime over his spouse. He chose an evil Führer over his child. He chose the Third Reich.

How cowardly and disgusting!

Who in their right mind would send their pregnant wife off to a concentration camp, for any reason whatsoever? Could there ever be any justification? No, it was obscene! Ava had come to realize, with a stabbing pain, that she had never really known Starholf Steiner at all. The man she had once believed, with all her heart, to be her happily-ever-after prince . . . was a monster as well.

The cab driver pulled up to a hotel in downtown Dresden. "This is a nice place; you'll like it," he said, turning to look at her. "Not too expensive, and it's safe."

Ava pulled out the money she had taken from Helen's playhouse. "How much do I owe you?"

He put his hand up. "Nothing; keep it. I was coming this way anyway, and you're going to need that money later."

She smiled at him. "*Danke* again for all your kindness."

"And *Fräulein* . . .," he said, giving her a fatherly, level stare.

"*Ja?*"

"Don't ever go back to an abusive man. They never change."

Starholf's face flashed before Ava's eyes. "Trust me, I won't."

❧❦❧

Outside on the street, Ava nervously looked around, taking stock of her environs. The city of Dresden was actively going about its business as if nothing extraordinary was occurring in the world, and she just stood there, watching the passersby for a moment. It was such a surreal feeling to be standing among the free after being a prisoner of war for what seemed like a decade.

A mentally unwell man, several yards away, kept scaring the birds off the sidewalk, laughing wildly as they scattered. When he saw Ava, he stopped and zeroed in on her, his eyes shining with glee. "A bird escaped from her cage!" he cackled. "A bird escaped from her cage!"

Ava gasped.

He ran up to her. "I know your secret, little bird!" he laughed, flapping his arms up and down as he encircled her, cawing like a crow in distress.

From the corner of her eye, Ava caught sight of two officers on horses at the end of the street. They were demanding to see a couple's identity papers.

"Did you know that crows eat little birds?" the deranged man asked, a toothless grin on his face. "Did you know that?"

Unnerved, Ava quickly turned away from the cretin and walked briskly into the hotel. When she looked back through the floor-to-ceiling window, he was still there, staring at her with his crazed eyes, his delirious shrieking reverberating through the air . . .

"I know your secret, little bird! I know!"

※

Inside the lobby, Ava again scanned her surroundings. A woman cradled an infant, waiting patiently while her husband checked them in. A young couple, clearly in love, hurried to the elevator as if they couldn't get to their room fast enough. An elderly man sat by himself in a leather armchair in the corner, leaning forward with both hands on top of his cane, gazing at nothing as if reminiscing of the past. And two men dressed in suits stood talking, shaking hands before going their separate ways, likely concluding a business deal. Yes, life for the lucky was still normal.

With no identification on her, Ava hesitated to approach the front desk. But she longed for the comfort of a hot bath, a decent meal, and a soft bed. Besides, she had come this far, and she was not about to stop now.

"*Guten Abend, Fräulein (Good evening, young lady),*" the concierge said, his Adam's apple sliding indubitably with each word.

"*Guten Abend*," replied Ava, avoiding eye contact. "I'd like your cheapest room, please."

"Of course. May I see your identification?"

"Well, sir . . . you see . . . I don't have it with me. I had to leave my home suddenly because . . . my husband . . . he was drunk again and about to hurt me."

With the red lipstick, mascara, and powder she had on; the new dress, wool jacket, and red beret she was wearing; and the cultured German she was speaking, Ava hoped that the concierge would see a good German woman and make an exception. Her father had also once told her and Shaylee that to portray confidence and command respect, you must always look the other person directly in the eye. And so she did, lifting her chin, giving him a level gaze with as much confidence as a king looking at his subject.

And yet the man didn't budge. "No papers, no room," he said flatly.

Ava's gaze softened to that of damsel in distress, and she put her arms protectively around her pregnant stomach, conjuring tears and quivering her lip like she was about to cry–a reflection of how she truly felt–manifesting an abused woman desperate for help. "I have the money to pay for the room, sir."

The concierge's wife came up behind him. "For goodness' sake, Klaus Müller, show some compassion and let the *Fräulein* have a room." She grabbed a key and placed it in Ava's hand, giving her a sympathetic look. "This one's got a nice view, and my husband is going to discount it for you." She glared at him; he just mumbled and walked off. "If you need anything else, please don't hesitate to ring the front desk."

"*Dankeschön (Thank you very much)*," said Ava, releasing an appreciative smile.

Once inside her room, Ava locked the door and pressed her back up against it, shaking uncontrollably.

She had made it!

From the horrible abuse at Ravensbrück, to the planned theft of her baby at the Johannmeyers, to the temporary shelter at Helen's playhouse, to the safety of her own room in this hotel. For a long moment she just stood there, breathing in and out, staring at the lovely space. Though it was small and basic, to Ava it was nothing short of a palace. The red curtains were open, letting the neon lights of the city shine through the large window. The queen bed with down and feather pillows, silky sheets, and soft mattress beckoned to be lain on. And the four-piece bathroom with fresh towels, soaps, and shampoos awaited its guest like a luxurious spa.

Ava gazed at the painting on the wall—a reproduction of Edmund Leighton's, *The Accolade*, depicting a beautiful redhead with long, flowing hair and regal gown standing before a kneeling man, knighting him with a sword. The woman displayed power, strength, and authority in a time of oppression where men ruled and women were subservient, defying the norm. It invigorated Ava, as she in some way identified with it, knowing she too had displayed power, strength, and authority during her struggle to survive, coming out the victor in a time of great oppression. It gave her a new appreciation for art, too. One that she previously never had, regrettably, having always dismissed her sister's many attempts to educate her on it. If she were ever given the chance, Ava swore she would never make that mistake again.

A bowl of fruit—apples, oranges, and bananas—sat on the table. Ava bee-lined to it, biting into a ripe Belle de Boskoop apple, savoring a crescendo of acidic, tangy juice. She devoured a Tarocco blood orange, rejoicing in its sweet nectar. And she consumed a Lady Finger banana, delighting in the creamy texture and saccharine flavor with notes of honey.

With her tastebuds now percolating, she then ordered room service, reveling in a wonderful meal of Bavarian pot roast and Fränkische bratwurst with sauerkraut—the exact same traditional German feast Shaylee had cooked when everyone came over to the Wolff farm for dinner that one evening. It surprised her that the hotel still had such foods, given the wartime rationing.

The last thing Ava did was what she had longed to do for so long: soak in a hot bath. The blisters on her feet stung as they hit the soapy water, but she barely noticed, focusing instead on the whole-body experience. It was heaven.

Afterward, curled up like a kitten in the soft bed, Ava fell asleep. Whatever miracles or curses were yet in store for her, whatever fate had meticulously planned, and whether she and her child would live or die . . . were all unknown.

But she had made it to safety.

For now.

"How much will you give me for this watch?" Ava asked, standing behind the counter in Milo's Pawn Shop.

It had been a week since she had been at the hotel, and Ava felt confident enough to venture out, attempting to sell the piece. A few blocks away–the bellboy had given her directions–and as eccentric as its owner, the intriguing shop was cluttered with the remnants of a thousand lives, each item, from the tarnished silverware to the dust-covered guitars, bearing a story that whispered to anyone who cared to listen.

Milo, a funny-looking man with a lazy eye and fringe of black, oily hair, put his monocular loupe against his good eye and examined the watch. "Real diamonds around the face and eighteen karat gold–a splendid piece, *Fräulein*."

"*Ja*, it belonged to my father," said Ava with a straight face. "He left it for me after he passed."

"Why would you want to sell such a fine watch when it belonged to your father?"

Ava looked down at her stomach and back up at Milo, coyly grinning her answer.

"Ahh, *ja* indeed. I understand," he said with a chuckle. "Raising children is not cheap."

Buyer and seller settled on a fair price, and the deal was made. Ava now had enough money to stay at the hotel for over a month, if she wanted to. After tipping the bellboy, she went back up to her room, laid the cash out on the bed and counted it again, then took another hot bath, luxuriating in the heat of the water soothing her skin. For a fleeting moment, all seemed well, her troubles behind her. And yet, she knew full well they most certainly were not. Because the Jews were being rounded up and murdered across Europe like animals in a butcher shop. And though she was hiding from it all, in just two months, a new life would be wriggling in her arms.

Hiding herself was one thing.

But hiding with a newborn crying for its mother, was entirely another.

CHAPTER 38

Living at the hotel was uneventful for Ava, which is how she wanted it. She kept a low profile, leaving her room only when necessary, avoiding all contact with others. To conserve her money, she bought groceries, eating fruit and a bagel or croissant for breakfast, and more fruit with a sandwich at lunch. Dinner was her only luxury, ordering room service.

As she contemplated her next move–where she'd go and when–her mind would often wander, gazing out the window at the bustling street below, watching the cars driving by and the people coming and going. She'd imagine the lives of each person, observing their appearance, mannerism, and whom they were with, guessing at their vocation, marital status, and the like. It became a game to her, helping to ease the stress.

Nighttime was the hardest, as the darkness seemed to exacerbate her conundrum, ridiculing any plans she would attempt to make. How on earth was she going to navigate through all this? How and where could she deliver her baby without being reported to the Nazis? It was all so overwhelming that she'd cry herself to sleep.

No longer required to wake up at an ungodly hour and slave all day at Ravensbrück or the Johannmeyers' country home until exhausted, Ava had lots of time to think. That in itself was both a blessing and a curse, ruminating over her previous wonderful life and her present miserable circumstances. She imagined a time when the war was over and she was back at the Wolff farm, with the quaint farmhouse nestled among golden fields and emerald trees, the glistening pond frequented by swans and the serene Tauber River inviting a swim, Hanz tending to the animals in the barn and Shaylee reading a book under a tree. Again she prayed for them both, grateful her father's life had been spared and her sister had escaped. Yes, when this wickedness was over, they'd all be back at the farm together again, and she'd raise her child in the same loving environment she herself had been raised.

Ava put her hand on her abdomen and smiled. Despite the constant worry over her impending delivery, she couldn't wait to hold her baby in her arms and gaze down into its innocent face. Like a pearl within its shell, this child of war was precious–boy or girl, it didn't matter–and she swore she would protect it with her life, come what may.

A Hans Christian Andersen book–*The Wild Swans*–lay on the bedside table, probably forgotten there by the previous occupant with children. Ava picked up the fairy tale, and as she flipped through its pages, like she had when perusing little Helen's storybook, *Hansel and Gretel*, she reminisced about her dear Papa. Akin to her sister Shaylee, it no longer mattered to her that Hanz and Maria were not her biological parents. No, they were still her parents, and her thoughts, viewpoints, and love for them remained in situ.

Ava stopped reading. The word "swan" lay on her tongue like sun-warmed honey, thinking about how her father had always used that endearing moniker when referring to his beloved daughters. She remembered on her wedding day, when Hanz had walked her down the aisle with tears in his eyes, telling her that no matter how old she got, she would always be his precious swan. She recalled, too, her father relating his own first love, Josie Blum, and how their parents refused to allow them to marry because she was Jewish and he Catholic. That no doubt influenced his decision with Ava, allowing her to marry an SS officer out of a father's fathomless love for his daughter, unable to destroy her bliss, believing the secret was safe. The funny thing was, she had seen it in his eyes that day. His happiness for her, tempered with a certain fear. She often wondered why he seemed so uncomfortable around Starholf when they'd visit, and now she knew why. "Oh, Papa!" Ava cried. "It's not your fault! You allowed it because you loved me so!"

⟆⟆⟆

"B̲ang, bang, bang!" came through the hotel room door the next morning. "Bang, bang, bang!"

Startled, Ava froze, staring at the door.

"Open up, *Fräulein!*"

"Who is it?" she asked.

"The Schutzstaffel."

Ava panicked as a sudden terror seized her. This was the end; they had found her!

"Open up or we'll break down the door!"

With nowhere to run, Ava slowly opened it. Two SS officers stood there, menacing in appearance.

"Show me your papers," demanded the higher-ranking officer.

"Umm . . . I . . . I . . .," she stuttered. "I don't have them."

"Why not?"

"Because . . . like I told the concierge, I had to leave my home suddenly. My husband, he's . . . he's abusive and hits me."

The two officers exchanged glances, then started laughing as if Ava had told them the funniest joke. "Lieutenant Steiner, abusive? Really?" They kept guffawing, until seconds later they stopped, no longer amused. "*Nein*, Starholf is soft. You're a Jew rat, and he should have shot you through your belly!"

Ava's entire body started to shake.

"But since he failed to do so, we'll do it now." Both officers pulled out their Walther P38 pistols and pointed them at Ava's abdomen.

Wrapping her arms around her stomach, Ava let out a bloodcurdling scream as the bullets pierced her flesh . . . Immediately she woke and sat up in bed, gasping for air. Once more, it was just a bad dream.

With her heart pumping wildly and her body still trembling, Ava got out of bed and went to the bathroom to splash cold water on her face. She stared at the woman in the mirror, a shadow of her former self, her choppy haircut growing out, dark circles under her once dazzling green eyes and her ivory skin now sallow. When were these nightmares going to stop?

Another frequent dream she had was the Gestapo breaking into her room in the middle of the night and finding her wrapped in the very woolen blankets embroidered with the Star of David that she and Shaylee had been wrapped in as infants when left in the Wolff barn. As they'd search the room, they'd also find the letter from Abigail, arresting Ava and taking her back to the Johannmeyers' home or the vile commandant at Ravensbrück. Again, she would wake up screaming.

These nightmares were so perturbing because, though she had escaped her oppressors physically, mentally they continued to torment her. And to add to her emotional anguish, Starholf was usually at the center of them all, in one way or another.

A knock came through the hotel room door again, this time for real, but less aggressive.

Ava hesitated, staring at it.

"I heard a scream," said a woman's voice from the other side, unthreatening in tone.

"Everything's all right. I just had a bad dream, that's all."

"I'm the maid, and I'm here to take care of your room. May I come in?"

The bed hadn't been changed in a few days, and she needed clean towels, so Ava opened the door. "*Danke.*"

"*Gern geschehen (You're welcome),*" said the maid with a warm smile. She took fresh sheets and towels off her linen cart and entered the room.

Ava observed the small, wiry woman with discerning eyes, pointy nose, and small chin as she made up the bed. Her black hair, streaked with white and pulled back in a tight bun, matched her maid's outfit, and she had a persistent, worried look etched on her face, as if she knew something disconcerting.

"It's the pregnancy, you know," the woman said, her German laced with a strong French accent. "It can bring on terrifying dreams. I had them too, though that was a long time ago for me."

Ava nodded to be polite. Her dreams had nothing to do with her pregnancy. No, hers were the direct result of the heinous villainy she was fleeing.

Finished with the bed, the maid went to the bathroom to replace the towels. "You're due in a few weeks, no?"

"*Ja.* Another month to go."

"My daughter had a little one recently. *Ma mignonne pêche potelée (My cute chubby peach),*" she said in French. "She now owns my heart."

Ava smiled. "What's her name?"

"Cleopatra," said the maid with pride, returning from the bathroom, "after the famous queen of the Ptolemaic Kingdom of Egypt. Beautiful, no?"

Ava agreed.

"And what about yours? What will you name your little king or queen?"

"I don't know yet." So much had happened to Ava since being ripped from the Steiner mansion that naming her child was not a priority.

"Pick a name that means something. A name that will be remembered, because when we die, that's all we have." The woman's eyes seemed to shine. "Proverbs twenty-two verse one . . . *'A good name is rather to be chosen than great riches, and loving favor rather than silver and gold.'* I believe this to be true."

Ava recalled the priest in St. Jacob's Church in Rothenburg ob der Tauber citing that same scripture.

"Speaking of names, I am Margaux Beaumont. My daughter, Colette, works as a maid here too; my husband, Valentin, is one of the hotel cooks; and my son-in-law, Hugo, works in building maintenance." Margaux beamed, proud of her hardworking family, her worried expression vanishing momentarily.

Ava wondered why the maid was being so friendly with her, even talking about her family members, whom she'd never met. "I'm . . ." She paused, wary of using her real name. "I'm Maria Becker."

Margaux smiled, then looked about the room. "Is your husband out today?"

"*Nein*, we ahh . . . we quarreled, and I'm staying here on my own. He's very abusive, and I had to leave."

"That's too bad," said Margaux, her worried expression returning. "A man should treat a woman carrying his child as if she were the most precious vase. Life is a gift from God, and He chose women as the bearers of this gift."

Ava became nervous. Since arriving at the hotel, she had tried hard to avoid contact with people, staying out of sight as much as possible, and yet here was this woman in her room, chatting up a storm with her, getting to know details that Ava preferred remained private. The last thing she needed was the maid to start talking about her to the other staff, with word getting out that a pregnant woman was seeking refuge from her husband in the hotel. She hadn't come this far to sabotage herself now, knowing how lucky she was to have gotten away when countless others were still being worked to death, gassed to death, or shot to death daily. "If you don't mind," she said, giving Margaux a serious look, "please don't mention any of this to anyone."

"No problem," said Margaux, giving Ava a reassuring look back, as if she knew all about Ava's plight. "I'll leave you be, now." As she was about to exit the room, she stopped and turned. "Oh, I almost forgot. Every night there are leftovers in the kitchen, and my husband often brings them home. I'd be happy to bring some up to you, if you'd like."

This would save Ava some money, which she was running out of. "*Danke*, that's very kind. But only if it's no trouble."

"No trouble at all. And Maria . . ."

"*Ja?*"

"You can trust me, *ma chére (my dear)*. I am your friend."

⌘

O ver the next few days, Margaux introduced Ava to her daughter Colette, her husband Valentin, and her son-in-law Hugo. Each were very pleased to meet her, as if seeing a distant relative after many years, and none of them asked any prying questions. Colette even brought Ava some of her maternity clothes she no longer needed, having given birth to little Cleo already, and trimmed Ava's uneven hair into a lovely bob that curved above the collarbone. If it weren't for their genuine concern and kindness, Ava would have thought something suspicious was going on with this family.

One evening, after the Beaumonts finished their work, everyone gathered together in Ava's room, eating leftovers from the hotel kitchen. Ava had forgotten how healing it was to share a meal with friends, and for the first time since her arrival, she almost felt normal.

"This food is delicious. My compliments to the chef," Ava said, taking another bite of the French cuisine.

"*Oui, mon mari (Yes, my husband)* had a restaurant in Paris," said Margaux, again mixing French in with her German, as she often did. "That's why he's such a *gute* cook."

Valentin grinned. "It was just a little diner, really. But *oui*, it did well." His German was better than Margaux's, yet suffused with a French accent as well.

"What brought you to Germany?" Ava asked.

"Inheritance, I suppose." Unlike his wife, who had a slim, bony face matching her body, Valentin's visage was round, like his belly. His hairline was low on his forehead, his unibrow thick, and his gray mustache seemed to dance when he spoke. "My parents lived in Germany for a while, and I was born here. When I was seven, *mon père (my father)* took us back to France, and that's where I grew up, met Margaux, and got married. Then when my parents died, my grandmother's house outside of Dresden went to me. I could have sold it, but it's such a nice property by a lake, so I brought my wife and daughter here instead." He glanced mischievously at Margaux. "And unfortunately, my mother-in-law too."

"Ahh!" Margaux said, pretending she was going to hit him.

He ducked, and they all laughed.

"It's a large house, so we had room for dear Henriette," Valentin quickly said, redeeming himself as his wife shook her head, smiling at her husband's teasing. "When Colette married *this* guy," he added, nudging Hugo, "he moved in as well, and with the addition of our little princess Cleo, we're all together now, as a family should be."

"*Oui, c'est beau (Yes, it's beautiful),*" said Margaux, getting teary-eyed. "In Paris, we only had a little home, so it would have been impossible to live together."

"We have an extra room, too," Colette said. She was the spitting image of her mother, only younger. "You could stay with us for a while, if you want."

Ava's face filled with emotion. What a blessing! A home in the country, outside the constant purview of Nazi sympathizers, SS officers, and the Gestapo. She could deliver her baby there if she found a discreet midwife. Alas, if only she could afford it. "I would love to," she said, disappointment in her voice, "but I don't have the money. After this week, I can't even afford this room."

Valentin and Margaux looked at each other.

"*Ne vous inquiétez pas, ma chére. L'argent n'est pas important (Don't worry, my dear. The money is not important),*" Margaux said in French.

"Sorry, I didn't understand," said Ava.

"She said the room is free," Valentin translated.

Ava looked at them in disbelief. "You would help me like that?"

They all smiled.

⁓⦅⊰◆⊱⦆⁓

When the Beaumonts left the hotel to go home that evening, they took a heavily pregnant Ava with them. She paid her bill at the front desk, and off they drove into the night. The city's harsh angles of concrete and steel soon gave way to winding roads through rolling hills and sprawling fields, and forty-five minutes later they arrived at the country home.

Margaux and Colette showed Ava her room. A tribute to a bygone era, the quaint living space on the second floor had a brass bed with goose feather pillows and a thick quilt, a French chiffonnier, an antique escritoire, and a yellow velvet chaise longue. Ava cried, overcome with relief and gratitude. Colette hugged her while Margaux turned down the bed, and her new hosts bid her good night.

Lying there in the darkness, Ava thought of the Beaumont ménage. These unpretentious, salt of the earth people were in fact strangers to her, befriending her almost against her will, providing her a lifeline and asking nothing in return. How could this be? After encountering such wickedness in others, she had lost faith in humanity, in benevolence and altruism, and yet this family she had met by chance wore those qualities like a cloak. Was God's hand in this, finally answering her supplications in prayer, assigning her a guardian angel to protect her and her child?

Perhaps.

At least that's what she wanted to believe . . .

⤞⬥⤝

Ava awoke the next morning to a bright new day with a fat calico cat lying at her feet. The fluffy ball of fur reminded her of Felix, Bastian, and Axel as puppies, except the feline kind. It eyed her suspiciously, as if daring her to move, and when she did, the scaredy cat instantly jumped off the bed and scampered out of the room. How did it even open the bedroom door to begin with, she wondered.

With daylight illuminating her surroundings, Ava got up and walked across the wood floor to the large window. Opening the curtains, she gazed out at the beautiful meadow. Nothing but grass, wildflowers, and trees could be seen, with a small lake a short stroll away, and there were no visible neighbors. How fortunate she was, she thought, to be brought here. The Nazis would never think to look for her in this cloistered domicile.

Getting dressed, Ava left her bedroom and went downstairs to greet the Beaumonts, only to find they had already gone to work. Besides the fat house cat, she was alone. Margaux had left her a note, though, encouraging Ava to make herself at home, and so she did, starting with breakfast.

First she drank a large glass of goat milk, pouring some in a saucer for the shy cat who was now rubbing against her leg, purring as if they were the best of friends. Then she fried three eggs and ate them with the homemade croissant Margaux had left for her on the table, smothering it in creamy butter. And lastly, she made herself some coffee and went outside on the back porch to drink it. For the time being, she was free, and it felt so good.

As the country sunshine warmed her face, Ava pondered over what human beings can endure under extreme circumstances. How strong the human spirit is, defying all odds, learning to adapt and survive at all costs. The breath of life in us refuses to concede, no matter what. Like a moth to the flame, it never gives up, and all that matters is to keep breathing. To live another day.

Several chickens and goats meandered in the yard, clucking and bleating, and when the horned ruminants saw their new visitor, they ran up to greet her, their neck bells jingling. Ava smiled, her mind filling with fond memories of her childhood days with Shaylee and Luka on the Wolff farm. As she wandered out into the grassy field, the sweet fragrance of honeysuckle tantalized her olfactory receptors and the warm breeze caressed her epidermis, conjuring a euphoric sensation born of restored hope–the same sensation she had felt when escaping the Johannmeyers' grasp. Here she was, eight months pregnant, the summer zephyr pushing against her maternity dress covering what looked like a watermelon, the sunshine dispensing happy kisses on her pale skin, and the friendly Capra hircus encircling her, welcoming their guest. "Dear Lord," Ava whispered, "so many times I almost gave up. And look at me now."

When she walked around to the side of the house, to her surprise, Ava saw an elderly woman washing clothes in a metal tub, with a baby sleeping in a wicker basket next to a chair. That must be Margaux's mother, Henriette, and Colette's daughter, Cleopatra, she surmised. "*Hallo,*" Ava said.

The woman looked up but didn't reply.

Ava remembered Margaux saying that her mother didn't speak a word of German, and since Ava didn't speak French, she raised her hand and waved instead.

The language barrier didn't stop Henriette, and when she realized who Ava was, she immediately began speaking in French, coming up to Ava and taking her by the hand, bringing her to the chair beside the basket. "*Cleo a besoin d'être nourri (Cleo needs to be fed),*" she said, handing Ava a bottle of goat milk. She gestured to make sure Ava understood.

Ava smiled and picked up little Cleopatra, putting the bottle to the baby's mouth. The infant started suckling, even though she was still asleep.

Henriette was happy to see this and scrunched her wrinkled face into a wide smile void of half her teeth. *"C'est une bonne pratique pour vous (This is good practice for you)!"* she laughed.

Ava, having no idea what this woman just said, nodded and smiled back, whilst Cleo grabbed her finger as she suckled.

⁂

During her stay with the Beaumonts, Ava helped Henriette cook, clean, and babysit Cleo while the rest of the family worked at the hotel. When everyone was home, they would teach Ava French, pointing at things and naming them, with Ava repeating them back. Colette and Ava would go for long walks together, Colette carrying her baby in a sling and Ava carrying hers in her belly, and they'd practice through small talk. Colette would ask simple questions like, *"Comment s'est passée ta journée (How was your day)?"* and Ava would respond with, *"Très bien, merci (Very good, thank you)."* Before long, she could communicate in French in a rudimentary way, enough to get her meaning across.

The days seemed to melt by, and Ava's estimated due date drew near. Everyone in the Beaumont family was excited, anticipating the new life about to enter the world. Both Henriette and Margaux had delivered their own daughters at home, and had helped other women deliver theirs, so they reassured Ava there was no need for a formally trained midwife. Their combined knowledge and experience would more than suffice.

One Sunday, Margaux and Colette took Ava for a picnic in the forest next to the lake. Though they had just finished eating, they brought two baskets with plenty of homemade bread, cheese, and fruit, and found a lovely patch of grass to sit down on. Birds chirped their melodies in the trees, wildflowers scented the air, and a mild breeze rippled the water's surface. Ava lay on the blanket and stared up at the indigo blue sky, the white cotton candy clouds gently floating across the expanse like a groom's finger tracing the curves of his wife's naked form on their wedding night. Once more it harkened her back to the jocund days spent on the farm with her sister Shaylee, lying on the grass by the pond or on the bank of the Tauber River, talking and laughing without a care in the world.

"Do you have any baby names picked yet?" Colette asked.

Ava sat up and smiled. Now that she felt safe living with the Beaumonts, she had recently mulled it over. *"Ja,* I was thinking Ophelia if it's a girl, and Samuel if it's a boy."

"*Beaux noms (Beautiful names),*" said Margaux, her eyes fixed on her surroundings.

A little girl and her mother, both ragged in appearance, furtively showed themselves among the trees about fifty yards away. It set off Ava's alarm bells, noticing they weren't alone. "A child and woman are standing over there," she said nervously, pointing at them, making the little girl retreat into the bushes.

Margaux put her hand on Ava's arm and gently lowered it. "*C'est d'accord (It's okay).*" Without saying another word, she and her daughter got up and took the baskets of food to the woman. The three of them spoke for a minute, and the woman hugged her benefactors with sincere gratitude before disappearing.

Ava stared at the scene, realizing what Margaux and Colette were doing. They were feeding the Jews that were hiding in the forest! The ones she had heard about from the other Jewish maids at the Johannmeyer home. When they returned, she whispered, "You're helping the Jews."

Both women nodded.

Ava's eyes teared up, a soulful expression of awe on her face at the magnanimity of this family.

"Just like we're helping a young Jewish woman who's pregnant and hiding from the Gestapo," said Margaux.

The air caught in Ava's lungs . . . They had known all along! "But how . . . how did you know?" she asked, flabbergasted.

"The day I met you, the Gestapo came to the hotel asking the concierge questions. I overheard them. They said a woman by the name of Ava Wolff, pregnant with an SS officer's baby, had escaped her work assignment at a German home. The concierge, Monsieur Müller, doesn't like the Nazis either, so he didn't give you away. But I knew they would be back."

"That's why you befriended me, introduced me to your family, and took me in." Ava was now crying.

"*Oui, ma chére (Yes, my dear).*"

"But why risk your family like this? They will kill you if you get caught hiding a Jew."

Margaux smiled at Ava with a motherly aura, the same way her own mother, Maria, used to smile at her children. "Because, *douce enfant (sweet child),* I am Jewish too."

The revelation made Ava dizzy as intense succor swept through her entire body.

"We waited to tell you," said Colette, "because you needed to fully trust us first. Now you see that you can."

"Valentin created new identification papers for me," Margaux added, "and he will do the same for you." She reached out and touched Ava's hand. "So tell us, child, what is your story? . . . Your *real* story."

Shards of golden rays pierced through the clouds, illuminating Ava as if an actor on the stage, ready to deliver her heartrending soliloquy in a tragic Shakespearean play. She told Margaux and Colette everything. Her entire life story, summarized in a few hours, culminating in her ghastly imprisonment at Ravensbrück and her forced Lebensborn-like purpose at the Johannmeyers. She left out nothing, from her shocking discovery of her heritage and Starholf's heartless renunciation of their marriage, the hardship she suffered at the concentration camp and the heinous acts perpetrated against her by the commandant, to the anti-Semitic crimes and murders she had witnessed along the way.

Margaux and Colette cried with her the whole time.

Hugging and holding her.

Feeling her pain.

⁓⚜⁓

The following evening before dinner, gunshots ricocheted through the air. Colette's husband, Hugo, came barreling through the back door. "The Nazis are shooting at the Jews in the forest! Hurry, we must hide her!"

Margaux hastily ushered Ava toward a bookshelf in the living room. Except, like the wooden hutch at her father's farm, it was just a decoy. Behind the bookshelf was a small secret room, and by releasing the hidden latch, the unit could be pushed aside, allowing entry.

"You must be very quiet," Margaux implored, locking eyes with Ava, imparting the gravity of the situation without need for further explanation. "No matter what you hear, say nothing. I will come get you when it's safe."

Ava, wide-eyed and trembling, stepped inside, and Hugo slid the bookshelf back. From then on, all she heard were the muffled voices of the Beaumont family speaking to each other in an undertone. Fifteen minutes later, however, the Nazis arrived, boisterous in their bullying and intimidation.

379

They searched the house as a formality, suspecting nothing, believing the Jews hiding in the forest were their only concern. The Beaumonts played the role of country bumpkins to a tee, feigning ignorance of the vermin in the forest, professing to never have seen them. Ava's heart beat so hard she feared it would crack her ribcage, and she prayed fervently, beseeching God to assign her protectors a guardian angel like he had assigned her. For if she were discovered, they would not only take her away but also likely shoot the entire Beaumont family for their crime.

Though it seemed like forever, the interrogation was over quickly, and the bookshelf slid open. "All is clear, *ma chére*," said Margaux, cool as a cucumber. "You can come out now."

Ava looked down at the puddle around her feet. So terrified of the Nazi soldiers, her water had broken.

She was going into labor!

⚜

The contractions went on for three days. Margaux wouldn't leave Ava's side, speaking to her in a confident, reassuring way, and Colette made sure there were enough clean towels and hot water at the ready. Henriette remained nearby, the wise matriarch overseeing it all.

Ava kept moaning, hunching forward then lying back, trying to find a position that would bring relief; yet nothing worked.

"It's okay, child," Margaux said. "I have been through this with Colette, and she went through it with Cleo. You'll have your beautiful gift soon, and all this pain will be forgotten."

"*Cadeaux (Gifts)*," Henriette corrected. "*Il y en a deux (There are two).*"

Margaux's eyes shot up at her mother. "*Deux bébés (Two babies)?*"

"*Oui, elle va avoir des jumeaux (Yes, she is having twins).*"

Knowing her mother was always right in these matters, Margaux didn't question how Henriette could be so sure. And Ava, consumed by her discomfort, didn't catch what was said.

Meanwhile, the men were outside with Cleo, smoking and talking, deep concern etched across their brows.

"If this goes on much longer, we might have to bring her to the hospital in Dresden," Hugo said.

Valentin shook his head. "We can't trust the doctors. The Gestapo will have already informed them about a pregnant Jewish woman soon to give birth." He looked down at his granddaughter sleeping peacefully in her wicker basket. "And they would take Ava's baby away, then torture her until she died or gave us up."

Hugo frowned sorrowfully. "If she dies here in childbirth, at least it will be among those who love her."

Valentin nodded, patting his son-in-law on the back.

Inside the house, Margaux kept coaching Ava, conjuring up accoucheuse skills to assist with the birth. "You must push, *ma chére*. I know it hurts, but you must push hard."

Ava's lips were dry and cracked, her voice hoarse from the moaning, her complexion white. She was getting weaker by the hour. "I can't," she cried out, totally exhausted. "I have no more strength. Just let me die."

"*Nein*, child. Now you listen to me," Margaux said, firm in tone. "You are stronger than a lioness. You already survived *une expérience des plus terribles (a most terrible experience)* as a prisoner in a concentration camp, and a harsh environment as a maid forced to slave for a Nazi family. You had the courage to escape and use your wits to outsmart the Schutzstaffel and Gestapo. And you managed to remain free all this time, living in a hotel, avoiding capture. So, Ava Wolff, lioness of Rothenburg ob der Tauber, you will not give up now! Do you hear me? Push and give those twins the life you fought so hard to save!"

"Twins?" Ava asked, shocked.

"*Oui, ma chére* . . . Twins."

"I am a twin." Invigorated by the bombshell, Ava pushed hard. So hard she thought she would pass out.

"*Gute*, child! *Gute*! Keep pushing!"

Seconds later, the first baby crowned, and within minutes, slid out of the womb.

"*Une fille (A girl)!*" Margaux exclaimed. She cut the umbilical cord, handed the baby to Colette, and clamped the end of the cord coming out of Ava, knowing that twin babies sometimes shared a placenta, and the second baby could bleed through the cord of the first.

Ava filled with elation at the sound of her daughter crying as Colette cleaned and wrapped the infant snug in a towel. She wanted to hold her baby immediately and reached out for her, but Margaux said, "One more to go, *ma chére*. Keep pushing."

Soon the second baby crowned and came out.

"Un garçon (A boy)!" Margaux once more exclaimed. Again she cut the umbilical cord, but something was wrong with this newborn . . . He wasn't moving or breathing!

Henriette started speaking rapidly in French and took the child, holding him upside down by his feet. She slapped the baby's bottom and rubbed his back, until finally the infant expanded its lungs and exhaled a copious, booming cry.

Ava sobbed with joy as Colette placed both her babies in her arms. Staring down at her daughter full of life and color, she said, "Look at you, my little princess Ophelia. You're a lioness too, aren't you." She then gazed at her pinkish-blue son, still swollen from his ordeal. "And you, my brave little man, Samuel. You looked after your sister, didn't you, almost sacrificing your life for her."

Three generations of Beaumont women exchanged looks and watched in awe, knowing that if they hadn't helped Ava by bringing her to their home, she and her babies would have died in that hotel.

CHAPTER 39

Ava still loved Starholf.

Wait . . . What!

Yes, she still loved him, despite all that he had done to her.

But how was that possible?

Children. Innocent, adorable, precious children . . .

Ophelia and Samuel.

Though Starholf had abandoned her, causing her physical pain, emotional dolor, killing her spirit as if he had taken a razor and slit her throat, then stepped back and watched it slowly bleed out, the birth of Ophelia and Samuel changed things. True, only mere weeks prior, when she was in the cab driver's car, escaping from the Johannmeyers to Dresden, she had cursed his name, his memory, thinking him a cowardly, disgusting, obscene monster for allowing his pregnant wife to be sent off to a concentration camp when he had the power to save her. But now, as she gazed into the angelic faces of her newborns, a power beyond reason swept over her, miraculously transmuting her odium for him back into love. And she wished so much he could be here to see them. To hold them. To cherish them. Yes, she still loved her husband for who he was before her world had crumbled. Before he knew she was Jewish.

In the dead of night, as their children slept beside her, one on her chest and the other cradled deep inside the curve of her inner arm, she would lie awake and think of all the things they would never get to do as a family. Like walking along the beach of the Baltic Sea, picking up seashells and making sandcastles. Or gazing at the splendiferous sunset as the sky metamorphosed into a blend of bright fuchsia, flaming scarlet, and molten gold. Or snuggling under blankets on the porch during a cool autumn night, pointing out the constellations as they drank hot cocoa.

All these precious moments, and many more, were lost to the abyss of hatred driving man's inhumanity to man. Experiencing their children growing up in that beautiful Steiner mansion, witnessing their first steps, hearing their first words, the love, the laughter, the joy that would have been . . . all traded for Hitler's vision of the Third Reich.

What an unconscionable tragedy!

Though she was thankful for her current situation, safe in the solicitude of the Beaumont family, Ava still suffered emotionally. PTSD had taken hold, as it often does when one comes out of the firestorm and has time to reflect. She tried to keep busy to cope with it, tending to her newborns, helping around the house, doing what she could to be useful. But it was a daily struggle.

Henriette was Ava's companion while the others worked at the hotel. Besides the fellowship, it helped improve her French. The older lady would often ramble on about how the world used to be when she was young–peaceful, courteous, honorable–before the Great War started in 1914 that took her husband from her. And now, with a second world war scourging the earth, she was certain dark spirit forces were in control, unleashing a plague of men possessed. Ava didn't catch all that Henriette was saying, especially when the woman spoke fast, but she understood the gist of it.

"When I was a little girl in my grandmother's village," Henriette said one morning in French, "a wise older woman would threaten bad men with spells, preventing them from doing wicked things. In those days, people were superstitious, and a curse was enough to scare them. But now the Great Dragon, the one called Devil and Satan, has been cast down to the earth, and he is very angry, knowing he has a short period of time. He has brought a plague of death and destruction with him and has filled the earth with it."

"How long will this plague last?" Ava asked, goosebumps covering her skin.

Henriette's searing gaze stared into nothing. "*Seul Dieu le sait cette, ma chére (Only God knows that, my dear).*"

⁓⦁⦂⦁⁓

Ava stayed close to her new home. Unless she was with the Beaumonts, she'd hardly ever venture out further than the backyard. After the

Nazis had shot at the Jews in the forest, coming into the house to interrogate the family thereafter, she feared their return. She knew how determined the Third Reich was to eradicate the "Undesirables," and it was only a matter of time before they'd be back.

One afternoon, notwithstanding the risk, Ava became restless and desperately wanted out. Out of the house, out of her problems, out of her head . . . Anywhere but in. With the Beaumonts at work and Henriette looking after the babies, she put on her boots and a red velvet cloak Colette had given her, covering her head with the cowl. She waited until Henriette was distracted, and like Little Red Riding Hood, off she went toward the lake.

The air was fresh and fragrant, the ground soft from an earlier rainstorm, the birds chirping a mirthful song. Ava sauntered across the meadow, nervous yet excited to explore on her own, her heart thrumming a little louder with each step. She kept a close eye on her surroundings, and when she came to the forest edge, she hesitated for a moment, then boldly entered.

For weeks now, from her bedroom window, Ava had seen a church steeple sticking out from among the treetops. When the sunlight hit the apex just right, it shimmered like polished silver, as if God were inviting her for a visit. And Ava wanted to go. She wanted to inspect its interior, to see what this church looked like, and most importantly, to supplicate the Hearer of Prayer in his own house.

As she approached the front of the old church, the birds seemed to chirp more zealously, as if gossiping with each other about the visiting stranger. The towering oak trees and whispering pines suddenly stilled, as if dismissing the breeze to focus on her as well. And Ava became hyperaware of the sound of her footsteps on the forest mulch, as if they too had somehow personified.

Standing in front of the two oval wooden doors, she slowly pushed one open. The hinges groaned, weary from disuse, and a draft of musty, damp air escaped the nave. The inside of the church was smaller than the outside would have you believe, and it was empty. Ava walked down the center aisle between the pews, looking up and around at the architecture. Like St. Jacob's Church in Rothenburg ob der Tauber, the structure was medieval, elaborate, and impressive, possessing an aura of grandeur. Stone pillars rose majestically, holding aloft the arched ceiling that echoed with the silent prayers of centuries; and tall, slender stained glass windows reflected a kaleidoscope of vivid colors, each pane a meticulous craftwork depicting biblical tales and saintly figures.

Ava walked to the front of the church and gazed up at the sculpture of Jesus Christ dominating the altar. Crucified on the stake, his crown of thorns penetrating his skull and his blood seeping from his wounds, the realism of the image was startling, its presence overwhelming, compelling Ava to her knees. She bowed her head, clasping her hands tightly, and began to pray. She prayed to the Creator for the strength to carry on, for the safety of those she loved, and for the atrocities of the war to end.

But then, a sound . . . Someone else was there!

Ava's head snapped up, and she rose to her feet, scanning the shadows that clung to the corners of the church. Was it the Nazis, hiding and ready to pounce? Oh no! My children, she thought! With her heart pounding wildly, adrenaline surging through her veins, she rushed back to the entrance of the church in a panic. Just before exiting, her peripheral vision caught sight of a man standing behind the last pillar, staring at her.

Ava pushed open the door and ran, her crimson cloak billowing behind her.

⚜

"**I** went to the church today," Ava announced that evening at dinner.

The Beaumont family simultaneously stopped eating and looked up at her, somewhat alarmed.

"I know I shouldn't have, but I really needed to get out, and I thought a house of God would be safe."

Margaux gave her mother a scolding glare. "*Tu l'as laissée partir au la forêt (You let her go to the forest)?*"

"*Je ne savais pas (I didn't know),*" said Henriette. "*La fille m'a passée glissé (The girl slipped past me).*"

"You shouldn't be going out on your own," Valentin counseled. "It's too dangerous."

Ava lowered her gaze, her cheeks flushing with guilt. "I'm sorry," she murmured, the weight of their collective worry bearing down on her.

"Did anyone see you?" Colette asked.

"*Ja,* there was a man there, standing behind one of the pillars. Nearly scared me to death."

"That's Father Craven," Colette said. "He came from another church that the Nazis had expropriated, and he hides in the basement."

"Hides?"

"*Oui*," said Margaux. "The Nazis don't like priests, either. Many have been murdered or arrested, including Father Weber who had a small congregation there before the Schutzstaffel came and took him away."

"Why?"

"They feel threatened by organized religion," said Hugo. "Which is not surprising, being an ungodly organization themselves."

The Nazis' long-term plan was to de-Christianize Germany after winning the war. Their ideology would not tolerate any organization or group that did not swear complete allegiance to the Third Reich, superseding even God. Aggressive anti-Church radicals within the Nazi Party had made this a priority concern, with Hitler initially restraining them only insomuch as to prevent strengthening the Church from undue persecution. Clergy members were closely watched, denounced, arrested, murdered, and sent to concentration camps, with an estimated one third of all priests facing some form of reprisal during the time the Nazis were in power.

"We bring Father Craven food, just like the Jews in the forest," Colette said. "He probably thought it was us and came up from his hiding spot."

"From the look on his face, I think I gave him a fright too," said Ava, trying to lighten the mood with a small smile. As she recalled him standing there in the shadows behind the pillar, staring at her with intensity in his blue eyes, it reminded her of someone she knew.

❧

Three days later, a horrible tragedy occurred. Nazi soldiers had ambushed the Jews hiding out in the forest and shot them all dead. The slaughter was indiscriminate—men, women, children, and even babies, all gunned down without mercy. Hearing the gunshots in the distance, the Beaumont family wished there was something they could do, but like the victims, they were powerless, only hoping the casualties were low. To be safe, they hid Ava behind the bookshelf again and brought Samuel and Ophelia into Hugo and Colette's bedroom, pretending the babies were theirs. But thankfully, the Nazis didn't come to the house this time.

Ava was in her room that evening when she heard voices downstairs, tense and emotional. She was tending to Samuel who was cranky with colic; Ophelia was fast asleep in her crib. Placing her son next to his sister, she went to see what the commotion was about.

"No words can describe it," said a man with an English accent, his voice cracking in disbelief. He had his back turned to Ava as everyone huddled around the kitchen table, listening to him relate what he had witnessed. "Families with children . . . even babies . . . all shot in the head and left to rot where they fell."

Valentin shook his head. "It must look like the Apocalypse."

"*Ja*, except the innocent were the ones annihilated."

Margaux noticed Ava standing at the entrance of the kitchen. "Come, come, *ma chére*," she beckoned, waving her over. "This is Father Craven, the man you saw at the church."

When the priest turned around, he locked eyes with her, his gaze intense like their first encounter.

Margaux finished the introduction. "Father, this is Ava Wolff, the young woman I told you about."

He stood and extended his hand to her. "Nice to meet you, Ava."

As if a deer caught in headlights, Ava hesitated. The man, in his late thirties, his face no longer in the shadows, could have been Starholf's doppelgänger with dark hair! Eyes like sea glass, chiseled jaw, fair skin–the resemblance to her ex-husband was uncanny, and conflicting impulses goaded her to either run to him or run away from him.

"I won't bite, I promise," said the priest, releasing a charming grin–again, so like Starholf's.

Ava slowly reached out and slid her slender hand into his firm grip. Hypnotized by his gaze, it seemed as if everyone else in the room had disappeared, and the two of them were now in the Steiner mansion. Memories of her short-lived life with Starholf flooded her mind, again conflicting her with sensations of joy, devastation, happiness, and heartache. Releasing his hand, she kept the revelation about his appearance to herself, her skin becoming clammy over it.

Margaux pulled out a chair next to the priest. "Sit, *ma chére*. Father Craven was just telling us about *le terrible meurtre (the terrible murder)* of the Jews in the forest."

"*Ja*, a most heinous crime," said the priest. "God will not forget what they did."

"They'll likely be back soon to bury them in a mass grave," Hugo said. "The Nazis usually don't leave evidence of such shocking crimes out in the open."

"That's why tomorrow morning I will go back there and pray over the dead bodies," said Father Craven.

"That's risky. They could catch you."

"I'm a man of God, Hugo. To not pray over the deceased would be sacrilege."

Before the war on the Wolff farm, and as a married woman living a sheltered life at the Steiner mansion, Ava would have been distraught and in tears over what she was hearing. But now, after witnessing similar atrocities at Ravensbrück and Ingrid's murder at the Johannmeyers, and experiencing the brutal rapes by the camp commandant, all she could do was sit there, numb and in silence.

"I wonder if the ghost in the forest will now have company," Colette said.

That stoked Ava's curiosity. "Ghost?"

"*Ja.* A Jewish family who owned a cottage nearby was murdered by the Nazis six months ago. Their little girl, about twelve years old, has haunted the woods ever since."

Henriette began rambling in French about her unnerving encounter with the apparition, swearing she'll never go anywhere near that forest again without her crucifix.

"I've seen her too," Hugo said. "She appears, and then she vanishes. It's enough to raise the hair on your neck."

"A lost soul is what she is," said Valentin. "Perhaps you could pray for her too, Father, when you pray over the dead bodies tomorrow."

The priest nodded, though he didn't believe in ghosts.

"I'm coming with you," Ava said.

Everyone looked at her with surprise.

"I have to go in case my sister is among them."

"I thought you said she escaped with her fiancé," Margaux questioned.

"She did, but I don't know where they went. What if they were there, hiding with that group of Jews?"

"It's a very tragic sight," Father Craven said, sadness in his sky blue eyes. "I'm a grown man, and it jarred me to the bone. I strongly recommend you don't come."

Ava thought of Shaylee before the war, always so quiet and gentle, reading a book in Rothenburg's library or admiring the art in the town's museum. She was always telling Ava how much she loved her, and Ava was often too proud to say it back. How she regretted that now, wishing she could hug her twin sister and tell her how much she loved her. "I have to know," she insisted. "If Shaylee was there and is now dead, I have to know."

"What if you find her?" Hugo asked.

"Then I will bury her myself."

Margaux looked at her husband, and he nodded. Placing her hand on Ava's arm, she said, "All right, *ma chére*. But do it quickly and return right away."

"I will. I promise."

❧

Father Craven spent the night at the Beaumonts. Early in the morning, just before sunrise, he tapped lightly on Ava's bedroom door. She opened it right away, dressed and ready to go. For a moment they only stared at each other, paralyzed by a peculiar mixture of chemistry, odd familiarity, and angst over what they were about to do.

"I wasn't sure if you still wanted to come," he half-whispered.

"I do. Like I said, I must know."

He nodded. "Very well, then. Let's go."

Henriette was the only one up, sitting in her favorite rocking chair in the living room, knitting a scarf without even looking. Her creased eyes, full of wisdom and experience, fixed on Ava's emerald gaze with a chilling pathos, as if knowing everything she was thinking, feeling, hoping. "*Que Dieu Tout-Puissant te protège, enfant (May Almighty God protect you, child).*"

"*Merci (Thank you),*" said Ava, her anxiety level rising.

Henriette's mien instantly turned positive, almost jubilant, as if God had given her a glimpse of Ava's future. "*Tu survivras cette tribulation, lionne de Rothenburg ob der Tauber (You will survive this tribulation, lioness of Rothenburg ob der Tauber).*"

In the gray predawn light, Father Craven led Ava across the meadow to the edge of the woods. As if a warning not to proceed, the forest seemed to hold its breath, the trees standing as solemn witnesses to the horrors that had unfolded beneath their boughs.

"Are you certain you want to see this?" Father Craven asked one last time.

Ava nodded.

A chilling breeze whispered through the leaves as they ventured into the woods, carrying with it the faint, metallic scent of blood. The first rays of sunlight pierced the canopy, casting eerie shadows that danced over the ground like specters. And a mourning dove would not let up its sorrowful call. Half a mile from the medieval church, they came upon the massacre . . .

Ava immediately fell to her knees and vomited.

"I'm sorry," said the priest, not knowing what else to say. "I was sick to my stomach too when I first saw them all."

When Ava regained her equilibrium, she slowly walked among the dead bodies scattered across the ground like a macabre mosaic. The heavy pounding in her heart threatened to pulverize the other vital organs in her thorax as she looked into the face of each corpse, fearful she would recognize her sister. Thick tears streamed down like a river; her entire being shook.

"Go back to the church," Father Craven said, seeing the revulsion on Ava's face. "If I find your twin sister, I'll come get you."

But Ava forced herself to stay, continuing her search.

Some of the deceased looked only to be sleeping, others appeared wide awake, their lifeless eyes staring violently ahead. Some appeared to be shot execution style, others while trying to run. Ava knelt beside a young woman, her heart seizing within her chest as she brushed a lock of hair from the woman's face. Not Shaylee, and yet the relief never came. She rose and continued, each step heavier than the last, each face a new fissure in her already shattered heart.

Every time Ava came upon a dead child, her knees buckled. One little girl who looked like Zelda Applebaum when she first came with her sister Jeta to the farm, cute as a button with her two front teeth missing, clung to her mother, her face frozen in terror. Her little brother, covered in dried blood, lay next to them.

Just like the ghastly scene at Ravensbrück, where naked bodies lay piled on top of each other like rotting mannequins, it again reminded Ava of the hauntingly ghoulish painting Shaylee had once shown her–*The Raft of the Medusa*. Only this time, it was much worse because of the sheer numbers. When Ava came across a dead baby, a bullet hole through the infant's eye, she lost all control and screamed heavenward, "Why are you allowing this! Why!", then fell to the ground, sobbing.

Meanwhile, Father Craven was fervently reciting the Requiem Prayer over the dead . . .

"Eternal rest grant unto them, O Lord, and let perpetual light shine upon them. May the souls of all the faithful departed, through the mercy of God, rest in peace. Amen."

⚜

On their way home, Ava did not speak. The shock of it all had rendered her mute, and she could not get the gruesome images out of her mind. A cold chill wrapped around her like a wet blanket in winter, seeping into her bone marrow, causing her to shiver. And it seemed like they weren't alone, as if the souls of the dead Jews were now following them, still seeking refuge, attaching themselves to the living.

"It's like they're still with us," Ava whispered, an outré look on her face. "Why do I feel like they're here?"

Father Craven observed her, concerned over her mental and emotional state.

"Why do I feel like they're here, Father?" she repeated, looking all around. "I can feel their eyes on me."

"Ava . . . There's no one here. Just you and me."

But Ava didn't believe him, her wild stare searching intently through the trees. And that's when she saw it: The apparition of the twelve-year-old girl the Beaumonts had spoken of. Ragged clothes, dirty hair, pale skin—almost translucent, body emaciated, the young girl looked like a sickly fairy. Terrified, Ava raised her hand and pointed. "There!"

When the priest looked, he saw nothing. "I warned you not to come. You shouldn't have seen what you did. Now you're hallucinating."

"*Nein*, I'm not!" she rebuffed. "The little girl . . . she was just there!" And yet, the girl had vanished. Ava began to sob, frantically looking around, trying to spot her again. When she couldn't find her, she got angry and glared at the priest. "What *gute* is that God you worship, anyway! Why doesn't he prevent all this! How can he watch as innocent people are slaughtered by these monsters!"

Father Craven had no answers either, his own faith under test. Gripping his Bible firmly, holding it close to his chest, he stared at Ava as she transformed from a quiet, sweet woman into an erratic moonling, howling at the injustice.

Though Ava had not found her sister among the bullet-ridden bodies, she was certain Shaylee too was dead. How could she and Christian have survived their escape when God wouldn't even protect a multitude of Jews hiding in the forest? No, Shaylee was buried somewhere in a shallow grave. Or incinerated into ashes, floating out the chimney of a crematorium after being gassed at a concentration camp. What were her last thoughts as she died, Ava wondered? Did she think of me, her identical twin, originating from the same zygote before splitting into separate embryos? Did she hold her breath for as long as she could before inhaling the poisonous fumes? Did she scream out my name at the last?

Unhinged, Ava fell to her knees, her emerald eyes wide and wild, her visage deranged and demented. A crazed woman who had lost her mind, she catatonically stared straight ahead at nothing. Father Craven, perturbed by the look out of her glossy, trance-like gaze, recalled from the Scriptures how a Phoenician woman had come to Jesus, pleading for him to cure her demon-possessed daughter. He wondered if a demon had attached itself to Ava, too, reaping enjoyment from her suffering. Kneeling, he took Ava into his arms and cradled her, reciting a quiet prayer from the Psalms . . .

"Yea, though I walk through the valley of the shadow of death, I will fear no evil: for thou art with me; thy rod and thy staff they comfort me." – Psalm 23:4

※

Ava was now in bed. Still catatonic, having no recollection of Father Craven bringing her back to the house, she stared at the wall, her body floating aimlessly like a rudderless ship lost at sea.

"She had a mental breakdown," Father Craven said. He was talking in a low voice to the Beaumonts in the kitchen. "It was too graphic for her to see."

"How can you blame her," said Margaux, "after all she's been through. *L'esprit ne peut que prendre tellement (The mind can only take so much).*"

"Did she find her sister?" Colette asked.

"*Nein.* But she said she saw that ghost child. The little girl. That's when she went mad."

"Did you see her too?" Hugo asked.

Father Craven shook his head. "I think Ava was hallucinating."

"*Nein*, Father. We've all seen the ghost of that poor girl," said Margaux.

"Well, as a man of God, I don't believe in ghosts. Only angels and demons."

The Beaumonts looked at each other, but no one argued with the priest.

Ava slowly came out of her catatonia. In the quiet of her room, her consciousness wove itself back from the abyss. Recognizing where she was, a calmness embraced her, like the placidity she used to feel as a child when Hanz and Maria gave her a hug.

As she lay there in bed by the soft glow of a bedside lamp, Ava's mind wandered to a cherished memory of her father playing his violin for her and Shaylee, giving them a private recital at the Wolff farm. She could almost see him standing there, winking at his beloved swans as he ebulliently performed a violin concerto from one of the Renaissance greats. She smiled at the vision. Such happy times, they were.

Closing her eyes, Ava basked in the music caressing her pneuma. The melody became energetic, flamboyant, fortissimo, and she wondered if everyone else in the house could hear it too. Toward the end, as the final notes faded into a soothing pianissimo of tranquility, her eyelids grew heavy, and she slipped into the refuge of sleep.

Before long, Ava started dreaming she was in the forest again, walking among the trees. But the trees were distorted, like giant trolls and ogres, and the ground was an interminable mass grave. The sky was gray as clouds imprisoned the sun, and the land, lifeless and bleak, emulated the dark aftermath of a cataclysm.

Suddenly Ava had the feeling she was being watched, just like before. As she turned around, the apparition of the little girl stepped out from behind a grotesque tree. A prickle rippled down from the base of Ava's neck to the bottom of her spine as her body filled with terror. She tried to run, but a hand reached up from the mass grave and grabbed her ankle, tumbling her to the ground. In absolute horror, she found herself on top of a mountain of dead, decomposing bodies, the soil sucking her in like quicksand.

Desperately Ava tried to stand up, but the more she struggled the more she sank, bloodied arms and legs entangling her as if thorned branches from a Black Locust tree. When she looked down at the body beneath her, her heart stopped . . .

It was Shaylee!

"Neiiinn!" Ava screamed. Shot through the eye, just like the baby, Shaylee's beautiful face had been violently butchered by a 9mm bullet. Ava held her sister in her arms, caterwauling in utter anguish, unable to even breathe. Howbeit she had suffered immensely during this war already, nothing compared to finding her sister like this. The true depth of heartbreak, wretchedness, and despair became known to her, and she wailed and wailed.

"Hush, now, my sweet sister," whispered faintly into Ava's ear.

But she kept ululating.

"Shhhh . . . It's okay, Ava."

A soft hand gently caressed her cheek, and when Ava opened her eyes, a miracle transpired . . . "Shaylee! You're alive!"

In an instant, a glorious meadow replaced the massive mountain of dead bodies, the trees were lush and green, the sun shone brightly in a lazuline sky, and the two sisters lay on a blanket by the pond at the Wolff farm, holding hands. Swans floated in the tranquil water; butterflies drifted on by.

"I thought you were dead!" Ava cried. "I thought I had lost you!"

"We're identical twins," said Shaylee, her tone calm and sure, her beautiful face unmarred by even the slightest imperfection. "We share the same life force, so if I were to die, you would feel it right away."

Ava noticed the twelve-year-old girl, no longer a corpselike apparition but a happy, healthy child, playing in the field with Felix, Bastian, and Axel. She waved at Ava, giggling in delight.

"I'm still alive," Shaylee said, kissing her sister on the cheek. "And I'm waiting for you, Ava. Come find me."

Ava woke up in a sweat. "Shaylee's alive!" she exclaimed, shaking and crying. "My sister is still alive!"

CHAPTER 40

It had now been five months since Christian and Shaylee sought refuge in the abandoned Jewish mansion in the forest. What was meant to be a hiding spot for only a month, two at best, turned out to be the entire summer. The Nazis had not returned, and while the outside world was being tossed about like debris in a hurricane, the couple had managed to avoid the brutalities of war occurring all across Europe.

Now, however, they were running low on supplies, having eaten most of the canned food in the cellar. Christian had no choice but to venture out to the nearest town to get what they needed. Realizing they should have left for Sweden a long time ago, he shook his head, disappointed in himself. The beautiful home, the beautiful weather, his beautiful wife, the seclusion they enjoyed, basking in each other's love—it had all lulled him into complacency, ignoring the reality of their dire situation when he should have been diligently making plans for their escape from Germany.

Shaylee walked hand in hand with him to where his car was hidden. "I wish you wouldn't go," she said, afraid of being alone, even for just a few hours. "We're fine. All I need is my handsome man."

"You say that now with a belly full of canned peaches," he replied. "Tomorrow, when your stomach aches, I won't look so handsome."

She put her head on his shoulder. "I'm terrified you won't return."

Christian stopped and faced her, gently grabbing hold of her shoulders and looking deep into her eyes. "I will return, Shaylee. I promise. I'm German, and no one has any reason to suspect me of anything. I won't linger anywhere, either."

She loved how he always made her feel safe and secure. "All right," she ceded, wrapping her arms around him, squeezing him tight. Too bad Ava didn't have a husband like Christian, she thought. Please, God, protect my sister and her child; I beg of you. Looking up at Christian with tears in her shining, hazel green eyes, she asked, "Can you please get me a fashion magazine too?"

He chuckled. "A fashion magazine?"

"*Ja*. Or else a magazine about Hollywood movies and actresses. If you can find one."

"Why?"

"Because Ava loved them, and I miss her terribly."

⚜

Christian drove to the nearest town, a good hour away. Getting out of his car, he kept his head low and nervously looked around, then walked into the local grocers. Within fifteen minutes, he had everything he and Shaylee needed to get them through the next few weeks—fruit, vegetables, meat, cheese, and bread. And of course, a fashion magazine.

Thank goodness he had cashed his check that day in Nuremberg before he picked up Shaylee, he thought. Going into a bank now would be out of the question, since the name Christian Hoffmann, a traitorous Wehrmacht soldier helping a dirty Jew, would be on the Nazi's "Most Wanted" list. As he made his way to the checkout counter, a display of tortoiseshell combs caught his eye. Thinking it a nice surprise gift for his wife, he picked an elegant one to compliment her dark hair.

"A fashion magazine and a beautiful shell comb for your *Fräulein*," said the woman at the cash register, smiling at him as she rang up each item. With her blonde hair in curlers and apron high on her thick waist, she reminded Christian of his mother. "How romantic. Would you like to add some chocolates and flowers? She'll love you even more."

Christian looked at the small heart-shaped box she pointed out, along with the arrangement of freshly cut roses. "*Ja, bitte*. Add those too."

"She's a lucky girl to have such a thoughtful, handsome young man."

"Why aren't you in uniform, son?" barked her husband, sitting in a chair a few feet away, his stern eyes staring at Christian from above his Nazi newspaper, the *Völkischer Beobachter (People's Observer)*. He was reading about Operation Barbarossa, where 3.8 million German soldiers had been sent into the Soviet Union to fight along a zone of conflict 1,800 miles long, establishing the Eastern Front of the war. The five-month offensive, from

June 22 to December 5, 1941, was the largest and costliest in human history, with around 10 million combatants taking part and over 8 million casualties by the end of it.

"Leave him alone," his wife defended. "Do you think they always wear them when they're on military leave?"

Christian's pulse started racing. "It's in the wash, sir."

The man frowned. "A proud Wehrmacht soldier should never be seen out of uniform during wartime."

"Look at his sweet face," said his wife. "Can't you tell he's in love?" She winked at Christian. "Don't mind my grumpy husband. He's forgotten what it's like to be *jung und verliebt (young and in love).*"

Christian forced a smile, paid the bill, and was on his way. When he exited the store, he saw a Jewish man on his knees across the street, two SS officers standing over him, hurling disgusting insults about the Jews. Somehow the man had managed to hide in his vandalized shoe and leather repair shop, surviving right under the noses of the Nazis all this time. Knowing it was the end, he remained motionless, staring at the ground rather than pleading for his life, waiting to be shot. Seconds later, he fell forward, a bullet hole in the back of his head.

Aghast, Christian started walking, just like the other pedestrians who had become accustomed to Jews being murdered in the streets, glancing over but saying nothing as they went about their business. When he got to his car, he quickly loaded the groceries in the trunk, jumped in the driver's seat, and turned the ignition.

"Stop!" shouted the grocery store owner, putting up his hand as he stepped in front of the vehicle.

Startled, Christian stared at the man. Had the grocer figured out who he was? The two SS officers, hearing him shout, were now looking at them, and Christian began to panic. Caught in a hornet's nest, with a menacing-looking Nazi sympathizer in front of him and two SS officers behind, he didn't know what to do. Should he step on the gas and run the man over, fleeing for his life? The thought of being arrested, or shot right there like the Jewish man, not able to return to Shaylee like he promised he would, made his heart sink. "*Nein,* I won't let this happen," he mumbled under his breath, determined to go down fighting. And just as he was about to hit the gas, the grocer came over to the driver's side door and knocked on the glass. Christian rolled down the window.

"You forgot the fancy comb for your *Fräulein*," said the grocer. "My wife was still gift-wrapping it for you when you left."

"Oh . . . *ja*, I . . . sorry . . . I was in a bit of a rush," Christian stuttered. "*Dankeschön.*"

"And get back into uniform, son! Be proud of who you are and what you stand for!" The grocer tapped the roof of the car and stepped back to give the Sieg Heil salute. "Heil Hitler!"

"Heil Hitler!" Christian parroted.

As he made the long drive back to the abandoned mansion, Christian ruminated on many things. Seeing that Jewish man capitulate to his execution, murdered in cold blood in the street as if it were inevitable, even deserved, was unsettling beyond words. Alive one moment, dead the next. And for what? Nine months he had been carried in his mother's womb, woven like a precious blanket by the awe-inspiring miracle of life, loved and cared for by his parents as a baby, nurtured and schooled from a boy through to manhood, then likely married with children of his own. All that life—the memories and experiences, the goals and accomplishments, the learnings and triumphs, the sunrises and sunsets—snuffed out in an instant. The senselessness of it all was sickening.

Being in love with a Jewish woman himself, it weighed heavily on Christian. Though he had sworn to protect Shaylee, in truth, there was little he could do against an army. If only there were a way to guarantee her safety, even at the expense of his own. If only he could find a surefire way to get her out of the country. If only they could live out their lives together, away from the madness of it all.

If only a million things.

Christian turned off the main road, entering the narrow path leading through the dense woods to their hideout. Their sanctuary. He would be seeing Shaylee's beautiful, smiling face any minute now. Yet in his mind, he could not erase the image of the Jewish man, his life effaced from the earth in a trice.

⚜

Early the next morning, with the rising sun, a little bird sat on the bedroom windowsill, chirping a passionate song. It seemed to pose as it sang, as if it were Violetta, the high-class courtesan in nineteenth-century Paris, professing her love for the young nobleman, Alfredo, in Giuseppe Verdi's iconic opera, *La traviata.* The song woke Shaylee from her slumber, and she stared at the Bavarian avifauna, mesmerized by the beauty of God's tiny creature. This is what mankind should be focused on, she thought. The Creator, and the splendor of his creation.

Christian woke and pulled Shaylee's naked body into his.

"Listen," she whispered. "The bird . . . Isn't it beautiful?"

He kissed her forehead, and they lay there in silence, enjoying the melodious tune. But Christian's mind kept wandering, interrupted by the ghastly experience from yesterday, his quiescence vanishing. "I'm going to tell you something, Shaylee," he said, breaking the silence. The little bird stopped singing and flew off, as if frightened by Christian's thoughts, unable to bear them. "It might sound alarming to you, but I need you to know."

"What is it?"

He tried hard to articulate his words in the right way. "Once you deeply love someone, that bond is forever forged. It can never be broken."

Shaylee looked up at him, meeting his eyes.

"I'm usually just an awkward, bumbling nobody, trying to find meaning in this world like anyone else. But one thing I know for certain, is that when you love someone as deeply as I love you, it can never die. Even if the person dies, the love itself survives, transcending death."

Shaylee wondered where he was going with this.

"They say energy cannot be destroyed; it can only change, from one form to another. And it's the same with love. No matter what happens to me, my love will always be with you, Shaylee. Forever. I want you to know that. To believe that. With all your heart."

His words started scaring her. "What are you talking about? You'll always be by my side. Always. Promise me, Christian."

"Shaylee, I can't promise you that. It's a miracle we've even had this time together, given what's happening out there." The morning light started flooding the room, illuminating everything in its path, as if the angels in heaven were listening. "But what I can promise you, is that I'll die trying to protect you."

"Why are you saying all this? You're frightening me."

"Because I have to keep us in reality. People are being slaughtered daily, and I don't know what the future holds." Again, the gruesome image of the Jewish man, succumbing to his fate, flooded Christian's mind. But he had no intention of telling Shaylee what he had witnessed; it would only frighten her more.

"We can stay here until it's over," said Shaylee, desperately trying to maintain the delusion.

He shook his head. "Eventually we'll run out of money. Or the soldiers will return. Or a German family will be given possession of the home. I just don't know."

"We're going to die, aren't we," Shaylee said, starting to cry. "That's what you're telling me. That it's only a matter of time."

"*Nein*, my sweet Shaylee. That's not what I'm saying." He pulled her in tightly, wrapping his strong arms around her like an emperor penguin covering its egg. "What I'm saying is that no matter what happens to me, to us, our love will survive it all."

As Shaylee softly wept in Christian's arms, the little bird returned to the windowsill, continuing its seraphic song. So beautifully it sang that Shaylee abruptly stopped crying, listening attentively once more. If only we could live inside that song, she thought. Like a dream within a dream, disappearing into it forever.

✦

Two weeks later, Shaylee disclosed some alarming news while they were lying in bed. "Christian," she said nervously.

"What," he mumbled, already drifting off.

"I don't know if it's because I'm eating less, but my period has stopped."

He opened his eyes.

"It's been three months now."

Christian sat up and looked at her. "Are you pregnant?"

"I don't know . . . Maybe."

The color left his face. "But we've been careful."

"There were a few times when we weren't."

Though having a baby seemed like the most natural thing in the world for two people in love, it wasn't the time or place, and they both knew it.

Shaylee placed her hand on her stomach. "Lately I've been feeling nauseous in the mornings, too." She started crying. "How could we have let this happen? How can I have a baby now, Christian?"

The words leaving her mouth sounded strange in his ears. Like when a sound is made in a cave, echoing until it disappears. "Shaylee, don't cry. I'll figure something out, I promise. I'm going to get us to Sweden."

Neither one spoke after that. How frustrating and painful it was to be at the mercy of their circumstances. At the mercy of the war, the Nazis, the evil infecting the land.

Christian hugged Shaylee and whispered that he loved her, that everything will be all right and she'll be a wonderful mother.

Shaylee stopped crying, her fears calming, his firm embrace making her feel safe.

CHAPTER 41

Berlin, 1997

The landlady had been talking for hours, holding me captive to this most astonishing story. But then she abruptly stopped, and her tired eyes became sad and glossy. Tears started flowing down her cheeks. "Mrs. Kuchen, are you okay?" I asked.

She didn't answer, seemingly catatonic, staring into nothing.

"Mrs. Kuchen?"

When she still didn't respond, I turned off the tape recorder and looked at the grandfather clock that ticked in the hallway. It was now 3:00 a.m. Though wide awake and I didn't want her to stop, I also didn't want to exhaust her. "I could come back tomorrow, if you wish," I said. "To hear the rest of the story. I have to know what happened."

Moments later, Mrs. Kuchen came back from wherever she had gone. "This next part isn't just sad," she said, wiping her tears. "It's horrifying. Every time I tell it, I always wish it had happened differently."

Though she had already related many horrific tragedies up to this point, I could see in her eyes that this was different.

She lit a cigarette, the velvety smoke drifting in the air like a fog above the Tauber. "Please, would you be so kind as to get me my Jägermeister?"

"Of course," I said. Retrieving the green glass bottle from her liquor cabinet, I brought it to her.

She poured herself another double shot and downed it, then looked at me with an intensity in her gaze that was spine-chilling, her emerald eyes piercing into my soul. "Turn it back on," she said, motioning at the tape recorder.

I did, and she began again . . .

CHAPTER 42

Autumn, 1942

"Shaylee, they saw me!" Christian shouted as he ran into the house. "At the grocery store, a soldier recognized me!" He had gone into the nearest town again to pick up more food. With his wife now pregnant, they had no choice but to try to get to Sweden before winter, and Shaylee needed to build up her strength for the trip. The meager rations they had been subsisting on were not enough.

Shaylee was in the library when she heard him. She dropped the book she was reading and ran to the foyer.

"They chased me," said Christian. "When I veered off the main road into the woods, I lost them. But they won't give up. Eventually they'll find us, so we have to go."

"Can't we just hide in the secret room we found?" Inside the attic with the small balcony and telescope, they had found a hidden room behind a false wall. Much like the one next to the cellar at the Wolff farm where Hanz had been hiding Abigail, except much smaller.

"*Nein!* I'm a wanted fugitive! They hate me more than they hate you, because to them I'm a traitor. Now that they know I'm in the area, they'll tear through every abandoned home until they find us. We have to go! Now!"

Shaylee's heart pounded. This fairy tale existence in this beautiful mansion in the peaceful country, with the lovely rooms, impressive library, and splendid terrace leading into a stunning garden of flowering plants, stone sculptures, and glorious fountain, was now over.

Reality had come back with a vengeance, turning their paradise into quicksand!

It all happened too fast. Shaylee almost tripped as they ran to the car and drove off. But had they not left when they did, they would have surely been caught, for no sooner had they exited the dirt road leading to the abandoned Jewish mansion than the Schutzstaffel drove up that very same road.

Christian kept going, driving like a madman. His heart was pumping too, his face flushed. Never had he been so afraid, not for himself but for Shaylee and their unborn child. Hours later, when he finally thought they were safe, he turned off the main road and found another grassy path leading into the forest. Among a cluster of trees, he parked the car for the night. "We'll stay here until tomorrow," he said.

"And then?" asked Shaylee.

Christian ran his fingers through his wavy blond hair. "And then we keep going. That's all I know right now."

Shaylee stared at his profile. With his strong nose and emotive eyes, he always reminded her of Michaelangelo's statue of David, the Renaissance masterpiece carved out of a block of marble from 1501 to 1504, commissioned for one of the buttresses of Opera del Duomo, the cathedral in Florence. Reaching over, she ran her finger gently across his cheek.

Christian took her hand and kissed it.

After a long moment, he reached into the back seat and grabbed the bag of groceries he had bought using the last of his money. "At least I didn't drop this as I ran," he said, pulling out some cheese, bread, and a bottle of milk. "This should carry us through a few days."

Quietly the couple ate, staring into the trees providing their protective shroud. When it was dark, they lay in each other's arms in the back, a wool blanket keeping them warm.

❧❦❧

Early the next morning, Christian woke up to a familiar sound. The same sound demons make in the bowels of hell . . .

A Nazi jeep!

Like a fox trapped by a pack of hound dogs, he panicked and jumped into the front seat of the car. "Shaylee, wake up!"

She lifted her head, squinting to adjust her eyes to the morning light. "What's wrong?"

"They're here!" Seconds later, as he turned the ignition, a bullet hit the back window.

Shaylee screamed.

"Keep your head down!"

Another shot rang out, and this time it hit Christian in the shoulder, but his adrenaline prevented him from feeling it. He plowed through the forest, barely missing the tall trees as he searched for an exit back onto the road. For a distance he managed to stay ahead of the Nazi jeep, until suddenly his right tire hit a log and flipped the car. Stunned by the impact, the next thing they knew, the Schutzstaffel were pulling them from the vehicle.

For the next hour, four SS officers viciously beat Christian, forcing Shaylee to watch.

"This is what happens to traitors," one of them said, punching Christian in the face again.

"You abandoned the Wehrmacht to help a dirty Jew," said another. *"Unverzeihlich (Unforgivable)!"*

The beating continued until Christian was no longer conscious, lying bloodied on the ground. Then the men turned their attention to Shaylee, tied to a tree.

"Did you really think you could escape us?" the commander of the group asked. Pulling out his knife, he cut Shaylee loose. "Okay, *Fräulein,* go."

She ran as fast as she could.

The commander was using her for sport, letting her have a head start. But quickly the men caught up, and they each took turns raping her.

Shaylee left her body as the vile acts were done to it. Her eyes stared at the treetops high in the sky, and the fluffy clouds floating by. Her ears heard the birds sing their melodious song. And her mind was with Christian in the mansion, lounging on the terrace and strolling through the garden. Her soul was still hers, even as her body was not.

And then she thought of the dolls she would make when she was twelve years old. With little silk outfits, hats and ribbons, lace and bows. And the decorative masks she and her sister Ava would create in Aadan Omari's ceramic workshop. As the Schutzstaffel continued to abuse and ravage her flesh, her thoughts remained pure and childlike, thinking of nothing but those innocent, nescient masks and dolls.

When it was over, the men dragged Shaylee back to the Jeep. One of them kicked her in the abdomen so hard she could barely breathe, and blood ran down her leg. In that instant, she knew she had lost her child.

Lying on the ground, completely numb, the distinct sound of a shovel digging into the earth reached her ears. And then she overheard the men talking . . .

"Why bother digging a grave?" one of them asked.

"We're going to teach the traitor a lesson and bury him alive."

Filled with terror, Shaylee screamed out, "*Neiiinn!* Christian!"

The commander walked over and kicked her again.

"Papa," Shaylee moaned. "Papa, stop them . . ." She passed out.

❧❦❧

When Shaylee regained consciousness, the Schutzstaffel officers were congregated around a bonfire, smoking and drinking, joking and laughing. She crawled on the ground, trying to get a glimpse of Christian, but he wasn't there. As she crawled a bit further, a sudden horror hit her . . .

Christian's hand was sticking up from the ground, the rest of his body buried beneath the soil!

Shaylee screamed, and the men laughed as they watched her struggle to her feet and stumble to the shallow grave. Dropping to her knees, she grabbed Christian's hand, still warm to the touch, trying to pull him out. When that didn't work, she frantically started digging at the soil, sobbing hysterically.

The men watched for a moment, entertained by Shaylee's frenzied effort. And when she grabbed hold of Christian's hand again to pull him out, the SS commander walked over and hit her on the head with his pistol.

Shaylee collapsed over the grave, still holding Christian's hand.

CHAPTER 43

Berlin, 1997

The tape recorder clicked, interrupting the landlady. It had run out of tape and was no longer recording. Mrs. Kuchen once more appeared catatonic, lost in the past, her tears falling like rain. I wanted to get up and go hug her, but before I could act, she looked at me and said, "They buried Christian alive . . . That sweet man . . . They buried him alive."

We both remained silent for a moment. These people who had lived decades ago were now so real to me that when I found out what happened to Christian and Shaylee, I cried with her. They were not just characters in a story anymore but my dear friends.

"I don't think my sweet sister ever recovered from that tragedy," the landlady said. "She was never the same."

"Wait . . . Shaylee is your sister? . . . Mrs. Kuchen, are *you* Ava Wolff?"

The older woman smiled through her tears.

"But . . . But I thought you were Mrs. Kuchen."

"*Ja*, her too. 'Kuchen' means 'cake' in German, which my friends have nicknamed me because of the delicious pastries I make. Pastries my mother Abigail had taught me."

Another woman—clearly her twin—came around the corner, yawning and stretching, her gray hair messy, her eyes half awake. Holding a tray of coffee and Jewish pastries, she said, "I see my sister kept you up all night. She always does that, if you let her."

With tears of my own still glistening, I looked at her in disbelief. "Shaylee . . ."

"*Ja*, dear, that's me. Although I go by Shalom now." She placed the tray on the table and sat down next to her sister, taking hold of her hand.

"Ava can't tell our story as good as me. Turn the recorder back on. If you're going to write a story about us, you'll want to hear how it ends."

I placed a fresh tape in the recorder and pressed play.

Shalom continued where Ava left off . . .

CHAPTER 44

Autumn, 1942

Shaylee awoke, sitting in the back of the same military jeep that had chased her and Christian through the forest. She could hear the SS officers talking, joking and laughing again about burying Christian alive, only to move on to what they were going to eat for breakfast. Monsters, she thought, her hands tied behind her back. Demons materialized in human form.

Looking out the window, she realized she must have been out for quite a while because a new sunrise was on the horizon. A new day, another horror. Everything she had gone through in the last twenty-four hours washed over her like a decimating tidal wave, and she wanted to scream. She wanted to fight, to go hysterical, even if they beat her for it, or shot her dead. But she could not. Shock, exhaustion, and sorrow stole her voice, and her power. All she could do was quietly whimper.

"*Der Kommandant ist immer der erste, der Milch und Honig bekommt (The commandant is always first to get the milk and honey),*" she recalled one of the vile officers laughing before they took turns raping her. And poor Christian, now lying in that cold grave alone, dirt all around him, covering his beautiful, kind face as his eyes remained open in terror. How could this all be happening?

Finally they arrived at their destination—the medieval Wewelsburg Castle, built from 1603 to 1609 by the prince-bishops of Paderborn in North Rhine-Westphalia. Shaylee stared at it both in awe and fear. The Renaissance structure surrounded by a moat appeared sinister and haunted, as if something out of a dark fairy tale she had once read in the library of Rothenburg ob der Tauber—another Neolithic structure, except without the dark aura.

When the Nazis came into power in 1933, German Schutzstaffel leader Heinrich Himmler wanted to find something grand and impressive to house a retreat and training school for SS members. Consisting of three towers linked together by thick stone walls in a triangular layout, the seventeenth-century Renaissance castle in Wewelsburg was just what he was looking for. As World War II broke out, his plans expanded, envisaging a secluded, central meeting place for only the highest-ranking SS officers, with a huge complex of buildings and ramparts surrounding the castle. This was to be called the "Center of the World," and it would be where the victorious Nazis would rule over their vast empire.

Himmler didn't choose that area to be his SS headquarters by chance, either. Wewelsburg Castle stood near the Teutoburg Forest, where Germanic tribes defeated the Roman army in 9 BCE. As such, it was revered as a place of mystical power, and he wanted that historical connection to the past, believing that the Schutzstaffel were similar to the Germanic warriors, superior in both race and culture.

Obsessed with the medieval era, in particular the Saxon dynasty which conquered lands in the east–a feat Nazi Germany wanted to replicate–Himmler had the plaster removed and the moat deepened, making the castle appear more defiant and "castle-like." Ancient Nordic symbols characterized the interior, and a series of oak-paneled study rooms were constructed bearing the names of various Teutonic military heroes and kings, as well as those of King Arthur and the explorer Christopher Columbus. The centerpiece of the refurbishment was in the castle's north tower, where two ornate rooms were designed: The Hall of the Supreme SS Leaders, with a Nazi Black Sun wheel embedded on the floor in twelve spokes, surrounded by twelve columns representing both the leaders of the organization and the twelve Knights of the Round Table–the Nazi's version of Camelot. And a vault in the tower's basement, with an eternal flame in the center of the room surrounded by twelve pedestals and a swastika on the ceiling. This was the "Crypt" where the Nazis would honor dead SS men and, some believed, hold secret SS ceremonies and occult rituals. Members of the SS were issued rings engraved with skulls and mystic symbols, and when one of them died, their ring was brought to Wewelsburg and placed in a casket. No one knows where these 11,500 rings are now.

The vast majority of the construction work carried out at the fortress was done by slave labor from the dedicated Niederhagen-Wewelsburg concentration camp, established in 1940. The smallest camp in the Nazi empire, it housed, among others, the largest concentration of incarcerated Jehovah's

Witnesses in the prison system.

The Nazis regarded Jehovah's Witnesses as enemies of the state for their refusal to take an oath of loyalty to Adolf Hitler, to give the Sieg Heil salute and participate in Nazi rallies and parades, or to serve in the German army. Jehovah's Witnesses believed that military service violated the biblical commandment not to kill, and that God's Kingdom would soon be established on earth, ridding the world of false religion and human governments, iniquities, and injustice—all part of what the Bible refers to as Satan's "System of Things." Jehovah's Witnesses also engaged in missionary activity to teach interested ones about God's Kingdom, and how and when it would come about, as prophesied in the Bible, and the Nazis saw that as subversive to the opposing plans of the Third Reich.

Unlike Jews and Roma (Gypsies), whom the Nazis targeted for racial reasons, Jehovah's Witnesses had the option to avoid persecution and torture in concentration camps by signing a document renouncing their faith and submitting to state authority. Yet they refused to violate their religious convictions, putting their faith in God, even to the point of death. Bibles and Bible-based literature were smuggled into the camps, and those incarcerated continued to meet covertly with other Witness prisoners and interested ones to conduct Bible studies and pray, supporting each other and strengthening one another's faith. Ironically, because of that same godly devotion, many Nazi camp officers and guards used Jehovah's Witnesses as domestic servants, knowing that they were trustworthy and would not steal from them or run away.

Of the 3,900 prisoners who passed through the gates of Niederhagen, 1,285 died from the harsh conditions, exploited until they were totally exhausted, starving, and weak, with sickness and disease taking many. A further fifty-six were executed.

Shaylee now found herself a prisoner at the Niederhagen concentration camp. Hard labor became her daily life, a stark contrast to the days of leisure with Christian at the abandoned Jewish mansion in the forest. Her one and only respite was when they occasionally put her to work in the SS garden.

One day she met a kind man named Philip Abelman there. He encouraged her not to give up and spoke to her consolingly, making her think of her dear father. That alone strengthened her.

"Why is the patch on your uniform purple?" she asked him as they worked. "Mine is yellow."

"Because I'm one of Jehovah's Witnesses," said Philip. "They designate us with a purple triangle."

"Why did they arrest you?"

"Because I wouldn't raise my arm and say 'Heil Hitler', I wouldn't swear allegiance to the Nazi flag, and I wouldn't join the Wehrmacht."

"Do they arrest all Jehovah's Witnesses?"

"Most, *ja*. If they find you." Of the estimated 20,000 who remained active through the Nazi period, about 10,000 were convicted and sentenced, with at least 3,000 sent to concentration camps and nearly 2,000 murdered. "They target us just like the Jews, Gypsies, and others. Not for racial reasons but reasons of conscience."

Shaylee shook her head. "All this persecution and killing over race and religious beliefs."

Philip pulled up a clump of weeds and tossed them into his wheelbarrow. "It's disgusting, isn't it? They have this satanic ideology of racial supremacy where the Aryans are at the top of the tree, and at the bottom are the *untermenschen (subhumans)*: Jews, Gypsies, Blacks, and homosexuals. Jehovah's Witnesses and others who won't submit to their obscene regime are there too."

"If you did what the Nazis asked, though, they'd let you go, right? You could walk right out of here."

"*Ja*. But at the same time, I'd be going against God."

"Why?"

"Because as our Creator, he expects exclusive devotion from us. We must not pledge allegiance to or worship any man or country, only God. And we must not kill, either."

"Why is God allowing all this killing, then?" Shaylee asked, confused by his answer.

"God's thoughts are not man's thoughts," said Philip, using a shovel to uproot a more stubborn weed plant. "And there's an unseen battle going on right now between *gute* and evil. Unfortunately, we humans are caught in the middle." He discreetly handed her an apple from his pocket, picked up his wheelbarrow, and went to another section of the garden before the guards saw them talking.

Shaylee sunk her teeth into the juicy fruit. It tasted like heaven, sweet and delicious, the flavor making her eyes water. As she stood there devouring it, SS officers walked to-and-fro in front of the enormous, looming castle, where inside she imagined the gates of hell.

⁕

Lieutenant Caligula Nöster, a high-ranking Schutzstaffel officer, had noticed Shaylee working one day. He took a keen interest in her and brought her to his private trailer for supposed questioning. Once there, he violently raped her. So badly that she bled afterward for three days.

The Lieutenant was a wiry man with a 6 mm buzz cut. He had foxlike eyes and a menacing scowl, and when he smiled, his canine teeth shined with two silver veneers. Named after Caligula, the third Roman emperor from 37-41 CE and great-grandson of Gaius Julius Caesar Augustus, the founder of the Roman Empire, Lieutenant Nöster was just like him—self-indulgent, cruel, erratic, tyrannical, and sexually perverted. He sadistically enjoyed tormenting Shaylee.

The sexual assaults went on for weeks, and Shaylee grew to detest that crooked cross he wore on his arm, along with everything it stood for. She would fight him at first, kicking and screaming, even biting, but she was no match for the large man. Not only would he easily overpower her, but he'd punch her, too, if she dared to continue resisting. Eventually she gave up fighting and submitted, each time turning her head to the side until it was over.

Just as she had done when being gang-raped by the SS officers who had brought her there, Shaylee would leave her body and float on the ether, thinking about the masks and dolls she would make when she was twelve years old. Other times she'd imagine being back at the farm with the fluffy sheep and friendly goats, walking alongside them in the pasture. Keeping her thoughts pure and childlike was the only way to bear it.

Soon Shaylee realized she was not the only one who suffered from this degrading abuse. Other young women were victims too, each of them a plaything for the wicked lieutenant. When they saw each other, they'd share a lingering, wordless stare, understanding the hell they were going through. Before long, one of them couldn't take it anymore and hung herself.

"I asked about you," Caligula Nöster said to Shaylee one day, bringing her into his private trailer again. A tub of cold water waited for her, and he

414

pushed her toward it. "I found out you and your sister were raised by German parents."

Shaylee thought of Hanz and Maria, and her eyes immediately welled with tears. Such wonderful memories. She recalled how her father would open his long arms to her, like an eagle's wings spreading out over its young, and she would walk into his warm, safe embrace. Or how, even as a grown woman, she would lay her head against her mother's chest, and the statuesque Maria would kiss her forehead. At that moment, she could see Maria in her mind's eye, with her fiery red hair that, when not done in the customary braids, would flow long and wild down her back. She could see her mother's kind, blue eyes, too—the color of the sea at midday. Eyes that clearly displayed her deep love for her daughters. Shaylee would do anything in the world to feel her mother's protective arms around her right now, hugging her close. Anything.

"That's disgusting that they took two Jewish babies and raised them," the lieutenant continued. "What decent German couple would do such a thing?"

Shaylee only stood by the tub, looking down at the floor.

"Take off your clothes and get in," he ordered, his silver canines catching the light, appearing as if fangs. "You smell like a dead dog rotting in the sun."

She undressed and got into the water, mechanically taking the soap and washing her body, knowing what would come next. At one point, when the water stilled, she caught sight of her own haunting reflection, her face so lean that her cheekbones looked like two carved potatoes, her hazel citrine eyes sad and empty, and her dark auburn hair growing out in uneven tufts. Who was that starved and abused Jewish woman staring back at her? Where had the healthy and vibrant German girl gone?

"Have you been thinking about that lover of yours?" Lieutenant Nöster asked, pretending to look sad by sticking out his lower lip. "That pitiful boyfriend who tried to protect you by hiding you in that Jew mansion? They buried him alive, didn't they. *Wunderbar!*" he laughed. "The traitor deserved it!" He studied Shaylee's reaction to see if he was getting a rise out of her. "What was his name?"

She could barely say it. ". . . Christian."

"Christian and Shaylee—has a nice ring to it." He smirked. "But it's not really Shaylee, is it. It's Shalom, and that's what you shall be called now. Your real Jewish name. No reason to hide it anymore–isn't that right, my little rag doll?"

Shaylee gave no response, shivering in the icy water.

He kept observing her, continuing his harassment. "You and your sister are twins, aren't you. Identical, no?"

"*Ja,*" she mumbled.

"*Mein Freund,* Dr. Mengele, has a medical center where he takes twins and does interesting experiments on them."

Shaylee stopped washing.

"He injures one, then studies the other to see if they've been affected too. What do you think about that, my little rag doll?"

"Monstrous," she whispered under her breath, keeping her eyes down.

Caligula's chilling stare invoked a coldness in the room. "I also found out your sister was married to Lieutenant Starholf Steiner. A man of noble, Aryan birth, loyal to the Fatherland. What a travesty and embarrassment. Who would have thought his rat sister-in-law would end up here?" He took out a razor and began sharpening it. "If you're curious about whether she's dead or not, I can tell you that she is."

Shaylee's heart dropped, and she looked up at him, trying to read his expression to see if he was lying. But she had been warned to never maintain eye contact, and he walked over to her, slapping her so hard her nose bled profusely, scarlet droplets falling into the bathwater. "Don't you ever look at me like that again," he said, leaning over to speak directly into her face, his foul breath repulsive. "I'll cut your pretty little nose off if you do. Understand?" He flicked the razor at her, grazing her cheek.

Shaylee flinched and put her hands up to protect herself.

"Did you hear me!"

"*Ja! Bitte!*" She started crying.

Lieutenant Nöster grabbed her by the neck and squeezed, pressing the razor against her skin. "I could kill you right now, and not one person would care. All your blood would seep into this bathtub, and I'd watch the water turn scarlet as you lay there submerged in your own blood." He chuckled. "What a piece of artwork that would be."

Shaylee had both hands on his wrists, trying to pry his death grip away. But it was in vain, like an ant fighting a giant. "Mercy!" she cried out.

"You want mercy, do you? I'll show you mercy." He plunged her head into the bathwater and held it there.

Fighting for her life, desperately trying to come up for air, Shaylee could see his evil face through the water, cursing at her. Was this how she was going to die?

Suddenly he let her go, and Shaylee rose from the water, gasping for air and coughing over the edge of the tub.

Lieutenant Nöster went over to the sink and started shaving like it was an ordinary day. As he glided the razor along his jawline, he nonchalantly said, "You'll be fine. I didn't even hold you under that long."

Shaylee held her neck, terrified.

"So, my little rag doll, do you want to know how your sister died?" he asked, continuing his cruelty.

Still regaining her equilibrium, her heart thumping so hard against her bony chest that her ribcage vibrated, Shaylee's thoughts turned to Ava . . . My poor sister . . . Please God, she can't be dead . . . Please God, she can't be.

"Ava Steiner was executed against a brick wall along with a dozen other vermin."

The room spun. Shaylee almost fainted.

"They say twins have a special connection and know when something bad has happened to the other. Did you feel it when they shot her? When her heart stopped, did yours skip a beat?"

Trembling uncontrollably now, Shaylee's emotional pain heightened the lieutenant's sick pleasure. Once he finished shaving, he undressed and ordered, "Get out," motioning for her to come to him. "And don't be thinking I shaved for you. I'm going home to see my wife and kids afterward, and I need to look my best."

She stepped out of the tub, and he grabbed her thin arm, throwing her on the bed. "How did it feel when your lover was buried alive and your sister was shot?" he whispered into her ear as he crawled on top of her.

Shaylee said nothing, unable to talk.

"To know that your Christian suffered, gasping for air as the soil covered his face, and your sweet Ava is no more."

A flood of tears poured down her cheeks.

"Tell me!" he yelled as he began violating her. "How did it feel! Tell me!"

"Avaaa!" Shaylee finally screamed out, so loudly that her teeth hurt. "Christian!" She started pleading with God again. *"Hilf mir, Gott! Bitte rette mich! Gott, wo bist du! (Help me, God! Please save me! God, where are you!)"*

Lieutenant Caligula Nöster laughed as she cried.

When the assaults became more aggressive, with slapping, punching, and choking, Shaylee feared she'd soon end up dead. Yet she didn't want to die. At one time she did, with Christian gone and now Ava too. But something was happening inside her where she fiercely wanted to fight for her life. "If you're ever alone in the forest, you're never lost," she recalled her father saying to her as a child. "The forest knows exactly where it is at all times. All you need to do is remain calm and listen to the trees, because they're speaking to you. They're telling you to look at your surroundings, think, and be brave. The moss and the grass will show you the way."

Shaylee began to study the patterns of the delivery trucks coming and going at the Niederhagen concentration camp. Prior to the installation of its own crematorium, dead prisoners were taken to civil crematoriums in Dortmund, Bochum, and Bielefeld-Brackwede. As the truck would sit and wait for the last of its ghastly cargo, other trucks would pass by, having been emptied of their camp supplies. One in particular often stopped to chat with the driver of the dead, and this would be Shaylee's opportunity. If she could climb onto the truck destined for the crematorium and wait, perhaps she could quickly jump into the back of the other while the two drivers had their smoke and talked. She would have to time it perfectly, though, ensuring she wasn't seen or heard in the broad light of day. Risky, yes. Perhaps foolish, as they would execute her immediately if caught. But it was the only way.

On the day of the escape, Shaylee was working in the SS garden—another detail she had carefully planned, knowing that the guards there were inattentive. She watched as the two assigned prisoners loaded the dead bodies onto the truck, and when there were enough of them, she sprinted to it and climbed on. The smell was horrible, worse than the most putrid stench she had ever known, as some of them were already decomposing, and the corpses were cold, clammy, and stiff like marble. When the last body was thrown in, landing beside her, she nearly gasped . . .

Philip Abelman!

Shaylee wanted to burst out crying. This godly man, who had given her a wonderful hope from the Bible, strengthening her to endure, was now gone. At least he was no longer suffering, she thought.

Just then, the second truck pulled up, and its driver got out to have a cigarette and chat with the driver of the dead. As the two men talked, Shaylee quietly climbed over the pile of corpses and snuck into the back of the empty vehicle, covering herself with a tarp. Ten minutes later, it began to move, passing through the gates of Niederhagen.

She had escaped!

The delivery truck was on its way to Dortmund. Exhausted, Shaylee fell asleep under the tarp. But it was only an hour's drive, and her hunger soon woke her to the smell of freshly baked bread, instantly reminding her of Maria. The truck wasn't moving, either, and she panicked, peeking out the back to see German civilians and cars all around. The driver had stopped at a restaurant to eat.

Shaylee knew she had to get out, but she wasn't expecting it to be in such a public place. She still had her striped uniform on, and anyone who saw her would know she was a concentration camp escapee. And then she saw a dumpster at the rear of the parking lot. There, she thought! I'll hide there!

Waiting for her opportunity, she crawled out of the vehicle and ran to the dumpster, climbing inside. Luckily, no one saw her, and though the smell was unpleasant, it was nothing like the truck with the dead corpses. She even found some stale, leftover bread.

Full of garbage, cardboard boxes, and food scraps from the restaurant, the dumpster provided Shaylee with shelter while she tried to figure out her next move. She ate whatever she could find that was edible, and though she had planned to leave when it was dark, she fell asleep instead, still exhausted from not having slept the night before.

Deep in the night, she dreamed a terrifying dream. Philip Abelman was standing in the distance like an apparition, speaking although his mouth wasn't moving. His previous words to her echoed through the air . . . "They have this satanic ideology of racial supremacy where the Aryans are at the top of the tree, and at the bottom are the *untermenschen (subhumans)*: Jews, Gypsies, Blacks, and homosexuals. Jehovah's Witnesses and others who won't submit to their obscene regime are there too."

Suddenly she was back at the Niederhagen concentration camp, and all the prisoners were mutating into trees, including herself. Her skin became bark, her arms and legs grew into branches, and her fingertips sprouted leaves. She tried to run but her feet had turned into roots, adhering her firmly to the ground. She tried to scream but her mouth had sealed up shut. Before long there was nothing left of her that was human, while vicious Aryan birds from hell perched high on her branches, mocking her pain.

Shaylee woke up in a sweat, breathing rapidly, her heartbeat racing.

A black feral cat had gotten into the dumpster and was curled up beside her for warmth and comfort. It reminded her of Isadora, the kitten her father had given to Abigail that grew into a beautiful farm cat, and while it lay next to her, it purred as she stroked it. For the rest of the night, Shaylee slept soundly, feeling safe for the first time in months.

⁓ↄﴥꙅ⁓

Early the next morning, two restaurant employees came to the dumpster: A full-figured older woman, with steel-colored hair in braids wrapped up on both sides of her head, wearing a dirty apron tied high on her waist. And a short, stocky man, with tattoos all over his arms. She was carrying a fresh bag of garbage, and he a large pot of week-old stew that was now bad.

Lifting the dumpster lid, the woman tossed the garbage bag in and held it open while the man poured out the stew. It was still hot, and when it landed on Shaylee's head, she yelped.

"A Jew!" the lady yelled, looking inside. "There's a Jew rat living in the dumpster!"

The man stood on his toes and looked inside too. *"Dreckig Tier (Filthy animal)!"* He spat on her.

"Bitte," Shaylee begged. *"Bitte,* I'm not a filthy animal. I'll leave." She raised her arms in the air, letting them know she was no threat.

The commotion caught the attention of two SS officers who had come to the restaurant for breakfast. When they saw Shaylee crawling out of the dumpster in her striped uniform, they ran over and began beating her with their clubs.

Lying on the cold ground, curled up in a ball and covering her head, Shaylee saw the black cat who had shared her cardboard bed that night, staring at her from a distance as they beat her. When it scurried away, she wished so badly she could follow it and be free.

The officers dragged her to their jeep and tied her up in the back, then went for breakfast. Upon their return, they started cracking jokes at Shaylee's expense.

"You like the trash, do you?" one of them laughed. "Living in a dumpster suits you?"

"Well she's a rat, after all. Maybe we should go back and look inside. We might find the rest of her family there."

The first officer lit a cigarette and looked her over more carefully. "She's very attractive for a Jew, though. Skinny and smelly, *ja*. But still quite pretty."

"Is that so," said the other, grinning. "Maybe I should tell your new bride that. She might be interested to know that you found a pretty rat in the sewer. Perhaps she'll let you take it home."

"*Ja, ja, Klugscheißer (Yeah, yeah, smart-ass).*"

Shaylee just stared at them, noticing their fresh haircuts, pressed uniforms, and shiny boots. She was keenly aware of their smell, too—a mixture of mink oil from their black leather boots intermingled with aftershave. The scent reminded her of Christian, and a wonderful memory flashed through her mind as they verbally degraded her. A sacred memory of the night she offered up her virginity, and he took it with tenderness and love. Afterward, they lay in each other's arms until morn.

"Where did you escape from?" one of the officer's asked.

Shaylee didn't answer.

"Do you have a problem with your ears?"

Still, Shaylee didn't answer, afraid to be sent back to that evil castle, and that wicked man.

"I bet she came from Niederhagen," said the other. He looked at Shaylee. "How did you escape from there? Tell us or you're going back."

"I climbed on the truck with the dead bodies," Shaylee finally answered. "And then I jumped into another empty delivery truck while the two drivers talked."

The SS officers laughed at her audacity, if not ingenuity.

"Should we take her back there?" the younger man asked.

"*Nein*," said the senior officer. "That's out of our way. Let's just bring her with us."

By that afternoon, instead of being returned to Niederhagen and the Wewelsburg Castle, Shaylee found herself a prisoner at Sachsenhausen, the concentration camp in Oranienburg, north of Berlin.

CHAPTER 45

Summer, 1943

Ava was still hiding at the Beaumont home, very much alive. The sadistic Lieutenant Caligula Nöster had lied to Shaylee–neither he nor the Gestapo looking for Ava knew where she was. Her fraternal twins, Ophelia and Samuel, were now almost a year old, and life in the country was simple and pleasant.

Every morning after Margeaux, Valentin, Colette, and Hugo left early for Dresden to work at the hotel, Ava would wake to find Henriette up and about in the kitchen, cleaning the breakfast dishes. She'd help the older lady, engaging in half French, half German small talk, then make breakfast for herself and feed her children. The time she had spent at that home seemed almost like a dream, first arriving pregnant, scared, and desperate, now a mother, calm, and safe. Her gratitude to the Beaumonts could not be expressed in words.

One afternoon, as she gazed at her sleeping children taking their nap, Ava thought of Father Craven, the priest at the church in the forest. Leaving her babies in Henriette's care, she decided to go visit him.

Ever since she had gone with the priest to witness the massacred Jews in the forest, looking to see if her sister Shaylee were among them, Ava had cultivated a strong bond with the man. They would talk for hours about everything and anything. Life, family, religion, politics. Even God and His perceived absence.

"Do you think the genocide will end soon?" she asked, sitting with him in the empty nave, the light streaming in through the stained glass windows creating a prism of color throughout the room. She had brought egg salad sandwiches and ginger tea, and they were enjoying it together. "Will life ever go back to normal?"

"If it did, what would you do?" Father Craven asked, wiping his mouth with a napkin.

Ava leaned back in the pew. "I'd bring my babies to see my parents. My mother . . . the one who raised me . . . she would be so happy to see them."

Father Craven smiled.

Ava turned to look directly at him. "This sounds so silly, but to just walk down any street in any city, window-shopping without being afraid . . . I mean . . . that would be *wunderbar*. I can't wait to taste freedom again." She thought for a moment. "And to eat lunch with my sister. Oh, I miss Shaylee so much it hurts. Being twins, we've always had this special bond, and to be separated like this is horrendous."

Father Craven looked at her tenderly in return. "I'll pray for her tonight."

Ava smiled. "*Danke.*"

"Just before you came, I was thinking about you."

"You were?"

"*Ja.* I was thinking how you must have been so frightened in that hotel room in Dresden, all alone and soon to give birth."

"Actually, *nein*," said Ava. "I mean . . . *Ja*, I was stressed over what to do, but I had escaped the Johannmeyer's home, and that made me happy. They would have taken Ophelia from me, given Samuel to Starholf, and sent me back to Ravensbrück."

He reached over and held her hand, and she moved closer to him, laying her head on his shoulder. Father Craven put his arm around her. Notwithstanding his uncanny likeness to Starholf, Ava had developed strong feelings for the priest. She knew they would never amount to anything, but she entertained them, nonetheless.

"Just coming here and you holding me," she said to him, closing her eyes in his soothing embrace, "is everything to me. Everything." She kissed his cheek. "I'm falling in love with you."

The priest said nothing. There was nothing to say, so he only held her. He was a victim of his circumstance too, and tomorrow wasn't promised to either of them.

⁓⚜⁓

The following day, Ava went back to the church to see the priest again. She wanted to apologize if she had made him uncomfortable, saying that she loved him. When she arrived, however, she found a gruesome scene . . .

Father Craven had been shot by the Schutzstaffel!

His lifeless body lay sprawled on the cold church floor, his eyes still open in shock, his mouth wide as if to scream.

There was no time to cry, and Ava ran back to the Beaumonts in terror, stumbling and falling along the way. If they came to the church in the forest, they'd likely come to the house too!

As she neared the home, Ava saw Henriette in the window. The older lady saw her too, keeping an eye out for her, discreetly shaking her head. Ava stopped and crouched down in the field, watching to see what was happening. Horrified, she saw a Nazi SS officer come into view. But not just any officer . . .

Starholf Steiner!

And he was holding Samuel in his arms, smiling down at the child!

Ava panicked. How did he find me? No, he's taking Samuel! Please, God, no! She fell to her knees and wept, realizing Ophelia would be taken too and given to the Johannmeyers. Not knowing what else to do, she ran back to the forest to grieve.

When the rest of the Beaumont family got home, Valentin and Hugo went to find her. Valentin brought her back to the house, while Hugo buried Father Craven.

"I can't believe it was Starholf," Ava said that night. Everyone was sitting around the kitchen table, discussing the matter. "I thought for sure he had found us when I saw him holding Samuel."

"He was just enamored with the child," said Colette. "He doesn't know that's his son."

"But why was he here, then?"

"He wanted to make sure the murdered Jews in the forest were properly buried in a mass grave," said Hugo. "As I said before, the Nazis usually cover their heinous crimes of that magnitude."

"That's how they caught Father Craven," Margeaux added. "He must have let his guard down."

Ava felt terrible, thinking the priest may have thought it was her returning. "I can't do the same," she said. "I can't let my guard down, and yet that's exactly what I've done for a long time now. I've gotten too used to feeling safe." The falsified papers Valentin had created for her would be of no use if she were recognized, and being married to Starholf Steiner, she knew several SS officers who also knew her. "For the sake of my children, I have to leave."

The Beaumonts agreed. Ava should go to Sweden, and Colette and Hugo would act as Ophelia and Samuel's parents until she could safely return. However long that would be.

⁂

The next morning, Ava said a painful goodbye to the wonderful Beaumont family. She held and kissed her beautiful children until the very last minute, handing Margeaux a letter for them to read as adults, should she die. In it she expressed how much she loved them, and that they were the reason she fought so hard to stay alive. She explained that she had to leave them with a loving family for a while to keep them safe, similar to how her own mother had done when Abigail left her and Shaylee with the Wolffs. And she begged them to love and take care of each other, and never allow hatred and discrimination to grow in their hearts toward anyone.

Valentin drove Ava to the train station in Dresden. From there she would travel to Hamburg, and then the port city of Lübeck. She was instructed to go to a specific address on Sunday morning at 3:00 a.m., where a fisherman codenamed Elbe, after the Elbe River in Dresden, would take her safely across the Baltic Sea to Sweden.

Dressed in a modest outfit so as not to attract attention, Ava sat on the train with a single small suitcase, staring out the window. Her emerald eyes reflected her gaze as if Shaylee were on the other side of the glass staring back at her, and it made her sad. She couldn't help but think about her life, where she had come from, who she was, and all that she had been through. Born a Jew, raised a German, back to a Jew. Growing up on a modest German farm in the country, marrying a wealthy Schutzstaffel officer from a noble family, running for her life as a fugitive. The whole unbelievable ordeal was like looking through a kaleidoscope to fix a broken jigsaw puzzle made of hatred, heartbreak, and betrayal.

The train arrived in Lübeck on Friday at 6:00 p.m. Ava took a hotel room for the night, contemplating what Sweden would be like. Would she really be able to escape the Nazi plague and walk freely among civilians, no longer chased like a fox on a hunting ground? How wonderful it would be if she found Shaylee and Christian there, she thought. They could wait out the war together. After all, they had both worked for the Resistance, helping others escape, so maybe they made it safely there too. She now regretted chastising her sister about it in the past.

Sunday morning at 3:00 a.m., Ava went to the address she was given to meet Elbe, the fisherman. She paid his fee, and he took her to his boat where several other Jewish fugitives were already aboard. But just as the vessel was about to depart for Sweden, something went terribly wrong . . .

The Gestapo had been tipped off!

Preventing the boat from leaving, they herded all the passengers into a truck and brought them to a warehouse for interrogation. Ava, so ready for freedom, was shell-shocked. Treated like refuse, she cowered as they grabbed, pushed, and prodded her, yelling and threatening.

Hours later, she was on a train to Auschwitz!

❦

Exhausted. Malnourished. Weak.

Hauntingly silent, spirits broken, staring straight ahead with sunken eyes from trauma and lack of sleep.

These were the waiflike people Ava found herself on the train with, being transferred to Auschwitz-Birkenau from the Sachsenhausen concentration camp. Hundreds of them, crammed together like sardines, with no room to move, lie, or sit. The pungent odor inside the car was nauseous, with feces, urine, and vomit–remnants of its occupants–covering every square inch.

The woman behind Ava threw up on her shoulder, apologizing profusely afterward. A frightened young girl beside her lost control of her bladder, and an old woman her bowel. A little boy, all by himself, wailed in Yiddish for his mummy, and Ava wanted to go to him, but there were too many people, making it nearly impossible to get to him. Cries, whimpers, and prayers were uttered everywhere.

Suddenly the train began moving, and within minutes the boxcar began to oscillate. It lulled Ava, making her eyelids heavy, closing in search of sleep. That's when she heard her father's calm, loving voice, singing a lullaby he always used to sing to her and Shaylee when they were little girls, coercing them to slumber . . . "Darling swans, oh darling swans, where have you gone? Down to the Tauber to swim in blue waters. Darling swans, oh darling swans, when will you return? Bright and early in the morning."

Ava opened her eyes, looking all around. "Papa? Papa, is that you?"

But only gaunt, sad faces stared back at her.

Remembering the happy days on the Wolff farm, with Hanz and Maria, Shaylee and Luka, the sheepdogs and the animals, Ava covered her face in her hands and wept. She knew she'd never see them or her children again.

"I think you might have a relative in here," an older woman said to her.

Ava looked up and wiped her eyes. "What did you say?"

"I never forget a face. You have a twin sister, no? . . . I saw her."

Staring at the woman, Ava thought she was hallucinating again, just like moments earlier, hearing her father's singing.

"There's a *Mädchen* on this train who looks exactly like you, only smaller."

Ava's heart started pounding. "Where?"

"Over there in the back," said the woman, pointing.

"Shaylee!" Ava screamed. "Shaylee!"

Seconds later . . . "Ava! Ava is that you!"

"Oh my God, Shaylee! Shaylee, it's me!" Ava immediately started pushing through the crowd of people, making her way toward the back of the boxcar. "Shaylee!"

"Ava!"

"Oh, God! Thank you, God!" Ava cried out. A sudden vigor entered her body, giving her the strength to push forward, forcing her way past those who wouldn't or couldn't move. One person after another she slid through, reminding her of the nightmare she had at the Beaumonts, when she found herself on a mountain of dead, decomposing bodies, struggling through bloodied arms and legs entangling her as if thorned branches from a Black Locust tree. But she would not be stopped. Her sister was here, in this very boxcar!

"Ava!" Shaylee screamed out again.

"Shaylee!"

And then Ava saw her . . .

The light streaming in through the wooden slats of the boxcar seemed to illuminate her sister as if a beacon of light shining down from heaven. She was smaller and skinnier than Ava remembered, her eyes large and defenseless, her face gaunt, her body frail.

When Shaylee saw Ava, she reached out her arms and wailed, "Ava! My sister, Ava! I thought you were dead!"

All the people still between them somehow moved aside as if Moses spreading the Red Sea, and the two siblings fell into each other's arms, trembling so hard their entire bodies shook, their knees on the verge of buckling, sobbing and sobbing. Ava and Shaylee Wolff, twin sisters born Jewish but raised in a German family, had survived their own private Armageddons, and now found the Promised Land . . . each other.

"What miracle has brought us back together?" Ava asked, thick tears of her own streaming down her face. She raked her eyes up and down her sister. Shaylee was filthy, her pallid skin stained brown, her clothes stained black, her teeth yellow and her fingernails dark as if she had been digging her own grave. But still she smiled, and there in that mask of suffering, Ava could see her sweet, precious sister.

But Shaylee couldn't talk, so overwhelmed with emotion that the words would not exit her mouth. All she could do was sob. Reaching up with quivering hands, she placed them on Ava's cheeks to make sure she was real. Ava took one and tenderly kissed the back of it.

"My sister was killed," a woman mumbled, watching them. "Why should they get to reunite? Why did God bless them and not us?"

An old man wiped his eyes. "In the womb they were made," he said in Yiddish. "God Almighty split the one and made them two. And now they are reunited. I have seen a miracle."

Other people watching couldn't help but praise God too for what they saw.

Shaylee finally found her voice. "Christian is dead," she cried. "They killed him, Ava."

A sharp stab of sadness pierced Ava's heart. She loved Christian too, for the young man he was, and the way he loved her sister. "I'm going to marry Shaylee someday and be the best husband in the world to her, and the best brother-in-law to you," she remembered him saying.

Shaylee kept weeping while Ava rocked her. And there they stood, twin sisters among countless other Jews, holding each other and crying over their miraculous reunion.

⁓⊱✦⊰⁓

Hours passed. Or was it days? Ava and Shaylee didn't know. They lost track of time on that filthy train, and when it finally screeched to a halt, they couldn't wait to get off. That is until they did . . .

The boxcar doors flung open like razor blades slicing through flesh. SS officers with vicious German Shepherds immediately started barking orders, demanding everyone exit the train. Frightened prisoners poured out into the night, exhausted, confused, and crying.

The sorting process began immediately. Men in one line, women and children in another. Like sheep to the slaughter, most were destined for the gas chambers, while the younger, healthier ones for grueling forced labor.

Gunshots rang out, elevating the fear. An older man, too slow for the officer's liking, fell to the ground with a bullet in his head. A woman clinging to her child, refusing to let him go, met the same fate. And a pregnant woman going into early labor, along with the older one helping her, both collapsed, each with a bullet to the chest.

As the moon cast an eerie glow through a thin veil of clouds, adding to the sinister atmosphere, Ava held her sister's hand, her grip vice-like. Shaylee's menses started, despite her malnourishment, and as the blood ran down her leg, she thought of their adoptive German mother. Imagining she was a little girl again, listening to Maria sing to her and Ava as she bathed them in the warm water scented with vanilla and lavender, she quietly cried, "Oh, Mama," feeling like the little boy who had just been ripped from his dead mother.

An SS officer with a scarred face, crooked rotting teeth, and bulbous nose singled Ava and Shaylee out among the crowd of terrorized prisoners. "Are you twins?" he asked, pressing his rifle firmly against Ava's sternum.

"*Ja,*" she said, praying he wouldn't pull the trigger.

A second Schutzstaffel officer approached, his gaze scrutinizing the siblings as well. "Of course they're twins, you fool. Look at them." His eyes lingered with fascination, a twisted smile playing on his lips. "And such pretty green eyes."

Both girls felt as if they were staring into the soul of a demon. A cold shiver ran down their spines.

More gunshots rang out, adding to the cacophony of death and despair, and two more men fell to the ground, only feet from where the sisters stood. One of them had previously given Shaylee his jacket in an act of kindness, and now his body lay lifeless in the mud. The other had been shot for mere sport.

Unfazed by the atrocities happening around him, the Schutzstaffel officer motioned for Ava and Shaylee to follow him. "You two are special," he said. "I'm taking you to a place where I can examine you closer."

Stepping over dead bodies and through pools of blood, Ava and Shaylee clung together as they walked. Little did they know, they were following a merciless man known for his monstrous medical experiments on Jewish twins!

⁂

"My name is Dr. Mengele. Don't be afraid. Nothing is going to happen to you."

Spine-chilling words indeed!

Dr. Josef Rudolf Mengele was one of the most infamous perpetrators of the Holocaust. Serving as the Chief Camp Physician at Auschwitz-Birkenau, he conducted inhumane and often deadly medical experiments on unwilling prisoners, particularly twins. As a result, he earned the nickname, "Angel of Death."

A highly trained doctor and medical researcher, Mengele used Nazi racial theory to justify his wide spectrum of experiments. These included testing methods for mass sterilization, inflicting wounds and injecting chemical substances and diseases to study the effects and potential treatments, unnecessary surgeries and procedures without anesthetic for training purposes, and dissecting murdered victims for anthropological and medical research. Additionally, he sent blood, body parts, organs, skeletons, and fetuses to his colleagues in Germany, supporting their research projects.

Dr. Mengele wasn't the only one who engaged in such abhorrent experiments in Germany's 44,000 concentration camps and incarceration sites. Many other Nazi doctors did too, all in the name of research for the Third Reich. Experiments centered around three main goals: survival of military personnel, testing of drugs and treatments, and the advancement of Nazi racial and ideological goals.

At Dachau, for example, physicians collaborated with the German Experimental Institution for Aviation to conduct high-altitude experiments on prisoners, trying to determine the maximum altitude from which crews of damaged aircraft could parachute to safety. Scientists also used prisoners to conduct freezing experiments to determine an effective treatment for hypothermia. And they used their victims to test various methods of making seawater drinkable.

At each of Dachau, Sachsenhausen, Buchenwald, Neuengamme, and Natzweiler-Struthof, camp inmates were used to test immunization compounds and antibodies for the prevention and treatment of contagious diseases, including malaria, typhus, tuberculosis, typhoid fever, yellow fever, and infectious hepatitis. At Ravensbrück, physicians conducted experiments in bone-grafting and tested newly developed synthetic antibiotics to treat bacterial infections. And at Sachsenhausen and Natzweiler-Struthof, prisoners were exposed to phosgene and mustard gas to test possible antidotes.

Experiments to further the tenets of Nazi racial theory were conducted at Auschwitz-Birkenau, Sachsenhausen, and Ravensbrück. Gruesome tests included how different races withstood various contagious diseases; effective, efficient, and inexpensive mass sterilization methods; and of course, the infamous Dr. Mengele's experiments on twins.

Mengele usually used one twin as a control subject while performing his experiments on the other. Those who died were dissected and studied, and the surviving twin would be killed and subjected to the same scrutiny. Of the 3,000 twins forced into unspeakable experimentation at Auschwitz-Birkenau, only 200 survived.

Ava and Shaylee were first taken to a shower room and cleansed, then brought to the examination room. "Wait here," said the assistant.

Moments later, Dr. Mengele entered the room. He carefully measured their arms and legs, height and weight, and other physical characteristics, taking detailed notes. "Very interesting," he said when done, his smile growing more fiendish. "Identical with only subtle differences. Perfect."

"Which one do you want to start with?" asked the assistant.

Dr. Mengele looked up from his notepad. "The smaller one. We begin tomorrow."

⁓◦⟡◦⟡◦⁓

That night in the barracks, an older Roma woman who had been at Auschwitz-Birkenau for over a year, saw how terrified Ava and Shaylee were. Her own twin daughters had been killed at the camp, and the Wolff sisters reminded her of them. "Don't be afraid," she said. "Lift your chin up and be brave."

Ava looked at her. "How can we not be afraid?"

"You've gotten this far, haven't you? Don't give up now."

431

One woman was sobbing and on the verge of a mental breakdown. "I'm sorry, baby. I'm sorry," she kept saying over and over in Yiddish. On arriving at the camp, she abandoned her five-year-old son in the line, hiding from him to save herself, knowing the Nazis usually sent mothers and their children directly to the gas chambers. Now she regretted it immensely.

"You chose to hide, now live with your choice," said an unsympathetic woman in the darkness.

Another Jewish woman was eyeing Ava and Shaylee from the top bunk. She knew enough to claim her spot above the others, as those in the lower bunks were often soaked in urine by morning from those above them who couldn't hold it in or leave to the latrine in the middle of the night. "You two are lucky," she said. "Very lucky."

"Why?" asked Ava.

"Because that doctor picked you from the line. I saw it. If he hadn't, you'd be dead right now."

Both sisters looked at each other.

"That line was leading straight to a gas chamber. They tell you you're going to take a shower, but instead of water, poisonous gas comes out of the showerheads. Once everyone inside is dead, they throw their naked bodies into a furnace like they're shoveling coal. That's what you see coming out of those chimneys. The ashes of their murder victims."

"How do you know all this?" asked Shaylee, aghast at what she heard.

"Because I was there, in that same lineup when I first arrived."

The woman went on to explain how the Nazis first humiliated everyone, forcing them to strip naked in front of all the officers and each other. Men, women, children, young and old—it didn't matter. As they waited to be crammed into a large shower room, one of the SS officers saw her and smiled, ogling her naked body. "Blonde hair and blue eyes—this one looks Aryan," he said to another, pulling her away from the line.

"Why are you telling them this?" the Roma woman asked. "They just got here, and you're frightening them. Leave them alone."

"*Nein*, they must know the truth. The only way to survive this place is to learn how."

The woman continued her traumatizing story. Perhaps talking about it to strangers, as if talking to her psychiatrist, was how she coped, trying to remain sane. "My frightened little sister wouldn't let go of my arm, screaming as they ripped her from me. My mother knew it was a *gute* thing that they were taking me, though, and she begged them to take my sister too. But they didn't, and that's the last time I saw either of them."

"That's terrible," said Ava. "I'm so sorry."

Shaylee was now crying, clinging to her sister, just like that little girl. It made her think of Christian again, how his hand was sticking up in the air after they buried him alive, as if desperately reaching for her.

The woman paused for a moment, once more wondering if it would have been better for her to have been gassed along with her loved ones. She did not go into detail over what happened to her next, but that SS officer did not save her for nothing. "Thank God I had hugged my little sister and kissed her cheek, and my mother too, just before they took me," was all she said, turning over and closing her eyes.

"This is all awful, so awful," said the Roma woman, staring into nothing as tears fell from her tourmaline eyes. "All of us are woven in our mother's womb like a quilt, our precious hearts beating like an intricate clock. Tick, tick, tick." She smiled, on the verge of delirium. "And then we're born alone in the arms of ourselves, our lungs desperate to breathe, that first cry of life ringing like a church bell. From that moment on, we continue to fight all our days for that sweet breath of life." She became animated, her dark eyes widening as she kept going. "Somehow we're kept alive by this natural wonder. This incredible machine that is gifted to us, connecting us to everything beautiful in the world. The sights and sounds, smells and tastes, the touch of love. But then these devils come along and try to destroy it, reaching inside our chest with their disgusting hands, squeezing the life from our *wunderbar* clock until it stops ticking. It's murder, is what it is! Cold-blooded murder!" The Roma woman paused, becoming reflective again. "The miracle of life is reduced to ashes by fire-breathing dragons, and we leave this world as we entered it—alone, again in the arms of ourselves. How can this be? It's like the sun being shot from the sky."

The others in the room listened attentively. They had become accustomed to the Roma woman's nightly outburst in her moments of despair. Some thought it was just the babbling of an old woman, while others found her words poetic and profound, wishing they had a pen and paper to write them all down.

Morning came quickly, and the barracks *Kapo (captain)* woke everyone, hitting his baton against the wall. "Rise and shine, you filthy pigs!" he yelled out. "Time for work!"

Ava and Shaylee were taken to the medical building. They held hands as they walked and kept looking at each other for comfort, bracing themselves for what was next. Like brave little soldiers heading to the front lines.

⁕

The barracks throughout Auschwitz-Birkenau were overcrowded way beyond capacity, and infested with lice, bedbugs, and rats. Contagious diseases erupted frequently and spread rapidly. Those selected for experiments in the medical building, however, lived in separate quarters and received better food and treatment. But it came at a high cost.

Ava and Shaylee were put in different rooms while the experiments took place. Shaylee was the guinea pig, Ava the one they observed. Whatever they did to Shaylee, they wanted to see if and how it affected her twin sister.

First they injected Shaylee with various experimental drugs. Then they moved on to chemical compounds. Every time the needle went into her pale, thin arm, she would flinch, and then scream as the unknown fluid burned her skin.

Often she would get sick to her stomach, other times she would lose consciousness. Afterward, she'd find herself in the infirmary to be examined, monitored, and documented. "Where's Ava?" she would whimper, half awake. "Why can't I see my sister?" Nearby, Ava would do the same, after being poked, probed, and tested to see what, if any, symptoms her sister displayed were also evident in her.

One night, a little seven-year-old boy was crying on the cot beside Shaylee. He too was a twin, and they would inflict various forms of pain on him to see if his brother could feel it. That day they continually hit him on the forehead with a metal object until he bled. The little boy's head was black and blue from bruising and covered in bandages.

"Do you want to lie next to me?" Shaylee whispered to him.

He nodded.

Shaylee lifted her blanket. "Come on, then."

The little boy climbed into her bed and curled up close, laying his head on her chest.

"What's your name?"

"Daniel."

"I'm Shaylee," she whispered, tenderly kissing his forehead. "Pretend these monsters that hurt us are dragons and trolls, and we are fairies. Soon a prince will come save us."

In the morning, Daniel was dead.

The medical torture went on for weeks, during which time Ava and Shaylee did not see each other. At the end of each day, instead of being sent to the quarters where they kept the prisoners undergoing experiments, Shaylee was too sick to leave the infirmary. They continued with other experiments on Ava, but eventually they sent her back to the regular barracks because without her twin sister, she was no longer of use to them, other than for forced labor.

Ava, along with a group of other prisoners, was instructed to go to one of the buildings where a photographer–a prisoner himself and photographer before the war–was forced to take pictures of them for camp records. The motivation was to create a visual aid to identify runaway prisoners or those whose identity had to be confirmed during their incarceration. Cruel and inhumane conditions at the camp, however, soon made the photo documentation system ineffective, as the prisoners' emaciated physique and facial features made them unrecognizable.

The photographs were taken in a laboratory of the *Politische Abteilung Erkennungsdienst (Political Department Identification Service)*. Tens of thousands of them between 1941 and 1945, of which only 38,916 would eventually survive and be archived in the Auschwitz-Birkenau Memorial and Museum established in Oświęcim, Poland, after the war. The Nazis had tried to destroy the evidence by ordering prisoner photographers Wilhelm Brasse and Bronisław Jureczek to burn the photos, but they bravely sabotaged the attempt instead, cleverly suffocating the fire by depriving it of oxygen, thereby preserving many.

While waiting in line, Ava met Yael, a ten-year-old girl whose mother had hid her in the lavatory prior to being taken to the gas chambers. She reminded Ava of Seraphina from Ravensbrück, only two years younger. Ava bonded instantly with Yael as if she were her little sister.

"Do you know what Yael means?" the little girl asked proudly.

"*Nein*," said Ava.

"Oh, it has such a marvelous meaning." She clasped her hands together, making Ava smile. "It means 'mountain goat', symbolizing bravery, agility, and strength. God's strength. In the Bible, the prophetess Deborah sent the Israelite men to defend against the invading Canaanites, but it was Yael, a heroic Israelite woman, who saved her people instead."

"A brave woman, she was," said Ava. "Like you." Earlier, she had witnessed Yael being beaten by a guard for not understanding the instructions given to her.

Yael smiled and nodded.

Each prisoner was photographed in three poses—a profile shot, an en face shot, and a head-covering shot with a headscarf (women) or a cap (men). In the bottom left corner were the camp number, nationality, reason for being there, and the "KL Auschwitz" reference. Ava went first and sat for the photographer, stoic in expression, her large green eyes both haunted and hunted, her gaunt face shadowed, her once alabaster skin now translucent with veins showing beneath the surface like a newborn baby bird. As she posed for each photo, it reminded her of when she and Shaylee had posed for their father as he painted their portrait in the barn. She remembered complaining about it, too, having to sit still for so long—another regret from the past.

The photographer stared at Ava after the photographs were taken. He had seen her before. She had won the Rothenburg ob der Tauber beauty pageant a few years back, and he was there as a photographer, hiding his Semitic background like hers. The realization shook him. How quickly the world had changed, he thought. This once beautiful young woman, winner of a beauty pageant, was now a prisoner in a notorious concentration camp.

Yael was next.

"My name is Wilhelm," the photographer said. "Don't look into the camera directly. Just look to the side. And don't smile or cry."

Yael posed for the pictures with bravery and strength—God's strength—her bright blue eyes hiding her fear.

"Such a pretty little *Mädchen*," the photographer mumbled to himself. "What a crime."

Afterward, Ava and Yael walked back to the barracks, hand in hand, just like Ava and Shaylee used to do as children. From then on, the little girl would not leave Ava's side during the day, and would nestle up close to her like a kitten at night.

"If we're ever freed from here, can you please take me with you?" she asked one night, her voice pleading in tone. "Please? I have no one else. They've all been killed."

Ava lifted her chin so Yael could see her eyes. "I promise you that when we leave this place, you will always be with me."

"Forever?"

"*Ja*, my darling swan," said Ava, tears welling in her eyes as she used her father's endearing term. "Where I go, you go. Now and forever." As she caressed Yael's cheek, the little girl closed her eyes and fell asleep, comforted that she would never be left alone.

All around them in the overcrowded barracks were countless other women, crammed side by side in the bunks. Some were crying, others moaning, many staring lifelessly into nothing. These were the ones most in trouble. The ones who had given up. Once the spirit is dead, the body quickly follows.

Ava stared down at little Yael for a while. Even with her shaved head, swollen lip, and bruised face from the vicious guard who had beaten her earlier, she looked like an angel. Knowing that they'd both probably die soon, she held the child closer, a hot tear running down her cheek.

～⦁～

One day Ava met someone else she never thought she would . . .
Her birth mother!

As she was walking with Yael, she heard her name being called. Turning to see who it was, a Jewish woman stood only a few feet away.

"Ava . . .," she said again, almost in shock.

"*Ja?*"

"I'm Abigail Katz . . . I'm your mother."

There, standing before Ava, was the woman who gave her life. Ava froze. "You're the Jewish woman who worked with us as housemaids for the Wagners in Rothenburg," she said, in shock herself.

"*Ja*. I worked there so I could see you and your sister up close and talk to you. Before that, I'd often watch you as children while I hid in the woods."

"I remember," said Ava, her tears flowing like the Tauber River. "Sometimes we'd see you too. We called you 'the woman in the forest.'"

Even in that horrendous place, a celestial feeling washed over them. With shaved heads and dirty clothes, the two women embraced and wouldn't let go.

Ava and Abigail had found a joy in each other that could not be described, and could not be taken from them. Though it was under the most grievous of circumstances, imprisoned in that hellish camp, they saw it as a true blessing. Strangely, it wasn't awkward for either of them. Abigail became Ava's mother, and Ava became her daughter. Not just biologically but in their hearts. Yes, Maria was still Ava's mother. But now so was Abigail. Sharing not just blood but also their pain, undergoing the same persecution, struggling to survive.

When Shaylee was released from the infirmary, she rejoined her sister and Abigail. Fortunately, Dr. Mengele had moved on to other twins, leaving the Wolff sisters alone. Shaylee embraced her birth mother just like Ava, with no hesitation or animosity. The reasons Abigail gave for her desperate decision to give up her babies all those years ago, were accepted with empathy and love.

Whenever she could, Abigail taught her daughters about their Jewish heritage, customs, and beliefs. Ava and Shaylee listened, eager to learn. The women talked about the foods they loved to eat and the recipes they used to cook, which somehow, paradoxically, helped cope with the hunger. And they conversed about their plans for the future, which importantly, helped foster hope.

It was a beautiful bonding experience shared between mother and daughters, three-cord strong, trying to salvage something normal in an abnormal world.

❧

Soon after Shaylee's release from the infirmary, she became very sick. Fever, chills, diarrhea, and weakness were consuming her fragile body. The chemical injections Dr. Mengele had forced on her were having long-term effects, breaking her vitality down.

"Tomorrow I'm going to ask them to bring you back to the infirmary," Ava said, concerned over her sister's health. "This has been going on for too long, and you need medical attention."

Shaylee had tried to be strong, not whining or complaining, even as she had a myriad of reasons to do so. And the last thing she wanted was to go

438

back to the infirmary. "*Nein*," she said, curled up against Ava in the bunk, wrapped in her sister's arms. "I can't go back there. I've seen what happens to those who appear too sick or don't recover quickly enough. Dr. Mengele takes them away, and they're never seen again."

Nazi physicians throughout Germany's concentration camps often conducted periodic selections in the infirmaries and barracks, looking for those who were injured or had become too ill or weak to work. The SS used various methods to murder these prisoners, including lethal injections and gassing. Dr. Mengele himself routinely carried out such selections at Auschwitz-Birkenau, which contributed to his epithet, "Angel of Death." Prisoners in the infirmary were terrified whenever he'd appear, fearful his visit meant their end.

"You would never know it by looking at him," Shaylee said. "Or speaking to him. Dr. Mengele is handsome and talks like he's your *Freund*, but really he's a monster. A gargoyle from the depths of hell."

Just like Starholf, Ava thought, remembering his sky blue eyes and chiseled face. A handsome monster. A gargoyle from hell. And yet, because of her children, she still loved him.

Ever since she and her sister were reunited, Ava continually gave Shaylee positive reinforcement. Kind words, hugs, reassuring smiles, encouragement to keep going. But that night she feared it wouldn't help. Shaylee was suffering and fighting off death. A couple of times during the night, she soiled herself, and Ava had to clean her with a rag she found, wiping her bony legs. And when the muscle spasms started, she massaged her sister, making them subside. She did everything she could to make Shaylee comfortable.

Panicky thoughts were going through Ava's mind, watching her sister deteriorate. Will she even make it through the night? How can I save her, what can I do? If she dies, will I die too? Maybe they knew something about twins, about our special connection, and when they gave her those horrible injections to slowly take her life, mine would follow.

Ava started to examine her past, thinking that perhaps this was somehow her fault. What if God were punishing her for what she had done with her adopted brother Luka? She thought back to that strange summer when she was a curious teenager on the cusp of womanhood, allowing him to be overly affectionate with her, even kissing, soon leading to forbidden conduct. True, they were not biological siblings, but it was still wrong, a sin, and Luka was badly hurt by it. Though she didn't know it yet, his broken heart, precipitating confusion and anger, had triggered the firestorm that exposed her, Shaylee, and Abigail's Jewish heritage, almost had her father executed, and ended Luka's life by suicide.

Please forgive me, God, Ava silently prayed. Forgive me for playing with Luka's heart, and please don't punish Shaylee for it. I beg of you.

"Ava, tell me a story," Shaylee said, interrupting her sister's regrets, her body sweating and her breathing labored.

"What kind of story?"

"A happy one. Something about the farm."

"There are so many."

"Tell me something about Mama's garden." Shaylee loved that glorious patch of earth. It was small, modest, but oh so lovely, with resplendent flowers, latticework, a wrought iron table and chair, and the pond nearby where the swans would visit. Hanz had made a wooden signpost at its entrance that read, *"Maria's Himmel (Heaven)."*

Ava thought for a moment. "I once saved a fairy in Mama's garden."

"You're telling me a falsehood, Ava Wolff." Shaylee weakly looked up at her sister and smiled, showing all her front teeth missing. A guard had hit her in the mouth with the butt of his rifle recently because she was walking too slowly from being sick. With a mouth full of blood, she spat out her teeth, and Ava could do nothing but watch. Abigail had witnessed it too, falling to her knees and grabbing handfuls of dirt, clutching them as her knuckles turned white. When something happened to her daughters, it happened to her.

Now whenever Ava saw her sister's toothless smile, all she could think about was how precious Shaylee was. How childlike and innocent she looked. Shaylee was not just her twin sibling but also her baby, her best friend, and her dear loved one to take care of. Yes, Shaylee was all those things wrapped in one.

"Did you really save a fairy?" Yael asked. She had been cuddling against Abigail, fast asleep, and was now awake and listening.

"*Nein,* my darling swan," said Ava, smiling at her. "It was a bumblebee. But it might as well have been a fairy."

Yael was fascinated, and she moved in closer. "What happened?"

"I was in the garden one day, watering the flowers and admiring how pretty they all looked. And then I noticed a little bee had fallen into a large bloom full of water. I poured it out and let the bee dry in the sun, hoping it wasn't dead, but the little thing wasn't moving."

"What happened next?" another woman asked, listening from the bunk above.

"*Ja*, what happened?" asked another.

The green in Ava's aventurine eyes brightened as they always did when she felt a flicker of joy. "The bumblebee lived. The sunshine had dried it out, and I watched in disbelief as it flapped its iridescent wings and caught the breeze, lifting into the air. But that's not the most amazing part."

"Oh, tell me what happened next!" said Yael.

"Later that day, the bumblebee came back and landed on my arm. I could see its tiny face staring at me, and I knew it was thanking me." Ava became excited as she spoke. "I knew in that moment that all living beings have a soul. Even a little bumblebee. Now isn't that something?"

"*Danke*, Ava," Shaylee said, closing her eyes full of tears. "I can see the farm now. I can see Mama in her garden, and Papa standing at the edge of the vineyard, smoking his pipe. I can see them together on the porch swing, and they're waving us home."

Ava turned her face away and bit back a sob.

All the women in the bunks who were close enough to hear Ava's story, and Shaylee's vision, were also brought to tears. Each of them had lived their own wonderful lives before the Nazi apocalypse decimated it. Sickness, starvation, humiliation, beatings, rape, murder, death. This was their reality now.

The vision in Shaylee's mind didn't last, though. Like a dream when one wakes, it vanished as soon as she opened her eyes again. Thoughts of everything she had gone through, and was still going through, replaced it, creating a division in her soul, separating psyche from flesh and splitting her in half. "All this suffering has changed me, Ava," she said quietly, weeping in her sister's embrace. "The old me is dead. Now a stranger is in my sick body, struggling to survive."

Ava only listened, holding Shaylee close, her heart breaking.

"It destroyed me when they murdered Christian. And at the castle, every time that monster raped me, another piece of me died. Now the injections they gave me have poisoned what's left." The life from Shaylee's eyes appeared to be slowly draining as she stared off into nothing. "I was naïve. I didn't realize what true suffering was like. What ongoing torture was like. What tasting death was like. Humans were made to be nurtured, to be held and cherished. Our entire existence, meant to be loved." Closing her eyes, she moaned and shuddered. "I didn't know, Ava. I didn't know. But now I do. God forgive my innocence."

As Ava looked down at her fragile sister, an image shined brightly in her mind, like a star beckoning her home. The memory was from that wonderful summer day at the farm when they were fifteen, where Shaylee floated in the pond in a lavender dress, arms to her sides, palms up, staring at the sky as Ava, wearing a similar dress and crown of wildflowers, tossed petals on her. They were reenacting a scene from *Ophelia*, the famous painting by British artist Sir John Everett Millais, created in 1852. Ophelia from Shakespeare's *Hamlet* was floating in a stream before her tragic death, her delicate body adorned with the wildflowers she had picked. This was how Shaylee looked now, personifying it—only worse—her skin so pale and sickly, almost glowing in the semi-darkness; her lovely eyes closed sweetly, resembling the back of two rose petals; her lips slightly open, waiting to be kissed. Kissed by the angel of death.

"I can feel a coldness come over me," Shaylee said, her voice sounding foreign and weak. "I am a butterfly with only a short time left. I came out of my cocoon, and I saw the sun and sky. I saw the miracle of life, and just as I was beginning to know this wondrous world, it's my time to die." As Shaylee spoke, Mozart's *Requiem* entered her consciousness. The haunting piece grappling with the mystery of death, composed by a man on the precipice of his own, willing his last creation into life with his final breaths, was a mournful plea for compassion and a humble request for God to have mercy, allowing for the peaceful repose of the dead. "Where is God's mercy?" Shaylee asked, hearing Mozart's *Requiem* in her mind. "Where is his mercy?"

"There is no mercy for us," said a woman listening.

Several others slowly nodded, as if in a trance. And like a ripple, then a wave, more women spoke up, agreeing, creating an echo of voices ricocheting among them.

"Can you hear it, Ava?" Shaylee asked, her breathing now shallow. "The Requiem Mass . . . it's chilling."

Ava caressed Shaylee's cheek, never wavering her eyes from her. And though they were surrounded by a multitude of emaciated women, with sad stares, shaved heads, and spirits broken, everyone in the barracks faded.

The filthy, weathered bunks and walls did too, and even their bloodthirsty Nazi captors outside. Only the twins remained, as if back in their mother's womb, alone in each other's embrace, comforting each other.

Abigail could only watch her daughters with great sadness, remembering them as tiny babies crying for her when she left them in a wicker basket in the Wolff barn. Helpless then, helpless now. Leaving her bunk, she went to them, kissing the back of Shaylee's hand and caressing it tenderly, humming a Jewish song: *Elohim Lanu Machaseh Va'oz (The Lord is Our Refuge and Strength)*. Others joined in, and the space around them became soft, shadowy, and intimate, like the scene in Eugène Carrière's 1889 painting, *Intimacy*. A sentimental portrait of the artist's wife and daughters, the artwork reflected the same love between Abigail and *her* daughters.

Silent tears chased one another down Ava's face as she stared at her precious sister, knowing she was dying. It made her think of the famous quote from Edgar Allan Poe, written in 1846: *"The death of a beautiful woman is, unquestionably, the most poetical topic in the world."* As Shaylee grew weaker and weaker, the sense of her imminent passing circulated the room like witches dancing around a cauldron, taunting and laughing. The whole world seemed to pause, and a golden glow surrounded the sisters as they whispered to each other, feeling every word. And then Shaylee's body went limp, her arms flailing to her sides. She no longer spoke, and the silence turned to an all-knowing awe.

Ava would not let Shaylee go, holding her tight, tucked in her embrace like a duckling in the feathers of its mother. Fate had brought Gemini's twin stars, Castor and Pollux, back together, and Ava would keep her other half until the very end. Until the Nazi demons came to take her.

❧◈☙

"I'll tell you a secret," said a woman lying in the bunk above Ava that night. The woman's name was Agnieszka, and recently she had come back from the infirmary like Shaylee. The Nazis had performed medical experiments on her too because she had heterochromia—one eye was brown and the other blue—something that intrigued Dr. Mengele.

Agnieszka's husband had been shot between the eyes in front of her, and her infant son ripped from her arms and thrown into a refuse fire. She wanted to die too after they forced her to watch her child scream and burn,

443

but the Nazis sent her to Auschwitz instead.

Soon after arriving at the camp, Agnieszka gave birth to a baby girl. She had hidden her pregnancy during the selection process; otherwise, they would have sent her straight to the gas chambers or, like many other women, perforated her uterus to force an abortion, which often resulted in subsequent death. They didn't even let her see her newborn, drowning it in a barrel of water and tossing it into the building's heating stove. Sterilization came next, after which a nurse told her to be grateful she was still alive, knowing the fate of most pregnant women at the camp.

After losing both her children in such unimaginable crimes, Agnieszka wouldn't speak for days. And when she finally did talk, only nonsense and gibberish came out of her mouth.

"What secret?" Ava asked, looking up at the woman. She was having trouble sleeping that night, infected with lice that caused her head to severely itch.

"The air around us is breathing," the woman whispered, a crazed look in her eyes. "It's breathing like a ferocious animal. An evil, invisible monster. When it enters your lungs, it slowly eats you alive, and that's why everyone is dying." She pointed her bony finger at Shaylee sleeping in Ava's arms. "She will be gone soon too."

"*Nein*, that's not true," Ava defended, protectively holding Shaylee's skeletal body closer. She could feel her sister's faint, labored breath on her chest. "She will recover."

Agnieszka continued as if in a trance. "These creatures are the ones controlling the bad men, telling them what to do. Telling them to commit their demonic crimes. They live inside them, thriving like a virus."

Ava stared at the woman with pity, knowing she had lost her mind from the trauma of what they had done to her husband and children, exacerbated by the gruesome medical experiments they did on her eyes—the brown one was severely damaged from the chemicals they injected into it—and the months of malnutrition and further abuse.

"*Ja*, each one of us is being eaten alive, one by one, fading away until we're gone forever. That's what happened to my poor little Bazyli, and my baby girl. I didn't even have a name for her yet."

"Why don't you close your eyes and try to sleep," Ava said. "It will keep the monsters away."

"*Nein*, I can't!" Agnieszka looked at Ava as if she were the crazy one.

"Sometimes my babies return to me, looking for protection from the monsters. That's why I refuse to die, even though they're eating me. Because if I do, who will hold and comfort Bazyli and my little girl?"

Ava thought of her own children, and her heart ached. Their smiles, the way their eyes would light up when she played with them, the sound of their cute giggles and sweet voices calling her "Mama." All those memories haunted her, but they also gave her hope to stay alive; to persevere so she could see them again.

Agnieszka became more delirious. "One day I looked up into the sun, and I saw them there, floating on its rays."

"You saw what?" asked Ava.

"The monsters. There were three of them, twelve feet tall and very frightening. Half dragon, half ox, with wings of an eagle and wide mouths full of sharp teeth. But it was their red eyes that terrified me most. Evil eyes, not from this world."

"What a horrible thing to have seen," Ava said.

"Do you know what they call themselves?"

Ava slowly shook her head.

"One is Misery, another Hopelessness, and the third one Despair." A single, glistening tear fell from Agnieszka's blue eye, leaving a trail down her dirt-stained cheek.

Ava could not look away. In her weakened, emotional state, sandwiched between countless filthy, starving women—one lost to insanity—she wondered if there truly were such creatures.

Hours later, deep in the night, Ava had a nightmare about one of them. The creature—a huge, massive beast exactly as Agnieszka had described—hovered above her, floating like a shadow, its teeth shining in the moonlight, its cold breath down her neck, its eyes not from this world.

"I am Misery," it whispered in her ear, its voice deep and coarse. "I have come for your sister." The creature was deciding what to do with Shaylee . . .

Eat her or let her live.

※

The following morning, a true miracle took place. Was it from the love of a sister, a mother, and a little girl?

Yes, I would say so.

Shaylee's fever broke, her stomach settled, her body strengthened, and her color returned!

She survived!

"Ava, tell me another story," she whispered, curling up into her sister. "About fairies, elves, and leprechauns. A happy one with a secret garden. A story so magical that it transports us far away from here."

Ava started crying with joy, Abigail and Yael too, recognizing the unlikely reprieve from the Divine. A powerful surge of hope washed over them all like a rogue wave, recalling the little bumblebee again, how it too had survived what seemed like certain death. The force of life in living beings has strength, Ava reminded herself. God's strength, like the meaning of "Yael." In her mind's eye, she saw that little bumblebee recovering, lifting up and catching air, flying away into the bright afternoon light of the blazing sun.

Later that day, still fragile but alive, Shaylee stood out in the sun and let the rays warm her skin.

"Where is God!" she heard a woman wail. "He has forsaken us!"

But Shaylee disagreed. He's all around us. Suffering with us. Not just as a spectator but experiencing everything we experience, holding our hands as we together endure. Every time an evil man hurts us, he pokes the Almighty in the eye.

Shaylee ambled along that day, thinking deeply. She had heard the death angel calling her, tormenting her, singing his evil lullaby, stinging her ears and sticking thorns in her heart. But she made it through the night, and he fled. I'll make it through today, too, she thought. And tomorrow. Just like Ava's bumblebee, I will survive this. I have my sister, my mother, and little Yael. I have my memories, and I have God.

These things will sustain me.

I will survive.

CHAPTER 46

Autumn, 1944

As night follows day, Hanz had tried to return to his life after Ava, Shaylee, and Abigail were taken. But he could not. He struggled with even the simplest things, only feeding the animals and letting the rest of the farm go. Severin had visited often during this time, taking military leave whenever he could to work on the farm. He had to, otherwise it would be lost.

One night, Hanz had a strange dream about the Irish prisoner who had harassed and provoked him at the jailhouse in Berlin. "I have seen you before, Blondie," the deranged man had said to him. "*Ja*, I remember now. At the insane asylum."

Hanz of course denied it then–he had never been to a mental institution. But when the Irishman said, "If it wasn't you, then it was someone who looks exactly like you," Hanz knew in his gut what the answer to the riddle was. The face the madman remembered must have been his older brother Andrew.

In his heart, Hanz had always questioned the story of Andrew's suicide, believing that he might still be alive somewhere. His parents had always been so vague about his death, other than to say he had shamed the family. Even as a young boy Hanz could tell something else had happened, something clandestine. And now that his two-year house arrest sentence was over, he decided to make the trip back to Berlin to find out what.

The mental hospital was as one would expect–depressing, eerie, even frightening. Cries, moans, and screams echoed in the air; sedated, zombie-like patients void of expression walked the hallways; and medical staff in white lab coats occasionally appeared, some reading reports on clipboards and others running to quell a sudden patient crisis.

Dressed in his Sunday best, Hanz went to the reception desk and asked if a patient named Andrew Berchtwald Wolff was hospitalized there. The medical clerk looked at him, asked to see his identification, and then told him to wait while she went to inquire.

Hanz didn't know what to expect. As he stood in the lobby, he wondered if his gut instinct had been wrong. The Irishman in that prison cell was a sick lunatic, after all, and it's entirely possible that Andrew did commit suicide after shaming the family. But why was it always swept under the rug? Why would his parents never talk about it? Footsteps broke his cogitation as the clerk returned with the chief psychiatrist, a medical file in his hand. "I'm sorry, Herr Wolff," was all he said, giving the document to Hanz and coldly walking away.

As he opened the file and read the first page, a feather could have knocked Hanz over. "Andrew was here," he said under his breath. "My *Bruder* was here. For decades." What he read next nearly buckled his knees, and he had to sit down . . .

Andrew Berchtwald Wolff had not committed suicide but was instead committed to the mental institute in Berlin by his own father because of his homosexuality. Considered deviant, sinful, and even criminal, they attempted to cure him of it through barbaric treatments, including chemically induced convulsions, nausea-inducing drugs, hypnosis therapy, and eventually, a new medical procedure called a lobotomy. Invented in 1935 by the Portuguese neurologist, Egas Moniz, it was considered a miracle cure, for which the doctor would later receive the Nobel Prize in Medicine.

When none of that seemed to work, however, they transferred Andrew to the Hadamar Psychiatric Clinic in 1939, and there he mysteriously died of an unknown cause. But Hanz knew the truth. "Patients in that mental hospital never leave," Enzo Grimaldi, the great-great-grandson of Joseph Grimaldi—a legend among clowns—had told him in that prison cell. And everyone knew why . . . His brother was murdered! Gassed and cremated the very day he arrived at that killing center.

Hanz wept as he read through the notes, written by several treating psychiatrists over the years. "I'm sorry, Andrew," he said aloud as if his sweet and loving brother were sitting next to him. "Forgive me for not knowing. For not being able to help." He sat there for a long while, then numbly left.

Once home, Hanz went into the barn and began drinking vodka, staring at the medical document on the wooden work bench until everything around him dissolved. Until it was only him and the paperwork. Opening that file was as if he had let out a ghost to roam free, and he wasn't sure if that was a good decision or bad. His brother's black-and-white photo, like a prison mug shot staring back at him, was now forever etched in his mind. All those years, all that life . . . stolen.

Hanz grabbed the file and threw it to the ground, dousing it with gasoline and lighting it on fire. He didn't want to ever read it again, tell anyone else about it, or see his brother's face so tormented and lost. He wanted to remember Andrew as he was when Hanz was a boy—kind, soft-spoken, and always good to him.

Now angry and disgusted, Hanz grabbed his vodka bottle and went outside. He made his way aimlessly toward the Tauber River, stumbling in the darkness of the night. "Secrets, ghosts, and lies—they're all around me!" he yelled out to no one. "What is real anymore! What is true!"

In his inebriated and distraught state, Hanz didn't see the stump in front of him and tripped over it, hitting the ground hard.

"Crack!"

A pain shot up his bad right leg. He fractured it.

Lying there in agony, Hanz yelled at the sky. His daughters and their birth mother were in a concentration camp, his wife was deathly ill in a tuberculosis clinic, and his older brother was murdered in a psychiatric killing facility.

And now the Wolff family patriarch was a fallen warrior.

A slain Viking.

A broken man.

Emotionally buried while still alive.

⁂

A week later, Severin came back to the farm. "Is this how it ends for you?" he asked, standing in Hanz's bedroom in full military uniform, meticulous and immaculate. With his *Schirmmütze* in his hands, his hair newly shorn, and his face so clean-shaven his skin still had a pinkness to it, he was the embodiment of a Nazi officer. Like a stone, emotionally removed and aloof. "You going to die a drunk in your bed?"

Hanz now had a cast on his leg. "A heartbroken drunk," he mumbled, his voice a mix of anger, bitterness, and despondency.

Severin stood over the bed and examined his older brother. The strong, vibrant man he knew seemed to have aged decades in the span of months. Hanz had lost a significant amount of weight, and he was starting to resemble the Jewish prisoners at the Nazi concentration camps. "When's the last time you've eaten, *Bruder?*"

Hanz didn't answer. His eyes were closed, his sandy blond beard threaded with silver had grown out, and he was clutching an empty vodka bottle. Several other empty bottles were scattered about on the floor like discarded candy wrappers. And his three loyal sheepdogs—Felix, Bastian, and Axel—lay at the foot of the bed, protecting their broken-spirited owner. Every so often, one of them would growl at Severin, only to start wagging its tail.

"The farm, the animals, the vineyard—everything is suffering," Severin said, sitting down in the chair in the corner. "Everything, Hanz."

"I don't care," he responded. In his drunken state, crushed under the weight of grief and helplessness, he began to quietly weep.

The two brothers remained silent for a moment. One a high-ranking Nazi officer who had fathered twin girls by a Jewish woman when they were both teenagers many years ago, running away from his responsibility. The other a simple farmer who had found them in his barn and raised them as his own, unaware of his brother's folly.

Severin glanced around the familiar room, memories of happier times flooding his mind. It seemed only yesterday that the little girls in pigtails ran about, barefoot and holding their dolls, singing little German songs, wanting him to pick them up and read to them. And little Luka, their adopted brother, following him around like a puppy everywhere, wanting to be just like his uncle. It pained Severin how it all turned so tragic. Who knew this beautiful, blended family would end up in such despair? "I'm sorry I brought this sorrow into your life," he said, his head shaking with regret. "It was all a terrible mistake, and . . ."

"*Nein!*" Hanz interrupted. "It was not a mistake. My beautiful swans brought life back to this farm, and to Maria. And when Maria got sick and had to be sent to Arizona, their mother brought life back to me."

"*Ja.* But now you must move on, *Bruder.*"

"Shaylee loved horses," Hanz said, ignoring his comment. "Especially the wild ones. She was always asking me to leave a bale of hay out for them in the field. And her books–she was never without them, always reading and learning about things, dreaming of traveling to different lands. She loved Ireland and Scotland. I wish I could have taken her there." He smiled as fresh tears began to fall. "And Ava, my little movie star. She wanted more than anything to go to America and become an actress. She would have taken Hollywood by storm, setting the screen on fire." He paused, thinking next of their beautiful mother. The woman he had fallen in love with, hiding her from the Nazis until she was ripped from his home. "Abigail was special too. She would weep when I played the violin for her."

"Hanz, you're romanticizing things," Severin said, listening to his brother languish. "You can't keep living in turmoil like this, wishing everything could be the way it was." He stood and walked over to the window, staring out at the picturesque view. The sky was clear and so blue it appeared to be turning a deep purple; the sheep were scattered about, munching on green grass; and a peaceful ambiance settled over the land. But inside the gloomy room, sadness radiated from his brother, thick and palpable. It made his skin crawl. "What can I do for you, *Bruder?*" he asked, turning around to face him.

"Get them back for me."

"You know I can't do that." Although Severin knew from his military contacts that Ava, Shaylee, and Abigail were at Auschwitz-Birkenau, his hands were tied. He loved his brother and would do it if he could, but no Jew would ever be released at his word.

"Then I have no need of you," Hanz said, rolling away from him, hiding his face in his hands.

Severin sighed. "All this pain and anguish over three Jews."

Hanz immediately sat up and glared at his brother, his expression as if fire were behind his eyes. It unnerved Severin. Somewhat frightened him, even, having never seen that look from his brother before. "Forgive me," he said. "I didn't mean that."

"If you ever say something like that again, I swear I'll kill you," Hanz said slowly, his demeanor fierce and convincing. "*Bruder* or not . . . Do you understand me?"

Severin nodded.

Hanz got out of bed and retrieved another bottle of vodka, taking a long drink.

Severin frowned. "I'm worried for you, *Bruder.* If you go on like this, you'll die soon."

"I'm already dead," he replied. With the vodka bottle in hand, he left his brother standing there, picking up his crutch and stumbling to his make-shift art studio in the barn, longing to gaze at his paintings of his beautiful swans and their mother.

⁕

Word had gotten out about Ava and Shalom and how Hanz Wolff had been harboring a Jew. Many Germans in the area shunned him, as did those who knew him in town, except for Ollie van Heinz. But Ollie wasn't around because he had been called up to serve in the Wehrmacht and was now stationed at the Western Front. With Germany losing the war, they were desperate for any able-bodied man, regardless of age. Sadly, Ollie would not return.

Hanz didn't care about the local scorn and spent his days at home in seclusion. "There has to be something I can do," he kept mumbling to himself at 3:00 a.m. one morning, drinking vodka, his sheepdogs by his side. Minutes later, he exclaimed, "I'm a damn fool! I'm a damn fool to think I could take on an army!" seething, hoping, thinking, obsessing about how to save his daughters and their birth mother.

At one point he sobbed, "Ava! Ava!" and shouted out to no one, "Shaylee! Shaylee, my darling, how can I save you from this nightmare!"

A crackling noise and the smell of smoke interrupted his moaning. Hanz went outside to investigate, only to find his crops on fire. Yet there was more. A creepy and bizarre shrine had been made from cornstalks. A scarecrow wearing a Nazi uniform, standing in front of the burning flames. One of his neighbors had played a cruel joke by constructing this monstrosity.

Hanz poured gasoline over the disgusting figure and lit it on fire too. Dropping his crutch and falling to his knees, he stared up at the repulsive effigy in rage and watched it burn until the uniform blazed and wilted, withering away, sitting there until the only thing left was smoke and ashes.

⁕

A German man and his wife had moved into the vacant property adjacent the Wolff farm. They were sympathetic to Hanz, and as a neighborly gesture, she brought over some meat pie and bone broth soup. Severin, who had come back to see his brother again, heated it up, arranging two place settings on the kitchen table while he waited for Hanz to return from his makeshift art studio in the barn–his place of solace. When Hanz came back, without saying a word he sat down across from Severin and began eating.

"*Gute,*" Severin said, happy to see it. Hungry himself, he dug in. "Mmm . . . She's a *gute* cook, your neighbor. Nice to have people like that next door."

Hanz looked up at him with an acrid scowl. "A Jewish family lived in that home before them. Malachi and Ursula Applebaum, and their two daughters, Jeta and Zelda. They were *meine Freunde,* and those Nazi bastards shot the parents in their own yard and took the girls away."

Severin inwardly cringed, regretting his attempt at small talk. Though he hated the atrocities of the Third Reich, he didn't want to engage with Hanz over it. Now was not the time. Cutting himself another piece of the meat pie, he said, "I'm going to stay here for a week," giving his brother a level gaze. "The fire did a lot of damage, and you need help to get this place back in order before it all goes to hell."

Hanz noticed a new military pin on his brother's uniform. "I see they gave you another shiny medal. What's that one for?" he asked sarcastically, returning to his food.

Severin hesitated. A man conflicted between his career and his moral compass, he often wondered what he was doing in the Nazi Party. Many times he thought of quitting, but that would come with some form of punishment, least of all being stripped of all his accolades. He had heard rumors of others who refused their duties, only to be shipped off to the Russian Front without cold weather gear and little or no ammunition, literally being used as cannon fodder, or sent on suicidal assaults across minefields. "If you must know, I led a team who successfully dismantled an operation to assassinate Hitler. They honored me with the Knight's Cross of the Iron Cross for exceptional bravery and leadership in the face of the enemy. Hitler himself presented it, and he even invited me to have dinner with him soon."

Hanz's head snapped up. "Is that so."

"*Ja,* we spoke at length. One on one, you wouldn't think he's the leader behind all this madness. He's actually quite cultured like you."

"He is nothing like me," Hanz scoffed. "He's an evil monster."

"Regardless, the man enjoys classical music and art. He always wanted to be a painter, and he wants to show me his collection at the Berghof."

An electric shock ran through Hanz. So powerful it seemed as if someone had just electrocuted him, giving birth to an incredible idea. God himself must have planted the epiphany in his brain, he thought. Where else would it come from? Smiling, he asked his brother, "Would you be able to give Adolf Hitler a gift for me?"

"A gift?"

"*Ja.*" Hanz put down his spoon. "A painting."

"You want to give the Führer a painting? Why?"

"An offering of my respect."

"Hanz, you just called the man an evil monster."

"All I ask is that you give it to him when you meet him for dinner."

Severin was completely confused. "A painting of what?"

"Of him, of course," said Hanz. "A portrait of Adolf Hitler so mesmerizing he'll be in absolute awe!"

CHAPTER 47

Hanz immediately went to work. Using a photo of Adolf Hitler from the front page of the *Völkischer Beobachter (People's Observer)*, and a picture of the 1796 oil painting, *Bonaparte at the Pont d'Arcole*, by French artist Antoine-Jean Gros, he painted for hours each day, meticulously engaging in his craft. Hanz knew that by placing Hitler in a similar setting, on par with Napolean Bonaparte in that famous painting, where the French dictator led his troops to storm the bridge in the Battle of Arcole, it would stroke the Führer's ego. That would move Hitler to want to reward him for such a flattering portrayal, and since Hanz had also been called up to serve in the Wehrmacht once his leg had healed, he'd request a position at Auschwitz-Birkenau as a guard. That's the only way he could get into the concentration camp and close to Ava, Shaylee, and Abigail.

With hands covered in paint, clothes covered in paint, deliriously laughing for no reason at all, then crying for reasons too numerous to count, Hanz feverishly worked. "You must do the thing you think you cannot do," echoed in his ears–something his father always used to say when Hanz didn't want to help him prepare the dead bodies for burial.

One month later, he was done. Just in time for the dinner Severin and his team were about to have with the Führer at the Berghof, his mountain retreat in the Bavarian Alps.

Hanz stepped back and stared at his creation. Through the semi-darkness of the barn, Adolf Hitler stared at him in return, as if the German dictator were right there in the room with him. Though he despised his subject, he had to admit it was his finest work yet.

Nevertheless, an unsettling feeling overwhelmed him, staring into the eyes of evil.

The following month, Hanz got the invitation he was praying for. Hitler wanted to meet the talented artist who had painted his portrait in a way that exuded unmatched strength, manliness, and vision, leading the Fatherland as its *Führer und Reichskanzler (Leader and Chancellor of the Reich)*!

That evening, as he sat on his porch, Ingomar paid him a visit, coming closer than usual. The black crow dropped a shiny object at his feet, as if offering a gift of his own. An emerald ring.

"What on earth?" Hanz said, picking it up. "Where did you get this, Ingomar?" And then it dawned on him . . . This was a piece of Constance Bodnar's stolen jewelry!

Hanz followed the crow as it flew back to that massive linden tree in the woods, where they had hung the masquerading priest who committed those terrible crimes.

Ingomar, sitting high on a branch, squawked at Hanz as if trying to tell him something.

Sliding his eyes down the tree, Hanz noticed a small hole in the trunk. Reaching up, he stuck his hand in it, and to his shocking surprise, he found the stash that was hidden all those years ago.

A bag of money and jewels!

The drive to the Berghof was long, and when Hanz and his brother pulled up to the building, he stopped and stared at it for a moment, anxious over what was about to take place. This meeting with the Führer would determine the fate of those he loved.

After passing through security, Hanz and Severin were greeted by the butler. An older man named Oz, he looked like a graying Saint Bernard, and led the men to the Great Room.

As they waited for Hitler, Hanz walked over to the enormous picture window with the panoramic view of the Untersberg Mountain in Austria. The day was clear, so Fortress Hohensalzburg, the centuries old medieval castle overlooking the city of Salzburg, was visible in the distance. What stunning scenery, he thought.

When Hitler entered the room, his German Shepherd Blondi by his side, Hanz and Severin gave the Sieg Heil salute.

"So this is the talented artist who painted my portrait," Hitler said, walking straight up to Hanz to shake his hand.

"*Ja, mein Führer (Yes, my Führer),*" said Severin. "My *Bruder*, Hanz Wolff."

An intense revulsion swept over Hanz as the two men gripped hands. He wanted to pull his away.

Hitler's looming, heavy stare remained fixed on Hanz, testing his mettle. When Hanz didn't blink, Hitler said, "Such exemplary German stock. You are the perfect example of the Aryan man."

Hanz forced a smile. How ironic that this puny dictator looked nothing like the Aryan ideal he so revered. "I'm honored that you liked my gift," he said. "I believe it to be my finest work."

"*Ja*, looks like a photograph," said Hitler. He looked at it hanging on the wall, mounted next to *Venus and Amor* by Paris Bordone, the Italian painter of the Venetian Renaissance. "Eva loves it too. She said it's the best picture of me she's ever seen."

"*Danke,*" said Hanz.

"I used to be an artist myself, you know. But that was a long time ago."

The three men sat down for dinner, and as Hitler spoke, all Hanz could think about were the people who had suffered by this monster's hand. The atrocities, the murders, the rapes; the families torn apart, including his own; and the attempted annihilation of an entire race of people. All of it was by his design. He was responsible. Sitting there, Hanz felt as if he were having dinner with Satan the Devil himself, in his preferred lodging in hell.

At the end of the evening, Hitler said, "Tell me, Herr Wolff, what can I do for you? Your gift has pleased me greatly, and I would like to do something for you in return."

"*Danke, mein Führer,*" Hanz said. "But I do not need anything." Hanz knew Hitler would not accept his humility.

"Nonsense. Tell me what I can do for you."

This was the moment Hanz had waited for. The pinnacle of his ruse. "Well, *mein Führer*, previously I had not been conscripted into the Wehrmacht because of the injury to my right leg, suffered during the Great War. And then I broke it recently. But now I have been ordered back to active duty, and I would like to serve the Reich as a guard at Auschwitz-Birkenau. There, I can help the Fatherland rid itself of the Jewish problem." Just saying those words made Hanz feel sick.

Hitler seemed pleased with this request and grinned. And yet he appeared somewhat skeptical at the same time. "You want to go where the vermin are? Among the filthy rats?"

"*Ja.* Very much so," said Hanz.

Hitler stared at him for a long moment. Too long. Those evil, dark blue eyes, boring into his, trying to get into his mind to read it. Sweat formed on Hanz's brow and lip, his heart elevating as he awaited the Führer's answer.

Smiling, Hitler shook Hanz's hand again, and said, "I will personally make sure you are sent to Auschwitz-Birkenau. I believe you will be a great addition there."

⁂

As soon as he arrived home, Hanz prepared to leave his farm. He didn't know how long he'd be gone, or if he'd even return alive, as the plot he was about to attempt was full of uncertainty and risk. Leon Dreisler, his neighbor to the east with the Jewish mail-order bride from Hungary, agreed to tend to his animals, crops, and vineyard during his absence. Leon had been honorably discharged from the Wehrmacht after losing an arm in the Battle of El Alamein in North Africa under Field Marshal Erwin Rommel, nicknamed the "Desert Fox" for his mastery of desert warfare; and his wife had been fortunate enough to escape the Gestapo scourge with convincing, falsified ID.

On the day of his departure, Hanz walked about his property to say his final goodbyes, talking to the land and the animals as if they were his good friends. He patted Agatha, his gluttonous cow with the large brown eyes and long lashes, remembering how she had faced away from her hay to carefully watch over the wicker basket she had found in the barn that morning, seemingly excited over the tiny new Homo sapiens sleeping inside it. "*Danke*, Agatha," he whispered to her. "*Danke* for looking after my swans."

Next he spoke to Bucephalus, his beloved horse who had also been there that wonderful day that changed his and Maria's lives. "I must go away for a while, *mein Freund*," he said, pressing his forehead into the black stallion's velvety muzzle, his hands holding either side of it. "I have faith Ava and Shaylee are still alive, and I'm going to find them and their mother."

Hanz left the gravesites until the end. As he placed flowers on the soil where he had buried Nila, his thoughts, difficult as they were, reminisced of the happier times with her, Randolph the Bull, and Ollie, joking and laughing together at The Devil's Needle. The Three Musketeers and their D'Artagnan. He could almost hear Nila's voice from the grave, whispering to him to not give up, to not lose hope, her reassuring words floating softly in the wind. It once more reminded him of the 1796 poem, *To A Primrose*, by Samuel Taylor Coleridge, celebrating the beauty and resilience of the first spring primrose and comparing it to the feeble yet hopeful signs of recovery from illness or despair. "I miss you, Nila," he said. "*Danke* for your encouragement and friendship."

The gravesites of his stillborn son, and his adopted son Luka, were saved for the last. Standing there by their tombstones, buried side by side, Hanz didn't know what to say at first—the emotion was too strong. But then his sentiments started flowing.

"I would have loved to have known you," he said to the stillborn child. "*Mein Sohn.*" His eyes burned as tears started to fall. "I would have loved to watch you grow up, to play with you, teach you, and love you. To see you become a man."

Hanz wiped his eyes and stared at the earth covering Luka, a stabbing pain shooting through his heart. He remembered that little boy with wavy blond hair so blond it almost looked white, shyly emerging from behind his father's back, staring up at him like a fragile bird. "*Ist schon gut, Luka. Ich bin jetzt dein Papa (It's okay, Luka. I'm your papa now),*" he had whispered to him, feeling the frightened child's grip tighten around his shirt. "This will be your home—a place of love and warmth. You'll be happy here." Hanz's voice cracked as he spoke. "You were always loved as my own blood, Luka. *Mein Sohn.* I'm sorry I failed you."

Just then, Ingomar flew overhead. As the black crow squawked, everything seemed connected, everything seemed right. Not right in the sense of being good, but in that he was on the right course, as if God himself had breathed courage into him, giving His divine blessing over what must be done. It was a strange feeling, too, as if some supernatural energy were saturating his entire being, flowing from the heavens above through the top of his crown to the bottom of his feet, driving into the dirt beneath him, continuing for eternity. And it jarred him, as if he were being held under the frozen Tauber River, only to break through the ice gasping for air; or sleepwalking for years, only to be jolted awake.

Hanz put on the Nazi uniform Severin had given him, despite his hatred for it. With his *Schirmmütze* on his head, he picked up his suitcase containing a few items, including the bag of money and stolen jewels that Ingomar had shown him. Getting into his car, he began his perilous journey to Auschwitz-Birkenau near Oświęcim, Poland, not knowing if he would ever see his farm again.

Bucephalus ran along the fence line as Hanz drove away, releasing a distressful nicker. Hanz tried not to look. The beautiful beast kept up with him until the road disappeared into the forest, and when Hanz glanced in the rearview mirror, Bucephalus stood at the end of the fence line, throwing his head back and kicking the ground.

"*Verabschiedung (Farewell), mein Freund*," he said to his beloved stallion. "I wish I could take you with me into this battle. But I am a one-man army."

CHAPTER 48

Winter, 1945

Ava was reassigned to work in the *Effektenlager (Securities Warehouse),* or Kanada section of Auschwitz-Birkenau. These were the buildings where the confiscated belongings of those arriving at the camp each day–usually their most valuable and sentimental possessions–were stored and sorted, then used in the camp itself or sent elsewhere throughout the Reich. By the time the sorting was done, most of the previous owners were already dead, murdered in the gas chambers.

The warehouses became known as "Kanada," or the land of plenty, because Canada symbolized wealth to the prisoners. Those who worked there were called the *Aufräumungskommando (Clearing-up Commando),* or "Kanada Kommando," and they viewed it as one of the best jobs in Auschwitz because they could sometimes secretly procure goods for themselves and other inmates in the flourishing black market.

But Ava had no interest in these valuables. The very sight of them disgusted her. Piles and piles of stolen property from people gassed and cremated not a stone's throw away from them. Jewelry, coins, furs; expensive coats, shoes, and handbags; clothes, spectacles, and personal items. Even gold fillings from teeth, destined to be melted into ingots and sent to Berlin for deposit in the safes of the German Reichsbank.

Her eyes often lingered on the mound of teeth sitting on a table, waiting for the dental workers to remove the precious metal. Of all the things taken from the unsuspecting murder victims, that was what repulsed her the most.

Once again, Ava wondered how human beings could do all these horrific deeds to other human beings, and why God was allowing it. The cruelty, depravity, and wickedness. And what was the point of all the discrimination, hardship, and public humiliation that took place for years prior, if the Nazis were only going to exterminate them anyway? The answer, she came to realize, was conditioning. To carry out such demonic policies, to commit such monstrous acts, the perpetrators had to be conditioned to lose their humanity and turn into beasts, not only ready but also eager to treat their victims as animals fit to be put down.

One day, Ava was told to go to the kitchen and bring back some food for the SS officers who supervised the work. The aroma of cooked meat, roasted potatoes, and vegetables under the silver cover of the large food tray she carried made her tongue salivate and her knees weak, tempting her to sneak a bite of it. But she knew that if she were caught even lifting the cover to take a sniff, she'd be severely punished. Beaten, or perhaps even shot. So instead, she just pretended the food was poisoned and her captors would soon die from it.

When she reentered the Kanada warehouse, Ava walked up to the table where the SS officers sat, her eyes to the ground, awaiting further instruction. They all stopped talking and stared at her, as if a den of snakes gazing at a mouse who accidentally entered their lair.

"Why are you just standing there, you stupid wench?" one of them barked. "*Legen Sie es auf den Tisch (Put it on the table).*"

Ava obeyed, head still low, knowing that for any reason he could shoot her, and no one would care.

"She's not bad looking, that one," another officer said, scanning her up and down with a lewd grin on his face. "Come here, woman."

Ava slowly walked over to him.

"Look at me."

She raised her head, her emerald eyes in fear.

"*Ja*, quite pretty, in fact, even with a shaved head and Jew stench."

The other SS officers at the table laughed.

"Now lift your dress."

She raised the hem above her knees.

"Higher."

Ava started trembling, lifting her dress a few more inches.

"Higher."

Tears burning in her eyes, falling down her cheeks, she exposed her underwear.

"Lift it higher."

When she hesitated, the SS officer stood, towering over her with a threatening glare. "I said lift . . . it . . . higher!"

Ava lifted it nearly over her head, her bony frame and small breasts fully exposed.

A superior officer walked in and scowled at the men. "You're supposed to be supervising the workers, not playing games with them!"

Ava let go of her dress, and as her frightened, teary eyes looked up at him, she recognized his face. He was one of Starholf's good friends–Fritz Köhler–and had even been to their house before.

Fritz recognized Ava too, staring at her for a moment, as if she were once again on stage at the Rothenburg ob der Tauber beauty pageant where he and Starholf first saw her. Then he slapped her so hard she fell to the floor. "Don't you ever use those emerald eyes to seduce an SS officer again," he said, glaring down at her. "Now get back to work!"

Ava ran to her workstation and began to separate leather goods, one from the other–wallets, purses, belts, gloves, and coats.

❧

"I saw Fritz Köhler today," Ava said, her lip still swollen from the blow he had inflicted on her. "Starholf's *Freund*." She, her sister, and Abigail were lying in their bunks at the end of the workday.

"Is that who hit you?" asked Shaylee.

"*Ja.*"

"Do you think he recognized you?"

"I know he did. That's why he hit me, telling me never to seduce an SS officer again. The men under him thought he was talking about them, but we both knew he was talking about Starholf."

"He'll no doubt tell him," Abigail said. "Starholf will want to know where his children are, and he'll have them interrogate you."

Ava looked at her sister and birth mother, the fury in her eyes trumping the fear. "I'll never tell them. Even if they kill me, I never will."

❧

"I'm so tired and hungry," Shaylee said to her sister one day. "And my period started again. It's running down my leg."

The twins had worked all day and now sat filthy and exhausted on the floor in the barracks. Their bodies were being pushed to their limits, stressing the functions intrinsic to a woman while feeling subhuman.

Shaylee rested her shaved head on Ava's bony shoulder. They had lost so much weight that it was surprising they still menstruated at all. But they did, and the old blood mixed with dirt trailing down their legs was always discomfiting. Usually they had small pieces of cloth to use for their menses, but someone had stolen theirs.

The women in the camp would rip the undergarments given to them into little pieces and hide them as if they were precious garments. They'd clean them as best they could, and reuse them when needed. They used them as currency, too, to barter for other things.

"I'm tired and hungry too," Ava said, closing her eyes. "That Bavarian pot roast you made at the farm before would be heaven right now."

"Or just a warm pretzel with mustard," said Shaylee.

"And for dessert, Mama's hot *Lebkuchen (gingerbread)*."

"Or her famous blueberry pie."

The sisters sat in silence for a moment, dreaming of all the delicious foods and desserts they used to enjoy and take for granted. Then Shaylee started to cry.

"What's the matter?" Ava asked.

"I just wish we could go back home."

Ava wrapped her arms around her sister and rocked her. "Me too, Shaylee." She remembered years ago at the farm when she found a little injured bird that had fallen out of its nest. The poor thing was trying desperately to climb back up the tree. Now she and her sister knew what that little bird felt like, desperately wanting to be home.

"Ava," Shaylee whimpered.

"Hmm?"

"The other day, I looked at another woman's arm, and my mouth watered. I know it's disgusting, but when I saw the muscle fiber move, it made me salivate."

"We're starving and abused in here, Shaylee. It's not surprising to have abnormal thoughts like that."

"We're going to die here, aren't we."

"*Nein!*" Ava said. She lifted her sister's chin to look her in the eye. "Don't say that again. We're going to survive until it's over. And then we're going to live a *wunderbar* life again."

"But the suffering is too much. I think I just want to die now. Let me die, Ava."

"Shaylee, stop! I won't let you die!"

Abigail was with a Roma woman, and they both overheard what the girls were saying.

"They remind me of grace and suffering," said the Romani. "When a person is suffering, there is a wicked whisper that they won't survive."

Abigail agreed, finishing the woman's thought. "*Ja,* but then it's answered by grace."

The Romani's dark eyes lit up. "The sorrow and the grace face off against each other. And in the depths of despair, we hear the voice of hope, like a light leading us out of the darkness, giving us the strength to hold on a little while longer."

Ava and Shaylee listened, and seeing the vigor in the eyes of the Roma woman, they both suddenly felt stronger.

"But you still must make a choice," said the woman. "Which voice will you listen to? The wicked whisper, or the voice of grace?" Her dark eyes shined as she looked intently at them. "Pick grace, my young ones. Pick grace. Because in grace is courage. In grace is perseverance. In grace is love. And love never fails."

It was an emotional moment for the women, and they all held hands and cried, encouraging each other to choose courage, perseverance, and love. To choose grace.

Little Yael walked up to the group of women and sat in Abigail's lap. "Grace," she said in her soft voice. "What a beautiful word."

⁂

Hanz had strategically woven his way into Auschwitz-Birkenau, serving as a guard for a month now. Each step of his plan had been well thought out and calculated, from painting a portrait of Hitler and meeting him for dinner, to avoiding the front lines and instead being sent to work at the camp, to finding the stolen money and Constance Bodnar's jewels required for future bribes. It had all worked out up till now, but unfortunately he hadn't yet seen Ava, Shaylee, or Abigail. It wasn't surprising, considering the monumental task. First he had to become familiar with the camp layout, administration, and procedures. Then he had to befriend the right staff who would be susceptible to the bribes when needed. And lastly, he had to find three people in a crowd of well over 100,000 prisoners, with constant churn in and out.

The emotional toll on Hanz was severe. He was so close, working in the very concentration camp where his beloved swans and Abigail were being held. But he had to be very careful. It wasn't like he could just go around, calling out their names. And he had to ensure he didn't raise any suspicions by snooping around or asking the wrong people the wrong questions. Instead, he acted jovial and friendly with the other officers, covertly trying to learn more about the camp, its subcamps, and its prisoners.

The adrenaline never left him, but neither did the worry. What if he were too late, he constantly wondered? Prisoners were dying every day, either being shot or gassed, or from abuse, starvation, and disease. The longer it took him to find his daughters and their birth mother and get them out, the less likely he would.

Each day, as Hanz served at his post or walked the grounds, dressed in the full Nazi uniform that disgusted him, he witnessed brutality beyond belief. If the world only knew what was happening in these camps, he thought. To see human beings treated this way, their pain and suffering etched into their expressions like a mask they could not remove, was extremely distressing. Especially knowing Ava, Shaylee, and Abigail were somewhere among them.

One time, when Hanz witnessed an elderly prisoner fall, he quickly grabbed him by the collar and lifted him back to his feet. The man likely would have been beaten or shot had the attending SS officer noticed. Looking up at Hanz in shock, he couldn't believe that a Nazi guard would help him. Hanz simply kept moving, acting as if nothing had happened.

In the SS barracks one night, as the men lay in their comfortable beds, one of the officers called out in the dark, "*Jemand eine gute Geschichte (Anyone have a good story)?*"

Hanz thought for a moment. He recalled an African fable his good friend, Aadan Omari, had once told him around a campfire, and decided to alter it for his audience. "*Ja, ich habe eine (Yes, I have one).*"

"*Lasst es uns hören (Let's hear it).*"

"It was a freezing, bitter night, just like this one," Hanz began. "The sky was so black it looked like a bottomless pit, and the air so cold it burned your lungs."

"Great, remind us how we freeze our asses when we guard the vermin," someone echoed back.

"Let the man tell the story," said another.

"Seven Schutzstaffel officers were lost in the forest when a blizzard started. They knew that if they didn't find shelter soon, they'd all freeze to death."

"Why would they be lost in the forest?" the same dissenting officer asked.

"Damn it, let him tell the story!" said the other.

Hanz continued. "They had traveled all night, their faces, hands, and feet blistered and frostbitten, their bodies exhausted, their spirits giving out. None of them could feel anything anymore, or even think straight. Losing all hope, they realized they were going to die."

"Nein!" exclaimed an SS officer, upset by this story.

"But then a faint light appeared in the distance," Hanz said. "A small cabin, aglow with life, warmth, and promise."

The upset officer felt better. *"Ja, gute."*

"The *SS-Oberführer (SS-Senior Leader)* thought he was hallucinating, but all the men saw it too and cried out for joy. Using all the strength they had left, they ran through the deep snow to get to the cabin. When they finally arrived, they didn't even have to knock–the door opened automatically."

All the officers were now enthralled, listening attentively.

"Inside were seven beautiful *Fräulein*, all sisters. The men thought they were dreaming, but the young women welcomed them in with big smiles, fed them, tended to their blisters and frostbite, and even bathed and put them to bed as if they were *ihre Kinder (their children).*"

"Ja, ich glaube ich mag diese Geschichte (Yeah, I think I like this story)," one of the men chuckled.

"The seven officers stayed in the cabin with the seven sisters for three whole days in total bliss as the blizzard kept howling. But when it finally stopped, revealing a clear sky full of stars and a full blood moon, something very strange happened to the *Fräulein*." Hanz paused before continuing.

No one made a sound, wanting to know what happened next.

"The eyes of each sister turned from glass blue to horrifying red, their teeth grew into large white fangs, their fair skin became covered in fur, and their feminine bodies transformed into nine-foot-tall muscular beasts. *Ja,* each *Fräulein* became a vicious, bloodthirsty werewolf!"

"Holy shit, what happened then?" asked one of the men.

"What the Schutzstaffel thought was their savior became their doom. First the ravenous beasts ate their livers, then their kidneys, then their hearts, all while the men were still alive. The SS officers screamed in pain, suffering like the prisoners in this camp, begging for mercy. But none was given. It was a complete blood fest."

"That's enough!" said Lieutenant Lutz, the highest-ranking SS officer in the barracks. "What kind of story is that! We are Schutzstaffel too!"

Hanz rolled over on his cot, closed his eyes, and smiled.

⁘

The following night in the SS barracks, Hanz was forced to fraternize with the enemy again—something he never got used to. Here he was, in the center of the storm among men he hated, still unable to locate his daughters and their birth mother, and he had to have a friendly card game with them before bed.

With cigarette in hand, he took a long drink of vodka, wincing from the strength of it. The radio was playing in the background, and as he waited for the other men, he listened to Hitler's voice—a rerun of a 1938 speech in Munich—blaring from the speakers. Hanz had been to that rally in person with his neighbors Leon Dreisler and Günther Nachtnebel, and he remembered parts of it before leaving early, unable to stand any more of the hateful vitriol spewing from that madman's lips . . .

"Once you understand my true intentions, my true loyalty to Germany and its people, you will see what I am trying to create: A new civilization without blemish or imperfection! My final goal is to eradicate the enemy and improve not only the Fatherland but also humanity as a whole! I have meticulously planned this! I have managed and executed this! I have taken clay and formed it into gold, creating a thousand-year Reich that will rule with its enemies at its feet! The next stage is to cleanse the Fatherland of the ignorant, the deficient, and the weak. An extermination of the vermin and the immoral! And this cleansing shall spread throughout the world!"

Hanz clenched his jaw as the audience cheered and applauded. Were they asleep? In a trance? Did they not fully understand what the man was saying? He remembered seeing the frenzied mass of people at the rally that day, celebrating as if under a spell, and even now it gave him shivers.

Hanz glanced around the room at the other men. One officer was shining his leather boots, another lying on his bunk flipping through a girlie magazine, and several more smoking, drinking, and talking. Before long, a group was sitting at the round table playing cards, sharing stories again, this time about war.

"I'll tell you a *gute* one," said an officer eager to share. He pulled an expensive cigar from his front pocket that he had gotten from the Kanada warehouse and lit it, puffing on it with pride. "My grandfather told me about his time serving under Kaiser Wilhelm, when he was sent to the German territory of Southwest Africa to squash a native uprising."

Hanz's ears perked, listening intently. His good friend Aadan Omari had once told him a story about that period in their country's history. But it was no African fable told around a campfire. No, the story Aadan related was the *Vernichtung (extermination)*, when the Second Reich engaged in genocide, wiping out the Herero and Nama indigenous tribes after they dared to fight back against the exploitation and injustices perpetrated against them.

The officer gleefully continued. "When they first arrived, my grandfather and his men gave shirts to the native women to cover their naked bodies and be decent. Well, the next day, all the women were wearing the shirts, sure enough. But they had cut holes in them, allowing their breasts to be exposed again." He slapped his knee, laughing hard.

The other officers joined in.

"I've got a war story too," said the youngest of them, wanting to fit in with his older peers. "About soldiers who came across mermaids out at sea. They called them Sirens."

Hanz, hearing the word "Sirens", thought about his wife Maria, when she had run out into the rain one night, undoing her bun and shaking her head to release her fiery red curls, the wind whipping them to-and-fro like threads of scarlet ribbon. What an unforgettable sight! "You are a wild, red-headed Siren, Maria Wolff," he had said to her, pulling her in close, gazing into her cerulean blue eyes before kissing her in the pouring rain. "But I caught you out at sea, and now you are mine."

At that moment, a strong melancholy gripped Hanz's heart, wondering how Maria was doing at the tuberculosis clinic in Arizona. He hoped she was getting better, and he longed for those tranquil days of sitting with her on the porch at their farm, watching the sunset, and lying in each other's arms in bed at night.

"I have heard of those Siren stories too," one of the officers said. "Beautiful maidens out at sea, but deadly, singing hypnotic songs to lure the men to their death by causing their ship to sail into rocks."

Lieutenant Lutz, the commanding officer, scoffed. "That's not a war story, you idiot. That's a myth. But I'll tell you one that's true." He downed his shot of vodka and poured himself another. "As a young man during the Great War, I was on a ship in the Indian Ocean. It capsized during a storm, and all of us were stranded out in the open sea, bobbing up and down in our life jackets. When it got dark, the terror started, and by morning, more than half the men were gone, blood and body parts everywhere."

"What happened?" the young officer asked.

"Sharks," said Lieutenant Lutz. "The ocean itself is not the only thing you have to worry about. What's just as dangerous are the creatures deep below it."

Another officer shook his head. "Imagine being eaten alive by a massive shark. *Was für ein schrecklicher Tod (What a terrible death)*. It's like being swallowed whole by a fire-breathing dragon."

"*Ja*," said Lieutenant Lutz. "I was lucky enough to find a piece of wood to float on, but then the waves tossed me about like a piece of paper, nearly breaking my back. It threw me from the wood, then threw me back onto it, knocking my teeth out in the process." He smiled, flashing his silver implants to the men. "The sea is a powerful force, but it's no man's *Freund*."

"War stories!" scoffed an officer with a psychopathic look out of his eyes. "You all sound like a bunch of old men in *die Kneipe (the pub)*. Let's talk about killing Jews." He grinned, his chipped teeth showing under a blond, handlebar mustache. "I've got a *wunderbar* story for you. Before I came to Auschwitz, we trapped a bunch of them in a barn and set it on fire. That thing lit up like a Christmas tree, and we all stood and watched, drinking and cheering as they screamed inside. To kill so many in one shot made us feel like gods."

"Child's play," said the officer flipping through the girlie magazine on his bunk. "I used to work in the *Einsatzgruppen (task forces, or mobile killing units)*."

All the men at the table turned and looked at him.

"We didn't just kill a barnful; we killed tens of thousands. Jews, *Zigeuner (Gypsies)*, communists. Men, women, and children. All of them."

The officer bragged about his time serving in the *Einsatzgruppen*, relating how they'd follow behind as the Wehrmacht advanced deep into Soviet territory in 1941. They rounded up entire towns, stripped them naked, and marched them to open fields, forests, and ravines where they shot or gassed them in special gas vans, dumping their bodies into mass graves. Sometimes they even made the victims dig the grave. By the spring of 1943, these mobile killing squads throughout the Third Reich had murdered more than a million Jews and tens of thousands of other innocent people.

"We were killing machines. We killed morning, noon, and night. It was like shooting birds on a fence."

All the men laughed.

Hanz's stomach tightened, repulsed by the company he was forced to keep. Rage started building inside him, from the bottom of his soul, working its way up to his heart. Sitting at that round table among the SS officers in Nazi uniforms, each taking turns telling a gruesome story about murder, rape, and torture, each more repugnant than the next as if trying to top one another, was sickening beyond belief. It reminded him of the terrible nightmare he had all those years ago. The one where the monsters in medieval armor were fighting in a valley while the kings of the earth sat at a round table, dipping their bread in a bowl of blood from the innocent. So shocking were the crimes he heard that it caused a sudden urge in him to pull his gun from its holster and shoot each one of them in the face, wiping off their smiles and laughter. He even placed his hand on it, finding it warm to the touch. Inviting.

But then something jarred Hanz back to why he was there. In his mind's eye, he could see Ava and Shaylee running in the meadow at the farm, the midday sun shining on them as they happily laughed and called out to him, "Papa, Papa, come find us!" The image, so clear and real, flooded his entire body with emotion.

"Hanz, what are you holding?" the officer with the handlebar mustache asked him.

"Huh?" He was still lost in his own thoughts.

"Your hand. What are you holding?"

"Oh, *ja.*" Hanz glanced around the table at the men, seeing all their faces staring back at him, waiting, their SS uniforms and military pins seemingly glowing through the smoke-filled air and dim lighting. He looked down at his cards, then placed them face up on the table. Scratching the new scruff on his chin, he said. "Whaddya know. I have a winning hand."

A week later, chaos and commotion ran through Auschwitz-Birkenau. For no apparent reason, the SS officers began frantically rounding everyone up, almost in a panic. Rumors started spreading throughout the camp as to why—Germany's military force was collapsing, and the Allied armies were closing in on the Nazi concentration camps.

With the Soviets rapidly approaching from the east, the Schutzstaffel were given orders from above to move the prisoners out of Auschwitz and its satellite camps and take them to the town of Wodzislaw in the western part of Upper Silesia, Poland. From there, they were to be put on freight trains and deported to other concentration camps within Germany.

It was bitterly cold that morning on January 17, 1945, when the evacuation on foot began. Nearly 60,000 prisoners were forced to march the thirty-five-mile trek under harsh conditions, with little or no food, water, or rest. Those who could not keep up were shot. Those who tried to escape were shot. Those who simply did or said something displeasing to an SS officer, no matter how trivial, were shot. All told, more than 15,000 would soon die, either from exhaustion, exposure, or a bullet, on what would later become infamously known as a "death march"—one of many the Nazis would force upon their helpless victims, moving them from camp to camp as they sought to prevent them from falling into Allied hands. With tens of thousands of corpses lining the routes, each death march was only missing a ghastly requiem.

The path the prisoners traveled was slush and mud, caking on their feet like wet concrete up their ankles and calves. Despite their fatigue, like the walking dead they kept trudging along. A Roma woman mumbled something in Romani to herself; an old Jewish man did the same in Yiddish. Everyone had their own horror story to tell, their own tribulation. Their misery was a living, breathing thing, inhabiting every fiber, pore, and cell in their emaciated bodies. Men didn't feel like men; women didn't feel like women; children didn't feel like children. In truth, no one even felt human anymore. The abuse, suffering, and torment for so long, and to such a severe degree, had transformed them into something unrecognizable. Something with no name, gender, or identity, other than the serial number tattooed on their flesh.

In the confusion of leaving Auschwitz-Birkenau, Ava, Shaylee, Abigail, and Yael were separated from each other. They had bonded while in the camp, helping, encouraging, and looking after one another, preserving themselves alive. And now that they were separated and on their own, it seemed to them as if they had been dismembered and flung out into a raging sea.

When the twin siblings had first arrived at the notorious death camp, everything was so traumatizing. Seeing someone humiliated, beaten, and killed would instantly make them shake and cry. Ava quickly learned that witnessing a murder in real life was much more horrific than it was in the movies; and Shaylee came to know that it was much more graphic than in a book. Watching a person's life force slowly fade while fighting to hold on, lingering in their breath, in their eyes, desperately grasping at anything to survive, is something you will never forget. An indelible image that makes you sick to your stomach. That is until you see if often enough that your mind becomes desensitized to it. Then you just numbly wonder about the victim's last thoughts. What were they, you speculate? Did they see the innocent faces of their children, laughing as they played in the yard? Did they hear the tranquil voice of their mother, smiling at them with love and pride? Did they think about their beloved spouse, or a kiss from a lover, the sweet taste still on their tongue? Or perhaps their last thoughts were not their own but those of the Creator, fulfilling his final promise from the Book of Revelation . . . *"And God shall wipe away all tears from their eyes; and there shall be no more death, neither sorrow, nor crying, neither shall there be any more pain. For the former things are passed away."*

The eyes of a person about to die reflect all the things inside them and more, right before they pass. Ava and Shaylee knew the look well. And while Ava was determined to keep going and survive no matter what, her sister was starting to break down, emotionally crumble, staring into nothing with a strange, vacant look on her face. And it wasn't just her; all the prisoners were beginning to have that same, hopeless look. As if a virus had infected them, and they were metamorphosing into zombies, slowly turning into something nightmares were made of. The Grim Reaper, with his black cloak and shiny sickle, was waiting, smiling, standing behind every man, woman, and child, ready to issue his kiss of death.

One of Ava's worn-out shoes got stuck in the mud and came off her foot. The blister on her heel had burst, and when the wet sludge made contact with the wound, it stung so badly she grimaced in pain. As she stopped to retrieve her shoe, an SS officer saw her and yelled, *'Bleiben sie in bewegung! Bleiben sie in bewegung! (Keep moving! Keep moving!)"* But Ava took a step back, leaning down to pull it from the mud.

"Bang!"

A bullet whizzed past her head, so close she felt its deadly trajectory. And yet it still took an innocent victim—the elderly man who had been walking alongside her fell to the ground. Horrified, Ava tried to lift him up, but his wife pushed her away. "*Retten sie sich selbst (Save yourself),*" she said. "*Gehen sie weiter (Keep walking).*"

Ava quickly grabbed her shoe and marched forward, staring at the officer who kept his gun pointing at her before slowly lowering it down.

As she kept walking, and walking, and walking, with no end in sight and no respite, Ava tried to convince herself that she, and hopefully her sister, Abigail, and Yael, would survive. That there was a reason she had not been killed yet. A reason she had escaped the hardship of Ravensbrück and the heinous sexual assaults from its commandant. A reason she had escaped the unthinkable plans of Starholf and the Johannmeyers, saving her children from them. And a reason she had survived the notorious Auschwitz-Birkenau, and the horrific experiments performed on her and her sister by the "Angel of Death," Dr. Josef Rudolf Mengele. *I'm a warrior,* she thought as she walked, *and I can survive this too. I will survive this!*

Ava remembered things her father had told her about the mind and body, and what amazing creations they are. A brilliant dichotomy of God's hand. Fragile yet resilient, weak yet strong, with blood, muscle, bone, and flesh covered only by a beautiful veneer of skin, and organs that complement each other, working together like stars in a galaxy. "The mind is master of the body, and the body obeys," he had told her. "A miraculous machine with an innate desire for survival. When it wills itself to endure, it can endure just about anything."

Hanz's words resonated through Ava's mind, fortifying her. *It will take more than beatings, abuse, starvation, and exhaustion to kill me,* she thought as she continued to put one foot in front of the other in the wet, muddy earth. *They will have to use a bullet, maybe two. Until then, I'm pushing forward, no matter how sick, hungry, or tired.* And oh, how sick, hungry, and tired she was! Coughing continually, stomach aching, sometimes nauseous, knees and feet hurting, her entire body freezing. Yet still, she was determined; she would not give up. *Tomorrow will be better,* she kept thinking. *And if not, then the next day. Or the next. Or the day after that. Yes, soon I will have a good meal, a hot bath, a soft bed, and a firm hug from my loved* ones. I can keep going until then.

Her mind wandered further, stretching beyond the arduous trek, the cold slush and mud, the sick and broken people all around her, and the SS officers with their steely guns and icy eyes, looking for a reason to kill. She remembered seeing that pretty woman in a yellow dress, with her hair done in loose curls and a stain of red on her lips, standing on the other side of the gates of Auschwitz that day, talking to her SS officer husband. It reminded Ava of who she once was, and who she would be again, wearing her own pretty yellow dress, hair done in curls, with her scarlet red lipstick and Chanel No. 5 perfume. And Shaylee, too, reading her many books, drawing sketches and taking notes, wearing her own lovely perfume–Coty L'Aimant. Yes, there is life outside this monstrous hell, she thought, and we're going to reach it. My sister and I both are. We will fall in love again. We will marry and have more children. We will live life!

Yes, we will live life, long and free!

Just then, Ava caught sight of Shaylee up ahead. As she excitedly ran to reach her, an older woman beside Shaylee struggled to keep going and fell down. She got back up and tried to march again, but an SS officer came from behind and hit her on the back of the head with the butt of his rifle so hard that she toppled, blood splattering everywhere, including all over Shaylee.

Shaylee froze. Slowly she reached up and touched the blood on her face, shaking all over. "I'm German," she said under her breath. "I'm not Jewish like them. I shouldn't be here."

The SS officer heard her and laughed. "*Bleib in Bewegung, oder du bist der Nächste (Keep moving, or you're next)*."

Ava arrived and quickly came to her sister's aid, putting her arm around her. "C'mon, sweetheart, keep walking." She looked at the SS officer. "She's fine. My sister's fine."

But Shaylee clearly wasn't, now hyperventilating. "My parents are German! I know nothing about Jews!" She tried to push Ava away. "I don't know you, either! Get away from me!"

"Shaylee, stop!" Ava said, shaking her sister. "Stop, or they'll shoot us!"

The SS officer laughed even harder, amused by the spectacle.

"Christian, where are you!" Shaylee yelled, looking behind her. "Tell them I'm German!"

Ava slapped her. "Christian's dead! Now keep walking!"

Shaylee abruptly stopped, like a crying baby calms when receiving a bottle of milk. "Have you seen Christian Hoffmann?" she asked in a small voice, as if Ava were a stranger. "He's my husband. Do you know where he is?"

Ava realized her sister had mentally broken down, and she too felt her sanity under attack. The ground suddenly seemed to rock back and forth like a rudderless ship in a rough sea.

"I'm going to have his baby," Shaylee said, smiling through tears.

The SS officer kept watching and listening, still amused by the show.

Ava tried to get her sister to move. "If you want to see Christian, come with me."

"You . . . You know where he is?"

"*Ja*, I do."

Shaylee looked confused, then deranged. "But you're lying! You're a liar, because they buried him! They buried him alive, and they beat me so hard I lost our child!" Falling to her knees, she began to sob uncontrollably.

Ava grabbed her sister's shoulders and tried to yank her to her feet. When she failed, she slapped Shaylee so hard the SS officer almost rolled on the ground in laughter. A second officer came over to watch the comedy as well.

When Ava went to strike Shaylee a second time, what she saw in her sister's wide, terrified eyes, terrified her in return, forcing chills up and down her spine . . .

She saw death.

Ava saw death in her sister's green eyes, staring back at her from the bowls of some unholy grave. Cold, horrible, evil death. It contaminated her, seeping deep into her skin through osmosis, straight from her hands that held her sister's bony shoulders as sure as someone had injected her with the same poison used on Shaylee in Dr. Mengele's labs. The sensation crawled down her throat and into her lungs, her kidneys, her liver, circulating through her blood, consuming her, just like the Roma woman at Auschwitz had warned: "Once the sorrow demon gets a hold of you, its black hole sucks in your soul. You die while still alive. Your eyes stay open, and you just die."

The look on Shaylee's face was wretched. Gaunt, pale as a corpse, head shaved with uneven regrowth, mouth slightly open with missing teeth, chin and cheekbones void of flesh, sunken eyes staring up at her sister. She was a helpless, heartbroken bird, imprisoned in a cage. A desperate, tormented soul. Filled with pity and pain seeing her sweet sister this way, Ava knelt and held little Shaylee in the mud while the other Jews continued to march past them. She kissed her cheeks, her cold forehead, her eyes damp from crying. "Please get up, Shaylee," she pleaded. "*Bitte*, sister. If you die, I will die too. Don't let the black hole of the sorrow demon consume you, after all you've been through."

The SS officer finally had enough and shot a bullet at Ava, grazing her left arm. She gasped in pain, as if a red-hot iron had seared her flesh, tattooing a new serial number over the old. But still she clung to her sister, protecting Shaylee with her body.

"The show is over. Now get that dirty Jew off the ground and start moving, or the next bullet is in your head," the SS officer threatened.

Ava didn't want to die, yet she was prepared to for her sister. But then Shaylee stood, and numbly, mechanically, started walking. Both sisters leaned on each other, pushing forward, marching, focusing ahead and not on the dreary, gray sky above, or the bullets whizzing by, killing other Jews who weren't as lucky, dying like flies all around. As they walked, Ava hummed the same song Maria used to sing to them as children, bathing them in a hot bath scented with vanilla and lavender, singing as she washed her daughters' hair.

❧

With Auschwitz-Birkenau now being evacuated, Hanz panicked. Using the last of the stolen jewels he had found in the linden tree by his farm, he bribed Lieutenant Lutz, the senior SS officer he had previously befriended, asking him to write an authorization to collect several Jewish prisoners for a work detail.

Lieutenant Lutz laughed. "Work detail? We're evacuating this camp, *mein Freund*. There's no work detail." But knowing the Third Reich was losing the war, he did it anyway, taking the jewels.

Hanz jumped into a Nazi truck and raced toward the marching line of prisoners to search for Ava, Shaylee, and Abigail.

This was his last chance to find them.

If he didn't, he never would.

❧

As the line of prisoners came into view, Hanz's heart pumped wildly in his chest. Never before had he been so frightened. Not for himself but for the lives he was trying to save. Pulling his truck up to the first SS officer guarding the line, he said, "I have orders to retain several Jews for work," showing the man the signed document. Inside, he was shaking.

The officer looked down at it, examining the order, then Hanz. "You don't have a cigarette, do you? I'm stuck walking these filthy Jews and *Zigeuner (Gypsies)* all the way to Wodzislaw, and I'm totally out."

Hanz reached into his pocket and retrieved his Sturm cigarettes. "Here, keep the pack."

"*Danke,*" said the officer, delighted. "Heil Hitler!"

Hanz saluted the soldier and drove on.

The bodies lying along the marching path made the place look like a war zone. Men, women, and even children, scattered about like flies, dead from sickness and exhaustion, or a bullet. Hanz drove the truck slowly, scanning the faces of both the living and the dead, desperately trying to locate any of the women. But what if he didn't find them? Then what? He would save some, he decided. He would take as many strangers with him as he could.

And that's when he saw a somewhat familiar face, traipsing along. At first he wasn't positive, but being an artist who paid attention to detail, he quickly recognized her as he got closer. Sure enough, it was Josie Blum, his childhood sweetheart and first love. Barely a reflection of her former self, her beautiful, waist-length hair–black as night, flowing over pale shoulders like a silken waterfall–was now replaced with a shaved head. Her ebony eyes, large and innocent, were now sunken and tormented. And her small, feminine frame, completely emaciated.

"It's my gift to you, Hanz," he remembered her saying in Stanley Horowitz's jewelry store when he was short 6,000 Marks for Maria's sapphire wedding ring. He had told her he couldn't accept her gift, and she responded, "*Ja*, you can. Maybe someday you'll return the favor."

Hanz stopped the truck. "You, there!" he called out, pointing at her. "I'm here to take a handful of workers, and you're one of them. Get in the truck."

At first Josie didn't recognize him, thinking he was just another Nazi officer. And then when she did, she practically ran to the truck and got in.

"Say nothing," Hanz instructed as he kept driving, resuming his search.

Moments later, among a group of prisoners, he saw another woman he would recognize anywhere . . . Abigail! Oh, how his heart rejoiced! A little girl was with her, and they were holding hands. "You, there!" he repeated, pointing at her. "I'm here to take a handful of workers, and you and the girl are selected. Get in the truck."

Abigail froze, staring at Hanz. She could not walk, talk, or even cry.

Yael tugged on her dress. "That man is calling you," she said in a small voice.

"I need workers; you and the girl, get in!" Hanz said again. Releasing a discreet smile, he waved her to come.

Once she and Yael were in the truck, Abigail let a flood of tears loose. "*Danke*, Hanz. *Danke*," she cried, shaking violently. "I thought I was dreaming."

"Have you seen Ava and Shaylee?" he asked desperately. "Do you know if they're here?"

"*Ja*, they were with me until we got separated. I think they're up ahead."

Hanz wanted to burst out crying too. But he had to maintain his composure and stay in character, so he kept driving. Along the way, he saw a man walking with a familiar gait. He knew that walk. It was someone he hadn't been looking for, nor expected to see . . . Randolph the Bull! Stopping the truck, he called out, "You, there! The man who looks like a Bull."

Randolph stopped in his tracks. No one had called him that in years, and he certainly didn't have the physique of a bull anymore, severely undernourished with his back slightly curved. Slowly he turned and stared at his friend in disbelief.

"I'm here to select workers, and I need someone with strength. Get in the truck."

Randolph didn't need any coaxing and pushed through the line to the vehicle. Once inside, he began to pray.

Before he continued, Hanz noticed another man in the line. Someone who reminded him of his older brother Andrew, who had been murdered in the Hadamar Psychiatric Clinic. Moved by the memory, he called out to the stranger, telling him to get in the truck. The man obeyed, not knowing why he was being singled out, and not caring, either.

It wasn't long before Hanz saw another familiar face among the crowd—Malachi and Ursula Applebaum's daughter, Jeta. He ordered her to get in the truck too, and once she recognized him, realizing she was being saved, she begged, "My sister Zelda, she's back there somewhere! *Bitte*, Mr. Wolff, we have to go get her!"

"*Nein*, I cannot," Hanz said. "I have to find my daughters. Keep quiet or you'll give us away."

"*Bitte!* She'll die!"

But Hanz had no choice. He couldn't go back and bring attention to himself and the others, and he was losing precious time to save his daughters. He had to keep going. Jeta kept crying in the back of the truck.

After another mile, his heart dropped . . .

There they are! Up ahead, Ava and Shaylee, walking arm in arm!

Absolute joy filled Hanz's entire being, and when he got close, it took everything he had not to stop the truck and run to them, hugging and kissing his daughters. Instead, he held strong and did something unusual. Leaning out the window, he whistled the unique tune he used to whistle when they were young, playing in the yard. The one they loved so much that sounded like an exotic bird, always running to him when they heard it. What happened next, he would remember for the rest of his life . . .

Ava was the first to stop and listen. When she realized it wasn't another hallucination, she turned around and saw him. Oh, what ecstasy filled her body!

When Shaylee saw him too, the euphoria knocked her to her knees.

Hanz put his finger to his mouth so they wouldn't scream out to him, then waved them over. "Don't say anything," he instructed. "Just get in the back of the truck."

Both daughters climbed in, bursting into tears.

"Hey, what's going on!" an SS officer barked, walking up to them. "What are you doing!"

Hanz remained calm and handed him the authorization paper he obtained through the bribe. "I'm ordered to retain these eight workers."

The officer looked at the document, then inside the truck. "That one is a child," he said, pointing at Yael. "Get her out and pick another."

"*Nein,*" said Hanz. "She stays. They need someone tiny who can climb into small spaces."

The officer stared at Hanz for what seemed like an eternity. Then he waved him on.

As they drove away, nobody spoke. They couldn't; all they could do was weep, each of them in shock, ecstatic over this sudden, unbelievable divine providence. Ava, Shaylee, Abigail, and Yael huddled close together, just as they had in the bunks at Auschwitz. Randolph reached over and put his hand on Hanz's shoulder.

Hanz, not looking back, laid his hand over the Bull's.

The fugitives slept in the truck that night, safe from the storm. In the morning, they boarded a cargo train that Hanz had prearranged prior to coming to Auschwitz-Birkenau, bribing the station master with some of Constance Bodnar's stolen jewels. Once they passed German security lines, everyone jumped off.

It took another day of travel through the forest on foot, but Hanz led them to a small town where he had reserved a bed-and-breakfast in advance. The owner, an elderly man sympathetic to those persecuted by the Nazis, had helped many others before, and even provided new identification papers for Ava, Shaylee, and Abigail based on older photos Hanz had provided him. Because he didn't know he'd be traveling with five more, Hanz also asked the man if he could do the same for Randolph, Josie, Jeta, Yael, and Nathaniel—the stranger who had reminded him of his older brother Andrew. The man agreed, but it would take a few days.

No one spoke much that evening, as they were still in Germany, with Schutzstaffel, Gestapo, Wehrmacht soldiers, and Nazi sympathizers everywhere. They simply rested, ate, showered, and changed into the civilian clothes the elderly man gave them, including hand-knitted wool berets for the women to cover their ragged, short hair.

A few days later, early in the morning as a rooster crowed in the distance and the stars still shined above, Hanz brought everyone to the passenger train station where he purchased their tickets with the last of his money. Waiting for the train to arrive was nerve-wracking, each of them anxiously looking around for soldiers. When it finally did arrive, they hastily boarded and found their seats. But it wasn't until the locomotive began moving that everyone started to relax. How thankful they all were to have made it this far! And when the train eventually crossed the border into Switzerland, the relief was overwhelming. Yes, they had escaped and were now free!

Free!

Was there ever a more beautiful word?

And yet, despite the elation, trauma and shock still clawed at their souls like a hungry beast, refusing to let go. It had barely been a week since they were prisoners in a grotesque and nightmarish concentration camp, witnessing people—men, women, children, and even babies—dying as easily as boots stomping on ants, wondering when they would be next. And Hanz, too, living in his own private purgatory, suffering torment day and night, watching the same atrocities while working as a guard at the camp, planning the great escape. A daring, courageous, inconceivable if not ludicrous plan, risking everything he had, including his life to save those he loved. Though they should have been celebrating, reveling, even dancing in the aisles of that passenger car as it rumbled down the tracks through the countryside of Switzerland, they all remained seated in silence, staring blankly at nothing, occasionally looking at each other with eyes speaking unspoken words only they could understand. But the somber mood was also accompanied by a strange sense of peace. A peace that sunk deeply, as if God himself were quietly sitting with them, holding each of their hands.

Oh, if only I could have saved them all, Hanz internally lamented, remembering each haunting face that gazed at him in that death march as he drove along the line. And poor Zelda, left behind, even as her sister Jeta begged him to go back for her. But he could not. He could only rescue a select few, and that would haunt him to his dying day.

Abigail placed her hand on his, as if reading his tortured mind. "You saved us," she said, barely a whisper, her voice soft and sweet, meek and humble, so genteel. "You saved us, Hanz."

He stared at her for a long moment, hypnotized by those alluring, ebony eyes, now filled with pain. And then he stared at Ava and Shaylee. Both girls were terribly thin, matchsticks for arms, shoulders bony like the back of a child's chair, looking more like anorexic teenagers than vibrant young women. Their once clear, radiant, fair skin now sallow. Dark shadows under their eyes. Eyes that hid the pain and trauma of ten lifetimes. It hurt him immensely to see his darling swans in such a weak and sickened state. But then they turned and smiled at him, and his entire world froze. When he saw their faces light up at him, he could no longer hold back his tears.

Oddly enough, at that same moment, Hanz heard his wife's voice in his mind. Something she had once said to him, giving him great comfort. It was about the albino deer he had saved all those years ago. "Because you saved that white buck, its offspring will one day fill the forest," she had told him. "Your kind act has saved many. Through the one, generations will flourish."

The irony of her powerful words was not lost on him, the meaning resonating deep into his very bones.

PART THREE

CHAPTER 49

Nine Months Later

Hanz had a cousin who owned a charming hotel in the beautiful town of Lucerne, Switzerland, right on Lake Lucerne itself. He had given all of them modest rooms along with jobs. Randolph the Bull and Nathaniel were cooks; Abigail and Josie Blum waitressed in the restaurant; Ava and Shalom—she now wanted to be called by her birth name—worked as maids with Jeta; Yael tagged along with Ava; Hanz did building maintenance and in the evenings, for extra money, played his violin for the guests. It was a simple life, but they were happy, safe, and secure.

And yet, all of them were still trying to recover from the trauma of the past. Many times, Ava would wake in the dead of night, crying for her children, and Shalom would console her sister. Or Shalom would wake and cry for Christian, and Ava would rock her back to sleep. The nightmares continued, too. Demon soldiers marching through pools of blood—just like Maria had dreamed years ago when the girls were young—beating, raping, shooting, gassing, and burning them, shrieking unholy words in some blasphemous ancient language, vivid and horrifying. One of them would invariably wake up screaming.

Despite the nocturnal plague, everyone continued fighting for normalcy. "This sounds so silly, but to just walk down any street in any city, window-shopping without being afraid . . . that would be *wunderbar*," Ava recalled telling Father Craven at the small church in the forest. "I can't wait to taste freedom again." And now that the war had ended, she did. They all did, savoring every last morsel of it.

Living like a family, rejoicing in this newfound liberty they never dreamed would come, the group walked leisurely in public with their heads held high. They ate in restaurants and shopped in stores. They hiked the trails and picnicked in the parks. Yes, there was still some prejudice and backlash from ignorant people who maintained their disdain for Jews, Roma, Blacks, and others they deemed inferior, but towering Hanz made sure they could no longer hurt those he loved.

Hanz had also started writing Maria again, keeping his letters upbeat and positive while she still convalesced at the tuberculosis clinic in Tucson, Arizona. He left the worst out, as Luka's death and everything else that happened could not be explained with a mere pen. Those were conversations that had to be had in person, when he could look into her eyes, cry with her, and hold her.

Abigail would occupy herself with whatever she could, focusing mostly on her daughters, making up for lost time. When Hanz played his violin for the hotel guests in the evenings, she would hear something different in the way he played. A great sadness in the melody born of the suffering they had all endured, sending shivers down her spine.

It was during this period that Randolph the Bull and Josie Blum's relationship blossomed. Heartbroken over Nila, Randolph sought comfort in Josie's arms, and before long they fell in love. They married in the local synagogue, with Hanz the best man and Abigail the maid of honor, then moved back to Poland when the travel restrictions lifted. As for Nathaniel, he left for America—something he wished he had done years ago. And Jeta set sail to New Zealand, wanting to get as far away from Europe as possible. Tragically, however, she would not recover from what she had endured. Witnessing her parents' murder and suffering in the concentration camp was horrific enough, but having to leave her sister Zelda behind while she survived, haunted her day and night. She became addicted to morphine, overdosing one night.

Once Severin had been discharged by the Allies, having been found not guilty of any war crimes, he burned his Nazi uniform and returned to the ebb and flow of life in Germany before the war. He missed his brother immensely, hoping he'd come home, and wrote to Hanz to tell him he had married and now had a son. Severin also wanted to talk to Ava and Shalom, and Abigail, to apologize and beg their forgiveness for abandoning them when he was a scared, immature teenager. To somehow make amends, and start anew with his daughters as their father instead of their uncle. But none of the women were ready for that, and it would take years for this anomalous family reunion to eventually happen. With the horrors they had been through, they wanted nothing to do with anyone who had once worn a Nazi uniform. Severin included.

As hard as it was, Hanz knew it was time for him to travel to America, to say goodbye to his darling swans and return to his wife. He was very much looking forward to seeing Maria again. It had been nearly four long years since he last saw her lovely face, and the thought of lying in her arms tempered the sadness of leaving his daughters.

"This won't be forever," he said to them as they all hugged and cried together. "I'll be back, I promise." Kissing their foreheads, he left them with their mother.

❧❦❧

Abigail went with Hanz to the train station; she had insisted on seeing him off alone. That day, the magnificent periwinkle mountains topped with whipped alabaster caps stood tall and proud, jutting into the sky as clear as a blue sheet of paper. Standing on the platform, the two dear friends reflected on their special bond as they stared at each other, saying nothing but feeling everything, knowing this was goodbye.

They had been through so much together, and apart, that it almost felt as if they shared the same bloodstream now. The same lungs, liver, kidneys, and heart. The emotional covenant they shared, sealed by the gift of twin baby girls who grew into beautiful young women owning their souls, made "goodbye" seem impossible.

"In another life, we could have been more than friends," they both thought but did not say. "Yes, in another life . . ."

As Hanz looked at Abigail, for a moment his mind flashed back to how he had found her in that death march. Head shaved, body starved, dark circles under her eyes, on the precipice of succumbing to the death angel who led it. He blinked, and instantly the woeful image vanished, replaced with who she was now. Hair growing out, thick and healthy, with a sheen so black it almost appeared blue, again reminding him of the coat on a black stallion he had once owned. Soon it would be long, cascading over her silky olive skin like it did that night in the secret room, appearing as if the whorls of the Tauber River. And her eyes, no longer sunken and destitute but shimmering like two black diamonds under the bright Swiss sky. Now, as then, he wished he could paint what he saw.

Abigail handed Hanz a small item wrapped in brown paper and tied with a ribbon picked intentionally to match the color of his azure blue eyes.

"What's this?" he asked, his smile circumscribed by a Viking blond beard in full glory.

"Open it, you sweet man."

"Ah! *Oliver Twist.*"

"One of the nights we ate dinner together in the secret room, you told me it was your favorite book."

"*Ja*, I remember."

"I read it too. It's a classic tale, not only of orphans but of *gute* conquering evil."

Hanz agreed, and as he opened the book, he thought of when Maria had come down into his small library in the cellar wearing her nightgown, bringing two hot teas and Choco Leibniz biscuits. She was worried that he spent hours down there because she was deaf and couldn't communicate like normal people do. It reminded him of why he was at the train station, and where he was going. "*Danke,*" he said, his eyes brimming with tears.

The conductor called out, indicating the train was about to leave. As the remaining passengers rushed to board, Hanz put the book in his coat pocket and picked up his suitcase. "I suppose we're all orphans in some way or another," he said, his gaze unwavering. "Like Oliver Twist, we're all searching for love, redemption, and a safe place to call home."

Abigail reached over and held his hand. "And that no matter what, we must endure the struggles of life, and always remain kind and decent toward others."

"Indeed. *Auf Wiedersehen, Abigail.*" He gave her a brotherly hug and walked away. But just before he stepped on the train, he stopped.

Abigail wondered what was wrong. Did he forget his ticket?

Hanz put his suitcase down and ran back to her as if he were desperate and in great need, his hat falling to the ground. Reaching out, he held her face in his hands like the black pearl he had once found with the most beautiful hue—a mixture of onyx, deep purple, and a touch of some color with no name—and pressed his lips tenderly onto hers. So gently he kissed her, it was as if he were handling fragile glass.

Pulling her into his embrace, holding her tight, he whispered in her ear, "There are many kinds of love, Abigail," the same way he had said there are many kinds of light when she was dancing in the rain and a brilliant rainbow arched across the horizon, juxtaposing with the rising sun, painting the sky with hues of pink and gold. "Agape, storge, philia, eros . . . Unconditional, familial, affectionate, romantic . . . And God's divine love."

"I know, I know, I know," was all Abigail could say against his cheek, weeping like a heartbroken child who lost her cherished doll.

"I feel all of them for you. All of them, and I always will." He let her go and briskly walked away, picking up his hat in the process, then his suitcase, embarking on the train.

Abigail watched it depart, smiling and waving through tears, so happy he kissed her farewell but not sure why. Perhaps it was because it sealed the bond they had started all those years ago, when a frightened young Jewish teenager trusted a kind, German farmer with her tiny infants, leaving them in his barn wrapped in woolen blankets embroidered with the Star of David.

❧❦❧

Before crossing the Atlantic Ocean, Hanz went to Africa to see his good friend, Aadan Omari. Aadan and his family had moved back to Cameroon soon after fleeing to Switzerland in 1940, and Hanz had received a letter from him with an open invitation to visit any time. So he did.

He spent a month with Aadan and Chiumbo, and told them everything that had happened in Germany after the couple left, including all the horrors experienced by his daughters, the tragic suicide of his son Luka, how he found out about Severin being Ava and Shalom's biological father, and the fact that Abigail was their real mother. It was therapeutic for Hanz, and he found himself letting go and crying in front of Aadan, releasing his pent-up emotions in a way he could not in front of Ava, Shalom, and Abigail, who had always relied on him to be their emotional rock. Aadan, as always, listened empathetically and gave his fatherly, wise counsel, which Hanz took to heart.

The visit was also a time to relax, reset, and recover for Hanz, now that he had no one to look after but himself. He enjoyed authentic African cuisine prepared by Chiumbo, went on safaris with Aadan to see the beautiful land and intriguing animals his friend had always told him about, and played his violin while Aadan played his slit drum.

"When you play that drum, I can envision a leopard staring up at the moon," Hanz said to him during their first session, grinning ear to ear. "Or an elephant getting ready to charge, protecting its young."

Aadan smiled, recalling the last time they had played together under the European beech tree at his former home outside of Rothenburg ob der Tauber. "And when you play that violin, I see the leprechauns dancing."

Both men laughed.

Finally Hanz headed to the United States of America, where his wife had been treated at the Desert Sanatorium, the tuberculosis clinic in Tucson, Arizona. Though she had mostly recovered, the dry climate was still advantageous for maintaining her health, and that's where she stayed to prevent a relapse. Besides, where else would she have gone while the war raged on?

As he got off the train, Hanz put his suitcase down and looked around. Nestled in the Sonoran Desert of Southern Arizona, the foreign town was so different from Rothenburg ob der Tauber. The sky was large enough to swallow you whole, the sun hot enough to burn you alive, and the landscape strange enough to make you think you were on another planet. As far as the eye could see, funny-looking, giant cacti dotted the parched land, just like in Ollie's comic book, making him laugh. It was much slower there, too, than it was in Germany. Calmer, with fewer people–most wearing cowboy hats and boots–all unaware, or perhaps didn't care, that a horrible war had just occurred. He liked it.

After checking into a motel, Hanz ate at a small diner, then spent the rest of the day looking for a vehicle. He bought a used Chevy pickup truck–quite different from the vehicles in Europe–and the following morning mapped his way to the clinic located on the edge of town. Surprisingly, he felt nervous as he drove, just as he had when going on his first date with Maria back in Austria. After all, he hadn't seen her in close to four years, and so much had happened.

In her letters, Maria had always expressed how excited she was to return to Rothenburg, to their farm, and to the life they once had. She couldn't wait to hug and kiss her daughters and son. It pained Hanz just thinking about what he had to tell her, that Ava and Shalom were now living with their birth mother in Switzerland, Severin was their real father, and Luka was gone. Not to mention that they wouldn't be returning to Germany any time soon. The doctor had made it clear that, for the sake of her health, she would have to remain in a dry climate permanently.

As he walked into the sanatorium, Hanz's heartbeat elevated. The nurse led him down the hallway to Maria's room, and when he saw her sitting there in a chair, eyes closed from dozing off while reading a book, he stood still in the doorway for a moment, staring at her. Suddenly Abigail felt like a strange dream he once had, the war no longer existed, and the suffering never occurred. Before him was the same angel he saw on that endless field of green back in Austria years ago. "Am I dreaming?" he asked himself, just like he did that glorious day.

"*Nein,*" echoed the elderly man's voice in his head, the one who had overheard him, sitting on a rock. "You're not dreaming, son. That there is a rare *Fräulein*. Only the Austrian Alps could produce such beauty."

Hanz smiled, recalling everything about that elysian time. And here she was again, his Maria, looking so beautiful in that lovely yellow dress. So healthy, skin aglow, color in her cheeks, fiery red hair flowing down her back. *Mein Herr, sie ist wunderschön (My lord, she's beautiful)*, he thought again—déjà vu. Slowly he walked up to her and placed his hand on her shoulder.

Maria opened her cerulean eyes and gasped . . . "Oh my God! Hanz, you're here!" She leaped out of her chair and threw her arms around his neck. "You're finally here to take me home!"

Hanz hugged her tightly. Husband and wife wept and kissed.

After the euphoria of their reunion, Hanz pulled up a chair next to hers. In so many ways, he was now a different man, and Maria sensed it. Having buried their stillborn son was nothing compared to the heartache that came later, and Hanz was grateful Maria had been spared.

"There's so much to tell you, *meine Liebe,*" he said to her, intense emotion washing over him. He took her hand. "While you've been here, many things have happened, many things have changed. Before I tell you, though, you must remember that we are family, you and me. We are strong, and together we can overcome anything."

Maria's eyes filled with tears as she carefully read his lips. "What's wrong, Hanz? I want to see Ava and Shaylee and Luka."

Hanz loved her so much that he omitted much of the gory details while still explaining everything that had happened to their daughters and their son. They talked and cried and held each other tight. Hanz told her they must live in Tucson for the time being, but promised he would take her to see Ava and Shalom in the future.

As the Arizona sun was setting, casting its rays through the window, warming their skin, Hanz reflected on his life with Maria, and on humanity. So many scholars, professors, scientists, and learned people from all over the world have tried to explain the meaning of life, but not one of them could add to what he already knew. The simple truth, uncomplicated, unadulterated, handed down from God himself, that each life was precious. Each person mattered, and each human being was valued and loved by the Creator. In the end, man's inhumanity to man mattered none, as the Ancient of Days would have the last word.

The sun was now behind the Tucson Mountains, and as it sank into tomorrow, it dragged with it what once was . . . a German farmer and his wife, their two adopted Jewish daughters, and their adopted neighbor's son, living together outside the peaceful medieval town of Rothenburg ob der Tauber . . . giving birth to what will be: A couple starting over in a new land, on a new path set before them.

Hanz kissed Maria on the forehead, and at that very moment as he held his wife, though far away from his birth country of Germany, he knew he was finally home.

CHAPTER 50

Berlin, 1997

When Shalom had finished the story, all three of us were in tears. It took us a moment to compose ourselves before anyone spoke.

"Did Hanz and Maria stay in Arizona for the rest of their lives?" I asked.

"*Ja*," said Ava. "They lived on a desert farm and raised goats, and they visited us every summer."

"And Abigail?"

"She eventually married a lovely man named Isaac Goldberg," Shalom answered. "He had lost his spouse and child to Nazi barbarity too."

It was then that I noticed something on Shalom's wrinkled hand. An emerald ring, like the one Ingomar had dropped at Hanz's feet on the porch, leading him to discover the money and stolen jewels that bought the freedom of the Jews he saved. "That emerald ring your wearing . . . Is that the same one?"

Shalom nodded. "It was precious to our father. And now my sister and I take turns wearing it as a symbol to remember what he did for us."

"And your children?" I asked Ava. "Did you get them back?" I had to know.

Ava smiled, her tears glistening in her green eyes. "*Ja*, I did. As soon as it was safe to travel after the war, I went to Dresden and got them from the Beaumonts. What a beautiful day that was." She paused as the emotion overtook her, stealing her breath away. "I had lost hope in Auschwitz of ever seeing them again. And when I held them, I felt heaven. Now they are grown and thriving with families of their own."

I wanted to ask about Starholf, but wasn't sure if I should mention his name. I didn't have to, though, as Ava did it on her own.

"It's too bad Starholf couldn't have seen his beautiful children grow up," she said. "Despite what he did to us, I'm sad over that. After the Nuremberg Trials, he feared he was next and committed suicide, not wanting the Steiner family name to be soiled."

Ava's love for him still showed in her eyes. Remarkable. "Did either of you ever remarry like Abigail?"

"We both did," said Shalom. "But it wasn't easy. Neither of us fully recovered from what we suffered."

"I used to say that if you licked my heart, you'd be poisoned from all the pain it held," said Ava. "And sometimes I still feel like that."

Shalom agreed. "I was full of trauma and anger for years. Thankfully, my husband was a loving, understanding man, and we still managed to create our own happiness. I couldn't have children, though. After what they did to me during those experiments, I was sterile."

"I'm so sorry," I said.

"My husband was kind and gentle too," said Ava. "He knew he had to be. I had three more children with him, and we gave one to Shalom and her husband." Ava squeezed her sister's hand. "We named her Grace."

"That's an incredible gift," I said, moved by her generosity.

"It is. And I would do it all over again."

"Whatever happened to little Yael?"

"In Auschwitz, I promised her, 'Where I go, you go. Now and forever.' She stayed with me until she grew up and got married herself. She and her family live not far from here and visit often."

Shalom had a mischievous grin on her face. "I'll tell you another secret," she said, her hazel green eyes twinkling.

Ava let out a giggle, knowing what it was, and in that moment I saw them as they once were. Two beautiful twin girls, so full of life.

"Behind the portrait our father painted of Hitler was another painting," Shalom almost whispered. "A second canvas. Papa had painted Hitler's face as a grotesque monster, labeling it, 'The Wicked Führer.'"

Despite the seriousness of it all, we laughed.

"In reality, that's what he was," I said, shaking my head in disgust. "He took so much away from you. And those Schutzstaffel officers did too."

"They were not officers," said Shalom. "They weren't even men. They were sadists. We were filthy from living like animals, but they were filthy on the inside. So filthy that the demons who directed them could not stand their stench."

Ava agreed. "After what they have done, they cannot wash off their crimes. And that fancy uniform they wore, it's part of their skin now. They can't take that off either. They have sinned beyond forgiveness, and Almighty God is now their judge and jury."

Though I nodded, I could never fully understand the depth of what Ava and Shalom had gone through. How could anyone, unless you were there? "And the albino buck," I said. "What a powerful symbol of its own. Through Hanz's kindness, its offspring flourished. And through his love and courage, generations of the eight Jews he saved will now live on."

Both women smiled, and Shalom said, "Some around Rothenburg ob der Tauber still see a white deer in the forest from time to time. Even after all these years."

I left that morning with my tapes and a slice of delicious cake from Mrs. Kuchen–Ava Wolff. And more importantly, I left a different man. I came to Germany as a journalist looking for my prize-winning story, and found so much more.

"Have you ever been heartbroken?" Ava had asked me when she first began.

"No," I had told her. "I haven't experienced that yet."

"You will after the story I'm about to tell you," she replied.

Ava was right.

And yet, I found myself inspired, too. Inspired by the human spirit, and the will to survive. "What makes a man a man is his tolerance for his fellow neighbors, and his love and kindness for humanity," I could hear Hanz Wolff saying as I walked back to my apartment. And then, "What does it cost to save a man or a woman's life? A painting and a bag of stolen jewels."

Suddenly I could see Hanz as if I had personally known him. I could see him in the barn that beautiful sunny morning, standing over two Jewish baby girls wrapped in woolen blankets embroidered with the Star of David, smiling and gently taking them to their new mother. Their new family, their new world. And I was hit with an astonishing awareness of what that meant. A German couple, raising Jewish babies as their own, proving that at the heart of us we are all just human. One race–the *human* race–no different from one another. Brothers and sisters under God, our Heavenly Father.

But there was still more that I had learned from these two Jewish women. I was naïve about history, and I was flooded with emotion over what the Jews and others had suffered during that horrific time of the Holocaust, having a newfound compassion for them, not only for the ones who died but also for those who survived and lived with the agony of what they had endured.

Ava and Shalom's story, like all the other stories of hatred and discrimination in mankind's history, had to be retold.

Retold and never forgotten . . .

AFTERWORD

The Holocaust was Nazi Germany's deliberate, organized, state-sponsored persecution and genocide of approximately six million European Jews. They also persecuted and committed genocide of more than 250,000 Roma (Gypsies), killed over three million Soviet prisoners of war, nearly two million Poles, over 250,000 people with disabilities, almost 2,000 Jehovah's Witnesses, hundreds of men accused of homosexuality, and other victims.

In total, between 1933 and 1945, the Nazis killed twelve million people. Twelve million too many.

My Final Thoughts . . .

"And then the last sentence is written, and I sit still in my creative space, ruminating over the story. The sensation electrifies me, then slowly calms like the ebb and flow of the ocean tides until it gently fades away. In that special moment, I knew as a writer, the story was ready to share." – Kate Birkin

When the entire manuscript for *Ava and Shalom* was completed, I went for dinner with my dear friend, editor, and coauthor, Mark Bornz, to celebrate. We sat tucked away at the back of our favorite French restaurant and talked about the experience of writing the book. From the meticulous and thorough research to the many months of writing and editing, it was hard, stressful work.

But oh, so worth it!

We knew we were creating something important. Something that wasn't just a novel about the Holocaust but a collection of stories about real people who lived real lives during that most harrowing and epoch time in mankind's history. This was a responsibility we did not take lightly. And a great honor.

As we continued our discussion that evening, we imagined being inside our own story, transported to that quaint medieval town of Rothenburg ob der Tauber in Bavaria, Germany, living as neighbors and friends of Hanz and Maria Wolff and their two daughters, Ava and Shaylee (Shalom). We both knew without a doubt that had we lived during that time, we would have been part of the Resistance, helping whomever we could, concealing as many Jews and others hated by the Nazi regime as we could. We would have risked our lives to do the right thing.

"Can you imagine someone barging into your home, tearing you away from everything you know, beating, raping, and murdering you and your loved ones because of your faith or ethnicity? And then, if you're still alive, taking you away to a horrific concentration camp?" When I asked that question, we both stared at each other, slowly shaking our heads.

I often soliloquized those thoughts when alone, writing out the story. Many times, as I played out the more gruesome scenes in my head, capturing them in print, I cried, even sobbed, knowing that what I was writing was not mere fiction. It was sometimes difficult to keep writing, and I'd have to take a break. "How could this have happened?" I asked more times than I can count. "How can someone do such horrible things to someone else?" Not only did it make me sad, but angry too. Angry toward those who committed these heinous crimes back then, and angry toward those who deny them now.

Outrageous!

After a few glasses of wine, I put my old leather folder on the table and pulled out the manuscript, laying it down in front of us. The sounds in the restaurant faded all around us, and we both stared at it in silence.

It was an emotional moment, happy and sad, and as we sat there, my editor and coauthor reached over and touched my hand. "We gave them a voice," he said, looking at me with his gray-blue eyes. They seemed to turn metallic, approaching silver as the tears formed. "A story. A legacy that will never be forgotten."

I nodded, tears rolling down my cheeks. "They weren't just victims, staring hauntingly into the camera lens. They were beautiful human beings who had lives, loves, and dreams."

And that was the original goal of this work when we first started, to not just write an account about the Holocaust but to write about their lives before it. To give these people a voice, a story, a legacy before the tragedy stole it. Ava and Shalom, Hanz and Maria, Abigail and little Yael, Nila and Randolph and Ollie, Christian and all the others who were kind, moral, and good—they are real people to me. Through the course of this journey, they have become my very dear friends. I have lived with them, laughed with them, wept with them, and wept for them. I have cherished my time with them, and I will never forget them.

I wrote a book about a community of friends and neighbors around a small town in Germany—Jews and others—who lived together peacefully before the horrors of history. A book that changed my life, opened my eyes and heart, and made me a better person. And although I couldn't save the ones who lived through that nightmare, it was so fulfilling to create someone who could.

Hanz Wolff stood up to the evil dragon. He protected those he loved, and even those he didn't know. The weak, the innocent, the ones with no helper. If only the world were full of men like him, the Holocaust would have never happened, and millions more would be alive.

In my mind's eye, I could see Ava and Shalom and their birth mother Abigail, starting over in Switzerland. I could see Hanz Wolff and his wife Maria on their goat farm in Arizona. And I could see hope for a new world.

As I smiled through my happy tears, a beautiful and meaningful song started playing in the background. It was *Imagine*, by John Lennon, and the lyrics made me cry. When the song ended, I couldn't help but think of another courageous man like Hanz Wolff. Another hero, a legendary man who changed the world, making a huge impact on humanity with his brilliant mind and beautiful heart—Martin Luther King Jr.

How fitting it is, then, to conclude my final thoughts by encouraging everyone to listen to his speeches, read his writings, and meditate on his powerful words he left behind.

Dear Reader,

I hope you enjoyed *Ava and Shalom*. It took much research, effort, and care to write this story about Jewish twin girls living in a most harrowing time of mankind's history, and it impacted me immensely. If you have a moment, I would be very grateful if you shared your feelings too, by leaving your feedback/rating via the retailer's review link where you purchased this novel. Even just a few words would be greatly appreciated.

Ready to time-travel again? . . . I invite you to embark on another dramatic and heartbreaking journey with me, taking you back to the 1930s Australian Outback, where you'll experience the #1 Bestseller, *The Consequence of Anna*. This story, inspired by actual events and soon to be a Major Motion Picture, was submitted for the Pulitzer Prize and was a semifinalist for the Kindle Book Award. You can find it at your favorite bookstore.

Lastly, if you'd like to receive free giveaways, insights into writing, and updates on my current projects and new releases, you can join my exclusive Readers' Club mailing list on my website at: https://katebirkinbooks.com

Thank you so much!
Kate Birkin

www.ingramcontent.com/pod-product-compliance
Lightning Source LLC
Chambersburg PA
CBHW030330010826
48973CB00004B/950